The
Haighdlen Chronicles
Books 1-3

The Laurille Legacy

Restoring the Throne

The Final Entry

~To my precious children, Adam and Elizabeth.~
Mama loves you both so much.

HAIGHDLEN CASTLE
CLARA
LAURISHIRE
LAKE LAURIE
MAJESTIC OAK
ALLEGIANCE GULF
VACILLIAN SEA
HAIGHDLEN

The Trawley Isles
Rozathian Ocean
Iadaen Ocean
Pladian Ocean
Lockessbarrow
Vynchia
Merchant Gulf
Haighdlen
Vacillian Sea
Leafbrooke
Sapience Sea
N
The Four Kingdoms

The
Laurille
Legacy

CHAPTER 1

An obsessive unwanted thought entered an otherwise pleasant dream.

Elise Laurille was all too familiar with the cyclical symptoms of a panic attack that came with having anxiety. Jerking awake, she sat up and scanned the darkened bedroom. Nothing seemed out of the ordinary. Everything was still except her overactive brain tricking her into thinking she was in danger. She looked down at the opened yearbook on her lap. When that didn't help, she shuffled through her college applications on her end table and checked her phone. Her attempts to distract herself failed, of course, and the inevitable attack snuck up on her.

Like clockwork, her chest froze, and she struggled to breathe. She jumped up and began pacing by the foot of her bed. Anything that kept her moving to get rid of the building adrenaline made her feel productive while her thoughts raced in circles.

Her eyes checked the time. *12:28 a.m.*

It was nearly impossible to hold on to any clear thought, let alone which one had actually brought on her panicked state.

She wiped her clammy palms along her pajama pants and took a steadying breath.

I have nothing to be afraid of. I am safe. I am safe. I am safe. This will pass. . .this feeling will go away.

Her foot stomped into the carpet as shameful tears poured relentlessly down her cheeks.

What is wrong with me? Why can't I control this?

She feared one day she'd go insane. At some point, people were going to notice how unhealthy this was and carry her off to an asylum. The imagery alone was enough to shake her unsteady state of mind.

This feeling will go away. Just breathe and wait.

This continued for the next five minutes or so, until she felt her chest clear, and the dark clouds within her mind began to subside.

That was the irony of panic attacks. Every time felt like the first time all over again.

She walked into the bathroom and looked at her reflection in the mirror. Being wide awake now, she was thankful it wasn't a school night. The year was almost over, and graduation was the following weekend. Everything familiar was coming to an end, and the idea of college was overwhelming. Maybe that was what woke her up. She couldn't be sure. . .

As she passed her mother's room on the way to bed, she was jolted back to reality by the sound of her mother's cell phone ringing. Elise saw her mother sleeping and let it go to voicemail. Until it rang again.

And again.

She tiptoed into her mother's room and peeked down at the screen.

Uncle Ian. . .why's he calling this late?

It went to voicemail for the third time. Then the phone buzzed with her uncle's incessant texts.

Ruby? Are you awake?

. . .

Ruby, this is important. Pick up the phone.
Ruby. NOW.
It's Mother. We have to go now.

Was her nana sick? Her mom never mentioned her and always became irritable when Elise did. She didn't even know where any of her family lived except her uncle. They visited with him and his family often enough, but never the others. Ruby had always excused it away as a simple falling out but would never go into any detail.

If her nana was sick, surely her mother would want to know.

Elise looked at the empty wine glass next to the phone. Her mom's eyeliner was smudged, and her mouth hung open deep in sleep. This occurred often enough for Elise to know it had been a busy night at the diner.

The phone vibrated again.

RUBY!!!!!!!!! Answer me or I'm calling Elise's phone and telling her EVERYTHING.

Before Elise could question his meaning, another text came in.

We can't hide it from her anymore. It's finally happened. PLEASE call me.

Unable to contain her curiosity, she risked her mother's wrath and gently shook the other woman's shoulder.

"Mom?"

Ruby made a noncommittal noise. Elise shook her again.

"What? What is it?" Ruby growled. "Elise? Do you have any idea what time it is? Do you know what kind of day I had?"

"Yeah, Mom, I can see that," Elise said, nodding towards the empty stemmed glass before she picked up her mom's phone. "Ian's been trying to get in touch with you. Your phone has been going off like crazy."

"Ugh, let me see that." She snatched the phone away, easing it back at arm's length for her eyes to adjust. When she got to the last message, her eyes widened.

"You didn't read any of this, did you?"

"No," Elise lied. "Is everything okay?"

As much as she hated being left out of something, Elise knew cornering her mom was a recipe for disaster. She'd have to play her mother's game strategically to get any information.

"Just get dressed," Ruby snapped as she swung her legs over the side of the bed. "Pack a small bag. We'll get a motel if we need to. You drive."

"Where are we going?"

The only reply she got was the sound of her mother's bathroom door shutting. She didn't know why she expected an answer to her question. Ruby avoided confrontation at all cost, and judging by the seriousness of Ian's texts, this was going to be no different.

***

"We're only going to be there an hour. Do you hear me?" Ruby asked as she took some Tylenol.

"Mom, I don't even know where 'there' is," Elise argued as she merged to pass someone.

Ruby moaned as she put on her sunglasses to block the oncoming headlights.

"Not so fast!"

Elise ignored the criticism and continued to stare ahead. She had been listening to her mom complain about her grandmother for almost an hour.

She eventually started paying more attention to the pattern of the swishing wipers to block out the rant about her supposed unreliable family.

"If it were up to me, we wouldn't even be going there at all." Ruby reclined her seat back.

"And yet here we are," Elise grumbled. "I still don't know what the big deal is. You complain all the time, but you never tell me *why* you don't like them."

"It's not that I don't like them," Ruby said. "I have to love them, but it's complicated. I'd rather not talk about it."

"And yet that's *all* you've done." Elise sighed. There was a brief awkward pause before she continued. "You know that excuse is getting old, right?"

Elise knew that she was giving her mother an attitude, but she was so frustrated, she really didn't care at this point. "I'm eighteen, Mom. You have to start including me at some point."

When she got no response, she rolled her eyes and slumped back into her seat.

It was times like these she wished she had applied for an out-of-state college. At least graduation was around the corner, then maybe her mom would start treating her like an adult and not some little kid who couldn't keep secrets.

"It's just off here. Make a right." Ruby pointed towards a long winding driveway that Elise hadn't noticed.

"Are you serious?" Elise asked. "You told me they all lived far away. We've only driven for forty-five minutes! We've been this close to Nana all this time?"

Her mother ignored her. Of course her mother ignored her. Elise bit her tongue and squeezed the steering wheel until her knuckles turned white. *Keep it together, Elise. If you want to know anything, don't blow up.*

She parked beside her uncle's car in front of a large two-story house. The coffee-colored vinyl siding and decorative stone exterior were covered in vines. Faded blue shutters, which had probably once added charm, now needed repairing. A struggling garden had long been taken over by weeds, and a tattered rope swing drooped from a nearby oak tree. The stepping-stones leading around the side were beginning to crack along with an empty cast stone three-tiered fountain.

Ruby cursed under her breath.

Elise looked up and saw what looked like several shadows in the upstairs windows.

"That better not be them."

"Who?"

"Never mind." Ruby huffed and sneered as she stepped into a puddle of mud that stained her shoes.

Elise gritted her teeth and turned the car off. She jumped out and huddled to stay under her mother's umbrella until they got to the front door.

Ruby banged on the knocker until a tall middle-aged man answered.

Her mother barged in before he could greet them. "Hello, Joseph. Where's Mother?"

"Welcome, your high-," Joseph said, but was stopped by Ruby's severe expression. "Erm, I believe that you will find her in the living room."

Her mother thanked him and hurried inside.

Was he about to say "highness"?

Once Joseph had taken their coats and umbrella, they made their way into the spacious living room.

"Ruby!"

A woman she assumed was her grandmother jumped up from the couch and walked up to them. She opened her arms wide only to pause a moment later, unsure if Ruby would be open to her embrace. She hovered awkwardly before hugging her anyway.

Elise was surprised to see how. . .*healthy* her grandmother was.

Joranna Laurille had an elegant flair about her that Elise absolutely loved. She was dressed in a billowy blouse that flowed as she walked with impeccable posture. Almost regal. Her dark red hair, that Ruby and Elise inherited, was frosted with gray and pulled back by a pearl clip. Her makeup was flawless and completed the overall polished appearance. Elise felt underwhelming with her ponytail, faded jeans, t-shirt and muddy sneakers.

"Hi, Mother," Ruby said. "Ian said you were sick."

"Oh, I am, dear, but never mind that now."

"He made it sound severe."

"Well, how else was I supposed to get you here? It's been at least ten years since you've visited me." Her eyes traveled over to Elise. "This can't be little Elise!"

Joranna didn't waste any time squeezing her, and Elise was comforted by an aroma of mint and vanilla.

"You are so beautiful."

"Thank you. . .Nana."

"I bet you don't remember me. You spent an entire summer here when you were eight. We had tea parties every day and played princesses. Do you remember?"

Elise tried jarring her memory.

"Um. . .a little."

Joranna scoffed. "I blame your mother."

"What else is new?" Ruby muttered before speaking up. "Anyway, we need to talk about the other thing."

"Oh, yes, we will. There's plenty of time."

"We need to talk about it *now*," Ruby said. "Elise and I are not staying."

The room grew cold as Joranna pulled her mouth into a thin line and invited her daughter to sit on the couch. Ruby made sure they only spoke in whispers so that their voices didn't carry.

Elise rolled her eyes and busied herself by walking around the room admiring the trinkets her grandmother had collected over the years.

The first thing to catch her eye was a crystal bowl with carved mermaids around the exterior. She reached out and grazed a finger along one of the tails.

"Ah, I see you have found my favorite gift," Joranna said, cutting Ruby off. "It was given to me by Eugena, the Mermaid Queen."

"Sorry?" Elise asked, thinking her grandmother was trying to pull her leg in a childish joke.

The older woman didn't seem offended and walked over to a nearby closet. She pulled out a long silken pink scarf.

"And *this*," she said, running the cloth lovingly across her cheek, "was given to me by Horanis, the Fairy King. It was sewn by the fairies of—"

"Mother," Ruby said, a chill in her voice, warning her mother not to complete her sentence. Elise watched her grandmother's lip twitch in annoyance. "I think it's time for you to go to bed."

"I'm not going to be told *when* to do anything," Joranna snapped. "Especially by a daughter who won't acknowledge my calls or letters."

The air was thick with tension that was only broken by the sound of running footsteps above them.

"Mother," Ruby said through a tightened jaw, "who else is here?"

Joranna hesitated and wrung her hands. "Everyone."

"I knew it. Elise, let's go."

"Now, hold on there, Ruby. Don't you go storming off. You just got here. Don't you think Elise should get to meet her family?"

Elise's curiosity was piqued, and she glanced down the hall hoping to see someone walking past.

Was she finally going to meet her mother's sister and older brother after all these years? Maybe her cousins, too?

"Mom, I want to meet them!" Elise said, ignoring her mother's signals to drop everything and leave. Getting back in the car without finding out what was really going on was the last thing she wanted to do.

"Of course you do!" Joranna said, sending Joseph to fetch the others and invite them down into the living room.

Ruby slumped down on the couch to pour a cup of the tea Joseph had brought in moments earlier.

"Mother, it's after two in the morning. What're they all doing awake?"

"We can hardly expect them to sleep after what they've just been through!" Joranna exclaimed.

The first ones to appear in the doorway were Ian and Morgan's twin daughters, Olivia and Naomi, who sported dark-brown pigtails and toothy smiles. They raced around the room until Joranna chastised them for running through the house. They settled for playing with their dolls in the corner of the room.

"I know you've visited them quite a bit, so you'll already know that Ian's wife Morgan is expecting again."

Elise didn't think that needed to be explained once a *very* pregnant Morgan came in with Ian a few moments later. The twins definitely favored their mother with the same thick hair and fair complexions. Her uncle was very charming, too, sporting brown hair and a short goatee. He smiled as he hugged Ruby and Elise.

Elise immediately felt comfortable around him, but the same couldn't be said about her other uncle, who entered next.

Richard was taller than Ian. His thick brown beard was trimmed to perfection across a strong jaw. His eyes, however, seemed sunken and blood-shot, and Elise wondered if he had been crying or sick recently. He sank into a nearby armchair and muttered a slurred greeting.

Two more women followed him, and Joranna introduced them as Richard's wife, Gwendolyn, and Elise's Aunt Sarah. Both sat down and adjusted their pants as if they had never worn any.

The family reunion concluded with Sarah's two boys, Paul and Eric, and Richard's and Gwendolyn's daughter, Madelyn. All three, teenagers just a few years younger than Elise, stayed near each other at the far side of the room muttering under their breaths.

The back of Elise's neck grew hot under everyone's stares.

The room seemed a lot smaller now that it was holding this rather odd group of characters. The air was once again thick with tension, and Elise wished for someone to say something. *Anything*.

"Well," Joranna said with a bright smile, "I must say it is wonderful to have everyone under the same roof again. It's been too long since we were a proper family."

Ruby groaned from across the room.

"Ugh, are we really going to do this, Mother? Pretend that we're all here by choice?" It seemed by the reaction on everyone's faces that Ruby was saying what was on everyone else's mind. Richard cleared his throat and asked Joseph to bring him a drink. "Why are all of you here anyway? She doesn't look that sick to me. And will someone please explain what Ian meant by 'it's finally happened'?"

"Oh, Ruby, for once in your life, can't you be considerate?" Sarah snapped at her younger sister.

Elise gulped. She had never heard anyone talk to her mother like that, and she honestly didn't know how she felt about it.

"I *am* being considerate," Ruby said. "I'm here, aren't I?"

"Yes, until things get hard, and then you'll probably leave again." Sarah clicked her tongue and pushed a brownish-blond strand of hair away from her eyes. "Look at you now. Are you drunk?"

"That's enough, you two," Joranna said as she walked to stand between her two daughters. "Not in front of the children." Both women moved away from each other. "Now, the reason we are all together is because something terrible has happened, and it has nothing to do with my cold."

She turned expectantly to her eldest to fill everyone in.

Richard took the last swig from his glass and took a deep breath.

"Haighdlen has been attacked. . .and taken over," he said, "by Rona."

Ruby gasped and Elise was filled with even more questions.

The other adults nodded grimly, their faces full of grief and confusion.

Elise was once again reminded that she was being watched when she heard more whispers from across the room. Her cousins didn't appear to be shocked or confused, and she was left to conclude that she was the only one left in the dark.

"Can someone please tell me what's going on? I don't know what you're talking about. Where's Haighdlen?"

"Oh, honestly, Ruby!" Sarah huffed again. "You really kept all this a secret from her?"

"It was working out fine until *you* all showed up, throwing her into a world she doesn't belong in!"

Both started to argue at the same time, and it was difficult to make out what each was saying to the other. What were they talking about? Where was her family from? She was genuinely confused and started to pay more attention to the others.

Richard seemed uncomfortable in his stiff blue jeans. Gwendolyn and Sarah didn't seem to be faring any better with their outfits. Madelyn and Paul sat very still on the loveseat while Eric had chosen to stand near the twins. Elise adjusted her posture to match theirs and hoped it was subtle.

"It doesn't matter now!" Richard bellowed, bringing his sisters' argument to an end. "Don't you see? No one is to blame here but me."

"Richard, that is not true," Joranna said. "We know you did everything you could."

"But it wasn't good enough, was it, Mother?" he asked, his voice breaking. He paused for a moment to gaze at her. "I failed my kingdom. . .Father's kingdom. So many lives were lost due to my poor leadership."

"I don't want to hear you talking like that," Joranna said as she took the glass out of Richard's hand. "You have been a strong and just ruler since your father passed, and I won't have you doubting your choice to leave."

"But it wasn't my choice," he said. His eyes closed, and he frowned as his mind wandered. "I wanted to stay there. . .to die for my kingdom. For my people."

"Richard, Liam and Charles pulled you out before you were killed," Sarah said, resting a hand on his arm.

"And now they're dead. They're both *dead*."

Ruby gasped and paled before them.

"Liam died doing what he felt was right." Sarah's voice sounded strained as she comforted her brother. "He made sure the boys and I were safe, and his duty was to protect you as well. And I know how much Charles meant to you. I'm so sorry."

"They were my best friends," Richard said. "I could've been there to save them. I should have stopped Rona before she ever grew to be as strong as she is now. The people are doomed now. She finally accomplished what she set out to do all those years ago when she killed Father."

Elise interrupted him.

"Okay, someone *please* catch me up. Mom, is this what you've been keeping from me? Is this the 'big secret'?"

Her chest felt constricted again as the reality of the conversation set in. Whatever was happening, it was serious enough that people were dying, and her family was right in the middle of it all. Her clothes and posture didn't seem like such a big deal now.

Ruby recognized Elise's anxious state and walked over to her.

"Elise, I don't want you mixed up in all of this. As you can see, nothing good comes out of it. Please, let's just get out of here."

"Yes, Ruby, leave. *Again*. Right when your family needs you," Sarah said.

"Okay, that's it," Ian said, speaking for the first time since he had greeted them. "I'm not going to sit here and watch you two rip each other apart. Ruby, what you chose to tell or not tell Elise was your choice. The point is you can't hide it from her now. She deserves to know. All of our children deserve to know where they come from. I'd love to take our son there when he's born. . .if there's anything left. So, what can we do?"

Richard shook his head.

"There's nothing to be done."

"All right, I've had enough," Gwendolyn snapped, pulling her husband up out of his seat. "I have seen you do too many great things to give up like this. You have trained your whole life to be the king that Haighdlen deserves, and I will not see you abandon it when it needs you most because of a lack of confidence. This is your chance to be great and save everyone. It isn't too late."

"But what can be done?" Sarah asked.

"We'll need a lot of magic," Joranna said. Elise watched her mother's face fall. "Maybe there's something in here." Joranna took a worn purple book off her shelf, opened the cover and leafed through the stiff pages.

"What is that?" Elise asked, once again feeling like she was the only one left out of a secret.

"It's my diary," Joranna said and stroked one of its pages. "I kept it all those years I was the Queen of Haighdlen."

Elise shook her head and waved her hands. "Okay, so. . . you're all some kind of royalty? *Actual* royalty? Like the Queen of England?"

"For the most part, yes," Joranna replied. "The Laurille family has ruled for many generations, but we were threatened by a powerful sorceress named Rona. It appears she has finally won and taken over the kingdom."

"I've never heard of Haighdlen." Elise frowned. "I don't remember seeing it on a map."

"And you never will on the maps of this world," Ian said. "The magical kingdoms are in another realm. Kind of like a comic book."

"Nice reference," Ruby scoffed as she dabbed her face with a tissue. "Elise, you don't need to be involved with all this magical nonsense, and I need to be alone."

"Don't keep her in the dark just because you're jealous," Sarah said.

"You know, I'm getting really tired of your holier-than-thou attitude." Ruby closed the distance between them. "It isn't bad enough your husband just died, but you have to drag me down with you?"

"I just thought you might want to be responsible for once and actually help Haighdlen and all those people who looked up to us."

"And look where it got them!"

There was a hush throughout the room, and Ruby immediately looked to Richard. Elise could tell her mother regretted her words as soon as she had said them.

Ruby walked over to her brother and touched his shoulder. "Richard. . .I didn't mean—"

"Don't trouble yourself," he said, shrugging her hand off. "You're not wrong. I'm not fit to rule. Look at us. None of us are. We'd rather fight each other."

What is going on here? Another realm? What happened to make them so angry with each other? I hate being left out!

Elise wiped her hands along her pants again as her thoughts ran away like they often did. Up until twenty minutes ago, Elise had only thought magic existed in fairy tales and movies. Now it sounded like it was all around her.

"I think I better get the children off to bed," Morgan spoke up, using Ian's hand to help her stand as she held her belly. "Keep me informed. I'll see you all in the morning." She kissed Ian good night and walked the twins and other teenagers out.

"Why don't we just take the obvious route?" Joranna said. "One of you can use magic to send someone back through the diary and alter what happened. They can defeat Rona before she gets this powerful. Think of all the lives that could be saved!"

"How would we pull that off?" Sarah asked. "We'd risk running into ourselves. Even with a disguise, it's dangerous."

Silence filled the room.

"What about her?" Ian asked. Elise's throat dried when she noticed Ian staring at her from across the room. "What if she went?"

What!

"Are you crazy?" Ruby spat. "Ian, she's never even been out of the country, let alone out of this realm. She knows nothing about Haighdlen or its customs. She'll be found out immediately!"

"Give her some credit," he argued. "Think about it. None of us would recognize her at that time in our lives. A simple spell could alter what our past selves remember so as not to risk recognizing her later as she ages."

A spell? What spell? Why isn't anyone else freaking out?

"And how do you expect an eighteen-year-old outsider to defeat the most powerful sorceress the world has ever seen?" Ruby argued.

Elise could hear her heart beating. Her breath quickened, and for a moment she thought she was going to have another panic attack.

I take everything back. I think I just want to go home now and forget all of this.

"Why don't we let Elise decide for herself?" Joranna suggested. Her eyes warmed as she looked at her granddaughter. An involuntary shiver ran down Elise's spine. "It's a lot to process right now. Take all the time you need to think about it." She handed Elise her diary. "Read through this, and hopefully it will help you get to know our world a little better. But please be careful with it. It's very dear to me."

Elise ran her fingers over the aging cover and could tell a lot of love had been placed inside. She knew her family needed her help, but at the moment, she really didn't see what she could do to help them. One minute she was coming to visit her sick grandmother, and now she was being asked to travel back in time through a book. She wanted someone to pinch and wake her up. None of this could be real. She didn't believe in magic like this. Were they trying to play a trick on her?

"Why don't you sleep on it?" Joranna offered again when Elise didn't reply. "Things may look different in the morning. Keep the diary as long as you wish."

Ruby's protests were ignored, and Elise was escorted to a bedroom on the second floor. Her bag had been brought in, and she saw that she was sharing a room with Paul and Madelyn, who were still awake.

"Wasn't there another boy?" Elise asked.

"Eric is sharing with the twins," said Paul, who was very tall and gangly with brownish-blonde hair and acne.

"Sorry for all the staring." Madelyn smiled. "You've just always been the *secret* cousin, you know? We've only heard about you, but never actually got to meet you."

Madelyn had inherited Gwendolyn's thick red hair and several freckles on her small face. She looked to be about thirteen years old while Paul was most likely fifteen or sixteen.

Secret cousin? I don't like the sound of that.

"What kinds of things have you heard?" Elise asked as she slipped into her bed.

Her cousins exchanged glances before Paul spoke again.

"That you haven't been to Haighdlen since you were a baby. Your mom is the only one besides Nana without magic, and that's why she left and hates the family. And that makes you the best candidate to go back and stop Rona." Paul blushed with a smile. "I eavesdropped from the stairs."

"Wish someone would've thought to tell me all this." Elise sighed. "I've never done anything magical either. What can the others do, and why are we the only ones without magic?"

"No one knows why." Paul shrugged. "She just took more from Nana's side, who is from this world, too. Nana moved back here with Ian and Ruby after our grandfather passed before we were born."

"As for magical talents," Madelyn added, "my father can make items levitate, Sarah can heal people, and Uncle Ian can turn invisible."

"Really?"

Why didn't Mom get any magic? Why did they move back here?

Elise scooted to the edge of her bed and wiped her palms again.

"They can do more, of course. We all have magical energies too, but our parents have more singular talents with their magic," Paul said.

This was all too much for Elise to take in for one night. Part of her was still waiting for the big joke to be revealed. Feeling her adrenaline building again, she looked for an escape. She feigned a yawn and rested her head on her pillow.

"Not to be rude, but I think I'm just going to lay here and think awhile. I kind of just got thrown into all this and haven't really gotten to process it."

"We understand," Madelyn said. "We don't want you to do anything you don't want to do, but. . .Haighdlen is our home. We'd really love if you'd help save it."

Save what exactly? None of this is making any sense!

"Maybe even save my dad from having to sacrifice himself?" Paul cleared his throat to stop tears from falling.

Not knowing what to say, Elise nodded and rolled over.

She used her cell phone light to glimpse at some of the entries at the beginning of the diary while she waited for the other two to fall asleep.

So, to recap, I'm some kind of princess from this strange place called Haighdlen. Everyone has magic except Mom, Nana, and me. Mom hates the family, and now they want me to travel through a book to save an entire kingdom. No pressure at all.

CHAPTER 2

Her family's request continued to weigh on Elise's mind as her mother dropped her off at school two days later.

"Have a good day," Ruby said. Elise nodded and tossed her backpack over her shoulder. "Don't look so depressed. You did the right thing."

Elise said goodbye and watched the car pull away from the curb before heading inside.

The usual crowds of students were gathered in the cafeteria awaiting the bell.

She took in all the students laughing and signing yearbooks, excited about the next chapter in their lives. She should be among them. Before her encounter with her family, she probably would have been. For years, it felt like her world hadn't branched further than her home and these halls.

Now all she could think about was the image of her relatives' disappointed faces when she had told them she didn't think she could go through with it.

Did they have any idea what they were asking her to do? How was she supposed to go back in time, supposedly interfere with some witch's plan, and save her family? She couldn't even believe she was entertaining the thought. It sounded so bizarre to say out loud that she hadn't told anybody about it. Not even her best friend.

Darcie Pickard was a confident young woman who seemed to know everyone. Her messy brown pixie-cut hair framed her thin face well and matched her eyes. She always seemed to have some type of dangly jewelry on that announced her arrival. Slightly taller than Elise with a smaller build, she was also meddlesome to a fault.

"Elise!" she said as she approached her friend. "I've been texting you for the last hour. Everything okay?"

"Ugh, I forgot to charge it last night." Elise glanced down at her now dead cell phone. "I've had a lot on my mind."

"You can fill me in during study hall. It's not like we'll need it now that finals are over. At the same time, it'll be the last chance you'll get to pretend you're not staring at Gavin for forty-five minutes straight, and I don't want to get in the way of that."

Elise forced a laugh as her eyes located him across the room.

She had developed a crush on Gavin Striess over the last two years since his family had moved there.

Darcie had informed her that his dad was in the military and had been stationed in the area. He had been immediately accepted by the popular kids, which meant that Elise didn't really get a chance to interact with him. Not that she'd know what to say anyway. Past the occasional shy hello, she didn't say much to him.

"You know you can talk to him, right?" Darcie asked. "It's not hard. Just say hi."

"And then what?" Elise scoffed. "Let's not forget how nervous I get, and words don't really come out."

"Which I find hard to believe," Darcie said. "When we're together, you don't have a problem talking all the time."

"Well, I *know* you. In my head, I can talk to him about anything, but here. . .I can't. I just choose to watch him. That way it doesn't get weird."

"Yes, because staring at someone and obsessing all the time isn't weird at all." Darcie crossed her arms and rolled her eyes. "You can keep playing stalker or you can do something about it. It's the last day of school. This way you won't have to wonder 'what if'."

The bell rang, saving Elise from having to respond, and she prayed that Darcie would drop the issue as they headed to study hall.

Unfortunately, Darcie was very persistent when it came to things she wanted, and she wasn't about to let Elise have any regrets.

Darcie chose two desks near Gavin and his friends. She didn't seem to care that everyone had used the same seats all year, and she knew Elise wouldn't sit by herself for the next forty-five minutes.

Elise slumped down into the chair beside her friend and pretended to look for something in her backpack.

"Hey, Gavin?" Darcie asked. Elise's heart began to race. "Could you sign my yearbook?"

Good, maybe I'm off the hook.

"Oh, and my friend's too? Elise, get yours out."

Elise reluctantly pulled her book out of her bag and chanced a look up at Gavin.

He was so good-looking and perfect. No wonder he was a popular kid. His skin was unblemished, his dark medium-length shaggy hairstyle fell into his chocolate brown eyes, and she didn't think his smile could get any dreamier.

She answered with an awkward grin of her own and hoped that she didn't have anything caught in her teeth.

"Oh, sure," he said as he turned to face them. He jotted something down in each book before handing them back. "Ready for graduation?"

Elise nodded, already feeling a lump forming in her throat.

"We're *so* ready," Darcie said, bubbling with excitement. "We were just wondering if we were going to see anybody here afterwards. Maybe at a party?"

"Same here," Gavin said. "We're all trying to plan something."

"Maybe Elise could throw a party?" Darcie suggested.

Gavin looked over, and it looked like he had forgotten she was sitting there.

Ugh, Darcie, shut up!

"Uh. . .maybe," Gavin stammered, and Elise wished she could crawl under a rock and hide. His face brightened as he addressed her again. "Hey, thanks for letting me look at your paper for that last test, Lisa. I didn't know a thing!" He chuckled before turning back to his friends.

Elise put her head down, hoping her hair would hide her from the world.

"Next time you want to help me, please don't," she muttered.

"Oh, come on," Darcie said. "I thought it went really well."

Elise opened her yearbook and plopped it onto Darcie's desk.

Have a great summer, Lisa. —Gavin

"You were saying?"

"He's just a guy. Anyway, what were you going to tell me earlier?"

For the next half hour, Elise spoke in a whisper, even going so far as to write some words down so she wouldn't gain attention.

When she finished, she glanced up to gauge her best friend's reaction. If Darcie didn't believe her, then nobody would.

"Wow. . ." Darcie took a deep breath and read the notes again. "And so. . .they're all at your grandma's house right now?" Elise nodded. "And you just *left*?"

"Well, what was I supposed to do, Darcie? Mom was with me and demanded to leave the whole time, and I couldn't process the idea that they had magic, let alone that they wanted me to time travel!"

Darcie shushed her as a couple of people looked over at them. Once the buzz of conversations resumed, Darcie spoke up.

"Elise, this is your family!"

"I know. . ."

"You've always said you wish you knew your family, and now you can!"

"And you believe all this?" Elise's brows furrowed. "Just like that?"

"Are you kidding me? Of course I believe it! How awesome is this? We have to go back to your grandmother's house and tell them you've changed your mind!"

". . .but I haven't."

"Well, you have to grow a backbone sometime, and this will help with that," Darcie said, smacking her desk. "Give me one good reason why you shouldn't."

Elise didn't have a response. Guilt twisted in the pit of her stomach. She knew that going was the right thing to do, even if she didn't have a plan. Her cousins wanted to go home, and if she was the only one who could help them out, then she should at least try.

"You're right."

"Great!" Darcie exclaimed. "We'll pack and head out after school."

"We?"

"You're not going without me! I'm not going to miss this."

"We don't have a way to get there," Elise reminded her. "Neither of us have a car."

"I know someone who will give us a ride," she said. "Tell your mom you want to have a sleepover at my house."

"Darcie, I'm not taking a group of people on this trip with me. My own mother wouldn't tell me this secret and I'm part of the family."

Darcie was too busy texting to hear any more arguments.

"Just trust me. Go home and pack. And charge your phone!" she fussed.

Why did her friend have to be so confident? Elise knew she needed to stop her pity party and 'grow a backbone', but sometimes Darcie's meddling was downright obnoxious.

When the final bell rang that afternoon, Elise didn't even have time to feel sentimental about high school ending. Her head was filled with too many questions about what she was going to do, and how she would get away with it.

CHAPTER 3

It was easy to get her mother's permission to stay at Darcie's for the night, but Elise was finding it harder to stomach the guilt of lying.

This would all be so much easier if I just had a car, she thought as Ruby backed out of the Pickard's driveway after dropping her off. Elise threw her bag over her shoulder and took in the sight of the familiar yellow two-story house ahead. She thought back to all the fun pool parties they'd had here over the last couple of years. She smiled as she remembered the late-night candy headaches, laughter, and mindless internet videos.

Her heart sank when she realized they probably wouldn't have too many more sleepovers once college started.

Darcie had just finished her cosmetology course. Elise remembered how nervous Darcie had been leading up to her state boards. Her friend would be applying for jobs soon, and that would take up most of her time. Everything seemed to be moving so fast.

Darcie walked outside to meet her while scrolling through her text messages.

"Okay, it's all set up," Darcie said after she replied to one. "Mitch will be here in about ten minutes."

"Mitch?" Elise asked. "Mitch who?"

"Mitchell Peterson. You know, the red-head in my history class?"

"Darcie! *Gavin's* best friend? Are you seriously trying to start something? I told you not to!"

"Relax, I'm not meddling. He owes me a favor."

"Oh really?" Elise asked, crossing her arms. "What kind of favor?"

"I helped him out last month. He showed up right before prom with a botched haircut his mom had given him." She chuckled. "He said he'd do *anything* if I helped him out on such short notice."

They walked into the house and found Darcie's mom sitting with her feet propped up enjoying a glass of wine.

"You girls having fun?" she asked with a smile.

"Yep. Are you glad the school year is over, too?" Elise asked.

"Yes. I love teaching kindergarten, but I need the break. My Littles have a lot more energy than I do!"

Darcie's parents were so much fun, and their house always had some kind of noise and excitement going on. Elise loved coming over whenever possible.

"We're going out for pizza and a movie. Mitch is coming to pick us up. He's the one who came over for a haircut that one night," said Darcie. Once they had Mrs. Pickard's permission, they hurried upstairs. "An hour drive there, an hour or two at the house, and then back. That story should keep us covered."

"I don't like lying to everyone."

"I don't either. I never lie, but we're doing this to help your family."

Elise knew her friend had a good point, but it didn't stop the shame from settling in.

"So, what are you going to tell your grandma?" Darcie asked as she checked her phone.

Elise plopped down onto the bed.

"I've been going through all kinds of scenarios in my head," she admitted. "I just can't forget the looks on my cousins' faces. . ."

"They must be so scared," Darcie said.

Elise pulled her grandmother's diary out of her bag.

"This is what I was telling you about. It's how they want me to travel. I had given it back, but I found it in my bag when Mom and I got home. I think my nana snuck it in there to make me reconsider. I just don't know what they want me to get from this. It starts when she met my grandfather while she worked as a waitress. He came here from Haighdlen, they fell in love, and then they just went back to rule the kingdom, I guess. Most of the entries are just boring old recaps of trips and birthdays."

"You can just ask her when we get there. Bring it with you." Darcie's face lit up as she received a text message. "Great! Mitch is here. Let's go!"

***

As they walked outside, Elise saw a red car jerk to a stop in the driveway. Hard rock music blared from inside. The window lowered, and Mitch waved them over.

Mitchell Peterson was long-limbed and almost too tall for the car he was driving. His short red hair was a lighter shade than Elise's. He was pale with his fair share of acne. His hazel eyes twinkled as he lowered his sunglasses to greet them.

"Heard you ladies needed a ride."

"Give it a rest, Mitch," Darcie said as she called shotgun.

"Darcie, we barely know him." Elise considered her words. "Okay, *I* barely know him."

"Look, Elise, I get you're nervous, but it's fine!" her friend assured her. "Live a little! We need a car; he has a car. We can trust him, and I don't want to waste this favor. Get in!"

Elise placed her hand on the handle but didn't open the door right away. Whispering a quick prayer, she opened the door and climbed into the backseat.

Mitch blasted the music again as he glanced over his shoulder to back out of the driveway. He avoided her gaze. Was he just as uncomfortable about this as she was?

About five minutes had passed when she noticed that he still hadn't gotten onto the highway. Instead, they pulled into another residential neighborhood. Elise leaned forward.

"Where are we going?"

Mitch shrugged.

"Oh, I told Gavin he could tag along if he wanted to. He was bored, and so I invited him."

"You what!"

Darcie turned in her seat and grinned without making eye contact. "Okay, *now* I'm meddling. I just figured Mitch could use someone to talk to and hang out with. It's not like it's a long road trip. They can wait outside while we run up and talk to your family."

Heat rushed to Elise's cheeks as the car slowed down in front of a gray one-story house.

I can't believe I'm actually looking at where he lives. It looks perfect. . .like him. What am I going to say?

She was pulled out of her wandering thoughts by the sound of the front door slamming.

"I said I got it!" Gavin yelled over his shoulder as he tossed his hands in the air. If someone in the house said anything else, he ignored them as he approached the car.

She had never seen him worked up like this before.

I wonder what made him so mad.

"Looks like his dad is giving him crap again," Mitch said. "He's always on Gavin to make something of himself. It really drives him crazy. Don't say anything," he said as Gavin opened the back door and sat down next to Elise without a word.

She pulled out the diary and wondered what was going on inside his mind. She wished she were braver and could tell him how she could relate to having a difficult parent. She knew how it felt to be hassled all the time and never heard or understood. She wanted to take away that line on his forehead. Elise avoided staring by leafing through the pages on her lap.

The silence was only broken twice when Mitch entered her grandmother's address into his GPS and when Gavin laughed out loud to a text he received.

He was obviously talking to someone who could put two words together around him.

Maybe he has a girlfriend. Why wouldn't he have a girlfriend?

Elise tried imagining what it might be like to date Gavin Striess, but she couldn't see what she had to offer him that was exciting. He always seemed so outgoing at school. She had overheard him once talking to his friends about how he played guitar in his garage. She didn't really have any hobbies that stuck out like that and would come across as boring compared to whoever he was texting.

Don't start the pity party again, Elise. You're going to annoy people. Suck it up and focus on why you're here. Think about your family.

She put all of her energy into the diary and came across an entry that piqued her interest.

April 26,1961

Dear Diary,
That boy keeps coming into the diner. I wish I was braver and could ask him what he's doing here. Maybe if I looked like the women he's been meeting it would be easier. They're so beautiful and confident.

He has a smile that makes me weak in the knees. Even though we've never spoken more than the usual greetings, I find myself fantasizing what it would be like to be with him. There's just something that draws me in.

I definitely feel sorry for him though. He's obviously looking for something and always comes back to the diner alone after his dates.

There was no way her grandmother had ever felt like this. The Joranna she met seemed so sure of herself. It was hard to imagine there was ever a time where her grandmother felt so small and helpless.

There's hope for me then. Maybe I can help them after all. Maybe I'm not making a mistake coming back.

"We're here!" Mitch announced, pulling Elise out of her thoughts.

The same winding driveway led them to the house, which looked less haunted in the early evening hours.

"We'll just be a minute," Darcie said as she invited herself. "You guys just hang here."

The walk to the front door seemed longer this time, and each step seemed to echo in Elise's ears. She took a steadying breath and calmed her nerves before knocking.

CHAPTER 4

Elise had been so preoccupied with how she was getting to her grandmother's house, that she hadn't thought of what to say once she got there.

Luckily, she was saved any humiliation when Joseph remembered her and allowed both girls to enter the house. He bowed and left to announce their arrival.

"This is so cool!" Darcie took in the foyer. "Your life literally became a fairy tale overnight."

"I still don't know what I'm going to say," Elise said.

"Relax. You're not time traveling or anything right now. You're just coming to tell them you changed your mind. You'll have plenty of time to make a plan and catch up on everything later."

Darcie's advice made her feel better.

"I should've just called Ian. It would've been easier."

"Yeah, but then I wouldn't have gotten to tag along and see it for myself," Darcie teased. "It's better that you're doing it in person anyway."

Elise doubted that as her grandmother came into view and greeted them.

"It's so good to see you again so soon! I was afraid we had scared you off."

"I think you did at first." Elise then introduced Darcie and the two ladies exchanged pleasantries. "So, Nana, I've been doing some thinking, and I really think I'd like to help after all if I can. I also brought this back."

She handed her grandmother the diary.

"Thank you," Joranna said. "I'm so glad you came. Now it'll give Ian and Morgan a chance to be involved before they go home tomorrow."

"Where is everyone?" Elise asked.

"Most of them went into the living room after dinner. Are you hungry? I can have plates made for you two."

"No, thanks. We're not staying long. I just wanted to tell you I changed my mind and to make a game plan."

"We had a friend drive us here, and he's waiting outside," Darcie said.

Joranna's cheerfulness dwindled.

"Elise. . .Does Ruby know you're here?"

The silence that followed answered her question. Joranna nodded and walked towards the telephone on a nearby table.

"Please don't call her!" Elise begged. "I figured I'd plan everything for now and come back later when I have more time. I'm staying at Darcie's like I told her, so I *technically* haven't lied."

Joranna didn't seem convinced.

"I just want to do this before I convince myself I'm crazy for believing any of it." She bit her lip and hoped she had made her case.

Joranna's gaze softened.

"As a mother, I can't condone this. However, we are running out of time, and I agree with Ian that you are the perfect one to go."

Clearly, her grandmother didn't know about her anxious nature.

Elise was startled by an unexpected knock at the door.

Joranna didn't wait for Joseph to answer and greeted Gavin and Mitch on the other side.

"Hey," Mitch said, "We're sorry to interrupt, but could we use your bathroom before heading back?"

Elise introduced them, and Joranna stepped aside to let Mitch go first. She directed him down the hall before turning back to Gavin.

"It was so nice of you to drive Elise here."

"It's Mitch's car." Gavin shrugged. "I'm just hanging out."

"I see." Joranna's eyes flickered between him and Elise.

"We'll just be a minute," he said.

***

Somehow a minute turned into an hour.

Elise fidgeted on the loveseat between Joranna and Darcie. All four of them were provided dinner after all, and the rest of the family had made their way down when they heard there were visitors.

Elise didn't have to worry about entertaining Mitch and Gavin, who had now made themselves comfortable on the floor with Sarah's boys, Madelyn and the twins. The adults shared the couch and various chairs.

Joranna had purchased a PlayStation system at some point to help entertain the children, but only Ian and Morgan's twins had ever seen one before. Mitch and Gavin were playing and teaching Paul, Eric and Madelyn about it. Joranna joked that she had no idea what it was she bought and hoped that the random games she picked up were good enough.

"That's weird you've never seen one of these before," Gavin said to Elise's cousins, not taking his eyes off the racing game they were playing. Mitch agreed and both boys grumbled under their breaths as their characters were attacked.

"We. . .are just stern about the types of games the children play," Sarah said.

The boys seemed to take this as a reasonable excuse and passed the controllers to Paul and Madelyn for the next race. The twins whined about wanting turns and were promised the next game.

Joranna motioned for Elise and the other adults to join her in the kitchen while the children were distracted. Elise cast a wary look over her shoulder, but Darcie waved her onward.

***

Once inside the eat-in kitchen, Elise took a seat at the table and waited for her uncles and aunts to enter.

"I'll start," Joranna said. "We're so thankful that you've decided to go, and we know we are throwing you blindly into this. Do you have any questions for us?"

Elise looked at all of their expectant faces and felt three inches tall. *Run! Head for the car. You could probably make it!*

She didn't know where to begin.

"I just have no idea what I'm doing, and I don't know why my mom is so against all of this."

"Ruby has always felt. . .left out," Joranna said. "As much as we've told her she belongs, she's doesn't believe us. Even when she found out she was expecting you, she tried to run away instead of telling us."

"But why?"

Joranna shrugged. "It's just her way. If she would've just come forward without trying to hide it or leaving, we could've shown her that a lot sooner."

"What am I supposed to do once you send me back? I feel like I should have a million questions, and I want to help, but I'm not sure where to start."

"We'll send you to the beginning. Find me," Joranna said. "The rest should play out as needed, and the diary will keep you on track as you learn more. Make sure Derek and I make it to Haighdlen and take you with us."

"Why would you do that?" Elise asked. "You won't know me. Why would you take a stranger?"

"Let's just hope we trust our instincts and go with it," Joranna admitted. "I know it's a stretch, but it'll be the only way to get through the portal and barriers around the castle."

"Try and learn everything you can about Rona as well," Richard grumbled, speaking for the first time since Elise had arrived. He looked better than he had during her last visit but still seemed withdrawn. "Find out what you can about any weaknesses she has and use them to your advantage without giving too much away."

"And be on the lookout for any spies," Sarah added.

"Spies?"

"Yes," Ian agreed, "A lot of Rona's power comes from her spies, and father was always looking for one. If you could find proof of a spy back then, we could probably find her faster."

The pressure was building inside Elise's head. *Don't they know I'm just a kid? This is a serious political mission that I have no business being a part of. I should've followed my fear and stayed home.*

"You've got this," Ian said, and his wife nodded in agreement. "You're strong, Elise. The Laurille family has always been strong. Believe in yourself."

Clearly, they don't know me. They're putting their futures in the hands of a spineless coward. Can't they sense that?

"So. . .if I get lucky enough to get to Haighdlen, what do I do?"

"Stay as close to the castle as you can," Richard said. "There won't be a reason to venture too far off at first. If such a spy existed then, they would want to stay local and close enough to learn any valuable information from the family."

"I say we leave it at that for now. She has her instructions," Joranna said. "Help us find the spy and keep Ruby from leaving when the time comes. The rest can wait until later."

Elise's mouth grew dry, and she found herself regretting not calling first. She excused herself to use the bathroom.

Splashing cool water on her face, she took a steadying breath and regarded herself in the mirror.

Why does it have to be me?

When she came out, she heard everyone back in the living room and was surprised to find her grandmother leafing through the diary again.

"So, I guess we should set a date for when we're doing this," Elise said.

"Oh, there's no need to do that." Joranna smiled and turned to a page near the beginning of the book.

Elise didn't hide her confusion.

"Well, you don't think we'd let you run off once we finally got you here, did you?" Sarah asked.

The blood drained from Elise's face as understanding sank in.

"Wait a minute!" Darcie jumped up from the couch. "She's going *now*?"

"Going where?" Mitch asked.

"We can't risk waiting for the perfect moment," Gwen said. "It's best if you start now."

"That wasn't part of the plan!" Elise spluttered.

"Where is she going?"

Mitch was ignored again.

"This is the opportune moment," Morgan said. "Trust us."

Joranna wrapped her arm around Elise and squeezed. "Besides, you won't be alone, so I have faith this will all work out."

Richard, Ian, and Sarah held out their hands as the diary was placed at their feet. Joranna took a step back with Gwen and Morgan.

"Good luck to you all, and thank you again," said Joranna.

You all?

Elise was unable to argue as she began to feel lightheaded. Everything started to spin, her vision clouded, and she felt like she was choking. She tried calling out for help, but the last thing she saw before everything went black was her grandmother blowing her a kiss.

CHAPTER 5

Elise awoke on the ground to discover every joint ached. She lifted her arm to block the sunlight and struggled to stand.

"Oh good! She's up!"

Darcie? That can't be right.

Elise's panic spiked when she realized she wasn't alone. Darcie really *was* with her. . .along with Mitch and Gavin!

Gavin stomped over to close the distance between them.

"Do you want to tell us what's going on here? Where are we?"

"This wasn't meant to happen." She looked around and saw that they were in some sort of alleyway in the middle of the day. "It was just supposed to be me going."

"Going *where*?" Mitch demanded.

"What wasn't supposed to happen?" Gavin asked. "You're not making sense!"

"It's a long story," she said. *How am I ever going to start telling them the truth?*

"That apparently concerns us," he argued. "How is this even possible?"

"My family is. . . different." When Elise realized he was waiting for more, she began pacing and wiped her hands on her jeans. "They need me to help fix something."

"In an *alley*?" Mitch exclaimed. "Did they want you murdered along the way? This makes no sense. How do we get back?"

"That's just it," Elise said. "I don't know. It was just supposed to be me going on a trip. Not everyone else."

"Guys, leave her alone," Darcie snapped. "Can't you see she's just as confused as we are?"

Gavin snarled in response.

"But it's her fault we're even here! There has to be more she's not telling us. Just tell us, Lisa!"

Elise didn't like his tone and felt her own temper flare up.

"First of all, my name is Elise. Not Lisa. *Elise*. Second of all, I'm just as lost as you. I was sent on this trip to help save my family from some sorceress who's trying to take over their kingdom."

"Kingdom?" both boys yelled.

Crap. Why did I let that slip out?

Darcie sighed.

"You might as well tell them everything, Elise."

They deserved the truth, but she didn't know how they were going to take it. Lying was useless at this point, so she took a deep breath.

Here goes nothing.

"The family staying at my nana's house is from another land called Haighdlen. I don't know much about it, but they ruled there. All of Nana's kids have some kind of magic except for my mom, which is why she never told me about it." She paused to gauge their reactions. When no one spoke, she continued, "But now it seems like this evil witch, Rona, has taken over, and a lot of people are getting killed. They want me to go back in time to find Rona's spy and save the family."

Elise knew it was heavy information to process, but at that moment, she would've given anything for one of them to speak. Only Darcie seemed convinced while the boys had yet to blink or move.

"Dude, we should've just stayed in the car," Mitch muttered.

"I know you don't believe any of this." Elise frowned. "I'm not asking for anything. You guys weren't supposed to be here, but for some reason my nana sent you back with me."

"Back where?" Gavin asked.

He had a good point.

How far did we go back?

Elise could make out the sounds of distant car horns and chatter from a nearby city. The air was damp, and the only movement came from a few pigeons walking around a dumpster a few feet away.

Elise perked up and rushed over to throw the dumpster lid open. She held her breath and rummaged around until she found what she was looking for. She pulled out an old newspaper and scanned its contents.

"We're really at the beginning of Nana's diary!" she said, wiping sludge off her hands. She realized at that moment that the diary hadn't traveled with them but continued her explanation. "She had no family and worked as a waitress at a diner in the city. It's where my grandfather met her. See for yourself."

She smoothed out the pages and pointed to the date printed at the top.

June 20, 1961.

"No way," Mitch said as he pulled out his cell phone to check the calendar. He tapped angrily at the screen, but the device wouldn't turn on.

Gavin huffed.

"So, what're we supposed to do?"

"Nana said to find her and make sure that she and my grandfather take us with them to Haighdlen."

"And let me guess," Darcie said, "We're not allowed to say who we are or what we're doing?" Elise nodded. "Perfect."

"Do you believe any of this?" Elise heard Mitch whisper to Gavin as they started walking towards the noises ahead.

"Not at all."

Gavin must have thought she was some kind of freak show. So much for staying invisible and watching him from a distance.

She prayed they would find Joranna and prove that this was real. Perhaps she wanted to prove it more to herself.

The cars and bicycles that passed them, as well as the fashions of the nearby pedestrians, were a definite indication that they were in the 1960s.

"This place looks like an old movie set," Gavin said. "Are you sure we're not just on some prank show?"

"There it is!" Darcie pointed to a diner across the busy intersection. "Come on. Let's go!"

***

The diner was full with the lunch hour crowd. Several teenagers were grouped around the barstools, and Elise could just make out the sound of a jukebox playing over the excitable chatter of patrons.

The four fought their way to the only empty booth in the back and sat down.

"So, why are we sitting?" Gavin asked. "We don't even know if this is the right diner."

"It's the only one around, and this is where that diary decided to drop us off," Elise reasoned.

"You might not want to say that too loudly." Mitch took his phone out. He checked to make sure no one was watching before he tried turning it on again. Fed up with it, he tossed the device by his side only for it to land on something soft. He looked down and pulled a suit jacket off of the bench seat. "What's this?"

"Excuse me, I believe that's mine," said a man approaching their booth. "I'm afraid I was saving this seat."

Elise and the others muttered quick apologies and stood to leave. They looked around for another empty table, but when they found none, the gentleman sighed and checked the clock before allowing them to stay.

Once they had scooted back in, he studied their appearances, and Elise half expected him to leave out of embarrassment.

"Thank you," she said. "Are you sure?"

"Yes, it's fine," said the man, putting on his jacket.

A waitress came by to drop off the man's coffee and take their orders.

All four realized they didn't have cash between them and ordered water.

Lifting the coffee cup to his mouth, the man offered to get them something to eat. They declined out of politeness until he insisted. The group muttered their thanks before ordering and returning their menus to the waitress.

"I'm meeting my fiancée here," he announced to break the silence, "but it doesn't look like she will be ready for quite some time." He leaned forward and extended his hand. "I'm Derek. Derek Laurille."

Elise's voice caught in her throat, and all she could do was stare at the grandfather she had never met. Darcie mouthed to the boys who Derek was. Elise wished she hadn't, because now they just stared at him like he was an alien from outer space.

His brows furrowed as he cleared his throat. "I'm sorry. I'm afraid I'm new to this country. Is this not how you greet strangers here?"

Elise nodded and offered her hand. She kicked the others under the table to do the same, and they introduced themselves one by one.

Derek was handsome with soft brown hair, broad shoulders, captivating blue eyes and a strong jaw. He spoke properly and had an inviting smile. He looked to be in his early twenties, and Elise was not at all surprised that this man had stolen her grandmother's heart.

Talk about your Prince Charming.

"Everyone is staring at us," Gavin muttered through gritted teeth.

Sure enough, Elise could see others sharing looks towards them and whispering.

She also noticed that there was a lack of. . .diversity in the occupants of the diner. She chanced a glance out of the window and saw the horrifying divisive signs that she had only seen in her textbooks. It made her stomach turn.

"Well, think about *when* we are," Darcie whispered, "1961. . . Let's just say not everyone was. . . *is*, comfortable with people's differences yet." She caught one man looking at her shorts and scooted further into the booth.

"That is a strange concept here." Derek frowned. "Where I am from, people's color and appearances aren't a judgmental matter."

"Where are you from?" Gavin asked, but Derek didn't seem to hear him as he sipped his coffee.

Darcie cleared her throat and crossed her arms on the table. "So. . . you have a fiancée? That's great! Congratulations."

"Thank you," he said. His expression grew wary when he caught the boys staring again.

"So, when is the wedding?" Elise asked.

"We don't have everything settled just yet. We are leaving shortly for my parents' home so that they can meet her."

"Meeting the parents, huh?" Mitch smiled. "Always awkward. Am I right?"

"Agreed." Derek chuckled. "Her parents are deceased, but mine will certainly be intimidating to her. I hope she doesn't change her mind."

"I think you'll be fine," Darcie said as she waved away his comment.

The food was delivered soon after, and the entire table ate in silence.

"Forgive me," Derek said after a few minutes, dabbing his mouth with a napkin, "but I cannot help but sense you are not from around here either."

"We. . . are traveling from. . .out of town. We just got here," Elise said. The others nodded in agreement.

"You're traveling with no luggage and no money?" The flatness of his tone expressed his disbelief.

"We travel light." Mitch shrugged. "We're drifters."

If Elise could have smacked him, she would've. She was thankful for his willingness to play along, but he wasn't helping. And why hadn't Gavin said anything? He was just sitting across from her and Derek staring like an idiot.

Say something!

"Well, let us hope my Joranna travels lightly," he joked. "It will not be a quick and easy trip home."

"Where is that?" Elise asked, hoping she could get more out of him.

"It is a long way away," he said, unwilling to give more explanation than that. "She will be provided with everything she needs there." He checked his pocket watch. "We should be leaving shortly if we are going to prepare for the engagement party in time." He lifted his chin as he searched the diner. "There she is."

His eyes lit up when he saw her coming their way. He stood as she arrived at the table and pecked her on the cheek.

Her eyes fell to the four of them and lingered on Elise.

"I'm sorry I ran late," she said. "They needed help to finish up some orders. What's all this?"

She looked to be about seventeen or eighteen years old, and her hair was pulled back into a thick red ponytail.

Gosh, she looks like Mom.

"Quirky travelers. . .like myself," Derek said with a crooked smile.

"I don't believe we've met. Hi, I'm Joranna."

Skeptical about their presence, she reacted the same way as Derek had about their clothes.

"Joranna, darling, this is Darcie. . .Gavin. . .Mitch, is it? And this is Elise."

Once again, Joranna kept staring at Elise with an odd expression on her face. She shook her head to clear her thoughts.

"I'm sorry," she said to Elise, "but you just look so familiar to me. Have we met before?"

"No, I don't think so."

"You remind me of someone. I'll think of it eventually." Joranna looked up at Derek. "I'm sorry you had to wait so long. My suitcase is just in the back. I'll meet you around there. It was nice to meet you all."

She excused herself and pecked Derek on the cheek before heading through the kitchen door again.

Darcie smiled.

"She's very pretty."

"Yes, she is." Derek watched her retreating figure. He turned back to the table and paid the bill. "Well, it was lovely to meet you all. I wish you the best."

He nodded and left the diner to meet Joranna around the back.

Elise panicked.

This is the only chance I have to get to Haighdlen. How are we going to get Derek and Joranna to agree to take us?

"Guys, we have to follow him," she said. "We'll be stuck here if we don't go."

"How do you plan on doing that?" Gavin asked. "He already thinks we're weird. I don't see him letting us stick around."

Her heart pounded in her ears, and she almost tripped racing around the corner where she saw her grandparents meeting.

"Excuse me!" she called as she approached them, "Um. . .I know this is kind of sudden and strange, but. . .we'd love to come with you. It's like you said, Joranna. It feels like you know us, right?"

She held her breath.

"I'm afraid that isn't possible," Derek explained. "The trip is simply too—"

Elise lunged herself forward and cut him off.

"We don't care how far it is! We can carry things or do whatever you need." She looked around for any more bags but was surprised to see that Joranna had only brought one.

For once in her life, she didn't care about making a scene or embarrassing herself. She *had* to go with them, or all of this would be for nothing.

"Please take us with you!"

Please change your mind. Please take us with you. Please.

He opened his mouth to decline again but suddenly stopped. Elise held her breath and continued to plead with her eyes. He hadn't given her another direct no for an answer.

He seemed to be struggling and looked between them and Joranna. Several moments passed like this. Elise became troubled by thoughts of what would happen if they were stranded there. Numbness spread down her arms and legs, and she concentrated on Derek's face. It looked as if he wanted to say no, and she prepared herself for it, but finally he sighed in defeat.

"Perhaps we should take them with us."

His fiancée's eyes widened, and she whispered in his ear.

"We may not know them, but they need our help." Joranna spoke inaudibly again. "There will be safety traveling in numbers as well. We can let them come to the party and then see to it that they head back home unaware of anything."

Unaware of anything? What did that mean?

"You're too trusting," Joranna said with a scowl. "It's taken weeks for you to let *me* see your home and tell me everything, and yet you're just going to invite these strangers after *five minutes*?"

"I can't explain it," Derek said, puzzled by his decision as well. "I just. . .we can trust them, Joranna. I just have this feeling."

Elise's chin trembled, and her brows arched in hope, until Joranna agreed against her will to go along with Derek's decision.

Out of the two, Elise didn't expect that it would be her grandmother who would have an issue with them.

Thanking them, Elise let out a massive sigh of relief as she and the others followed Derek and Joranna towards the edge of town.

We did it! I don't know how, but we did!

As fear of the unknown slowly replaced her initial excitement, she did her best to quell the approaching nausea. The feeling was coming back to her other limbs, and she took comfort in the fact that they were at least heading in the right direction.

Elise only wished now that she had read the diary a little further to know exactly where they were headed.

CHAPTER 6

Very little was spoken over the next half hour, and Elise knew it was due to their presence.

She kept replaying Derek's reaction in her head. It was as if he had said yes against his will, but she couldn't figure out why he had agreed so suddenly.

And then there was his other comment. . .making them unaware of what would happen.

What did he mean?

The group slowed as Derek paused to adjust his grip on Joranna's suitcase. He reached with his free hand to take hers and continued walking.

Elise chanced a glance towards Gavin, but when their eyes met, she returned her gaze to the ground.

She wondered what was going through her friends' heads about all of this. Especially Mitch and Gavin. They had only signed up to give her and Darcie a ride, and yet now were following perfect strangers into an unknown land without a plan of getting home. She was surprised she was the only anxious one, or perhaps she was just the only one who allowed it to show.

"Here we are," Derek announced as they entered a small batch of trees. He chose one in particular that seemed to be off by itself and turned to face them. "This is the last opportunity you will all have to change your minds," he warned, "including you, Joranna."

"No, I'm ready." Joranna's voice caught in her throat as her nerves betrayed her.

When no one else objected, Derek smiled and took his fiancée's hand once more. He set the suitcase down and placed his palm against the rough bark.

Blue light began to trace Derek's fingers. Elise stared in disbelief as the glow spread beyond his hand. In a brilliant flash, the bark darkened and revealed an entrance into the tree.

"We're not going *into* that, are we?" Mitch asked.

"Looks like they are," Gavin said as Derek and Joranna stepped through.

Elise hesitated by the entrance and hoped one of the others would go first.

Why didn't I just listen to my mom and stay away? Now it's too late to go back, and the only way we're ever getting home is to follow them.

Before her grandparents could get too far ahead, she stepped down into the underground tunnel.

She relied on the sound of Joranna's breathing since everything was pitch black in front of her. The uneven earth was soft under her shoes and made it even more difficult to walk. She put out her arms to keep her balance. Moist soil coated her palms, and the air smelled heavily of fresh grass and rain.

Elise wiped the sweat from her face and wondered how much of the dirt had been smudged on her skin or fallen into her hair. She could hear the other three struggling behind her and felt a little less embarrassed when Mitch tripped for the third time.

"We're almost there," Derek said. He too sounded winded.

Elise could feel the ground inclining under her feet. Her thighs grew heavy under the strain, and she made a mental note of how out of shape she was.

The tunnel continued narrowing until she felt her arms graze the sides.

Everyone waited in silent anticipation as Derek instructed them to stop.

A spec of sunlight broke through the soil above them, and Derek placed his hand over it. The familiar blue light surrounded his hand, and another door was crafted.

Derek lifted himself out and turned back to help Joranna.

Elise was able to halfway hoist herself up before Derek helped her. She turned and saw that they had come out of a similar tree and now stood at the top of a steep hill. The others emerged one by one, and everyone took a moment to catch their breaths.

"I wanted you to see it from the best view," Derek told Joranna as he intertwined their fingers and kissed her hand. "Welcome to Haighdlen."

Vast forests covered the land before them like an emerald blanket that stretched as far as Elise could see.

Haighdlen seemed to come alive before them. Various birds sang and swooped in and out of the treetops, and the air was sweet and fragrant. A distant waterfall poured into the winding river below, and just off to the distant left, Elise could see a picturesque castle.

The midday sunlight glistened off its ivory towers, and the royal flags proudly waved against the peaceful blue sky.

Not far from the castle grounds, Elise could see rich farmland and what appeared to be a village or town.

"What are those?" Darcie asked, breaking Elise out of her trance.

Small fireflies were zipping about, chasing each other in a way that Elise had never seen bugs behave.

"Fairies," Derek said. "They're best left alone."

"I thought they were friendly and did nice stuff like grant wishes," Darcie said.

"Some do, but more often than not they're very mischievous. Best to leave them be."

"And *all* of this. . ." Joranna's voice trailed off, "is yours?"

"*Ours*," Derek corrected as he squeezed her hand. "If you'll have me."

Elise's heart swelled at the sight of them. She could only hope for a romance half as perfect as theirs one day.

Joranna blew out a long breath and avoided anyone's gaze until Derek suggested they continue on. He lifted the suitcase and led them down the hill.

***

"So, what else do you have living in this crazy place?" Mitch asked once they had reached the bottom and found the forest path.

Elise couldn't tell if Mitch actually believed where he was or if he was just trying to humor them.

"There are all different sorts of creatures in our world," Derek replied. "Fairies. . . mermaids—"

"*Actual* mermaids?" Joranna perked up at the idea and stopped. "Could we see them? Please?"

Derek cleared his throat and shrugged. "I can understand the appeal, and they live just off this path, but they are very private creatures."

"That's code for no," Gavin joked as he and Mitch started snickering and suggesting Joranna better get used to hearing that.

"Ignore them," Darcie whispered to Elise, picking up on her mood. "You have to lighten up, Elise. Whether they believe this or not, they're here. Let them figure it out for themselves."

Darcie's right. I should just ignore Gavin and keep to my mission.

"I can try to arrange a meeting, but I wouldn't expect too much hospitality," Derek warned as they entered a quiet clearing near a rather large lake.

Elise shivered involuntarily as they left the forest's protective covering.

Derek took a few steps forward before turning to stop them.

"It's best to keep your distance here," he said. "This is legally their territory."

"Are they coming up already?" Gavin asked.

"You have to call them," Derek explained. "They don't come up much during the day. They prefer to be left alone unless you're acquainted with them."

He bent to lower his hand into the water and stirred until enough ripples were created to cross almost the entire surface.

Everyone was quiet. Elise half expected for the ground to shake, or have the water burst out and drench them all. She tried squinting her eyes to see the other side.

The only response came when they saw the top of a woman's head emerge to the surface.

She kept the lower part of her face hidden, and her jet-black hair floated like snakes around her. She met each of their eyes before settling on Derek with a calculative stare. Not a word was spoken as she dipped below the water again and all signs of life were nonexistent.

"Stay calm," Derek warned as he shielded them with his arms. "No sudden movements."

Before anyone could question him, the water began to ripple, and they all took an involuntary step back.

"I don't understand," Darcie said. "Isn't *anything* gentle around here?"

Her question went unanswered as a dozen or so heads came out of the water.

Their skin colors and features seemed to spread across ethnicities.

Elise located the one who had come up alone and got a good look at her. Her soaked black hair rested down her back and covered her breasts. She rose until the water level rested at her waist, and Elise could see that her tail was a continuation of her skin, only covered in flesh-colored scales. She was truly an exotic creature to behold.

"I wish to speak to Eugena," Derek announced with a bow.

That name sparked a memory, and Elise was reminded of her grandmother's words during her first visit just days earlier.

It was given to me by Eugena, the Mermaid Queen.

"I'm afraid Queen Eugena is not available for simple calls," a deep and stern voice called out from their left.

They all turned towards the voice that belonged to a large merman. His skin was dark brown, and his head was shaved. His face sported a thin goatee and bright green eyes. He was very muscular and adorned with a shield across his chest. In his hands he gripped a spear, and Elise could sense she wasn't the only one intimidated by his appearance.

"I beg your pardon," Derek said, "I am Derek Laurille, the Crown Prince of Haighdlen. My parents accompanied me during my previous visits. I only wished to—"

"To show us off to your visitors?" he snarled. "To make a mockery of our kind? You tread too closely, young prince," he threatened. "Should we consider this a breach of the contract?"

"No! No!" Derek answered, ushering them all further away back towards the trees. "Forgive the intrusion. It will not happen again without a proper invitation."

"See that it doesn't," the merman growled, pointing his spear in their direction. "Lanai," he called over his shoulder to the mermaid Elise had admired before, "escort everyone back now."

He waited until the merpeople were below the surface before easing back under the water himself.

"I'm sorry," Joranna apologized when the water was still again. "I shouldn't have asked. You tried to warn me."

"No, no, the fault is mine," Derek confessed. "I shouldn't have changed my mind. We should've kept walking."

"What is their problem?" Gavin asked. "We didn't even do anything."

"To be honest, their tribe has been threatened by my ancestors before. It goes back to a time when the royal family wasn't so accepting of different kingdoms within their own. They wanted to rule everything that lived, and so war inevitably broke out. I'm sure you're wondering how they can pose a threat from under water, but they too have magic of their own. My father was the first to try and make peace with them."

They returned to the forest path.

"What contract was he talking about?" Joranna asked.

"The war wasn't an ongoing slaughter, but it took many years before a treaty could be made that both kingdoms agreed on. Only the royal family is welcome near their land, but if anyone else should cross their path or try to drink from their water, they consider it a threat. That wasn't even all of them. To tell you the truth, if I hadn't been with you. . ."

Derek didn't need to finish his sentence for them all to understand. Elise suspected that if the boys didn't believe in anything before, they did now.

"They were so beautiful though," Elise said. "Well. . .I guess we can skip any other creatures then."

"I know it's not all that you had imagined," Derek said, more so to Joranna. "But don't judge all of Haighdlen on the merpeople. They're only hostile because our people never gave them any reason to be otherwise. It has always been a sensitive relationship."

"So, are they in all the waters here?" Mitch asked. "I don't want to get too close to any of them."

"No, just a couple of the lakes. As you get closer to other kingdoms, however, you'll find tribes that aren't so willing to make peace."

"And those back there *are*?" Gavin asked in disbelief.

"That was Lake Laulie," Derek said. "Eugena was very hesitant to form any alliance and was advised by her counsel not to, but she gave us the benefit of a doubt. Other tribes aren't so forgiving."

He used the suitcase to push away some longer branches that blocked their path.

"Lake Mirage, for example, has its name for a reason. Its mermaids often kill humans who come near it on sight. They tempt the intruder with their desires, and it's almost impossible to escape before they torture you."

"I wouldn't mind being tortured if they look anything like those other mermaids." Mitch smiled. "Am I right, Gav?"

The boys chuckled and joked for the next several minutes.

"I'd like to show you the town before we make it to the castle," Derek said to Joranna. "I want to show you off to the world."

"Derek, I don't look good enough to be presented or shown off," Joranna whispered. "My uniform is covered in food, there's dirt in my hair and on my face. . .they'll think you've lost your mind. I'd like to freshen up."

"I wouldn't recommend any of the water here," Gavin teased.

"And shouldn't you have guards?" Joranna asked. "It can't be safe for a prince to wander around without protection."

"Now you're sounding like my parents." He chuckled and kissed her forehead. "They wanted to send an entire fleet to get you, but I insisted against it. We're perfectly safe, and we can avoid the town for now if you want to. Besides, most people will see you tomorrow night at the ball. There will be guards there. I just didn't want to scare you off with a bunch of royal protocol."

"Next time. . .maybe bring the guards?" Joranna suggested.

"As you wish." Derek bowed his head with a grin.

Elise didn't care for Derek's trusting disposition, but right now it was the only reason she and her friends had made it this far.

"So, what happens next?" Darcie asked.

"I'll arrange for the rest of you to stay with us tonight, and you'll be properly fitted with more appropriate attire."

"Are you sure that's such a good idea?" Joranna glanced over her shoulder at Elise. "Should we *all* be showing up so casually?"

Heat rushed to Elise's cheeks and she once again felt unwelcome. Her eyes searched Derek's for any wavering.

They were so close. . .if he dumped them now, they didn't stand a chance of finding out about Rona or the spy.

"Trust me, darling," Derek comforted her. "My parents will be fine with it."

There was a silent exchange between them that made Elise want to forget the whole plan. Elise would have to make sure she didn't become too trusting of her grandfather.

Derek waved them forward.

They must have walked another hour or so before the castle walls came into view.

"Stay close. We're approaching the back gates." Derek panted. "There's a protection barrier that requires magic to bypass. Members of the royal family are able to escort others, and you'll be granted the same privilege, Joranna. We'll go around the garden into the back doors, so we can change before meeting Mother and Father."

Elise half expected an alarm to go off or another blue light to flash.

However, the prince simply walked along the wall until he came to the gate where four guards stood in formation. They bowed and addressed their prince before one unlocked the gate. Derek whispered instructions to them and beckoned Elise and the others forward.

Elise avoided the guards' eyes as she and her friends followed her grandparents into the castle gates.

CHAPTER 7

An extra set of guards surrounded them once inside the gates, but Elise didn't know if she felt safer by their presence.

At their quickened pace, she struggled to take in everything around her.

They were not permitted to go through the vast garden, and Elise could only make out the outer landscaped walls and what appeared to be the top of a fountain.

Derek pointed out the various entrances to the garden and stables in the distance.

Ahead of them they could see the back courtyard where several well-dressed men and women walked in hushed conversations with one another. Servants bustled around going about their duties. Elise felt like she was on the set of a movie. No less than seven tables had been set with fine china and linens, and another servant walked around adjusting the placement of cups and utensils. Even the napkins were turned to certain angles to achieve the image of perfection.

All eyes soon became glued on their party.

"Now," Derek whispered, "all we have to do is sneak in and—"

"Derek, you've returned!"

Derek closed his eyes and gave Joranna a lopsided smile and shrug.

They all turned their heads to see the king and queen walking arm-in-arm towards them.

"We were expecting you a bit earlier, darling," said the queen.

"Yes, well, we were detained a bit by our new acquaintances," Derek said as he gestured towards their group. "Joranna, may I present my parents, King Theronde and Queen Avalyn."

King Theronde looked the part of a king. He was tall like Derek with streaks of gray through his brown hair and goatee. Small wrinkles surrounded his eyes, yet there was kindness behind them.

The queen was draped in pearl earrings, several jeweled necklaces and rings on each finger. Her welcoming smile was betrayed by disapproving glances at their soiled clothing.

"I would like you to meet Joranna Kensington," said Derek.

Joranna staggered as she curtsied and blushed when a few specs of soil fell out of her hair.

"Your majesties." She wiped her dress and dusted herself off. "I'm sorry about my clothes. I wanted to change before being introduced to you. We just got here and—"

"Derek, I am disappointed in you!" The queen stopped as one of her ladies approached to whisper into her ear. She nodded and sent the lady away before continuing. "I told you not to go out without protection. You could have been met by bandits along your journey."

Derek only smiled and kissed his mother's cheek.

"It's hard to get away with anything around here," he whispered.

"And what are *you* wearing, son?" King Theronde asked as he took in their clothes with the same distasteful frown as his wife.

"I'm quite well-dressed for Joranna's land, Father."

The king made a disapproving sound in the back of his throat.

"Did you take them to the town dressed like that?" Queen Avalyn asked.

Elise felt flustered again under her scrutiny and wanted to get Joranna out of there as soon as possible to save her any more embarrassment.

"Actually, no," Derek said. "Joranna insisted that we wait until she was properly dressed."

"She has some sense about her then." Theronde nodded towards Joranna. "I'm sure you are all rather nice looking once you're all cleaned up."

"Nevertheless, we have heard great things about you, Joranna," Queen Avalyn said. "Your land seems very strange, but we are willing to open our minds if it means our son will be happy."

Joranna took Derek's cue and thanked them.

"And who are your companions?" Queen Avalyn inquired. "You didn't mention bringing any others."

Derek introduced them all one-by-one, and once again, Elise saw their eyes linger on her the longest.

They sense something. I'll be found out before I can even learn anything at this rate.

"Strange land indeed," the king repeated before clearing his throat.

"I've invited them to stay the night and accompany us to the engagement ball," Derek said. "With your blessing of course."

The king and queen exchanged uncertain looks.

"You all are certainly welcome." The queen smiled, but Elise suspected it was only to not make a scene.

"Yes." King Theronde nodded. "Why don't we have one of the maids give our visitors a quick tour on the way to their rooms where they can change for dinner? Surely, we can see to it that they receive proper garments. Shall we meet in the dining hall in an hour?"

"Sounds wonderful. See you then," Derek said.

Elise and her friends thanked them as a servant was summoned to take them inside.

***

The courtyard doors led directly into the ballroom. Several maids were busy dusting and preparing the room for the upcoming party. From there the group was led into the main hall. Every window was trimmed with elegant designs, the curtains were drawn back to allow for maximum sunlight. Antique tables were decorated with priceless vases and bouquets.

They were led up a grand staircase into another long hallway. The walls were lined with portraits on either side, and Elise was overcome with emotion as she took in the faces of her relatives. It was incredibly humbling to look upon the years of greatness that had occupied these halls.

But where would I fit in with all this?

One particular painting caught her attention, and she stopped walking.

It was of Queen Avalyn playing with a young Derek in the royal garden. He looked to be no older than three or four-years-old.

Elise was mesmerized by the vivid colors and serenity of the picture. The brush strokes seemed so effortless and precise, and she wanted to ingrain this painting to memory. A loving mother with her child. They both looked so happy playing together, and she felt something twist in her stomach.

She was pulled away from admiring it as Darcie tugged on her arm to catch up with the rest of the group who had already rounded the corner.

They caught up just as Joranna was being shown her room.

Elise and Darcie were assigned two adjacent rooms while the boys were escorted by a male servant to a separate hallway. Elise wished that they could just share a room. She didn't know how she was expected to spend the night alone after all of this.

A maid followed her into the guest room and provided her with a wash pitcher, basin, and a dress. She made to start undressing her until Elise jumped back and assured her that she could do it. The maid curtsied without a word and showed herself out.

Once the door was closed and she was alone, Elise collapsed on the bed and tried to wrap her head around everything.

What a rush this all had been. Just hours ago, she had been at Darcie's house, and now she was a guest of the royal family. *Her* royal family.

She had seen fairies, been threatened by mermaids, and had been introduced to her grandparents and great-grandparents all in one day.

Her head was spinning from it all, and she just wanted to reach out to her friends. With a heavy sigh, she supposed that she should start getting ready to meet everyone in the dining hall.

Elise sat up and lifted her shirt over her head. She crossed the room and poured water into the basin. The warm washcloth rubbed against her tired muscles. This time, a contented sigh escaped her lips.

She hadn't walked this much since she could remember, and her feet were killing her. She stood in front of the mirror and made sure to remove every smudge of dirt off her skin before continuing down her body.

Elise stepped out of her jeans and continued until she felt fresher. She would've been more satisfied taking a long hot bath, but because of time constraints, this would have to do.

She picked up the dress and held it against her body. It was a simple teal color, nothing too extravagant, with a square neckline and sheer flowing sleeves. It would definitely be better than jeans and sneakers, she mused.

I wonder if Gavin will like it.

Her fingers caressed the silky material, and she prayed that it would fit.

Elise jumped and cried out as the door opened behind her. She jerked up the dress to hide her bra and underwear from view.

Panic flooded through her brain as Mitch walked in. Upon seeing her, he jumped as well.

"Whoa," he said putting his hand up over his eyes. "I'm sorry, Elise."

"Mitch, get out!" she shouted. "What are you doing?"

"Calm down, calm down. I was just looking for the bathroom."

"This isn't it!" Elise snapped, looking down to make sure the dress covered everything as she pressed the material against her.

"I can see that."

She watched as he peeked through his fingers.

"Mitch!"

"Okay, okay," he said, closing his fingers again. "I'll go."

As he turned to leave, however, something caught Elise's eye.

"Mitch? What are those?"

"What are what?"

"Around your neck. Are those your headphones?" she asked in horror.

"Well, yeah." He shrugged, still hiding his eyes but using his other hand to grasp them. "I'm trying to get something to work around here."

"You're going to get us caught!" she said. "Take them off *now*!"

He sighed.

"Fine, fine."

He tucked them into his pocket and his playful grin returned.

"By the way," he said as he backed out of the room, his eyes covered. "Don't worry. You look good."

Elise rushed over and slammed the door.

Without wasting a single second, and not wanting to risk another intrusion, she stepped into the gown and fastened it.

She smoothed out the fabric and had to admit that it fit her well. Now that she was calmer, she chuckled in disbelief at what had just happened. She straightened her posture in front of the mirror. Her face was still flushed, and she hoped that Mitch hadn't seen *everything*.

Normally she only had negative things to say about herself, but as his words replayed in her mind, she smiled and admired the way she looked.

She jumped at the sound of someone knocking and was relieved when it was the same maid returning to pull her hair up and provide shoes. Elise didn't mind getting help in those departments.

***

Once all of them met again in the hall, they were led into the dining hall and shown where to sit.

Joranna was seated next to Derek and his parents, while Elise and the others were positioned further down the table beside the council members.

Elise was impressed by everyone's new clothes. She had to admit that they certainly looked the part now.

Well-dressed servants began to carry trays of food around.

As everyone else began to eat, the four teenagers looked at each other and wondered who would go first.

"So, what now?" Darcie whispered, and all four leaned in so that they could hear better. "This is *insane!*"

"I don't even know what's going on," said Gavin. "Some guy came in and helped me dress. It was weird. Can we just go home now?"

"Sure," Darcie jeered, not bothering to hide her sarcasm. "Do you have any ideas, smart guy?"

"Well, Elise said she had to learn something," Mitch mumbled as he nodded for the servant to scoop out extra potatoes and ham. He didn't mind continuing to talk with his mouth full. "So, it's probably going to be up to her to get us back. Nothing we can do."

Elise glared at Mitch.

"Gee, thanks."

He swallowed the bite he was chewing and winked at her with a smile.

She sighed in frustration.

"It's not like I want us all stuck here. I just don't know where to go."

"Well, you may want to actually *talk* to someone in your family," Gavin said. "They told you to learn what you can about that witch or whatever. Bring it up."

"Right now? Are you crazy?"

"Yeah, she's right. They'd probably lock us up and think we work for Rona," Darcie said. "You can't just bring it up out of the blue like that. And look at some of these guys. . ."

They all glanced at the severe-looking men sitting around them. A few were even eyeing them from across the table.

"Let's just say I doubt they're dying to help us out," Darcie said.

"Maybe I can talk to Joranna." Elise watched her grandmother smiling and making small talk with the royal family. "She might be the only way I can get any information."

But for now, that would have to wait as her stomach growled and brought her attention back to her plate.

***

The four of them declined an invitation to visit with everyone in the drawing room after dinner. Because they were all so exhausted, they muttered quick good nights to each other before going to their own separate rooms.

Elise's frustration grew as she lay restless in her bed despite her fatigue. Every time she closed her eyes, her mind raced with unanswered questions.

When can we go home? How am I supposed to gain my family's trust? What does Gavin think about all this? I wonder if the others are still asleep. Why can't I sleep? I wish I had my phone.

She sat up when the door opened and visibly relaxed when she saw Darcie enter in her nightgown.

"I wanted to see if you were asleep," she whispered as she crept across the room and sat on the foot of Elise's bed.

"Ugh, I wish I was." Elise groaned. "I am *so* tired, and I just can't sleep."

"Well, you know I've always had trouble sleeping, so it's nothing new to me," Darcie muttered. She looked down at Elise and sighed. "I wanted to say sorry for earlier."

"About what?" Elise asked.

"We kind of just put you on the spot at dinner about getting home. Especially the guys. We all know you're just as lost as we are."

"Thanks," Elise said. "Believe me. . .I've been regretting ever saying yes to helping. I would've really liked more directions than just 'find us'. You know?"

Darcie nodded.

"I'm scared, Darcie," Elise confessed. "I really am."

Darcie crawled under the blankets, and Elise turned to face her.

"I just have this awful feeling that something is coming, and I don't know how to prepare for it. If anything happened to you guys, or we got stuck here. . ."

"Elise, you can't think like that," Darcie said. "Believe me, I'm freaking out about getting home, too. We were just supposed to visit your grandma's for an hour. But we're right here with you. Even Gavin and Mitch. They just don't know how to say it."

"I'm sorry you're all stuck, but I'm also glad in a way that Nana sent everyone with me. If I was alone. . ."

"I know. And by the way." Darcie paused to yawn. "Gavin doesn't hate you, you know."

"Well, let's just say I don't see myself being one of his favorite people right now," Elise said. "He didn't ask for any of this. It's not fair to him."

"And yet he's still here," Darcie offered.

"Well, what choice does he have?" Elise asked. She shook her head. "Believe me. I'd love to tell him how I feel. I've thought about writing him a note so many times, the things I would say in it, and how I would give it to him. I see it all play out like a movie in my head. Then I see him and choke."

"You've just got it bad, that's all," Darcie teased.

"What about you? What about Mitch?"

"Mitch is a moron," Darcie said, waving off her friend's comment. "I'm not thinking about him."

"Liar."

"I saw him wink at you about something. What was that about?"

"Nothing."

Elise didn't want Darcie getting the wrong idea about them.

Neither spoke for the next few moments and just enjoyed each other's company.

Elise could finally feel herself growing drowsy once more.

"All right." Darcie yawned again, causing Elise to do the same. "I guess I'll head back to my room. I just wanted to make sure you were okay."

Elise nodded and wished her friend a good night. It wasn't long before she was able to get comfortable and drift off to sleep.

CHAPTER 8

Elise ran through a garden as fast as her feet could carry her, although she wasn't being chased.

She was carefree as the wind rushed past her, and somewhere in the back of her mind she realized that she was a child again.

Her mother sat on the grass a few feet away.

Ruby's hair blew freely around her smiling face, and she reached down to swing Elise around before they collapsed in a fit of giggles on the ground.

Elise couldn't remember when she had felt so happy. After placing a flower in her mother's hair, Ruby leaned down to kiss her.

Her mother's hair was soft against her cheek, but when she pulled back everything changed.

In an instant, Elise was eighteen again and alone. She called for her mother, but the garden was abandoned and overgrown. As she ran further down the path, everything around her became distorted and colors flowed together like paint.

The ground was no longer solid and pooled beneath her feet. She fought to free herself, but it became too heavy and she sank deeper and deeper until she was forced awake covered in sweat with her heart pounding.

Her body was crippled with anxiety, and her mind felt fuzzy. She struggled to remember where she was.

She steadied her breathing, recognized the guest room she was in, and allowed her heartbeat to regulate. She was safe in the castle.

Elise had never been a big believer in the meaning behind dreams, and rarely even recalled them afterward, but something about this one seemed strange. Had it been just a dream or a memory?

She searched for her jeans and t-shirt but saw that another casual dress had been placed out for her at some point. She put it on before a maid, or anyone else, could interrupt and settled for her signature ponytail before walking out.

The hallway was empty as she crept over to Darcie's room and cracked open the door. Her friend was still asleep. She didn't want to bother either of the guys and figured they would find her when they all woke up.

On her way towards the staircase, the painting of Queen Avalyn and a young Derek caught her eye. She admired it for several minutes before placing her fingers over the brush strokes on the boy.

A sudden shock jolted through her hand, and she jumped back.

What was that?

She stared at her palm and touched it with her other hand. Checking to make sure she was still alone, she tapped the painting near Avalyn.

Nothing happened.

She moved her fingers across Derek's image, and once again, an electric shock coursed through her arm.

Without waiting another moment, she took off running towards Darcie's room, but was cut off when two maids rounded the corner.

Taking advantage of their distracted conversation, Elise spun around and hurried down the staircase before she was seen.

She had barely reached the bottom step when she heard her great-grandmother's voice.

"Oh, Joranna, there you are. I was just about to. . .oh, I beg your pardon."

Elise looked around for Joranna and realized the queen's mistake.

"For a moment there, you looked just like my son's fiancée. Are you her sister?"

"Uh. . .no." Elise gave her a quick curtsy. "Just a friend. No relation."

The queen shrugged and beckoned Elise to follow her.

"I am having tea with Joranna this morning. I thought we could have some time alone to really get to know each other. I take it you're very good friends for her to bring you along."

Elise feigned a smile and nodded.

Avalyn looked over Elise's shoulder.

"There you are!" she cried.

Joranna looked delicate in her light blue gown, but the suspicious look she now gave Elise said that she was anything but fragile.

"You're welcome to join us if you like, Alice."

"My name is Elise, Your Majesty, and I don't want to intrude on your private meeting."

"No, no, it's all right," Joranna said. "The more the merrier."

The queen smiled in approval and walked ahead of them through a gorgeous set of French doors towards the garden.

"Thank you," Elise whispered.

Joranna turned sharply on her heel.

"*Listen*, I don't know who you are. I don't know why you asked to come with us, and I *don't* know what you plan to get out of it. As if you couldn't tell, I'm trying to learn how to fit in, and I don't appreciate you and your friends tagging along trying to snoop into our business."

Elise was frozen in shock and didn't know how to respond. Clearly talking to Joranna about anything was off the table at this point. Avalyn's beckoning voice cut through the silence, and Elise kept her distance while following Joranna outside.

Another setting was placed at the small tea table, and Elise admired the fine china and delicious looking pastries in front of her.

The queen wasted no time starting a conversation about royal duties and all that Joranna would be responsible for. Elise would have felt sorrier for her grandmother if she hadn't just cut her down.

Joranna was growing paler by the minute, and it wasn't long before Avalyn shifted her attention to Elise.

"I still feel like I know you from somewhere," she said. "It'll come to me sooner or later I suppose."

She lifted a delicate cup to her lips and encouraged them to do it the same way.

"The kingdom will be excited to see so many guests of honor. They've been very eager to see Prince Derek settle down. You all will open the ball with the first waltz."

Elise's shoulders fell, and she felt a lump form in her throat. Not only did she not dance at all, but the thought of Gavin or Mitch dancing seemed very unlikely as well. They'd be exposed in no time.

"I don't think we'll be able to," Elise said as she looked down into her teacup. "You see. . .none of my friends dance. We don't know how, so I think it'd be best if Prince Derek and Joranna did it. It's all for them anyway."

"I don't know the steps either," Joranna confessed.

"That is quite all right," the queen replied. "It would have been helpful to know this earlier, but I shall have dance lessons arranged for you all after breakfast. We can't have you all embarrassing yourselves. First impressions are *everything*."

Joranna and Elise exchanged anxious looks.

Elise was thankful for her ability to blend into the crowd, but poor Joranna didn't stand a chance at being ignored.

"Shall we have a walk in the garden? I'd be happy to give you a tour myself." Avalyn stood up, ending the tea party.

***

The royal garden covered most of the land from the castle to the black iron gates. The ground was rich with vibrant colors and lush greenery. Stepping stones led to a wooden vine-covered arbor that was lined on either side by rose bushes.

Once through the arched entrance, the garden came alive with nature. Birds chirped and traded songs between one another while butterflies danced from bloom to bloom.

"I often come here when I need guidance or to be alone," Avalyn said. "It is my favorite place."

Along the edges of their path Elise could not see the ground through all the various types of flowered bushes. The outer landscaped walls made it feel like a small, secluded forest.

Elise closed her eyes and inhaled the sweetness of the rich fragrant air. She had no desire to ever leave.

Why did mom want to keep me away from this place?

Avalyn led them over a small bridge that crossed a pond near a stone waterfall.

Elise could make out an ornate white gazebo a few feet away, and her eyes were drawn to a wooden pergola and swing. Ivy and plants had been trained to grow around the woodwork, and she imagined herself reading on the swing with the sounds of nature as her only company.

"I hope you've talked about children."

Elise couldn't hear Joranna gulp, but she imagined the queen had taken her grandmother by surprise.

"I used to love bringing Derek out here on our many walks together. Oh, how I wanted more children." She cleared her throat and composed herself before walking them past the gazebo. "It's my wish to see this garden full of little ones before too long."

They stopped only once more beside the large stone fountain Elise had seen from afar the day before.

In the center was a statue of a woman holding coins in one of her outstretched hands. She had a full figure and long wavy hair. She also wore a crown of leaves and stood proudly as water streamed from beneath her sandaled feet.

"Would you give us a moment, Alice?"

Elise nodded without correcting her and walked a few feet away.

Avalyn gestured towards the statue and talked with Joranna for several moments in secret.

In the meantime, Elise tried to distract herself with thoughts of how she was going to handle dance lessons, or worse, even tell her friends that they had to participate.

All of the different scenarios ended with her going alone. She would just have to hope that Gavin and Mitch believed in all of this.

CHAPTER 9

Unfortunately, the guys took the news about dancing the way Elise had anticipated.

"Yeah, right," Gavin scoffed. "Sorry, but I don't dance. Let's just show up at the stupid ball thing and leave. Okay?"

"Uh. . .not okay," Darcie corrected. "Elise said the queen expects us all to dance the first dance with *everybody* watching. We wouldn't be able to sneak out before that."

"Are you serious?" He huffed and stabbed his fork into his eggs. "It's just one thing after another, isn't it?"

"I'm with Gav," Mitch agreed. "It's one thing to expect us to dress up in these funny clothes, which pinch by the way." He took a bite of his toast and continued talking, spitting crumbs on his lap. "But now they want us to parade around as ballroom dancers? Are they trying to get us to confess?"

"Shh!" Elise said. "Keep it down. We can handle this, guys. It should just be a quick lesson. Let's just flub our way through it and no one will notice."

"Well, yeah, you'll probably have a dress that hides your feet," Gavin scoffed.

Elise could only hope she'd be so lucky.

Despite their collective groans and excuses, they were escorted by Derek into the ballroom after breakfast. A trio of musicians were already waiting and bowed to them as they entered.

Joranna made Derek promise that he would stay with her during the lesson.

"I won't go anywhere, but you're in excellent hands. Mother has arranged for Dalton to be your dancing instructor. He's the best," Derek said as the man entered the room.

Dalton was most likely in his late twenties. He was very handsome with dark brown skin, short hair, and a warm smile.

He introduced himself, had them do the same, and suggested that they get started right away. He paired them off and positioned their arms to create the proper hold.

"The first thing you want to do is know which foot to start on," he announced, explaining that the boys would start forward with their left foot while the girls would step back with their right. He demonstrated the steps and movements for each role.

Elise was partnered with Mitch first and groaned when he approached her.

Was he going to embarrass her any more than he already had?

"It's important that you all have the correct frame from the beginning all the way to the end of the dance," Dalton instructed, walking around to adjust the couples as they were moving to the music.

Elise felt stiff and awkward once she was in the correct hold. How did this come naturally to some people? She was definitely going to look like an outsider that night.

Mitch had already stepped on her feet twice.

So much for staying invisible.

"Why does Gavin keep looking over here?" Elise asked. "You didn't tell him anything, did you?"

"No."

"Mitch, I'm serious."

"I swear I haven't said anything!" he replied. "Maybe he's just trying to see if he's doing it right. They can't all be as good as we are."

"No, Mr. Peterson." Dalton interrupted them to correct Mitch's footing. He reviewed the box step once more.

Elise suppressed a laugh until he stepped on her foot for the third time. She wondered if that time had been on purpose.

After a few more minutes of practice, Dalton had the couples switch.

Derek stepped up with a polite smile and offered his hand to Elise. She shuffled forward and held her arms up. When their skin touched, Elise felt the same shock and jumped back. It appeared Derek felt it too. He apologized and offered his hand once more. When it happened again, Elise pulled away and hid her hands behind her back.

Derek's calculative stare made her feel guilty. He checked over his shoulder to make sure none of the others had noticed before he took her wrists and forced her arms up into a hold. He squeezed her hand to suppress the shock. After a few seconds, the zapping feeling faded and was replaced with a warming sensation.

Derek began leading Elise, while Mitch was paired with Darcie and Gavin with Joranna.

"Do you want to tell me what you're *really* doing here?"

His tone was hardened, cautious, and it was clear by the way he stared over her head as he spoke that he didn't want anyone else in the room to know that something was amiss.

"We just wanted to see the kingdom."

He didn't reply.

Elise swallowed and counted her steps before her curiosity got the better of her.

"Are you still going to erase our memories after the ball?"

He seemed surprised by her bluntness and checked to make sure they weren't being overheard.

"I don't believe I ever acknowledged any such plan." He turned them around and smiled at Joranna to encourage her before he spoke again. "But I think my fiancée's first instincts about you all were correct. I believe there is some deception on your part. Between trying to understand the moment I agreed to bring you here and this," he paused to shake his tingling fingers, "There is something about you four that I don't trust. For that reason, I can't allow you to stay or remember our world past this evening. Now what have you to say?"

"I guess I don't understand why you're still letting us go to the party. Why wouldn't you just erase our memories now and get it over with?"

"Is that a request?"

"No! This place is perfect. I'd never want to forget it. I guess I'm confused why you're letting us stay until the ball."

Dalton praised their form and Derek thanked him before turning back to look at her.

"The process of making you forget this place isn't some simple spell that I can conjure. It will be arranged after the ball to avoid any disruption or scandal before then."

He cleared his throat and suggested to Dalton that they switch couples again.

This time she was going to be led by Gavin. She felt his hand pull her in and stop on her shoulder blade. This was the closest she had ever been to him.

They kept their attention on anything besides each other, and Elise worried that the awkwardness would eat her alive.

Say something, Elise!

"You're good at this," he said to break the silence.

"Thanks. You are, too." When he disagreed, she continued. "At least you haven't stepped on my foot. I feel bad for Joranna now." At least it appeared that Mitch hadn't hurt her grandmother yet.

"So, what is the plan tonight?" Gavin asked.

"I'm going to try and talk with Joranna," she said. "I don't think she knows much about Rona yet, but she's our safest option at the moment. Derek *is* planning to wipe our memories tonight, and if that happens. . ."

"We'll never get home," he finished for her. "Yeah, we can't let that happen."

Dalton clapped his hands and announced the end of the lesson.

"I believe you all are ready, and I cannot wait to see you all tonight. Remember which foot and hand you start off with and keep your frames. The rest will come naturally to you. Men, make sure you are leading your partners and setting the direction. And most importantly, when in doubt, count in your head. Do not get ahead or behind the music. It was a pleasure to teach you all this morning."

Elise was surprised to find that she wished the lesson hadn't ended so soon.

Dalton bid everyone farewell and kissed the ladies' hands before exiting the room.

Elise's heart sank a little when he was gone. Dalton had eased her anxiety and made what could have been terrifying more tolerable.

Once the four friends were alone in the drawing room a few minutes later, Darcie groaned and massaged her feet.

"I hope there aren't any more lessons today," she said. "Let's try to be productive. What's Joranna doing today?"

"I overheard her telling Derek the queen is going to have her in etiquette lessons all afternoon, so there goes my chance to talk to her before the ball."

Elise went on to tell them about Joranna's harsh words from that morning.

"That doesn't sound like the nice lady who greeted us at the house," Gavin said.

"Yeah, she invited us in with no problem and didn't even know us," Mitch said.

"She's just scared right now," Darcie said. "This is the beginning of the diary. She's just learning about this place like we are, but *we* get to leave. . .I hope."

The room fell silent.

"You guys *do* believe in all this, don't you?" Elise asked.

"Yeah, sure," Mitch said. "Gav?"

Gavin shrugged.

"I don't know," he said. "I think I would've woken up by now if I were dreaming, and I don't usually dream of people helping me dress and learn to dance. . .so, I guess so. I'm ready for it to be over though," he said. "I kind of have plans that don't involve time traveling to different dimensions."

All four jumped as someone knocked on the door.

A maid informed them that the king and queen had arranged fittings for them with Edith, a fabriwitch. Seeing their confused expressions, she went on to explain that Edith specialized in creating garments.

"Oh, how exciting!" Darcie squealed as she bounced up and down. "Can you imagine what she could make for *us*? I wonder if she'll take requests!"

"And on that note, I think I'll just wait in my own room," Mitch said as he and Gavin said goodbye and left with the maid.

"We better go to ours, too," Darcie said, talking much faster now that she was all worked up. "I wonder what kind of accessories we'll get. Do you think she'd do layers?"

Elise couldn't get a word in between her friend's excitable chattering all the way to their rooms.

"Can you believe this, Elise? A real ball! You officially have the coolest family ever! Do you think she'll be here soon? I hope she can do something for the guys. They need all the help they can get. Maybe you and Gavin will even share a special moment or two."

Elise rolled her eyes at her friend's wink.

"Goodbye, Darcie." Elise chuckled as she entered her bedroom.

***

Edith was a tall slender woman with gray hair pulled tightly away from her face. Her cheeks were rosy pink, and she had a friendly disposition.

She bustled around Elise taking measurements and talking to herself.

"You are a similar size to His Majesty's fiancée," Edith muttered. "Are the two of you related?" Elise replied that they were simply friends. Edith asked a few more questions and had her put her arms straight out and turn. She took the last of the measurements. "I think you're going to be *very* pleased with this."

The fabriwitch waved her hands around, and Elise saw a similar light surround Edith's hand that had outlined Derek's at the tree.

She winced, not knowing what to expect, anticipating pain, pinching, or something uncomfortable. When she felt nothing, she opened her eyes, and stood back to admire Edith's work in the mirror.

Edith had chosen a ruffled midnight blue gown with embroidered jewels that complemented Elise's figure. The fabric draped off her shoulders and accented her feminine features. She was also given long matching gloves, and her dark red hair was pulled up except two soft strands curled on either side of her face.

Long diamond earrings dangled from each ear and caught the light when she turned her head. Her eye makeup was darker than she was used to, but she had to admit that it suited her. Her blushed skin appeared softer, and for once she felt like she was worthy enough to stand alongside any other woman without envy.

Edith smiled as she clasped a diamond necklace around her neck.

"You'll have his attention tonight," she said with a knowing glint in her eye.

Who's she talking about?

"You are beautiful, child," said Edith. "I can tell from your posture you don't believe it but stand tall. You're officially a guest of the royal family."

Elise thanked her as the fabriwitch left and concentrated on her mission for the evening. She would have to find time to talk with Joranna and Derek about Rona and somehow not get all their memories erased. She had decided that afternoon that having Derek there would be a necessary risk if she were going to get any useful information.

After pacing for several minutes, her chest threatened to burst with anticipation and her palms felt moist beneath her gloves. This was really happening. Nothing could've prepared her for this, and yet here she was dressed for a ball.

Elise practiced a couple of the steps Dalton had taught her and allowed herself to fantasize about that moment when she would get to dance with Gavin again. Darcie had promised she'd make it happen.

Perhaps her friend was right. Maybe she could have a special moment with him. Anything was possible at this point, and if he turned her down, it'd be no different than where they were now. She was never going to look as good as she did tonight, so she might as well go for it.

She took a deep breath and walked over to Darcie's room just as Edith was working on her friend's gown.

Darcie's was a wine-colored sleeveless gown with a sweetheart neckline. It also had ruffles and suited Darcie very well. Her normally spiky brown hair was pulled back and pinned with pearl clips, and she was given small pearl earrings, a necklace, and a bracelet over her matching gloves.

"You look *beautiful*," Elise said.

"You do too," Darcie said. "Is that mascara? Look at you," she teased. "If Gavin doesn't look at you now, he's an idiot."

Edith informed them that she had dressed the gentlemen earlier, and they were all ready to go. The two thanked her again before they made their way down the hallway.

As they approached Gavin's room, Darcie put her finger over her lips and pressed her ear to the door. Elise smiled and followed her friend's example. At first, she could only hear muffled sounds before she could make out their voices.

". . .come on," she heard Mitch say. "She's not that bad. She's probably just shy. That's all."

"Dude, no matter what we say or do, she just acts scared all the time. It's annoying. And what sucks is she's our only chance at getting out of here."

Elise pulled away from the door.

Oh no. They're talking about me.

She glanced at Darcie, who was looking back at her. Her heart pounded in her chest as the truth sank in. Gavin didn't like her after all. She didn't expect him to want to date her, but it didn't sound like he liked her at all in *any* way. She reluctantly put her ear to the door again but was only able to make out every other word.

". . .not even supposed to be here. . .not even real. . ."

"I think she'll surprise you. . ."

"What am I supposed to say to her?"

". . .I think she really likes you."

Mitch!

Elise was horrified. Humiliated. She thought she had been a fool around him before. Now it was going to be worse. She closed her eyes and willed the floor to open up and swallow her.

". . .and how can I. . .she's always so afraid. . ."

She grunted in frustration as she could only make out half of what Gavin was saying.

". . .like I said. It's getting old. Isn't it bad enough we're all stuck here? Let her have her little crush. It's not like she's going to relax and have any fun."

"I don't know about that. . ." Mitch trailed off.

Gavin took the bait, but Elise couldn't hear Mitch's reply.

"No way!" Gavin exclaimed. "You're joking. There's no way."

What are they saying?

Now Elise was just aggravated and hated herself for listening in on their conversation. She would've much rather just wondered what Gavin was thinking rather than know the truth. Her shoulders fell in defeat as she pulled away from the door.

"Let's just go," she said.

Darcie grabbed her into a fierce hug until the door opened.

Both girls stood in shock. Elise locked eyes with Gavin over Mitch's shoulder and saw his eyes widen.

Mitch leaned against the doorframe and winked at them.

"Come to party early?"

Elise didn't stay to hear Darcie's candid response and hurried towards the ballroom while making a mental note not to trip in her heels. The last thing she needed was for the guys to see her trying not to cry or ruin Edith's hard work.

She had been looking forward to tonight, and she wasn't going to let Gavin's opinion of her ruin it. . .at least she was going to try.

After taking a deep steadying breath and dabbing the corners of her eyes without smudging her makeup, she momentarily forgot all about Gavin as she entered the ballroom. Her mouth dropped in awe at the spectacle in front of her.

CHAPTER 10

The room was extraordinarily lit with no less than half a dozen crystal chandeliers. Large floor to ceiling windows were draped with rich golden curtains that complemented the cream-colored walls.

The tables that lined either side of the room featured formal place settings and oversized centerpieces. There was a long head table for the royal family, and her gaze fell on another table across the room filled with the most delicious selection of food she had ever seen.

Elise chose to ignore the taunting dance floor and busied herself by watching the guests mingle. She saw every color and fabric, all extravagant, and was thankful that Edith had taken care of designing her gown so that she could feel hidden among them.

Several well-dressed attendants waited on a grand staircase for the family's arrival.

As the musicians finished a piece, polite applause sounded and Elise perked up, having seen her friends enter the ballroom.

Avoiding Gavin's gaze as he approached, she felt a pinch in her chest when she saw his elegant coat and combed hair. A nearby servant showed them to their table and Elise glared as Darcie arranged for her to sit by Gavin.

Fate seemed to be on her side as the horns announcing the royals' arrival saved her from having to make conversation.

King Theronde and Queen Avalyn were the first to be announced and descended the grand staircase together. They took their places at the center of the floor before Derek and Joranna's names were called.

Derek wore a handsome navy-blue dress coat with golden epaulettes and buttons. He nodded out of ceremony and offered an arm to his lady.

A hush fell over the room, and several of the guests craned their necks to see the engaged couple.

Elise's heart melted at the way Derek gazed at his bride-to-be. She hoped to receive that look someday and thought that her grandmother was the luckiest woman in the world.

Joranna twisted her gloved fingers together as she took in the great room and shifted under everyone's gaze. She slipped her hand around Derek's arm and allowed herself to be escorted forward.

Elise's eyes fell to her grandmother's champagne-colored gown. The fitted bodice and sleeves were sewn with a laced floral design. Her hair was pulled up and adorned with three laced orchids. She wore simple teardrop diamond earrings and was in every fathomable way the perfect image of a princess.

Murmurs of approval rippled throughout the room, and Joranna began to visibly relax.

Once both couples were in position, the announcer invited the honored guests to join them for the first waltz.

Elise felt like she had swallowed ten ice cubes at once and hesitated until Darcie pulled her out of her seat.

By the time she reached the dance floor, Elise had already lived through every worst-case scenario in her mind. She took a deep breath.

Do I have an awkward dance with Gavin or possibly lose a toe with Mitch?

She decided that she would choose Gavin but noticed he didn't join them on the floor.

"Where's Gavin?" Elise asked.

Theronde cleared his throat to get their attention.

Following their previous instructions, Elise and Darcie curtsied and Mitch bowed to the family.

As Darcie pulled Mitch into their starting hold, Elise hoped she was just imagining the confused murmurs from the crowd. Her heartbeat drummed in her ears and she began to feel heat radiating along her hairline.

Don't cry, Elise. Not here.

"There you are!" a familiar voice said. "You are quicker than me."

Elise turned as Dalton stepped up in a strapping formal coat and pulled her into a strong starting hold.

As the first notes began to play and their feet began to move, Elise suppressed the cry in her throat.

"Thank you," she whispered.

"Don't trouble yourself, my lady."

His smile immediately put her at ease. She was grateful to her savior.

As the music swelled, Dalton led her in gentle twirls, and Elise felt safer than she would have with Mitch or Gavin. Dancing came as natural as breathing to him and she knew she was in good hands. He whispered little reminders in her ear throughout the dance, keeping her mind distracted from their audience.

As immersed as she was, the nagging concern about where Gavin had sneaked off to threatened to ruin her good time.

Why isn't he here? Why did he leave us like that? Leave me like that?

"I knew you could do it," Dalton whispered.

His voice was smooth like silk, but her distracted expression gave her away.

"I saw him make a dash out into the hall and couldn't leave you there."

Her heart fell.

He didn't want to dance with me so much that he would rather humiliate me in front of everyone.

The more she saw how he talked and behaved, the less perfect he seemed.

I wish he hadn't come with us at all.

Elise fought the urge to hug Dalton as the music finished and curtsied along with the other ladies as the men bowed. She thanked him as he kissed her hand before disappearing in the crowd of approaching dancers.

The royal couples thanked them and made their way to the head table.

As they approached their own seats, Elise saw that Gavin had returned.

He looked up with an unreadable expression as she took her place beside him.

"Where were you, man?" Mitch asked.

"I had to use the bathroom."

Liar.

Elise crossed her arms and leaned back in her chair, choosing to watch the dancers. Out of the corner of her eye, she watched Darcie nudge Mitch and nod in her direction.

She rolled her eyes as Mitch straightened his posture and cleared his throat.

"Man, I love this song," he said as he attempted to bob his head to the classical tune.

"Mitch, you don't even know this song," Gavin said. "Seriously, I went to the bathroom. No big deal!"

Elise whirled around in her chair.

"Actually, it *is* a big deal. You just left me out there! You were so afraid to screw up." She shook her head and scoffed. "You know, for someone who was just complaining about me doing the same thing, you certainly jumped at the chance to run scared, too."

Before anyone could reply, two young gentlemen stepped up to the table.

"Hello," the first one greeted. "You must be the prince's visitors. I'm Wyatt, and this is my friend, Finlay."

They bowed.

"Would you two ladies like to join us for the next dance?"

Elise interrupted Darcie's decline and encouraged her friend to leave the boys at the table. She didn't feel like hearing what Gavin had to say and was enjoying the attention she was receiving.

"We'd love to," Elise said. "Come on, Darcie."

Her stomach felt like a million butterflies trying to escape, and her throat grew drier at her newfound confidence. It was easy to hide her bad dancing skills with Dalton, but Finlay probably didn't know what he had gotten himself into.

Elise mentally patted herself on the back. She would've turned away the offer, not that many ever came, but she was getting a little tired of being scared all the time.

This will show Gavin there's more to me than just being anxious. I can have fun.

"You look very lovely this evening," Finlay said.

"Thank you."

"I don't believe I caught your name."

"Elise."

Finlay smirked and heat rose to her face.

"Counting your steps?"

She smiled up at him before concentrating once more on the floor.

"I used to do the same thing when I first started, but don't worry. You are in good hands."

His confidence sent shivers through her body that encouraged her eyes to leave her feet.

She chanced a look at Darcie, who was already babbling away with Wyatt, before checking on their table.

"So, is he your suitor?" Finlay asked.

Elise glanced over at Gavin.

"No, not at all."

The next few minutes passed in silence.

"He keeps watching us," Finlay said. "Perhaps he's jealous?"

Doubt it.

"Why don't we have a bit of fun with him then?"

Before she could ask, he twirled and dipped her in one fluid motion.

Dalton definitely hasn't taught me that step yet.

Finlay pulled her upright against him as the music stopped and she could feel his breath on her ear. Adrenaline raced through her veins as she struggled to catch her breath.

"We'll see if that will get him on his feet and act like a proper gentleman. If he's smart, he will ask you for the next dance."

As the couples dispersed, Finlay bowed and led her back to the table.

"It was an honor to meet you, Elise. I really enjoyed our dance. Have a pleasant evening."

Darcie beamed.

"Wasn't that so much fun?" she squealed. "Let's do it again!"

"It actually was," Elise said. She wasn't ready for the fun to stop. All of this would be a memory soon.

Maybe an erased memory.

Gavin fidgeted with something on his shirt and didn't look like he would be moving any time soon.

She decided to take matters into her own hands.

"Do you want to dance?"

It seemed her blunt request took him by surprise, too, but putting him on the spot worked to her advantage.

"Um. . .Sure."

I don't believe it. He actually said yes! And he's still here. I can't mess this up.

"We're dancing, too," Darcie said as she pulled Mitch up from his seat.

Once they were out on the dance floor again, Elise felt Gavin's hand reach around her lower waist.

"I think your hand is supposed to be a little higher," she reminded him.

"Oh. . .sorry," he muttered, lifting his hand up to her shoulder blade.

The great and popular Gavin Striess actually looks flustered for once. I'm going to milk this for all it's worth.

She watched his mouth as he counted and lost count a couple of times herself. He definitely wasn't as graceful as her last two dancers had been.

"I'm sorry," he said.

"It's fine."

"No, I could tell I really made you mad," he said. "I didn't mean to. I just didn't want to mess up with everyone watching."

Elise shrugged.

"I'm just glad Dalton came when he did. He really saved the day."

"Better him than me," Gavin said. His expression soured. "I would've just ruined it."

Elise fought the urge to feel sorry for him.

"It's okay to be scared," she said, helping Gavin to turn them so that they didn't bump into another couple.

"Yeah, but I shouldn't have said those things about you."

"I shouldn't have been eavesdropping. So, let's just forget it."

"Sounds good. Just tell me when I'm being a jerk. I don't always realize it. Darcie's been nagging me a lot about it."

Elise rolled her eyes.

"Gavin, look, you know I like you. I'm too awkward to hide it, and Darcie can't keep to herself. But I'm really tired of her pushing and trying to make something happen. Let's just be ourselves, and maybe she'll quit trying so hard."

He smiled down at her.

"It's nice that you're at least talking to me now. We aren't doing too badly."

"You're right," she said. "You've only stepped on me once."

He looked down at their feet and she chuckled.

"It's fine. I feel sorrier for Darcie."

As the dance ended and dinner was announced, the remaining dancers returned to their seats.

Servants approached with platters and loaded their plates. Elise's stomach growled as her eyes devoured the food. She and her friends waited until everyone had been served and watched for what fork to use.

Before she could stuff her face, however, King Theronde stood and drew the attention of everyone in the room.

"Queen Avalyn and I would like to formally welcome you all this evening, and we are so thrilled that you could join us in celebrating Derek and Joranna. They will do great things for Haighdlen." He raised his glass and waited for everyone in the room to do the same. "We wish them nothing but the longest and happiest of unions. To Derek and Joranna!"

"To Derek and Joranna!" everyone chanted before drinking.

"Please feast, drink, and enjoy the rest of the evening!" Theronde said.

After the applause dwindled, the musicians began to play dinner music and a collective buzzing of conversations spread throughout the room.

Elise saw Darcie trying to gauge the mood between her and Gavin, but she wasn't going to help.

There was nothing there, and that was okay. She resigned herself to admiring him like she always did, only now they could talk. The pressure was off, and it felt like a huge weight had been lifted from her shoulders. She could be his friend.

"Did you get to talk to Joranna?" Darcie asked her.

"Not yet."

I forgot all about that.

"I don't know how to approach her," she confessed. "What am I supposed to say? Even if she knows about Rona, she's skeptical of us. And look how happy they are. . .Now isn't the time to spoil their evening."

"But if we don't ask or do something quick, we all lose our memories here or get stuck in the 1960s version of our world forever," Darcie said.

Elise slapped her cloth napkin on the table.

Fine. I'll do it, but it's going to blow up in my face.

As she stood, however, she made eye contact with her grandparents. Derek whispered something to Joranna, who nodded before the pair of them began walking over.

Elise's chest tightened and she whirled around to face her friends.

"They're coming this way! Derek's probably ready to erase our memories. What're we going to do?"

The other three dropped their forks and began looking around the room in a panic.

"We need to lose them in the crowd," Gavin said. "We'll run up to our rooms, grab our regular clothes and make a run for it out of the back doors to the courtyard."

"What if they send the guards?" Mitch asked.

"Then don't get caught," Gavin said. "Now go!"

Joranna and Derek were only tables away, and Gavin's idea was the best they had. Elise knew the couple wouldn't chase them in here and cause a scene at their own engagement ball.

She and the others rudely pushed passed guests and hurried towards the staircase.

Bursting into the guest bedroom, Elise tossed her jewelry on the dresser and pulled at the fabric of her dress. She hated to leave it wrinkled on the floor, but there was no time.

As they met up in the hallway, they could hear Derek's voice instructing guards to block all exits and search for them.

"We could try the window," Gavin suggested.

"Are you crazy?" Mitch shouted. "We'd never make it!"

"We don't have a choice!" Darcie cried as they heard footsteps coming up the staircase. "Quick, go to Mitch's room. It's the furthest away."

As they entered, Mitch ran over to open the window.

Elise locked the door but lost her footing on the way to the others.

"Mitch, why did you leave your shoes on the—"

"It's too far down," Darcie panted. "We don't have time to tie any sheets together."

"Wait!" Elise cried out. "It wasn't shoes I tripped over. Look! It's my grandmother's diary! It just showed up."

"What does that mean?" Darcie asked.

"I don't know. Maybe it's here to help somehow," Elise said.

A guard pounded on the door and demanded to be let in.

"Well, open it and find out!" Gavin shouted.

Elise fumbled with the book and flipped to a random page. Within seconds, she began to feel the familiar pull from the portal. Her chest tightened, but the excitement overrode her fear.

It'll all be over in a few minutes, and we'll be home! We'll get to keep our memories. Just wait it out.

Others were shouting from the hall as the pounding continued. Any moment now, they would bust the door down.

Hurry up!

She glanced down at the book as the booming voices outside threatened them. They had mere seconds.

As the guards burst in, she closed her eyes and welcomed the enveloping darkness.

CHAPTER 11

Elise opened her eyes to a swirling gray sky. Her shirt was soaked with dew and her muscles were stiff as she sat up. The others were lying next to her in the grass.

"Guys? We have a problem," she said.

They were still on the castle grounds. She recognized the gazebo and realized they were in the royal garden. She didn't see anyone but could hear faint conversations coming from the courtyard.

Did we do something wrong?

She looked and felt around for the diary, which was now missing again.

Elise yawned and rubbed her eyes. Smudged mascara coated her fingertips, and she realized her hair was still up. After removing the pins, she fished in her pocket for the extra hair tie she kept for emergencies.

The other three sat up one at a time.

"What's going on?" Gavin said. "Why aren't we home?"

"I don't know." Elise finished her ponytail.

"Are you sure you did it right?" he asked.

"What do you mean? All I did was open it up, and it sent us here. There's only one way to do it!"

"Obviously not or we'd be home!"

Elise glared at him.

"Okay, let's not panic," Darcie said. "We can just find someone to—"

"Who, Darcie?" Gavin snapped. "Did you forget about getting chased out of here and almost having our memories erased? We can't just walk up to ask for directions. If we get caught, who's to say they won't try again?"

Darcie sighed.

"We're lucky we landed inside the walls, because trying to get anything done from the outside would be ten times harder!" she said.

"No, believing in any of this is ten times harder." He raked his fingers through his hair and kicked at the ground. "What're we supposed to do now?"

Elise shook her head.

"I thought the diary was only supposed to show up if we learned something," she said. "We don't know who the spy is yet. If it was just going to keep us here, why did it show up at all?"

"And that portal thing definitely opened," Mitch said. "We all felt it. Didn't we?"

A frown flashed across Gavin's face as he shushed them. Someone was coming.

Queen Avalyn strolled into view a few feet away. She leafed through a book and hadn't seemed to notice them yet.

"Don't panic, Your Majesty. You're safe," Darcie announced.

Avalyn jumped and clutched the book to her chest.

"Very smooth," Mitch muttered.

"Don't come any closer!" the queen ordered.

"You can trust us." Elise extended her hands out and inched towards her great-grandmother.

"Stop there!" The four did as the queen commanded. Her brows furrowed as she examined them. "I've seen you before, but I can't place where. . ."

"We just left." Elise frowned. "We were at the engagement ball."

"Oh, that's right! You were Derek's visitors. That was such a lovely evening." She sighed and loosened the grip on her book. "I can't believe it's been two years already."

"Two years?" Mitch shrieked.

The queen nodded.

"Forgive me for not remembering you straight away. I recall seeing you there, but not too many details about your visit. You'll have to remind me of your names."

One by one, they introduced themselves again.

After the last of the four had spoken, the sound of Derek's voice calling made the hairs stand up on the back of Elise's neck.

"We need your help," she told the queen. "Don't let him take us. We're not a threat!"

Before the other woman could reply, Derek rounded the corner and spotted them.

Elise was thankful he couldn't erase their memories with his gaze alone.

He stepped in front of his mother.

"Are you all right, Mother? Have they hurt you?"

"Hurt me?" she asked. "Why would they hurt me? I don't understand what is going on."

"They're fugitives. What is your purpose here?" he demanded.

"We just want to talk," Darcie said.

"Mother, please go inside the castle while I handle this. Alert the guards, too."

Avalyn retreated down the path, and Elise lowered her gaze with a heavy sigh. A lone raindrop landed on her nose. Another fell on her shoulder and before long, a steady sprinkle came down around them.

Under Derek's scrutiny, Elise's mouth grew dry.

"How did you pass through the barrier?"

I don't know.

"How did you get onto the castle grounds?"

We were dropped off here.

The truth wasn't useful at this point. As the sound of clanking armor approached, Elise held out her hands for her friends' help.

No one spoke.

"Very well then," Derek said and ordered that they all be escorted to the king immediately.

Their pleas and whimpers went unanswered as they were ushered forward.

As the castle grew larger ahead of them, shivers spread through Elise's limbs at the thought of the king sending them to a cold dark cell.

***

Their arrival was announced outside the king's study. Elise recognized Theronde's deep voice as he ordered them inside.

Derek wasted no time walking up to his father's desk.

"Father, these were the fugitives who escaped that night at our engagement ball. They threatened us and the safety of this kingdom."

"Threatened you? When did we threaten you?" Gavin asked.

Derek glared over his shoulder before leaning down to his father's level.

"You know the story of what happened, and I find it highly suspicious that they should return. Their intentions can only be treasonous."

Elise interrupted him.

"That's not true!" She could feel a guard's breath on the back of her neck and was careful with her words. "We don't want to hurt anyone. We just wanted to talk and explain what happened."

"It's too late for that," Derek said. "We need to deal with this quickly and efficiently. I don't want to alarm Joranna in her condition."

King Theronde had yet to answer from his chair and continued perusing the documents in front of him. For several moments only the sound of shuffling papers could be heard. Elise saw a muscle in Derek's jaw twitch. At long last, the king sighed and regarded his son.

"Derek, until you learn to practice patience, you will never be ready to rule," Theronde said. "You have denied these travelers the ability to explain themselves and are ready to punish them without proof." His hand rose to silence his son's argument. "And may I point out that it was *you* who brought them here in the first place?"

"Yes, but I told you that I didn't want—"

"Whether you wanted to or not, the fact remains that you have to accept the consequences that come from your actions."

"I tried to handle it that night, but I don't see their reason in coming here now. It can't be for anything good."

"We're here to talk about Rona," Darcie said.

The room fell silent, and only the growing storm could be heard beating against the windows. All eyes turned to Darcie.

Why did she have to go blurt that out for?

"Do you see, Father? It's worse than I thought. They *are* spies! They disguised themselves among Joranna's world in order to gain access. How else would they know about Rona?"

The king studied Elise and her friends. His fingertips drummed together on top of the desk.

"My son makes a compelling argument." Theronde removed his glasses and stood with a sigh. His fingers stroked his beard as he paced the room. "If you do come on Rona's behalf, you are a great threat indeed, though I don't see any significance in your appearances. I should think we'd know by now if you possessed any *real* power."

"We came to warn you," Elise said. "She's planning to attack."

"And who precisely told you this?" he asked.

She looked into his stern eyes and longed to tell her great-grandfather the absolute truth. She didn't want to lie, but if she were going to get anywhere near her actual home, she had to try and stick to the plan.

"We can't tell you that," Elise said. "Our friend knows it's going to happen, and we want to know more about Rona in case. . ."

"In case she plans to attack our friend later," Gavin said.

Elise was taken aback by Gavin's unexpected aid and wished he'd make eye contact with her.

Theronde returned to his chair and placed his glasses on his nose. He tilted his face and glanced at the four of them.

"If what you say is true, then my kingdom is indebted to your. . .*friend*. However, if you are found to be lying, the charges against you will be *very* grave indeed. Do you understand?"

They all nodded.

"And you still stand by your story?"

When they agreed, Theronde dismissed the guards and called for two servants to escort them to the same rooms as before.

"You will stay with us tonight. I want to have a private meeting with the four of you at dinner to learn more about this threat, but do not get too comfortable."

Unwilling to argue or question the king's decision, they followed the servants out as Derek continued pleading with his father to reconsider.

***

Elise's eyes burned with tears as the bedroom door closed behind her. She wiped them away and breathed a heavy sigh of relief.

I could be in a cell right now. I can't mess this up. We need to talk about a plan, so our story stays consistent.

At that moment, the fabriwitch from before entered the room. "Edith!"

She wanted to thank the fabriwitch for her advice, but Edith did not look the same. Her face looked pale, and her mouth was drawn back in a tight line as she shook her head to silence Elise.

"What's wrong?" Elise asked.

"I am on strict orders not to speak to any of you," she whispered. "My instructions are to only provide you with more appropriate attire for dinner."

Elise wondered why the maids hadn't just brought extras like before.

Maybe they have other guests.

It didn't look like she was going to find out either way as Edith bustled around her taking measurements.

The older woman conjured a plain silver gown on Elise, and two similar styles folded themselves on the dresser. Edith curtsied without a word and left the room.

Elise's shoulders fell as she caught a glimpse of a guard standing outside before the door closed.

So much for talking with the others ahead of time.

***

"What's going on here?" Mitch asked after they had all been separately escorted to the dining room. "That fabric-whatever acted like she didn't even see me."

"Not to mention the guard that's staring at us," Darcie whispered. "Is he going to hover over us while we eat, too?"

"I have orders to accompany you for the duration of your stay," said the guard.

"Great. They think we're criminals," Gavin grumbled. "All because that stupid book didn't do its job."

He scoffed and twisted his fork back and forth between his fingers.

"That's the last time I go into a stranger's house to use the bathroom," Mitch muttered.

"Okay, guys, focus," Elise whispered. "We don't have a lot of time to get on the same page. So, we are four travelers who heard from a friend that Rona is planning to attack Haighdlen."

"And we volunteered to deliver the message since they already knew who we were," Darcie said.

"Silence!" the guard bellowed as a horn announced the start of dinner. "Not another word between you. Now stand for the royal family."

After rising, Elise clasped her hands together and lowered her head as the doors opened.

Derek ignored them completely as he helped Joranna adjust in her chair. She avoided their eyes as well and placed her hands around her bulging stomach.

Theronde and Avalyn also offered no greetings upon their arrival.

Their plates and glasses were filled, and the only noise came from the clattering of silverware against the china.

"Father, I don't see why we couldn't have handled all of this in your study," Derek fumed. "This is hardly a family matter. Joranna does not need to hear any unpleasantness."

"Derek, please," Joranna said. "I'm going to have a baby. I'm not a piece of glass that's going to break any minute. Let your father handle things the way he wants."

"Thank you, Joranna." King Theronde cleared his throat behind his napkin.

"And since this concerns the kingdom," Avalyn argued, "I believe it *is* a family matter."

Derek lowered his head and stabbed at his food.

"Now, several things concern me," Theronde said. "First, I'm curious about how you four penetrated the walls without being seen. If the guards didn't allow you access, our protective magic should've stopped you. Only our family can break through it willingly without assistance. So, that is something I am going to investigate personally."

Elise felt her ears grow hotter under his stare.

"Second, your actions are highly suspicious. Derek isn't one to be easily swayed, and yet you were able to con your way into our lives two years ago without a clear purpose. We provided you with hospitality and treated you with kindness, only to have you vanish without a trace."

"That wasn't our fault. He was coming to erase our memories!" Mitch said.

The guard behind them took a step closer to Mitch's chair.

"Which he was right to do," Theronde said before clearing his throat. "Had he succeeded, we wouldn't be dealing with this security concern." He gulped from his glass. "I want to know where this information comes from, and I want to know now. I will *not* be manipulated. If I am to take your word seriously, I need to know it has merit."

Elise looked at their expectant glances. She set her fork down on her plate, suddenly finding it difficult to swallow, and tried to spin the truth as best she could.

"We were sent here, because our friend has seen the future," Elise said.

She hoped that that was believable since magic technically existed.

"A war against Rona is coming, and your family will be forced to flee unless we can stop her early. It's too dangerous to share our friend's name. We had to swear not to."

She bit her lip and straightened in her chair.

"Did your *friend* give a timeline for these events?" Theronde asked. Elise shook her head and he nodded in defeat. "Very well."

She chose to ignore his curtness and tried her luck.

"Could *you* tell us anything about Rona?"

"Only that she is the biggest threat to any of the four main kingdoms. Our magic pales in comparison to what she has managed to acquire. I'll not give much more than that in the event that you are her spies. I'm still not completely convinced of your innocence in all of this."

Elise's stomach turned, and she was left with a bad taste in her mouth that prevented her from taking another bite.

I wanted more than just being told she has magic. I know that already.

"Are you all right, darling?" Derek asked.

Joranna put her fork down and took a deep breath.

"I'm fine," she said and waved her hand. "I just had a short pain that's all. Nothing to worry about. Please continue."

"We have to get the doctor."

"Derek, you can't keep calling the doctor for every little pain. It doesn't mean the baby is coming yet."

Derek eased back but continued to watch her out of the corner of his eyes.

"Have you decided on a name yet?" Queen Avalyn asked.

Elise was thankful for the subject change.

"Mother, I said we were going to wait…"

"We can tell them if you'd like," Joranna said. "I know we were going to save it, but I don't see it mattering very much either way."

Derek took Joranna's hand.

"If it's a girl, we're thinking Jane after Joranna's mother. If it's a boy, Richard."

"Those are lovely names," the queen said as she finished her dinner. "Oh, I get so excited thinking about having little feet running through the halls again. Don't you, Theronde?"

Theronde made a noncommittal sound in the back of his throat as one of his soldiers entered the room. The young man made no attempt at pleasantries and crossed the room to whisper into the king's ear right away.

Why are they looking at us?

"Thank you, Brahm," he said. "I expect to be informed of any updates. Good work."

As the soldier nodded and left, Theronde turned his attention back to them.

"Rumors are spreading through the kingdom about a possible spy or *spies* placed within my court and an impending attack."

"So, you *are* spies," Derek shouted, "and liars as well!"

"Derek, please," Avalyn said.

"They've been the only change, Father," Derek countered. "You said so yourself. It's too suspicious."

"I know what I said," the king said, "but we must try to—"

Joranna dropped her fork and cried out as she pushed herself away from the table. This time she didn't fight Derek away when he took her hand.

"I'm fine." Her head fell back, and she gritted her teeth.

Derek called for a servant to fetch the doctor and helped Joranna stand. His father came to help on her other side.

"Take the travelers to the library, and hold them there after they finish dinner," Theronde ordered.

Once the commotion died away, and the royal family disappeared down the hall, Elise looked around at her friends.

"Well…that wasn't scary at all," Mitch said. He raised his hand for another helping of food.

"Man, that's crazy that you're here right when your uncle is being born," Gavin said.

"That's probably why it sent us here," Darcie said. "Maybe it's not just when you learn about Rona." She leaned forward and whispered. "Maybe it's to help you see what's all at stake."

Elise shrugged.

"It makes sense, but I don't know what the diary wants me to do. We keep getting ourselves into trouble, and Derek won't let us get anywhere near learning anything more about Rona."

"At least the king didn't send us away in handcuffs," Gavin said. "Looks like the whole innocent-until-proven-guilty thing holds up here, too."

I hope so.

Considering the proximity of the guards who led them to the library, Elise couldn't be too sure.

CHAPTER 12

"So, they're letting us stay the night. That's a good thing. Right?" Darcie asked.

"Only because they don't know what to do with us." Elise sighed. "I'm surprised we're not in jail or whatever they have here. I just want to know about those rumors that guard came in with. It's too convenient that the king should get *that* kind of news when we get here."

"Do you think that's what we were supposed to see?" Gavin asked. "Maybe the diary could show up now."

"I don't know. I mean, the rumors are about Rona, but I thought we were supposed to see my uncle being born."

Mitch groaned and slumped into an armchair.

"I hope not. We're going to be here forever. I heard a woman can be in labor for days."

"Let's pray that doesn't happen," Darcie said. "We can't stall that long."

"I wish I could read the diary. If I could just get my hands on it and actually *read* something that happened. . ." Elise placed her hands on her hips and paced back and forth in front of the fireplace. "I was so confused that first night that all I could do was leaf through it. I just kept seeing random stories about their kids, and every now and again Rona's name would be written. Now it's just going to transport us whenever we touch it, but who knows when it's going to show up?"

"I'm telling you, what if it's already here?" Gavin asked. "We're in a library. There are a ton of books in here. It could just be sitting right here waiting for us to find it."

"I tripped on it last time, because it literally appeared in front of me. Why would it be hidden if we're supposed to easily find it?"

"You never said it had to come easily," Gavin replied. "And from the way we're getting sent from one place to another without any explanation, I don't think '*easy*' is a requirement with your family."

"Should we start looking?" Darcie tilted her head to inspect some of the titles on the shelves.

"I'll check to make sure no one will catch us going through their stuff," said Elise.

She peeked into the hall and immediately made eye contact with the same guard from the dining room.

"Your Majesty!"

Elise turned as a short, white-bearded man approached her. His eyes fell to her stomach and then her face again. He sighed in realization. "I beg your pardon, my lady. I thought you were Princess Joranna, and I had given strict orders for her to stay in bed."

"Oh, you must be the doctor," Elise said. "You're not the first to make that mistake about me. Is there anything we can do to help?"

"I'm afraid all we can do is wait." He sighed. "I've given her something for the pain, but the little prince or princess will get here in due time."

He bowed his head and hurried towards the staircase.

Elise closed the door.

"We should be good for a while. There's just that guard outside."

"He creeps me out," Darcie said with a shiver.

***

Elise jerked and grasped the arms of her chair, causing the book on her lap to crash on the floor. She yawned and picked it back up. According to the clock, they had been searching for over two hours.

"Anybody find anything yet?" she asked.

Her friends moaned back at her.

Elise rubbed her eyes, looked down at the purple cover, and leafed through a couple of pages.

She yawned and decided to give her eyes a break by examining the room.

At least it's more comfortable than a cell.

Dark brown bookshelves lined three of the walls. Two enormous crimson couches faced each other combined with armchairs scattered throughout the room. Two tables with chairs were in the corner, and the fireplace burned against the fourth wall. More family paintings decorated this room, as well as different maps of explorations.

Elise walked over to one of the maps that showed four kingdoms.

Haighdlen. . .Leafbrooke. . .Vynchia. . .Lockesbarrow. . .I wonder what the others are like.

Darcie stepped in front of her carrying a stack of books as Elise turned to scan the last bookshelf for any other purple covers. When she didn't find any, she grabbed an atlas and went back to her chair.

We're never going to find Nana's diary in here, but at least this will help pass the time.

Swinging her feet over the side, she began to study. It didn't take long before her eyelids drooped again. She pinched the bridge of her nose and decided to distract herself.

Gavin sat facing her at one of the tables. His head was propped up on his hand as he turned a few pages in his book.

The flickering firelight made shadows dance across his face and a few locks of hair had fallen in front of his eyes.

She slouched so that she could peek over her book. Her mind took off with possibilities, imagining the same room with just the two of them. The confidence she always yearned for now threatened to spill over. Her book was cast aside as she approached his table. She didn't fear his rejection and instead slipped in front of him so that she had his full attention. She sat on the table and was rewarded with that perfect smile. His long fingers slid up her thighs and around her waist. Heat rushed through her body as his lips came closer to hers.

Gavin glanced up from his book and Elise jerked back to reality in her armchair.

Did he see me staring?

She focused on anything else besides him. Darcie was perusing titles at the other table, and Mitch was asleep on one of the couches.

Elise jumped as the guard opened the door and announced King Theronde's arrival.

Darcie walked over to wake Mitch, then all four stood up as Theronde entered.

"I certainly didn't expect to keep you waiting this long, but it seems I will have to postpone our meeting. You will stay tonight and be summoned first thing in the morning. We will come to a decision then. Goodnight."

No other explanations were given as they were led to their guest bedrooms upstairs. With their new chaperone, there was little chance of sneaking into other rooms, and so Elise was forced to toss and turn until the early morning hours.

When she finally felt herself drifting off to sleep, two maids entered. The first delivered a wash basin and pitcher while the second set out a clean dress. The curtains were opened to let the morning light in, but Elise groaned and pulled a pillow over her head.

"His Majesty requests your presence in the dining hall," the first said.

Elise felt like a zombie as she was dressed and led over to the vanity where the second began styling her hair into a relaxed updo. It wasn't as elaborate as Edith's ballroom look, but it was more fitting than a ponytail to meet with the king.

Elise thanked both ladies and stepped out into the hall. The escort was waiting, as expected, and standing at attention.

"Do you ever sleep?"

He didn't reply.

Elise stifled a yawn with the back of her hand.

"Has the baby been born yet?"

"The young prince was born during the night," he said.

She smiled.

Maybe now the diary will show up, and we can go home!

Darcie was the next to exit. After Elise was able to relay the news to her, she threw her arms around Elise's neck and hugged her best friend.

"What did I miss?" Mitch asked.

"Joranna had her baby!" Darcie said.

"You will address her as 'Her Royal Highness' or 'Princess'," the guard corrected.

"Dude, chill, it's not like she's here," Mitch said with a yawn. When the guard took a step closer, Mitch put his hands up and apologized. "Okay, okay. So, will 'Her Royal Highness' be joining us?"

"I doubt it," said Elise.

She looked over Mitch's shoulder at the sound of china crashing. Gavin's door opened and he backed out of the room in only trousers and a white shirt.

"I said I can dress myself! Thanks, but no thanks," he called before turning to face them.

Elise's eyes fell to his opened shirt, and she stared a moment too long at his bare chest.

"I'm all for the royal treatment," Gavin said, "but I draw the line at helping me dress."

He's going to kill me.

He put an end to her suffering by buttoning his shirt and throwing on his vest.

When they arrived, Theronde and Avalyn were already seated and waiting for them. Once they were settled, their guard walked over to join three others standing against the wall near the king.

Servants began to bring trays over. One served the food while another filled their goblets.

Elise cleared her throat.

"I heard that the baby was born. Congratulations."

"Thank you," said Avalyn. "He is so precious. I'm afraid you'll be seeing little of me once I finish eating. I just can't stay away."

"Yes, he's quite extraordinary." Theronde beamed and cut into his ham before taking a bite. "He will be a fine ruler one day and do great things for Haighdlen."

Elise focused on her plate and moved her food around with her fork. She let her great-grandparents relish Richard's birth and had no intention of ruining their dreams with the truth about Haighdlen's fate.

"And how's Jor. . . I mean, the princess?" Darcie asked.

"She's doing well," the queen said. "Joranna is going to be a terrific mother. She has such a caring nature."

They all looked up as Derek entered the room.

The nearby servants bowed and bustled to have a plate filled for him.

"I'm so glad you decided to come down after all," Avalyn said. "I take it Joranna has eaten?"

"She has." He glanced in their direction before continuing. "She's resting now. Poor thing is exhausted."

"Well, I suppose there's nothing left to do but address your visit," Theronde announced to Elise and the others. "I have put my best men out to address this threat. If there is a spy in our midst, I have faith that they will soon be discovered." He set down his fork and regarded them. "Having said that, no evidence has turned up to incriminate any of you, and I'm happy to say that you are all free to go once you're finished with your meals. Brahm and his men will escort you to the castle gates where you may begin your journey home."

The four teenagers thanked him, and Elise felt a weight lift from her shoulders.

"Now the diary can show up!" Darcie whispered.

Elise nodded and looked around.

If that's all, then where is it already?

She glanced under the table and heard Derek clear his throat.

"Actually, Father, there is one more matter of business to take care of," he said. "The birth of our son has helped Joranna and me to see things more clearly. Father told me of your innocence earlier this morning, and Joranna and I wanted to offer a personal apology for our behavior towards you all. We judged you too quickly. You could have stayed away, but you risked coming back. You also could have kept the threat a secret, but you didn't."

The king dabbed his mouth and nodded.

"Please accept our apology as well, as we consider you to be allies to Haighdlen."

"Perhaps to make amends," added the queen, "they could accompany Derek on his trip to receive Eugena's gift on their way home?"

Eugena. . . Oh, the Mermaid Queen!

"That's a wonderful idea, Mother. Eugena wishes to present us with a gift honoring Richard's birth. I should be happy to give you a tour of the nearby town as well if you'll join me."

Elise's only option was to nod since her mouth was full.

I like this Derek much better.

"Well, it's settled then!" Theronde said. "Brahm, prepare some men to escort Derek and our visitors down to Clara and Lake Laulie."

"Yes, Your Majesty." The guard bowed and exited the room.

Theronde's brows furrowed as a thought occurred to him.

"One last thing. There is only one part of your visit that I can't figure out. How did you get to the garden undetected?"

Elise looked at Gavin, Mitch, and Darcie for support.

"There have been so many deliveries coming in and out of the gates these last few days in preparation for Richard's arrival. I could see it being a simple oversight," Avalyn said.

They know something. I can see it in their eyes. They must know I'm related by now. They're probably just waiting for me to confess it. If I agree with the queen, maybe I can buy myself some more time.

She nodded and smiled.

"A potentially dangerous oversight, but it seems we are spared of any malice this time. Very well. Enjoy the tour and perhaps announce your arrival next time."

They definitely know something. We're getting an awful lot of preferential treatment.

"Please tell Joranna congratulations and we're glad she's doing well," Darcie said.

Derek nodded.

"I will meet you in the courtyard in an hour."

CHAPTER 13

As promised, Elise and the others soon found themselves being led by carriage towards Lake Laulie. Derek and his guards rode on horseback ahead of them.

Elise's stomach turned as they hit another bump in the road.

I should have taken one of the forward-facing seats.

"This place is so beautiful," Darcie said, leaning her head against the glass. "I can't wait to see the mermaids again."

"I'm surprised they want to give Joranna anything. I figured they'd just see a new prince as another threat," Mitch said.

"Maybe it's a tradition in their culture," Darcie reasoned. "I'm glad we get to see it!"

Gavin leaned his head out of the opening above the door and made sure they couldn't be overheard.

"Don't you guys think it's weird that Derek just apologized out of the blue?"

"You heard him. He said they talked about it and didn't think we were a threat," Elise said with a shrug.

Should we not believe them?

"Yeah, but hours before that he was ready to put us on trial."

Gavin had a point.

"We probably have Joranna's hormones to thank for that," Darcie said.

"I won't argue." Mitch grinned. "I'd rather see more hot mermaids than be locked in prison. Let's just take our luck and roll with it."

Their conversation dwindled as Derek slowed and came to ride beside them.

"The lake is just up ahead in the clearing. We'll walk from here."

His horse whinnied as he pulled on the reigns, and the guards followed his lead.

The carriage slowed as Derek dismounted and addressed his men. "I will lead them from here. The rest of you stay and guard the carriage and horses please." He turned and assessed Elise and her friends. "Hopefully, your appearances will be better received this time."

They followed Derek off the path and into the clearing by the lake.

Sunlight glistened along the tranquil waters. There wasn't a single cloud in the sky, and Elise squinted against the brightness.

"Once we have Eugena's gift, we will tour Clara," Derek said.

"Clara?"

"Yes, Elise, it is our biggest and most profitable town in the entire kingdom. It's named after my great-great-grandfather Claramond."

I wonder if his portrait is one of the ones I saw in the castle. I'll have to check when we get back.

"This land had been plagued with many wars for years before treaties were made between the kingdoms. Mostly over goods and territory. Claramond was not a blood-thirsty ruler and saw this land for what it could be. He established trade with our nearest neighboring kingdom, Vynchia, first. It spread to the others in time, but Vynchia still remains our closest ally. Claramond took a special interest in this area and ultimately built Haighdlen into the great kingdom that it is now."

I have so many questions now. I wish I hadn't wasted so much time in the library last night. She glanced at Gavin. *Maybe I can look for a history book later.*

Derek held up his hand to stop them. He crept to the lake's edge and stirred the water with his fingers.

When the ripples spread too far for their eyes to follow, a lone head emerged.

Elise recognized his shaved head, piercing green eyes and dark muscular body as he rose out of the water. It was the same merman who had threatened them before.

"Good morning, Erumann," Derek said with a cordial nod. "I am here as requested."

"Queen Eugena is expecting you."

Erumann stared at Elise and her friends before descending again.

"Well. . .that seemed to go better than last time," said Mitch.

The water bubbled violently as thirty or more merpeople broke through the surface. At Erumann's command, they all eased back from the shore's edge.

Elise felt goosebumps dance across her skin and stood on her toes. She and Darcie smiled at each other in anticipation.

The merpeople bowed their heads as their captivating queen rose from the depths of the water.

Eugena's skin was dark brown like Erumann's, and her long hair was a swirling combination of blue and green that covered her breasts. A crystal circlet adorned with small, jeweled starfish and tassels on either side framed her face. Her striking eyes were the iciest shade of blue that Elise had ever seen. In her hand she carried an ornate scepter topped with a jewel that matched her eyes.

She stared at each of them in turn before looking directly at Derek.

"Welcome to Lake Laulie again, Prince Derek." She nodded her head towards him. "I believe congratulations are in order for you and your wife."

"Thank you."

"I am so in love with her hair!" Darcie whispered into Elise's ear. She was about to reply when Eugena looked over in their direction.

"We did not expect other visitors."

"The princess invited them on her behalf as our honored guests," Derek explained.

Elise noticed a small gash on the queen's cheekbone and a few scars on her upper arms. When she caught the queen's gaze, she looked down at her feet.

"They are to keep their distance. Let's get on with it then," Eugena said.

She handed her scepter to Erumann and cupped her hands together as if to pray. She dipped them and scooped up a generous amount of water.

Eugena closed her eyes and inhaled deeply.

For several moments, nothing appeared to happen.

Elise chanced a look at her friends, who shrugged. Derek had his back to them, but Elise wondered if he could see any better.

None of the merpeople moved and the water had stilled.

The only sound around them was birds flying overhead and from within the trees.

Just as Elise considered sitting down, the queen opened her eyes and held out her hands towards Derek. Her mouth lifted in a half smile as he stepped forward.

The water in her hand had solidified into crystal.

It's Nana's bowl!

Eugena pressed the tips of her fingers against it, and several images of mermaids appeared to be carved into the crystal.

Glimmering in the sunlight, it was just as breathtaking as the first time Elise had seen it in her grandmother's house.

Eugena held the bowl out with one hand while using the other to take her scepter back. She swam to the water's edge and offered it to Derek.

The jewel on her scepter began to glow. She waved it over the bowl in his hands, and the carvings began to shimmer.

"To show our willingness to continue to live in peace with your family, we offer you this gift in honor of the future queen and birth of your child. Please inform Princess Joranna that, should she ever need it, she can fill this bowl with water and communicate directly with us."

Elise should've known it was more than a decoration.

I wonder how many times Nana has used it.

"We are deeply honored by your gift and generosity." Derek bowed. "Please know that we are always at your service as well, Your Majesty. Thank you."

"Until we meet again," Eugena said. Her eyes traveled to Elise and her friends before settling on hers a moment longer. A shiver ran down Elise's spine as the icy stare seemed to penetrate through to her soul.

Why is she looking at me?

Elise made sure to look at anything except the queen's gaze and prayed she would move on to someone else. At long last, she turned to glance over her shoulder and nodded at her subjects, who all began to descend into the lake.

"Farewell," she said before she retreated back into the water.

Assessing the area one last time, Erumann nodded to them all before joining his queen.

No one spoke until the lake was as calm as when they first arrived.

"Shall we be off then?" Derek asked them as they headed back towards the carriage and horses. "You all are very fortunate to have witnessed such a ceremony. On to Clara!"

***

The four friends waited until the carriage was in motion before they all began speaking at the same time.

"Can you believe what we just saw?" Darcie asked. She giggled and waved her hands to fan herself.

"I can't even breathe!" Elise bounced in her seat and matched her friend's energy. "Who knew that bowl had so much history? I saw it at her house but just thought it was an ordinary bowl."

Mitch chuckled.

"I'm learning that nothing about your family is ordinary."

"You know," Gavin said, "I think I'm officially past the point of waiting to wake up." The others chuckled and nodded. "I mean, I can only try to convince myself for so long, but a mermaid just made a telephone bowl out of water to give to Joranna for having a baby. I'm not creative enough to make that up on my own."

"You think we'll find the diary when we get back to the castle?" Darcie asked. "Do you think we've seen enough to report anything to your family?"

"I don't know. I mean, she had the bowl in her house so she's aware of it and what it does. We still don't know who the spy is. We may still have to do more."

Maybe we could ask someone who works in the castle.

Elise's face fell and she twisted her fingers together.

"What is it?" Darcie asked. "You only play with your hands when you're worried."

Elise sighed.

It can't hurt to tell them.

"I've been thinking about Dalton."

Gavin tensed in the seat across from her.

"He helped me out so much last time, and I haven't seen him since we got here. I really liked him. Not like *that*, but I wanted to say thanks."

"You should ask your family about him when we get home," Darcie suggested.

"Or ask while we're here," Mitch said.

Elise shrugged.

"They only just stopped accusing us of everything. Mom and Nana never mentioned him before. I don't even know if they'd remember him."

"I don't know why they couldn't have helped you out a bit more," Mitch said. "Like 'here's a map of the kingdom. Go find the bad guy and come tell us how it went.'"

Elise laughed.

Mitch definitely had a way of saying what they were all thinking.

"If it were that easy, they could've just done it themselves," Elise muttered.

"Y'all know I'm right," Mitch said. "They just threw us all into this crap with nothing to go off of. Don't get me wrong, the mermaids were cool, and I'm with Gavin on finally believing all of it. But we're not finding out anything about this Rona chick, and even with an apology, we're still somewhat suspected of being spies. I don't see an end to it. No one is going to tell us anything."

"He's right," Gavin said. "It's not a lot to go on."

What do they expect me to do about it? I didn't control any of this!

She wiped a loose strand of hair out of her eyes and felt heat rush to her face.

"Look, I know it's frustrating!" Elise leaned back against her seat and crossed her arms. Her jaw tightened as tears threatened to form. "You think I'm not frustrated? I'm sick of being accused, too, and I hate all these dresses and rules. I hate the secrecy. I want my jeans. I want my phone! I'd love a manual that explains what to do, but the truth is, this is what we have to work with. So, the sooner we all try to accept it and stop complaining, the easier all this will be. I could really use your help."

"Whoa, Elise. Calm down," Darcie said. Elise glared at her. "I know you hate when I tell you that, but they're just venting a little."

"I'm sorry." She turned her head and blinked away her tears. *Get it together, Elise. You're overreacting.*

"I just feel like it's my fault you're all here, and I want to get us all home. I want things back to normal."

Elise chanced a peek out of the window. In the distance she could see farmland and distant cottages. The carriage began to slow.

When they were helped out a few minutes later, she saw that they were just outside of the town's entrance. Derek removed his dress jacket and placed it inside the carriage. Two guards stayed with him while the rest took the carriage and horses to the stables nearby.

"Are you ready to see Clara?" Derek asked. His smile eased Elise's nerves and she couldn't remember the last time she had seen it.

They stepped underneath an ornate stone archway engraved with the town's name. Long vines grew and twisted up against the faded stone. The pathway led into the heart of the marketplace where the townspeople were shopping and going about their business. Carts lined the sides of the path, selling different products from eggs, spices, and wine to custom made jewelry. There were also several adjoining shops a few feet away behind the carts. Each looked almost identical with pointed roofs, reddish-brown shingles and stone walls.

As they walked for the next several minutes, Elise saw the signs for a butcher shop, a bookstore, a tailor and bakery before the shops continued down the next road. A numbing buzz sounded as all of the ongoing conversations overlapped and people bustled around them. She could hear chickens clucking as well as children laughing and playing nearby. A couple of the kids ran past them, and for a moment Elise felt everything was quite chaotic.

Derek, however, seemed perfectly at ease. Wearing only his white linen shirt and dark blue vest, he seemed quite cheerful as he mingled with those around him. The guards were careful to keep near him, but Derek felt no threat here. This was where he was at his happiest. . .among people. He navigated the street without effort, smiling at everyone who was close enough as they stopped and bowed to him. He thanked them and even gave a few coins to some who were begging on the street.

"Around the corner on the next street, there is the cobbler, the inn and a pub, as well as the carpentry shop," Derek said. "The blacksmith is on the other end and up the road about a mile is the church. The town continues from there, but it's better to avoid some parts, especially after dark," he warned.

Elise's stomach growled as rich smells wafted through the air. She was relieved when Derek gestured to the nearest shop where most of the smells were coming from.

"I have a need to step into the bakery if you'd care to join me," Derek said. "You won't find better delicacies in the kingdom."

Upon entering, Elise closed her eyes and inhaled the mouth-watering scent of freshly baked breads, cakes, and sweet frosting. Sunlight poured in through the small windows on either side of the door. A man working at the back counter was kneading a large pile of dough and smiled when he saw them.

"Good morning, Your Highness!" The man laughed and excused his appearance before grabbing a towel to wipe the flour from his hands. "Let me just get cleaned up and I'll be right with you." He bowed, then rushed up a small wooden staircase.

"Go ahead and have a look around," Derek told them.

All four walked in different directions around the shop.

Elise felt like she could gain five pounds just by looking at the inventory.

The front counter had three shelves filled with an assortment of cookies and pastries. The tops of the counters displayed five tiered platters with the most enticing cupcakes Elise had ever seen with frosting of every color. Along the sides of the shop, wall length shelves showcased various golden-brown rolls and croissants.

The baker returned and greeted them all again. He was a rather cheerful man, possibly in his early thirties, with a plump clean-shaven face and sandy-brown hair.

"Good morning, Mr. Baxter," Derek said. "How are you this morning?"

"I can't complain, Your Majesty. This is a pleasant surprise since I normally do business with the king's steward. How might I help you all today?"

"I wanted to personally come and announce that my son has been born." Derek couldn't hide his smile.

"Ahh, a happy day indeed, Sire. I am very glad to hear it. And how is the new mother doing?"

"She is doing well. Thank you. Tired, as to be expected, but both are healthy and happy. I'd like to have a special cake made to celebrate and I know that you make the best around."

"I'd be honored, Sire."

Elise watched from across the shop as Derek became animated talking about his son and the presenting ceremony that he wanted to hold to introduce Richard to the kingdom. He described the cake while the baker took notes. When Derek had finished, Mr. Baxter turned to address Elise and the others.

"I imagine your guests are hungry. Please select anything you like, free of charge."

Mitch didn't waste any time before picking an éclair. Darcie walked to the other end of the counter and picked up a cinnamon twist roll.

Elise felt Gavin's eyes on her, and her heart began to race.

Maybe I should pick something small, so I don't look like such a pig.

A nagging voice in the back of her mind told her not to worry what he thought. She was starving and should get what she wanted. Deciding to listen to her conscience, and her stomach, she reached out and selected an oversized vanilla cupcake with strawberry icing that she had been eyeing for several minutes.

Gavin smiled and reached around her to grab an oatmeal raisin cookie. His eyes closed and he moaned in the back of his throat. The sound stirred something in Elise's stomach that definitely didn't come from hunger and she longed to hear that sound again. She returned to her own cupcake and walked over to stand behind Derek. He held out money and insisted that he pay for the cake and the treats. They thanked him through their full mouths and exited the shop.

"You've got some frosting on your lip." Gavin gestured to his own lip for her to see. Elise wiped her mouth and muttered her thanks. Once he had joined Derek and Mitch ahead of her, she waved Darcie over and asked if anything was in her teeth. Darcie chuckled and assured her she was fine before asking the same question and smiling at her.

When both had deemed one another decent, they hurried through the crowd to catch up with the boys.

Both girls jumped as an old woman came in between them and approached Mitch. She carried an oversized basket full of richly colored blooms.

"Excuse me, kind sir," she said, startling him as well. "Why not buy a flower for your lady, sir?" She held out a small white flower towards Darcie and raised an eyebrow at him.

"Oh no," they both replied.

"We aren't…"

"Not like that," Darcie said.

"Well, how about you, sir?" She turned to Gavin with a toothy grin.

"Here, allow me," Derek said. He stepped away from his guards and smiled as he gave the woman a handful of coins. He handed two long-stemmed roses to Elise and Darcie, then bought a small bouquet for Joranna.

"Bless you. Thank you kindly, Your Majesty."

Elise had never seen anyone look so relieved as Gavin and Mitch did, and she chuckled as she buried her nose into her rose's soft petals.

"This place is so beautiful."

"I've been coming here since I was a boy," Derek said. He smiled and nodded at a couple of townspeople who called out to him. "I hope my children grow to love it here as I do. As you can see, we enjoy most of these products in the castle and have come to know these wonderful people well."

Elise took this as her opportunity.

"Um…speaking of people in the castle, do you remember a man named Dalton?"

Derek squinted his eyes against the sun and looked puzzled.

"He gave us all the dance lessons for your engagement ball."

"Ah, yes," Derek said. "Truth be told, we have so many servants and people in the castle it's hard to remember every single one. I know that sounds terrible, but yes, I remember who you're referring to. He actually received an invitation to the Vynchian palace about a year ago. While there, he met his bride and asked to relocate permanently."

Elise felt disappointed but overall relieved to hear that he was happy even if she couldn't thank him again.

They strolled under a smaller stone archway and approached a crowd watching a nearby street performance.

Positioned near a small stone fountain, three musicians played lively music on a mandolin, violin, and flute. A few couples danced along to the upbeat music, while Derek and several others laughed and clapped. The mandolin player cavorted around the couples and grinned when he saw Derek.

"Let it be known that we have a most honored guest in our audience today, His Majesty Prince Derek!" he said with a bow and caused others who hadn't noticed him to bow as well.

Derek smiled, but it didn't reach his eyes, and Elise suddenly felt the mood change.

The musician appeared to be no more than twenty or twenty-one years old with tousled hair and a roughly shaven face.

"Shall we not entertain him and his guests during their visit? For he is a most *generous* prince and will one day be a most valued ruler."

Elise glared between the man and Derek. His smile and kind words were thrown out like knives more than compliments. As his mockery continued and laughter began to radiate through the crowd, Derek shifted under everyone's gaze and grew uncomfortable. The guards reached for the hilts of their swords, but Derek stopped them.

The mandolin player plucked a few more notes and danced around the guards.

"Have I ever told you all the tale of a foolish prince who chose greed and fortune over love? A man whose vanity cost him all that he cherished at the expense of his beloved? And yet, history has *romanticized* this man? Made him out to be a hero that we should adore?"

He returned to the fountain and nodded for his companions to join him in a new melody. A few upbeat notes played before he broke out in song.

> *"There was once a foolish king,*
> *Whose heart and mind were small,*
> *If he couldn't have everything,*
> *He sought to quash it all."*

He danced around the crowd, avoiding Derek and the guards for the moment as he gained admirers.

> *"Some called him a founder,*
> *They claimed this land he saved,*

But he really was a bounder,
Can't excuse how he behaved.

His queen bore every king's wish,
A bouncing baby son,
But he chose instead to be selfish,
His vanity, it won.

He didn't give them any time,
Though his attention they both yearned,
The boy grew up, resented him,
And yet he never learned.

Only when his sweetheart queen
Was failed by her draining health,
Did he realize how he'd always been,
And had no one to share his wealth."

Derek turned on his heels and pushed past the crowd and the player.

"Was it something I said, Your Majesty?" A few people laughed while others began to disperse. "Do you not care about history, Your Majesty? Are you not entertained by your lineage and so-called *values* you live by?"

What's this guy's problem?

Derek took the high road, but Elise was ready to punch this musician in the face.

The player was not at all intimidated and called out to Derek once more.

"Your family sits high and mighty in your plush castle while we all sit down here awaiting Rona's army. And it is coming."

His tone took a somber turn as he addressed the crowd. Derek stopped walking and looked over his shoulder.

"We will not be fooled by feigned assurances. Hear me, everyone! Rona *will* rise again. And when she does, let us not be sitting ducks. Arm yourselves! Hold your future king accountable! What will he do to protect us all?"

"Enough!" Derek called back. "Seize him!"

A guard grabbed the man and escorted him away through the crowd. A few apologized to Derek as they passed while several others began to engage in a panicked chatter.

The other guard ordered the crowd to disperse as Derek stormed off. Elise and the others had to jog to catch up with him.

He didn't speak until they turned the corner onto the main street.

"The nerve of some people!"

"What was that all about?" Gavin asked.

"He's mocking the very creator of this town. Yes, Claramond was known to enjoy the finer things in life. And yes, a lot of time and effort went into building this kingdom. Rather than praise and give him credit where it is due, they tear apart his character."

"Sounds like any other kind of politics," Mitch muttered.

Elise hesitated.

"Was any of it true?"

Derek sighed.

"It's possible," he admitted. "There was a diary found from my great-great-grandmother Queen Eleanora that expressed much heartache during her marriage. Claramond was often preoccupied with projects. Their son went on to do great things to keep the kingdom growing and eventually reconciled with his father on his deathbed." He shook his head and quickened his steps. "But I will not sit idly by and let someone defame his character. This town owes him everything, despite his shortcomings."

"What will happen to that guy?" Darcie asked.

"I can't arrest him based on blasphemy against the crown alone. He is free to say and believe what he wishes but causing a disturbance and possible riot is a criminal offense. Knowing my father, he will probably receive a minor punishment and be released."

"Was that stuff about Rona true?" Elise asked.

When Derek sighed again and stopped walking, Elise immediately regretted her question. They had only just gained his respect and favor and she didn't want to jeopardize that within hours of earning it.

"Father has been getting more letters from neighboring kingdoms and tensions are rising. We have no leads at the moment, but I urge you if you hear a whisper to continue your promise to Father and report it immediately."

There was the same underlying threat to his tone that King Theronde had used when he had asked the same of them.

They approached the same shops near the entrance and once again Elise could smell the bakery.

"I'd rather not let that musician spoil our entire visit. Is there anything else you'd like to see before we return home?" Derek asked.

"I wouldn't mind looking in that bookshop," Darcie said. "I'm curious to see what kind of books you guys have here."

Elise nodded.

Maybe I could find that history book and learn about Claramond.

"Feel free to visit it. I will see that the horses are prepped and meet you at the entrance shortly," Derek said.

Darcie led them over to the bookstore.

Elise was surprised how small the shop was. All the books were crowded together on shelves that reached the ceiling. There were also tall standalones that lined the middle of the shop. Lanterns were positioned along the ends but were not lit due to the sunlight that poured in through the small windows.

A handful of people were already in the shop, and when she couldn't find the shopkeeper, Elise wasted no time walking over to the rolling bookshelf ladder.

"Man, he is pissed off," Mitch said, looking back through the window. "I don't see the big deal. It was just a stupid song about a dead guy."

"Mitch, that's his family!" Darcie's comment came from behind one of the middle shelves.

"That singer had it coming," Gavin said as he leaned against a shelf and loosened his collar. "That song was rehearsed. He couldn't have come up with that on the spot."

"I agree," Elise said. "I could've strangled him myself. He humiliated Derek out there."

She stepped off the ladder and walked down the next aisle. She brushed her fingertips against the countless spines, and the titles blended together.

She grabbed a random book and opened it, only to realize it was in a different language. When she looked up, she was startled to find Gavin standing beside her.

"Sorry," he said. He waited for her to put the book away. "Look, um. . ." He glanced over to make sure Darcie and Mitch couldn't hear him and ran his hand along the back of his neck. "I wanted to talk about that Dalton guy from earlier. I didn't want to do it with anyone around, but I wanted to say—"

"It's here!"

Darcie squealed, jumping up and down. Mitch hurried to her side as she waved a book above her head.

It was the diary!

We can leave!

Elise ran to Darcie and Mitch.

"What are you waiting for? Give it to Elise. Use it!" Mitch said.

Darcie shoved it into Elise's hands. Both eagerly waited for her to open it.

"I can't just use it here," Elise said as Gavin joined them. The shopkeeper came out of a back room and greeted them. The other patrons frowned at them from a distance. Elise lowered her voice. "Derek is waiting for us. We'll look guilty if we leave now. We don't know where it's going to take us!"

"But we agreed we'd take the tour on our way out of town. They didn't know we still needed the diary. We can get away with it," Darcie argued.

"I know, but let's at least say bye one more time. We shouldn't let Derek go back angry and alone either."

Darcie rolled her eyes and nodded.

"Okay, fine, but then we are leaving."

I also want to see if I can find Claramond's portrait.

"Tell them we'll come back when we hear some stuff," Gavin said. "That should work. Not to mention they have a new baby. They'll be too busy to worry about us."

Elise nodded and clutched the book to her chest. "We need to hide this."

She looked at the shopkeeper, who had his back turned.

We can't let him think we're stealing this.

Gavin waved for her to hand it over and tucked the book under his vest between his waistband and undershirt. The shape was still visible through the material, so they stood close to block his chest from view. Elise's heart was racing a mile a minute as they made it out to the street where they met Derek and the guards.

At the carriage, Darcie offered to hold Joranna's bouquet and handed Derek his coat. He was only too happy to allow them to return.

Gavin pulled the diary out from his vest so that he could adjust his position. When the carriage began to move, he relaxed against his seat and handed it to Elise.

She spent the better part of the trip feeling like a kid on Christmas morning. Her knees bounced the diary on her lap, and she drummed her fingers on the cover until Mitch grunted and reached across the carriage to take it. Elise scowled at him before turning her attention to the window.

How much longer is it? Maybe we should've left when we had the chance. I wonder if it would disappear if we didn't use it fast enough.

Now all there was left to do was give Joranna her bowl, say a proper goodbye, and hope for the best.

CHAPTER 14

Once they were back at the castle, Derek was happy to oblige Elise's request to see the portrait hall.

Elise was once again drawn to the painting of Avalyn and Derek playing, but she was careful to keep her distance this time.

"I'm sorry you all had to witness that shameful display today," said Derek.

He paused about halfway down the hall in front of a large family portrait. He nodded towards the plaque beneath it.

King Claramond, founder of Clara, Queen Eleanora and Prince Eamon

King Claramond looked far more severe than Elise expected. His thick shoulder-length hair was black as ink and his expression came across stern and cold. Elise thought that he resembled a villain from a fairy tale. This didn't match the picture in her head based on Derek's family stories. Queen Eleanora had beautiful blonde hair wrapped in pearls and was painted in a powder pink gown with white lace. A small blonde-haired boy sat on her lap.

"A strong family unit," said a voice behind them. King Theronde crossed the hall and joined them. "I trust Derek told you of the town's origins?"

"Yes," Elise said.

"If you'll excuse me," Derek said, "I'm going to give Joranna her gift and the flowers." He gestured towards the bowl and bouquet in his hands.

Once he had left, Theronde turned his attention back to the painting.

"A lifetime achievement indeed. He is a ruler I respect very much. We owe our prosperity to this great man."

"They don't look happy," Mitch said.

"Life may not always be filled with happiness, but it is always filled with purpose," Theronde said. "Sometimes duty has to come first."

Elise was careful with her next words and hoped she'd get more information out of her great-grandfather.

"Derek got upset when someone mocked the way King Claramond treated his family."

"It's a lesson to be sure," he said with a sigh. "Eleanora's diaries suggest their family's relationships were strained, but we can't let that overshadow all the good that he did for this kingdom and its people." The mention of diaries brought Elise's attention back to the one hidden under Mitch's shirt. "Was there anything else? I hardly see Derek stewing over some light jesting."

They all shared an uncomfortable glance. Derek came around the corner and walked towards them as Theronde repeated his question.

"He said Rona will return and everyone should hold you accountable, Father," Derek said. "Needless to say, he was apprehended before he could stir up too much trouble."

"I see…" Theronde sighed again and stared at the painting. "Could I see you all in my study, please?"

Gavin cleared his throat and looked at the other three for support.

"We were about to leave actually."

"Yeah, we need to get going, but didn't want to leave without saying goodbye this time," Darcie said.

"We were just about to go change, but we promise to bring you any news," Elise added.

The king frowned.

"This will only take a moment. It's not a conversation I feel comfortable having in the hall, and then I'd be happy to provide you with a proper escort out. Derek, you'll join us, too."

"Yes, Father. Let's allow them to change and we'll all meet in ten minutes."

The king nodded and excused himself. Derek did the same and left to see Joranna again.

***

Elise closed her eyes and smiled as she stepped into her jeans. She would never take them for granted again. As she began to fix her hair, however, the tie broke and fell on the floor.

Crap! Not now.

She groaned, picked it up and threw it on the vanity in front of her, then stared at her reflection.

Her hair had a mind of its own. When it wasn't tied back, it usually preferred to thicken and frizz up.

Elise quickly wet her fingers with the leftover water from the pitcher on the dresser and tried to tame her unruly locks. She parted it on one side before pressing down. Anything to make it look like she didn't just roll out of bed. Picking up the hairbrush one of the maids had left on the vanity, she yanked it through without any luck. She jerked open the drawers to find them all empty. Elise finally sighed and stared at herself again.

Okay, calm down. It should only be for a few minutes. With any luck, we'll go back to Nana's, and I can borrow one there.

She opened the door and heard her friends talking in the hallway. Maybe if she just played it cool, it wouldn't be a big deal. Elise ran her fingers through the parted side one more time and tucked a few strands behind her ear before she joined them.

"Darcie, do you have a hair clip I could use?"

She ran her hand along the back of her neck and tried not to look at the boys.

Darcie fidgeted in her pockets and shrugged.

"Sorry, they're all in my purse in the car. Don't worry about it though. I've always said you look great with your hair down. Doesn't she look good, guys?"

She was going to have to talk to Darcie about how subtle conversations worked at a later time. Mitch shrugged and said she looked fine and Gavin nodded.

"I didn't realize your hair was so long. Looks good," said Gavin.

"Thanks."

Quit touching it, Elise. You're just bringing more attention to it. See? He's looking again!

"Elise?"

They all turned as Joranna came into the hall. For someone who had recently had a baby, she looked breathtaking. She had on fresh makeup and her hair had been done. They all bowed and curtsied as she approached with Richard in her arms.

"I'm so glad I caught you. Derek told me you were about to leave, and I hate we didn't get to talk this time."

"It's okay. You had a good reason," Elise said. She looked down at the sleeping infant. "He's beautiful."

"Thank you." Joranna rocked her arms back and forth gently. "Would you like to hold him?"

Elise thought back to what happened when she touched Derek and didn't want to chance hurting the baby by touching his child. She politely declined and was satisfied watching from a distance.

"Thank you so much for going with Derek to get my gift. How was Eugena?"

"She's intense," Darcie said.

"I've heard. I plan to go visit in person and thank them when I'm able. How did you like Clara?"

"I wish I lived here," Elise said.

Joranna smiled.

"I'm glad to hear that. I don't know if Derek told you everything, so I wanted to come apologize to you all in person."

"You really don't have to," Elise said. "We're just glad you're not angry at us. We'd like to come back and visit again."

"I'd like that. In some weird way, you've become friends of ours. I know we got off on the wrong foot, but maybe we'll get to spend more time together during your next visit. I hope it doesn't come with terrible news, but I know you'll do what it takes to keep Haighdlen safe. Maybe I'll have gotten some sleep before then."

They chuckled, and Elise was caught by surprise when Joranna hugged her. Knowing that her grandparents weren't mad at them anymore took a huge weight off her shoulders. Once Joranna had returned to her bedroom, they made their way down to the king's study.

***

To their dismay, the four were met at the bottom of the stairs by the same guard who had been instructed to chaperone them.

"I can't deal with this guy right now," Gavin whispered. "We've already had the diary for almost two hours. Let's just open it and make a run for it."

Elise rolled her eyes at him.

"I'm not too happy about the babysitter either but leaving right now could mess everything up!"

He leaned in closer to her.

"I'm just sick of getting delayed. I want to go home."

King Theronde's voice called them inside.

The guard stepped around and opened the door to the office.

Elise was surprised to see Derek and Queen Avalyn already there. The king looked up from his document and beckoned them forward to be seated.

A fire was lit despite the early afternoon hour.

Elise corrected her posture when Avalyn took a seat beside her.

"I'm saddened that you have to be off so soon," the king said. "I should have liked to introduce you to my council, but I will share your revelations with them and discuss further security measures."

"Can you really not share anything else?" Avalyn asked. "A name? A date?"

Elise's hands were tied at this point. She wanted to give more information, but without knowing who the spy was, little could be done. She didn't want to risk everyone's futures. They were early enough in the diary that a simple warning was their safest bet. She shrugged and shook her head.

"Any luck finding a spy?" the queen asked.

Theronde shook his head and reclined back in his chair.

"We'll catch the spy soon enough, Mother," Derek reassured her.

"If there even is a spy," she mused. "What better way to instill fear than by having us all on the lookout for something that doesn't exist. A wild goose chase to keep us busy before she strikes."

I hadn't thought about that.

"No, there is a spy," Theronde said. "But the question remains if we will find him in time. That performer was correct about one thing. Rona is coming. A war is coming, and we must prepare for it."

His chilling declaration made Elise feel like she had swallowed a bucket of ice.

"What can I do, Father?" Derek asked. The urgency in his tone could not be mistaken. "Please give me something to do."

"You need only be there for your bride and young son. My men are out searching for possible suspects, as well as interrogating the man arrested today. The kingdom must not see us panic. We will remain calm and strong."

He turned his attention to Elise and her friends.

"You may thank your *friend* for the warning and remember your loyalty must remain to Haighdlen."

"Yes, Your Majesty," Elise said.

"And when can we expect a follow up report?"

Elise searched her friends' faces. If all went according to plan, and the diary sent them back to her grandmother's house, Elise would return alone and couldn't make promises on their behalves.

"We haven't been given our next instructions," Darcie said.

"But I promise that I will report to you as soon as there is more news," Elise added.

The king didn't appear satisfied by the empty promise, but he nodded and granted them permission to leave.

An odd sensation came over Elise as she exited the study. Half an hour earlier, she couldn't wait to open the diary and take a chance getting home. Now that the opportunity was here, she was reluctant to leave.

King Theronde made good on his promise to provide them with an escort through the gates and to the entrance of the forest.

Once he verified they were alone, Mitch pulled out the diary from the back of his tucked t-shirt, then shook the fabric loose to straighten it.

"Here, take it."

Elise hesitated.

"What if it doesn't take us home?"

"You're really going to do this now?" Gavin snapped. "Just open it!"

He's right. Don't pull a you right now. Just get them home.

She said a silent prayer and peeled back the cover.

CHAPTER 15

Elise awoke to a beautiful twilight sky.

A few birds flew overhead, and the humid summer air smelled sweet. Crickets sang nearby and a car honked in the distance.

A car?

She bolted upright and felt relief wash over her. They were on Joranna's front lawn. She chortled and shook her head.

We actually made it!

Everything appeared the same, and there was no sign of her mother's car yet.

I'm safe.

Her smile fell, however, when she saw Mitch's car parked in the driveway.

Now they're going to wake up and leave.

She looked down at Gavin and realized she probably only had a few minutes left to be this close to him. She doubted their paths would cross much after graduation. Elise double checked that Mitch and Darcie were still unconscious before she reached out to intertwine her fingers with his.

Her other hand brushed the hair out of his eyes.

He's such a peaceful sleeper.

She grazed the back of her hand against his cheek and admired his features, fighting the urge to lean down and kiss him.

A sudden dinging sound made her jump and pull away from him. The sound repeated a couple more times before she realized it was coming from Mitch's pocket. As all three of them started to stir, she scooted further away.

Mitch's eyes shot open and he fished his phone out.

"Hey, my phone works again! I have ten texts already. What about y'all?"

"We left ours in the car," said Darcie. "Are we really back?"

Gavin stood to adjust his clothes and ran his fingers through his hair.

"It looks like it. This is great!"

"I'll say!" Mitch exclaimed. "Elise, go say bye to your family, and let's get on the road."

"You guys go ahead and head home."

They turned to look at her and Darcie stepped closer.

"Elise, what's going on? We made it back. You're coming home with us."

"I can't. I have to go back to Haighdlen."

"That makes no sense," Gavin argued. "Why would you do that when it's taken us this long to finally get home?"

Elise felt her stomach churn under his gaze, and she fiddled with her hands. She looked down at her twisting fingers so she could collect her thoughts better.

"Joranna gave us. . .I mean, me, two missions. I'm supposed to find the spy and then stop Mom from running away." When no one responded, she continued. "Well, we didn't find the spy, and the only one I've seen born is Richard. So, clearly I've got to go back."

"Maybe they changed their minds. Let's go talk to your family," Darcie said.

"No, don't be stupid," Elise said. "We've risked everything to try and get you guys back here. Y'all didn't ask for this, and the car is right there. I can handle it. Go."

"You don't have to tell me twice," Mitch said. He finished a text and gestured for Gavin to follow him. "Make up your mind."

Darcie shot her friend a glance that she hoped would send the message to reconsider.

"If you're nervous about telling them you want to go home, I'll go in and help you."

"That's the funny thing," Elise said. "For the first time, I'm not really afraid. I want to do this."

"Then I'm coming, too."

"Darcie, no. The guys are ready to leave, and I'll need you to cover for me with Mom."

Darcie looked over at the guys waiting outside the car and back at Elise. Elise wrapped her arms around Darcie and squeezed.

"Thank you for all your help. I'll be home as soon as I can."

"And how will you get home?" Darcie blinked back a couple of tears and cleared her throat.

"I'm sure Ian could drive me," Elise said. "Seriously, go. You don't have to protect me. I'll be home before you know it. We'll have a real sleepover."

Darcie wiped her cheek and stomped her foot.

"And what about Rona? Elise, you can't face her alone. What if they send you right into battle?"

"Then it'll just be me, and I'll know my friends are far away and safe."

She looked over Darcie's shoulder as Gavin walked back up. Elise ran her hands through her hair and pulled out a couple of leaves.

He pushed his hands into his pockets, rocking back and forth on his feet.

"You coming, Darcie?" he asked. He sensed the mood between them and put his hand on Darcie's shoulder. "Come on. She's made up her mind."

"In a minute. You go ahead," she said. When he was far enough away, Darcie placed her hands on her hips. "And what about Gavin? You're just going to let him get away?"

"I never had a chance with him," Elise said. "Anything we had was due to your meddling. It wasn't real. He doesn't like me like that." She sighed. "It's better this way. I can go back to being 'Lisa' to him."

"I don't believe that," she said. "I think there *is* something there. You should've seen his face when you came out with your hair down. He couldn't stop watching you in the king's office."

Elise's heart swelled at the possibility. She watched Gavin get into the passenger seat and shook her head when Mitch honked the horn.

She would say anything to get me in the car.

"You need to go."

Darcie scoffed and stomped all the way back to the car. She climbed into the backseat and slammed the door shut.

Elise turned to hide her own tears and walked up to the porch. She paused outside the door to watch Mitch turn the car around. Darcie was on her knees, facing her out of the back windshield. Elise waved and felt her heart sink as Mitch drove away down the winding driveway.

I'm sorry.

***

Elise's guilt eased as Joranna's smiling face answered the door.

"You're back!" she cried, pulling Elise into a tight squeeze. "Oh, it's so good to see you! Come in, you must tell me everything you've seen. Where are the others? I thought I heard a car horn."

Elise stepped into the house.

"They left."

Joranna closed the door and pressed her hand to her chest.

"Elise, I'm so sorry."

"No, don't be. I sent them home. It's better this way."

"I doubt that," she said. "Let me get everyone down here, then you can tell us everything."

Elise sat in the living room while Joranna went upstairs to collect the family. Her cousins were already crowded around the room's television playing video games. Joseph brought in a tray with tea as Elise watched her aunts and uncles arrive one by one to welcome her back.

Joranna paused on her way down the stairs and coughed heavily into her elbow. After she cleared her throat, she walked over to sit beside Elise on the couch.

"Children, go upstairs and take a break from that nonsense. You've been on it all afternoon," Gwen scolded. She ushered them out of the room before walking over to stand next to Richard.

No one spoke while the children made their way up, and Morgan checked to make sure the older ones weren't eavesdropping.

Elise studied her grandmother's face.

"What is it?" Joranna asked. She ran her fingers along her cheeks and teeth. "Do I have something on my face?"

"No." Elise smiled. "I'm just not used to seeing you like this."

"Old?" Ian said into a cough. Morgan punched his arm and he laughed. "She knows I'm kidding."

Joranna chuckled and turned back to Elise.

"Tell us everything!"

Elise looked at their expectant faces and paused on her Uncle Richard's still sour expression.

"I don't know anything yet." She shrugged to hide her insecurity and began to fidget with her fingers. "We didn't find the spy, and Mom isn't born yet. I figured the only reason it brought us back was to send the others home, so I did."

"So, what *did* you see?" Sarah asked.

Elise smiled as she relived the memory.

"I got to meet my grandfather."

Joranna's eyes glistened as Elise retold the diner adventure and how they all fumbled through the engagement ball before being chased out.

"He loved you so much," Elise said.

Joranna wiped her eyes with a handkerchief. "He loved his family more than anything."

"And then we traveled forward a couple of years. We had to convince you all that we weren't the spies. We got to meet Eugena when she gave you your special bowl, and Derek took us to see Clara after Richard was born. The diary appeared while we were in the bookshop, but we had to wait to talk to King Theronde before we could come home."

Her brow furrowed.

"Wait. . .if everything we just did altered the past, wouldn't you remember us coming?"

"There is a faint memory of visitors coming," Joranna said. She closed her eyes and tried to make it clearer. "But our spell altered our memories of the visit to the family, and only your names stick out at the moment."

"Besides, it's so early in the diary, and you said so yourself that you haven't really learned anything new," Richard reasoned.

"It makes sense that nothing has changed yet and why you would return to this spot in time," Ian said. "But if you go further, and continue to change the past, we can't promise you'll return to the same version of the present."

"How long were we gone?" Elise asked.

Joranna looked up at the clock on the mantle.

"About two hours."

"Two hours? We were there for four days!"

"You're also going in between different time periods in another dimension." Her grandmother paused to cough again. "The diary will see that you leave and arrive when you're needed."

"So, you knew exactly where we were going to go?"

"I knew where you would land," Joranna said, "but where you all go during a specific time is up to your choices."

"So, Mom still doesn't know I'm here?"

"She hasn't called any of us," Ian said. "I'd say you're still safe."

Elise gasped and felt around her pockets.

My phone!

Her things were still in Mitch's car. What if her mom was texting her? If she didn't reply, her mother would certainly think something was up and come looking for her. She prayed if that happened that Darcie would answer.

Joranna placed her hand on Elise's knee.

"Relax. We'll deal with Ruby if something comes up."

"Go back for a moment," Richard said. "You said our grandfather wanted to talk to you before you left. What did he say?"

"He wanted us to thank whoever tipped us off. He was also finally convinced we weren't spies, but he made us promise to be loyal to Haighdlen. We said we'd bring any news that we found about Rona or a spy to him."

"Are you sure there's nothing else? I would hardly consider this useful."

"Richard," Joranna scolded.

"She's only been to a couple of places," Ian pointed out. "Give her time."

Elise struggled to find anything else they could find interesting.

"The only other part I can think of is King Claramond."

"The founder of Clara?" Sarah asked. "What's he got to do with anything? He was dead long before any of this happened."

There was a knock on the door that made Elise pause.

Joseph stepped out to answer it. When he returned, Elise's heart leapt into her throat as she saw Darcie, Mitch, and Gavin enter the room. Joseph bowed and excused himself.

"What're you guys doing here?"

"You forgot your phone," Gavin said. He reached forward and handed it to her.

No missed calls or messages. I'm good for now.

"Thanks. Was my purse in there, too?"

"I knew we forgot something," Darcie said.

Gavin turned to walk back outside for it, but Darcie stopped him.

"Just wait. That's not the only reason we're back."

Gavin rocked back and forth with his hands in his pockets, Mitch ran his hand along the back of his neck, and Darcie fumbled with her own phone in her hands. Elise raised her eyebrows and shook her head for more.

"It wasn't right," Gavin said. "Leaving you wasn't right."

"If you're not ready to come home, then we're with you until you are," Darcie said. She turned and stared at Mitch until he looked up from his phone, where his eyes had been glued since she began their explanation.

"Oh, yeah." He shoved the device back in his pocket. "We came this far with you."

"And we want to help your family," Darcie said.

"Bless you," Joranna said. She stood and hugged each of them, then turned to face Elise. "What a fine group of friends you have. Rona could only wish for loyalty like this."

"It'll take more than loyalty and luck from a few kids," Richard grumbled. "Excuse me." He turned and walked out of the room. Gwendolyn apologized for his behavior and followed him.

"Don't listen to him, dear," Joranna said. "We know you can do this and now that your friends are back, you're even stronger."

Elise nodded but Richard's words still stung.

"Let's get back to Claramond," Sarah suggested. "Maybe that can help us."

"I'm going to go to the bathroom first," Elise said, excusing herself. She walked down the hallway and noticed that the bathroom door was locked. Joseph spoke up from inside, so she decided to use the one upstairs.

Hearing Joranna offer her friends something to eat, she jogged up the stairway so she could join them faster. As she reached the landing, however, she heard whispers coming from one of the bedrooms. The door down the hall was cracked, but she could clearly make out Richard and Gwendolyn's voices.

"The man I met in Clara was fearless," Gwendolyn reminded him. "A noble prince who valiantly took on any threat."

His answering tone was cold, distant, and emotionless.

"That man is dead."

Elise's curiosity got the best of her and she crept closer until she could see them through the small opening.

Gwendolyn ran her fingers through his hair and crossed her arms around his neck. His arms wrapped around her.

"It's all right to be afraid, Rich," she said. She leaned her forehead against his. "It's perfectly fine to lose a battle."

"I lost a kingdom."

Gwen gripped his chin and forced him to look down at her.

"Yes, but it is *not* okay to give up. This family is looking for you to step up and be a ruler. Your kingdom *needs* a ruler."

"And look what I did to them, Gwen. I nearly got them all killed. My best friends died saving me. I can't live with myself knowing that I caused all of this. I let it happen, because I was too proud to ask for help. I failed my kingdom, my family. . .and my father. All he did, all he gave up, was for Haighdlen. I failed everyone."

"And you can sit here feeling sorry for yourself." Gwen slapped his arm. "Or you can accept what has happened, own up to your mistakes, and move forward to help this family. It's not fair to expect that poor girl to clean up all our messes. It wasn't right to expect this of her in the first place."

"I doubt much good can come from it. If our entire family was forced to flee, what chance do those kids have?"

"You can doubt all you like, but I for one will not sit in this house a moment longer while you pout in the corner and drink yourself to death. I *will* fight for this family, regardless of our losses. I want to equip that young woman with anything she will need. The fact she's not quitting is a sign she can do this. Your family's blood runs in her veins." She jabbed a finger against his chest. "Now, you have a choice. You can continue down this path of self-loathing, or you can clean yourself up and do what you know in your heart to be right."

Richard took her hand into his and nodded.

"Tell her what she needs to say to persuade a younger you to make different choices. You have a chance to change the fate of our kingdom, and I *won't* let you waste it."

He reached up and stroked her hair.

"You're right," he admitted. "I haven't been much help to anyone. I will talk to her." He kissed her and rested his head on hers. They held each other and rocked for a moment in an embrace. Elise heard them kiss. "You are an exquisite queen and Haighdlen is lucky to have you."

"Someone has to keep you in line." Gwen giggled and Richard closed the door. Elise heard it lock and took the hint to go ahead to the bathroom.

After she washed her hands, she squealed when she opened a drawer and saw a hair tie. Her family probably wouldn't care if she took it. She splashed a little water on her hands and tamed her frizz before pulling her hair back into a ponytail. There wasn't any hairspray in sight, but anything was better than how she arrived.

***

She made it downstairs in time to join her friends in the kitchen. Joranna had a plate ready for her and she dove in.

"Thanks for bringing me my phone," she said to Gavin.

"Don't mention it." He stood to take his dish to the sink.

Elise looked over at Darcie.

"Any word from your mom?"

"Only a text and I replied. So, we're good."

"Thanks for making them turn around."

Darcie checked to make sure Gavin couldn't hear them.

"I wanted to turn around from the beginning, but it was actually Gavin who spoke up first."

"What?"

Elise glanced at Gavin.

That doesn't make sense. He was so eager to get home. Why would he do that?

When he turned around, she avoided his gaze.

Darcie smiled and nodded with a mouthful of food.

"And Mitch?" Elise asked.

When he didn't look up, Darcie kicked his foot under the table.

"Well, they made good points," he said. "You did leave your stuff in the car."

Darcie glared at him.

"And we couldn't leave you hanging."

This seemed enough to get him off the hook as Gavin came back to sit by Elise.

"What're we talking about?"

"I think Elise was going to finish telling us about your meeting with Theronde," Joranna said.

Richard and Gwen walked in and took seats around the table. The kitchen had seemed spacious until everyone crowded around.

Richard appeared to be in better spirits. He had also showered and shaved. Without his beard, Elise couldn't believe how much he resembled Derek.

"So, you were saying something about King Claramond?" Sarah asked. She seemed just as confused as she had been earlier.

Elise shrugged.

"While we were in town, there was a street performer who was singing and taunting Derek about him. Derek got really upset and made us leave. The family said he was a great ruler and did all these great things, but there were apparently some people who thought he chose fame over his family and weren't okay with it."

"The guy said Rona would come back and they'd need to hold the king responsible," Darcie added.

"They were right," Richard mumbled. "They just had the wrong king in mind."

Gwen shot him a warning glance. Richard shrugged and reached for a cookie from a plate in the center of the table.

"But we're talking years before anything really happened," Morgan said. "Ian, didn't you say you were a teenager when she attacked?"

"Yes, but she spent years generating fear and spreading rumors. It wasn't until much later that she actually formed her army."

"Then why didn't we just go there?" Gavin asked.

"You will," Joranna said. "I had just hoped we could find something about the spy sooner than that."

She opened her cupboard and pulled out the diary.

"It arrived a few minutes before you did." She leafed through the pages.

"So, we're going to when Rona attacked then?" Mitch asked. "Do we get to vote on it, or is that the official plan?"

"Not quite yet."

"What are you thinking about, Mother?" Sarah moved to look over Joranna's shoulder.

"The uprising," Joranna whispered. "I sent you where I thought would be the most useful for finding information. But the uprising was years later after all the children were born. I didn't think we were going to skip that far ahead yet."

Sarah reached over and shuffled a couple of pages.

"Wasn't that around the time of the fire? Have you passed it?"

As her stomach churned, Elise regretted eating so much. *Uprising? A fire?*

"That's what I'm looking for," Joranna said. She ran her finger down the length of each page. "That was the first uprising. That should lend us an opportunity for answers. And perhaps after that, we should just dive into the main event."

"Main event? What main event?" Darcie asked.

"Where Rona first attacked us. It led to a large and bloody battle, but it was the turning point for our family. Haighdlen was never the same afterwards. Rona retreated, but she was not defeated. I was saving it for the end of your journey anyway to make sure you were ready."

"Ready for a battle?" Gavin asked. His face paled. "Are you crazy?"

"We're fighting?" Mitch shrieked. "I thought we were just getting some information about this witch lady. Nobody said anything about fighting."

Elise reached for her water. She couldn't tell if she wanted to throw up or pass out, but either felt like a better choice than heading back through the portal at the moment.

They probably regret turning the car around now.

"Let's pray they find the spy. If they do, they'll return home. Any fighting can probably be avoided," Ian said.

Well, that's a relief.

"Listen to you." Sarah smiled and walked over to her brother. "Where is that young boy who wanted to slay Rona himself and charge head on into battle? I think living in this world all these years has made you soft." She nudged him on the arm.

"Will we really need to fight, Nana?" Elise asked.

"I won't say one way or the other. Too many unknowns. But if your journey is going to start altering our memories and lives, we need to be precise in our decision in case it doesn't bring you back here."

"So. . .we're heading out, most likely to a battle, and we don't even know if we'll make it home?" Gavin asked.

"The battle won't be for a while from where you'll land." Joranna reassured them that it would most likely be unnecessary to venture that far into the diary. "You'll have plenty of time to get acquainted with the family and the situation. I'm sure you'll be a great help."

"They'll need a story," Gwen suggested. "They can use the fact that they have information on Rona as a reason they showed up, but what about their appearances? They won't have aged."

"Maybe a potion? An aging curse?" Morgan offered.

"But why would someone want to curse them?" Ian asked. "It's going to look really suspicious. We don't want them to waste time trying to stay out of trouble. Right?"

"He's right," Sarah agreed. "Is there any harm in them disclosing that they can time travel? I mean aside from the obvious altering memories part."

"I don't think that would be worth it." Richard walked over to the liquor cabinet but was blocked by Joranna.

"There could be something to Morgan's idea about an aging curse," Sarah said. "Perhaps we could link it to Rona somehow. That could get them an advantage to learning about her."

There were murmurs of agreement throughout the room.

"Wait," Gwendolyn said. "And how will they explain when and how they were cursed?"

Silence spread through the room as no one had a reply.

"You know what? They're just going to have to sell it the best that they can." Joranna coughed into her arm again. "Please excuse me. At the time we're sending them, Derek would've received word of several small attacks from Rona and her followers throughout the kingdoms. If anyone asks why they were cursed, they could simply say they were trying to protect Haighdlen and got caught. It would not be too far-fetched of a story."

"So, Rona would curse them to be young and beautiful for the rest of their lives?" Richard raised an eyebrow at his mother.

"I know it has its flaws," Joranna said. "And if you have something better, please share it, but we don't have much time."

"Um, can we maybe get some different clothes? More Haighdlen-ish?" Darcie asked. "It's getting really awkward to show up in the same outfits and needing more to blend in."

Richard, Gwendolyn and Sarah went upstairs to find some clothes that they had managed to bring with them. They returned to the living room a few minutes later with a selection of outfits, and the four took turns dressing in the bathroom.

"You'll have to forgive their condition," Gwendolyn said while smoothing some wrinkles out of Darcie's pea-green dress. "When we left, there wasn't time to pack them properly."

Elise ran her fingers along the fabric.

"It's okay. Thanks again."

She glanced down at Gwendolyn's burgundy gown that wasn't quite a perfect fit but would do. Richard's shirts and vests were slightly too big on the boys, who didn't have Richard's broad shoulders.

Anything is going to be better than jeans and t-shirts.

Richard cleared his throat.

"Elise, can we have a moment?" He gestured for his brother and sister to follow him back into the kitchen. "Have a seat, please."

Elise braced herself for any bad news he was about to tell her.

What now?

Richard cleared his throat.

"I admire what you have done up until now, but you'll need more information if you're going to get ahead of Rona. We want to help you in any way we can. Do you have any questions?"

Where do I start?

Elise looked at her Uncle Ian and asked the question that had burned in the back of her mind for some time.

"Why did you choose me? Was it just because I was the only one there at the time who didn't exist?"

"That did play a large part of it," he replied. "But we also did it because we see something in you. Maybe you don't see it in yourself yet, but we do. This family has seen its share of battles and trials, and through it all we have prevailed. We are strong. We are loyal. We can fight. You possess all of these qualities."

Elise scoffed.

Clearly, they don't see the anxiety disorder sign flashing above my head at all times.

"Don't underestimate your qualities," Richard said.

"We just want to help you be ready," Sarah explained. "We weren't our best selves during your first visit, but we love you and Ruby very much. Please know that."

"I know you guys want more from me," Elise began. "I don't think I'm really good at all this. I just feel…like we're stumbling through and finding things by chance."

"And that is perfectly fine," Ian said. "We want to give you some advice and answer any questions you may have."

Elise took a deep breath.

"What fire were you talking about?"

"There was a fire in the castle once and we never found out who was responsible," Sarah explained. "We always wondered if it was one of Rona's followers. It started in Ruby's bedroom during her birthday ball. Whether you find the person or not, we all believe that it is an excellent time to get more information."

Ian sighed.

"The biggest piece of advice I can give you, Elise, is to trust your instincts. They will never steer you wrong. That will be your biggest weapon."

His brother and sister nodded in agreement.

"Try to have a little fun, too." Sarah's brothers looked at her with skeptical expressions. "Yes, *I* said it. It's all right to have some fun. I know it doesn't sound like me, but Haighdlen is a wonderful place to explore and I hope that you get to see it."

"But beware of traps and people who may be untrustworthy. It began to get very unclear who you could trust after a while." Richard opened his mouth to say more and paused. "Elise, I may be one of your biggest challenges later on. All of my life I have wanted to be my father. I have wanted to be what he stood for. I don't know how far into my mother's diary you are going to travel, but as I grow older, I will become arrogant. I will not fear anything, and that is dangerous. Do all that you can to convince me of my weaknesses. It is the only way I can get stronger. Convince me that I am not him." Richard cleared his throat and straightened up. "Very well. You had best be off."

Elise and her friends gathered in the living room and said goodbye to everyone.

As Joranna turned to the diary entry she needed, Elise felt so grateful that her friends were by her side.

Her aunt and uncles joined hands with Joranna, and she turned the book outwards towards them.

"Good luck. We love you."

Elise's reply went unheard as they were once again whisked away into a suffocating portal of darkness.

CHAPTER 16

Elise stirred, squinting against the sunlight in her eyes. She lifted her hand to block it and realized she was on the ground with scratchy grass beneath her. The air was warm and sweet. She could hear birds in the distance and her friends talking nearby.

"Is she awake yet?"

Gavin sounded muffled and far away. She focused harder to wake herself up.

"I think so."

Darcie's here too.

Elise sat up and rubbed her face. When she opened her eyes, she saw that they were sitting in the middle of the forest.

"Why did we land here?" Her voice sounded hoarse and her muscles felt stiff. She stood to dust dirt and twigs off her dress, then after a good stretch she felt like herself again.

"That's what we were wondering," Darcie said. "How are we supposed to get near your family if we didn't land on the other side of the castle walls?"

"Maybe it didn't work," Mitch muttered.

Elise stepped forward and looked around. Nothing in particular stood out to her. No matter which direction she turned, everything looked the same.

I don't understand.

Mitch grunted, raking his fingers through his hair.

"How are we supposed to find our way back now?"

"Well, splitting up is out of the question," Gavin said. "I say we just pick a direction and chance it until we find something else to go on."

Mitch and Darcie agreed.

"Wait! Before we go, I wanted to say something." Elise tore off a twig from a low hanging branch and twisted it in her hands as she spoke. "I never got a chance to thank y'all for coming back. It really meant a lot. Thank you."

"We were happy to do it," Darcie said.

"Now help us not regret it." Gavin smiled and held out his arm. "Ladies first. You pick which wrong turn we take."

Elise chuckled and stepped onto the path in front of them. She closed her eyes, trying to concentrate on the sounds around her. When that didn't give her any leads, she looked up into the trees.

A darting light shot from one tree to another. At first, she thought it was a trick of the sunlight, but then two more chased after it before disappearing.

"Hey, what're those?" She pointed.

"Oh, are those the fairies Derek told us about?" Darcie squealed and bounced on her feet. "How exciting! I wonder if they'll land so we can get a closer look."

They watched as only one light returned, whizzing through a few more trees before hovering.

What's it waiting for?

Elise stepped closer.

"I think we should follow it."

"Are you crazy?"

Gavin sure likes asking that.

"Elise, it's not trying to lead you anywhere," Gavin said. "It doesn't even know what you're looking for. It's just flying around."

"I just have this feeling. I think it wants us to follow it."

The light twirled in circles and hovered again. When none of them moved, it took off at a quicker pace.

"Don't let it get away!" Elise shouted. She lifted the hem of her dress and took off down the forest path after it, the others following close behind her. She ducked under branches and moved brush out of her way as fast as she could, careful not to get her clothes caught on any bushes.

For a moment, she thought she had lost it. Then it popped out of a bush in front of her face and darted off away from the path.

Before she could follow, Gavin tugged on her arm.

"Elise, I don't think we should leave the path. We don't know where we are. At least we stand the chance of getting help at some point if we stay here. Someone will probably come by."

"We can trust it," Elise insisted.

"But even Derek told us to leave them alone," Mitch reminded her. "It could be a trick."

"No, wait, listen!" Elise held up her hand to quiet them. Somewhere close by they could hear laughter. Her face lit up and she stepped carefully off the path. Pulling back a few thick branches, she saw a lake, one that was slightly smaller than Lake Laulie. Sitting next to it, she saw Joranna on a large blanket with three children. Elise felt like her chest would burst with excitement, and she fought the urge to call out to her grandmother. She looked up, but there wasn't any sign of the fairy.

"Thank you," she said towards the treetops. "See, guys? I told you—"

Something whirled through the air behind her, and Mitch was knocked to the ground. He cried out and clutched his arm as he rocked back and forth.

What just happened?

Darcie fell to her knees beside him.

"Mitch! What's wrong? Let me see!"

He resisted her attempts, but when she finally pulled his hand away, they saw blood on his ripped sleeve. "Did anybody see anything?"

Gavin looked around them.

"There's nobody else here! Does anybody know how to treat it?"

Mitch shrieked when Darcie pushed on it.

"Anything but that!" Mitch screamed. He squeezed his eyes shut and tried preventing her from touching it again.

"I'm trying to stop the bleeding." Darcie threw her hands in the air. "I don't know what I'm doing!"

"Who shot him?" Gavin asked.

"I didn't see anybody." Elise looked around. "Maybe we can find help."

"Something tells me they wouldn't have painkillers," Mitch spluttered.

Gavin shuffled through the brush a few feet away before finding an arrow. He tapped the pointed edge with his finger, checking for blood.

Movement in the trees nearby made them freeze.

"Is everything all right over there?"

Crap! What're we going to do? We can't carry him.

Heat rushed to Elise's face as she wondered how they were going to run with Mitch injured. Several scenarios flew through her head as her heartbeat raced in her ears.

She jumped when Derek stepped out from behind a line of trees.

Elise tensed as he regarded each of them, then relaxed when she saw him smile.

"It's you! What an unexpected surprise. I must say I lost hope of seeing you four again over these last few years."

He hadn't aged much, but his face had filled out more and he sported a thin beard.

Mitch grunted and held his arm.

"That's great. Can we play catch up later?"

Derek knelt down to assess the bleeding. Mitch sucked in air through his teeth with a sharp hiss. "What is it? A bullet?"

"I was worried about this when we heard someone scream," Derek said. "I'm afraid Richard made a poor shot with his bow, and the arrow grazed your arm."

"Just *grazed*? You make it sound like a paper cut. It feels like it went straight through my arm!"

"I assure you it's a graze, but it's a pretty good one. If it had pierced all the way through, you'd be in a lot of pain."

"I *am* in a lot of pain!"

Gavin stepped around Mitch and handed the arrow to Derek.

"It's not quite the welcome back treatment, is it?" Derek apologized. "My family and I are having a picnic nearby. Please join us. We will tend to his wound before an infection sets in. This way."

Gavin helped Mitch stand, then the four of them followed him towards the clearing. Not far into their walk, Derek stopped.

"Come on out, Richard."

A teenaged boy, perhaps twelve or thirteen years old, hesitated behind a tree trunk. When Derek called again, he hung his head low and shuffled forward with his bow.

Seeing Richard gave Elise an idea of how far they had traveled in the diary.

"I believe more practice is in order." Derek handed Richard his arrow. "And an apology, young man."

"I'm very sorry, sir."

"Don't sweat it," Mitch said as he panted and leaned against Gavin for support. "Can we just fix it, please?"

The blood had spread down his arm and soaked his sleeve.

Nodding, Derek patted Richard's shoulder and turned him in the direction of the lake.

***

Joranna ran up when they came into view, but there wasn't time to give them a proper greeting. She ushered them over to a clear spot away from the food where they could lay Mitch down.

Derek walked over to one of the three horses that were tied up nearby to pull bandages and a couple of washcloths from the satchel. He soaked the washcloths in the lake and brought them over.

Turning her head away as Derek worked, Elise tried to concentrate on anything else around her. She winced when she heard Mitch groan and hated that her friend was in so much pain. Joranna wiped the sweat and dirt off of Mitch's face while Derek cleaned and washed the wound.

Distant laughter caught Elise's attention and she turned to see the other three children playing tag.

Her breath caught in her chest when she saw her mother. Ruby was a petite little girl with red curls that bounced when she ran.

She struggled to keep up with the other two, but that didn't stop her from trying.

"Is that your mom?" Gavin asked. "It must be weird to see her like that, huh?"

Elise nodded.

"She looks happy though." Elise couldn't look away from the dimpled cheeks and twinkling eyes. "I think the weirdest part is seeing someone and already knowing what their life is going to be like."

"Yeah, that's got to be tough. So, does she have depression now or something?"

"Not officially," Elise said. "She never goes to the doctor, but I think she has some form of it. She just chooses to self-medicate."

"We don't have to talk about it if you don't want to."

"No, it's fine. The confusing part is figuring out what happened that made her hate it here so much. It seems so perfect."

"There now," Derek announced. Turning, Gavin and Elise watched Joranna wipe the remaining blood off Mitch's hands. Derek had ripped Mitch's entire sleeve, and now all they could see was a bandage wrapped around his bicep. Derek wiped his own forehead and regarded the rest of them. "It's nice to see you all again. Perhaps it could have been under better circumstances."

"Will he be okay?" Darcie asked.

"He will be just fine. I know it still hurts, but the threat is gone. We can have the doctor check it over when we return to the castle."

"Darling?" Joranna nodded towards the other children, then back at Mitch's arm. Elise was confused, but Derek seemed to understand perfectly.

"That's a great idea," he said. "Sarah, darling? Would you come over here, please?"

The children paused their game and ran over to join the group. Sarah seemed to be about eleven; Ian may have been seven or eight; and her mother couldn't have been older than five.

Sarah's smile fell when she saw Mitch's bandage.

"Oh, Father, please don't. Not again. I'm not ready."

"Nonsense. It will be good practice for your talents."

"But I'm so nervous."

"Yeah, me too," Mitch said, looking back and forth between the two. "Let's be done playing doctor."

"You can do this, sweetheart," Joranna coaxed her.

Ian and Ruby both started encouraging Sarah.

The young girl sat down beside Mitch and adjusted her dress.

"This is our daughter Sarah," Derek introduced. "She also possesses magic like me and is able to heal."

"I'm not very good yet. I've only done some bruises and scrapes."

"There's no need to be afraid," her father said. "I've got it far enough along now that you should be capable of this."

"What if I hurt him more?" She took a deep breath and tucked a piece of brownish-blonde hair behind her ear.

"Have faith in yourself," said her mother. "You could make his pain go away entirely. Focus on that."

Derek crouched down behind her and instructed her to close her eyes. He rested her hand on Mitch's bandage. Mitch looked ready to run away himself, but Darcie held him down. "Concentrate all your thoughts on what you're trying to do. Control the magic and where it goes."

Joranna hushed the younger ones, and for the next several minutes, the only sounds around them came from the forest.

Sarah huffed, pushing his arm away. When Mitch whimpered, she crossed her own arms.

"I told you I can't do it. Father, please just do it already."

"I can help his pain a little, but only you could heal it entirely. You'll never learn unless you do it yourself. Now try again."

"Block out the world and focus on his wound," Joranna said. "You've been doing so well in your lessons."

"Yes, just try not to take his whole arm off, Sarah," Ian teased.

"Shut it, will you?" Sarah cried.

Joranna led the two youngest back over to the picnic blanket despite their fussing to stay.

Sarah placed her hand on the bandage again and closed her eyes.

As Mitch made a straining noise in the back of his throat, Sarah closed her eyes tighter, wrinkling up her freckled nose.

"What is she doing to me?" He writhed and buried his face in Darcie's lap. "It hurts. . . it hurts. Wait. . . it doesn't hurt anymore. Did that actually work?"

Sarah smiled as Derek leaned down to assess her magic. After the bandage was unwound, and the remaining dried blood was wiped off, he held Mitch's arm up for them to see. There was no longer any sign of a cut or abrasion to the area.

"Well done, Sarah." He hugged his daughter as they all congratulated her. Mitch laughed in astonishment and thanked her. He twisted his arm back and forth, admiring her work. She blushed from the attention and excused herself to join Joranna and her siblings.

"I'm so sorry again, sir," Richard said. "I will make sure to be more careful."

"It's all right." Mitch stood, towering over Richard. "It was an accident. Let's just be glad I handled it as well as I did."

They chuckled and Derek sent Richard to join the family.

"Well, I think that's quite enough excitement for now," he said. "Would you all like to join us for lunch? I'd love to properly catch up and introduce you all to the children."

They agreed and followed him over to their picnic site.

***

It was a beautiful summer afternoon in Haighdlen, and Derek had chosen the perfect spot to take the family for a picnic. He assured the teenagers that no mermaids lived in this particular lake.

Once everything had been set up, they were introduced to the children, then everyone gathered around to enjoy a beautiful spread of tea, ham, rolls, fresh fruit, cheese, and cake.

"You're probably wondering why there aren't any servants here," Derek said. "I feel like we're always surrounded by servants, guards, and council members. I wanted to spend some time with my family. Don't be alarmed though. There are guards in the perimeter to make sure this area is secure, but they'll keep their distance."

This is a lot better than the stiff royal dining room.

The family seemed more relaxed outdoors as well. They definitely smiled more. It was nice to see them be. . .normal. She smiled at their light banter before the attention was returned to them.

"You haven't aged at all," Joranna said, "although you seem to have found some more appropriate clothes than you used to wear."

"We were cursed." Mitch took a large bite of ham and didn't seem to notice his friends' silent pleas for him to shut up. "By Rona."

Elise closed her eyes and tried to think of a supporting statement. They hadn't had time to discuss which idea they were going to go with, but now Mitch had decided for them.

Darcie jumped in next.

"We were spying and heard there were attacks, so we investigated more."

"But then one of her soldiers found us and that's when she did it," Gavin said.

"Our memories were wiped afterwards so we don't know what happened after that," Elise added.

That was pathetic. There's no way they're going to believe any of this.

"There has to be more to it," Derek said. "I don't see her stopping you from aging and that being it. Doesn't seem like much suffering to me. Not many people face Rona and live to tell the tale."

"But she took their memories," Joranna said. "Who knows what else she could have done to them? I'm sure they suffered."

Stuffing a piece of bread in her mouth to avoid answering, Elise only nodded and shrugged.

"That is true. Perhaps they were tortured."

"What's torture?" Ruby asked.

"Let's talk about something else," Joranna said. "We came for a nice picnic to celebrate our little girl. Ruby, tell them how old you are today."

Ruby held up five fingers.

"Yes, and we're having a ball tonight. It's her first big girl party." Joranna tucked Ruby's hair behind her ear and pulled her into her lap. "I must say you four have always had remarkable timing. You seem to show up when we're celebrating something. You must think we throw parties all the time. Anyway, we'd love for you to come and stay with us tonight if you can."

"Yes, you must," Derek said. "I'd love to discuss the circumstances surrounding your encounter with Rona as well. The parts you remember, of course."

Elise was thankful when Richard changed the subject by asking his father if they could go out on the lake.

"We keep a few small boats moored here in the summer," he informed them. "It looks like we'll be taking all of them out today. Richard and I will prepare them and call around for you when they're ready."

Joranna pulled out a book from the picnic basket and Ian crawled over to join Ruby on her lap. Darcie convinced Sarah to let her braid her hair, while Gavin and Mitch helped themselves to more cake. Everyone listened to Joranna's story.

Elise leaned on her hands and tilted her head back to enjoy the warm sun against her skin. Her mind swirled with questions.

What are we going to do when we get back to the castle? Are we going to learn anything else about Rona? Will there be a fire? Are we expected to dance again tonight? What will I wear?

Drifting off to sleep at the sound of Joranna's voice, Elise jumped awake when she finished reading and Richard returned.

"The boats are ready!" he announced. Everyone helped tidy up the picnic blanket and followed Richard down to the edge of the lake. "Father said we'll have to pair off to fit everyone."

Five small boats with oars floated side by side before them. Each looked big enough to hold about two people.

"Darcie is my partner!" Sarah said with her hand raised. She bounced up and down and pulled Darcie into the first boat. Darcie looked back towards Elise and shrugged.

"Mitchell," Richard said, "would you go with me? I'd like to make up for the arrow incident."

"Sure, but I get to row."

He and Richard climbed into the second boat.

Derek rested his hands on his knees and leaned down to Ruby's height.

"Want to go out with me, Birthday Girl?"

"No, I want Mother," Ruby pouted and buried her face into Joranna's dress.

"What else is new? Number one as usual." He kissed Joranna and turned towards Ian. "Ian still loves me. Don't you, son?"

Ian agreed and hopped around his father. Derek helped him calm down enough to step into the next boat.

"Come along, sweetheart," Joranna said. She picked Ruby up, then lifted her into the fourth boat. "Now sit down and stay very still. You don't want us to rock too much." Joranna stepped in after her and got situated.

Oh no.

Elise's heart pounded as she looked at the final boat. Gavin had already gotten in and was now waiting for her. His hands rested on the oars. She was thankful he didn't laugh when she took a moment to gain her balance and sit down.

Watching the other boats spread out around the lake, she wiped her palms on her dress.

What am I going to say? I have to say something, because he's just staring at me. I must seem like such an idiot.

She licked her lips and twisted a piece of her sleeve with her fingers. Feeling the familiar signs of a panic attack, she screamed for her mind to turn off.

I can't have one right here in front of him. He'll freak! Why does he make me so nervous?

"Are you okay?"

She nodded and took a deep breath.

See? He's noticing. Turn it off. Turn it off!

But she felt herself escalate to the point of no return. Whenever she got to this level, it was easier to ride out the panic attack than try to fight it. Normally, she'd reach for her phone, but since she couldn't, she tried staring at the water to distract herself.

"Hey, what's wrong?"

"Nothing."

She wanted to stand up and pace. Run. Anything to move and get the building adrenaline out.

It's a good thing he doesn't like you like that, she told herself. *This could be a romantic moment, but you'd ruin it. You always have to panic and ruin everything. Control yourself already! Everybody else is calm and enjoying themselves. Why can't you?*

She looked around and tried to find an escape. If she were at home, she'd go to her fool-proof plan of finding a bathroom to hide in. Her body urged her to get away so no one would see her at her lowest point.

Jump out of the boat. Swim for the shore.

She wanted to scream until it was over. Her thoughts spun like a tornado inside her head and she couldn't pick out just one. A wave of nausea rolled within her stomach, which started a new fear of getting sick in front of him. She wiped her palms again.

What must he think of me? I can't look at him. It'll go away. This has to go away. Breathe. I am safe. I am safe. I am—

Gavin released the oars and leaned forward to grab her hands. His touch brought her focus back to him, and the tornado stopped swirling. With her heartbeat still uneven, it felt like someone was playing a drum inside her chest. Another wave crashed within her belly.

"Hey, breathe," he said. "Look at me."

"No, really. I'm fine."

Her gaze flickered to him and back on the water.

He squeezed her hands and kept his eyes on hers.

"You need to breathe. You're safe."

Elise checked the other boats to make sure no one else had seen her.

"Don't worry about them. Look at me."

She took a deep breath and exhaled slowly. He made her do it again. Little by little, she felt the suffocating cloud lift from her mind and was able to come back to reality.

Fighting the urge to cry, her fight-or-flight response was replaced by the familiar feelings of shame and embarrassment.

When she visibly calmed, he let go and began to row them again.

"Thanks," she said. "I'm sorry."

"For what?"

Isn't it obvious?

"For letting my crazy out in front of you. I bet you're regretting turning around to come back and help me."

"I never thought that."

She scoffed.

"You don't think I'm some psycho that should be carried off and sedated?"

"You used the word psycho. Not me." He smiled while they rowed for a couple of minutes in silence. "Do you ever try to talk it out with someone when it happens?"

"No, I usually just distract myself until it goes away. I have an anxiety disorder, so it's pretty much here to stay." Even with a ponytail, she had to pull her hair off of her neck. She twirled a lock around her finger. "I might even have to take medicine eventually. Then I'll really be crazy, right?"

"I wouldn't say that." He shrugged. "Nothing's wrong with medicine, and there's probably more techniques you could learn to help. Talking it out might help you clear your head and stop so many from coming."

"How do you know so much about panic attacks?"

"My mom has them sometimes. So, what're you afraid of?"

You.

"You're asking me now?" she asked. "We're really doing this?"

"What else are we going to talk about? Come on. It might help."

"What am I *not* afraid of?" She laughed under her breath and fidgeted.

"Then pick one."

What you think of me.

"Being there for my family," she said, playing it safe. "They're so happy here, but they're going to end up resenting and fighting each other. I just met most of them a few days ago. I guess I just want to be there for them so there doesn't have to be any drama."

"You can't escape family drama. It's what makes up a family."

"So, your family is crazy, too, huh?" she asked.

He leaned back and rested his arms. The boat slowed, letting the others go further ahead.

"Mainly my dad." He squinted as he gazed up at the sky and reclined back on his hands.

"Mitch told us he's in the military."

"Yeah, he has been since before I was born. He's always on my case."

"He probably just wants what's best for you."

"He does, but that's the thing. He never asks what I want to do. He usually just tells me what I need to do. He's been on me about joining after graduation."

"You don't want to?"

He shrugged.

"I don't know yet. I'm still figuring things out. So, when I get stressed and try to relax with my guitar in the garage, he just loses it. He says I need to be more responsible and get my life on track." He smiled at her. "I bet you don't have that problem. You probably already have a scholarship and know exactly where you're going."

"You'd be surprised." She let her hand hang freely over the side and dip in the water. "I'm going to go to the community college for a couple of semesters and knock out some general ed courses. Save some money."

"Makes sense. Any ideas on what you'd like to do someday?"

"I want to help people, but I just have to figure out how. I don't have the stomach to be a nurse, but I'd like to help in some way. You?"

"Let's keep this on you," he said. "This is your therapy session."

"Oh really? You're my therapist now?"

"Yeah, and I'm not cheap either." They shared a laugh and he picked up the oars again to get them moving. "Personally, I think I'm killing it."

She leaned forward and crossed her arms over her knees.

"Then what's my diagnosis, Doc? Is it pretty serious?"

She gasped when he released the oars and leaned in, too. The boat rocked back and forth under the sudden movement and she had to grab the sides to steady herself. He was mere inches from her as he studied her face.

"You worry too much."

"*That's* your big discovery? Wow, thanks for enlightening me."

"It's because you care so much. You love your family. There's nothing wrong with that."

"It will be when they wake up one day and realize I'm the wrong one for this job," she said.

"Well, you're the only one here who thinks that."

His eyes flickered to her mouth, as she resisted the thought to jump in the water again.

Her cheeks flushed and a shiver ran down her spine. She didn't know if it was due to her anxious state or Gavin's proximity to her.

"Shouldn't we be getting back?" Joranna called to Derek's boat.

Gavin and Elise straightened up and he picked up the oars again.

"Yes, if we hurry, we can squeeze in a quick game before we need to get ready," Derek said and turned to call out to the other boats. "We'll arrange for you all to share horses with the guards on the way back. The three over there will only be enough for my family. No worries though. It's not a long trip."

Elise doubted it would be as enjoyable as Derek tried to paint it, but she was willing to try anything to get some distance from Gavin and clear her head.

***

Once they returned to the grounds, Derek invited everyone to play a game of cricket. He promised proper gear and extra servants to make up the teams. Elise was thankful for the invitation, but she and Darcie opted for helping Joranna inspect the ball preparations. Joranna sent the youngest three children to rest before the evening's festivities, and so it ended up just being a boys' game. Elise had no regrets turning down his offer. Gym was her least favorite class and she was in no way athletically inclined. Darcie dabbled in a few sports here and there, but helping to plan a party outweighed any game offer.

Servants were busy bustling about the room carrying food, flowers and decorations. The musicians were positioned in the corner and were tuning their instruments. Tables were already placed in positions that were similar to how they were for the engagement ball. Pink and silver streamers hung around the room, and everything was fit for a princess.

"I believe all is in order," Joranna said. "There will be pony rides outside, an acrobatic performance, and a magician."

"That sounds fun," Elise said.

"I'm also opening the doors here to lead out into the garden since it's such a warm night," Joranna added. "Lanterns will be hung throughout the entire area and I'm going to have a few fountains brought out to liven it up."

"Do you have a lot of guests coming?" Elise asked.

"A little over a hundred are planning to attend. I've invited some children from the village as well."

She paused to smell a bouquet of freshly arranged flowers.

"That's bigger than any party I've ever had," Darcie said with a chuckle.

Elise looked around the room.

"Are the king and queen going to help you prepare anything? I haven't seen them since we got back."

Joranna lifted her head away from the blooms and continued walking.

"I'm afraid they've passed away. King Theronde suffered a heart attack soon after Ruby was born. Queen Avalyn wasn't the same after that. Sadly, she started getting sick a couple of years later and passed about six months ago."

Both girls apologized.

"Thank you. It's been extremely hard on Derek. They were so involved in our children's lives. We've had trouble adjusting. Derek has kept very busy and lately has become determined to spend lots of family time together, hence the picnic this afternoon. I think this ball will help him escape the stress he's been under."

Elise pictured her great-grandparents in the study. Theronde had promised a feast the next day they met.

If I had known it would be the last time I'd see them, I wouldn't have been in such a hurry.

"How do you like being queen?" Darcie asked.

"It's been a challenge," Joranna confessed. "Lucky for me, Avalyn paid a lot of attention to me and made sure that I was educated and rehearsed in the royal ways. There are still plenty of days I feel like I fall short."

"I think you're doing a fantastic job," Elise said.

Darcie nodded.

"Yeah, this ball you put together is amazing! The people are lucky to have you."

She smiled.

"Well, thank you, ladies. I hope it all runs smoothly."

Elise was prevented from reassuring her grandmother by the sudden commotion out near the garden. The boys had returned from their game and were laughing as they entered all sweaty and worn out.

Joranna laughed as Derek kissed her. She fussed at their lateness before sending him and Richard to wash. Elise, however, could only notice how see through Gavin's shirt had become. The fabric clung to his heated skin and sweat glistened along his exposed chest. He and Mitch greeted them before Joranna suggested they also clean up. Elise's eyes followed Gavin.

"Elise?" Darcie asked.

Gavin glanced over his shoulder at her on the way out.

She gasped and turned around.

"Do you think he saw me looking?"

"Elise, I think the guards outside saw you looking," Darcie chuckled. "He's probably going to tease you now. It's your own fault for getting caught. . .again."

"Yeah, yeah." Elise rolled her eyes as a maid came to whisper into Joranna's ear.

"Thank you," she said and turned towards them. "Edith has arrived and is ready to fit you both in your rooms."

Elise and Darcie walked down the hallway and caught up with Mitch and Gavin at the staircase.

Mitch tapped Gavin on the shoulder and made him stop.

"Hang on. We need to wait."

"For what?" Elise asked.

"Well, I didn't know how long you might want to have a look at this." He pointed at Gavin's body. "If you follow him you might see more."

"You guys are such jerks," Darcie said.

"Yeah, leave her alone." Gavin laughed, patting Mitch's back to keep him walking.

I'm so humiliated!

***

"I can't believe I did that!" Elise exclaimed as she threw herself on the guest bed a few minutes later. She peeked out at Darcie from underneath a pillow. "Is it possible to die from embarrassment?"

"Come on, it wasn't that bad. You just had a movie moment. That's all."

"A movie moment?"

"Yeah, that part in the movie where the hot guy comes in and everything goes into slow motion. All you were missing was a fog machine and a killer soundtrack."

Elise laughed and hugged her best friend.

"You're awesome. Thanks. I feel better."

"Just doing my job."

A knock at the door broke their hug and Edith poked her head in.

"Good evening. May I come in?"

"I'll see you later in the ballroom," Darcie said and headed to her own room.

Edith entered, closing the door behind her.

"It's good to see you again. It's been a long time." Edith began to circle Elise and take measurements. "You look like a day hasn't passed since then."

Elise thanked her and made a quick change of subject by asking about what ideas she had for her gown.

"This is a lovely color on you already." Edith ran her fingers along Gwendolyn's borrowed burgundy gown. "I think I'll keep the color and make some adjustments."

The familiar blue light surrounded Edith's hand and there was a flash. Elise opened her eyes and looked in the mirror. She now wore an embellished gown of the same color with sheer cape sleeves.

"Perfect! It's stunning yet subtle for the occasion. Not over the top. And the sheer sleeves will keep you cool in the warm summer air," Edith said. Elise turned around and admired the fabriwitch's work once again. "And now for your hair!"

She led Elise over to sit in front of the vanity mirror and got to work. She gently pulled out Elise's ponytail and brushed through it. Once all the tangles were removed, she twisted it around her hand.

"I'm thinking of pulling it up with more embellishments!"

Elise cleared her throat.

"Do you think you could maybe style it down? Please?"

Edith stared at Elise in the mirror for a moment and shrugged. She released her hair and brushed through it a few more times. She clicked her tongue and parted a good portion to one side before there was another blue flash. Elise watched all the frizz disappear as if she had added product to it. Her hair even curled at the bottom and rested just below her shoulders. She was reminded of an old Hollywood actress. After Edith added the finishing touches of makeup, Elise was once again stunned to see how mature she looked.

"That should get his attention," she said with a wink. She tapped Elise's shoulder and bid her farewell as she headed to Darcie's room.

As fireworks boomed outside, Elise stood up to walk over to the window. Cheers rang out from the crowd below as she fiddled with the necklace around her neck.

She couldn't let herself get distracted by Gavin tonight. It was a child's birthday party, they were on a mission, and it wouldn't be appropriate. They had had a fun day with her family, but it was time for her to get serious. She recalled her aunt Sarah's present-day warning.

"There was a fire in the castle once and we never found out who was responsible. We always wondered if it was one of Rona's followers. It started in Ruby's bedroom during her birthday ball."

There was going to be a fire tonight. Someone was going to cause it on purpose. She needed to remind her friends so they could be on the lookout for anything suspicious.

Taking one last look at herself in the mirror, she smoothed out her dress and headed down to the ballroom.

CHAPTER 17

Guests filled the ballroom, and the party was in full swing. Servants walked around serving drinks and appetizers, while children ran through the crowd giggling. The tables were garnished with pink runners and matching bouquets of roses as well as fine china place settings. The musicians were playing dinner music, and everyone was enjoying themselves. She noticed that there was a line of guards on either side of the room, but there were also several officers in formal uniforms mingling among the guests.

The French doors were open for guests to come and go in the sweet, fragrant, warm summer air. The sun was almost completely set and the lights in the garden illuminated the area brilliantly.

A table was positioned at the front of the room that displayed a large portrait of Ruby. On one side of it, Elise saw a five-layered cake with pink icing and white flowers on top. Dozens of elegantly wrapped gifts piled high on the other side.

She avoided the wine and opted for a glass of punch that came around. As she sipped, she saw Darcie enter the room and joined her.

"I love your dress," Elise said as she admired Darcie's violet gown. "Edith did a great job."

"She did with yours, too. And your hair is down!"

"Just trying something different."

"For Gavin?" Darcie smiled in a way that told Elise that she saw right through her.

"I did it for me." Elise looked down into her glass and knew she didn't get away with the lie. "He saw me have a panic attack today. It was definitely a low point for me."

"You didn't say anything earlier. What did he do?"

Elise traced the rim of her glass with her finger and smiled at the memory.

"He was actually really nice. He talked me through it."

"I told you he wasn't so bad. You guys were really chatty today. It's all going according to my plans."

"Yeah, well, you can stuff your plans tonight," Elise said. "We need to stay focused and see what we can find out about a fire starting. Keep your eyes out for anything suspicious and pass the word on to the guys when they get here."

She paused when Derek and Joranna approached.

"You both look lovely," Joranna said. "We're so glad you could be here."

"Hope we didn't wear you out too much today," Derek added. They were interrupted as two uniformed gentlemen approached. "Ladies, allow me to introduce you to Captain Brahm and. . ."

"This is Sanders, Your Highness," Brahm introduced. Both men bowed their heads.

"Sanders, yes," Derek said. "I trust you both are having a good time?"

"Very much, Sire," Sanders replied and turned his attention to Darcie. "I was just telling the captain here that there was a beautiful young lady that I would love to dance with. Could I persuade you to join me for a dance after dinner?"

Darcie hesitated until the officer reached out to kiss her hand. She accepted with a smile and asked when dinner would be served.

"Ah, to be younger and impatient again," Brahm said. They shared a chuckle and Derek informed them that the dinner call would only be moments away. "You have done a spectacular job, Your Majesty. The children especially seem to be having fun."

"Thank you, Brahm," she said. "Please enjoy the festivities and we will talk soon."

She and Derek excused themselves and continued to mingle through the crowd.

"Brahm?" Elise asked. The captain looked down at her. "I've heard that name. Did you work for King Theronde, too?"

"Yes, I've been serving the Laurille family for the last seventeen years. And you must be the famous travelers. You both look splendid this evening."

They thanked him before Elise continued.

"Can I ask you a question?" She looked around until he picked up on the hint, leaning down to hear her better. "The last time we were here everyone was looking for a spy. Did they ever find anyone?"

He straightened and took a sip from his glass.

"Ever the detective," he said. "The rumors fortunately dissipated and we're no longer concerned about an inside threat."

"So, you just stopped looking?" Darcie asked. "Isn't that what the spy would want?"

"I'm glad to see your loyalty is strong for Haighdlen," he said. "I have the finest men who have sworn allegiance to keeping this family and kingdom safe. Please don't trouble yourself with such matters. Enjoy the occasion and know you're in good hands."

He bowed his head and excused himself.

"I'll collect you after dinner then?" Sanders asked. Darcie smiled and nodded just as dinner was announced.

A servant helped Elise and Darcie find their seats as the first courses were passed around.

"Where are the guys?" Elise asked as she folded her napkin in her lap.

Darcie leaned forward to see the entryway.

"There they are, and it looks like Edith is doing her own meddling."

Elise saw Gavin and Mitch looking for them. Both were very well dressed in formal attire and she noticed Gavin's vest was the same shade of burgundy as her gown.

"You're right. Looks like you have a partner in crime."

When will the meddling end?

Elise shook her head and held up her hand to motion them over.

***

The dinner hour passed smoothly enough, and Elise was able to give the boys the same instructions to keep a look out.

"Do we even know if it's the same ball?" Mitch asked. "Seems like the family does this sort of thing a lot."

"Sarah was very specific when she told me. She said Ruby's birthday ball. I don't think it's a coincidence that we got sent to this one."

"But it sounds like there's not even a spy anymore," Gavin said. "So, who exactly are we looking for?"

Elise sighed.

"I don't know. The fact there's a million people here makes it that much harder. It could be anybody."

Mitch moaned in approval as the dessert course was served.

"I'm glad your family's not poor." He looked up at their startled expressions and shrugged. "What? So far, it's worked out great for us. Good food, big bedrooms. . .all I'm saying is it could be worse."

The band finished their last dinner piece and began to play a lively tune. Several couples and children approached the dance floor. Elise immediately located Sanders and saw him making his way over to their table. Darcie saw him, too, and didn't wait for another formal invitation before she stood.

Mitch looked up from his plate.

"Where are you going?"

"To dance with that guy." She tossed her napkin on the table and smoothed her gown.

"Do you know him?"

"No, but he asked me, and I want to." Darcie patted her hair and asked Elise to look at her teeth. When everything checked out, she met Sanders in the middle of the room. He smiled and offered his arm before leading her to the dance floor.

Mitch slouched and finished off his pudding.

"Where did he come from?"

"He's one of Derek's soldiers," Elise said. "We met him and the captain earlier before you got here."

"Which one is the captain?" Gavin asked. Elise pointed him out across the room. "Have we seen him before?"

"Yeah, he was a soldier when Theronde was king. He gave the king the tip about the rumors circulating. But he said that the rumors went away a long time ago and not to worry about it."

"You're not capable of doing that," Gavin teased. "I take it you're already coming up with a plan?"

"There may not be a spy, but something dirty is going on. Rona wouldn't just go away, so I'm sure there's been stuff happening since our last visit."

"It really sucks someone would start a fire and ruin the kid's party," he said.

"It would suck more if she were actually enjoying it." Mitch pointed their attention to Ruby, who was sitting in a chair by the open doors and coloring on some paper.

"She looks so lonely," Elise said. "Do you think I should go talk to her?"

She didn't wait for an answer and headed over to the little girl.

Ruby was the perfect image of a princess in a powder pink gown. Her hair was pulled back, and she wore a small tiara.

"Ruby?" The child jumped and a few crayons rolled onto the floor. "Oh, I'm sorry." Elise picked them up and laid them next to her again. "I'm Elise. I'm a friend of your parents. We had the picnic together today. How are you?"

"I'm fine," she said without looking up from the paper.

Elise glanced down.

"That's a nice drawing. Is that a unicorn?" Ruby nodded. "I thought so. You're really good." It didn't seem like Ruby was going to talk anymore, so Elise tried again. "Why aren't you playing with the other kids?"

"They were mean to me."

"What do you mean?"

"Charlie Fenton made the other kids start ignoring me, and then he cut in front of me for the pony ride."

"I'm sorry," Elise said. "Did you tell a grown up?"

"Yes. He called me a tattle tale and took my tiara."

Elise wanted to find this little Charlie Fenton and put him in his place.

"Where is he?"

"He's outside with Richard."

"He's Richard's friend? I thought he was a little kid."

"No, he and Richard tease me all the time."

"Ruby, I'm sorry." Elise took a seat next to her. It was strange having this conversation with her mom. "I get teased, too. I know it's not fun."

"You do?"

"Yep. You should stand up for yourself and tell this Charlie to leave you alone. If he's friends with Richard, he's too old to be doing that anyway."

Ruby smiled and finished her drawing.

"Here. This is for you."

Elise took the drawing and saw that while they had talked, Ruby had drawn two people on the unicorn. While it was mostly scribbled, Elise could make out two girls wearing the same color dresses they were.

"Is this us?" Ruby nodded. Elise reached out and hugged her. "Thank you. I'll keep it safe."

Ruby ran outside, and Elise smiled as she folded the picture carefully. She looked for a good place to put it and finally settled with tucking it into the front of her gown.

When she approached her table, she saw it was empty and looked around for her friends. Darcie was still dancing with Sanders, but she couldn't find the boys. Stepping through the crowd, she was relieved when she saw Gavin across the room with his back to her.

When she got closer, however, she paused because he was standing among a group of people. Elise took advantage of her distance to assess them. One member of the party was a beautiful young blonde woman. Her voluptuous figure was evident in a sky-blue gown. The surrounding group of men seemed enthralled with her, and she even held her glass in a way that oozed class. One of the other gentlemen made a joke, and as they laughed, she rested her hand on Gavin's shoulder.

Suddenly, Elise felt less like a Hollywood actress and more like the unknown understudy.

As she turned around to leave, she saw Derek walk inside holding Ruby's hand. As the musicians began to play a soft piece of music, he helped the little girl onto his shoes and swayed them both to the music.

I wish I had a camera.

Ruby had cheered up and was enjoying being the center of attention. Joranna watched from nearby and dabbed her eyes with a handkerchief. Derek helped his daughter down and twirled her a few times. The room erupted into applause when the music ended. Joranna held up her hand and announced it was time for everyone to sing.

Elise sang along to the birthday tune but scanned the room for anyone or anything that might seem off.

Am I just being paranoid?

Perhaps Brahm was right and something had changed since their previous visit that prevented the fire.

Derek held Ruby up so she could blow out her candles. Applause rang out and he sat her down at the head table to enjoy a slice of cake.

Once the dance music started up again, Elise watched as Darcie decided to stay with Sanders for another song. She turned back to see Gavin talking with the same group.

I don't want to interrupt. It looks like he's enjoying himself.

The decision was made for her, however, when the blonde saw her. The woman tapped Gavin on the shoulder and nodded towards Elise.

Gavin turned around and smiled.

"Oh, hey, Elise. Everything okay?"

"Yeah." She attempted to stand straighter and hold herself together as the other woman and gentlemen sized her up. "I was just wondering if you knew where Mitch went."

"Oh, he was just here. They came around offering tours of the castle and armory."

"They're offering tours?" Elise asked. Her thoughts began to race.

That means not all the guests are here right now. Someone could be slipping by undetected.

"Are you feeling well, my dear?" the woman asked. "You look quite pale."

"No, I'm fine." Elise stared between Gavin and the woman. "You two have fun."

She turned on her heel, and her eyes darted from person to person until she found Brahm. She made a bee line for him through the crowd and interrupted his conversation.

"Captain, something is going to happen! I really need to talk to you."

He laughed and excused himself from his group of guests. When he turned, his smile was replaced with a scowl.

"My dear, I don't know how polite society conducts itself where you're from, but I insist you get a hold of yourself before you make a scene!"

"There's no time for that." She tugged at his elbow and tried to get him to follow her. "We have to stop those tours. Someone's going to try and hurt people."

He pulled away from her touch. Once he assessed that they weren't being watched, he smiled and leaned down so only she could hear him.

"I've already told you that the perimeter has been checked and is being heavily guarded. Nothing will get past me. I must encourage you to return to the party without creating a scandal."

"But—"

"Do I need to alert His Majesty that your sole purpose in being here is to spread fear and ruin his daughter's birthday in front of his peers, councilmen, and subjects?"

She stomped her foot and pushed her face closer to him.

"No, that's not what I want. I'm telling you I think someone is going to try and hurt people!"

"I've heard enough, young lady." He bowed and slipped away through the crowd.

I need to talk to the guys. Someone has to do something.

The hallway was heavily guarded. Mitch must've been with a group. She couldn't talk to Darcie yet, and Gavin was perfectly preoccupied with his new friends. Her anger threatened to erupt, and she wanted to kick something. Before she could embarrass Derek and Joranna, she turned and walked out the French doors to be alone.

She passed the line for the pony rides. The magician and acrobats were surrounded by a cheering crowd. Now that night had fallen, the only lights came from the lanterns and torches.

I wish I could enjoy the party more.

Elise admired one of the fountains, but when she looked down at her reflection, she saw that the summer heat was causing her hair to slowly frizz again. She dipped her hand in the water and put it all back in place before chuckling to herself.

It doesn't really matter at this point. There's no one to show off for.

She needed to take a walk and cool off. She didn't want to wait for tragedy to strike, but without any help, she knew there was little she could do.

Only a handful of people seemed to be walking through the garden, so she decided that that would be the best place to be alone.

At least no one would see her if she cried, but she told herself that she wasn't going to let that happen. This wasn't time to feel sorry for herself. It was time to get control, wait for the party to die down a little, then try to speak to Derek and Joranna privately.

They'll want to know where I got my information.

That's where she was stuck, because she couldn't give anything away.

If we don't play our cards right, we'll be blamed for anything bad that happens.

She crossed over the small bridge past the pond and the stone waterfall. The area around the gazebo was very well lit and only a handful of people had ventured this far. Elise was thankful to find the gazebo empty and took a seat on one of the benches inside. The paper crinkled against her skin, so she pulled it out and unfolded the page.

She ran her fingers over the drawing.

"You okay?"

She jumped and looked up as Gavin stepped into the gazebo.

"How did you know I was out here?"

"You looked upset when you left, so I followed you to see if you were okay."

"I'm fine." She folded the paper and stuffed it down into the front of her gown again. He stayed on the other side of the gazebo and leaned against the railing.

He looked absolutely irresistible in his formal clothes.

Edith did such a great job tonight.

"Do you want to talk?" he asked. "I saw you speaking to the captain."

"I was trying to warn him, but he wouldn't listen to me." She looked down and toyed with her jewelry. "I just can't stand sitting around knowing something bad is going to happen and feeling helpless."

"It has to be hard. Being so close to your family without being able to tell them the truth."

She nodded and felt the first threat of tears form. She inhaled deeply and chose to pace to keep them from falling.

The last thing I need is for Gavin to see me have a panic attack and bawl my eyes out in the same day.

"You look nice by the way." The compliment caught her off guard and she stopped pacing. "I didn't get a chance to tell you earlier."

"Thanks. You do, too."

He looked over his shoulder at another couple walking by. He bowed his head at them and turned back to face her.

"So, how long are we going to hide out here?"

"You can go in whenever you want. I'm sure your friends are missing you. One in particular."

"Shut up," he said with a laugh. "She was just standing there with everybody else. They invited Mitch and me for one of the tours."

"Why didn't you go?"

"She tried to get me to stay for a dance first, but I wasn't interested."

"I don't see why not. She's clearly your type."

"Oh, and you know my type?" Gavin crossed his arms and leaned against a beam.

She got distracted when a lock of his hair fell into his face, then continued pacing.

"She looks like all the other girls you walked down the halls with at school. She has a little more class." Elise cocked her head to one side. "Definitely has more of other things, too."

"And that bothers you?"

"What? No," Elise said. "Like I said. You don't have to stay out here with me. I'm fine."

He moved without making a sound, and she jumped when she found herself face to face with him.

"And what if I want to stay out here with you?"

Shadows bounced across his face from the flickering torches. She kept waiting for him to break into laughter, but his expression remained serious. A chill ran down her spine despite the warm weather. She waited for the adrenaline-infused tornado to sweep away her thoughts.

But it didn't come.

In fact, she didn't feel any sort of panic. Her thoughts were crystal clear about what she wanted. She studied every curve of his face before settling on his mouth. Surprising herself, she closed the distance between them and waited for him to back away. When he didn't, she leaned up and touched her lips to his.

It was soft and brief, unlike the kisses she normally fantasized about with him. The clouds didn't part; fireworks didn't shoot off behind her eyes, but in its own way, it satisfied an ever-growing curiosity within her. Opening her eyes, she tightened her mouth into a thin line and looked down at her feet.

"What's wrong?" he asked.

She smiled.

"I've wanted to do that for so long."

"Was it everything you dreamed it'd be?"

They laughed and she slapped him on the arm.

"Don't spoil it," she said. As their laughter faded, she scrunched up her face. "Was it lousy?"

"Not at all." He reached out and interlocked his fingers with hers. "I've wanted to for a while, too."

Is this really happening? This is too good to be true. Maybe I'm traveling through the diary and about to wake up any moment.

She couldn't look away when he locked his eyes on hers.

"Want to do it again?" he asked.

Without waiting, he leaned down and she met him in another kiss.

His lips were smooth but confident. He released one of her hands and cupped her face as the kiss deepened. His fingers tangled in her hair. She gripped his sleeve, feeling weightless in his embrace. As they pulled apart, his crooked smile made her chest tighten. She giggled and ran her fingers through his hair to fix it.

Distant screams startled them, and they jerked apart. People were shouting and sounds of panic were coming from the castle. Calls for order could be heard over the chaos.

"Fire!" someone shouted. "Fire!"

Elise felt the blood drain from her face. It had actually happened. She had told herself not to get distracted. The guilt would have to wait. Without a word, she took off running towards the castle with Gavin hard on her heels.

CHAPTER 18

More and more people ran out into the courtyard as Elise and Gavin approached. She stood on her toes to look over the crowd for Mitch, Darcie, and her family.

"There they are," Gavin shouted. She followed his finger and saw her family exiting to safety. Joranna ushered her oldest three out of the doors with Derek following closely holding Ruby, who was crying. He passed her into Joranna's arms and turned to one of his servants.

"Get me my horse! Quick, man!" He ordered for all the carriages to be searched. "Have them available, but no one leaves until we have assessed the cause and get the situation under control."

Two guards were ordered to block the doors to prevent anyone reentering. Elise looked around at all the unfamiliar faces and felt her fear growing by the minute.

"Elise!"

Seeing Darcie's hand raised above the sea of people, Elise and Gavin made their way over to her. She threw her arms around her friend's neck.

"We're so glad you're safe," Elise said. "Where's Mitch?"

"I still haven't found him. Sanders got called to help with the fire and I've been looking. Where were y'all?"

"We'll explain later. What if he's not out here? We need to get in to look for him."

She stepped up to the guards, but a well-dressed gentleman blocked her.

"Excuse me, Miss, but no one is allowed in. King's orders. The fire is still spreading, and it's not yet under control. You will need to stay here with the others."

"But we can't find our friend!" Darcie cried. "Someone has to go look for him."

"The castle is being diligently searched. He will be found, but for now, I'm going to ask you to wait here."

The king walked back over to assess the situation.

"What is the problem?"

"We need to get back in," Elise said. "We can't find Mitch and we think he might still be in there."

"Your Majesty, I have given them your orders that no one is to go in," the man said. Derek turned to head back into the ballroom. "Sire, I must insist that you leave as well for your safety."

"I shall be the last one to leave, Ballard. I will assist with the search. See to it no one gets away. When the fire is under control, I want to find who is responsible. Don't let any carriages leave the grounds. Elise, I want you all to wait with my family. We will find Mitchell. My steward, Ballard, will help in any way he can. Excuse me."

"Yes, Your Majesty," Ballard said. He straightened his waistcoat, smoothed his blond hair and turned to Elise.

Derek hurried back into the castle while Ballard led them over to where Joranna and the children waited.

The entire courtyard was filled with people anxiously chattering back and forth while children cried throughout the crowd. Members of the staff were huddled near the royal family. After a sole window was opened in one of the bedrooms, the onlookers below could see and smell the smoke floating into the night sky. Just behind it they could make out movement. Commands could be heard coming from inside, but no one could be identified.

"Are they going to be okay?" Elise asked.

"They just have to be," Joranna said. "We can only pray they can contain it." She kissed the top of Ruby's head and held her close. "I'm just thankful we're all here together."

"We're still missing Mitch," Gavin said.

"No, look!" Sarah shouted. She pointed through the crowd and they all turned to see the blonde woman from before escorting Mitch over.

"Mitch!" Darcie threw her arms around him, not letting go for several moments. When she pulled back and assessed that he was unhurt, she slapped his arm. "Where have you been?"

"When the tour got interrupted, the soldiers brought him and the others to us to wait out here. Dreadful turn of events," the woman said and gazed up at the castle. "Glad to see you all made it out safely. I'm so sorry, Princess." She bowed to Ruby and excused herself to join her party near the closest fountains.

"I don't like her," Elise muttered. She watched the other woman slip in and out of the groups of people like a snake.

Gavin raised an eyebrow at her.

"Why not? She brought Mitch back and everybody's okay."

"This is crazy. Am I right?" Mitch asked. "I mean, you tried to warn us, Elise, but I didn't think it'd be this big of a deal."

"You knew this would happen?" Joranna asked.

Elise froze and looked at her family's questioning eyes, struggling for what to say. Ruby lifted her head from her mother's neck and looked at Elise. The fear and confusion on the child's face tore at her heart. She glared at Mitch.

"I said I was worried something like this *could* happen."

The sound of someone coughing distracted them, and they turned to see Derek exit through the same doors where his horse stood waiting for him to mount. He took the reins and walked the animal over to his family.

"It's out." He coughed into his arm again. "As of right now, it looks as if it was started in one of the guest bedrooms." He glanced at the teenagers before kissing Joranna and checking on the children.

A guest bedroom? I thought it was supposed to be Ruby's room.

"Elise here seems to have some knowledge of tonight's incident," Joranna said. "Perhaps we should talk privately in your office?"

Elise waved her hands in front of her.

"I didn't start it! I don't know how it happened."

"That's what we're here to find out," Derek said. "I know you were in the ballroom long before it was started. Nevertheless, I should like to speak more about your insight once the rest is settled."

Elise's stomach sank in dread.

Great. Now we have to come up with more lies to cover ourselves.

She marveled at the fact that within a matter of minutes she had gone from fearing for Mitch's safety to wanting to punch him in face for getting them cornered again.

Derek brushed his thumb gently across Ruby's cheek.

"I'm sorry about this, darling. We'll fix this. Don't be frightened." He turned to his other children. "Everything is fine now. The rest of the wings seem unaffected, so we'll give the castle time to air out before we go back in to sleep."

He turned and mounted his horse before addressing the crowd. After he called everyone to order, the buzzing of conversations dwindled.

"The castle has been searched and the fire has been controlled. My captain has reported that someone set fire to the curtains of one of the guest bedrooms. The fireplace was not lit so this appears to have been intentional." Several people gasped in horror and surprise. Whispers began to circulate, and Derek held up his hand for silence. "We are fortunate no one was hurt and that it was discovered as quickly as it was. This deliberate threat to the safety of my family, servants, and guests, as well as to the structure of this castle, is unforgivable." His expression hardened as he surveyed the guests in front of him. "I want to know who did this. Who will step forward and claim responsibility?"

There were whispers and murmurs among the guests, but no one spoke up. Derek gritted his teeth and squeezed the horse with his lower legs to move forward. Several guests cried out and moved out of the way.

"I will not ask again!" His guttural inquiry pierced through Elise's heart and conscience. Had there been anything else she could've done? "Do I need to interrogate the entire kingdom? You know the penalty if you withhold information on this matter."

Elise gazed around at the silent magicians, acrobats and animal handlers. The upper-class guests also looked around for anyone to speak up. Elise's eyes settled on the musicians, who stood together in a group holding their instruments. The mandolin player had his body turned from her. He spat on the ground and visibly did not seem very interested in Derek's threats. As he turned back to face the king, Elise gasped.

"What? What is it?" Darcie asked.

"I know him. . ." Her brain tried to remember where she had seen his face before. She didn't recognize his thick black hair or beard, but she couldn't push away the thought that he looked familiar. Then it clicked. "How did we not notice *him* before?" She gestured with her head towards the musicians. "Look at the mandolin player."

"Is he the guy that was teasing Derek before?" Gavin asked. "He doesn't look like it. Are you sure that's him?"

"Yes!" Elise said. "I don't blame Derek for not recognizing him. To us, it was like yesterday. To Derek, it's been what, thirteen or so years?"

Gavin shook his head.

"You don't think that guy would hold a grudge that long, do you? Wouldn't they have his name from when he was arrested last time?"

"Not if he changed it or lied," Elise whispered. "And he's clearly disguised himself."

"He was smart to get hired with the musicians. How else would he have gotten through the protection spell to get close to the king?" Mitch said. "Looks like we found our spy."

Everything certainly did point to that conclusion.

"Isn't it obvious, Your Majesty?" a voice rang out, causing everyone's attention to turn towards an older musician standing by the mandolin player. He was shorter, heavier and had gray wispy hair along with a pair of mutton chop sideburns. His own violin lay on the ground next to him, forgotten. "No idiot started this fire and only a fool would fess up. You can talk until you're dead but keeping us out here will get you nowhere."

"How dare you!" Derek turned his horse to face the musicians. "What is your name, sir?"

"Kinden, Sire," the older man said with a poor attempt at a bow. "And if you ask me, whoever did this was right to do so."

Echoing gasps and shrieks rang out through the crowd.

"You, sir, are on dangerous ground!" Derek warned.

"Your threats are empty, Sire, just like your father's before you." He turned and addressed the crowd. "There was just an attack on Vynchia by Lockesbarrian soldiers. No doubt ordered by Rona herself. They're our allies, our closest neighbor, and yet he doesn't send aid. It's only a matter of time before it's our turn, or perhaps this is it! Who's to say she's not about to strike us all down here and now?"

"Guards! Seize him!"

Elise felt the hair on the back of her neck stand as a group of guards descended upon the musicians. Kinden was restrained and handcuffed.

"Can't handle the truth then, Sire?" the mandolin player taunted. "You haven't changed! The entire monarchy is a bunch of cowardly dogs! My father is only pointing out facts. You'd all be fools to ignore him!"

"Seize them both!" Derek ordered. The two gentlemen were brought forward. "Until proven innocent, you both are being held responsible for this evening's events. Take them away!"

"We didn't start that bloody fire!" Kinden barked over the roar of the crowd as he and his son were taken out of sight. The people rejoiced and many cried out for their punishment.

Derek raised his hand.

"You will all be questioned and searched upon your departure tonight, but the initial threat seems to have been removed. Again, I apologize for the inconvenience this evening."

Applause rang out among the people before Ballard stepped forward to establish order.

Derek trotted over to where Elise and the others stood.

"When we're cleared to reenter, come to my office. Joranna, have the children put to bed and join us."

He didn't wait for a response before galloping off to meet with his officers.

***

Ballard took it upon himself to escort them to the king's office once all the guests had been sent home. He entered alone to announce their arrival and moments later returned to invite them in.

The room appeared unchanged from when Theronde ruled. Crimson drapes still hung on the windows, the couch and chairs remained in the same positions, and the intimidating oak desk was covered in documents.

Upon their entry, they found Joranna seated on the couch and Derek perusing the bookshelf on the opposite wall. Ballard told them where to sit and waited behind Derek's chair for the king to proceed.

Derek crossed the room to sit behind the desk with a sigh. He placed a book on the only empty space left before picking up a pile of papers. His bloodshot eyes scanned the contents before he finally gave up and set them aside to massage the bridge of his nose.

"Darling, you're so tired," Joranna said. "Why don't we have this talk in the morning?"

"Because we need to have it now." He stared at each of the teenagers. "Do you have anything you'd like to tell me before I go further?" When he received no answer, he cleared his throat. "You must see the coincidence between the time of your arrival and tonight's events. I have yet to absolve *anyone,* and the four of you always seem to turn up when there's trouble. You claim you're here to help, and yet you bolt in and out of our lives as quickly as you please."

"And let's not forget the *endless* hospitality and kindness Your Majesty has shown them," Ballard added.

Who is this guy?

The smug way he smiled made her skin crawl, and he lingered near Derek like a pet.

A pet rat.

"Precisely, Ballard. I cannot sit idly by while so much suspicious behavior lies before me."

"I thought the musicians did this," Mitch said. "If anyone is a spy around here, I'd put money on those two."

"They are the prime suspects," Derek replied. "But we haven't had the chance to discuss your purpose for this particular visit."

Joranna turned towards Elise.

"Didn't you say you knew something about tonight's fire before it happened?"

Elise had never felt her mouth become drier than it was in that moment. She decided to protect herself by combining her present-day knowledge with the musicians' information.

"We knew that an uprising was possible. When Vynchia got attacked, there was a rumor that you would be next."

The last part may have been a lie, but whatever helped their reputation at this point was all that mattered.

Derek asked Ballard to summon the captain and waited until he left to continue.

"And you have no connection to Kinden and his son?"

They shook their heads and swore they were innocent.

"I believe them," Joranna said. "I know you want answers, but I don't think they're guilty."

He scoffed.

"So, what do you propose we do, Joranna? Let them go? *Again?* It will only label us as weak and gullible!"

"Better than hasty and unjust. I think your father would agree."

No one dared to break the silence that followed. The crackling fire produced the only movement and sound until Ballard and the captain arrived. The king and queen struggled to compose themselves as the door opened.

The captain bowed to them and raised an eyebrow as he saw the other occupants.

"You summoned me, Your Majesty?"

"Yes, Brahm." Derek straightened up in the chair. "Did you by chance ever come across any rumors predicting tonight's events?"

The captain shook his head and replied that he had not.

"That's interesting," the king said. "Elise was kind enough to share with me that after the events that transpired in Vynchia, we became the next target. I would think you and your men would have been made aware of this."

"Majesty, any hint of a threat would be reported to you immediately."

"Then why didn't you tell him when Elise warned you earlier?" Gavin challenged.

"What?" Derek bellowed. "Brahm, is this true?"

The color drained from the captain's face and he let out an uncomfortable chuckle. With all eyes on him now, he began to stumble over his words.

"Your Majesty, you simply had to be there in that moment. It was mere speculation on her part. I made the decision on your behalf. There was no need to involve you and your family in a potential scandal that would cause panic."

"And what would you call what *did* happen tonight?" Derek asked.

Elise suppressed her smile and watched him squirm under the scrutinization.

"I can only offer my sincerest apologies and vow that it will never happen again."

The next minute, Elise felt him lean over her chair and could feel his breath on her neck.

"But have you asked her who her source is?" he asked. "After all, wasn't it *her* room where the fire was started?"

"What?" Elise squeaked.

Why was someone in my room?

"I may have made a wrongful choice in not believing her, but you should've seen her tonight. She was practically in hysterics and could not be reasoned with. Surely that type of unstable behavior warrants a closer examination?"

"That's crazy!" Darcie shouted. "Why would Elise try so hard to warn you if she was the one who started it?"

"Yeah, why would she turn herself in?" Mitch asked. "Fess up, man. You messed up, and now the real criminal is still out there somewhere."

"They were with us all day, Derek," Joranna reasoned. "When would they have had the chance?"

"By that logic, we could excuse the musicians. They played all evening." Derek rubbed the back of his neck and stretched. "So, we have nothing."

"I wouldn't say nothing," Brahm said with a smile, and his hands came to rest on Elise's shoulders. She jerked away from his touch. "I recall a time this evening when they separated. That could've allowed one of them plenty of time to sneak away."

"I'm telling you, we didn't do anything!" Elise slumped back in her chair. "Maybe if we could talk to Kinden, we could figure out if he knew anything."

"I have no doubt that he's linked to this, even if only by ideology," Derek said. "I cannot condemn him on beliefs and speech alone, but if he is found to be guilty of tonight's crimes, he will pay for it."

"How bad was the damage?" Elise asked.

"Whoever did it intended to send a message rather than harm anyone. The fire was small and containable, but the room will need complete renovation."

"We'll set you four up in a different wing of the castle away from the smoke damage," Joranna said.

"Your Majesty!" Ballard cried in horror. "You're not seriously letting them stay the night? Surely, with the evidence presented, they should be in the dungeon with the musicians until they are cleared!"

"I agree with Ballard," the captain said. "The culprits who attacked Queen Arymei were never found. Given the timing of their arrival, we could very well be staring at them."

"Queen Arymei?" Darcie asked.

"An attempt was made to assassinate the new Vynchian queen at her coronation," Joranna said. "She was tricked by undercover spies who infiltrated her army and gained her trust long before the event even took place. She was completely blindsided, and no one can figure out how they escaped."

Elise looked back over at Derek.

"And you think Rona is behind all of these attacks?"

"It would seem so," Derek said. "They all send a message of power and evoke fear. Rona feeds off the fear of others. These attacks come after a long quiet period, which leads me to believe she has followers. She's getting bolder. As long as we have protestors like Kinden rioting in the streets, we are leaving ourselves distracted for an attack. That's just what she wants."

"Talk to him," Elise suggested. "Or let us talk to him. Maybe he'll open up to someone else."

"Kinden and his son had no trouble undermining my authority out there. If they had something to say, I believe it would be shared. The guards will question them enough, and if we can't find sufficient evidence, they'll be let go."

"What about us?" Gavin asked.

"After hearing your testimonies, I'll appease Joranna and let you stay the night."

A wave of relief washed over Elise.

Brahm made to argue, but Derek held up his hand.

"Now, I don't want to hear anymore tonight. Elise made every attempt to warn you about a threat. In the future, Elise, please bring any news to me directly. It would appear luck is on your side yet again."

Both Brahm and Ballard looked as if they had swallowed something sour.

Derek instructed Ballard to lead the travelers to their rooms and dismissed Brahm, who turned on his heel and stormed out.

Ballard waited until all four were lined up before he led them into the hallway.

"You know, I don't remember King Theronde having a 'Ballard'," Mitch muttered.

"Every king has a steward," Ballard explained. "Our roles can vary based on what the king needs. His Majesty is newly king and therefore requires more assistance. I play many roles at present."

Elise only half paid attention to their conversation. Her mind was still in the office. Her heart ached to beg Derek for another chance. It felt like they were giving up, but she also didn't want to press her luck and put them in danger.

Somebody who isn't out for a conviction needs to talk to Kinden.

She waited for Ballard to turn the corner and stopped. Darcie paused when she noticed, but Elise put a finger up to her mouth and waved for her friend to keep walking. Darcie sent her a look that told her she wasn't off the hook but followed her friend's wishes and turned the corner.

Elise tiptoed back down the hall to Derek's office, where she discovered the door was open a crack. She lifted her hand to knock but stopped when she heard the king and queen arguing inside.

"I've let them stay the night, Joranna. Why aren't you satisfied?"

"Because I still don't think you're convinced they're innocent."

"The fire was set to one of their rooms! Who else knew of their arrival until the last minute? This took planning."

"Why would they incriminate themselves?" Derek only groaned in response. "I agree they should have told us as soon as they got here, but the fact of the matter is, she made the attempt to warn us. What unsettles me is how complacent you are towards Brahm's decision to play king. If anyone deserves a night in the dungeon, perhaps it's him."

"You know I can't do that. Tonight's scandal alone will cause enough rumors. I don't need anyone thinking I have trouble in my ranks."

"You need to talk with him. This can't be over. What's to stop him from making other decisions behind your back? If there is still a spy out there, we need Brahm to be sharp and reminded that only the strictest loyalty will be accepted from his position."

"I will talk to him, but can you agree that those four coming in and out of our lives, years apart, is unsettling, too?"

"It is," Joranna conceded. "And I don't really believe they were cursed. I think something deeper is going on, but their motives have always been driven by what will keep Haighdlen safe. Doesn't that improve your opinion of them?"

"My opinion doesn't mean much at the moment." He frowned. "I have to do what's best for the kingdom. Right now, that would appear to keep listening to them. We keep giving them chances that we wouldn't give to anyone else and I can't really explain why. They could prove to be a great weapon to finding out Rona's weakness, or they could be manipulating us and we're willingly playing the pawns."

She walked over and began to massage his shoulders.

"You know it's the smartest choice to keep as many pieces on the board at a time. Don't make any sacrificial moves unless it's necessary."

He reached up and caressed one of her hands.

"You're right. We can keep them in our good favor for now, but I'll say this given their history. Should their departure feel like an escape, or several years pass without any correspondence, they will be shown the dungeon rather than a comfortable guest room if they arrive again. Luck can only get them so far before they will have to answer for their unorthodox tactics."

Elise jumped as a hand pulled at her gown. Whirling around, she didn't see anyone. She looked down to discover Ruby standing in her nightgown. She sighed and lowered to her knees.

"Ruby, what are you doing?" she whispered

"I was afraid."

"About what?"

"What if there's another fire?" She hugged her teddy bear and rocked back and forth. "I want my mother."

Elise made to answer but was interrupted as Ballard came around the corner. Out of breath he looked ready to boil over as a vein bulged in his neck. He huffed at her and crossed his arms.

"I suppose we have trouble following simple instructions," he said. "Perhaps a chaperone is necessary?"

The door of the study widened, and light flooded into the hall. Derek and Joranna stood in the doorway.

"Elise?" Derek asked. "What's going on? Ruby, why are you out of bed?"

"Should I tell His Majesty that you snuck off to eavesdrop? I'd be happy to secure a chaperone for their rooms tonight, Sire."

Ruby ran forward and tried to hide in her mother's gown. Joranna stroked her daughter's hair.

"I didn't come to eavesdrop," Elise said and looked down at her young mother. "I saw Ruby in the hall after you walked away. She wanted her parents because she's afraid about the fire. I was just helping her find them."

"I'll help Ruby back to bed," Joranna said. She excused herself and lifted Ruby up into her arms.

"Thank you for helping," Derek said. "We're off to bed."

Elise nodded, knowing that now was not the time to question him about Kinden. It was a close call as it was, and she still wasn't sure that she had convinced Ballard. At least once she was in her room, she could sneak over to Darcie's and talk.

I might get to see Gavin before he falls asleep.

"On second thought, Ballard, a chaperone couldn't hurt," Derek said. "With everything unsolved at the moment, a little extra security for everyone couldn't hurt."

Or not.

Her shoulders slouched as she said goodnight and followed the steward. A guard came to monitor the corridor, and Elise couldn't shut the door fast enough on Ballard once she was in her room.

After changing into the provided nightgown, she carried her mother's drawing to bed. As her eyes grew heavy admiring it, she folded and tucked it under her pillow while her thoughts drifted.

So much had happened in the last few hours that it seemed surreal the picnic had only been that afternoon. Elise relived the conversation in the boat, her frustration at the ball and finally the kiss. She smiled into her pillow and pinched the blankets tighter around her body.

Darcie is going to flip when I tell her.

She wanted to burst into her friend's room that moment but knew that a guard would only be there to stop her. It would have to wait until morning, along with any chance of questioning Kinden.

Why was my room chosen over Ruby's?

An uneasiness spread through her. That would also have to be something for tomorrow as her body demanded she rest.

CHAPTER 19

Elise awoke to the sound of a light knock on the door. She opened one eye to see two maids enter with a gown, pitcher, and basin.

"Good morning, Miss," one said as both curtsied.

Elise threw her arm up to block the sunlight that streamed in as the drapes were thrown open.

"We're here to dress you, Miss."

"Oh, don't worry about that." Elise yawned. "I can dress myself. You don't have to."

The maids looked at each other.

"We've been instructed to help you dress and escort you to the dining room for breakfast, Miss," the first one said.

Helping me dress and another escort. . .I probably have the extra security measures to thank for that.

They were going to be chaperoned at all times. Elise groaned and swung her legs over the side of the bed.

"I have the water here to wash your face unless you'd rather take a bath," said the second maid. "I can prepare it for you."

"Could I at least take a bath by myself?" When they looked at each other again, she scoffed. "I'll just wash my face then."

She grabbed the cloth and soaked it before scrubbing her face and body. She was provided perfume and helped into her gown. While the first helped her dress, the second began making her bed.

"Wait!" Elise cried and lunged for the bed. She scrambled about until she found the crinkled paper folded under the pillow. She smiled at their perplexed expressions and tucked the drawing into the front of her gown. Someone had already tried to burn down one of her rooms. She didn't want to risk losing the drawing.

The next few minutes passed in an awkward silence as one maid did her hair and makeup while the other took care of the bedding and laundry. Elise didn't think she'd ever get used to such an invasion of privacy. She longed for a nice hot shower, but not if someone was going to be watching her to make sure she did it right.

***

Once they arrived downstairs, Ballard met them at the entryway to the dining room.

"That will be all, ladies. Thank you." The maids curtsied and left. "I trust you slept well, Miss?"

"I did until I wasn't allowed to anymore," she grumbled. "I guess I have you to thank for the wake-up call?"

"His Majesty will be having breakfast any moment. I feel it's only appropriate that his guests join him promptly."

She groaned in response and stepped around him. Her sour mood only lifted when she saw the other three waiting for her. With Mitch and Darcie sat on one side of the table she chose the empty seat next to Gavin.

"You look like you got the same wake-up call we did," Darcie said. She rested her face against her palm and yawned.

"So much for trusting us," Mitch said. "We can't leave our rooms and when we do, we have chaperones. This sucks."

"Not to mention the first-class treatment," Gavin grumbled. "A guy should be able to get himself dressed without a witness."

Elise rubbed her face but was careful not to smudge her makeup. She doubted there was enough foundation in the world to hide the bags she probably had under her eyes.

"I want to talk before anybody else comes in." Darcie looked to make sure Ballard was still by the doorway and that the other guards were far enough out of earshot. "Somebody's onto us."

"I was thinking the same thing last night," Elise said. "History didn't repeat itself. We changed something somehow and they chose my room instead."

"It's a warning," Mitch agreed. "Whoever did this is trying to send us a message. I'll bet it's our spy."

"But who could it be?" Gavin asked.

"Maybe that blonde woman had something to do with it," Elise said. "She was sketchy."

"I don't know." Mitch shook his head. "If they're targeting us, then they would have to recognize us from before. I never saw that woman until last night."

"Something else is bothering me…" Darcie took a long pause. "What if it wasn't a coincidence that we were separated last night? What if someone arranged for it to happen?"

They sat in silence and processed her theory.

"It makes sense." Gavin leaned in so they could hear better. "It allowed whoever did it time to get away and make us look guilty."

"Did we meddle too much without realizing it?" Elise shifted in her chair. "Did we change something? What if we're being punished?"

"I don't think that's what happened." Mitch pointed a finger at Elise. "Besides, your family sent us back to change things."

"Yeah, but this is major. There was always supposed to be a fire, but we changed the target. What if that throws off everything else from here on out?" When they didn't reply, she continued, "This is why we need to get to Kinden and straighten some of this out."

"You're not still hung up on that, are you?" Gavin rolled his eyes. "You heard Derek. It's not going to happen. You need to stop obsessing about it."

"It's our only option! What if we snuck down and interviewed him?"

"And how do you propose we do that?" Darcie asked. "Just waltz past security?" Mitch suggested a distraction, but Darcie shook her head and pinched the bridge of her nose. "Yeah, sure, because four outsiders could easily distract well-trained guards and sneak into the dungeon. This isn't a movie, y'all. This is real!"

"Well, what is your smart idea?" he shouted.

Elise hushed them as a couple of guards looked in their direction. Ballard glanced over his shoulder but was distracted when Ruby came into the room carrying a book under her arm.

He bowed and greeted her. The little girl bypassed him and waved at Elise's group. Climbing into her seat, she opened her book on the table.

"Good morning, Ruby," Elise said. "Are you making more drawings today?"

"Maybe later." She busied herself by leafing through the pages that she couldn't read yet.

"How does it feel to be five? Do you feel any different?"

"I'm just sad about my party." Ruby sighed. "I didn't even get to see the magician and he's my favorite part. I always get called up to pretend I have magic like my family."

Elise's heart fell. She looked down at the angelic face before her. Even at such a young age, Ruby felt left out.

Gavin reached out and squeezed Elise's hand under the table.

"What are you reading?" Darcie asked.

"I don't know. I found it on the stairs, but I can't read it."

"Well, here, I'll help you." Elise reached for the book, closing it to check the title.

Frozen, she stared at the familiar purple cover. Her friends were transfixed as well, and all four had to contain their excitement. Mitch mouthed for her to open it.

"Ruby, can I borrow this?"

The princess shrugged. "Sure. There aren't any pictures though. I've already checked."

"Good morning, everyone." As Joranna entered the room with Derek, Ballard signaled for the others to stand. Once the royal couple was seated, Elise slid the book on her chair and sat on it. "I was wondering where you had gotten off to, Ruby. Are you hungry, sweetheart?"

The other three children staggered in and after everyone was seated, the servers began to bring around the platters.

"How did everyone sleep?" Joranna asked. "I'm afraid I tossed and turned myself. Ruby even climbed into our bed at one point."

"I didn't have to because I'm brave," Ian bragged. "I'm not afraid of anything!"

"There's nothing wrong with being afraid," Joranna said. "Besides, Ruby, I was thinking that after breakfast we could open your presents. Won't that be fun?" Ruby's face lit up and she tried to slide out of her chair, but Joranna placed a hand to calm the child. "After breakfast."

Ruby slumped back and pouted.

"I don't want it. I'm not hungry," she whined. "I want to open my presents now!"

Joranna tried to whisper her corrections until Ruby's tantrum grew louder and Derek bellowed his daughter's name. She sniffled and took a bite while quiet tears streamed down her cheeks.

The servers finished loading their plates with scrambled eggs, savory sausages and croissants. Fresh fruit was added to the table and everyone was invited to begin.

"Ian, dear, take smaller bites." The boy took a slow bite for his mother's benefit but continued to shovel in humongous bites the moment she looked away.

Richard looked up at his father reading the morning documents.

"Are there any I can read, Father?"

"Not this morning, Son. There's nothing of interest for you."

Richard's face fell and he stabbed at his food.

"Quit trying to be Father," Sarah whispered. "You're not the king."

"I will be!"

"Darling, maybe you could set the dispatches down just this once," Joranna suggested.

"Joranna, I'm sorry. I'm a bit overwhelmed here if you haven't noticed."

"And it can wait long enough to have breakfast with your family and guests." She huffed as he continued reading. Elise was relieved when he picked up on her anger and set the papers aside to eat.

"Ruby, watch this!" Ian whispered. He glanced up to make sure his parents weren't watching before he pulled back on his spoon and sent a bite of jam flying across the table into Sarah's hair.

Sarah screamed when it landed and fell onto her lap. Richard chuckled as Sarah scrubbed at her dress.

"You little halfwit!" she cried. "Oh, Mother! Do something. Look at this stain. Look what he did!"

Ian and Ruby joined Richard in laughter.

The commotion was enough for Derek to stand and scoop up his papers.

"Can I not get *one* moment of peace and quiet around here?" he shouted as he stormed out of the room.

There was a hush at the table and Elise watched to gauge her grandmother's reaction.

"I'm so sorry." Joranna's face was flushed, but she took a moment to compose herself. The children had stopped laughing and could read their mother's body language well enough to stay silent as she called one of the servants over. "Please find Gracie and have her help Sarah get cleaned up and changed." Sarah threw her cloth napkin on the table and glared at Ian on the way out.

"You've come at a rather tense time once again," she informed Elise and her friends. "Forgive Derek. He's under a lot of stress this morning."

"Are all the letters about last night?" Elise asked.

"Some, but not all. There's no point in hiding the fact now. He tossed and turned all night as it is, but he awoke to find several important letters missing this morning. Letters between himself and other prominent leaders containing valuable information. If they landed in the wrong hands. . ."

"He thinks someone stole them?" Gavin asked.

She nodded. "He knew where they were, and we went to bed very late. I think he's more upset at himself than anything."

Mitch glanced at the door.

"He doesn't think we did it, does he?"

Joranna chuckled in spite of herself.

"I believe for once, you're not at the top of the list. You had all gone to bed far long before we did, and a chaperone was put into place. I hope that didn't offend you, but precautions had to be taken. It turned out to work for your favor because you couldn't be falsely accused." She placed her napkin on the table and looked at everyone. "Don't judge Derek right now. He's not himself. I don't think he will be for a while." She waited until everyone had taken their last few bites and looked down at her son. "I need to be left alone with Ian. If everyone is finished, would you excuse us, please? Ruby, we'll open your presents when I'm finished. Go play for now."

Everyone began to shuffle out of the room, and Elise turned away from Joranna in order to hide the diary from view.

***

"What are you waiting for?" Gavin asked once they were in the hall. "Open it!"

"He's right. Things are getting really sketchy," Darcie agreed. "Let's get out of here while we're not in hot water."

Elise hesitated and looked down at the book.

"We need to help them find the spy. We know they're here because his papers were just taken early this morning."

"The diary wouldn't have shown up unless we were done learning everything we needed for now," Gavin said.

He has a point. It would be easier just to open it.

"Do you think you know who it is?" Darcie asked.

Elise couldn't say the name out loud. She looked to her right and nodded towards the doorway where Ballard waited.

"Let's go out to the courtyard and I'll explain," she whispered. However, as they turned to leave, Ballard cleared his throat.

"Not so fast, if you please. I strictly remember orders for a chaperone to be used for you all."

"That was last night," Mitch exclaimed. "You're really going to send a guy to follow us around?"

"Absolutely. You may have mysterious ways to poison His Majesty's judgement, but so long as I'm around, I will see to it that nothing suspicious comes from your visit."

"Doesn't this place have a butler or housekeeper? You should let them do their jobs, man," Gavin said.

Ballard ignored him and snapped his fingers for one of the guards to walk over. The requested guard arrived, and Ballard gave him brief instructions to stay near them. He straightened his jacket and brushed a waxed piece of hair back into place. "I have to tend to business matters with His Majesty. I trust you can stay out of trouble while I'm gone." He turned on his heel and walked towards Derek's office.

Mitch glared at the steward's retreating figure.

"I'm with you, Elise. Something isn't right about that guy. He's in a hurry to get somewhere."

Elise looked down at the diary.

I need to tell them about Derek's threat if we leave for too long.

She also wanted to relay her thoughts on Ballard, but the guard's presence put a wrench in her plans for now. If Ballard's instructions were followed, they wouldn't even have enough space to whisper.

Derek came around the corner from the staircase.

I thought he was in his office.

Her thoughts raced with possibilities and she gasped.

"It's definitely Ballard!" She turned to the guard. "You need to go to the king's office."

"I don't take orders from you," he sneered. "I have my orders and they are to keep my eye on you."

She stomped her foot and wanted to strangle him.

"There's no time for that! He's probably in there stealing stuff right now!"

"Elise, what's going on?" Derek asked. The guard bowed as he approached.

She whirled around to face him and felt the accusation on her tongue.

"There you are, Your Majesty!"

They turned to see the captain approaching from the courtyard.

"I've just come from the tower, Sire, and I wanted to inform you that the interrogation is complete."

"Excellent work, Brahm. And?"

"And we got a full confession. Everything from planning to infiltrate the band to starting the fire."

"Then it is done." Derek sighed. "Issue a kingdom announcement and summon the council."

"Wait!" She bit her lip and sighed. "I don't think they did it."

"Elise, now is not the time for this," Derek said. "You just heard the captain. They confessed. It's over."

"There's more to it. I think you have a spy in the castle."

Their stunned expressions gave her hope that at least she'd been listened to. Derek gestured for her to follow him.

She asked for one more moment and shoved the diary in Gavin's hands.

"*Don't* open that yet."

"Elise, what are you doing?" he said. "You haven't even told us anything yet. What's going on?"

"We need to leave now!" Mitch reached for the diary before Elise stopped him.

"Believe me. At least wait until I give a signal before you open it." She waved her hands around trying to reach an idea. "I'll. . . nod my head when I'm done. Then you can open it and we'll go, but let me do this first!"

She didn't wait for a reply as she hurried over to where Derek and Brahm had stepped aside. When she caught up to them, she paused to catch her breath and nearly spit out the words.

"Well?" Derek asked.

"It's Ballard. He's your spy."

Derek and Brahm exchanged glances before both burst into laughter. It wasn't the response she had expected, and she felt her inner hero shrink by the second.

What's so funny about that?

"Do you see what I was saying, Sire?" Brahm chuckled. "Do you understand now why I had dismissed her before?"

"Elise," Derek said, "I don't think you know what you're saying." He smiled before he collected himself. "Now, I'm sorry for losing my temper at breakfast and I didn't intend to get you stirred up. However, Ballard has been a loyal member to this staff and kingdom."

"I'm telling you, he's guilty!" As they continued finding her warnings amusing, she grew hotter. Her skin burned and her hands curled into fists. The spy was right in front of them and they were choosing to ignore it. "He's in your office right now! He lied and said he was doing business with *you*. Well, you're not in there. He's probably stealing more letters!"

The mention of stolen letters caused the smile to leave Derek's face. His brows furrowed and she saw the confusion play across his face as to how she knew about that. Before he could ask, however, Brahm stepped in.

"Young lady, why don't we call the doctor. Perhaps he could give you a tonic for your nerves. You're clearly in hysterics."

"No, I'm fine!" she snapped. "Look, he's the perfect person to do this. He's using his position to manipulate you, and he has access to all your stuff. You can't let him get away with it!"

How can he be so calm about this?

She was presenting his spy on a silver platter, yet he looked as if she were giving him a simple weather report. Elise ran her fingers through her hair and felt it pull loose around her face. If she could just slap the smirk off of Brahm's face, she'd feel somewhat gratified. "You better do something now, or—"

"Are you about to threaten the king?" Brahm asked. He stepped in front of Derek and towered over her. She shrank away from him and lowered her eyes. She didn't know where her confidence had come from, but it was now replaced with her old companion, fear. She had overstepped and now tried to form an apology in her mind.

"I can handle this, Brahm." Derek stepped around the captain and looked at her. "Elise, I truly believe your intentions are honorable, but you're trying to be involved in something much bigger than yourself. Now, the captain has received a confession; my council and I are meeting to discuss further actions; and all will be well. Ballard is a good man and loyal friend. Now, I won't have any more outbursts to defame his character. Is that understood?"

She opened her mouth to argue, but he repeated his question louder. She closed her mouth and nodded.

"That will be all then. Come, Brahm, we have much to plan."

The two turned around the corner and proceeded down another corridor.

Elise stepped forward to follow them but was stopped in her tracks by an all-too-familiar feeling. A heaviness crept into her chest and she became lightheaded.

Oh no. Not yet. Please tell me he didn't!

She spun around, gazing in horror at the open book in Gavin's hands. Unable to fight it, she watched everything around her crumble into darkness.

CHAPTER 20

Elise awakened to a persistent chirping above her. She opened her eyes and saw the handful of birds calling to one another in a tree. Sweat soaked through her back in the thick humid air. They had once again landed in the royal garden.

Why didn't it take us back to Nana's? Did it not work?

She found a renewed energy as a bee flew too close for comfort. Elise scrambled to her feet to gain distance from it before looking around.

Mitch was still unconscious a few feet away by the pergola, while Gavin and Darcie were talking near the gazebo.

She replayed the sweet memory of her kiss with Gavin in the gazebo. The warm and fuzzy flutters in her stomach shifted, however, as she remembered him opening the diary. Pure rage coursed through her veins as she closed the distance between them.

"What did you do that for?" she shrieked. Her hands pushed against his chest and he stumbled back a step.

Darcie stepped in between them.

"Elise, what's wrong?"

"I wasn't ready to leave yet! Why did you open it?"

Gavin tilted his head to see around Darcie's shoulder.

"You nodded your head."

"I was answering his question!"

"Elise, stop yelling. Someone's going to hear you," Darcie whispered.

"Too late." Mitch groaned and made his way over. "What's wrong?"

Darcie continued, "You gave the signal, so he opened it. What's the big deal?"

We're dead. We're so dead. There's no way he's going to let us back in now.

Elise tried to run her fingers through her hair. When they caught in the pins and tangles, she ripped at them until her hair fell around her shoulders. She paced and steadied her breath, knowing inside she was angrier with herself than any of her friends.

"I didn't get the chance to tell y'all before." She lowered her head and was unable to look them in the eyes as she spoke. "I overheard Derek tell Joranna that if we ever left without warning or skipped a bunch of years again, we'd be thrown in the tower."

She braced herself for their outbursts, and when none came, she glanced up.

Darcie took a step forward and grabbed her hands.

"Well, we should be okay then. You were talking with him for a while and at least got to tell him we were leaving, right?"

Elise shook her head.

The reaction she expected occurred as they all began questioning what she had been thinking. She took the verbal beating, knowing that she deserved it.

"Well, I hope it was worth it," Gavin said, shaking his head. "I'm glad you felt strong enough about Ballard that you've doomed any chance we had of finding the real spy and getting out of here."

His disappointment in her stung the most.

"I don't like the guy either, Elise, but why are you so sure he's the spy?" Mitch asked.

Unwanted tears streamed down her face and she wiped them away with a shrug. Everything she had been convinced of before now seemed trivial.

"We weren't getting anywhere with trying to talk to Kinden, and Ballard was being shady. I thought he was sneaking into the office to take more letters. I tried to warn Derek, but he just laughed at me." She didn't expect their pity and she didn't want it, but she couldn't bear having all three angry with her. Her own irrational feelings had long gone. "I'm so sorry. I thought I was doing the right thing."

She turned and walked further into the garden until she came to the fountain. The imposing statue made her feel even smaller, something she didn't even think was possible at that moment.

"Elise?" Darcie walked over to the statue's stone base. She motioned for Elise to sit next to her and patted her on the back. "You okay?"

"I'm sorry," Elise said. "I was just so sure we were going to find something."

"And we still might, but you can't blame us for being upset. We don't know what we're walking into now." Elise nodded and wiped her nose on her sleeve. "You and Gavin are acting different, too. Is something going on?"

There wasn't any reason to hide it from her friend, and she had been itching to tell her already.

"Yes. . .no, I mean. . .I don't know," Elise said. She lowered her face into her hands. "We kissed."

Elise sat up and brushed her hair out of her face. Darcie looked like a little kid who walked into her living room Christmas morning to find out Santa had visited. She tapped her feet and let out a poorly contained squeal as she wrapped her arms around Elise.

"I knew it!" she cried and squeezed her friend. "I knew something happened. You guys have been so weird. You could cut the tension with a knife! So, what else?"

Elise shrugged and watched Gavin and Mitch talking in the distance. "Nothing. I figured he told you when I saw you talking."

"He should have! But seriously, what happened next?"

"That's it. The fire started right after, then we had to run back to the castle. We really haven't had a minute alone since."

"I can help with that!"

Elise grabbed her friend before she could sprint away.

"Darcie, not now. I just lunged at him. I doubt he's wanting to reminisce that kiss right now."

"He's got a temper, too. He's probably over it," Darcie said with a wave.

"Yeah, but one minute he's a jerk, then the next he's sweet. He drives me *crazy*," Elise growled, running her fingers through her hair again, making the tangles worse.

Darcie stifled a laugh.

"You've got it so bad. Come on, let's get moving and see how far we traveled."

Elise dipped her hand into the fountain and smoothed her hair out. She checked her reflection one more time before she allowed herself to be led over to where the guys were waiting.

Where do I even start?

"Gavin, I'm sorry. You didn't do anything wrong. I was just angry."

"Hey, I get it. I mess up, too."

He looked as if he wanted to grab her hand, and she also wondered what to do next.

Darcie was only too happy to step in as the hero and took it upon herself to lead them towards the castle.

"Okay, great, we're all made up. Let's go."

***

When they neared the arbor, Elise ducked behind one of the rose bushes and waved her friends over to do the same.

It appeared luck was on their side. Her family just happened to be sitting outside at a table having afternoon tea. She recognized Derek and Joranna right away, though both had once again undergone changes. Derek had a thick and polished beard that resembled Richard's in the future. His face had filled out further. His eyes seemed worn. Joranna whispered something into his ear and his hearty laughter rang out throughout the courtyard. Joranna's figure had filled out somewhat as well.

At least they look happy.

Elise was drawn to the four young adults at the table. She located her mother first and estimated her to be about fifteen or sixteen years old. Sitting beside her was Ian, who reminded Elise of Mitch. He was thin and gangly with a dark mop of hair. Sarah and

Richard had their backs to them, but it was clear that they weren't the same children Elise and her friends had visited before.

"Mother, may I please be excused?" Ruby placed her cloth napkin on the table.

The conversations around the table came to a close as everyone's eyes turned to her.

"Ruby, it's been a while since you've joined us for tea. Can't you stay a few more minutes?" Joranna asked.

"I'm tired. I'd like to lay down."

"You have taken naps every day for the last two weeks," Sarah said. "If you're ill, please stay away from me. It could be contagious."

"I don't have the energy to argue with you." Ruby stifled a yawn and pushed her cup away.

"I hope your mom is okay," Darcie said. "We were sure gone awhile."

"Yeah, Richard is older than we are now," Gavin whispered.

"I bet he has better aim, too," Mitch said with a grimace.

Their chuckles were silenced as they found themselves covered by a shadow. The next few seconds consisted of clanking armor, grunts, and struggling pleas, before they were seized and escorted towards the royal family.

Forced from her hiding spot, Elise felt her pulse racing as they approached the table. She had never felt more alienated from these people as she did now.

Her family looked up at the commotion. Sarah cried out as she rushed to the other side of the table to stand behind Ian and Ruby. Richard stood to face them, but Derek stepped forward and assured him he would handle it.

"What are you doing here?" Joranna asked.

"They were found in your garden, Majesty," the guard holding Darcie announced.

"Trespassers," Elise's guard said. "We're not sure how they crossed the barrier, but you're no longer in danger."

"They're not dangerous," Joranna said. When a moment of silence passed, she looked at her husband. "Derek, tell them."

Elise watched a series of emotions play across Derek's face that ranged from confusion and hurt to anger.

"Arrest them."

Darcie cried out and Elise couldn't stop her tears from falling. Mitch and Gavin tried to reason with Derek, but he only put his hand up to silence them.

"What's going on? Who are they?" Ian asked.

"Derek, let's handle this inside and talk to them. This is unnecessary," Joranna said.

"I vowed that if I ever saw the four of you again, that I would not be trifled with. You have come in and out of our lives for years unannounced and I have since been convinced of your unreliability. I have played the fool for too long. Now you will pay for your secrecy. Take them to the tower."

"Who convinced you of that?" Elise asked. She struggled against her guard's hold, but he only squeezed her tighter. "We haven't done anything wrong. Please! Please don't do this. We're only trying to help!"

Her pleas and the family's questions fell on deaf ears as Derek ushered his family inside. Joranna continued to protest, but followed her husband and children in.

Elise hoped they could have avoided this fate if they were able to approach at the right time, but it seemed their luck had finally run out. Their wrists were clasped in iron handcuffs.

Panic flooded in and her thoughts raced out of control.

What's going to happen to us? What will happen to the family? What if Rona shows up? Are we going to be stuck here forever?

She wilted in the guard's arms and lost all hope for their mission and futures.

***

The door to the tower was unlocked and they stepped into a dark entryway. Elise expected to climb the countless steps ahead of them but grew confused when one of the guards unlocked a hidden door on the floor.

"Aren't we going up in the tower?" Mitch asked.

The guards chuckled until the one by the door answered him.

"You're not going up it. You're going underneath it."

Elise felt her insides grow cold even before entering the underground chamber.

The stairs, if they could even be called that, were narrow and steep. Elise pulled up the hem of her dress so she wouldn't step on it and fall. She followed the flickering light of the torch carried by one of the guards ahead of her.

"These are worse than the ladders on my dad's ship," Gavin said behind her.

"Silence!" a guard barked from the back.

Rather than being helped off the steps, Elise felt herself be pulled by her arm.

The torches on the walls and in the guards' hands provided the only light. It took Elise a few minutes for her eyes to adjust.

This dungeon seemed to consist of several tunnels and archways. They were led in so many directions that by the time they arrived at their destination, Elise couldn't tell where they were or how deep they had gone.

Cells lined both sides of this room and various sizes of chains hung along the walls and ceiling. The sound of dripping water caused a shiver to run down Elise's spine. The firelight flickered along the walls, creating shadows that further gave Elise the feeling this place was haunted.

As they were led forward past the cells, voices called out for mercy and food. Dirt and blood covered arms reached out of the bars.

Elise's scream echoed throughout the chamber when one arm got close enough to grab her gown.

A guard whirled around, pulling his sword. He grabbed the person's wrist to force it away from Elise.

"Reach again and I'll make you unable to do so!" He used the hilt to smash the prisoner's hand. The faceless inmate cried out and vanished back into the cell. The same guard continued forward to unlock two cells that faced each other. Elise and Darcie were forced into the right one, while Gavin and Mitch were thrown in the left.

The sound of the key turning in the lock twisted Elise's stomach and she lunged at the bars.

"Please, don't do this. Let us out. We aren't spies! We're innocent. If you'll just get the king, we can—"

But the guards walked out. Despite hearing another door in the distance being shut and locked, Elise continued calling out for someone.

"Elise, it's no use," she heard Gavin grumble from across the room. She squinted her eyes in the dim light but couldn't make out their cell.

"What're we going to do now?" Mitch's voice betrayed that he was crying. He cleared his throat. "There has to be some way out of here. There always is."

"Again, this isn't a movie!" Darcie snapped. "This is *real life*. Dungeons are meant to lock people away. It's not going to have any secret passageways, and there won't be any fairies or genies to let us out."

"Well, there are fairies in this world," he said.

"And do you see any, genius?"

Mitch didn't reply.

"Okay, let's not turn on each other," Elise said. "They'll come back eventually to talk to us. So, we need to have a plan by then."

"Don't count on it," said a voice to her left. "This is where people go to be forgotten."

"Who's there?" Elise walked over to the far wall and didn't see anyone. The voice was coming from the cell next to theirs. "Who are you?"

"Don't bother trying to break free," he continued, "This place is a labyrinth of tunnels."

"They'll need to bring us food, won't they?" Darcie said. "We could try then."

"You won't see anyone until after sundown. They'll throw you a bit of water and supper before disappearing until the following day. Otherwise, they're outside guarding the door. So, don't even waste your time trying to escape."

"That's easy for you to say. I have to get up to find my family!" Elise cried.

"That's what I said when I first got put in here. It's been so long that I'm sure my family has long forgotten about me."

Elise's heart ached for the man, but her mind was still set on getting out of their cells. Even if it was hopeless, she had to try.

"I'm really sorry for what happened to you, but we can't just stay in here. This isn't how this was supposed to happen!"

"We knew this *could* happen though," Gavin said. "I'm sorry I sent us here before you could warn us."

"Well, we can't worry about that now." Darcie continued to bang on the bars. "We have to focus on how we can get through to anybody."

"Too bad this isn't a movie. If it were, we'd create a loud distraction, then we would take out the guards when they came to see what was up. Then one of us would steal the keys and we'd run out. But now that I'm in the scene, I just don't see that working."

Gavin scoffed at his friend.

"I'd like to see you 'take out' a guard."

"Guys, focus please!" A heroic escape might not be possible, but Elise's heart skipped a beat as another idea came to her. "What about Kinden?"

Gavin growled.

"How many times are we going to have to hear that name?"

"Just shut up and listen. He and his son were arrested that night. Maybe they were brought here. They could even still be here." She turned her face towards the prisoner's cell. "Hello? Are you still there?"

"Can't really go anywhere, can I?"

Elise pressed her face against the bars.

"Do you know if there are any musicians in here? Maybe a father and son?"

"It's hard to tell who people were before they came in here. We're all suspects of spying and treason."

"Can you just give us a straight answer?" Gavin griped.

Elise tried again.

"They were brought in after the castle caught on fire. I don't know how long ago it was, but—"

"Ahh, I do recall that fire," the man replied. "It was long before I was arrested, but I thought everyone knew what happened after that."

"Tell us!"

"Two men were arrested at the castle that night and charged with treason. They were accused of working for Rona and the people demanded justice. The two were sentenced to death a few days after the council met."

Kinden and his son are both dead. Now how are we going to find out about Rona or figure out what really happened?

"Well, let's look on the bright side," said Darcie, "Your family is still ruling, and there's no sign of any attacks yet."

"Yeah, but did you see the way Derek jumped down our throats in the royal garden?" Mitch asked. "Something else was up."

"You talk so informally about the royal family," the prisoner observed. "He has his castle guarded and changes his protective barrier spells every week. If you got through that, I'd call you suspicious myself."

Crap! We should probably be more careful about what we say in front of him.

"It's complicated," Elise explained. "But we're not dangerous. It's all been a misunderstanding."

"Well, they've heard that one a million times. We all say it when we come in. I doubt any of the ones who get put in here actually did anything. Everyone is so terrified of Rona that anyone thought to even be thinking about her gets arrested. Can't blame them, really. There have been so many kidnappings and assassination attempts throughout the last few years that no one trusts anyone anymore."

I didn't know it had gotten that bad.

"Who's been kidnapped?" she asked.

"Mostly young men. It is believed that Rona is building an army. Once she has the soldiers she needs, she will be no match for any of the kingdoms. She wants them all."

"How do you know all this?" Mitch called from his cell.

"One hears things during other people's torture sessions. These walls carry screams and pleas as well as confessions."

"So, what's your story then?" Gavin asked. "How'd you get in here?"

The prisoner coughed and wheezed for a moment before he spoke again.

"A young man was seeking shelter one night and we let him stay in our barn. The following day we found out he was a fugitive from Lockesbarrow, and I was accused of being a spy, of harboring a fugitive. The captain tortured me personally for information that I didn't have. I tried to tell them that I was a simple farmer trying to make a living with my wife and two daughters, but the truth wasn't what they wanted to hear."

Tears streamed down Elise's face, and she wished she knew what to say. This had to stop. All of this paranoia and chaos wasn't what Haighdlen was supposed to be. She didn't want her grandfather remembered like this. She had to get to him before Rona actually did show up. Sinking to her knees, she leaned against the door.

"I'm so sorry," she whispered.

He made a non-committal noise.

"Do not trouble your mind over my fate. I only hate that yours has been decided so young."

Elise glanced over to where she knew the boys' cell was. Her thoughts wandered to how they had all gotten here.

What I wouldn't give to be back in that gazebo right now.

She mouthed the words *I'm sorry* to him even though she knew he couldn't see. As one last escape plan failed in her mind, she sighed and pressed against her chest to make sure her mother's drawing was still there. She turned to Darcie.

"We have to tell the truth."

"What?"

"We have to tell them who we are."

"Are you crazy? We can't do that," Gavin argued. "They'll hang us just like those other guys."

"And there's the whole space-time continuum thing," Mitch added. "They sent us because they wouldn't recognize us."

"The guys are right," Darcie said. "We can't tell them how we got here."

Elise sobbed into her sleeve. At this point, she didn't care how much the prisoner heard.

"Then how do you suppose we get out? We're just kids! We can't take on a whole army and escape a dungeon. We don't have magic of our own and right now we have nothing to lose. Maybe if we tell the truth, we can actually get somewhere, and I think I know how we're going to do it."

***

As hours passed, Elise lost all track of time. There hadn't been any signs of guards, and the never ceasing cries and groans of the other prisoners echoed through the chamber. She was filthy from sitting on the ground so long and could feel dirt in her hair and beneath her fingernails.

Elise rehearsed how she could break the truth to her family, trying to anticipate their reactions. The false hope she had attempted to rally faded within her and she began to lose confidence in her plan.

"I'm sorry about all of this," she said, hoping the boys could hear her, too. "This is all my fault."

"Hey."

Elise looked up at the void where Gavin's voice was coming from.

I wish I could reach out and touch him.

"We are going to get out of here."

"He's right," said Darcie. "This was always going to happen at some point. We kept saying how we were surprised he didn't lock us up sooner. As much as it sucks, I don't think Derek would be a good king if he kept letting us walk in and out of their lives and not feel threatened. We can't expect a grand party and fancy dinners every time."

"I could go for one of those right now. I'm starving."

Elise agreed with Mitch and her stomach growled in reply.

I wish we were back in the castle. I want a hot meal and a bath. I'd even let a maid help me at this point.

"I just hoped we could avoid this part." Elise twisted the fabric of her gown between her fingers and sighed.

"I'm scared, too," Darcie said. "But the last thing your family needs is for us to give up. We're going to figure this out."

Elise jumped as a door opened and footsteps could be heard coming down the tunnel. The cells creaked open and shut one by one as food was delivered. Guards barked orders to each prisoner as they passed.

As the echoes grew closer, Elise's heart beat against her chest. When she heard the keys jingling in the cell beside her, she threw herself against the door and wrapped her fingers around the bars.

"Sir, please listen," Elise begged.

"Stand back!" a second guard barked. Elise and Darcie backed away as the cell was opened and a tray was delivered. Elise looked down at the loaf of bread and small pitcher of water. They were locked in once again and the guards walked across to Gavin and Mitch's cell. She leapt at the door and cried out to them. When they didn't turn back, she mustered every ounce of courage she had left.

"We're ready to confess!"

CHAPTER 21

The guards moved swiftly once she made her declaration, and it took only minutes before the door jerked open with a deafening creak. An additional guard joined them. Two large dogs snarled and barked against the leashes in his hand.

Despite the savage growls, Elise tripped over the water pitcher as she raced to the cell door. She twisted her neck to catch a glimpse of Derek as footsteps approached, rehearsing her confession one more time. In anticipation, she bounced on the balls of her feet.

Her smile vanished, however, when she noticed it wasn't Derek standing in front of her.

"I have waited years for this," Brahm purred and gestured to the guards behind him to silence the dogs. He reached down to scratch one behind the ears. "Imagine my excitement when I was told that, not only had His Majesty had you arrested, but that you had a confession as well."

Brahm hadn't aged like the king and queen. The captain's graying hair was covered in oil, plastered to his head beneath his hat, and he wore more medals and honors on his immaculate uniform. His face was worn, scratched, and featured a rather noticeable scar across his cheek. Perhaps he had seen a few battles since their last meeting.

"It's a pity, really." He reached through the bars and dragged a finger down Elise's neck. She stepped out of his reach. "I imagine you'd be quite fetching during torture."

Gavin slammed his fists against the bars of his cell.

Brahm smirked, looking her up and down before crossing his hands behind his back.

"I shall take your confession now."

She wiped her palms along the sides of her dress and avoided his gaze.

"I wanted to confess to Derek—"

"*King* Derek will not hear your confession as that duty falls upon me. Now do you wish to confess or not?" he spat.

"Look, man, we're only confessing to the king," Gavin called from behind him. "And you better keep your hands to yourself!"

Ignoring him, Brahm took his time sizing up both young women. Elise clenched her legs together and kept her distance from the cell door.

Ugh, please just go away. Leave us alone.

"Perhaps you will need the night to think about it."

He turned on his heel to leave. She stepped forward to argue, but one of the dogs was released and lunged at the bars. Darcie pulled her out of the way as Elise felt saliva land on her face. The beast snarled and scratched at the bars, causing Elise and Darcie to cower at the far end of their cell.

"We have information!" Mitch called. He saw Brahm's distant shadow pause. "Yeah, you heard me. We have information about Rona and we're only sharing it with the king. So, you can either go get him or be charged with treason yourself for knowing about it and not doing anything."

"You wouldn't want to make that mistake twice, would you?" Gavin added.

Brahm snapped his fingers and the dogs were taken away.

"I will *not* be threatened," Brahm growled, "especially by the likes of four children. Haighdlen will be protected at all cost. You *will* tell me what information you have or have it forced out of you."

"Don't tell him anything, children," said the nearby prisoner.

"Silence!" Brahm barked before composing himself. "I give the orders around here, Mr. Archer."

"We swore to the king that we would come to him, and we're only going to talk to him!"

Elise was shocked by her outburst and thankful the shadows hid the fear in her eyes.

If only Derek would come. I know I could convince him.

"And that's your final decision?"

His deep voice penetrated her thoughts and she shivered. She was as good as dead with whatever she decided. If she told him, they would be killed. If she didn't, they would be tortured to the point of wanting to be killed.

She prayed for a way out. Maybe a moment alone with Derek. As another round of tears threatened to spill, she longed with all her might for an escape. As she made to answer, a door creaked opened.

Brahm jerked his head and strode over to see who had arrived.

"Your Majesties, this is highly uncalled for!"

Elise thanked the Lord at the sight of Derek and Joranna. Guards escorted them on either side down the tunnel towards Elise and the others despite Brahm's objections.

"Are you all right?" Joranna asked.

"Joranna, please, they are still our prisoners. We are simply here to hear what they have to say."

"These are children, Derek. The fact you have left them in here this long is inexcusable. They're the same age as our own children."

"Treason doesn't see age."

"How did you know we had something to share?" Darcie asked.

"One of the guards told Ballard," said the queen.

"Which guard?"

Derek ignored Brahm and stepped closer to Elise.

"We're innocent. You have to believe us," said Elise.

"Then pray tell me, why did you vanish all those years ago when we were looking for suspects? You couldn't have made yourself look guiltier than if you had turned yourselves in. I vowed then and there that I would not let you slip through my fingers again."

"We had to leave," Gavin called from behind Derek. "We had a lead on who the real culprit was and wanted to investigate for ourselves."

Derek turned on his heel and walked over to the boys' cell.

"And what did this investigation yield?"

"Nothing, but by the time we found that out, it was too late to come back."

"It's the truth," said Darcie.

"Yeah, we'd never hurt your family," Mitch added. "Everything we've done is to help. Elise worries herself sick trying to do the right thing for you all."

Joranna looked over at her.

"Why do you care about us so much, Elise?"

This was her moment. The one she had rehearsed in her head. She didn't know how it would affect the space-time continuum or whatever, but she knew that this was their only chance to get free. She was going to have to take it.

"We were sent here to protect Haighdlen. Rona's going to attack, and our family will be forced to flee the kingdom."

"*Our* family?" asked Derek.

She took a deep breath and tried to choose her words carefully.

"I'm. . .related to you. And I was sent here to find the spy and protect you."

Brahm stepped in front of the royal couple. "Your Majesties, I cannot watch this any longer. You are being manipulated by a criminal. I've seen it before. People will say anything to earn their freedom."

"Why do you think you brought us with you from that diner all those years ago?" Elise challenged. "You can't explain it. It was just a feeling you had, right?" They didn't reply. "Everyone confused me with Joranna when we first got here because we look so alike. *Queen* Joranna, sorry." She smiled at her grandmother and turned her attention back to Derek. "And you keep talking about us getting past your barrier."

"Yes, that only blood—"

"Only *blood* relatives can get past. I *am* your relative, and the last thing I want to do is hurt this kingdom. Even if it means erasing everyone's memories at the end."

"Who exactly are you?" Joranna asked.

"My name is really Elise. I've been sent to learn about what happened to the family and to help prevent Rona from taking it over for good."

Derek gestured towards the other three.

"And your companions?"

"They were sent to help me. We travel through a diary that was kept during this time. The people who sent us believe that we have a chance to fix what's been happening and to stop Rona for good."

"Suppose you are telling us the truth—"

"Sire!" Brahm cried before Derek silenced him again.

"Suppose you were sent here to help us. What is your plan for stopping Rona?"

"We. . .we don't know yet."

"A mark of a liar," Brahm insisted. "Sire, they're only talking like this to confuse you. No good can come of this."

Elise pressed on.

"We just want to find the spy! Whatever is coming is coming soon."

"I can't say I haven't wondered about her connection to us in the past," Joranna said. "Time traveling would explain their aging better than a curse."

"Yeah, that was my bad," Mitch apologized.

Gavin cleared his throat.

"Everything Elise is saying is true. It took me too long to believe her. Don't make the same mistake I did. There is a spy, but it's not us. We'd just like the chance to help you find them."

Joranna was the first to answer.

"I believe them."

"Your mind has been poisoned, Your Majesty!"

"Do not disrespect the queen!" Derek frowned at the captain. "Her instincts have never been wrong, and everything they have said makes sense. Whether or not I can justify it in my head, I believe what they're saying."

"Then you'll let us out?" Mitch asked.

Please, please, please!

Derek looked down at his wife and nodded.

Elise and Darcie broke into grateful tears as they hugged one another. Derek called the guards to unlock their cells. Once the boys were freed, Elise ran over and wrapped her arms around Gavin's neck. She squeezed like he was her lifeline and melted against him when he did the same. Mitch and Darcie joined them in a group hug as Brahm huffed and stormed off.

"Don't worry about him," Derek said. "He is severely loyal to the kingdom and abhors any type of change. Let us get you all cleaned up and properly fed before we talk further."

"Derek, wait," Elise said before catching his raised eyebrow. "I mean, *King* Derek. I think that the prisoner next to us is innocent."

"Elise. . ."

"I know how it sounds, but I really think he's innocent. He told us about his family and what really happened. If you'll just hear him out, you'll see for yourself."

"Kind child," said Mr. Archer. "I do not expect the same blessing that you have received, but seeing you get yours is enough to restore my faith in the world."

Elise walked over to where she could see him. His feeble body was covered in rags and rested against the wall. Dirt and blood were mixed in his white hair and covered most of his skin. He gave her a toothy smile and nodded for her to go on.

She turned back to her grandparents.

"I will look into it," Derek promised. "It's late. Let's get you back."

The dungeon was the last place she ever wanted to be but leaving Mr. Archer behind filled her with guilt.

Are there others who are innocent like him?

"Goodbye, Mr. Archer, and thank you."

***

Elise sighed when she was able to step into the bathtub. She clutched her robe against her chest and waited for the maids to leave the room. When it was clear they weren't going anywhere, she bit her lip and avoided their eyes as they took her robe.

Why do they have to see me naked? What if they laugh at me?

If there was anything wrong with her body, they didn't comment. She plopped down into the bubbles to hide herself and apologized when some of the water splashed into the floor. The first maid approached with a bar of soap.

"Please let me do it."

"As you wish, Miss." She curtsied. "I'll bring the water to rinse once you've finished." Both maids walked over to stand by the doorway.

Realizing she wasn't going to get any time alone, Elise resolved to enjoy the moment anyway and count her blessings.

Inhaling the sweet scent of her bath, she reclined and adjusted the bubbles to hide the parts of her that were exposed. Her eyes closed as the hot water relaxed her stiff muscles.

Because she didn't know how much time had passed while she was lost in her thoughts, she was eager to talk to her friends. Especially Gavin. They hadn't had much time since being released, and she longed for his touch again.

I hope we don't get into too much trouble from sharing everything. What if Derek asks for more information?

And then there was the matter of Mr. Archer. He had become another goal of hers besides finding the spy.

Shaking her head to get a grip of herself, she washed her body. One maid poured fresh water over her to rinse the soap off while the other provided a fresh robe.

After being dried off, they fitted her in a beautiful forest green gown. Anything was preferable to what she had before, and she thanked them as she tucked her mother's drawing into the same spot. It wasn't in the same condition and showed wear and tear, but she refused to get rid of it.

The last of the buttons on her gown were secured and her hair was pulled back.

Why are they doing my makeup? It's late, and we're probably going to bed soon.

It did no good to argue. Elise thanked the maids one more time before walking out into the hallway. Darcie had also just finished getting ready.

"Wait for me!" She closed her guest room door and caught up to Elise. "You look great."

"You, too. I guess the boys are already downstairs."

"I can't believe we got out!"

"Right? Mitch was incredible today the way he stood up to Brahm like that. Pretty brave stuff. Don't you think?" Elise asked.

Darcie smiled.

"Yeah, brave. Not a word I'd usually use to describe Mitch." They chuckled. "He and Gavin did a great job putting the captain in his place. I still can't get over Derek and Joranna showing up the way they did."

Gavin and Mitch were waiting at the bottom of the staircase. They stopped their conversation and watched both girls come down.

Elise felt Gavin's eyes on her and she broke into a smile, then looked away. She noticed Mitch's eyes glued on Darcie and nudged her friend.

Darcie rolled her eyes and greeted the guys.

"You boys clean up nice."

Mitch pulled back his coat and sniffed.

"Hey, anything beats dungeon funk, am I right? I hope they saved us some food. My stomach is growling so bad right now."

Gavin smiled at Elise.

"It's good to see you. You look beautiful."

"Thank you." His hand reached for hers and squeezed.

Mitch turned to lead them into the dining room, and she saw Darcie's smile falter before following him. Elise tried to reach for her friend, but Darcie waved it off.

***

Derek and Joranna were already seated with Ruby, who was picking at her food beside her mother. Elise and the others were shown to their seats, then a few platters were brought to them.

"Forgive us for not joining you. We ate earlier," Derek said.

Elise tried to remember her manners and use self-control as her dinner was placed before her. Once everything was plated, her fork couldn't get the food into her mouth fast enough. It felt so good to eat a proper meal. None of them spoke for the next ten minutes while they ate. Derek read the papers and Joranna spoke in whispers to Ruby. They were only disturbed when Richard walked in laughing with another young man about the same age.

"Sorry to interrupt everyone," Richard said as he struggled to contain his laughter. "We came to see if there was any dessert. Didn't know we'd have our visitors down here." He came around to them and reached out his hand. "I know it's been awhile since we last met. How do you do? Allow me to introduce my good friend, Charles Fenton."

Charles smiled and bowed to them all before the two joined the group.

Elise and Darcie smiled to each other as they took their last few bites of food. Charles had brown hair, a bit of stubble on his face, and a smile that probably got him what he wanted most of the time.

He really gives off a bad boy vibe.

"Good evening, Majesties," Charles said. "Hello, Princess. You're looking lovely this evening."

"Thank you," said the princess.

Something seemed familiar about him, but Elise couldn't place it. She did notice, however, that he glanced over at Ruby quite often.

Charles Fenton. . .Fenton. Charlie Fenton!

"I saw him at Mom's birthday party," she whispered to Darcie. "He was teasing her."

"He's completely hung up on her."

"It's just funny. She's never mentioned him before."

Elise stared at the young man until he caught her gaze and she looked away.

Once dessert was served, Derek cleared his throat and asked for everyone's attention.

"In light of your recent confessions I have issued a full pardon for the four of you. Your reputations are fully restored, and you are hereby welcome in Haighdlen. That being said, is there anything else you need to divulge?"

"We were told that there have been attacks," Elise said. "Is there any pattern to them?"

"They all appear to be done at random," Derek replied. "Rona has only been sighted a handful of times throughout the last few years, which has caused paranoia to spread. She's extremely powerful. I've met several times with the other leaders. We aren't handling this situation with any levity."

"I think I may head to bed after all," Ruby said, stifling a yawn as she excused herself.

"You've only just gotten here. Would you like me to come with you?" Joranna asked. Ruby declined and stood to leave. Charles rose as she exited and waited until she was gone before he sat to continue his dessert.

"I'm actually glad that she has left because we'd like to offer you a mission, should you wish to take it," Derek said.

"We do?" Joranna whirled around to look at her husband. Her brows lifted as she frowned. "What mission is this?"

"You said yourself earlier that we could give them a task to test their loyalty," Derek said.

"Yes, but I thought that we would discuss the type of test first. What did you have in mind?"

"Richard, Charles, would you excuse us, please?"

When both boys had left, Derek turned to Elise and her friends, lowering his voice.

"We have reason to believe that Ruby has been sneaking out in the middle of the night. No one can seem to locate her for hours at a time. Yet she mysteriously shows up again the next morning as if nothing happened."

Elise's mouth opened and her own eyebrows threatened to disappear into her hairline.

"You want us to spy on her?"

Is he joking?

"Derek, that is hardly an appropriate answer to this problem. We are her parents and should be there for her."

"But she won't talk to us, dear. We are the last people in the world she wants to confide in right now, and we're both exhausted from worrying about her whereabouts and trying to catch her. Whatever methods she's using are working, and we need to stop her before she gets herself hurt."

"I don't think she's going to like being followed," Mitch muttered.

"It's a direct invasion on her privacy. She'll never trust us again," Joranna argued.

"What choice have we, Joranna? She has found a way to sneak past the guards without raising alarm. She knows how to get through the walls and go who knows where undetected. If we don't stop her now, anything could happen. She's already coming home ill as it is."

"It's just a cold." Joranna shifted in her chair, not meeting their eyes, and cleared her throat. "I want to know where she's going just as much as you do, but we need to try talking to her about this."

"This way is much more efficient." Derek turned to Elise. "And if you're really family, you'll want what's best for her and her reputation, too. Am I right?"

Elise stammered and couldn't get a full answer out.

He continued.

"Something tells me now that she's feeling better, she's going to try and sneak out tonight. I'd like you to follow her to see where she's been getting off to."

Joranna's mouth tightened as she shot a disapproving glance at her husband.

"I have to apologize for Derek. He doesn't seem to remember that you all have just spent your entire day in prison and are exhausted. To ask you to go on such a mission is highly inappropriate. I would understand if you don't want to."

"No. . .we'll do it," Elise said.

"Wonderful!" Derek smacked his palm against the table with a smile. "It's decided then. Wait in the library until we've all gone to bed. Then make your way to the back courtyard. We shall consult with you all in the morning for a full report if anything happens."

Joranna remained silent until Derek kissed her and left the room. Her face paled and she fiddled with a handkerchief in her lap.

"I don't agree with this plan. I can't believe he has the audacity to suggest it, but I am anxious to know what she has been getting herself into. I think someone is helping her. Please let us know if there's anything we can do. We just want her safe." She dabbed the corner of her eye and smiled.

She looks so tired.

"You'll understand one day when you have children. And please don't think badly of Derek. He really just wants what's best and he's a very good man. We just want to help her." She bid them goodnight and they were left alone as the servants began to clean the table.

"Guys, this is messed up." Elise hid her face in her hands. "I just agreed to spy on my mom."

"Let's try not to freak out yet," Darcie said. "Maybe it won't be so bad. Maybe she's just meeting some friends in town. It might be nothing."

"I hope so." Elise groaned, tilting her head back. "I just didn't expect something like this to fall under finding the spy and helping Mom."

Gavin glanced over at the servants within earshot of them.

"Let's talk in the library."

***

Upon entering the library, they noticed a fire had already been lit. Elise took a seat on one of the crimson couches and was comforted when Gavin sat beside her. Mitch draped himself over a chair while Darcie browsed the shelves for a book to read.

"Just do me a favor," Elise called over her shoulder, "Don't open any purple ones this time, okay?"

They chuckled and Darcie promised to do the best she could.

Gavin rested their joined hands on his knee.

"Are you nervous?"

"A little. I guess I'm just worried about what I'm going to see. I feel like I'm about to learn a piece of her story that she's kept hidden on purpose."

It might even explain why Mom and I don't have the closest relationship.

She sighed.

"I just don't know if I'm ready."

Instead of answering, he only pulled her in close and wrapped his arms around her. She closed her eyes and leaned against him. Hours ago, she wouldn't have thought this would be possible, and she doubted that Gavin knew how much he was helping her.

He's so warm. I could fall asleep like this.

When her body jerked, she pulled away with an apologetic yawn. He shook his head and smiled.

"What is it?" she asked. She checked her mouth for any drool.

"I want to kiss you again."

His statement caught her off guard and she looked over her shoulder at Darcie and Mitch.

"Right here? In front of everyone?"

He leaned forward and took her hand again.

"I would be in a cell right now if it weren't for you. Who knows where I'll end up later because of you?" She failed to contain her laughter until he became serious again. "I don't care who sees."

Her eyes searched his face. With one last look over his shoulder, she nodded and leaned in.

CHAPTER 22

The grounds were not as inviting at night when not lit for a party. The angelic statues looked more like gargoyles poking out from behind the hedges, and the warm breeze through the trees and bushes gave the illusion of someone moving around them. Elise was thankful for the full moon's light amidst all the darkness.

"Are we sure she's even going to come out this way?" Gavin whispered.

"If I were sneaking out, I don't think that I'd just walk out the front door, and she doesn't strike me as the type of person to tie sheets together to climb out the window. So, how else would she leave?" Darcie asked.

"But there's a guard by the door! I know Derek told them to let us come and go tonight, but I doubt Ruby would be able to sneak past him."

A clock inside the doors chimed ten times.

"Gav is right. It's late," Mitch said. "Maybe she isn't going—"

Elise held up her hand.

"Shh, wait. Someone's coming!"

They saw movement from around the side of the castle.

Is Mom already on her way back? Did we miss her?

Elise's heart drummed so loud she was sure her friends could hear it as her eyes bounced between the approaching shadow and the guard. Would her mother be caught? As the shadow stepped into the moonlight, her heart fell as she saw that it was only another guard.

Maybe we are waiting for nothing.

"You're late again, Porter," the first guard growled. He removed his helmet and glared as he shoved the key into the other man's hand. "That's twice in a month!"

"Sorry," the second muttered from beneath his own helmet.

"See that it doesn't happen again, or I'll report you to the captain!"

The first continued his muttering as he stomped off towards the tower.

The night grew still, and all appeared as it had before. Unable to stifle a yawn, Elise finally agreed with Mitch and Gavin.

She's probably not going anywhere tonight.

Porter stepped away from his post and peered through the glass panes into the darkened ballroom. He pulled out the key and checked over his shoulder before pushing it into the lock.

"What's he doing?" Mitch whispered.

The guard cracked the door and muttered into it. Elise squinted her eyes and tilted her ear closer.

Their questions were answered when a petite hooded figure emerged into the courtyard and kept watch while Porter locked the door back. Both made their way towards the garden, prompting Elise and the others to duck further behind the hedges.

"I don't think it's such a good night tonight, Princess."

"The threat is the same every night," Ruby replied.

Porter reached out and turned her around before taking her hands in his. The intimacy caught her off guard, but she didn't pull away.

"What I mean is, I can't do this for you anymore. I know there's something out there you want, but I can't stand back and let you risk everything time and time again. It's not safe for you to leave the castle grounds, let alone the kingdom."

The kingdom! Where's she been going?

Elise held her breath and eased closer. The branches scratched her face, but she didn't care. Why was her mother leaving the kingdom?

"That's not for you to decide." She pulled away from him. "I have to do this."

"Wait, I—"

"Charles, please." Elise's heart skipped a beat as he removed his helmet. Ruby pulled her hood around her face and looked over her shoulders. "What are you doing? Put that back on!"

"Not until you let me finish," he said. He pushed the hair out of his face and looked down at her. "I thought helping you this way might improve your opinion of me, but I've let it go on for too long. If I'm caught aiding you, not only is your reputation ruined, but I could be banished from court."

When Ruby gave no answer, he dropped his helmet and reached for her hands again. He waited for her to look up at him.

"I love you. . .Ruby." She stiffened and looked down at her feet, causing him to do the same. "Perhaps it's common of me to admit it so openly, and I am fully aware that you may not return my feelings. My friendship with your brother also complicates matters, but if my confession helps you stop seeking something elsewhere, then it will have been worth it."

Why had her mother never mentioned this man before? He seemed to be the whole package. Elise grew impatient at the amount of time it was taking Ruby to answer. She rolled her eyes and wondered what her mother had done to mess this up for herself. She couldn't see why Ruby wanted out of this family so badly. Not inheriting magic seemed a pretty shallow reason to give up a royal lifestyle and the love of a good man. Nothing about their present-day lives was worth leaving this.

Ruby sighed. When she did speak, her voice cracked beneath her tears.

"I have wanted to hear those words for so long." She brought up one of his hands and nuzzled her face against his palm. "But I'm afraid you're too late."

As his formality returned, he pulled his hands away before clearing his throat.

"You're engaged then?"

She shook her head and wiped her face with the back of her hand.

"I'm not engaged, but thinking along those lines will help your feelings to pass."

He scoffed.

"Forgive me, Princess, but you claim to have both waited to hear such words from me and wish them away. Surely, you can understand my confusion. If you're not engaged, I cannot see why I'm too late."

"You'll see soon enough and want nothing to do with me." She held up her hand when he tried to argue. "But you'll be happy to know that this is the last time I'll need your help. We won't speak of this again." She walked towards the garden entrance.

"And what will I get for my silence?"

Elise watched uncertainty play across her mother's moonlit features. Ruby's eyes shifted in alarm, then she whirled around.

"You'd blackmail me?" She froze as he crossed the courtyard. Gathering what courage she could muster, she stood her ground and gazed up at him. "H-how much?"

"Not money." Ruby took a tentative step back, wrapping the fabric of her cloak tighter around herself. "I'd die before I ever did that, Princess." Her shoulders relaxed, and a visible shiver ran through her body as he closed the distance between them. "But if I'm to continue pretending after learning you feel the same, I'd like to ease my suffering a bit." His thumb caressed her bottom lip and tilted her chin up.

They were close enough for Elise to reach out and touch them, and witnessing such an intimate moment filled her with mixed emotions. On the one hand she knew she should look away since this was her mom, but the heat between the two drew her in. She couldn't look away.

It was unclear who leaned in first as the two shared a kiss. Elise saw that her friends were just as mesmerized.

Charles wrapped his arms around Ruby's waist and pulled her out of the moonlight. Her arms wrapped around his neck as they stumbled and bumped into the hedges, causing Elise and the others to scoot out of the way. Leaves were shaken loose and fell to the ground.

The couple pulled apart to catch their breaths. Elise could just make out their figures over her shoulder as she strained to hear them over a nearby cricket.

Her mother spoke first.

"Will that payment suffice?"

"It'll have to. . .for now."

He elicited a moan as he placed kisses along her neck. Her fingers snaked through his hair and brought his face back up to meet hers.

"We should get going," she whispered.

He groaned, dropping his forehead to her shoulder. As the two pulled apart and stepped away from the bushes, Ruby shook leaves out of her now lowered hood, while Charles combed his fingers through his disheveled hair. He walked over to retrieve his helmet while Ruby straightened her cloak.

"You there!"

Jumping back, the princess stumbled into the darkness behind a tree. Charles turned away from the voice and adjusted his helmet. Ballard came from around the side of the castle.

"Have you by chance seen Lord Fenton?"

Charles disguised his voice to reply that he had not.

"Carry on then," Ballard panted, as he rested his hands on his knees. "If you should find him, please let him know the prince is looking for him. I'm afraid my duties have been reduced to carrying messages and looking after headstrong children. And by the way. . ." He straightened and leaned in close to Charles. "I know the king is allowing those pesky visitors to go wherever they wish while they watch for the princess. They could even be out searching now, but if you *do* see anything, report to me first. Do you understand?"

Charles nodded. Ballard stared between the guard and the door until Charles got the hint, then fumbled for the key to let him inside.

"Why would he want to be told instead of Brahm?" Darcie whispered. Elise shrugged, wondering the same thing.

Charles locked the door again and looked around until Ruby stepped out from her hiding place.

"Your father has sent out those visitors to follow you. We need to get you inside now."

Ruby growled and stomped her foot into the ground.

"Ugh, this isn't fair!" She paced in silence and drummed her fingers on her hips. "I'm just going to have to risk it."

"But, Princess—"

"You don't understand."

"I would if you would just tell me! What is so important out there?" When she made no answer, his voice softened. "Ruby, please."

"If he's already sent out spies, then I won't have many opportunities left. I have to finish this."

"Finish what?"

Turning on her heel, she entered the garden. His hands curled into fists as he followed, and Elise knew his frustration all-too-well. Ruby Laurille always ignored things that made her uncomfortable.

***

Elise and the others waited until Charles and Ruby were far enough ahead before they began to follow. At the speed they were having to walk to keep up, the garden seemed smaller. Before she knew it, they had passed the gazebo, pond, and the fountain until they came to a large tree near a secluded spot by the back castle wall. Very little moonlight reached this spot, and Elise had to rely on the noise of the couple's movements to know where they were.

"Let me join you this time."

"There's no need."

"Don't be so reckless. You should have an escort," he said. Ruby turned away, shimmying something out of her cloak. "You've made all the arrangements you need then?"

"I have." Ruby held on to one end of a rope before passing Charles the rest. "Like I said, this is the last time. Good night, Charles. Thank you for everything."

A low branch on the tree shook and a few leaves rustled.

She isn't doing what I think she's doing, is she?

One by one, each branch shook under Ruby's weight. She slipped only once, but he steadied her, and at last her figure could be seen in the moonlight again as she reached the top. She threw her end of the rope over the wall and looked down to make sure Charles had his half.

"Be safe, Princess."

Once she had thrown her legs over and begun to climb down, he pulled his end against her weight until she reached the bottom of the other side.

Elise felt a panic bubbling in her stomach. How were they supposed to run to the gate and keep up with her in time? They would lose her.

Charles sighed and lowered his arms.

"Are you still there?"

Elise looked around and at her friends. His voice wasn't loud enough for Ruby to hear.

Is he talking to us?

"You can come out now. She's gone."

Elise was frozen on the spot. How had he known they were there? Her doubt of whether or not he actually saw them was answered when he looked in their direction.

"She's faster than you think. You had better go."

Elise couldn't hold in her curiosity.

"Why are you doing this?"

"And how long have you known we were following you?" Darcie asked.

"I've known long enough, and someone has to help her. Simple as that."

Elise's heart sank.

I wish Mom hadn't been so selfish.

"Won't she be mad that you're helping us?" Gavin asked.

"Something's different this time." He pulled until Ruby's half of the rope fell back over their side of the wall. Picking it up off the ground, he held it out to them. "She shouldn't hear you now. Are you going or not?"

"You don't mean. . ." Elise pointed up and Charles shrugged. "I can't do that."

"Then you'll have to wait here until sunrise when I meet her again."

"Elise, we can't sit here all night," Darcie said.

"But I can't climb over that wall! I couldn't even do a chin-up in gym."

Gavin rubbed his hand on her back.

"We'll help you. You can't quit now."

Mitch pushed through to the front.

"Let's go, guys. She's probably almost at the town by now. I'll go first and help on the other side."

He took the rope and climbed like a cat to the top branch.

How does he do that? Is he even touching the branches?

Elise tried to silence the voice in her head that delighted in body-shaming her. She wasn't heavy, but she was too out-of-shape for this sort of thing. The sinister presence in her mind was kind enough to share every possible worst-case scenario, where no matter how she got over that wall, Gavin wouldn't be attracted to her anymore and she'd look like an idiot.

It took no time for Darcie to swing over the wall next. Elise felt a lump in her throat when the rope loosened, and Charles turned towards her.

"I'll be right behind you," Gavin whispered in her ear.

She tried swallowing the lump away as she grabbed the lowest branch. With her sweaty palms, she couldn't fathom how she was supposed to keep a tight hold on a rope without slipping. Despite her awkwardness, Charles lifted her weight easily and helped her up the next two branches. She wrapped her arms around the trunk as she looked up at the top of the wall.

She was transported back to class on Rope Climbing Day. The ceiling of the gymnasium seemed higher than ever, and the other girls giggled behind her while the coach scribbled on the clipboard. Her trusty sidekick, anxiety, made sure to only bring her focus on the students who *could* do it until the whistle was blown. The coach gave her a comical swing as she did with the others who couldn't complete the task before she was asked to jump off. She shook her head to escape from the memory, and her saving grace now was that no one could see her cheeks burning.

If Mom can do this, then so can I.

She took it one branch at a time until she couldn't get any higher. She tugged against the rope and felt Mitch or Darcie pull it tight while Charles held his end. It was only a short distance from where she stood to the top of the wall. She knew if she could just get her body over it, then gravity would handle the rest.

Why is it taking me so long? Just do it. DO IT.

She eased out onto the exposed part of the rope and gripped it as tightly as her wet palms would allow.

Her mind kept screaming out what would happen if she fell. Would someone catch her? Could she die from this high up?

Do it for Mom. She needs you.

Elise tightened her arms and legs around the rope, pulling herself to the wall.

"That's it, Elise. You got it!" Darcie called from below.

"You can do this!" Mitch said.

Elise lunged forward and swung a leg over. She clung to the wall and gazed down into the darkness below. Her vision blurred.

There, you did it. The hard part is over, and you did it in a dress! Now for the easier, probably more painful, part. Just get it over with.

She pivoted her body, and even with her feet gripping, she found she slid more than actually climbed down.

Her sidekick retreated when her feet touched the ground and she realized what she had done. A smile broke across her face as Darcie clapped her on the back. They didn't have to know that her palms were on fire or that her arms felt like they were about to fall off.

She had just steadied her breathing when Gavin lowered down. He tugged on the rope and the four watched as Charles pulled it back over the wall. Gavin took a couple of deep breaths to recover.

"Charles just said we should follow the main road. Ruby will cut through the thicker part of the forest to stay hidden, and it'll help us save time. Let's go."

***

By the time they reached the arched entryway of the town, Elise had long been wishing they would've taken a carriage.

Shivering against the evening breeze, she stood closer to Gavin as they walked deeper into the town. This visit didn't fill her with the same sense of wonder it had before, and she caught herself checking her surroundings every few seconds. It was quieter at this hour. Shop windows were dark, but some carts were still open to straggling patrons. In the torchlit street, light chatter and laughter from the crowd did little to ease Elise's wariness.

"Do we even know if she's going through here?" she asked. "What if she stays in the forest?"

"This is where Charles said she goes," Gavin said. "We wouldn't have gotten that much ahead of her, so she's probably just blending in."

Elise made a point to focus harder on the people around her. She took in every dress, hat, and cloak trying to find her mom.

"Is that her?"

Elise followed Darcie's finger and caught a glimpse of Ruby just as she made a left to the next street. At some point she had acquired a lantern to carry with her.

"Isn't that the way Derek said to avoid after dark?" Mitch whispered.

The farther they walked, the more Elise wanted to turn around and wait for Ruby at the castle. She grew uncomfortable seeing people sitting on the steps of shops asking for money. In the distance, they could hear horses whinnying and more lewd laughter. Gavin and Mitch sped up when a couple of provocative women called out to them.

Elise was further confused when Ruby headed into a residential area of small cottages. Some still had windows lit and a baby could be heard crying in the distance. Their questions were answered as Ruby crept up to a dark and quiet home. As she checked over her shoulder, Elise and the others ducked behind a pile of chopped firewood. Ruby tapped her knuckles against the window three times before walking to the back door.

It took only a moment for a candle to be lit and carried outside by another young woman, who had untamed fiery red hair and only appeared to be slightly older than Ruby. As the door creaked shut behind her, she pulled her shawl tighter against the cool night air.

"You're later than usual. I thought you might have changed your mind."

"Do you have it?" Ruby whispered.

The woman pulled a small vial from her pocket and handed it to Ruby. Elise strained her eyes but couldn't see what was in it. In exchange, Ruby gave her a small pouch of coins.

"It's getting harder to come by," the woman said. "Fairies aren't generous, you know. I wasn't able to barter for much this time."

"This is more than enough. Tonight is my last trip."

"I'm glad to hear it." The woman leaned against the door. "Can't really say it's proper for a princess to be sneaking out of the kingdom. You don't want it to come back and haunt you if you become queen."

Ruby scoffed.

"Being fourth in line, I doubt it. Besides, I have no plans on ruling Haighdlen. *You'll* be queen before I am." They shared a chuckle before Ruby put the vial into her pocket. "I better be going. Thank you, Gwen."

"Safe traveling, Your Majesty."

Gwen? It can't be the same person.

As Gwen turned to enter the house, the candle lit her face, and Elise's mouth dropped when she recognized a younger version of her aunt. She was Richard's future wife.

"Now *there's* a story I want to hear," said Darcie. "I wonder if she's even met Richard yet."

"I didn't know she and Mom knew each other when they were younger."

Her head was spinning with new questions and possibilities, but they would all have to wait as Ruby was on the move again.

"Was it just me, or did it look like Elise's mom was scoring drugs?" asked Mitch. He and Gavin snickered as they followed Ruby to the edge of town.

Elise was thankful to be out of Clara but wasn't so thrilled about having to enter a dark forest in the middle of the night. Even with the moonlight, several areas were pitch black. They slowed their pace so they wouldn't be discovered and had to fully rely on the lantern in Ruby's hand.

Why did her mother have to act so stupid? She was literally going into a dark forest, alone and unprotected, and didn't seem to take any warnings from others seriously.

Elise found herself lost in thought for most of their hour or so of walking.

"Do you still think Ballard is the spy?" Darcie's question brought Elise out of her reverie. She shrugged. "Because I'm starting to agree with you."

"I can't put my finger on it, but I just don't trust him," Elise said. "What made you change your mind?"

"I've been thinking about it ever since he warned Charles. You already saw him do some shady things, and then to want to bypass the captain for secret information? He's up to something. The question is, do we bring it up to Derek and Joranna again?"

"They won't believe us," Gavin said. "Not without enough proof."

"We could try and get Charles to disguise himself again and question him," Mitch offered.

"Charles wouldn't have any reason to do that. He said he's done sneaking around anyway," said Elise.

Something caught her eye, and Elise looked over to see the moonlight reflecting off the water in that direction.

"She's not going near the mermaid lake, is she?" Gavin whispered.

Elise shook her head.

"No, look, she's staying to the other side of the path, away from it."

"How big is this kingdom anyway?" Mitch shuffled his feet and whined. "Shouldn't we be getting close to a border or something if she's leaving?"

"I don't think she's going to another kingdom. . ." said Darcie.

They stopped to watch as Ruby began climbing up a steep grass-covered hill.

"Wait a minute, that's not what I think it is, is it?" Gavin asked.

Elise's eyes followed Ruby's trail up to the top and saw the same tree they had come out of when they arrived in Haighdlen.

"She's going to our world. That's where she's been sneaking off to!"

"Like father, like daughter," said Mitch. It was trickier to follow her at this angle without being seen, but the four did their best to creep several feet behind. Not long after they began their ascent, the four were out of breath and struggling to keep up. "You know, it was a lot easier when we came here. At least then, we were going *down* the hill."

Ruby staggered her way up to the top and didn't seem to be having an easy time of it herself. Elise and the others stayed around the middle of the hill as Ruby reached the peak. The princess rested against the tree trunk for several moments to gain her bearings, while the four friends crawled around the side out of her direct view.

Ruby fished the vial from her pocket and pulled the cork out, pouring a generous amount of blue potion into her palm. When she touched it to the bark, the same light appeared that Derek's magic had created.

After Ruby lowered into the tunnel, Darcie sprinted forward.

"Come on, let's catch up with her before it closes!"

The boys took off at an eager pace, but as she raced after them, Elise came to a realization that made her pause.

CHAPTER 23

Gavin was the first to notice that she didn't follow them. "What's wrong?"

Darcie and Mitch stopped to wait near the top, but when she didn't move, Gavin turned towards her.

"Elise, come on! We're going to miss the portal!" Darcie cried.

An inner battle raged inside Elise as her friends' calls went unanswered. This was her chance to find out where Ruby was sneaking off to and what changed her life. Yet, something urged her not to follow her mom in. It wasn't a voice or spell, but something stronger that Elise couldn't put her finger on. She thought it might be her conscience, but it felt different.

"If you're tired, I'll help you," said Gavin, offering his hand.

Making up her mind, she shook her head and turned back as the blue light vanished. Darcie stomped down towards her. As Elise reached the bottom of the hill, she prepared herself for the inevitable lecture.

"Why did you do that!" screamed Darcie. "Now how are we going to know where she went?"

Elise sat down on the grass and brought her knees up to her chest.

"I couldn't do it."

That wasn't a good enough answer for Darcie.

"No, you *wouldn't* do it! It's always something with you, Elise. You're afraid of everything! We're not going to get any of your answers just sitting here. We should be following her and figuring out what's she's up to!"

"Hey, ease up on her." Gavin crouched down to Elise's eye level. "Why didn't you want to go through?"

She shrugged.

"I don't know why. Something told me not to. Every instinct I had was to run away from it."

"That's your anxiety! You've done this before," Darcie said.

Mitch looked around to make sure they weren't being overheard.

"Guys, what're we going to do? We can't go back yet. Charles won't have the rope ready for a few more hours. We should've gone in."

Elise was too busy mulling over Darcie's words to pay Mitch any mind. Each attack dug deeper under her skin until she stood and sidestepped Gavin.

"It wasn't just my anxiety. This was different!" She gritted her teeth when Darcie didn't look at her. "Did you ever think of what would happen if we got stuck over there? She said it's her last trip. If something went wrong, we couldn't get back!"

Darcie only scoffed and rolled her eyes. She gestured towards their surroundings.

"Oh yes, because *this* is much better. Let's sit and wait for Ruby to come tell us where she went. I'm sure the spy will come walking out and reveal who he is, too. Then we're all set. Everything will just fall into our laps." It was Elise's turn to roll her eyes as Darcie circled. "We have followed you willingly without question. And when we finally get close to figuring out what it all means, you get scared and bolt!"

"I didn't ask you to follow me! You could've done your own thing. You're so good at meddling anyway that I'm surprised you didn't take over to drag me down the portal." Darcie's eyes widened and she opened her mouth to argue, but Elise was boiling at this point. She didn't want to hear it. "And don't look surprised. You walk around acting so confident like nothing bothers you, when deep down you're *just* as scared as I am. The only difference is I show it. That doesn't make it wrong."

The heated exchange came to an end as both girls glared at one another. Elise didn't regret her decision. She was convinced something much worse would've happened if she had followed Ruby, and nothing Darcie said was going to change that.

Darcie spun on her heel and stormed off.

"Where are you going?" Elise asked.

"Away from you!"

"Fine!"

After Mitch followed Darcie, Elise felt Gavin's hand on her shoulder.

"You okay?"

She crossed her arms and watched her friend's retreating figure. It took several deep breaths before she felt her rage begin to melt away. There was a bitterness to her tone when she replied.

"Do you blame me, too?"

He kissed the top of her head, which should've been comforting, but only made her feel like a child.

"You had your reasons. She's just mad. She'll come around."

She tensed when he hugged her from behind and tried to think of a way to ask for space without hurting his feelings.

Fortunately, he sensed this and suggested she take a walk to cool down.

Having nowhere to safely go on her own, she chose to climb the hill. She could hear Darcie in her mind berating her for only now choosing to do so.

She watched Gavin walk over to where the couple was sitting and for the first time felt truly alone. She knew from their perspective, she had betrayed them. Whatever Gavin's good intentions were, she knew that on some level he must blame her. The truth sounded ridiculous when she repeated it in her mind. It seemed like an excuse that she would use when having a panic attack, and she couldn't blame Darcie for flying off the handle.

Elise plopped down against the tree, looking around for any signs or clues that Ruby had been there. When she didn't find any, she wilted.

How am I going to convince them that what I did was for the best?

As her mind drifted with different scenarios, she tried to find comfort in her surroundings. The breeze was stronger from this height, but it felt good against her heated skin and smelled sweet. Examining the blanket of stars, she marveled at how Haighdlen was just as breathtaking at night as it was during the day. Being here now reminded her of the first time Derek had ever introduced them to it.

The ivory towers of the castle seemed so far away that it was hard to believe that they had started there. Unseen animals of the night called out from the blackened forest because the moonlight illuminated only the treetops and waterfall. She could see a glimpse of the town's torches, but it was enough to remind her that they were going to have to eventually walk all the way back.

She smiled in spite of her mood as several fairy lights zipped in and out of the folds of the trees.

I'll never get tired of this place.

A few more minutes passed before Elise felt calm again. She knew she'd have to apologize to her friends. When she adjusted herself to get more comfortable, she felt something poking her chest. Elise pulled out the piece of paper that was folded in her dress.

She had studied her mother's drawing so many times that she didn't need any light to know what was on the paper. Her fingers trailed over the waxed lines before tucking it safely back in at a different angle.

Despite worrying about what her friends thought of her, she knew deep down that she wasn't giving up on her mom. There had to be another way to find out the truth without risking leaving this world. But before she could figure any of that out, she had to set things right.

***

Her friends hadn't gone far, and she found them sitting by the edge of the forest. They stood when she approached, but no one spoke at first. Being in front of them now made Elise forget what little she had rehearsed on the way down.

"You guys deserve a better explanation of what happened. I know what it looked like, and I wish I could describe what I felt better. I felt like something terrible was going to happen if we had followed Mom." When they didn't answer, she twisted her fingers together and continued. "But something that was in my control was how I acted afterwards. I know I get scared about a lot of things, but you really hurt me, Darcie. I hate that you see me that way and I wish I could change that part of myself."

She tried to keep her voice from cracking.

"I'm not sorry about what I did, but I am sorry for slowing us down. I know the answers won't magically appear and we probably have more work to do now, but I won't get anywhere without you guys."

Goosebumps trickled down her arms as she awaited their response. Gavin seemed sympathetic while Mitch gauged Darcie's reaction. Elise readied herself for rejection when their silence extended long enough for the air to grow thick around them. She allowed herself to hope when she saw Gavin smile at her. The guys accepted her apology, and while Darcie still showed mixed emotions, she stepped forward and hugged Elise. She also apologized for her words.

"I'm sorry for embarrassing you in front of Gavin, too," Darcie whispered in her ear.

Elise squeezed back and felt the weight lift from her shoulders. When they pulled away, the question came up of what to do while they waited for Ruby to return.

"This clearing is lit pretty well right now. It's kind of romantic," Darcie said. She looked between Gavin and Elise. "And don't worry. I can watch Mitch while you're gone." She chuckled at Mitch's pout. "If y'all are going to label me a meddler, I may as well live up to it."

With her mind cleared, Elise was open to Gavin's touch again. He led her to a more secluded spot.

The two walked in silence for the first few minutes, content with just being together. His hand was warm against hers. She thought back to the shy girl who couldn't bring herself to talk to him. Maybe Darcie was rubbing off on her.

"It's nice to finally be alone without any interruptions."

She agreed with him. It was one of the first times they weren't being followed by a guard or chasing after the diary. Time was on their side for once, and she wanted to soak in every calm moment.

They spent the next half hour asking questions and getting to know each other better. She learned his favorite color was navy blue, that he hated mushrooms, and favored music and technology over sports. In return, he learned her favorite color was turquoise, that she loved a variety of music, and could pretty much quote every line from any romantic comedy.

"You're probably more into action and horror movies," she said.

"You're so quick to label me." He chuckled. "I could be into period dramas or musicals like you, too." She raised her eyebrows and lowered her chin in disbelief. "Okay, action movies it is. Guilty as charged, but not horror. That's more of Mitch's thing."

They turned around to start heading back when Elise failed to stifle a yawn.

"I hadn't planned on staying up all night."

He yawned in return and they paused to rest.

"Yeah, who knows when we'll actually get to sleep once we get back?" He leaned against a low hanging branch as they listened to the deafening crickets and frogs within the forest. "We can sit here. You can nap on my lap if you want."

His offer was tempting considering how heavy her eyes were, but she shook her head.

"I don't want to waste time sleeping."

She let her eyes do the talking until he caught on.

He leaned in gently, but her lips soon grew eager against his mouth. She gripped the fabric of his coat and pulled him against her.

Gavin turned them so that her back rested against the trunk of the tree and his hands lowered to her hips. Draping her arms over his shoulders, she placed a couple of playful kisses at the base of his neck. He pulled away only long enough to warn her.

"You don't want to do that."

The huskiness of his voice encouraged her to continue. He permitted her three or four more before his mouth found hers again with the same fervor. Elise felt her hair tangle on the bark, which was already painful against her back, but she didn't care. His hands felt so good and she longed for him to explore with them. She allowed his kisses to spread along her skin as sweet sensations pulsed through her. His body responded in return. Pulling free of her tangles, she ignored the pain as he found a particularly sensitive spot at the base of her neck. She was in no hurry to give him a warning of her own.

Her eyes shot open, and she gasped as a snapped branch fell at their feet. They broke apart and looked at one another before hearing someone snicker above them.

CHAPTER 24

Gavin called up for whoever was in the tree to show themselves. Elise's cheeks burned, and she stepped away to adjust her gown.

Someone saw us. We're being watched. Ugh, I'm so humiliated!

"Who's there?" he called again.

By the third time, Darcie and Mitch caught up with them.

"Who're you yelling at?" Mitch asked.

"There's somebody in that tree spying on us," said Elise.

All four heard the snickering continue from above their heads.

Who's up there? What's so funny?

Gavin stepped back and craned his neck.

Darcie screamed, staggered and thrashed as a bright ball of light pulled her hair. She tried to shake it loose, but it only gripped tighter.

Mitch danced around trying to swat it off.

"Leave her alone!"

The fairy dodged his attempts and blew dust into his face. Mitch howled, scratching at his eyes.

Darcie squealed and rubbed the back of her head against a tree trunk. Gavin tried to smack it from a distance while Elise poked at it using the fallen branch.

With their combined efforts, the fairy finally released Darcie's hair and whizzed past Elise and Gavin, who ducked out of the way. Its light bounced in amusement until it dimmed on a low hanging branch.

Darcie whimpered and massaged her scalp.

"How can something so tiny cause so much pain?"

The fairy's snickering rolled into full twinkling laughter as two other balls of light joined the first on the branch. They looked like whimsical flames on a candle.

Elise and her friends crept closer. When the other two fairies dimmed their brightness, they could make out all three of their small, illuminated bodies.

It appeared to be two boys and a girl, the latter being the one who had pulled Darcie's hair. She wore a hunter green tunic with brown tights and boots. Her mouse-like face was full of freckles, and she had pointed ears in front of a stringy brown ponytail. Her wings were folded, and in her belt she carried a miniature knife that Elise knew better than to underestimate.

"Thinking of going into the forest, eh? I'd think again if I were you." Her voice was squeaky yet assertive.

"We weren't going in," Elise said. "But we've been in there before."

"With protection," the second fairy replied. He had tousled black hair, a broad chest and wore similar attire. "Where are your guards and weapons this time?"

"I'd say they're too small to be a threat, but I'm rethinking that now," said Mitch. His eyes were bloodshot from the fairy dust.

Elise noticed that the third fairy didn't join in with his friends.

"Who are you guys?"

"I am Thicket," said the first fairy with a dramatic bow. She gestured to the other two. "This is Hemlock and Sage. And consider this your warning."

"Warning of what?" Gavin asked.

"Of what we do to people who cause trouble in our forest!" Hemlock spat.

"So, you're not the ones who grant wishes?" asked Darcie. Thicket snorted.

"Did it feel like I was granting you a wish?"

Sage, the smallest of the three, had yet to speak. With blond hair and a pale complexion, he had a meekness about him.

Although she spoke to all three, Elise kept her eyes on him.

"But the royal family comes through here all the time, and they've never mentioned any trouble with you."

Thicket's voice turned shrill.

"That's because they leave us alone!"

"We didn't mess with you either," Mitch said.

"Maybe not you two," said Hemlock, gesturing to him and Darcie, "but *these* two bumped into our tree while we were sleeping."

Gavin scoffed and shrugged his shoulders.

"Big deal. We'll leave then."

"Not so fast!" Thicket screeched. Her light brightened as she flew off the branch and hovered in front of him with her dagger pointed at his nose.

"Hey, calm down," said Mitch. He wasn't afraid of the tiny weapon, but it was clear he didn't want to antagonize her. "And if you're mad at these two, why did you attack Darcie?"

"Because I felt like it. We don't take disturbances lightly. Accident or not, we still like to have a little fun."

"It sounds like it was just a misunderstanding," said the third fairy.

Thicket's shoulders sagged, and she growled as she flew to his side. Sheathing her knife, she dimmed once more upon landing.

"Sage, you *always* do this! Every time we're lucky enough to find stragglers, you show them mercy. How can you call yourself a fairy?"

"But they aren't a threat to us."

"You don't know that!" Hemlock snapped. "You think because you helped them once long ago that they're not a threat? Humans are fickle and we told you to stop meddling in our fun."

"It was you?" Elise asked Sage. Had this little fairy really been the one to lead them to her family's picnic that day they were lost? She leaned in to see him closer and felt her heart swell. "Thank you."

"Enough!" Thicket cried. "We get hunted too often to place any trust in humans. Consider yourself lucky it was Sage to find you and not me."

"Or me," Hemlock added. "To help a human with no payment in return is a disgrace to the name of fairy as Sage will soon learn."

Payment. That was the key. It was the only tolerated interaction between fairies and humans, and Elise began looking around for something to give them.

"We could use your help again."

"Is she even listening?" Hemlock asked. "I thought we were quite clear."

"We're waiting for someone. Someone who is using fairy magic right now. Maybe you could tell us more about it?"

"Absolutely not," he replied.

Gavin took her arm and eased her back.

"Forget it, Elise. They're just wasting our time. They don't know anything."

Thicket took off again in a twinkling ball of light before she disappeared near Elise.

"You scared her off," Elise said.

"Ha! As if any of you could scare me," came Thicket's voice.

Elise looked down and felt the cheeky fairy's movement on her shoulder.

"We're only our brightest when we fly, but we control our light when we land. It just shows what an outsider you are."

"You're wondering about the princess. I'll tell you," said Sage.

Elise whirled around and rushed to the smallest fairy's side.

Thicket jumped from Elise's shoulder to the branch and clapped her hand over Sage's mouth.

"Don't you dare say a word until they offer something in return!"

Elise bent forward and grasped the branch.

"Please! Tell me everything you know. It's important!" The fairies wobbled back and forth under her weight, causing Elise to release it with an apology.

They hovered in midair until the branch stilled before landing again.

"I want to tell her," Sage said. His voice was calmer and more child-like than the other two.

"Have you even assessed her? How do you know she is worthy?" Hemlock asked.

Sage seemed to heed Hemlock's suggestion and gestured for Elise to come closer. His round blue eyes searched hers while Elise hoped she wasn't being tricked. Thicket and Hemlock didn't hide their displeasure but stayed quiet. Sage placed his hand on the tip of Elise's nose.

He closed his eyes, and all became still. Nobody dared to make a sound except the creatures in the forest. Their calls seemed amplified in the silence. It went on like this for so long that Elise was starting to cramp from her crouching position. The strain on her neck urged her to pull away, but she fought against the impulse and prayed that it wouldn't be much longer.

At long last Sage lowered his hand and Elise was free to relax.

"You have a caged power hidden inside you. The princess you're seeking does not share this quality but has a special tie to you." He informed the other fairies that she could be trusted.

Elise blew out a sigh of relief and thanked him.

"I need to know more about her, but I don't have anything to give you."

He held up a hand and shook his head.

"It is payment enough to help you in your endeavor." He ignored his companions' objections. "The princess has been traveling back and forth only a short time. She first acquired magic by bartering her own belongings, but as her family grew suspicious, she began finding other ways to get it."

"Like Gwen?"

Sage nodded.

"Gwendolyn provided us with protection and supplies but with Rona's growing power we cannot risk ourselves or our magic by having it used to open barriers. We have warned that we will not aid any longer."

Thicket crossed her arms and huffed at the whole situation.

"Well, I'm glad she can't get her hands on anymore. She had to learn the hard way tonight that it took more than usual to get out, and there's barely enough to get back. She'd bleed us dry if she had the chance!"

"Why did it take more?" Darcie asked.

"She's not alone and since she isn't supplying the magic, it requires a stronger amount to travel," said Hemlock.

"But we stayed back," Mitch said. "We watched her go in by herself."

"The princess is expecting," Sage explained.

Elise grew uncomfortable under his stare and a numbness spread throughout her body.

Why hadn't she realized before? Ruby's illness and fatigue all made sense now.

That's why she won't let Charles love her.

Elise's heart raced and she all but lunged at the fairies.

"I need some of your magic. I've got to get to her!"

The fairies chortled and shook their heads.

"We don't just *give* magic. Didn't you hear the story?" Hemlock asked.

"Sage may be stupid enough to share his secrets, but even he won't supply magic for nothing," Thicket said.

"We don't have any money." Elise pleaded for them to make an exception, but the three didn't budge.

Sage pointed to the bracelets on Elise's wrist.

"What about those?"

"The maids dressed me with these. They're not mine to give."

Thicket squeaked.

"Then neither is our magic."

I wish we had gone through that portal now.

Elise fidgeted with the jewelry and looked at her friends. They were just simple bracelets after all. Maybe Derek and Joranna wouldn't even notice they were gone. If they were willing to have them put on guests, they couldn't hold any special meaning.

"Okay, fine."

Gavin and Mitch stepped in between her and the fairies.

"We just got out of the dungeon!" said Gavin. "Don't go giving away their stuff and get us thrown back in!"

Mitch nodded.

"Gav's right. I don't want to end up back in there."

Elise didn't want to start any more fights that night, but this was the only way to help her mom.

She shouldn't be out there pregnant and alone. She could be in real danger. Why would she even leave knowing she was pregnant? I have to find out.

The force trying to stop her would just have to be ignored. Gavin's disapproval hurt the most when she slid the bracelets off.

It took all three fairies to carry the bracelets between them to a higher branch for inspection.

"What do you guys even need them for?" Mitch asked.

"That's not your concern! A deal is a deal," Hemlock spat. He rubbed his palms together as he examined the jewelry. Once approved, the bracelets were carried to the top of the tree, and everything became still.

"Did we just get tricked?" Darcie asked.

Mitch clicked his tongue.

"I'd love to know what else they store up there."

A pool of dread rippled in Elise's gut when she still heard no movement above them. Had they been robbed? Gavin turned his back to her and kicked a nearby trunk.

As possible cover stories began forming in her head, a rustling sound pulled her from her thoughts. A glass vial was being lowered between the three balls of light. It was twice their size, but they managed.

The fairies landed on the same branch as before and balanced the vial. Demanding silence, they placed their palms over the opening.

Their magical energies radiated from their hands as a blue light wafted through the air like smoke. It twisted and pooled into the vial before solidifying into a syrupy substance.

After assuring it was secured, the two male fairies flew back through the leaves, then returned with a cork to plug it up.

Elise waited until they nodded before she took it.

"Thank you." She held the bottle in front of her face and shook the illuminated substance. "Now we can go after her."

"Oh, I wouldn't use it to go after her now," Hemlock said. "She'll be coming back within the hour."

"And you're just *now* telling me! Why even give it to us in the first place?"

"I told you we like to have fun." Thicket giggled. "Besides, a deal's a deal. It's bought and paid for, so you might as well hang on to it, and don't do anything stupid!"

Gavin lunged forward but was unable to catch them as they flew away.

Elise sat down and crossed her legs beneath her gown. She rested her head in her palm and shook the bottle.

What am I supposed to do with it now? What was the point?

"Don't let them get to you," Darcie said, taking a seat next to her. She picked a leaf off her dress and wrapped an arm around her best friend. "You got the magic. That's all that matters."

"Yeah, but what good does it do if I can't travel after her? A part of me still wants to try, but I know we probably wouldn't find her in time."

Darcie pulled in tighter, and Elise rested her head on her friend's shoulder. Gavin settled down on her other side, while Mitch took a seat in front of them. His eyes widened as he pointed over their heads.

One of the fairies was returning. The bright light hovered above their heads before it went out above Elise's knee.

"Do not mind the others," Sage whispered. "They care very little for personal quests and human emotion."

He jumped off and landed by their feet.

Elise followed the rustling grass and path of his voice.

"Why did you come back?"

"I sensed more than just a hidden power before, and I can't ignore it. There's a greatness in you that is strong enough to conquer the darkness heading your way." Elise was glad he couldn't see her roll her eyes. Strong wasn't a word she ever used to describe herself. "I know you do not agree, and that self-doubt will be your downfall if you don't learn to believe in yourself."

She jumped as he lit up and floated in front of her.

"We gave you plenty of magic. It can be used for more than just allowing you four to travel through worlds. It's enough to grant you one powerful act. Only you can decide when the time is right. Whatever you do, don't waste it. Farewell."

He darted into the trees before she could thank him, and the four sat processing what had just happened.

"The magic isn't wasted after all. It's good for anything we want to do later!" Darcie said.

Elise wished she shared her friend's enthusiasm.

"Yeah, but what will 'later' look like?" Elise felt a mixture of emotions battling inside her without a clear victor. She wanted to cry, scream, run and sleep all at once. She had an urge to punch something or just chuck the vial into the woods and be done with it altogether.

Why didn't I just ignore my feelings before and jump through the tunnel? Things would've been so much easier.

Why did everything have to come back to her in vague encrypted messages? There was a greatness in her. She was more powerful than she knew. All would work out in the end if she just believed in herself.

She was sick of it. All of it.

Why do I have to be the savior and only hope for my family? Can't they save themselves? Even if they can't, is it such a big deal to expect them to live in a different world? Joranna, Ruby, and Ian learned to do it. It can be done.

She didn't like the path her thoughts were taking, so she tried to remind herself why she agreed to do this in the first place. It was time to admit the truth to herself.

"I'm a wreck, you guys. I've been angry at my mom for so long that there's a part of me that's been wondering if I even want to help her. Isn't that awful?" She sniffled and tucked a piece of loose hair behind her ear. "But something changed when they told us she's pregnant. I knew she was young when she had me, but I just didn't put the pieces together. Now I keep wondering if I only want to help because it's me inside of her and that sounds selfish, doesn't it?"

It was refreshing to say it out loud, and she laughed through her tears in spite of herself.

Gavin doesn't need to see me ugly cry. My face must be a blubbering wet mess.

She was doing a decent job of hiding it until he wrapped his arms around her. This time, she didn't want to pull away. She leaned into his touch and cried into his shoulder.

"She must be so scared. Why didn't I follow her?" Her shoulders shook with uncontrollable sobs and her tears soaked into his sleeve. "She didn't deserve this. Any of it. I must have been the last straw that made her run. I ruined her."

"Elise, that's not true!" Darcie said. "You can't believe that."

"I should've figured it out sooner." She wept more. "And I'm so angry. Where's my dad in all this? I never met him, but he's got to be around somewhere. Maybe even over there. But why is she alone? Is that my fault too?"

"I think you're overthinking it. From what we've seen, your mom has had trust issues long before this," Gavin said. He ran his hand up and down her back. His voice was comforting. "And your family doesn't even know she's pregnant yet, and they live with her! Cut yourself some slack."

She held him closer as another wave of tears came to the surface. When she felt somewhat under control of her feelings, she pulled away and wiped her eyes.

"I just didn't expect to feel this way when the time came. I'm supposed to help her through this and keep her close, but I don't even know where to start. A few days ago, I just wanted to graduate! Now I've got us all stuck here, wondering whether Rona will or won't attack; we still haven't found the spy; and now I have to make sure Mom doesn't do anything stupid. Things just sounded so much simpler in Nana's kitchen."

Mitch surprised her by putting his hand on her shoulder. He eased her away from Gavin so that she could see him better.

"Hey," he whispered, lowering his face until she looked at him. "That fairy wasn't making stuff up. If he saw something, that's because there's something to see. Your family saw it too. It's okay to be scared, but you've got this, and you've got us. Whatever happens, nothing changes that."

She leaned into his hug and was thankful to have the three of them by her side. Mitch was right. Even if all went wrong, she'd still have them and that gave her a great comfort.

"Why don't we take a nap while we wait?" Gavin suggested.

Elise shook her head and yawned in spite of herself. She used her sleeve to dry her lingering tears that had grown cold by the cool night air.

"I can't fall asleep. I don't want to miss her coming back."

"Then we'll take turns. One of us will be a lookout while the rest of us sleep, then we'll switch," he said.

Mitch offered to take the first shift.

"I'll watch. I'm not that tired."

Settling against the nearest tree, Gavin offered a spot for Elise to sit in his lap. She nestled between his legs, resting her head under his chin. She marveled at the perfect fit and soon felt her eyes drooping. When exhaustion took over, she drifted off to sleep in his arms.

CHAPTER 25

Elise stirred but didn't open her eyes. She felt Gavin's heart beating against her ear and nuzzled her face into his shirt. Inhaling his scent, she began drifting off again until she heard a chorus of birds chirping. She peeked up at the sky with one eye. The sun had not risen, but already the forest was full of sounds signaling a new day.

Any hope of sleeping longer was gone as a nearby movement startled her.

Her scream awoke the others. When she was alert, she recognized her mother a few feet away. Startled, Ruby nearly tripped over the lantern she had burning behind her. Elise scrambled to her feet.

"What're you doing?" Elise shouted.

"I should ask you the same thing. So, it's true that Father sent you after me."

Mitch rubbed his face and looked at the princess.

"And you could've gotten away while we were sleeping. Why'd you sneak up on us?"

"Why were *you* asleep?" Darcie asked him.

Ruby didn't reply, but Elise followed her glance to their feet where the vial had dropped out of Gavin's pocket.

Elise picked it up, watching Ruby fixate on the blue concoction.

"Were you trying to steal this?"

"You idiots just left it out in the open. I overheard you're not even from here, and fairy magic is extremely rare to come by. I would put it to better use than whatever you're going to waste it on. Now hand it here!"

Elise held it out of reach, but Ruby's stare never left the vial. Frowning, she extended her hand for Elise to give it to her. The flickering light from the lantern exposed the crazed look in her mother's eyes.

"You're addicted to it."

You'd do anything for magic, wouldn't you, Mom?

"Don't be ridiculous. I just know how to appreciate it."

"What were you doing in the other world?" Elise asked.

Ruby didn't reply.

Now's not the time to be stubborn, Mom. Just tell us!

"Shouldn't you be getting back before your family wakes up?" Gavin asked.

"What's the hurry if you're just going to turn me in anyway?"

"I don't want to get you in trouble," Elise said. "Besides, you said this was your last trip, so you won't be needing magic anymore."

She gave it back to Gavin to place in his pocket.

Ruby grunted and straightened her gown and cloak.

"So, what do you expect will happen? That we'll just stroll up to my parents and have a cheerful chat over tea? Once they know I've been leaving the kingdom, I'll never hear the end of it."

"I don't think sending us was the right thing to do, but they're just worried about you," Darcie said.

"Why did he send you instead of guards or something?" "So we could show them they could trust us. We've known your family since your parents got married," Elise said.

"How can that be?" Ruby asked. "You look the same age as me."

"It's a long story." Gavin shook his head. "Seriously, it would take too long. But the king wanted us to prove our loyalty and make sure you were safe at the same time."

"We all agree with you though," said Mitch. "It's not right to spy on you, but it's also not right to hide that you're pregnant from them either."

He shrank under his friends' stares and Ruby's mouth dropped open. She eased away as the air around them thickened. Elise watched her mother's defensive walls go up. This wasn't going well.

"How dare you! How do you know? Why would you say that? Who do you think you are?"

Elise took a step towards her.

"Ruby. . ."

"You will address me as *Princess* Ruby or Your Highness. Do not claim a close acquaintance with me. I have no reason to believe you care the slightest bit, and I refuse to hear any judgement from you."

"We're not judging, Ruby." Her mother jerked her head to look at her. "I mean, Princess Ruby.

"We just want to help you," Darcie said.

Ruby seethed and picked up her lantern.

"I should've left sooner when I had the chance."

"Running away isn't going to solve your problem," said Gavin.

"What do you know?"

Elise felt her own temper surge and took another bold step forward. If she couldn't reach her mother through reason, she'd have to do it using Ruby's own stubbornness against her.

"I know that you live in a huge castle with servants to meet your every need. I know you have a family who is worried sick about you even if they don't know how to say it. If you run away now, you'll only regret it. I know you don't want to hear this, and you can try to shut me out, but people love you. Running away and hiding isn't fair to you, them, your baby, or even Charles."

"Now you go too far," Ruby snapped. "Don't bring him into this. One night of spying doesn't give you the right to make such statements about how I live my life. I will do what I want. I always have."

And look where it's gotten you.

Elise knew to hold that last thought to herself. This was only pushing Ruby further away, and if they weren't careful, her mother would be sneaking off for good and their interference would be for nothing.

"What if I could prove how much you mean to people?" Elise took Ruby's hesitation as invitation enough and pulled her aside.

Elise pulled out the crinkled drawing for Ruby to see. Her mother held her lantern up.

"You probably don't remember, but you drew this for me. I've kept it ever since." She handed it over for Ruby to examine. "I know you don't trust us yet and our ages don't make sense, but we've known your family a long time. They'll want to help you."

"It's not that simple. My reputation will be ruined. The castle will be enveloped in scandal. Our family name will be tainted. Better to have an estranged daughter than a soiled one."

That seems really extreme.

Elise had a hard time believing that a pregnancy could ruin an entire kingdom and ignored the rising guilt that tried to come back. Her friends were right. This wasn't her fault, but she was determined to fix it, nonetheless.

"You don't have to be so tough all the time," she said. Elise resisted the urge to hug Ruby and instead settled for placing a hand on her shoulder. "I know you're scared, but it probably won't be as bad as you think. We can go with you and help find a way to tell your parents."

Ruby shoved the paper into Elise's hand.

"You're kind to want to help, but I wouldn't waste your time."

Elise wasn't giving up. She folded the paper back into her gown and stomped after her mother.

"We're all going back to the castle anyway, so you might as well go in at the same time as us."

Ruby scoffed.

"Why? To make you all look like the heroes for catching me?"

Elise waved for the others to follow them.

"I know everything seems like a big deal right now, but if you don't face it, you'll mess up your whole life!"

"I'm done listening."

How many times had Elise heard Ruby end arguments that way growing up? Blood rushed to her face and she curled her hands into fists.

"Well, I'm not done talking!" Elise caught up and grabbed Ruby's shoulder.

"Don't you dare touch me! Do you know who I am?"

"I'm not worried about who you are. I'm worried about who you'll be," Elise snapped.

Years of torment and silent treatments erupted within her and Elise allowed her pain to flow out.

"You're going to regret this one day. Years from now it will eat away at you, and your pride still won't let you ask for help. You'll take it out on other people and push them all away just like you did with Charles." Ruby made to argue, but Elise had heard enough arguing for a lifetime. "You think you're helping your family, but you're only thinking of yourself when you should be focused on that baby. It's going to look up to you. You're going to be its whole world until you screw that up, too!"

Her heart thrashed inside of her chest, and she felt a wave of pride wash over her for the first time since she could remember. Her spirit cheered her on for more, but watching the perplexed expression on Ruby's face caused Elise to relent.

The problem was this was the wrong Ruby. Elise could only be half-gratified.

"I don't have to sit here and listen to this!"

Darcie tugged on Elise's sleeve.

"Elise, let's go. You tried."

"Yeah, we'll tell them we couldn't find her," said Mitch.

Her friends had a point. She needed to know when to give up, to move on. Pulling out the drawing, she looked at it one more time before letting it fall at Ruby's feet.

Still fighting a wave of guilt, she walked with her friends in the direction of the castle.

Gavin reached out to squeeze her hand.

"That was awesome, by the way."

***

It didn't occur to any of them how much they had relied on Ruby as a guide through the forest, and the four soon found themselves standing in front of a fork in the path.

"Did we get turned around?" Darcie asked.

"How could we? There's one path and we just walked straight last night the whole time. I don't remember any forks before!" Mitch exclaimed. He walked over and sat on a nearby stump.

"Well, clearly not. Now, which way do we go?" she asked.

"This is Elise's mission. Let her choose."

"Oh no, you're not pawning it off on her every time something gets hard. Be helpful for once, Mitch. Get up!"

Mitch rose with a groan and rolled his eyes as he stomped over to the path. He glanced in both directions, then pointed to the left.

"I like this way."

"You just guessed! You didn't even think about it!"

"Darcie, I told you I don't remember there even being a fork, so how am I supposed to pick the right one? Either way, there's a fifty percent chance this one is it."

Their banter continued to escalate until both were arguing over one another. Unable to make out what either was saying, Gavin came to stand between the two.

"Let's all agree we're lost and not try to put all the pressure on one person."

The two glared at each other but complied.

"Well, if we go this way," Mitch said, pointing to the left, "we'll follow the path through a bunch of trees, and if we go that way, we'll go past a bunch of trees. Tough call."

Darcie scoffed and began leading everyone towards the left path.

"Where are you going?" They all turned to see Ruby approaching. She nodded her head towards the right. "The castle is that way."

The sky was beginning to lighten, and Elise could make out a piece of paper in Ruby's other hand that wasn't holding her lantern. Ruby followed her gaze and held out the drawing.

"I was hoping I'd run into you before we got back," she said. Elise took the paper from her and tucked it into the front of her gown once more. "It doesn't hold the same value to me, but I'd hate to see you throw it away." Her mom sighed and lowered her head. "I've been thinking about what you said. . .about how this isn't just about me anymore." Elise remained silent but felt a flicker of hope ignite in her chest. "And while your methods are questionable, and I still don't really know who you are, I do believe you care about what happens to us."

"Does that mean you'll go with us to talk to your parents?" Elise asked.

Ruby nodded.

"I think I need to talk to more than just them about my selfish behavior lately."

Elise once again fought the urge to run up and hug her mother.

This will be the change she needs! She'll talk to my grandparents and Charles, and all will work out.

The diary couldn't be too far away from returning and sending them home now. She beamed at Ruby and they stepped out of the way so the princess could lead them down the right path.

"Just curious," Mitch asked Ruby, "what's down that left path?"

"The Bedeviled Swamp."

It took everything in Elise not to burst out laughing at Mitch's stunned expression.

***

They arrived at the castle wall moments before the sun rose. Reddish-orange clouds floated against a periwinkle backdrop. The still air was perfumed by the garden on the other side. Elise's hem and shoes were wet from the dew-soaked grass.

Her stomach fell when she saw the expected rope dangling before them. It had been hard enough to do with a tree for help, but this was a straight climb with unreliable foot holds along the way.

"Let's use the gate," she suggested.

"That wouldn't really be sneaking back in then, would it?" Mitch asked.

"There's no need to sneak in. We're on our way to talk to Derek and Joranna anyway, and we have clearance from the guards to pass through."

"*You* have clearance," Ruby said. "I'm going up."

"You can't!" Elise said, snatching the rope from her mother's grasp. "You shouldn't be climbing like this when you're pregnant. I couldn't stop you before."

"And you can now?" Ruby pulled the rope back.

"What if you get hurt or something happens to the baby?"

"I've done this enough times." Ruby put the now unlit lantern on the ground. "Use the gate, and Charles and I will meet you in the ballroom. It will be unlocked."

Elise was reluctant to walk away. Her trusty companion, anxiety, was once again quick to join her side.

But what're you supposed to do? Catch her if she falls? What if you can't even make it up? Are you really going to make your friends wait around forever?

Even if her inner voice made sense, it still didn't make Elise any more comfortable as she watched Ruby test the rope and begin climbing. Her only comfort was that Ruby seemed to know which footholds were secure and outperformed Elise's ability within seconds.

"Are you sure you don't want to go up?" Gavin asked.

"Yeah, I'll save that for her."

***

Even with their clearance, Elise lowered her head and avoided making eye contact with the guard posted at the gate. Though innocent, something about this made her feel like they had done something wrong.

Should I have stayed with Mom?

She reassured herself that Charles was there and would make sure she was safe. This way would definitely save time.

The blood drained from her face, however, when she looked up and saw Charles watching them.

He wasn't alone.

A handful of guards stood on either side of him, and Ballard waited with the king and queen a few feet ahead.

I don't understand. . .if he's here, then who's holding the rope for her?

Had Charles ratted them out? Had he been so upset she turned him down that he confessed to the whole thing? If it weren't for the audience, Elise would march forward and demand to know what was going on. The shame on his face was enough to convince her of his involvement.

That shame turned to anguish, however, when a guard escorted Ruby into the courtyard. She was just as shocked and confused by the welcoming committee. Her eyes darted between Elise and the large party before settling on Charles. The two shared a silent exchange that only ended when Derek cleared his throat.

"Thank goodness you're all back safely. I wish to speak to the five of you in my office. Lord Fenton, you are dismissed until the council can determine the proper course of action."

Joranna held out her hand and waited for Ruby to cross over before following them inside. Ruby's eyes never left Charles until she passed through the glass doors.

Elise couldn't take her eyes off of him either. He had been so perfect but had let them down.

***

Sitting on the other side of Derek's desk felt like being sent to the principal's office. Guards stood by the door, but the family had yet to arrive.

Darcie cleared her throat and motioned for Elise to check her neck. Furrowing her eyebrows, she touched the side of her neck but felt nothing. Darcie nodded over to a mirror hanging on the wall.

Upon closer inspection of her reflection, Elise's eyes widened in panic as she saw the red mark on her skin. She gasped and clasped her hand over it.

Her friend bounded off the couch and came to her aid. The boys turned to see what the commotion was about as Darcie began pulling out the pins, adjusting Elise's hair around her shoulders.

Mitch winked at her.

"That must've been some romantic walk."

Elise groaned and rolled her eyes. She didn't have time to go upstairs to apply any makeup or powder on it. She made eye contact with Gavin in the mirror. He shrugged and mouthed an apology, but there was little to be done about it.

"There!" Darcie stood back. "Just don't move around too much until we can hide it better."

It wasn't the best, but Elise had to admit her friend was talented. If she kept her head still enough, her hair would do the trick for a short while.

She had just enough time to thank Darcie before Derek and Joranna entered with Ruby. Elise was surprised to see Ballard follow them in before the doors were closed.

Derek took his place behind the desk while Joranna sat with Ruby on the couch. Despite Joranna's whispering advice on posture, Ruby slouched back and crossed her arms.

"We have tried to talk privately. It seems that Ruby is not ready to disclose where she was," said Derek, "so I'm afraid you'll have to go first. Tell us about last night."

Elise wondered how on earth she was supposed to respond. She had promised her mom they could talk to her grandparents together, but this was more likely to exploit her. She looked at their expectant faces and felt particularly unsettled by Ballard's smug expression. With arms crossed behind his back, the steward stood near Derek looking as if he had just won the lottery.

"If none of you share, I shall have to assume the worst," he warned. Each of them seemed to be waiting for someone else to take the leap. "Very well. Ballard, I believe you had something you wanted to say."

"I'd be only too happy to, Your Highness." Ballard bowed. "I have been deeply concerned about the princess's safety, and while making my rounds last night, I couldn't help but feel something was amiss."

Ruby was careful not to show any emotion while he spoke, but Elise could sense her anger boiling just below the surface. She wouldn't give herself away and give him the satisfaction. She was too proud for that. Taking no notice of her, Ballard was too preoccupied with his heroic recollection of the night.

"Everything seemed in order, so you can imagine my surprise when I found the guard I had just spoken to outside unconscious in the kitchen." He didn't pick up on Derek's cue to pause and continued prattling on. "I often indulge myself with a morsel before bed, though this is the first time I've found a body in the pantry! I was able to revive the young man, but he was unable to tell me how he had gotten there and had no recollection of our conversation. I immediately set out to confront the imposter but found him to be missing. Naturally, I took it upon myself to stake out the area until he returned. And who should turn up but none other than Lord Fenton? When searched, we found the guard's key and a rope. Suspicious activity for someone in your court, Sire. I believe he should be charged at once for treason and being a possible spy."

Elise screwed up her face and gripped the armrests of the chair she was sitting in.

"He's not a spy!"

Whatever doubts she had had about Charles's loyalty were gone now. He was clearly stuck in this mess like they all were.

"Well, his actions *are* questionable," Derek said with a pointed look at Ruby. "If he wasn't disguised for spying, then please enlighten us to what he was doing there."

Elise wanted to smack the smirk right off of Ballard's face. She hadn't hated someone so much in her entire life as she did at that moment.

"Maybe we should talk about this in private," Joranna suggested.

"We tried that," Derek said. "Ruby, just make this easier on all of us and tell the truth." He followed her gaze over his shoulder. "That will be all, Ballard. You're dismissed."

If the room hadn't been so full of tension, Elise would've laughed at Ballard's pale, baffled expression. He spluttered and tried to argue, but Derek held up his hand, asking him to leave. Once the door was closed, the king turned back to his youngest daughter.

"Ruby, I know you don't like me right now, but please know that everything I have ever done has been for your safety."

"We only want you to be safe." Joranna gently moved a lock of hair out of Ruby's face. The princess leaned away from the gesture and stood up to start pacing about the room. "If you'd only talk to us."

Ruby whirled around to face them.

"What good will that do? I came home hoping to talk to you, but instead got a welcoming committee ready to chop my head off."

"Ballard only did what he did because Lord Fenton was out of line," said Derek.

"Ballard did what he did because he's a groveling, pathetic excuse for a man who's only out for his own self-gain."

"Young lady, if Lord Fenton's suspicious behavior has any ties to you disappearing—"

"Leave Charles out of this."

Derek was taken aback by her outburst and eased back in his chair. He muddled over her words, and it was clear he was getting a better understanding of the situation.

"I see."

An awkward silence filled the room. Elise wished Derek had dismissed them along with Ballard. She felt completely out of place and wanted to be anywhere else.

"I think what hurt the most is you sent out almost complete strangers to spy on me instead of just trusting me."

"Ruby, we tried!" Joranna said. "You became completely withdrawn. It's dangerous and you don't need to be traveling on your own. And how do you explain your recent sickness?" She glanced at

Elise and the others as if to censor herself but continued in a lowered serious tone. "We're not idiots, Ruby."

"Is it Lord Fenton's?" Derek whispered even though he couldn't bring himself to look at her.

Ruby didn't hide her shock but made no reply.

"We just want to hear the truth and stop you from sneaking over that wall," Joranna said. "We want to protect you."

Ruby crossed the room and stood between the two guards by the door.

"I don't need you to protect me, and Charles had nothing to do with it. I made him help me, so you can leave him alone. And you needn't worry about me sneaking over the wall. I'm done with that. The next time I leave, it will be right through the front gates for good!"

As she reached for the door handle, Derek's fist slammed against the desk.

"Ruby Jane Laurille, this impetuous behavior has gone on long enough. If you walk out of this room now, you will be restricted to the grounds!"

Ruby glared coldly at her father and Elise prayed that she wouldn't call Derek's bluff.

Please just sit down, Elise silently urged her mother.

In true Ruby fashion, however, the young princess turned and slammed the door behind her.

Joranna jumped up to follow, but Derek stopped her. He held out his hand for her to join him behind the desk, massaging the bridge of his nose. Joranna brought her hand up to hide her tears, and Derek's voice was strangled when he spoke again.

"Please," he begged. "Tell us what you know."

Elise stared into their tired eyes. Both looked pale. She wanted to protect her mother like she had promised, but her heart broke at the sight of her grandparents suffering. It was as if they were playing a game of tug-of-war for her loyalty.

I need to stick to the facts that they pretty much know already. I can't give away too much without her here.

"She went to our world, but we didn't go. We waited for her to come back and followed her here. Honest."

She left out the part about her mother's rendezvous with Charles and their encounter with the fairies. They were overwhelmed enough without her adding to their stress.

"I'm curious to know where she'd be getting magic from and how Lord Fenton ties in. I'm still not convinced he's blameless in all this," said Derek. He ordered one of the guards to approach his desk. "Inform the captain that Princess Ruby is restricted to the grounds until further notice, and have Ballard summon the council right away." The guard bowed before exiting to deliver the message.

Joranna couldn't stay still any longer and began pacing. Unable to vent properly, she stomped her foot as her face crumpled.

"How could she let this happen?" Joranna pulled a handkerchief from the front of her gown and wiped her eyes. "Did we do something wrong? What could have possibly compelled her to do this? Doesn't she know what this does to her reputation? To our family?"

"And how long can we possibly hide it?" Derek asked. "Tensions are high enough without a scandal. I can't even look at her right now. How could she be so foolish?"

Hearing them echo Ruby's own worries made Elise glad her mother had left after all.

"Avalyn would have had a fit if she knew I let people see me go to pieces like this. Forgive me," Joranna said. Her face scrunched again as more tears approached and Derek stood to hold his wife. Sobbing openly into his shoulder, she talked into his sleeve. "I hate this. She must be so scared."

Derek sniffed to control his own urge to cry and kissed the top of his wife's head.

"We're going to get through this. I think it's best if we retire and process this in private. We can't be of any use to her if we can't control ourselves. Then we can talk to Ruby again."

"We should let her sleep and get something to eat first," said Joranna. "She must be exhausted. You all must be."

"Quite right." Derek turned to face them. "Return to your rooms. Rest for a while. We'll take it from here." As they turned to leave, he called out one more time. "Is there anything else you need to tell us?" All four looked at each other. "I don't think I need to remind you where you spent the majority of yesterday."

A chill ran down Elise's spine. She would do anything to avoid going back in that dungeon again. Was there something she could say to comfort them without compromising what little trust Ruby had in her? When she couldn't figure out a way to do that, she even considered telling them about Ballard's suspicious behavior the night before, but now didn't seem like the right time for that either. Elise shook her head, knowing very well her grandparents were unconvinced, and led the others out into the hall.

Mitch sighed as the door closed behind them.

"Guys, should we just tell them your mom's using fairy magic? I don't want to go back in that cell."

"They know we're not telling them everything," said Gavin. "Is this really worth getting arrested again? Maybe we just use the magic in that vial and try to go home now. Deal with whatever happens then."

"So, just give up?" Elise asked. She looked over to Darcie. "Do you feel the same way?"

Darcie shrugged.

"This is bigger than any of us, Elise. This is something your family has to work out together, and maybe we're just getting in the way, messing it up more."

Elise weighed their advice with her own inner voice that wanted to fix everything.

That's what we were sent here to do, right?

"I'm going to talk to her. . .by myself this time. Maybe she'll open up more."

"You should probably just leave her alone," Mitch said. "She's so mad right now."

"I don't have time though," Elise said. "Every minute we waste, the spy is giving more information to Rona. And the diary hasn't shown up, which means we're not done. But I think it should just be me. All four of us can be a bit much. You guys go upstairs and get some sleep. I'll rest when I'm done."

It was clear none of them wanted to leave, but Elise wasn't going to change her mind. Mitch and Darcie eventually headed up to their rooms.

Gavin took her hand.

"Are you sure you don't need any help?"

"I'm sure. You wouldn't be allowed near her room anyway. Besides," Elise added with a coy smile, pulling her hair back and exposing her neck, "you've helped enough."

They chuckled and he apologized again before kissing her.

"Good luck."

***

Elise thought she had remembered where her mother's bedroom was, but now that she stared down a corridor of matching doors, she wasn't so sure. Once she had narrowed it down to a section of the hall, she stared at the five doors in question.

She tried to use the process of elimination by pressing her ear against the doors, which was working just fine until her aunt Sarah came around the corner and caught her.

"What are you doing?"

Elise jumped and felt like a child with her hand in the cookie jar. She stammered and tried to find the right thing to say.

"I'm looking for my. . .Ruby. Princess Ruby. Is this her room?"

Sarah looked Elise up and down.

"We haven't really been properly acquainted, but I know you're close with my parents. Do they know you're up here?"

Quick! Just lie.

"Yes."

Sarah wavered on the spot and was clearly fighting a battle in her head.

"What do you want her for?"

"Just to talk. I want to help."

Sarah scoffed.

"You're brave to want to face the dragon. She's got a temper on her. I heard you followed her last night. Is she okay?"

Elise could hear the sincerity in her aunt's voice, which was a tone that her mother probably wasn't used to hearing from her sister.

"She will be."

Sarah nodded and sucked her lips into a thin line before she pointed two doors down from where Elise stood.

"Tell her I. . .well, tell her we're here if she needs anything."

Elise nodded, reading into what Sarah wasn't able to say. She thanked her aunt and waited for the princess to leave before she knocked on her mother's door.

"Princess? It's me, Elise. Can I come in?"

"Not as long as you're working for my parents," came the reply from inside.

Elise tested the locked doorknob and blew out a deep breath. This was going to be harder than she thought. Pressing her ear against the door, she heard movement and rustling papers on the other side.

"I just want to talk. I'm alone." Again, no reply. "Ruby, you can trust me. I didn't tell them anything about last night. I'm not leaving until you see me."

She heard Ruby groan in frustration and the door flew open. Her mother ushered her in. The door slammed behind her, and the lock clicked. Ruby returned to bustling about her room.

Elise was momentarily rendered speechless as she took in the beauty of the room.

There was an extra-large bed in the center with a sheer canopy and engraved headboard. The domed ceiling was painted to portray a bright sky full of soft white clouds. White drapes floated from the open windows, and just between them was a polished curve-shaped writing table and chair. The doors of the table had been opened to unveil a writing surface haphazardly covered in papers. The ornate rug Elise was standing on covered most of the floor. A wardrobe and accompanying vanity completed the lush decor.

Elise was brought out of her wistful state of mind by the sound of Ruby lugging out a trunk from under her bed.

"Make it quick," Ruby said with a strain. "As you can see, I'm very busy."

"What are you doing?"

"I believe I made myself very clear in Father's office."

"Ruby, you can't leave." Elise crossed over to her mother. She saw a pile of discarded clothes in the corner that included Ruby's traveling cloak. Among them was a mini skirt and bright neon top. Elise wondered how many trips her mother had made altogether. "I know you're mad."

"You don't know what I'm feeling," Ruby said as she began to pull gowns from the wardrobe and fold them into the trunk. "You don't know anything about me. I wish you'd stop trying to push yourself into my life. I've said it before. I don't need anyone."

"Where will you go?"

Ruby scoffed and pressed down on the growing pile.

"Like I would tell you. You'll just run downstairs and rat me out like Ballard did."

"Don't compare me to that creep," Elise said. "I can't believe he sold Charles out like that."

"I can." Ruby continued about her packing. "But maybe this was how it was supposed to be."

"No, it's not." Elise stepped in front of Ruby and blocked her from adding another gown. "I think if you'd just talk to your parents again, you'd see they want to take care of you."

"Elise, my own father can't even look at me right now."

She pushed Elise aside and continued adding items to the trunk.

We're worried about you.

"They're just mad because they don't know how to help. They're processing it like you are."

"I can't face the shame and disgrace that this child will cause my family. I've damaged my own reputation. I won't damage theirs or disgrace the crown anymore."

Elise gritted her teeth to control her temper. As much as she loved Haighdlen and wanted to make it her own home, it was times like these she was thankful for the modern mindset concerning women.

A baby shouldn't be the end of the world for someone.

She tried to put herself in her mother's shoes.

What if she had been pregnant? Who would she trust? Would she feel safe? Would she want to run away, too? She and her mother definitely had two different demeanors, but growing up with her mother had given her experience in how to approach the other woman when she was in one of her moods. She had to break through her mother's walls.

Taking another deep breath to calm her tone, Elise stood in front of the trunk again. She shifted to prevent the princess from getting around her, holding her stance as the other woman glared. Elise didn't waver and pleaded with her eyes for Ruby to stop fighting.

She's not telling me something.

"Ruby. . .what happened last night?"

There was a stillness in the room as the power struggle came to a head before Ruby slumped down onto the chair by the writing table. A few letters from Charles caught Elise's eye, but she wasn't able to decipher any of the writing before Ruby snatched them up and folded them in her hand.

"You're really not going to leave me alone, are you?" When Elise shook her head, Ruby leaned her head back and closed her eyes. "I suppose it doesn't matter. By the time you do turn me in, I'll be long gone."

Ruby stood with a sigh, then paced the floor while twisting her fingers together. Elise didn't rush her and felt a glimmer of hope when her mother's icy stare melted away. Ruby opened her mouth several times to start but no words came out. Finally, she stopped to lean against the wardrobe. She gazed down at the gowns in the trunk, but her mind was somewhere else. Her eyes fluttered back and forth as she relived a memory. When she spoke, it was little more than a whisper.

"I went to tell him."

A lump formed in Elise's chest. She remained silent and let Ruby go at her own pace, but her mind burned with so many questions about the dad she never knew.

Ruby shook her head, grabbing her hairbrush from the vanity.

"Anyway, it's over. He's made it very clear he wants nothing to do with me. It's done. You can go now."

Elise took Ruby's hand before she could pick up a pair of shoes to pack. Ruby pulled away and stuffed them in anyway.

"What did he say?"

Elise wasn't about to be this close to finding out more about her dad and give up now.

She's going to do her best to put me through more misery!

Catching a glimpse of a letter from Charles that Ruby had missed, Elise snatched it off the table and held it up.

Ruby scowled at her.

"Give that here!"

Elise pulled away and lifted it higher.

"What did he say?"

"I'm not playing these games with you!"

Elise darted away from her mother's reach.

"What did he say?"

"So help me, if you don't give me back my letter—"

"No one is judging you, Ruby. Just spit it out. What did he say?"

"He said to find someone who cared to raise it!" she screamed.

The color drained from Elise's face, and she felt a numbness spread throughout her body. Her mother's words echoed in her mind. For a moment, time seemed to stop, and all thoughts of an argument were gone.

Regretting having pushed Ruby so far, Elise sat down on the bed in shock and held the letter out for her mom to take. It was added to the trunk with the others before the princess walked around to sit next to Elise. Neither spoke as the tension eased between them.

"I'm sorry," Elise whispered, catching a tear before it could fall as she looked over at the other woman.

"Don't be," Ruby said, calmer now. She shook her head and smiled in disbelief. "It was so humiliating."

Elise had heard bits and pieces about her dad growing up, but Ruby had always ended the conversation shortly after.

"Did he say anything else?"

Ruby shrugged. "He said he had a scholarship to worry about and couldn't handle this."

Ballard was no longer the most hated person in Elise's life now.

How can a guy just abandon his pregnant girlfriend like that?

Ruby wiped her own eyes and didn't look up as she spoke.

"Needless to say, we were pretty much done when a girl walked up behind him wearing just his shirt. That told me everything I needed to know. Guess it was a good thing I was planning for this to be my last trip."

This is what she's kept from me. That's why she's chosen to block out Haighdlen, my dad, her lack of magic. . .all of it. She's been hiding all these years. So many sad memories.

Elise now understood her mother in a way she never had before. She wanted to reassure Ruby that she and her baby would be okay. Ruby needed to know that this wasn't her fault, but running away would only add to her struggles.

"You need to tell your parents everything."

"Are you still on that?" Ruby asked. "I just said it's done. It's all taken care of. Dylan doesn't want me. The kingdom won't want me. My family will be better off."

"I know you don't believe that," Elise said. "And what about Charles? You're just going to forget about him?"

"Once he knows the truth, I won't be of any value to him, but I'll always have his letters. Now that I've confided in you, will you please just leave me alone and let me go?"

"I know I don't understand how you're feeling, and I know you feel alone," said Elise, "but they really just want to help."

"Don't you see how it'll play out though? Father will send out search parties for Dylan. Mother will be in hysterics. My brothers and sister will shun me even more and I'll be no better off than if I just leave now."

Elise reached out to lay a hand on top of Ruby's. She was thankful when her mother didn't pull away.

"Please don't take this the wrong way. You're strong, Ruby, but you can't do this alone. Yes, you *can*, but you shouldn't. It's not a smart choice emotionally or financially. Give your family a chance. They may surprise you."

Ruby sighed.

"If I agree to talk to them and they react as I know they will, would you promise to drop the matter and let me leave?"

Elise felt uncomfortable making such a promise, but at that moment, her options were slim. She'd have to rely on the hope that her grandparents would say and do the right things to keep Ruby at home. The only alternative was letting Ruby sneak out and repeating the original timeline. She'd eventually reconcile to a point, but the trust would never be the same. Elise had to be willing to take the chance that this could strengthen her family's bond. With a heavy sigh of her own, she nodded.

She accompanied Ruby to Derek and Joranna's bedroom. When the princess was invited in, she cast one last skeptical look at Elise in the hallway before closing the door behind her.

CHAPTER 26

Elise was able to nap for a couple of hours and only woke when a maid came to in to check on her. Upon finding her awake, the young lady stayed to help Elise bathe and change for the day.

Once dressed, Elise sat in front of the mirror, trying to ignore the growling in her stomach while the maid did her makeup and hair.

She pretended to scratch an itch so that she could hide her neck with her hand.

"Can you style it down please?"

Elise waited until the maid wasn't looking and scooped some powder on her fingers to dab on the blemish. If the other woman noticed, she didn't say anything and curtsied on her way out. Breathing a sigh of relief and checking her reflection one more time, Elise left in search of her friends.

She found them shortly after in the courtyard along with her uncles and aunt.

A table had been set with a delicious assortment of brunch options. Or was it lunch? Elise had forgotten to check the clock on the way out and didn't know what time it was.

She took a seat between Gavin and Darcie, then allowed one of the servants to fix her a plate.

"Are the others coming down?" Elise asked as she took a bite of her croissant. The buttery flavor of the flaky crust was enough to make her moan. She threw etiquette out the window by quickly grabbing another from the middle of the table despite the full plate in front of her.

"Ballard said they were detained and would join us for dinner," Richard said.

"Has he seemed off to you lately?" Sarah asked, dabbing the side of her mouth with a cloth napkin.

"What do you mean?" Darcie asked, exchanging a look with Elise.

Sarah waved as she waited to swallow her food.

"Oh, I'm sure it's nothing. He's just been very preoccupied with Father lately. More than usual, that's all."

Elise and her friends listened as Sarah rambled on about letters, trips, and countless meetings between the king and steward.

"Not to mention he's recently turned into some sort of governor to us all," Ian said. "He's so concerned about where everyone is throughout the day."

"And that doesn't make you guys suspect anything?" Gavin asked.

Mitch chimed in.

"Like maybe he's the spy everyone's looking for?"

The three of them burst into fits of laughter.

Sarah struggled to speak amidst her giggles.

"Could you imagine? Ballard of all people?"

"What's so funny?" Elise asked. "He could be putting your family in real danger."

"Trust me," Richard said. "The last person capable of treason is Ballard. The man has his faults, to be sure, but he's completely loyal to the family."

Sarah leaned forward.

"Speaking of possible treason, I heard they're investigating Lord Fenton," she whispered.

"Your best friend?" Ian asked his brother. "Why would they do something like that?"

Richard's glance flickered on Elise and her friends before he shrugged nonchalantly.

"I was only able to speak to him briefly before he was escorted home. The whole thing seems a terrible joke really. Charlie is innocent. This is just another stunt to make it look like they're actually doing something useful."

"Is it true he was helping Ruby sneak out? I overheard some of the maids talking," said Ian.

Richard shrugged.

"He wouldn't say. He apologized for any negative consequences it would cause, and he's not allowed back until the council meets."

"It's very sad, but I wouldn't be surprised. Ruby has a way of starting drama, attracting trouble wherever she goes," Sarah said, laying her cloth napkin on the table. Elise was glad her aunt couldn't see her fists curled under the table.

She has no idea what Mom is going through. Calm down, Elise. Making a loud scene to defend her won't solve anything right now.

Sarah looked up at the sky.

"Shall we go in soon? It looks like it's going to rain."

Her brothers agreed and finished their meal before excusing themselves.

"It's obviously Ballard," Darcie said when the others had walked inside. "I mean, why can't they—"

Elise shushed her friend as Derek and Joranna stepped out into the courtyard. They seemed to be in better spirits than the last time they had talked and Joranna greeted them with a smile.

"Good morning. It looks like we can make it after all. It's a shame we missed the children."

Derek greeted them as well and their plates were served.

"Let's eat before the weather turns on us," he said before taking a bite.

Elise looked between them and allowed herself to hope for the best.

"How is she?"

Joranna nodded and dabbed her mouth as she swallowed.

"She's sleeping now. We were able to have a good talk, and she even let me help her unpack her trunk. Thank you all for what you did. She told me of her conversation with you, Elise. I can't thank you enough."

It felt awkward to receive praise for doing what just felt like the right thing to do.

"There's a lot to adjust to," Derek said, "but the thought of her feeling like she needed to run hurt the most. I apologize for my methods of finding her out, but I think we're in a good place now to help her."

"What made her change her mind?" asked Elise.

"I think you had a great deal of influence," Derek told her. "She talked highly of your guidance and how you had to push for her to come to us. I'm afraid Ruby takes after me in that regard. I don't always show my emotions. It's not how I was brought up."

"I struggled to understand that when I first came here," Joranna said. "Avalyn always said it was important to hide strong emotions in public, and it took me a long time to learn. But, when we let Ruby hear how we were feeling, she started to understand our reactions better."

"You are all still too young to understand, but one day when you have children, you'll make plans for their lives. You'll want to shield them from everything," said Derek. "And the day you realize they aren't following that path is when the real power struggle begins. You want them independent, but the idea of them not needing you as much hurts in a way I can't describe."

"He's right," Joranna said with a heavy sigh. "Our baby is expecting a baby, and it will take a while to wrap our heads around that."

The four teenagers remained quiet while the king and queen finished their food. They moved inside once it started to sprinkle, so the table and food could be cleaned up.

Elise was dying to find out what was going to happen to Charles.

"Your Majesty," she asked Derek, "can I ask you something?"

But just as he turned towards her, Ballard met up with them.

"Your Majesty, the council is ready for you in your office."

"Thank you, Ballard." Derek turned back to the group. "I have important business to discuss at the moment. If you wouldn't mind waiting in the library for now, I can come find you and we can talk afterward." He called out to Ballard, who had already turned to leave. "Ballard, would you escort them please?"

The other man shifted back and forth and looked like he would've rather done anything else.

"Perhaps they'd be more comfortable waiting in their rooms, Sire? After all, your meetings are known to go on quite longer than expected." His eyes continued to check the hall behind them. "I have some business to finish in the library myself, and I could even have something sent up for them to—"

Derek had grown impatient listening and cut him off.

"The library will do just fine, Ballard. Now."

"Very well, Your Highness."

He bowed his head and glowered at them.

The feeling is mutual, buddy.

She didn't hide her pout and resented having another babysitter. They knew where the library was and could take care of themselves. She was even okay going up to their rooms. They would probably have more privacy. All four dragged their feet and dreaded the supervised waiting period that was to follow.

Ballard paused outside the library with his hand on the handle.

"What's wrong?" Gavin asked.

The other man spun on his heel to face them. He wiped a lock of hair from his forehead and hesitated.

"Allow me to go in and check to make sure everything is in order. I want you to be comfortable."

"Dude, what's going on?" Mitch asked. "Just let us in."

"You will stay here!" He blocked Mitch from stepping around him. "Let me see if any other members of the family are using the room and need solitude. I'll return in a moment."

He opened the door only wide enough for his body to fit through and shut it behind him.

"You were right, Elise. We've got to tell Derek about him again," Darcie said.

"He probably has a secret weapon in there or something. Maybe even hostages," said Mitch.

Elise tried to peek through the keyhole.

"He'd be more discreet than that, but something is up. He definitely doesn't want us in there."

"Well, that's where Derek wants us to wait, and he's in charge, so let's just go in," Gavin said.

A surge of courage rose in Elise's chest and she felt ready to catch the steward in the act. She braced herself for the accusation ahead and turned the handle.

***

From the doorway, they saw no weapons or hostages. The room appeared still until Ballard backed into view against a table. His fingers curled around the edges and his face had gone completely white. Sweat formed on his brow when he spotted them, and his shallowed breathing added to his haggard appearance. His lip quivered as if to speak, but he could only manage to use his eyes. He looked towards the corner blocked by the door. His hands trembled against the supporting wood, and he looked as if he would faint.

A wisp of smoke appeared near his hand as if blown from a cigarette, swirled about in circular motions before settling on the table, and puffed out into a cloud. When it vanished, the diary rested in its place.

Elise could feel her friends stiffen around her. Then her eyes widened as she looked at Ballard again.

You really are the spy.

She jumped out of her skin as a woman poked her head around the door and looked at them. Elise couldn't help but feel like she had seen this woman before.

While she appeared youthful enough, soft gray strands wove through her blonde hair and the lines on her face suggested an anxious existence. She turned to whisper over her shoulder before a familiar voice urged her to hurry them in.

"And close the door, Ingrid!"

Ingrid ushered them inside to stand beside the steward. She checked the hallway again before closing the door behind her.

Elise was startled to see Brahm standing in the corner. Seeing him and the other woman close to each other triggered her memory and she now recognized the woman from Ruby's birthday ball.

"I'm afraid your visit is once again ill-timed," Brahm said. While cordial, Elise felt patronized by his tone the same way she had at the party. He gestured to the woman next to him. "Allow me to introduce my sister, Ingrid. We were settling a few business matters while the king is in his council session. A little harmless research."

His demeanor suggested otherwise.

Elise's inner voice urged her to demand to know what was going on, but she felt paralyzed by fear.

"If you'd all be so kind as to go elsewhere, it would be much appreciated," said Brahm. "I'd be happy to suggest a more suitable location."

It didn't take a genius to hear the underlying threat and know where he meant. Brahm had thrown an absolute fit when Derek had released them from prison.

Gavin cleared his throat behind her.

"Well, Derek told us to wait here for him, so we're going to stay."

"How you have remained in His Majesty's good graces with such informality still baffles me."

"Shall I create a distraction to get them out?" Ingrid asked.

Brahm shook his head and stepped closer to them.

"That won't be necessary. If the king said he will meet them here, then this is where he will find them."

Each step he took seemed calculated and he spoke with such superiority that one would almost think he was the king.

The captain closed the distance between them and looked down at the tremulous man before him.

"There's nothing sinister going on here, is there, Mr. Ballard?" The steward made no reply. "In fact, I believe this good man could do with some wine to settle his nerves. Ingrid, would you be so kind?"

His sister crossed over to a small table that held several bottles and glasses, then prepared a flute, holding it out for Ballard to take. When he didn't accept, Brahm forced it to the man's lips. Ballard sputtered as the wine was poured down his throat. As the captain passed the flute back to his sister, the diary on the table caught his eye.

"What do we have here?"

Elise panicked and sprung for it, but he was quicker. After her hand slammed against the empty table, her pulse quickened as he pulled back the front cover.

She closed her eyes, bracing herself for the suffocating portal. Gavin and the others huddled around her in the same fashion. When nothing happened, they saw Brahm's puzzled expression.

"What sorcery is contained in this?" he asked. "It appears to belong to Her Majesty, but the pages are blank. Now why would you be cowering over an empty diary?"

He shook the book a few times and even ripped a page from it. When nothing happened, he threw the crumpled page into the fire.

"I should return this to the queen." He walked back and forth at a relaxed pace while perusing the book. "Then again, it's much too tattered and useless to be of any interest to her."

All four cried out, threw up their hands and stumbled over one another as he held it above the fire. The commotion only ceased when he paused. The smirk across his face made Elise shrink back.

"Rona will be most intrigued by this." He tucked the book inside his coat and looked upon them like a predator stalking its prey. "She has been asking about you for quite some time."

The name sent a flood of shivers down Elise's back. Rona knew about them already, and it had been Brahm spying all this time. Now that she thought back to the steward's suspicious behaviors, Brahm had never been too far away. The diary had been warning them.

"Why're you doing this, man?" Mitch asked. "The family trusts you!"

"Do you really expect me to stand here and confess everything I've done and plan to do?" He chuckled. His amusement subsided as he approached them. "But I will congratulate Mr. Ballard." His voice dropped to almost a whisper, then he moved within inches from the other man's face. "The king's little lap dog here has been tracking me for years, convinced of my guilt and wavering allegiance. Was it worth it, old man?" Brahm unsheathed his sword and placed the blade under the steward's chin, making him flinch. The captain ordered him to stand tall and stop being such a coward. Ballard composed himself and stepped in front of Elise and her friends. Brahm chuckled. "And now he's a martyr. A man of many noble qualities."

He pulled back and struck Ballard on the head with the hilt of his sword, causing the weaker gentleman to fall unconscious at his feet.

"That's better. Now," he said, holding his blade out towards them, "Ingrid and I were in the process of collecting some very important documents, and I will not be outed by a group of sniveling teenaged outsiders. You four have caused me many headaches over the years." He patted his chest pocket. "But now I know your secret, and if you want it to remain your secret, you will back out of this room and forget what you saw. Is that clear?"

Elise looked down at Ballard's unconscious body. Before she could talk herself out of it, she pulled the vial of fairy magic out of Gavin's pocket.

With quicker reflexes, Brahm's blade knocked it from her hands. It landed on the carpet and rolled several feet away still corked. Elise's relief of its condition was only short-lived as Ingrid walked over to pick it up.

"Looks like they have more secrets. This is rare magic indeed," she purred. She ran her fingers along the glass and gazed upon its contents longingly.

Her brother snatched it from her grasp.

"Don't forget yourself, Sister. Keep your wits about you and don't fall victim to its charms."

With his attention elsewhere, Gavin and Mitch exchanged looks before lunging forward. While Brahm was stronger in every sense, their force was enough to push him off balance, causing him to trip over Ballard's body.

Ingrid rushed to aid her brother, but Elise and Darcie grabbed her arms. Twisting against their hold, she stomped Darcie's foot with her heel.

Darcie cried out, releasing her grip. Before Ingrid could swing around to Elise, however, Darcie grabbed two fistfuls of the blonde's hair. Shrieking, Ingrid clawed at Darcie's wrists. Between the two of them, they were able to wrestle her to the ground with her hands behind her back.

Darcie straddled her, keeping a firm grip on her head, while Elise swung her leg over to sit backwards on Ingrid's hands. She used her feet to pin down the older woman's flailing legs. With Ingrid restrained, they watched the chaos unfold before them.

Mitch had somehow come to possess the vial and was now being chased. Brahm was only feet behind him, but his pace was hindered with Gavin on his back. Gavin wrapped his arms around the captain's neck and was trying to apply as much pressure as he could. He dug his heels into the man's ribs until Brahm backed him into one of the bookshelves. The force caused several books to tumble onto the floor. One thrust didn't shake Gavin, but by the fourth or fifth attempt, the wind had been knocked out of him. He fell on top of the pile of books.

Free of the extra weight, Brahm turned and lifted his sword above Gavin.

"Hey!" Mitch called out. He had climbed on top of a table and uncorked the vial. "Leave him alone or I will throw this at your face!"

Brahm weighed the threat.

It was at that moment that Ballard gained consciousness and upon seeing the captain at a standstill with Mitch, scrambled over to assist Gavin.

"So, what do you think happens now, boy?" Brahm called out. "You play the hero and win the girl?" Mitch's eyes flickered to Darcie, but he remained focused. "I was training to fight before you were even born, so don't be stupid."

Mitch looked around at his options. His fingers tightened around the glass, and he licked his lips. Ingrid had finally ceased resisting, but Elise and Darcie couldn't release her. With Ballard's help, Gavin was trying to push one of the shelves onto Brahm, but they were built in, unable to be toppled.

Mitch cleared his throat and tried to appear taller. He corked the vial.

"Give back the diary. Let us go. You can have the magic."

"Do it, Brahm." Ingrid strained against the carpet. "Think of what we could do with a spell of our choice! It's more useful than any paths we were planning. Let them have the stupid book. It's useless anyway."

"If it were useless, they wouldn't want it," Brahm said. "No one would give away fairy magic for nothing."

"Gavin, think fast!" Mitch called and tossed the vial over the man's head.

Brahm reacted too late, and his fingers only grazed the glass before it landed in Gavin's hands.

"You fools!" he bellowed as he considered which boy to follow. "I am not playing these childish games. You're toying with dangerous magic and it's going to get you killed."

Mitch leapt from the table and landed on Brahm's shoulders, effectively knocking the bigger man to the ground.

Ballard took the opportunity to run up and pull Joranna's diary out of the captain's coat, but as he was about to get away, Brahm grabbed his foot. The steward came crashing to the floor and had just enough time to throw the diary in Gavin's direction.

Mitch scrambled through the pile of discarded books on the floor and began smashing them over Brahm's head to give Gavin enough time to scoop up the diary.

Gavin was so preoccupied that he didn't see one of the thicker books slide across the floor until he turned his ankle on it trying to run away.

The diary bounced and landed a few feet from Elise, who attempted to grab it while still pinning Ingrid down. Gavin tried to stand but couldn't bear weight on his ankle and tripped again.

"Are you okay?" she called.

"Yeah." His voice was strained. "Just don't let him get it."

Brahm was already stumbling to his feet. Gavin tossed the vial back over to Mitch, who just barely caught it before it smashed on a table. He started pulling chairs and scooting tables to slow Brahm's path.

Elise's fingertips nudged the corner of the diary.

"I think I can hold her for a second. Go for it," Darcie said.

Elise leaned forward but Brahm's boot slammed down on the book. She looked up to see his sword in one hand and Ballard's collar in the other. The steward squirmed against his hold, but the captain pulled against the fabric, choking him into submission.

"You have the *gall* to try and overpower me? When will you learn that you are nothing but foolish children? There are forces in play here you couldn't possibly fathom."

Elise looked at Ballard groveling, begging for mercy. He hung his head. She had wasted so much time hating and accusing that now she could only pity him.

"Clearly, you can see I have my hands full," Brahm purred down to Elise and scooted the book to her without lifting his boot. "Be a good little girl and put it back where I had it."

When she hesitated, he lifted the blade to Ballard's neck.

"Don't do it, Elise!" Gavin cried.

Darcie shook her head while Mitch was steadily creeping up behind Brahm with the vial. He had even gone so far as to uncork it and was within throwing distance before Ingrid cried out for her brother to move.

Darcie clasped a hand over her mouth, but it was too late. In a fit of rage, the captain lunged Ballard forward into Mitch, knocking both to the ground before he spun around.

Elise felt a wave of relief that Mitch had at least been able to re-cork the vial in time. It hadn't broken. She grabbed the diary at the same time as Brahm, who lifted her to her feet. He jerked it from her hands. Once it was stuffed back into his coat, he wrapped a hand around her neck.

Darcie and Gavin cried out, as the latter began hobbling towards her.

Elise felt the thick fingers press deeper against her throat.

To her left, she heard a scuffle and watched as Ingrid rolled over to gain the upper hand with Darcie. Mitch, who had started running to help Elise, now looked between both girls. Gavin propelled himself into Brahm, giving Mitch the chance to help Darcie, but the larger man nudged him off with a blow from his shoulder. To her right, she saw Ballard slink out of the room and felt all of her hope disappear. Looking into the eyes of her killer, she tried her best to brace herself.

Her fear peaked in a way she had never experienced as a numbness crept into her fingertips that resembled electric shocks. She felt like her head was swimming. When he dug in his thumbs, her vision blurred before all turned black.

***

She didn't know where she was, but she was aware that she was lying down. Distorted voices called her name.

"Are you okay?" they asked.

I think so. My head just hurts.

Someone was shaking her shoulders and she heard crying. Her eyes opened. The library ceiling and the surrounding bookshelves swam into view before her vision settled on her friends sitting beside her.

"What happened?"

"Oh, thank God you're okay!" Darcie sniffled and threw her arms around her best friend.

Elise made to sit up, and Gavin moved quickly to help her go slower.

"Easy." He massaged her back and she noticed that his reddened eyelids betrayed he had also been crying.

As her memories came flooding back, she felt in her right mind again. She looked down at Gavin's leg.

"How's your ankle?"

He smiled and chuckled under his breath.

"You almost die, and you're worried about me," he said. "I'll be fine."

She looked around the room. Ballard was talking to Derek and Joranna near a handful of guards by the door.

"Where's Brahm and Ingrid?"

"Oh man, it was awesome!" Mitch said as if retelling the ending of a favorite action film. "Brahm had his sword up ready to kill you. Gavin was down for the count, and Brahm had us beat. I was about to dump the magic out of the vial when his sword levitated out of his hand!"

"Ballard was able to reach Derek in time. He used his magic to disarm Brahm," said Darcie.

Gavin jumped in.

"Yeah, then the guards came in and arrested him and Ingrid."

Elise looked over at the steward. The one she anticipated having arrested had saved them all. She stood with Darcie's assistance while Mitch helped Gavin stand against the wall.

She waited for an opportunity to interrupt. When Joranna saw her, she threw out her arms to hug Elise.

"You're all right!" she cried. The queen was practically in hysterics and began to assess her on the spot. "Is anything broken? Are you hurt?"

"I'm fine, but Gavin's ankle is in pretty bad shape." She bit her lip and took a deep breath before holding out her hand towards Ballard. "Thank you. . .for everything."

Rather than shake back, he turned her hand over and leaned down to kiss it.

"It was my duty, Miss. I'm glad to see you've recovered."

Elise thanked Derek as well before heading back over to her friends. She gasped and checked the floor around them.

"Where's the diary? The vial?"

"Taken care of." Mitch winked and lifted the flap of his coat to reveal the diary tucked away. Gavin patted his own pocket with the vial in it. "Should we get going then?"

"Going?" Joranna exclaimed. "You're not going anywhere yet! Not until his ankle is mended and you're all examined."

Knowing there was no use in arguing, the four allowed themselves to be escorted out while the doctor was promptly summoned.

CHAPTER 27

After being examined, Elise, Mitch, and Darcie waited outside of the guest room where Gavin was being treated. It didn't take long before Ruby had gotten word of the events from the library, and she soon sought them out.

"Ian just told me," she said. "So, it was the captain all this time?" They nodded. "Father must feel so betrayed. Where is your friend?"

"He's inside with the doctor. It's a bad sprain, but he said he has an ointment that will heal it by tomorrow morning," said Elise.

"The perks of living in a world with magic," said Mitch.

"Speaking of magic, why didn't my sister just heal him?"

"The king asked if she would, but she said she felt more comfortable having the doctor look in case she made it worse," Darcie said.

Mitch scoffed.

"If he's like me, he's probably skeptical of any magic touching him. I know I was when I got hurt. She probably would've done a good job, though. Then we could already be home."

"So, you're planning on leaving when he's healed?" Ruby asked.

They nodded.

"There's not much left for us to do. We need to get home," Darcie said.

Ruby turned to Elise.

"If that be the case, could I have a word with you for a moment?"

Elise followed her down the hall to where they would have more privacy. Ruby looked around to make sure they wouldn't be overheard and lowered her voice to a whisper.

"As odd as it sounds, I'm going to miss you. You irritated me more than anything." She chuckled. "But you got me to start thinking more clearly about the future. My family surprised me too."

"I'm so glad," Elise said. She wished she could lean forward and hug her mother, but Ruby was showing a vulnerable side that Elise didn't want to scare off. "Did you find out what's going to happen to Charles?"

Ruby's smile wilted and she looked down at the floor and nodded.

"Lord Fenton will receive a warning and get to keep his position in court. Richard hopes to make him his chief adviser one day, so that's what he will be working towards."

"Wow, just like that? That's great! Why do you seem so sad about it?"

She fiddled with her fingers and still made no eye contact. She took a deep breath to keep her emotions in check.

"He will be granted that lifestyle on the condition that he doesn't pursue any type of relationship with me. Otherwise, his title is stripped. A marriage will be arranged as soon as possible for me, and if I progress along normally, it will be excused as premature when I do deliver."

Elise's mind felt like it was going to explode. Her temper rose and she struggled to find her words.

No, this isn't how I wanted it to happen. It's not fair!

"But that's not right! Your dad got to marry an outsider. Charles is at least a lord, so there's nothing inappropriate about it. Why not let you marry him, then pretend it's his baby? At least that way, you can be happy!"

Ruby shrugged and smiled.

"A princess's duty is to follow and not question."

Elise gave her a look that said she didn't buy her reasoning.

"Ruby, no offense, but you've done anything but follow the rules lately. I don't see why this has to be an exception. You love each other. Why don't you fight more for it?"

"For the time being, this is just how things have to be," she said. "I made my choices and now I have to accept the consequences of them. Thanks to you, my options already look better than they might've had I left, and I won't let him choose me over this promised position that will guarantee him happiness. Don't feel sorry for us, Elise. We'll both avoid the scandal and eventually move on."

Elise didn't believe anything she was hearing and knew that neither would move on so fast. If this was the path that was supposed to be better thanks to her, she shuddered to think what her mother's original experience had been. She was caught off guard when Ruby leaned in to hug her. She wrapped her arms around her mother and knew she held on a moment longer than was necessary, but she didn't care.

***

Once they were permitted to visit Gavin, Elise gathered them all together by his bed and relayed what Ruby had just told her.

"What kind of backwards medieval crap is that?" Darcie fumed.

"If they're in love and there has to be a wedding, why can't they just marry each other?" Gavin asked.

"That's what I said," Elise said. "But enough people know about what happened now to stop any rumors. If they rush to get married, it makes the scandal worse."

"So, what did talking her into staying do to help any?" Mitch asked. "Weren't we supposed to guarantee her a fairy tale ending or something? It sounds like we made it worse."

"I thought the same thing, but the way she talked, this will be better. I'm not sure how much I believe her, but the fact she's talking with the family shows some improvement."

Gavin sighed.

"I guess we won't know until we travel back and see."

"I've been thinking about that, guys," Darcie said. Her expression soured and her tone grew serious. "What if we altered

Rona's plans so much that there are no present-day Laurilles back home? Now that Ruby's staying and getting married, they may not have to flee or start a new life. What will we actually be heading home to?"

There was a heavy silence between them.

"She has a point," said Gavin. "We never actually got to meet Rona to know for sure. Do you think she'll still be a threat?"

"I'm sure she'll find her ways," said Elise. "I mean, Brahm can't be the only spy she has out there. He was just the closest to the royal family."

"You guys are making it sound like we didn't do anything," Mitch said. "We did exactly what we were sent here to do. The spy was found, and Elise's mom stayed home. We even ended up with the diary and a vial of magic! So, let's just trust that the universe knows what it's doing and celebrate a win for once."

"The magic! Mitch, you're a genius," Darcie said. "We could use the magic to insure where we go. If we imagine your grandmother's house just the way it was, it would have to take us there, right?"

Elise chuckled.

"You're putting a lot of faith and possibility into one vial."

"But the little fairy said it's good for one powerful spell or travel. Maybe we can bypass your grandmother's altogether and just wish ourselves to our own houses!" Darcie bounced on the balls of her feet.

"I'd have my car back though, right?"

Darcie ignored Mitch's question and continued ranting on about how much time they could save by just going home to see what happened.

"We wouldn't have to risk getting back and no one being there," she said.

"That sounds like an easy fix, but I want to see my grandmother's house for myself. If no one is there, at least the car should be and we can drive home. If they are there, I want to see and tell them for myself."

"Won't they know since they lived it?"

Again, Mitch was ignored.

"It feels weird that it's over," said Elise. "We just weren't meant to meet Rona like we thought. I mean, the diary wouldn't have shown up if it wasn't ready for us to travel through it. Like Mitch said, we finished what we came to do, so I don't know why it would send us to a battle instead of home. The timeline is bound to have fixed itself. I don't know that I want to waste a fairy spell on something that could happen naturally."

"That makes sense," Gavin said.

We just have to trust the diary to get us safely back.

"It will be interesting to see what we can use that magic on later if we save it," Mitch said.

The conversation took a pleasant turn as they began sharing possible ideas before they were interrupted by a knock at the door.

Derek and Joranna asked if Gavin was up to more visitors. Two chairs were pulled up for them beside the bed, and they inquired how everyone was feeling.

"We heard that you have plans on leaving in the morning. I can't express our thanks enough and tell you how sorely you'll be missed," Derek said. "Haighdlen is indebted to you once again."

"So, what happens now?" Darcie asked.

"Brahm has obviously lost his position and honors, and he has been arrested with his sister. Both are being sentenced within the week," the king replied.

"I still can't believe it was him all along, lying straight to our faces. Is there anything we can do to repay you?" Joranna asked.

Elise assured them that their hospitality and free food was enough, but something else came to mind that still bothered her.

"Do you think now you could review Mr. Archer's prison sentence?" Derek looked uncomfortable. "I know it's not common to do, but I just have this feeling he shouldn't be in there."

Derek and Joranna shared a look before he sighed.

"Considering Brahm led most of the investigations, I think I have quite a bit of reviewing to do. Consider it done."

A smile broke across Elise's face, and she felt elated by his promise.

Derek cleared his throat.

"I feel like there has been enough doom and gloom around here for one afternoon. Shall we collect the children and all take a carriage ride through the kingdom to celebrate your last night in Haighdlen?" He glanced at Gavin's elevated ankle. "I'm sure I could get the doctor to release you for it."

"I think I'll stay here and sleep for a while. The doctor gave me something for the pain that's starting to work," Gavin said.

"Very well then. We'll meet the rest of you out front with the carriages," said Derek as he and Joranna left to find the others.

Elise turned back to look down at Gavin. Struggling to keep his eyes open, he smiled up at her uncertain expression.

"I'm fine." He laughed. "I'm just really tired. By morning, I'll be ready to go. I'll even hang onto the diary and keep it safe tonight in case you're out late."

"You sure, man?" asked Mitch. "We can stay here with you."

"I don't want to go without you," Elise said. She brushed a few locks of hair out of his eyes. "They can go, and I'll stay."

"There's no need. I have the doctor here, and they're offering you a fun night out before you have to leave this place. I don't want you wasting it sitting here. Now's your chance to go enjoy it without any guilt or to-do list." When she hesitated again, he pulled out the diary. "If you don't, I'll open it right now and you'll have to drag me to a hospital when we land wherever."

"Okay, okay." She giggled as he nudged her off the bed. "It just won't be the same."

"Glad to know I'm the glue that holds y'all together." They laughed before he addressed her again. "Take the vial with you. The doc may confiscate it if he finds it. And I mean it, have fun."

She nodded and leaned down to kiss him. He squeezed her hand and said goodbye to the other two before they left him to sleep.

***

As they stepped out of the castle doors, they found the royal family, mounted guards, and two carriages. The clouds had cleared, allowing the bright sunlight to be reflected off the ivory towers.

Derek and the princes mounted their horses. A footman helped Joranna step into the first carriage to join the princesses while another footman approached the four teenagers.

Once they had taken their seats, the door closed beside them. Derek called out, and with a lurch, the carriages began to move.

"Cheer up, Elise," Mitch said. "If Gav were here right now, he'd probably be drooling on your shoulder."

Darcie agreed.

"Yeah, he's probably already asleep."

Their sentiments cheered her up a bit, but Elise still wished that Gavin could be there with her.

She looked back longingly at the castle and resolved to enjoy herself as he had instructed her to do.

As they passed through the gates, her mind traveled back to their previous conversation. She wondered what they would find at her grandmother's house. Rona was still out there and even knew about them. That thought alone should've filled her with dread, but as she gazed out the window at her family's horses and carriage, she smiled.

She was surprised to realize that she didn't feel an inkling of fear about the future or the unknown. They had done what they set out to do, and come morning, they would be home. Those worries could wait for another day.

We did it. Everything is going to be okay.

She closed her eyes and let the cool breeze blow across her face. She imagined a great weight being lifted from her shoulders and relaxed back in her seat to enjoy the view. The three took turns pointing out the various sights and laughing together.

For the time being, they were safe, and that was enough.

Restoring
The
Throne

PROLOGUE

Haighdlen's former Captain of the Guard was now a prisoner in the dungeon beneath the castle.

After being accused of treason by the king himself, Brahm was locked away and the guards given strict orders to limit communications with him. The one on duty had yet to even make eye contact.

Slouching against the cold steel bars, Brahm scoffed at his predicament. The irony of being imprisoned within one of the cells he once filled with his own prisoners was almost laughable.

These fools are so blindly loyal to Derek Laurille, they are incapable of forming any real opinions of their own.

Admittedly, their willingness to conform had served him well up until his arrest.

Everyone in this forsaken hole knows that I'm the reason this powerful army is feared.

His life had been devoted to training the very soldiers who turned a cold shoulder to him. Now there was nothing to show for it.

And it was all because of *her*.

A stupid, meddlesome, red-headed brat.

Elise Laurille had swooped in with her companions to poison the minds of the royal family. By foiling his plans to aid Rona claim the throne, they not only succeeded in tarnishing his reputation, but that of his sister as well.

Closing his eyes, Brahm recalled his final moments with Elise only hours before.

The soft delicate skin of her neck had been warm against his hand. He could still feel Elise's racing pulse throbbing against his thumb. She was mere seconds from death.

If only I had acted quicker. . .

The sudden sound of a woman's cry brought him back to reality. A sorrowful, tortured plea—normally music to his ears—lost all of its pleasantness when coming from his sister.

Each of Ingrid's sobs twisted a knife further into Brahm's otherwise hardened stomach.

He squeezed the bars until his knuckles turned white.

If you hurt her, I will end you, he promised whoever was escorting her closer. Just a few more steps and he'd have a new victim.

Brahm was robbed of any satisfaction as Ingrid's body was thrust to the cold stone floor less than twenty feet in front of him. Grunting from the impact, she crawled, sobbing, into the cell across from his. Fading footsteps indicated whoever brought her wasn't going to be showing their face anytime soon.

The silent guard outside of Brahm's cell joined her, prompting Ingrid to tug at his leg—begging for mercy—only to be kicked off.

Ingrid cowered in the corner of her cell, whimpering as she watched the key turn in the lock.

Brahm's blood boiled.

"You're dead the next time you touch her! Do you understand?"

"Shut up."

Oh, now you want to talk.

"If they beat her—"

"Shut it, will you? You no longer have power here."

Brahm responded by spitting at the other man's feet.

The guard's sword was half unsheathed when an approaching man stopped him. Brahm recognized his friend, Sanders's, voice.

Sanders, my most trusted friend. It's about time.

Based on the look of his uniform and assertive tone, Sanders had recently advanced in rank.

"I'll take it from here," Sanders told the guard on duty.

"I'm on strict orders not to leave this post until morning, sir."

Rather than argue, Sanders cocked his head back and slammed it against the other man's. The guard's body fell with a heavy thud.

Brahm nodded appreciatively.

"You're getting better."

"Learned from the best."

"Well, hurry up then!" Brahm hissed.

Sanders struggled to loosen the keys from the unconscious man's belt.

Brahm glanced in the direction of the main doors, still hidden by darkness. They only had a few minutes to make this work.

When the cell creaked open, allowing his escape, he placed a grateful hand upon his friend's shoulder.

"Your loyalty has not gone unnoticed."

He kept watch while Sanders unlocked Ingrid's cell.

Throwing her arms around her savior's neck, Ingrid nuzzled her tear-soaked face against his stubbled cheek.

"When this is all over," she purred, "I can thank you properly for old times' sake."

Brahm cleared his throat.

"That's enough, Ingrid. We need to get going. I need a uniform from the office."

"Why not take his?" she asked, pointing to the body at their feet.

"We can't risk him regaining consciousness first. Help me move him," he ordered.

After locking the guard inside Brahm's cell, the three made their way towards the former captain's office. Knowing the main corridors would be monitored, Brahm took them through a secret passageway within the stone wall that opened just outside their destination. Knowing the castle better than anyone, he wasn't about to let a group of vigilante teenagers be his demise.

Once Sanders unlocked the door, Brahm was pleased to find the room untouched. He wasted no time throwing open the doors of his wardrobe for the extra uniform he kept there. After changing, he hid his face beneath a helmet. Removing any signs of his original rank, he turned towards a mirror on the wall before nodding with approval.

He collected several documents, as well as a hidden stash of money, from his desk. Crossing the room, he also retrieved a small velvet bag and a dagger from his safe.

"Where is His Majesty now?" he asked Sanders.

"Several guards escorted the royal family to town for some evening entertainment."

"Did the travelers join them?"

"All but one."

"The red-head?" He dared to hope it would be that easy.

"I do not know, sir. My sources tell me one stayed behind with the doctor."

While a swift escape was necessary, Brahm knew that he wouldn't get this opportunity again to possibly catch Elise on her own.

"We will go there first then."

He tucked the velvet bag inside his uniform jacket with the documents and money before concealing his dagger inside his boot.

Sanders's eyes widened in horror.

"But, sir! If you're caught—"

Brahm held up his hand to silence him before grabbing Ingrid's arm.

"You take her other side," he told Sanders. "If anyone asks, she's been summoned for further questioning. We are simply her escorts." He instructed his sister to keep her mouth shut as he led them out into the corridor again.

Hearing their footsteps echoing around them, as well as Ingrid's panicked shallow breaths in his ear, he attempted to get a grip on his nerves as he watched over his shoulder for any followers. They passed a total of six other guards along the way. Nothing appeared out of the ordinary. No one questioned their intentions until they reached the entrance. Two guards blocked their path as a third stood up from a nearby desk. Brahm recognized the latter as his lieutenant.

"What's all this then?" the lieutenant challenged. "This prisoner was already ordered back to her cell."

Sanders cleared his throat.

"I was sent to retrieve her for further questioning."

"By whom? I have received no news of this summons."

Brahm scowled at his friend.

Say something, you fool!

Sanders shifted from one foot to the other before clearing his throat. He tightened his hold on Ingrid's arm.

"An emergency council meeting has been called. The king entrusted the task to me personally. He wishes for the prisoner to be ready upon his return."

There was a long pause as the three were sized up.

Brahm was impressed by Sanders's ability to think on his feet. He held his breath as the lieutenant looked between them before his gaze settled on the keys hanging from Sanders's belt. Ingrid's lip quivered while Brahm held his breath.

Despite his obvious inner battle, the lieutenant tightened his jaw and nodded.

They had not taken two steps forward before the lieutenant cleared his throat.

"How many men will you be requiring?"

"I think we can manage, sir," Sanders replied.

The lieutenant sneered with disapproval.

"Standard protocol states that a minimum of six escorts be present for transfers and summons."

Brahm remained silent, knowing there were too many men present to do anything stupid. Sanders chanced a quick glance in his direction before stumbling his way through another excuse.

"I commend your loyalty to protocol, Lieutenant. However, the king wishes to avoid any more gossip and scandals where this investigation is concerned. He requested a more discreet approach."

"Then why didn't he—"

"Best not to question His Majesty's actions," Sanders warned, cutting the other gentleman off. "You wouldn't want to end up like the disgraced captain, would you?"

A tense moment passed between them.

Brahm's temper flared at the mention of his status, but they were so close to succeeding for him to throw it all away. He would let it slide. . .this time.

At long last, they were allowed to pass.

Feeling the lieutenant's eyes burning a hole into his back, Brahm hastened their pace. Sanders knocked on the low ceiling until a guard opened a hidden door above them. One by one, they were helped out of the dungeon into the dark entryway of the tower.

Almost there.

The walk from the tower to the castle was longer than Brahm remembered. A layer of sweat formed along his brow while he braced himself for any further obstacles. He released the breath he had been holding when they approached the courtyard entrance to the castle. Nodding to the guard on duty, with Brahm's identity still hidden, the three stepped through the French doors into the ballroom. In a matter of seconds, they crossed over the grand dance floor towards the main hall.

Brahm looked in both directions to see if the coast was clear. Only a handful of servants were present. If they were going to take any chances of reaching the doctor, now was it.

"There's no way we're going to get away with this." Ingrid wept as her knees buckled beneath her. She slumped against her brother. "We're as good as dead."

Brahm growled as he and Sanders straightened her up again.

"Woman, compose yourself at once! I did not bring you this far to hear your constant sniveling. Now, not another word."

His sister tightened her lips into a thin line to suppress another sob before being led towards the hall of guest rooms the doctor usually reserved for his visits.

After searching most of the usual rooms, Brahm felt a twinge of doubt. Perhaps he was mistaken. Maybe he had missed his opportunity.

Then, as luck would have it, the doctor stepped out of the last door and jumped when he saw them.

"I beg your pardon. You startled me there." He bowed before he stepped around them. "If you'll excuse me, I'm just off for more supplies."

Brahm waited for the doctor to be out of sight before approaching the door.

This was it.

His heart raced as he imagined what he'd find on the other side. Would Elise scream? Would she try to run? His hand twitched with anticipation as he slowly turned the knob.

The room was quiet when he stepped inside. The curtains were lowered, enveloping the room in darkness except three candles on the dresser. Brahm crept towards the bed in search of red hair.

Pulling back the blankets, he was disappointed to find Elise's troublesome suitor instead. He grunted, threw the linens back down, and spun sharply on his heel. He had wasted precious time for nothing.

What was that?

Something caught his attention in the mirror across the room. Looking back down at the bed, he noticed something sticking out from under the young man. Brahm removed the blankets once again and leaned closer.

Well, well, well. What is this?

Carefully sliding it out from under Gavin, Brahm instantly recognized the same diary he tried to steal earlier.

My time has not been wasted after all. Rona will be most pleased.

Gavin rolled onto his side with a groan.

Brahm inspected the tattered purple cover. Nothing seemed particularly extraordinary about it, but the way Elise and the others had reacted, he knew better than to be fooled by its plain appearance. While nothing happened the last time, he still couldn't fight the urge to open it again.

Just as he lifted the cover, he jumped when the door cracked open. Sanders poked his head inside. Seeing Brahm alone, he pulled Ingrid into the room with him before closing the door.

"Everything all right, sir?"

"What's taking so long?" Ingrid asked.

Brahm held up the diary. Ingrid's eyes widened as she clapped her hands together with a squeal. Brahm held a finger over his mouth.

"Brother, you did it! You must get it to Queen Rona at once!"

"What is it?" Sanders whispered.

"Protection," Brahm replied. "This will certainly keep us in Rona's good graces. I was hoping to find the girl with it."

All three looked down at the bed.

"Could he be worth something though?" Ingrid asked. "Surely any of them are better than nothing, right?"

Brahm weighed his options.

"Sir, we really must be going. The risk is greater now more than ever," Sanders reminded him.

Brahm tucked the diary into his uniform jacket.

"Ingrid is right," he said, pulling out the velvet bag he had retrieved from his safe. Taking her hand, he tilted the bag, pouring a small amount of powder into her palm. "Take this, Sister. Collect your daughter and go to Lockesbarrow. Await my instructions."

"Alone?" she asked. "Can't Sanders go with me?"

"We can't risk his absence being noticed as well. Go to my cottage. I will join you as soon as I can."

Brahm didn't want her traveling by herself, but she would be safer traveling to his cottage than to Rona's castle with him.

Ingrid hesitated and glanced up at Sanders, who nodded for her to comply. Taking a deep breath, she tossed the powder up in the air before vanishing.

"Will she be safe on her own?" Sanders inquired. He coughed while swatting his hand at the remaining powder in the air. "I would've gladly accompanied her."

"There is no need for that."

Stepping behind Sanders, Brahm reached down and removed the dagger from his boot.

Before Sanders could react, Brahm clasped his hand over the other man's mouth and stabbed the dagger into his neck in one swift motion. As Sanders fell to the ground, gurgling, the former captain frowned.

"I am sorry, old friend."

But I can't risk any loose ends here.

Gavin rolled over with a stretch as overlapping shouts came from the hall demanding every room be checked. Various doors were opened and slammed shut. The search party was getting closer. Brahm stepped over Sanders's twitching body towards the bed. He covered Gavin's mouth but wasn't quick enough to escape an elbow strike to the stomach. Despite Gavin's flailing body, Brahm was able to pin him down while fumbling with the velvet bag.

A moment later, the door burst open as the lieutenant entered with four guards. Floating dust particles wafted through air as the room was searched. Only one lifeless body was found inside.

Brahm's original guard, now freed from his cell, immediately began helping the lieutenant assess Sanders.

"Find and alert His Majesty at once!" ordered the lieutenant. "The royal family is in danger!"

CHAPTER 1

Gavin Striess jerked awake in complete darkness.

He became immediately aware that he was gagged with his hands and feet bound. Judging by the coarse texture, he assumed with rope. He bit down on the cloth between his teeth. Its thickness would stifle any attempts he made to call for help. After pulling against his restraints, he only managed to make them tighter.

Taking a moment to gain his bearings, he deduced that he was also lying blindfolded on a moving surface with squeaky wheels. A cart, maybe? That would explain the sounds of hooves, not to mention the way his body continued to bounce from what felt like a bumpy road. Chills coursed through him despite the warm breeze against his skin.

Where am I? How did I get out of the castle?

To prevent himself from panicking, he tried to assess the situation. If he were going to escape, staying focused was key. He had seen documentaries about how to escape car trunks, but horse-drawn carts never seemed to make it on the news.

He'd have to attempt rolling off. Gavin turned his ankle in a circular motion to confirm that it had healed. He could likely survive the fall if he knew he wouldn't be caught directly after. Despite being blindfolded, he closed his eyes. Taking a deep breath, he listened for any clues to help him. When that didn't help, he spent the next several minutes visualizing his options, each one ending in excruciating pain. As he let his thoughts wander, he remembered the diary he had been guarding.

Did it get stolen too? Maybe it's on the cart right now.
He thought about Elise, Mitch, and Darcie.
Do they know I'm gone? Are they safe?
He had to get back to them, even if he didn't manage to get the diary. Seeing his friends again was worth suffering any temporary injuries—though that didn't mean he was looking forward to a possible broken bone or two. He swallowed as best he could around the gag, bracing his body for impact. Even if the cart didn't have an open back, he hoped with enough force, he could break free anyway. Closing his eyes, he tucked his arms against his sides before hurling his body towards the other end of the cart.

After two or three rolls, however, the cart came to an abrupt stop and slammed him against the opposite end near the driver. He groaned as his shoulder was crushed from the impact.

Gavin perked up at the sound of a gravelly chuckle.

"Serves you right."

I know that voice. Who is that?

He wasn't given time to figure it out as someone grabbed his foot and pulled. His back slid smoothly against the bed of the cart until his legs hung over the edge.

"Stay still," the driver ordered.

Not trusting his chances of escaping at the present moment, Gavin had no choice but to comply with the command. He felt a strong hand grip him around one of his ankles before hearing the sound of a knife slicing through the ropes.

Why is he freeing me? This makes no sense.

Confused, he lay paralyzed with fear. When his feet were released, he heard more footsteps approaching.

Strong hands jerked at his collar, forcing him to stand. Gavin wobbled on the spot before being made to walk forwards in darkness.

The gruff voice barked orders for the horse to be taken care of. The animal whinnied as it was led away. As the squeaking wheel on the cart also faded, Gavin felt a renewed sense of panic rise within him.

The kidnapper dragged him by his shirt along an uneven path. Painful rocks crunched beneath Gavin's bare feet, causing him to stumble blindly multiple times. His groans and curses were ignored.

He could mentally picture his boots positioned neatly under the bed where the doctor had been treating him back at the castle. The memory sent more thoughts circulating through his mind about his friends' whereabouts.

Had something happened when they went to the town? Were they hurt?

He thought of Elise.

If anything happens to her. . .

Gavin tripped as the ground sloped downward. Hearing the creaking sound of a metal gate opening sent his heart hammering within his chest.

Is this some kind of prison?

The soaked gag caused drool to build up at the corners of his mouth until he couldn't help but cough. The stranger smacked him on the back, too close to his injured shoulder. Gavin winced.

"Straighten up."

Gavin did his best to comply. His wrists were rubbed raw from his previous attempts to pull free. His palms were freshly coated with new sweat. The rocks, now smaller and sharper, cut into his feet. He tried slowing down his breathing to hear better. Several deep voices talked nearby. Horses whinnied in the distance. The air smelled damp.

"Well, well, well," said a voice a few feet away. "I've seen everything now. Word's been around this morning that you were caught. Didn't think you'd be showing up here again. Come to get a beating from Rona herself, have you?"

Several other men laughed.

Is that Brahm?

It couldn't be. He had been arrested.

"Why have you come back?" a second voice asked.

"I have something for Her Majesty," came the reply as the same hand clapped against Gavin's shoulder, making him groan.

Gavin froze, knowing he was being sized up.

"Her Majesty is not expecting any new recruits. Especially a weakling such as this. You'd best be on your way."

Gavin's blood boiled. Had his hands not been tied together, he would've already connected his fist with both of their jaws.

"He's anything but weak. I believe she will make an exception," said his kidnapper. "I have some useful information for her as well." When no reply came, he growled. "You don't want to make an enemy of me. Open the gate."

The threat proved successful as the gate creaked open in front of them. Gavin was ushered forward by his collar once more. There was no doubt in his mind now. It was Brahm. He tried to wrap his head around how this could have happened.

There's no way Derek would've freed him. Not after everything he's done. How did he get away?

This man was dangerous. Gavin would have to tread carefully if he were going to have a chance of getting back to the others.

Another set of doors closed behind them. Gavin immediately felt that the air was colder here. It was also too quiet.

He shivered, making the hairs on the back of his neck stand up.

Where is he taking me? Are we even still in Haighdlen? Where is the diary?

A second set of doors were opened for them. Brahm's footsteps now echoed against a hard floor. Gavin was thankful for the cool surface against his bare feet. The sound of swords unsheathing made him and Brahm stop dead in their tracks.

Hushed whispers spread throughout the room. Gavin angled his head to catch what they were saying.

"Who is that?" someone asked.

"Disgraceful," replied another.

"Her Majesty will not be pleased."

The blindfold was suddenly ripped off of Gavin's face, causing him to turn away from the harsh light. When his eyes finally stopped burning, he opened them one at a time and blinked until they adjusted to the brightness of the room. Brahm nudged the back of his knees until they buckled so that Gavin now sat in a kneeling position on the floor. Brahm followed with his own bow before motioning for Gavin to turn his attention to the opposite end of the room.

They were in a massive throne room that rivaled Haighdlen's in architectural beauty. Four oversized crystal chandeliers hung from the tall cove ceiling. Warm sunlight poured in through eight wall-length windows that lined the room on either side. White marble beams positioned between each window matched the smooth floor.

Gavin could now see the crowd of well-dressed people looking at him. Several ladies were speaking behind their fans. All heads turned towards the center of the room where an elegant woman sat upon a lushly decorated throne.

"I have come with a gift for Her Majesty," Brahm called out above the murmurs.

All eyes turned towards the woman who made no effort to move from her slouched position.

"How dare you interrupt me while I'm holding court?" she scolded Brahm. "I should have you removed and whipped." She regarded the pair of them with a lack of interest. "Or perhaps whipped here. We could use the amusement to liven up this dull place." Forced laughter trickled throughout the gathered group. She rolled her eyes, growing irritable at Brahm's lack of response. "Why are you here? I certainly haven't summoned you."

"I have brought a gift for you, Majesty, along with news," Brahm said. If he bowed any further, his nose would've touched the floor. He didn't dare make eye contact. The room grew silent, awaiting her reaction, which put Gavin on edge.

At last, she stood. The courtiers parted to clear her path, and from his kneeled position, Gavin could properly see her for the first time. His initial thought was how beautiful she looked.

Her long sleeved, white-laced gown draped from her shoulders, accentuating her curves. A satin train dragged along the marbled floor. Her jet-black hair was embellished with so many jewels that, when hit with the sunlight, gave her the appearance of having a halo. Judging by the growing lump in his throat, Gavin knew this woman was anything but angelic.

"What could be so important that you felt the need to interrupt my court?" she asked Brahm.

"I was discovered—er, imprisoned— but managed to bring him for you as well as swipe this little gem during my escape." Brahm removed the diary from a pocket inside of his coat. "For you, my queen."

Gavin's body straightened with a jerk. Choking on the gag, he pulled against his restraints. Feeling desperate, he hobbled on both knees to get closer.

The pitiful display caused Brahm and the queen to turn their attention to him. Brahm snatched a handful of Gavin's hair, forcing his face down again.

"Bow before Queen Rona!"

This is Rona?

Rona shook her head, clicking her tongue.

"Be nice to him, Thaddy."

Thaddy?

Brahm stiffened. Instead of responding, he handed the book to Rona, who peered down at Gavin once again. With a wave of her hand, the gag vanished from his mouth along with the ropes around his wrists. Massaging his jaw, he looked up at her.

"You're Rona?"

"*Queen* Rona, you insolent boy!" Brahm spat.

Placing a finger under Gavin's chin, she had him stand. Rona studied him for a moment before she smiled with a hint of mischief behind her dark indigo eyes.

"You almost seem disappointed," she said, chuckling. When she spoke to Brahm again, her gaze never left Gavin's face. "Yes, I think he will do nicely, Thaddy. Thank you."

Brahm grimaced.

"If you please, Your Highness. I'd prefer my surname be used when we're in less intimate settings."

She ignored his request, turning her attention instead to the diary.

"Now, what is so special about this?" She turned it over to look at both sides, gauging Gavin's reaction.

"The meddling travelers I told you about. . . *he's* one of them," said Brahm, pointing to Gavin. "I shouldn't be surprised if the other three are already out looking for him right now. "And *that*," he nodded towards the diary, "is how their magic works. I haven't figured it out yet, but I know it's the secret to their power."

He looked quite pleased with himself.

"So, what you're telling me is that you're no longer able to perform your duties in Haighdlen, and that you lack the brainpower to outwit four adolescent drifters. Is that correct?" The color drained from Brahm's face as words failed him. Rona clicked her tongue. "I rather wonder if you're of any more use to me."

Gavin reached out as Rona made to open the front cover but was seized by two guards.

"Interesting," she said.

He watched as she opened it, but like when Brahm had tried in the library, nothing happened. Gavin's pulse raced as he stared at his only means of getting back to his friends.

Closing the diary, she tucked it under her arm and stepped closer to Gavin. "Do you want to tell me what you and your companions are planning?" When he didn't answer, she smiled at him. "Challenge accepted then. I have my own secrets too. I shall insure they don't find you until I'm ready." She turned to Brahm. "Have him taken to the closest regiment so that I may keep an eye on him. We'll talk again when he is ready. I'm leaving you in charge of his progress. See to it you don't let me down again. That will be all, Thaddy."

Gavin's protests were ignored as he was escorted out. At least this time, he could see where he was going. Brahm led them across the front courtyard to where a carriage waited. A thick set of iron handcuffs were placed on his wrists before the door was opened for Gavin. When he didn't immediately step in, Brahm nudged Gavin's back hard enough to make him fall onto the seat. He waited for Gavin to clamber into an awkward sitting position before taking the seat opposite of him. After instructing the coachman to take them to somewhere called Whistpore Camp, Brahm closed the door. As the carriage began to move, Gavin tried to wrap his head around what just happened.

What camp is he talking about? Where are they taking me? How am I going to get the diary back from Rona? She didn't seem all that scary to me. I don't know why everyone is so afraid of her.

Truth be told, whenever he pictured Rona before, he always imagined some old ugly witch dressed in black with a crooked nose and missing teeth. Certainly not the sensual, vibrant woman he encountered. He turned his attention to the man sitting across from him. Brahm had lowered his head, perhaps even drifted off to sleep. Gavin didn't know what Rona saw in him, but they definitely seemed to be well-acquainted. A few more minutes passed before Gavin couldn't stand the silence anymore.

"So. . .*Thaddy*, is it?"

If looks could kill, Brahm's answering glare would've stabbed him a thousand times by now. Gavin's poorly concealed smirk probably didn't help either.

"I suggest if you'd like to keep your tongue attached that you never say that name again."

Gavin slumped against the seat as he regarded Brahm with confusion.

"How did you even get away, man? Where are we going? Some kind of prison?" Gavin asked.

He looks paranoid. Why does he keep looking out the window?

"You've been fortunate enough to be recruited into the Whistpore Regiment. The training camp is only a few miles from here."

Regiment? Like an actual military camp?

"I'm not joining her army."

"It's amusing you believe you have a choice. This is a punishment for me as well. I have my own agenda, and I don't need to be seen." Brahm scoffed. "You're going to be a pitiful soldier indeed."

Gavin's stomach filled with dread. First his dad. . .now Rona.

Why does it always have to come back to the military?

He didn't want to be controlled and forced into anything, let alone a death sentence in an alternate dimension. He had to get home, but now that Rona took the diary, he wondered if the others were equally stranded.

What if they find an alternate way home? Some kind of magic that works without the diary. Would they leave me here?

He slouched further in his seat.

"Where are my friends?"

"Probably mourning your absence." Brahm chuckled. "Especially that pretty little redhead."

Straightening up, Gavin's temper flared as he mentally strangled the former captain. Sensing this, Brahm was quick to pull a knife from his boot. He spun it, tapping the sharp tip against his finger. Fear flooded through Gavin's veins at the sight of dried blood on the blade. He could risk kicking the knife out of Brahm's hand, perhaps even try knocking him unconscious, but he'd have no way of escaping his iron cuffs. He would most likely get a worse punishment when they reached their destination. For the time being, he would have to accept his current situation and be left to wonder what was in store for him.

CHAPTER 2

Back in the dining room of Haighdlen Castle, Elise stared at her breakfast plate. Twelve hours ago, they returned from town to hear about Brahm's escape with his sister along with the news that Gavin was missing. Derek ordered a full investigation into the guard who was murdered in Gavin's room while search parties were sent out for their friend.

But he was more than that to *her* now. He was her boyfriend. None of the attempts to cheer her—or any of them— up proved successful. Despite exhaustion, Elise's entire night had been spent tossing and turning, praying she'd wake to find it was all a bad dream.

Everything was supposed to be over—Brahm had been caught, her mom didn't run away, and the pregnancy scandal was in the process of being covered up. That was the only mission she and her friends had been given when they were sent back in time through her grandmother's diary. The diary, along with a vial of fairy magic they had received in the forest, would've given them enough power to get home.

Elise toyed with the vial in her lap under the table. Their part was finished. It was the family's job to take over so nothing else got messed up. No matter how many times she repeated all of this in her head, she knew that without Gavin or the diary, that plan was out. She was only sulking at this point. Angry. Confused. There were so many emotions swirling inside her that she hardly knew how to pinpoint a single feeling. One thing that she could focus on–obsess over, really— was how badly she wanted to find Gavin.

What if something happened to him? Why haven't they found him yet? What if they don't find him? Who knows where the diary is or if we'll ever get it back now? We'll all get stuck here for good!

She tried preventing her anxious thoughts from escalating into the third panic attack that morning. Feeling her adrenaline building, her palms growing sweaty around the vial, she tried redirecting her thoughts by focusing on the other people around her.

Along with Mitch and Darcie, the entire royal family was present around the table. Few words had been spoken since the food arrived. Joranna shifted in her chair, looking between her husband and children, while Derek was engulfed in reading his documents as usual. Their children— who Elise wouldn't call children anymore— avoided eye contact with one another. For several minutes, the only sounds came from silverware clinking against plates. Elise's attention drifted to Gavin's empty chair beside her until Joranna cleared her throat.

"I know you don't want to hear this," she told Elise, "But you really should try eating something."

Elise moved her eggs around a bit with her fork before taking a bite. She didn't bother trying to copy her family's impeccable dining etiquette this time. Eating was the furthest thing from her mind. With each bite her nausea only grew. Darcie—and even more surprisingly, Mitch—didn't seem hungry either. The latter had yet to crack a single joke the entire morning. Unspoken fears kept them all in a numbed silence that was only broken by Joranna again.

"Ian, straighten up please," she called to her youngest son, if anything to keep conversation flowing.

Rolling his eyes, Elise's uncle Ian, who she guessed must have been around her age, sat up long enough for his mother to look away before he promptly slouched back in his seat to continue eating.

"Haven't you had enough, dearest?" Joranna whispered to Sarah next, who was reaching for another croissant.

Elise's aunt dropped it back onto the platter with a huff.

"I don't see you saying the same thing to Ruby, Mother, and she's clearly on her third! Though I suppose now we all know why."

"Sarah! That's terrible. Apologize to your sister at once!"

Neither her mother's admonishment nor her sister's glare seemed to faze Sarah.

"There's no need, Mother, she wouldn't mean it," replied Ruby with a shrug before looking across the table. "If you have a problem with me or my *situation*, Sarah, please say it." Matching her sister's challenging stare, Ruby reached for the discarded croissant before taking a slow, oversized bite.

As Elise's mother moaned with approval, Sarah looked as if she was about to crawl across the table to pull her sister's hair out.

"Ladies, can we please talk about something else?" When both girls finally broke eye contact, the queen took a bite of her own breakfast.

"We could talk about Rona." Ian's wry smile in response to his mother dropping her fork suggested he received the reaction he desired. Derek even lowered his papers as all eyes turned to the youngest prince.

"Why would you even bring her up at a time like this?" Sarah shrieked.

Pushing his plate away, Ian rolled his eyes.

"Calm yourself, Sister. No need to get yourself all worked up. It was merely a change of subject to lighten the mood." Crossing his arms, he stretched his legs under the table. "You no longer look like you want to gouge Ruby's eyes out, so learn to loosen up. Have a laugh."

"Rona is *no* laughing matter." Derek's jaw tightened as he frowned at his son from the head of the table. "And I don't appreciate you bringing her up to unsettle everyone at the table. Not everything is a joke."

"So, we're all going to sit here pretending she has nothing to do with what's-his-name being taken?" Ian cocked his head towards Gavin's chair.

The mere mention of Gavin made Elise feel unsteady. She clutched the vial to keep her composure.

"We don't know anything for sure yet," Joranna replied.

Ian shrugged one shoulder, turning his attention to Elise, Darcie, and Mitch.

"All I'm saying is this isn't the first time a young man has been kidnapped in Haighdlen without a trace." He stood up, ignoring his parents' disapproving glances. "Although it is the first disappearance from castle grounds. Just something to think about." Throwing his cloth napkin on top of his plate, he left the room.

A moment passed before Richard cleared his throat.

"He has a point, Father."

"One that I'm not going to acknowledge." The documents were back to hiding the king's face. Richard exchanged glances with his mother before nodding towards Derek, encouraging her to intervene.

Joranna looked down at her lap, folding her napkin several times.

"It might be a good idea to talk about it a bit more." She was careful with her words as she spoke to the stack of papers. "We're assuming Brahm took that young man, but we don't know where or why. Not to mention the security measures that need to take place now."

"Charlie could help with that," Richard added. His gaze flickered to Ruby, whose shoulders tensed as she stared a hole into the table. "He knows the grounds well, and it will only give him more experience before he joins my council one day. I could write to him."

"Lord Fenton is lucky enough to have been sent home with only a warning. I forbid any contact with him at present while matters are being settled. I would also think his part in your sister's recent scandal would assuage any concern you feel for him."

Seeing Richard's and Ruby's faces fall, Sarah took her turn to try reaching out to the king.

"Father, surely you could—"

"No, no, and for the last time, NO!" Elise jumped as his fist connected with the table. Derek tossed the documents away from him, giving up trying to read anything else. "I want no more talk of this! Does everyone understand?"

Richard stood up from the table.

"Perhaps you haven't noticed, Father, but we aren't children anymore. We've grown up. Everyone knows there's a threat in our kingdom, and we aren't going to sit around waiting for you to tell us when we're allowed to care!" Before Derek could reprimand him, Richard held out his palm, causing the disheveled documents to levitate. With a flick of his wrist, the loose pages stacked neatly again before lowering in front of the king. "We need to take action, Father. You know as well as I do the answer is not in those stupid papers, but pour over them if you must."

No one spoke as the eldest prince left the room.

"I'll go talk to him," said Joranna before Derek stopped her.

"He's just spoiled. They all are. We're too soft on them." His dismissive tone didn't elicit a response. He stood, collected the stack, and kissed his wife's hand. "I have a meeting with the council."

Pausing at the doorway, Derek turned to address the three travelers. "When it is finished, I will update you on our attempts to recover Mr. Striess. You have my sincerest condolences. Please know that I consider this an important matter that will not be ignored."

When Derek was out of sight, Ruby scoffed into her cup before taking a sip.

"I've heard that one before."

"Your father means what he says," Joranna argued. "If you ask me, you all owe your father an apology."

"For what?" Ruby asked. "Richard's right. This is a direct attack that should be dealt with. War might be the only option."

"Honestly, Ruby, this is hardly a topic of conversation with guests here," said the queen, folding her napkin on the table.

"I'm only saying what everyone is thinking."

"Yes," Sarah replied to her sister, "but they have the good sense to keep quiet about it. You're the only one who appears to lack a filter *and* morals."

"That does it!" Joranna stood abruptly, glaring down at the princesses. All formality had vanished as a lock of hair fell into her face. Through gritted teeth, she berated her girls. "I want *both* of you to follow me right now. Forgive us," she added before they left the three friends sitting alone at the table.

As the table was cleared, Elise couldn't help but notice the strained look on Mitch's face. At any other time, she might have even found his sour expression comical, but in that moment, she knew his pain.

"Do you think your mom is in a lot of trouble?" Darcie whispered, bringing Elise out of her thoughts. "She and your aunt *really* don't like each other, do they?"

Before she could answer, Mitch interrupted.

"Can we skip the gossip, so we can figure out how we're going to find Gav, please?"

Fighting the urge to argue back, Elise looked around to make sure they weren't being overheard.

"I'm scared about what Brahm will do. I know it was him. He would love nothing more than to hurt one of us. What's worse is he stole the diary. What if he finds a way to work it?"

There was a silence as all three considered the possibilities.

"Maybe Gavin will get it back," Mitch offered. "If he opens it like before, we all get sucked through the portal, right?"

"That's how it usually works," said Elise. "But Brahm wouldn't be careless enough to let that happen." She rested her forehead against the table, speaking into her lap. "I wish we could get it."

"Even a page would probably work," Mitch muttered into his hand.

Darcie's eyes lit up, her fingers tapping the edge of the table with excitement while she searched for words. The loud noise and vibration across the table made Elise lift her head.

"I've got it!" Darcie's hands moved from the table to Mitch's sleeve. Gripping the fabric, she shook his arm until he jerked away, demanding to know what was wrong with her. "You guys just said it! We only need a page!" She looked between the two, waiting for them to understand. When it was clear they weren't following, she rolled her eyes. "Brahm ripped a page out of the diary, remember?"

"Yeah, but he threw it in the fire." Mitch shrugged. "It's gone."

"We wouldn't be able to anything now," Elise added.

"Maybe we don't need a whole page," Darcie countered. "If we can find a *piece*, it might still have the magic we need."

Elise knew better than to get her hopes up, but anything was more productive than sitting here waiting for Derek to finish his meeting.

Darcie didn't wait for a response before heading out towards the library.

Mitch shook his head, unconvinced, as he followed them.

By the time Elise and Mitch entered the library, Darcie was already crouched over on her knees, searching the unlit fireplace with an iron poker.

"Find anything?" Elise asked.

Darcie eased back onto her knees. Tossing the poker aside with a loud clanking noise, she dusted her hands on her gown.

"You missed a little." Mitch touched his nose to imply her own was smudged.

Darcie screamed into the fabric of her dress before scrubbing her entire face until it was red.

"It's hopeless!" she cried, standing up only to stomp her foot. "I'm out of ideas. There's nothing but ashes in there."

Mitch and Elise were smart enough to keep their "I told you so's" to themselves. Unable to think of anything useful to say, Elise was actually grateful when Ballard cocked his head inside the room.

"There you are!" He sighed in relief as he leaned against the door frame to catch his breath. "His Majesty requests an audience with you and the royal family in an hour."

That was fast. Maybe he's found something!

***

Sixty minutes had never seemed so long. Waiting to be called in, Elise paced outside of Derek's study, trying her best to ignore the guard by the door. Along with her friends, Ian was the only other person present. Besides greeting them with a nod, Ian had kept to himself. He leafed through a book, though Elise doubted he was actually reading since he spent no more than a few seconds on a single page.

Ruby was next to join the group waiting out in the hall. Elise was immediately tempted to bombard her with questions.

What did Joranna say? Are you and Sarah still mad at each other? Do you have any plans to sneak out to meet Charles?

She was trying to decide which question would be the least invasive when she noticed how pale Ruby looked. In the end, only one question seemed necessary.

"Are you okay?"

Ruby nodded before leaning against the wall. Closing her eyes, she took a deep breath before massaging her lower belly.

"Forgive me." She stifled a yawn. "My body is still punishing me for my little escapade the other night. I shouldn't have overeaten either."

"Do you want us to find the doctor?" Darcie asked.

Ruby shook her head.

"No, I'm fine, really. Mother has him checking on me every hour as it is." Her eyes gleamed with a hint of mischief as she smiled. "But a little discomfort is worth the look on Sarah's face when I took that bite."

Elise and the others snickered. It was such a welcome sight to see her mother joking. . .*laughing*. Not one to miss a good time, Ian pushed off the wall to join them.

"I'll put my money on Ruby every time." Draping his arm across his sister's shoulders, he winked down at her. "You definitely put her in her place. That skinny stiff needs to lighten up once in a while. I hope you're not in too much trouble."

Ruby shrugged, matching Ian's playful smile. "No more than usual."

The sound of approaching footsteps made the two siblings lower their voices. Within a few minutes, Joranna, Richard, and Sarah arrived. Elise was relieved when the door to the study finally opened, sparing them any awkward silence. They waited while the councilmen exited the room, each one looking more unpleasant than the one before. Not a word was spoken by any of them, but that's not what caught Elise's attention. The last member wasn't severe looking at all. Appearing no older than thirty, his features were smoother. His long silver hair was tied back, exposing his pierced pointed ears.

Is he. . .an elf? An actual *elf?*

He didn't make eye contact as Elise watched him turn the corner. She looked at her friends who sported the same awe-struck expression she did.

I didn't know there were elves in this world too!

More questions swirled around in her mind.

"Are you just going to stand there keeping Their Majesties waiting?"

Not realizing the family was already in the study, Ballard's question prompted the three to apologize and file into the room.

Once everyone was settled, Derek cleared his throat. The infamous stack of papers was set aside as he examined them all.

"I believe the first order of business," he began with a sigh, "is to apologize to you all." After a pause, he looked at his family. "You're not my subjects. You're my children. Richard was right. I can't expect you to sit by ignoring what is happening when it affects you as much as anyone else. I get so engulfed with kingdom affairs that I forget that you are all old enough to know what is happening." He squeezed Joranna's hand as his expression turned somber. "That is why I wanted you all to be the first ones to know that, as of today, we are officially at war with Lockesbarrow."

A war! Elise felt her pulse accelerate. Her thoughts raced a mile a minute. *What's going to happen to everyone? Was this how it happened before? Is this because Gavin was kidnapped?*

The king's declaration was met with mixed emotions. Joranna did not appear surprised—most likely kept informed by Derek—but the anxiety behind her eyes was evident.

"Excellent!" Richard exclaimed. "We'll make sure the Lockesbarrian throne is the only one to get stolen."

Let's hope he's right. Hopefully, we've changed enough to stop Rona from taking over Haighdlen.

"Who was in charge of Lockesbarrow before?" Darcie asked.

"Queen Prisha," Joranna replied. Judging by the neutral expressions on the Laurille children's faces, this story was well-known to all but the three travelers. "No one knows what really happened, but when Rona's brother was sentenced to death several years ago, Rona held Prisha responsible and vowed to seek revenge."

"But if she got her revenge by becoming Queen, why is she trying to build an army to come after you guys?" asked Mitch.

"For more power. Why else?" Ian shrugged. "I'd like to see her try taking over Haighdlen."

No, you wouldn't, Elise thought gravely.

"So, was it a unanimous decision, Father?" Richard inquired. Along with Ian, he looked ready to grab his sword right then.

"Only one was opposed. We can expect to have Vynchia as our ally, but not surprisingly, Leafbrooke will stay out of it."

Richard scoffed.

"Why do the Elves agree to have ambassadors if they're never willing to compromise?"

"You'll learn soon enough, Richard, that it's more than which side you're on during times of conflict," Derek explained. "There are other matters to consider; trade, treaties, beliefs. . .you can't just grab a sword or disregard an entire population because it doesn't benefit you. But enough talk about this. The decision is made."

"Am I the only one who disagrees?" Sarah asked.

"Usually," Ian quipped.

Sarah glared as Richard and Ruby snickered.

"Why does it have to resort to fighting, Father? You've said war goes against everything that Haighdlen stands for. Rona knows what she's doing. She's building an army of boys. I even heard of some being taken as young as twelve! You'll be slaughtering *children*!"

"She's counting on that scaring everyone off from stopping her," Richard countered. "When she sees the size of our joint armies, she'll have no choice but to surrender. There won't be a need for bloodshed."

Sarah turned her head away before slouching against her chair. It was the first time Elise had ever seen her aunt lose the prim and proper act.

"I wish I had your confidence, Brother, but you can keep your flawed, idiotic sense of logic."

"I am going to stop everyone right now before anything else hurtful is said," Joranna interrupted. "Regardless of our different opinions, the matter is settled. It will be much better if we appear united."

Sarah gripped both armrests of her chair until her knuckles turned white. Without a word, she stomped across the room before slamming the door behind her.

Joranna pinched the bridge of her nose, blowing out a long, calming breath.

"Let's move on to the other matter, please," she managed to say.

"Right." Derek folded his hands, clearing his throat again. "I wanted to apologize as I'm afraid there are no new leads on your friend. I don't take this lightly. Mr. Striess's disappearance weighs heavily on me, and I vow that we won't stop until he is recovered. Please know we are doing everything we can."

"So, what exactly *are* you doing?" Elise was shocked by Mitch's outburst. Derek's apology sounded heartfelt, but Mitch was past the point of pleasantries. He tried approaching Derek's desk until two guards blocked his path. "This is supposed to be the safest place, right? My best friend is missing. You've got guards out there, but y'all are supposed to have magic. You're telling me there's no spell or potion that can help?"

"Mitch—"

Elise closed her mouth at the death glare he sent over his shoulder.

"What are we supposed to do then? Wait? *More* waiting!"

He was shouting by this point. It would only take a word from Derek for him to be escorted out. Elise locked eyes with Darcie before nodding towards Mitch.

Do something. Make him stop!

"—who knows if Gavin is even still alive? Waiting around here isn't going to do anything! I'm so sick of you pretending like—"

Elise, who had closed her eyes from embarrassment, chanced a peek when he cut off his rant.

Towering over Darcie's small frame, Mitch furrowed his brows, regarding her with an unreadable expression. The hand she had placed on his chest rose and fell in time with his breaths. Despite the audience, it felt incredibly intimate, making Elise feel somewhat out of place.

Darcie shook her head, her not-so-subtle stare pleading for him to stop. Elise sighed in relief when Mitch's shoulders sagged in defeat. Raking his fingers through his hair, he turned away from Darcie's touch to have a seat again.

That was intense! What is going on with those two? I need to ask her later.

"Perhaps we all need to take a break to process everything," Joranna suggested. She encouraged everyone to exit as she announced her plans to take a walk in the garden. Derek offered to join her before leading the group out.

Against her better judgement, Elise waited until her friends and family had mostly exited the room before whispering to get Ruby's attention. When Ruby paused in the doorway, Elise waved her closer.

"I didn't want the others to hear. Have you learned any more about your parents' plan for you?"

"Why are you asking?"

"I don't want to see you marry a stranger."

"You don't need to worry about me," said the princess.

"Have you had the chance to talk to Charles? Maybe we can fix this." Ruby stiffened, but Elise couldn't give up now. "It's so obvious that he loves—"

"It's time for me to move on, Elise." The decisiveness in her mother's tone made Elise close her mouth. She nodded her head, pressing her lips into a thin line. Sensing her discomfort, Ruby's tone softened. "Let it go, please. You already have plenty to worry about. I am sorry about your friend. I hope they find him. Let me know if there's anything I can do."

Elise knew that Ruby only meant it as a cordial gesture, but she was suddenly filled with hope as she realized who she was talking to.

Maybe we *can find Gavin. . .*

She checked the doorway one more time before lowering her voice.

"Actually, there is."

CHAPTER 3

A lump formed in Gavin's throat again as the carriage slowed, tiny rocks crunching beneath its wheels. Although it had not been long since he and Brahm had departed Rona's castle, the sun was now hidden beneath an overcast sky. The surrounding area was blanketed in a fog so thick that Gavin could not see six feet in front of him. In the distance, he heard waves crashing against the shore.

Are we on a beach?

After exiting the carriage—being shoved out was more like it—Gavin shivered when the chilled damp air touched his skin.

"Where are we?"

"Your new home for the foreseeable future." Brahm let out a sharp whistle. Within seconds a young boy, no older than thirteen or fourteen years old, came into view. "Take us to your commanding officer at once."

Bowing his head, the boy led them forward. Gavin was ordered to follow while Brahm took the rear. Jagged pieces of rocks and shells pierced the existing scrapes on his bare feet as they made their way around a steep rock face. Due to the limited visibility, Gavin was unable to see the top. He questioned its massive width after they walked for over twenty minutes beside it. Trying his best to walk on his toes without falling behind, Gavin kept his attention on the boy so he wouldn't lose sight of him. It was a good thing he did, because in the blink of an eye, the boy ducked into an opening in the rock wall that Gavin hadn't noticed.

Grazing the top of his head on the rock as he entered, Gavin paused for his eyes to adjust to the darkened room. No less than eight mounted torches illuminated the otherwise bare circular space. At the opposite end was a door. Judging from the multiple visible locks and burly watchman, Gavin doubted anything—or anyone—locked inside ever came out. He watched as the guard's eyes flickered between his iron cuffs and Brahm. Without a word, he unlocked the door only long enough to allow the younger boy inside.

The awkward silence that followed was enough to put Gavin on edge. Shifting from one foot to the other, he blew out a large breath as his mind wandered.

What is this place? How do I get out? What if I don't see my friends again? Or my family? They'll never find me in here. I don't stand a chance getting away right now. This guy is three times my size. I wish they'd cut these cuffs off. Then I might get a punch in.

A gruff voice called out from the other side of the door, prompting the watchman to unlock it again. The same boy walked out ahead of a man in armor.

"You are the commanding officer, I presume?" Brahm asked. The formidable soldier removed his helmet. "Isaac, is that you?"

"It's good to see you again, Brahm."

As the two shook hands, Gavin was left to wonder how they knew each other.

Isaac was younger than Brahm by a number of years. Having the advantage in height—*and strength*, thought Gavin—Isaac embodied the perfect soldier. Although he had an impressive athletic build and a sharp jawline, it was his cold stare that commanded respect. Being on the receiving end of it, Gavin felt his stomach tighten, but he was determined not to lose his nerve.

Don't let him sense your fear. Don't let him get to you. Be strong.

"New recruit, eh?" Isaac sounded too friendly as he stepped closer. Gavin didn't buy the nice guy act for a second. He braced himself for any surprise attacks. "Which kingdom are you from, Boy?"

Brahm chimed in before Gavin could respond. "He's a special case. An outsider from an unknown world. Her Majesty has tasked me with overseeing his training at your camp."

"I'm intrigued." Isaac leaned forward to inspect Gavin. Up close, the flickering torchlight revealed tiny scars etched across the man's dark brown skin. With his thick black hair tied back, Gavin was able to see that one particular scar extended all the way across Isaac's ear.

"He looks healthy enough. Has he been given any former training?" Brahm replied that he had not. Isaac clicked his tongue. "Pity, though not much different from some others we've received. Fetch our new recruit his training garments. Meet us in the holding area." Pausing only to give Gavin an apologetic stare, the younger boy bowed to Isaac's command before disappearing through the foggy exit.

Holding area? Where are they taking me?

As if reading his mind, Isaac beckoned them to follow him through the door. Stepping around the watchman, Gavin was surprised to find a long ascending set of stairs on the other side. Identical torches were hung every ten feet or so. While the dark, spiraling walk did little to settle his impending sense of danger, the cool stone steps provided some much-needed relief to the soles of Gavin's feet. As he rounded the eighth flight of stairs, however, his feet were no longer a concern as he questioned whether his knees would give out beneath him. They had passed so many doors already and yet continued to climb.

Now I know why I couldn't see the top of this place before. . .

In the tight confinement of the stairwell, his stomach grumbled loud enough to be heard. When *was* the last time he had eaten? He got distracted from his hunger by the welcome sight of the last door. Upon its opening, his eyes squinted against the brighter, yet still cloudy, sky. In front of them lay a walkway leading to the other side of the mountain. As he followed Isaac across it, he took in his surroundings.

From this height, the wind whistled in his ears like an oncoming train. A flock of seagulls squawked overhead as the cool breeze blew through Gavin's hair. The smell of fish filled his nostrils.

Ocean spray misted amongst the fog as wave after monstrous wave crashed against the boulders below.

Surveying the area, Gavin saw five more mountainous cliffs around the scenic landscape. On the edge of one particular precipice, he saw a striking castle—no doubt the one they had just come from. It appeared to be built into the cliff itself as one monumental structure with multiple towers and balconies. Beyond this beautiful, yet treacherous coast, a fleet of ships docked at a port. From his moving position, Gavin was unable to count how many there actually were. Right before he entered the mountain again, he caught a glimpse of a quiet city in the distance.

Brahm closed the door, muffling the sounds outside. Producing a key from his pocket, Isaac unlocked the final door. Gavin wrinkled up his nose as a stench of body odor and sweat reached his nostrils.

No less than a hundred young men and boys were scattered throughout the rounded chamber. Some huddled together in groups while others chose to isolate along the walls. A handful of older men in uniforms patrolled the room.

Retrieving a key of his own, Brahm unlocked Gavin's cuffs before letting them fall to the floor with a loud, echoing clang that brought everyone's attention to Gavin. The hairs on the back of his neck stood up as he felt the countless sets of eyes on him. Massaging his freed wrists, he avoided eye contact with anyone.

Isaac stepped over to a nearby table with a piece of parchment draped across it. Picking up a quill from the inkwell, he beckoned Gavin forward.

"What is your name, Boy?" When Gavin didn't reply, Isaac's gaze flickered expectantly from Gavin to Brahm.

"His name is Gavin Striess," Brahm replied.

"Age?"

Brahm smacked the back of Gavin's head hard enough to make him stumble. Wincing, Gavin brought his hand up to massage the area before he answered.

"Eighteen."

After examining Gavin again, Isaac nodded with approval as he completed his registration notes. One of the men in uniform answered a knock at the door before allowing the same young boy from outside to enter carrying a pile of clothes and a pair of boots in his arms. Isaac waved the boy forward, instructing him to help Gavin change.

"Hey, man, back off!"

I'm not letting anybody here take my clothes off.

"There's no use resisting." Isaac turned towards the confused errand boy before nodding in Gavin's direction. "Dress him."

Gavin took a step backwards. Anticipating a struggle, three men—including Brahm— surrounded him. Scowling, Gavin jerked his own shirt over his head.

No one's helping me change.

After tossing the removed garment to the ground, he snatched an oversized burgundy tunic from the boy's outstretched arms. His body tensed as he swapped his dress pants for a tattered black pair. Although no one around him seemed fazed, Gavin repeatedly checked over his shoulder towards the other boys in the room. Only when he finished changing did he allow the boy to help put a belt and boots on him. While they were scuffed and a size too big, he was thankful to have something covering his sore, painful feet.

Looking around a moment later, Gavin noticed that the boy, along with his discarded clothing, were nowhere to be seen. The same could not be said about his three babysitters, who still flanked him.

"You'd better start behaving," Brahm growled in his ear as Isaac approached.

"Now that you are properly registered, introductions are in order. I am your commanding officer. You will refer to me as sir and sir only." All hints of friendliness had vanished from his features. He held out his arm, directing Gavin's attention to the entire chamber. "This is the holding area. When you are not training, you will eat, sleep, and wait here."

So, this is the barracks, Gavin thought. *I'm not about to eat or sleep here. There aren't even any beds. I've got to get out now.*

He scanned the perimeter of the bare, windowless room as Isaac led him forward. No exits were visible except the guarded door he had entered from. Growing paranoid from the countless sets of eyes following him, Gavin observed a mixture of expressions—fear, resentment, curiosity. . . He snapped back to attention when Isaac pulled a dusty brown mat from a disorderly pile of rags.

Isaac dropped it on the stone floor.

"That is where you sleep," he said to Gavin. "You will rotate between scheduled trainings along with standing watch. Your group's next session begins at sunset. The other officers will help with anything else you need to know." His smile returned as he regarded Brahm. "I believe that's all for now. Can I interest you in a drink, old friend?"

Brahm accepted the offer before shooting Gavin a look that told him he better not try anything stupid. Only after the door locked did Gavin realize the other two bodyguards had walked off. A hissing sound made him look down at a young man gesturing for him to sit.

"You better get to polishing before one of the guards flogs you," he warned Gavin, who watched the others on this half of the room scrubbing boots and weapons. Gavin caught the rag that was tossed to him by the other boy. "I'm Everett, by the way."

Everett had light brown skin, short black hair, and an easiness about him that made Gavin feel comfortable enough to give his name. After a brief, firm handshake, Everett cocked his head to two other boys polishing nearby. "This is Erick, and that's Tristan."

Erick, who couldn't have been older than fourteen, had a round face and a mop of black hair. He reached across Everett to shake Gavin's hand while the other young man didn't bother to even look up from his work. Tristan was older, perhaps twenty, with shoulder-length brown hair and a pasty complexion. His eyes were large compared to the rest of his face, and he looked malnourished. His only acknowledgement of Gavin was a scoff over his shoulder.

"Don't mind him," Everett whispered. "He hates everybody."

Ignoring Tristan's cold shoulder treatment, Gavin lowered his voice. "So, where are we exactly?"

"This is one of the Lockesbarrian training camps in the Whistpore Mountains." Gavin stared in confusion. Everett and Erick exchanged glances before the former tried again. "Lockesbarrow is one of the four main kingdoms. . ." He trailed off as if this were common knowledge.

"You're not from around here, are you?" Erick asked. "Which kingdom are you from?"

"It doesn't matter. I'm not staying. I need to get out of here."

Both boys shook with hollow laughter.

Gavin narrowed his eyes. "I have to get back to my friends. I think they might be in trouble."

"Having a good laugh over here, are we?"

Everett and Erick froze, their eyes staring over Gavin's shoulder.

Turning his head, Gavin came face to face with a uniformed guard whose mere scrutiny made Everett go silent and Erick tremble. He was close enough for Gavin to smell his horrible breath as he held up a fist. "Knock it off or there will be a good lashing in your futures. Get back to work!" he barked.

When the guard was far enough out of earshot, Gavin opened his mouth to ask a question, but quickly shut it when Everett's eyes widened with a tense shake of his head. Now was not the time.

These guys know something I don't. I need answers, but I can take a hint. He's warning me for a reason.

Growing more frustrated and hungrier, Gavin scrubbed vigorously at a boot that Everett had handed him. He would bide his time for now, but there would come a point where he saw himself cracking under the pressure. He just needed to be ready when that moment came.

I don't care what it takes, he thought. *I'm getting out of here.*

CHAPTER 4

Outside by the castle stables, Elise waited with Mitch and Darcie for Ruby to meet them. Seated inside a small carriage, the three felt like the late spring sun was baking them inside. With every passing moment, Elise grew more anxious.

What if she's changed her mind? How will we get out without her?

Her mother had been reluctant to help at first. When it was just the two of them in Derek's study before, Elise begged for Ruby's help to go after Gavin. The princess, while conflicted, was sympathetic enough to offer the use of a servant carriage as well as supplies. Though there were multiple ones available, the use of a royal carriage would receive too much attention. A master of bending the rules herself, Ruby knew which maids and servants were the most trustworthy at keeping secrets.

"Are you sure we're at the right spot?" asked Darcie. "Maybe you got your mom's instructions wrong."

"No, she said to meet her at the stables. A servant even led us to the carriage," Elise replied, craning her neck to see better from the window.

"I don't get it," said Mitch. "If your mom has all these connections to help get us a carriage, why did she go through all the trouble of climbing walls when she snuck out?"

"She was going at night when everyone was going to bed," Darcie answered.

Elise nodded. "Ruby said our carriage will just look like some servants are headed to the market in town. It'll be less conspicuous than decorative flags and mandatory attendants." Relief washed over her when she saw her mother approaching at last.

"Forgive me." Ruby was a bit out of breath from hurrying to join them. "I had hoped to use an afternoon ride on my horse as an excuse to get here sooner, but Mother took one look at my riding clothes and about had a stroke. There goes another fun activity for a while. Anyway, to avoid a lecture, I changed."

"That's okay," Elise said, scooting over to give her mother space. "Go ahead and get in."

"I can't go with you." The three teenagers didn't hide their confusion. "I'm restricted to the grounds, remember?" Elise recalled the meeting in Derek's study the day before when, while in a heated discussion about her pregnancy, Ruby had walked out despite her father warning her not to. "Besides, you'll need someone here to cover for you. Hopefully, they'll be too busy planning for the ball to notice too much."

Elise's brow furrowed. "What ball?"

"My parents are hosting a ball here in three days."

"They didn't tell us anything about that!"

Ruby chuckled at Elise's indignant response. "I didn't realize you were required to be kept informed of kingdom affairs. Tell me, do they need your approval *and* signature before making decisions?"

Elise supposed she had a point. They weren't important as far as the kingdom was concerned. She couldn't expect to be included on everything the family did.

"But why would they have a ball?" Darcie asked. "Didn't the king *just* say they were going to war?"

Ruby shook her head with a shrug. "Planning like that will take a while. In the meantime, they don't want to cause unrest by alarming the kingdom. A ball is the perfect distraction."

"I can see that," said Darcie. "Plus, they're fun and romantic. I kind of wish we weren't leaving now."

"Speak for yourself," Mitch muttered, slumping back in his seat.

"I agree with Mr. Peterson," Ruby said.

"You don't like them?" asked Elise.

Ruby paused before answering. "If I were merely a guest, I could see the appeal. As a member of the royal family, however, it's a simple game of politics. My parents are in a rush to see me married, and what better way to do it than by parading me around an event where the best eligible options will be in attendance?"

That isn't right, thought Elise. *A baby shouldn't be a life sentence.*

Rolling her eyes at the situation, Ruby perked up when a maid approached carrying what looked like a pile of brown blankets. "Thank you, Gretchen." Elise's mother turned to pass the pile through the carriage window as the maid walked back towards the castle. "These are traveling cloaks for you all to wear, and these," she added, giving Elise four identical letters, "are for safe passage across any borders. They're stamped with the royal seal."

"Why are there four?" Mitch asked.

Ruby looked at Elise. "You didn't tell them?"

Elise turned towards her friends' confused expressions.

"When we were planning this earlier, she said there was someone in Clara who might be able to help us. I didn't think to tell you guys, because I thought she was going with us." After skimming the papers, Elise looked up at her mother. "How will we find him if you're not with us?"

"I've sent word ahead already. He's expecting to meet you at the tavern. You'll be taken there directly. Give him the fourth copy in case you need to leave the kingdom for any reason."

"That reminds me," Elise said once they had thanked the princess. She pulled a folded piece of paper out from the front of her gown. "I wrote this for your parents. Hopefully after reading it, they won't be as mad about us leaving like this."

Nodding, Ruby's eyes widened as she too reached into the front of her gown. "Oh! I almost forgot." Elise watched with interest as something hanging from a chain was handed to her. "This is for you."

Elise held out her hand to accept the mysterious item. After closer examination, what she thought was an ordinary pendant turned out to be a small tear-shaped bottle with a corked top. It was a rather extraordinary necklace. Holding the ornate item up in the sunlight, Elise could see etched leaves and unfamiliar yet beautiful script.

"What is this?" Elise squinted at the foreign letters.

"It's an Elven bottle necklace. I bought it from a merchant during our last family trip to Leafbrooke," said Ruby, looking down at her feet. "It often came in handy when. . . well, you know." Elise knew her mother was referring to all the times she had traveled using fairy magic. Why she didn't carry it the night before last, Elise didn't know, but now didn't seem like the time to ask. The topic was clearly a sensitive one as Ruby rocked on the balls of her feet.

I know you don't like looking vulnerable, Mom, Elise thought, wishing she could speak the words aloud.

"Yes, well." Clearing her throat, Ruby straightened up and gestured towards the necklace. When she spoke again, her words were rushed with a hint of irritation. "You all are too inexperienced to be carrying around fairy magic, anyway, let alone in a cheap vial out in the open without protection."

"Thank you," said Elise.

She asked Mitch to hand her the vial he was keeping in his pocket. Darcie uncorked the potion bottle, holding it steady so that Elise could pour. Mitch held both of his hands out underneath them in case any spilled. As the bright blue magic oozed from one bottle to the other, Elise noticed that Ruby's eyes were transfixed on it. There was an unmistakable longing, even hunger, in her expression.

"You don't need it, Ruby," Elise whispered, remembering her mother's addiction to magic. "You're strong enough without it."

Heat rushed to the princess's face. Breaking eye contact, Ruby tucked a fallen strand of hair behind her ear. She stepped away from the carriage.

"It's getting late. You'd better put it on and get going. Ian's magic will wear off soon."

"Ian's magic?" Elise asked. "You told Ian what we're doing?"

"We can trust him." Ruby shrugged. "Besides, it'll help you get to Clara faster. We're officially even after all this."

After pushing the cork in, Elise slipped the necklace over her head before tucking the bottle down the front of her gown.

Elise opened her mouth to ask the name of their guide but was distracted when the same maid came running up to them again.

"Your Majesty," she panted, "you're needed straight away for your fitting."

"I'll be up in a moment, Gretchen."

"Your mother is asking after you and these three. What shall I tell her, Princess?"

Ruby sighed, casting one last look at the carriage. "It seems I'll be covering for you sooner than I thought. It's best if you get going. I'll give them the letter. Drive on," she called out to the driver.

The carriage lurched forward as Ruby and Gretchen walked in the direction of the castle.

"What did you say in the letter?" Darcie asked.

"I thanked them for all they did for us, but I said that we had to try finding Gavin ourselves. I also asked them to consider holding off on attacking Rona."

Mitch looked puzzled.

"Why'd you do that?"

"We need to focus on getting all four of us home. I don't want to add a war into the mix if we can avoid it. If they do eventually attack, maybe we can get out of here before they do. I just thought writing a letter was better than disappearing like we usually do."

I hope they won't be mad, but we're getting nowhere close to finding Gavin just sitting at the castle. Wait. . . I was going to ask mom something.

Elise tried to remember where her thoughts had been before she was interrupted earlier.

"So, what's this guy's name?" Mitch asked.

Elise felt a sinking sense of dread in the pit of her stomach.

That was it.

***

It was nearly sunset when they arrived in Clara. Fed up with the lack of information and small space, Mitch slid across Darcie's lap to exit the carriage first when it finally stopped outside of the tavern.

"So, let me get this straight," he said, stepping back so the driver could help the ladies out. "We're here to meet some guy, but we don't know his name or what he looks like." He scoffed. "This is like a nightmare!"

"I thought she'd be with us, so I didn't think to ask in time," Elise repeated. The three put on their traveler's cloaks now that they had space to do so.

Taking a step closer, the driver cleared his throat.

"I beg your pardon, Miss," he said to Elise with a bow, "I'm supposed to give you this." He pulled a small, yet surprisingly heavy, pouch from his pocket. Elise loosened the cord around it. There must have been twenty or thirty coins inside! "I need to be getting back. I can transfer the supplies to a rented cart while you're inside. Will you be all right?"

The reality of the moment sunk in, and Elise felt stupid. She hadn't thought any of this through. They would be completely on their own. She had believed that Ruby would stick with them in the beginning, yet here they were on a whim with no plan. Rather than show how she felt, Elise smiled at the gentleman while pulling out a pile of coins.

"We'll be fine." She held out her hand. "Please take however much you need to rent the cart for us. Keep a couple more for yourself. Once everything is moved over, you can go back. Please tell the princess thank you for us."

Expressing his gratitude, the man bowed before setting off down the street in search of their rental.

Mitch scoffed. "You're lucky he didn't take the whole bag and ditch us somewhere else."

"Mitch's right," said Darcie. "That guy *must* be loyal to give up a bag of money like that."

Elise looked around for the driver to ask if he knew who they were supposed to meet, but he had already disappeared amongst the crowd.

Mitch tucked his hands into his pockets. "Well, before you go praising him too much, let's wait to see if he *actually* does what he's supposed to do."

Looking up at the sign above the door, Elise braced herself for what—or who— she might find.

Once inside, Elise found that it was much larger than the outside suggested. Long tables with bench seats lined the walls on either side of them. Flickering sconces were mounted beside each one, illuminating the entire room with the help of a crackling fire on the back wall. A cluster of smaller tables and chairs were positioned in front of the bar where a middle-aged bartender was busy completing orders. Against the wall was a wooden staircase leading up to a second level.

It appeared to be a popular time of day as all but two of the smaller tables were filled with loud, drunken conversations and boisterous laughter. Three barmaids expertly navigated the room carrying trays while a young teenaged boy helped bus the tables.

"Are we old enough to be in here?" Darcie whispered.

"I'm willing to bet they don't have the same age laws here," Elise said, catching a glimpse of young men chugging from goblets at a nearby table.

Mitch was all too eager to blend in, suggesting that they find a seat at one of the smaller available tables. He even went a step further by offering to ask the bartender if he knew of anyone waiting for someone.

Sitting down at the vacant table, Elise kept her head low and arms tucked in as she scanned the room. All the seated patrons appeared to be with groups.

Mitch approached the table a few minutes later carrying three large mugs. He apologized when a few drops of whatever he had ordered splashed out onto Darcie's gown. Too busy enjoying the first chug to notice Darcie's glare, Mitch pulled his mug away just long enough to inform them the bartender didn't know of anyone waiting.

Wrinkling her nose at the smell, Elise chanced a quick sip from her mug before sliding it towards Mitch.

"Maybe he's just running a little late," Darcie offered, ignoring her mug as well. "I'm sure whoever it is. . ."

When Darcie trailed off, Elise followed her friend's stare to see someone walking down the creaky staircase. Impressed that anyone could make Darcie lose her ability to speak, Elise soon found *herself* rendered speechless as the stranger reached the bottom floor.

I'm with you, Darcie. If this were a movie, he'd be walking in slow motion right now.

Elise glanced over at her best friend, who also looked like she was in a trance.

Darcie eyed the gentleman like an all-you-can-eat buffet. Elise stifled a chuckle when it took three attempts for Darcie to answer to her name.

"What were you going to say?" Elise asked.

Crashing back to reality, Darcie replied that she had no idea. The two girls broke into laughter when Mitch asked what they were talking about.

"Do you think he's the one we're supposed to meet?" Darcie asked.

"Wipe your chin," Elise said with a chuckle. "There's no way that's him."

"How do you know?"

"Who are y'all talking about?" Mitch asked. When Elise nodded her head to the bar, where the man was now standing, Mitch scoffed. "Yeah, that's not him."

"It *could* be." Darcie failed to hide the hopefulness in her voice. "He's alone, isn't he?"

"Yeah, but he wasn't." Both girls waited for Mitch to finish his last sip to elaborate. He cocked his head towards the staircase where they saw an attractive young woman coming down while adjusting the straps of her dress. A few locks of tangled hair fell around her face as she wiped away a bit of smeared lipstick.

"You don't know that he was with her," Darcie argued. Mitch tugged at his collar before nodding towards the bar. Sure enough, there was a small stain on the other man's collar that matched the same shade of lipstick. "Maybe he brought his girlfriend with him."

Mitch made a sound imitating a buzzer. "Wrong again."

Elise and Darcie watched as the woman walked a lap around the room before she was welcomed at the table of young men Elise had seen upon entering.

Not accustomed to being proven wrong, Darcie huffed, pulling her stolen mug away from Mitch's lips.

"Well, so what? Go ask him if he's here to meet anybody else."

When Mitch replied that that wasn't going to happen, Darcie pulled off her traveling cloak and declared that she would do it herself.

Better her than me, Elise thought.

"This should go well," Mitch chuckled, grabbing Darcie's mug again.

It's a good thing Mitch isn't watching, Elise thought, because it looked like it *was* going well. She knew Darcie's flirtatious nature enough to recognize when her friend was succeeding. What Elise didn't know, however, was why the stranger's smile widened after looking over to her. *What is Darcie saying?* She didn't have to wait long before Darcie grabbed the man's hand to lead him over to their table.

"Guys, this is Vaughn," she introduced, ignoring Mitch when he choked on some ale. She looked quite pleased with herself. "He *is* here to meet someone." Instructing Vaughn to take the empty seat beside Elise, Darcie scooted her chair around the side of the table to be closer to him. "This is Elise and Mitch."

"Pleased to meet you," Vaughn said. "So, Darcie tells me you're trying to find someone."

"Yes, my boyfriend," Elise answered.

Vaughn followed up with a few questions, including what Gavin looked like along with his age. When Elise finished her description, Vaughn had a solemn expression on his face.

"He sounds exactly like her type."

"Who?" Elise asked. "Rona?"

Vaughn checked over his shoulder before lowering his voice.

"I'd be careful if I were you. That's not a name you want to be speaking of so casually, but yes. The abductions throughout the kingdoms all fit certain characteristics. Young, healthy, male. . .I'd be willing to bet a good deal that your friend is in Lockesbarrow."

Elise's worst fears were confirmed. She had always suspected Brahm of taking Gavin, but hearing from yet another person that he could be in Rona's kingdom made it all feel surreal.

"You may have a bit of trouble crossing the borders," said Vaughn. When Elise mentioned that they had four letters for safe passage, Vaughn looked impressed. "You'd better slow down, friend," he added to Mitch, who responded by tilting his head back to drain Darcie's mug completely.

"So, you'll take us there?" Darcie asked.

Elise shot her friend a knowing glare.

Meddling was Darcie's greatest gift, followed closely by her persuasion skills. Both types were on full display. Darcie leaned towards him, using a hand to cradle her chin.

Mitch hiccupped before excusing himself from the table.

Elise was left feeling like a third wheel while the other two flirted together.

"It's not exactly an easy journey," Vaughn said, leaning closer to whisper. "I'm not sure you'd be up for it."

Darcie hummed, sliding her hand across the table to stroke the back of his. "I'm tougher than you think."

Geez, Darcie. Down girl, Elise thought.

Something convinced Vaughn to accept the challenge. Elise had a feeling it had less to do with helping their cause and more to do with the suggestive way Darcie adjusted the neckline of her dress. Vaughn leaned back to look at Elise.

"For you ladies," he whispered, "I would brave a thousand Ronas."

Elise didn't have Darcie's perky laughter, but she thanked him, nonetheless. A nagging voice entered her mind, adding to the uneasy feeling in her chest.

Is this the right thing to do? We don't know this guy, but Mom said she wrote to him already, so he knows what he's doing. I can trust her, but can we trust him? Something doesn't feel right. I wish Mom were here. She'd know what to do. She's better at this than me.

Mitch returned to the table looking as if he no longer had any ale left in his stomach. His face was pale with a thin layer of sweat along his brow. Darcie didn't notice his return until he picked up her discarded cloak to wipe his face.

"Oh, you're back," she said, ripping the cloak from him to put it back on. "Come on. We're leaving."

"So soon?" Vaughn asked.

"Darcie, wait. I have to pay for Mitch's drinks," Elise said, pulling out the pouch.

"Allow me," Vaughn replied before walking over to pay the bartender.

"Isn't he amazing!" Darcie gushed to Elise.

"I don't trust him," Mitch said sourly.

Darcie rolled her eyes.

"Elise's mom arranged all of this. It's okay," she said.

"Did he mention my mom's letter?" Elise asked. Darcie replied that it hadn't come up. "How do we know it's the right guy then? Did he say he was here to meet *us*?"

Darcie waved away her questions.

"I asked if he was here to meet someone. He said it looked that way and then came to the table."

"Darcie, that just sounds like he was flirting with you. He may not be the guy my mom wrote to at all! What if he's a criminal?" Elise asked.

"He looks like one."

Darcie ignored Mitch's comment.

"Elise, do you want to find Gavin or not? This guy knows the way. I think we can trust him."

"Oh, please!" Mitch exclaimed. "The guy looks like a cover on the books my mom reads."

They stopped talking as Vaughn approached.

"We have a little daylight left," he said, glancing out the window. "There's enough time to make it to an inn by nightfall."

"And what do you get out of this?" Mitch asked. "We don't have enough money to pay you. You can just drop everything to go on this trip? Don't you have a job or something?"

"Mitch, don't be rude!" Darcie said. "He offered to take us. Just leave it alone. And look, there's a horse and cart waiting for us outside. Come on." Not bothering to hear anymore objections, Darcie pulled Vaughn towards the exit.

CHAPTER 5

Gavin's chest burned with each breath he took while running in formation. He expected his legs to give out at any moment, which surprised him given his usual endurance during school drills. Perhaps because during gym class, there was an end in sight. He had already lost track of how long they had all been running along the perimeter of the beach. His sole comfort was that he wasn't the only one struggling, but that didn't stop Isaac and the other officers from singling him out.

Already that afternoon, Gavin had been labeled an "inexperienced", "foul-tempered", "spoiled outsider". Judging by the whispers and laughter, it appeared that everyone in his company— except Everett and Erick—shared the same opinion. Being a military brat, Gavin shrugged off the attention. He was used to being the new kid. What he *wasn't* used to was being unpopular. Gavin had always been blessed with the looks and personality to fit in wherever his dad had been stationed.

The sweet sound of Isaac's whistle gave him the permission needed to collapse against the rockface. He wiped his forehead with the hem of his sweat-soaked tunic. The fabric clung to his skin like a wet towel. Staring off into the sea, he had half a mind to dive in for relief. Any other time, he would have marveled at the way the sunset reflected off the horizon, but for now all he could focus on was slowing down his heart rate until he could see straight.

How was he going to get out of here? This couldn't have been part of the royal family's plan when they sent him and the others back into the diary. He knew time passed differently while they were traveling, but he wondered what would happen if he didn't escape in time. How long would it be before his parents noticed? His mother's worried face popped into his mind. He missed his family. It dawned on him that the last conversation he had had with his dad was another argument on his way to Mitch's car before heading to Joranna's house. He wished things were different with his dad. After the last few hours, Gavin wanted nothing more than to call home and apologize for his behavior.

He thought of Elise. Was she safe? Gavin missed her. If he was being honest with himself, he missed his old life. . .his friends. . .even school.

"On your feet!" an officer barked down at him, pulling Gavin out of his thoughts. "Time to move out."

Each boy was given armor, a load of supplies on his back, as well as a lantern before following Isaac and his other men away from the coast. While the officers had the privilege of leading on horseback, the recruits were forced to follow on foot. Three horse-drawn carts followed behind the group. Gavin was surprised to find that the Whistpore Mountains stretched for miles.

If we're going to be hiking all this way, why not wait until tomorrow? It'll be dark soon.

He was given the opportunity to ask his question when Everett came to walk beside of him.

"Isaac doesn't care about that sort of thing," the boy replied. "He says we should always be ready, so we train at any time of day."

"How long have you been here?" Gavin asked.

"About four months. Erick's only been here three weeks. He's from Vynchia like me. I try to keep an eye on him."

"What about him?" Gavin nodded his head towards Tristan, who walked alone ahead of them.

"Tristan's been here longer than anybody. He's skilled at just about everything."

"Then why is he still at a training camp?"

"I've heard Isaac tell him he'd make a great commanding officer one day, but his insubordination keeps him from advancing."

"Then why not just kick him out?" Gavin asked.

Everett shook his head. "Isaac's too proud. He's not getting rid of a strong soldier for anything. He also wants to stay in the queen's good graces, so he puts up with a lot where Tristan is concerned. I've seen Isaac put him through some rough punishments, but he can't seem to break him."

I wonder what kind of punishments, Gavin thought as he pulled a canteen out of a side pocket on his pack. While it wasn't cold, the moment the water touched his lips, Gavin's dry mouth and dehydrated body practically sang. Interrupting his guzzling, Everett warned him to ration it out rather than gulp it all down at once.

Isaac held up his hand, signaling them to stop when the trail opened into a lush green valley. While abundant with wildflowers and trees, there were large visible patches of flattened brown grass, most likely due to multiple training sessions like this one. Flat rocks protruded from a winding narrow river that flowed through the center of the uneven terrain. Dense clouds covered the surrounding mountain peaks. The brisk mountain breeze caused Gavin to shiver, but he welcomed the clean chilled air into his lungs.

A group of younger boys, who were called runners Gavin had learned, unloaded the carts before hurrying to prep the training area. After being instructed to drop their gear, the recruits were guided to line up in front of six large trunks. Each trunk was flanked by an officer and a runner. Everett informed Gavin that they were grouped by skill level before taking his own place two lines over. Gavin was in the last line along with Erick and ten others.

At the sound of a whistle, the officers opened the trunks. Gavin watched, his head tilted for a better view, as the runners passed out swords to the recruits in their assigned lines. One by one, the boys in front of him dueled with the officer. Each turn lasted only between thirty seconds to a minute, but Gavin didn't think he'd last that long against the skilled swordsman. Intimidated by the officer's footwork alone, he felt the hilt of his sword slip due to the sweat on his palm. When his turn approached, the officer beckoned him forward. Gavin stared at his superior opponent, who was easily twice his size in weight and stature. Through his peripheral vision, he caught a glimpse of Tristan dueling his own officer across the field in the first line. He moved and struck with such ease that it was hard to tell at times who was more skilled.

Well, here goes nothing. Gavin lifted the sword the way he'd observed others do before him. Erick had told him while waiting in line that the blade was duller and more flexible than they would hold in actual combat. That still didn't stop the blows from hurting as the officer's blade struck his hands over and over. His turn lasted a mere twenty or so seconds before he was disarmed. Gavin heard poorly concealed chuckles behind him in line.

"Didn't your father teach you how to hold a sword, boy?" With a raspy chuckle, Gavin's officer tossed his swiped sword on the ground by his feet.

Gavin tightened his jaw. Picking up the discarded weapon, he visualized the damage he wanted to do with it. Fighting the urge to lunge forward, he took his place at the back of the line as another round began. It took a few turns for him to feel fatigued. While his sword was only three or four pounds, it didn't take long for him to feel the strain on his muscles.

The drills continued until nightfall with no measurable improvement on Gavin's part. Once the weapons were collected, Isaac informed them that they were to camp out there for the night.

Gavin wiped the sweat from his forehead as he rummaged in his pack for the supplies needed to set up his tent. Although his skin was warm from exertion, the temperature had dropped enough that his breath was visible in the cold mountain air.

"Do you want some help?"

Gavin looked up to see Everett and Erick standing next to him. Nodding, he thanked them before getting to work. He was grateful for the assistance that cut at least half the time off the task.

At least mine looks like everyone else's now.

"Aren't you hungry?" Erick pointed towards the crackling fire where other recruits were lined up to receive dinner.

"I'm good," Gavin lied. His stomach chose that exact moment to betray his hunger, but he ignored the skeptical looks both boys gave him. "I'm just going to bed."

"Don't be so hard on yourself," said Everett. "It was only your first day."

"Yeah, but I doubt anybody here sucks as bad as I do." He held up his hand when Erick tried to reason with him. "Guys, don't worry about me. It was a really bad day, and I have another one coming tomorrow." Isaac had already announced that they would be paired off the following day for more swordplay as well as archery. It was gearing up to be a second embarrassing display for him, something he wasn't used to dealing with back home.

Rather than argue, both boys left him alone. Gavin removed his armor piece by piece before stretching out on the ground. Any other time, he might have had difficulty getting comfortable, but he was so sore that exhaustion outweighed any concerns about comfort.

As he lay falling asleep, his thoughts ranged from Elise to his family and friends. Mixed in were possible scenarios of getting out of there. All were unrealistic without magic or super strength. He was pulled from the brink of sleep by an appetizing smell that wafted into his tent. Expecting to see Everett or Erick bringing him dinner, Gavin jumped when he heard Brahm order him to come out.

When Gavin managed to crawl out of his tent, he saw Brahm and Isaac waiting for him. His eyes fell to the plate of roasted chicken and boiled potatoes in Brahm's hand.

"Brahm came to check in on your first day," Isaac informed him. "He thought I was exaggerating when I told him it was one of the most pitiful displays I've ever seen. He said he had to see for himself before leaving in the morning."

Where is he going?

"My, how the mighty have fallen," Brahm said. "You look terrible. Well done, Isaac." The two shared a jovial laugh between them. "How does tomorrow look for him?"

"Not much better, friend. I think we might just kill the poor boy." More laughter followed, fueling Gavin's temper. "He'd make more progress if he wasn't so blinded by defiance. Within an hour of your departure this morning, he was already trying to escape."

"I would've loved to have witnessed that."

The two men continued talking as if Gavin wasn't there. Finally, Isaac cleared his throat to change the subject.

"In all seriousness, Brahm, I don't believe he's cut out for it."

"I'm with you," the other man replied, "but Her Majesty wants him close to keep an eye on him."

"And what becomes of us if he's not progressing as he should be?"

"We must do our best not to find out," Brahm said between bites. "I will return in the morning."

"Can you not be persuaded to stay?"

Brahm declined Isaac's offer. "I must visit my sister and niece."

Gavin watched as they walked away. His hands clenched into fists by his side. Even if he were punished afterwards, he would wager the reward of tackling one of them would be worth it.

"Leave it alone," Tristan said. Gavin turned to the other boy coming out of his tent a few feet away. "It's not worth it."

"You don't know what he's done," Gavin said through gritted teeth, watching Brahm cross the valley.

"It doesn't matter." Tristan's words were enough to bring Gavin's attention back to him.

What does he mean it doesn't matter? If it weren't for Brahm, I'd still be with Elise and the others. I'd be home by now.

"The sooner you conform, the easier your life will be." Tristan twisted a medallion between his fingers that he wore around his neck on a chain. His tone sounded as if he were bored.

Gavin was confused. "I heard the only reason you're still here is because *you* won't conform. So, why should I?"

"Because *I* can handle it."

Is that a challenge? He thinks he's better than me.

Gavin assessed the other man's size. He was all skin and bone. Gavin could snap him in half if he wanted. He had enough pent-up anger to do it. Especially since Tristan wasn't wearing his armor either. Gavin took the six or seven steps needed to reach Tristan before shoving him. Although the force would've been enough to knock most people off their feet, his assault merely made Tristan stumble back a step or two before regaining his balance. It was like hitting a wall. When Tristan didn't retaliate, it only egged Gavin on further. He threw punches left and right, but Tristan easily dodged them all before sweeping Gavin's legs out from under him. Gavin landed hard on the ground.

By this time, others had heard the commotion and were gathering to watch. Several cried out for Tristan to teach Gavin a lesson. In the distance, there were orders for them to break it up.

Tristan had yet to strike Gavin, using only defensive moves. Although having the advantage, Tristan waited silently. His composure only fueled Gavin's anger.

Blind rage and an entire day's worth of humiliation boiled to the surface. Wiping the dirt from his eyes, Gavin leapt up to punch Tristan's face.

Only it wasn't Tristan on the receiving end of his attack.

In his haste, Gavin had failed to notice an officer step between them. His anger now forgotten, Gavin watched the bigger man bring his hand up to dab his nose, which now dripped blood.

"Disperse! Everyone to your tents," Isaac called, breaking up the crowd. After assessing the situation, his eyes settled on Tristan and Gavin. "I should've known."

Gavin flinched as the back of Isaac's hand swiftly connected with Tristan's face.

This makes no sense. Tristan knows how to dodge that. Why did he let Isaac hurt him?

Besides a grunt from impact, the only indication that Tristan was in pain was the way he clenched his jaw. A vein in his reddened cheek throbbed, and his breathing was shallow, but the young man remained stoic in front of their commanding officer. Expecting the same strike, Gavin knew he wouldn't have the same ability to act as brave when Isaac turned towards him.

"I don't know what the queen sees in you, but I can tell you what I see." He spoke so quietly that Gavin struggled to hear him over the crackling fire and distant murmurs from the officers. "I see a coward—an impulsive, undeserving, coddled little boy not worth my time. If I teach you nothing else while you are here, it *will* be to respect authority." Gavin remained silent as Isaac took a step back to address the officer who had intervened. "I think we have found our first pairing for tomorrow." Gavin's stomach sank as he and Tristan exchanged glances. Isaac continued, pacing back and forth in front of them. "Now, I suggest you bury whatever problem the two of you have. Save your energy for the field. As of now, we will see what shape Striess is in after twenty lashes." Gavin looked around as the spectators chuckled, some even going so far as to say how much Gavin deserved it.

Lashes? Like, actual *lashes? They're going to whip me? He can't be serious.*

Before he could respond, two officers grabbed both of his arms. Gavin instinctively resisted until Isaac leaned in closer. "Don't struggle. You've already made yourself look enough of a fool for one day. Learn from this." He turned towards the bloody officer again. "I think it only fitting that Officer Flint do the honors." Terror rippled throughout Gavin's body as he looked up at the officer. The light from the fire flickered across Officer Flint's smile. His face, smeared with blood from his nose to his ear, lit up with anticipation. "Away with him!"

Gavin shot one more look at Tristan before he was escorted away from the campsite. Wondering how he had let himself get to this point, Gavin braced himself for the pain that awaited him.

CHAPTER 6

Stepping out of the tavern, Elise approached a small boy waiting by a horse and cart. Two flickering lanterns were mounted on either side.

"Is that for us?" she asked. Nodding, the boy held out his hand. Elise pulled a couple of coins from her pouch to pay him. "Thank you."

Mitch waited for the boy to run out of earshot. "You need to quit spending all of our money so fast!"

"He did his job. I had to tip him." Elise looked back at Darcie waiting by the door. Vaughn told them he needed to collect his essentials inside. He emerged carrying a tattered satchel across his chest and a sheathed sword on his belt. She leaned towards Mitch. "Do you really think that's the guy my mom hired to help us?"

His eyes lingered on the flirtatious pair. "I don't trust him."

Elise hated to admit it, but she didn't either. Something didn't seem right about him. Vaughn was at the right place at the right time, but she would need proof before she agreed to let him lead them anywhere. Waving the other two over to her and Mitch, she mustered up the courage to question him.

"I need some proof that you're the one we're here to meet."

"Elise," Darcie said, "This is a waste of time. Let's get in the cart and get going."

"We don't need him," Mitch argued.

"Oh really? Well, do you know how to control one of these things?" Darcie asked, nodding towards the horse. When Mitch didn't reply, she continued. "I didn't think so, but Vaughn *does*. Let's go."

"Wait." Elise stepped between Vaughn and Darcie. Momentarily losing her train of thought, she lowered her head so she could focus without looking into his eyes. "We were told to meet someone here who could help us find Gavin. The princess wrote a letter—"

"Do you mean *this* letter?" Vaughn pulled a crumpled piece of paper out of his pocket. She didn't see Vaughn's name anywhere, but Elise recognized Ruby's handwriting. A wave of relief washed over her.

He is *the right person. Thank God.*

"Shall we get going then?" he asked.

Shrugging at Mitch, Elise allowed Vaughn to help her and Darcie into the cart.

"We can't pay you," Mitch said, repeating the same arguments he had inside the tavern.

"It's been taken care of," Vaughn replied.

"See? Ruby took care of everything," Darcie said, watching Vaughn take his seat behind the horse. "Now, get in or we're leaving you here."

Mitch looked as if he'd almost prefer if they did. Losing an internal struggle, he huffed before climbing into the cart beside Elise.

There was a noticeable difference between traveling by carriage and riding on a cart. The bumpiness reminded Elise of childhood hayrides being pulled by a tractor. Her bottom had bounced off her seat twice already. Vaughn held the reins with ease, looking over his shoulder only twice to insure they were doing all right. Mitch and Darcie were avoiding each other at opposite ends of the cart. Elise spent the duration of the trip looking out in the distance at the vast farmland.

"How much farther until we get to the inn?" Elise asked, noticing that the sky was growing darker. Vaughn had promised they would be there by nightfall.

"About five miles or so." Vaughn shook his head.

"Are you okay?" Elise asked. "You keep shaking your head." This must have been the third or fourth time she had seen him do it.

"A slight headache. It'll pass."

Darcie handed him a canteen of water from one of their supply bags. Vaughn thanked her as he took a swig from it.

When Mitch mentioned he was also thirsty, Darcie tossed the bag onto his lap to get it himself. The lantern light flickered across his sour expression.

Lighten up, Darcie, Elise wanted to say out loud. *Mitch is trying to keep us safe. I can't say that I completely trust Vaughn yet either.*

Feeling a need to keep the conversation going, Elise decided to find out more about their guide.

"So, where are you from?"

"Lockesbarrow, but I've lived the last few years in Haighdlen."

"What brought you here?" Darcie asked.

"Rona." Sensing their shocked reactions and burning questions, he chuckled without turning around. Judging by his physique, Elise was surprised that Vaughn *wasn't* part of Rona's army based on the stories. "I was a stable boy in the town at the time. The night before Rona took the throne, I accidentally witnessed guards sending Queen Prisha into hiding."

"What happened?" asked Elise.

"One of the guards saw me. I thought I was as good as dead, but he took pity on me. Told me to run away as far as I could."

Gazing with admiration at the back of Vaughn's head, Darcie leaned forward. "And then you came to Haighdlen?"

Vaughn nodded. "I don't know how many days I walked. I crossed borders by hiding in merchant carts. By the time I reached Haighdlen, I was weak and starving. I met a farmer who told me I could stay in his barn." He got quiet for a moment, reliving the memory. "By that point, gossip had spread about a dangerous Lockesbarrian fugitive. The farmer asked me to leave, which I did. I later heard he had been arrested, so I stayed hidden a while longer."

Elise felt a cold chill radiate throughout her body. Her chest tightened as she mentally ventured back to the Haighdlen dungeon.

When they were imprisoned, she and her friends had had a discussion with one of the other prisoners, Mr. Archer. Closing her eyes, she could still hear his tortured, raspy voice when Gavin had asked him how he ended up there.

"A young man was seeking shelter one night and we let him stay in our barn. The following day we found out he was a fugitive from Lockesbarrow, and I was accused of being a spy, of harboring a fugitive. . ."

Vaughn was the Lockesbarrian fugitive responsible for his arrest. In the flickering light, she saw her friends' tense expressions. They must have made the same assumption. Elise wondered if Derek had released Mr. Archer yet since he had promised to revisit the matter after Brahm was arrested.

"What happened after that?" Darcie asked.

"I kept an eye on his wife and daughters—from a distance, of course. I felt I owed him that much. They're making a decent living selling their crops in Clara."

"So, what do you do now?" Mitch asked. "Do you even *have* a job?"

"Mitch!"

"What?" he asked Darcie. "It's a legit question. Just because Ruby trusts him doesn't mean I can't ask him stuff."

"It's all right," Vaughn said with a chuckle. "I work as a drifting farmhand. I go where the work is needed and am compensated per job that is done. I don't like to be tied down." He shot a wink over his shoulder. His answer seemed to satisfy Darcie. Elise couldn't help but think *any* of his answers would satisfy her friend.

At least that explains his availability to take us to Lockesbarrow, Elise thought.

While Mitch didn't look persuaded, Vaughn's answers were convincing enough to stop the interrogation for the time being.

It was hard to believe they had been hot in the carriage earlier that afternoon, given the way the evening breeze made Elise shiver now that the sun had set. She was eager to reach the inn, if anything to get a break from her friends' palpable drama. How long were they going to go without speaking this time? Growing nauseated from the constant back and forth rocking motion of the cart, Elise gazed up at the night sky. The moon peeked out between the passing tree branches. For about ten minutes, the only sounds came from the leaves crunching beneath the wheels and crickets chirping. Pulling her traveling cloak tighter, Elise hugged her knees close to her chest.

I hope Gavin is safe. What if he's scared or hurt? I wonder what Lockesbarrow is like. What if Rona finds him? I hope we can save him in time. I miss him so much it hurts.

Was he thinking about her? Did he miss her as much as she missed him? Elise felt like her heart was going to burst into a thousand pieces. How was it possible to miss somebody this much? Had it only been *one* day since she had seen him? Out of the corner of her eye, she saw Vaughn jerk his head again.

I want to trust him, Mom. He has your letter and answers every question so easily, so why do I feel so uneasy around him?

Her train of thought was interrupted by the sound of a loud crack as the cart dipped. Darcie cried out as she, Mitch, and Elise grabbed the sides of the cart to steady themselves. Vaughn called over his shoulder for them to stay calm as he struggled to gain control of the horse. Elise glanced over the side at the back wheel closest to her. It wobbled and bounced out of sync with the others until, inch by inch, it inevitably separated from the axle, lurching everyone off balance. Vaughn fell backwards into the cart. Both Mitch and Darcie toppled on top of Elise, unable to pull themselves up until the cart slid to a halt.

Elise's sides hurt under the weight of her friends. She remained frozen in shock, trying to assess if anything else hurt. Cursing under his breath, Vaughn gained his bearings before hopping out to separate the spooked horse from the cart.

Mitch scoffed as he pulled himself up.

"Well, this is just great. Now what do we do?"

"We continue on foot," Vaughn replied, patting the horse's neck. "The ladies can ride the horse."

"Can't we get it fixed?" Darcie asked.

"Once we get to the inn, I'll arrange to have it and the horse returned to town, but it will cost too much time to wait for the repair. We'll be better leaving on our own in the morning without them."

"You want to walk the *whole* way?" Mitch spluttered. "How long will that be?"

Vaughn shrugged. "Maybe four to five days to Vynchia. Then we can take a boat." He laughed at their expressions. "Not an adventurous lot, are you?"

"This is insane. Let's go back to the castle tomorrow and get another cart," Mitch suggested.

"You heard what he said, Mitch," Darcie argued. "It'll cost us too much time! Let's be thankful he's still willing to take us."

Feeling her fear and confusion peaking, Elise watched as her two friends argued over one another. How were they ever going to find Gavin if everything turned into a fight?

"Want me to give you a hand?"

Elise jumped. She hadn't noticed Vaughn step up behind her until his breath had tickled her ear. She nodded over her shoulder and thanked him once he had helped her up onto the horse. As if her luck couldn't get any worse, a mosquito chose that exact moment to fly too close to her mouth, causing her to splutter and duck away from it. Steadying herself, Elise hoped Vaughn was too distracted helping Darcie to notice. A nearby snicker let her know that Mitch had witnessed the whole thing. Luckily, no one could see her blushed cheeks.

Elise had to admit that her mom had chosen a knowledgeable guide. Within minutes, Vaughn managed to divide the supplies between them to carry. Even Mitch was unable to critique him anymore.

Taking the reins in his free hand, Vaughn walked alongside the horse. Elise would've preferred a flashlight to the lanterns she and Darcie held, but any light was helpful now they were entering a dense patch of forest. If not for the light, everything would've been pitch black. The crickets and frogs called out all around them. A chill ran down Elise's spine as she clutched the handle of the lantern tightly. Her mind was already playing tricks on her. Several shapes in the shadows morphed into what looked like figures about to pounce on them. What would happen if they were attacked?

In an attempt not to lose her nerve, she looked around for anything to start up a conversation.

"How's your headache?" she asked Vaughn.

"Much better. Thank you."

When he didn't offer anything else, Elise looked over her shoulder at Mitch, who followed behind the horse.

"Are you doing all right, Mitch?"

"Oh yeah. Doing great. I think I'm up to my thirtieth mosquito bite and I can't say enough about the view."

"Why did you even ask him?" Darcie whispered in Elise's ear. "He's feeling sorry for himself when he should be thankful Vaughn found a way to keep us going."

Elise didn't reply. She felt sorry for Mitch. She knew how much he was missing Gavin as well. It couldn't have been easy to watch Darcie throwing herself all over Vaughn either.

"Tell me," Vaughn said, adjusting the strap of his satchel, "How did you become acquainted with the royal family anyway?"

"I'm a distant relative," Elise said, unwilling to share any more than that on the subject. Sensing this, Vaughn changed his line of questioning.

"Have you ever been to Vynchia?" When they replied they had not, he continued, "It's a beautiful kingdom—an ally to Haighdlen. We'll use your safe passage letters to cross the border as well as for the boat to Lockesbarrow."

"Wasn't there a fourth kingdom?" Darcie asked.

"Leafbrooke, but we're going to leave the Elves alone. We'll be risking enough as it is without provoking *them*." Elise absentmindedly fidgeted with the bottle necklace around her neck at the mention of the Elven kingdom. Vaughn scoffed. "Besides, they're all so arrogant, it'll absolutely drive them mad when an unknown relative of the Haighdlen royal family defeats Rona instead of one of their own."

"Hey, we never said anything about killing her!" Mitch jogged forward to stand in front of Vaughn. "We just want to find Gavin and go home."

"Yeah, we really haven't gotten as far as killing anyone," Darcie agreed.

"Well, you *need* to get that far." Vaughn's eyes flickered between all three of them. "Because if you think that Rona is just going to let you slip in and take what she believes to be hers, then you can end your little childish quest here since you're as good as dead anyway."

A heavy, awkward, silence followed. Elise felt at odds with herself. She wanted to find Gavin more than anything in the whole world, but would Vaughn leave if they didn't agree to try killing Rona? There was no way they could reach Gavin without his help.

"Now," Vaughn continued, "if you're serious about this expedition, then we need to clear up any hostility." He took a step closer to Mitch as Elise and Darcie watched from on top of the horse. "You don't trust me. Why?"

Lowering his head—taken off guard—Mitch dug the toe of his boot into the dirt. "I still don't know why you'd blindly agree to lead us. You don't know us. If it's so dangerous, why do it?"

"I'm not doing anything blindly," Vaughn replied. "I've been compensated, it's safer to travel in numbers, and I know the lay of the land. Anything else?"

Gaining back some of his nerve, Mitch looked up. "Why waste time walking for three days instead of just waiting at the inn for a new cart? Or fix the one we had?"

Vaughn opened his mouth to reply before closing it again. He took his time forming his response. When he spoke, his explanation was slow and calculated.

"I'm not one for sitting around waiting for the unknown. Your only chance of saving your friend is following me. Staying put, or even going back, puts the princess's efforts helping you in vain."

Elise hadn't thought of that. She knew if Derek or Joranna saw them, they wouldn't let them out of their sights again.

"You *can* trust me, Mitchell," said Vaughn. "I *will* guide you and the ladies to Lockesbarrow. You have my word."

Sensing no reply, Vaughn turned and continued to lead the horse forward.

"Isn't he incredible?" Darcie whispered into Elise's ear.

Conflicted, Elise found herself siding with both of her friends. Like Mitch, she didn't completely trust Vaughn. He played the role of the swashbuckling hero a little *too* well. However, like Darcie, she believed he was their best chance to find Gavin.

Elise pulled the bottle necklace out from under the front of her cloak. The bright, glowing magic was mostly concealed by the design of the bottle. A few specs of blue light shown through. The fairy magic was good for one powerful spell. She and her friends had almost used it when they encountered Brahm in the library. Given the situation they were in now, she was glad they hadn't. While she couldn't think of an immediate need for it, Elise was thankful she had the backup plan. It gave her a small—perhaps false—sense of security.

"We're nearly there," Vaughn said after Elise yawned. Mitch groaned that his feet were killing him. "Better get used to it. This is but only the first part of the journey."

That got Elise thinking.

"You said Gavin's probably in Lockesbarrow," she said. "Do you know where exactly?"

"My guess is one of her training camps. She has them scattered throughout the kingdom for protection while her soldiers train." Elise was horrified. Vaughn continued. "If that is where he is, he'll be trained to use weapons, run, and fight."

"But none of us are prepared for that kind of training," Darcie said. "What happens to him if he sticks out?"

Vaughn shrugged.

"It's hard to say really. If he doesn't comply, he'll be punished. They won't kill him, though, so there's a silver lining."

Some silver lining, Elise thought. *Gavin's not from here. What if he's already targeted? What if they're hurting him?*

"Don't let it unsettle you," Vaughn said. "Rona's main tool is manipulation."

"What do you mean?" Mitch asked.

"She wants to bend others to her will. She makes them support her cause and hers alone. Thoughts of families or escaping are treated as weakness until they are no longer a priority. Her soldiers are taught to forget."

"Gav wouldn't fall for something like that. He'll resist," Mitch said.

"If your friend can withstand the mental game of it all, there's hope that you'll be able to save him."

"And if he can't?" Elise asked.

Vaughn's silence answered her question.

"You sure know a lot about how Rona works," Mitch said. "Were you in one of those camps?"

"Ugh, Mitch, will you stop attacking him about everything?" Darcie spat. "You're going to make him quit helping. Cut it out!"

Before Mitch could argue, Vaughn held his arm up to quiet them.

"Don't move." Looking around, he unsheathed his sword. "I heard something."

Panic flooded Elise's body. Was someone—or something—going to attack them? Vaughn's guarded stance and clipped tone was enough to keep them all silent. Although she and Darcie held their lanterns higher, it did little to reveal their surroundings.

All at once, three balls of light shot out from the brush near the horse's feet before circling around its head. Elise leaned away as one of the lights almost hit her nose. Spooked, the horse whinnied and reared up onto its hind legs. She heard Darcie scream in her ear. Unable to stay mounted, Elise failed to grab the reigns before crying out as she and Darcie fell to the ground. Vaughn made a desperate attempt to stop him, but all four watched as the animal galloped away in fright.

Despite some aches and possible bruising, she and Darcie were able to stand. It was only then that Elise could focus on the three lights, bouncing around Mitch's head until Vaughn's sword sent them back into a tree.

"It's the fairies!" Excitement welled up in Elise's chest at the sight of them. She hadn't seen them since they had given her the magic in her necklace while following Ruby through the forest.

They can help us!

Vaughn stopped her from getting closer. "What's wrong? They're just fairies."

"Precisely. Nasty, interfering, demonic creatures."

When he prevented her from passing again, Elise called up towards the tree.

"Wait! Please come back!"

"What are you playing at?" Vaughn growled. "Have you lost your senses?"

The way he looked down at her made Elise feel like a misbehaving child. When he lifted his sword towards the tree, however, she risked his disapproval.

"Don't! They can help us!"

A limb on the tree shook, sending leaves to the ground. High-pitched laughter rang out before the three lights returned as the fairies took flight.

"You see?" said one who, once landed, Elise recognized as Hemlock. Standing on her shoulder, he scowled and crossed his arms. "*This* is why we do not help humans. You're reckless and only think of yourselves."

"Yes," said the second fairy, Thicket, landing on Darcie's head. She clicked her tongue at them. "Always wanting more. Never satisfied."

"Where's the other one?" Elise asked, looking around for the third light that had vanished. "Where's Sage?"

"I am here." Elise turned at the sound of the youngest fairy's voice, locating him on the closest tree limb. "We sensed our magic nearby." He glanced down at her necklace. "Why are you all the way out here?"

"Gavin's been kidnapped," said Elise. "We think he's in one of Rona's camps in Lockesbarrow. We're on our way to save him."

Hemlock and Thicket howled with laughter.

"Just when I thought they couldn't get any stupider." Thicket chortled, holding her sides as she gasped for breath.

"We could use your help," Elise told Sage, ignoring the insults. "Could you get a message to Gavin?"

Before Sage could reply, Thicket flew to his side.

"The audacity," she murmured with disapproval. "Blatantly asking fairies for help, especially after trying to stab us." She shot a nasty glance towards Vaughn.

"Should we be able to locate him, what would you like us to tell him?"

"Sage!" Thicket exclaimed. "There is no way we are leaving this forest, let alone the kingdom."

"Disgrace to the name of fairy," Hemlock spat. "Should've clipped his wings after the last time."

"Agreed." Thicket turned towards Sage. "We *fool* humans. They're untrustworthy and dangerous. They deserve any kind of punishment we can summon. Especially ones as helpless as them. *Why* do you insist on breaking every rule for these mortals?"

"I've told you, she's different," he replied, keeping his eyes on Vaughn as he spoke. "I will do what I can to prevent Rona from becoming too powerful, but it will require payment."

"Typical," Mitch scoffed.

"Give him a couple of coins, Elise," Darcie whispered.

Vaughn stepped in front of Elise as she reached into her pocket.

"Elise, don't! You will not waste what little money you have on these conniving pests."

"At least one of you has enough sense to fear us," Hemlock said before growing quiet when Elise held out two coins. He and Thicket immediately pounced.

"Tell him we're on our way to get him and that we have someone leading us there," Elise said.

"Consider this transaction over," Thicket panted, struggling under the weight of the coins as she and Hemlock lifted them. "Sage, you're on your own for this little escapade."

She and Hemlock flew up and disappeared into the darkness with the coins.

"Pay them no mind," Sage said. "They can't resist gold or a good show. They'll accompany me, and we will do our best to get your message delivered."

"Thank you, thank you, thank you!" Elise said, feeling like she would burst from gratitude. The little fairy nodded before disappearing into the same tree as the other two.

This is amazing! Now Gavin will know we're coming. Hopefully it helps him stay strong!

Her rejoicing was short-lived as the reality of their situation hit her—their supplies had been strapped to the horse that they no longer had. She was further discouraged when she saw the expression on Vaughn's face.

"That was a mistake." Saying no more, he turned to continue walking towards the inn.

CHAPTER 7

Pain.

It was all Gavin's brain could focus on. While the whip had only contacted his back and arms, his entire body felt like it had taken a beating.

Alone in his tent, he had lost track of what hour it was. The sun had not risen, yet with each passing moment, Gavin dreaded when it would.

He was going to be partnered with Tristan. As if his physical punishment hadn't been bad enough, Gavin wished he were anywhere else. There was no way Tristan would go easy on him. How was he expected to train? He could hardly stand. Every whipped part of him felt like it was on fire. What scared him the most was that it had only been one day.

I don't stand a chance, he thought. *They'll kill me before I can get out of here.*

His thoughts wandered to Elise, Mitch, and Darcie. He would gladly take another punishment if it meant he could get back to them. If his first day had been any indication, it was that this was not the lifestyle he was meant for at all. He could almost guarantee he would not fulfill his dad's wish for him to join a military branch. He had no desire to travel. To follow. To be ordered left and right. Gavin wanted to make his own way. His own choices. Why couldn't his dad just understand that? He was tired of moving around from place to place. He wanted to stay with his friends. He wanted more time with Elise.

As he lay there, Gavin pictured her smile. He could almost hear her laugh. She filled most of his thoughts lately. The few memories they'd been able to share flashed through his mind. The conversation on the boat, their first kiss in the gazebo, their late-night walk in the forest. . .He remembered how scared he had felt when Elise lost consciousness at the hands of Brahm in the castle library. Even though they hadn't been a couple long, he was surprised at how much he already cared about her. Gavin couldn't help but think how little Elise would think of him if she could see him now. He had never felt so weak and helpless in his life.

I'm not good for her. I can't stay out of trouble long enough. He thought back to the time they made it home but willingly followed Elise back into the diary. *It would've been better if I hadn't followed her. Maybe I should've gone home when I had the chance. She could focus on her family and not worry about finding me.*

A cynical voice inside him pointed out that maybe she *wasn't* trying to find him. What made him so important to halt her entire family's mission? It was enough to fuel the sense of dread that had taken permanent residence in his stomach. Something would have to change. Perhaps he needed to quit sulking about the agonizing turns his life had suddenly taken and figure out how to stay alive. He didn't have a plan, but he once again reminded himself that anything beat lying alone in a cold, dark tent covered in blood.

Gavin drifted in and out of sleep. He wasn't sure how long, if at all, he slept. A poorly aimed ray of sunshine peeked through a hole in his tent. Squinting against the intruding light, he heard the other soldiers stirring. The sudden opening of his tent made him jump. He immediately regretted it as a blinding pain seared through his back and arms. When Gavin saw Tristan's face, he buried his own against the ground with a groan.

"Go away." The words were slurred with his face pushed against the dirt. Maybe that was why Tristan stayed put.

Doubt it, he thought. *He's probably here to gloat.*

"I brought you some breakfast."

Not expecting Tristan's response, Gavin turned his head to look at the plate of eggs and tomatoes.

Tristan grimaced at his back.

"That looks bad," he said, shaking his head. "I'll tell Isaac you can't train today."

"Don't!" Gavin growled as the sudden jerk of his neck sent more stabbing sensations down his body. He took a couple of deep breaths before continuing. "I'll be out in a minute. Just leave the plate there."

Tristan made to argue, but a sudden commotion made him look over his shoulder. Before Gavin could ask him what he saw, Tristan was gone.

"He's in here," Isaac's voice said.

Gavin heard footsteps approaching his tent. Even with a quickened pulse, his body failed to follow his urge to run.

Bracing himself for Brahm, Gavin felt his mouth grow dry as Rona darkened the opening of the tent. Even in a thick maroon traveling cloak, she was stunning. Removing her hood, she lowered to her knees by his side.

"Good morning, my little rebel," she said. He stiffened as she ran her fingers lightly across his shoulder blade. "I heard you had quite a long night. How do you feel?" When Gavin didn't respond, she dug her fingertip into one of his deeper gashes. A guttural cry escaped his lips as he dug his face into the dirt. "How about now?"

When she finally removed her hand, he pushed up on his elbows, panting. She raised an eyebrow, awaiting his response.

"You're sick! You know that?" he spat. Despite gasps from the eavesdropping recruits outside, her amused grin returned.

"Punish him, Your Majesty!" Isaac insisted. "Teach him a lesson of what happens to those who disrespect you."

Her eyes twinkled in a way that made Gavin's stomach turn.

"He doesn't need punishment, Isaac," she replied coolly, clicking her tongue as she examined Gavin's wounds. "He needs encouragement." Reaching into her cloak, she pulled out the diary. Instinctively, Gavin reached but failed to knock it out of her hand. He closed his eyes and clenched his jaw as his body seized in pain. "See?" Her answering chuckle taunted him as she held the book just out of his reach. "Now, are you ready to tell me what this does? How to use it?"

Receiving only silence, she nodded and returned the diary.

"He's a poor excuse for a soldier, Majesty. Quite possibly the worst I've seen," Isaac quipped.

Rona reached out and stroked Gavin's cheek, now covered in a fresh layer of sweat.

"Why won't you do what you're told?" she purred. When he pulled away from her touch, she smiled again. "Defiant until the end, I see. I'm intrigued. Let's keep our little challenge going, shall we? I want to see what you're capable of."

Furrowing his brows in confusion, he tensed as she lowered her hand to his back again. This time, instead of causing him harm, Gavin felt the open wounds sewing shut. Tugging sensations spread across his injuries until he could flex his muscles without pain. Sitting up in disbelief, he rolled his shoulders.

She healed me. . .

He followed her out of the tent to the other recruits' shock and amazement. Ignoring their gasps and whispers, he addressed Rona again.

"Just let me go," he called to her. "I'm clearly not a soldier. I don't belong here."

She smirked at him over her shoulder.

"And *they* do?" She gestured towards the group of teenaged onlookers. Gavin was met with a mixture of reactions, most of them anger. He located Everett and Erick in the crowd wearing unreadable expressions. Rona hummed to herself as she straightened out her cloak. "Be careful not to lose what few friends you *do* manage to make." Closing the distance between them, she brushed a lock of hair away from his eyes. "Take my advice. Forget everything before this. *No one* is coming for you. You belong to me now." Patting his cheek, she turned back to Isaac. "Should he have any more trouble adjusting, I shall deal with him personally. Try to see that it doesn't come to that, Isaac."

Isaac bowed, vowing to do his best. He walked her towards a grand carriage while the officers broke up the group of boys. Gavin took advantage of the quiet moment to eat his breakfast.

As he finished his last bite, he saw Everett and Erick approach his tent. Fearing they had misunderstood him about belonging there, he waited for one of them to speak first.

"I'm glad to see she healed you," Everett said. Gavin relaxed when neither looked upset. "Although I doubt it was out of kindness."

"It wasn't," Gavin said. "She has something planned."

"What do you think it is?" Erick asked. His round face looked as if he had seen a ghost. "Will she come back?"

Gavin replied with complete honesty that he had no idea.

"Are you going to train today?" Everett asked.

"I don't have a choice," Gavin grumbled. Their replies were interrupted as Tristan stepped up between them.

"Can I have a word?" He cocked his head towards his own tent. Unable to think of an excuse, Gavin reluctantly followed Tristan with his friends' eyes on him the whole time. Tristan checked over his shoulder outside of the tent, but didn't go in. When he was sure they wouldn't be overheard, he spoke in a whisper.

"What did Rona say to you?"

His question took Gavin by surprise. He had been expecting something about the training or his skills.

"Why do you care?" Gavin asked.

Tristan rolled his eyes.

"I'm serious." Gavin believed him, but he still didn't know why it was any of Tristan's business.

"I was traveling with friends. She wanted to know what our plans were. I didn't tell her."

"What kind of plans?"

Gavin scoffed. "If I wouldn't tell her, what makes you think I'd tell you?"

His answer was clearly not what Tristan wanted to hear. He paced in front of Gavin, fiddling with the gold medallion around his neck. Gavin had noticed him playing with it the night before but had never said anything. He tried to make out what was on it. Catching him looking at it, Tristan stopped pacing.

"It was my father's."

"Where is he?"

"You expect me to answer you, but you can avoid *my* questions? It doesn't work like that, I'm afraid."

He had a good point. Gavin had no right to expect any answers when he himself wasn't willing to share anything. For a moment, neither spoke. When the awkwardness became unbearable, Gavin muttered his thanks for the breakfast.

"You'll need your strength," Tristan replied. "We're doing sword fighting and archery today."

"Do we have to?"

"We'll start now. Lesson number one, quit whining. It makes you weak."

"We're not starting yet. We don't even have weapons!" Gavin exclaimed. "And I wasn't whining."

"Lesson number two, stop arguing. Just do what you're told and keep your head down."

"But you don't even do that. Is this because I won't tell you what Rona said?" Gavin asked.

The whistle blew as Isaac instructed everyone to gather for the training session to officially begin. Once he made his usual fear-inducing speech, and all the boys were paired off, swords were distributed to every recruit. When Tristan and Gavin were far enough away from the others, Gavin decided to give in. He didn't trust Tristan, but he wasn't going to make it through the day without his help either. He responded to Tristan's starting position by lowering his own sword to the ground.

"You're the only one who can help me, so I'll tell you," Gavin said, rubbing the back of his neck. "My friends and I came here through a magical diary after she hurt my girlfriend's family. We found out Brahm was spying on Haighdlen and helping Rona. We thought we stopped him when he was arrested, but he broke out and took me with him. I'm trying to get back to my friends and go home. She wants to know how the diary works."

"You won't tell her?"

"I couldn't if I wanted to," Gavin replied. "It's always just worked on its own, but now that she has it, I don't know how we're going to get home. Plus, I'm stuck here."

"And your friends?" Tristan asked.

Gavin shrugged, twisting the tip of the sword's blade into the dirt.

"I don't know. I think they're still in Haighdlen, but I have no way of getting in touch with them. They might even find a way to get home without me."

"Would they really leave without you?"

Honestly, Gavin didn't know the answer. He didn't know what he would want to do if the situation were reversed. He'd like to think his choice would be the honorable one.

"It doesn't matter," he said before tilting his chin towards Tristan's medallion. "What about you? You seem really interested in what Rona does."

Tristan lowered his sword before looking down at the piece around his neck.

"She hurt my family too." Tristan twisted the golden medallion. In the sunlight, Gavin could see a banner wrapped around an anchor engraved on it. "My father was the Lockesbarrian Ambassador to Leafbrooke. I used to go on trips with him and play with the Elven children. When Rona seized power of Lockesbarrow, my dad refused to follow her. You can imagine what happened next."

"She killed him?"

Tristan nodded. "Our house and goods were destroyed. I was captured and recruited as one of the first in her training camps. She visits from time to time to parade me around as an example of her power. It's why I hid when she showed up today. I thought she was looking for me."

Gavin struggled to find something helpful to say.

"Sorry about your dad."

Tristan, whose face had scrunched up reliving a bad memory, snapped out of his thoughts and shrugged.

"My dad was all I had. It's why I train so hard. One day I'll be ready to face her. Not only to avenge my father, but to prove that I'm no longer afraid of her or anyone else for that matter. They can't break me."

Gavin admired Tristan's passion. If he were honest with himself, he envied it. As much as he and his dad argued, Gavin didn't know what he'd do if he lost him.

"Enough talking." Tristan held up his sword. "Ready?"

It's now or never, thought Gavin, copying Tristan's stance. *Let's get this over with.*

"Ready."

CHAPTER 8

The wooden door creaked open as Elise and Darcie entered their room for the night. It was smaller than Elise expected, but she reminded herself that they just needed it to sleep for one night. Having only enough money to afford two rooms, Mitch was left no other choice but to share with Vaughn.

"I'm starving," said Darcie. "Let's hurry and clean up before we meet the guys downstairs." After tossing their traveling cloaks onto the bed, Darcie crossed the room to where a pitcher and basin sat on a table for them. Filling the basin, she picked up one of the folded washcloths next to it before scrubbing her hands and face. When Elise didn't immediately join her, Darcie peeked over her shoulder. "You okay?"

"I'm not really that hungry. I'll probably skip it."

Darcie dried off before giving Elise a look that told her she didn't believe one word she said.

"Spill. What's wrong?"

Elise rolled her eyes. Why couldn't Darcie drop it and go without her? Elise would've tried coming up with another excuse, but she was already fiddling with her fingers, which was always a dead giveaway that something was bothering her.

"Vaughn hasn't said two words to me since I sent the fairies. I think he's really mad at me, and I know Mitch isn't happy that we don't have any money left."

Darcie scoffed.

"Mitch needs to watch it. If he doesn't stop being an idiot, we'll never find Gavin. Ugh, I could've slapped him tonight."

"He's just trying to help," Elise offered. "I can't blame him."

"You too?" Darcie rolled her eyes. "Why can't y'all give Vaughn a chance? He's answered every annoying question. He has your mom's letter. What else do you need?"

Attempting not to have Darcie upset with her either, Elise shrugged and stayed quiet.

"Vaughn mentioned they usually have musicians in the dining hall at this inn," Darcie continued, using some of the water to fix her hair in a mirror on the wall. "I think I might ask him to dance. Or even better, maybe ask someone else to dance and see if that makes him ask me. What do you think?" When Elise didn't answer, Darcie huffed. "Elise? Are you evening listening to me?"

The truth was that Elise wasn't listening. She was on the foot of the bed lost in thought about whether the fairies would be able to reach Gavin and what she would possibly say to get the boys talking to her again once they reached the dining hall. Elise apologized when she saw Darcie staring at her.

"Try to have a little fun tonight."

"*Fun?*" Elise asked. "Darcie, we're not here to have fun. We're trying to find Gavin!"

"Yeah," her friend said, finishing her hair before looking at Elise, "but we have to stop to eat and sleep. Why does that have to be uneventful? If we have to be here, let's live a little."

"You're on your own with Vaughn." Elise wanted no part in her friend's added agenda.

"Some gal pal you are," Darcie teased before striking a pose. "How do I look?"

"Like you lost your horse and you've been walking in the forest all night."

"Shut up." Laughing, Darcie slapped Elise on the arm before pulling her friend towards the door.

Vaughn and Mitch were already waiting for them in the dining hall. Once the ladies were seated, a waitress came over to offer ale. Vaughn took two mugs, holding one out for Mitch, who declined by referring to his overindulgence only hours before. Elise also shook her head, leaving Darcie to lean across the table to take the second mug with a smile. The waitress sat cups of water in front of Mitch and Elise before leaving to fetch their dinners. It was only when they were halfway through their meal of boiled chicken, potatoes, carrots, and rolls that Vaughn spoke.

"Make sure you get plenty. This is probably the last heavy meal we'll have on our journey."

"You don't have to tell me twice," Mitch replied.

Elise dug into her own food. While bland, it satisfied her hungry belly along with the cool, refreshing water. She hadn't realized how much she needed it.

When they were full and their plates had been taken, the innkeeper's wife came over with plates of —what she referred to as— her famous pie. Vaughn hummed in approval, confirming that her pie was, indeed, delicious. Darcie was quick to agree with Vaughn. Elise was too full to accept a piece but thanked the kind woman for her offer.

The one positive thing that came from Darcie being preoccupied was that it kept her attention away from meddling with Elise. Right on cue, Darcie perked up when the aforementioned musicians began playing a new set. As a handful of couples headed for the dance floor, Darcie turned to Vaughn.

"Want to dance?"

"You've discovered my weakness." His eyes flickered to Elise before looking back at Darcie. "I was born with two left feet, I'm afraid. I wouldn't dream of shaming you or subjecting anyone else in the room to such a horrific display."

Despite being rejected, Darcie stared at Vaughn as if he had just spouted a romantic sonnet.

The guy has a way with language, I'll give him that, Elise thought. Mitch looked unimpressed, cradling his face with one hand while stabbing his pie with a fork.

With a dramatic pout, Darcie pulled on Elise's arm, beckoning her to dance with her. When Elise tried to argue, Darcie looked pointedly at her, as if to say, "don't embarrass me". Rolling her eyes, Elise shuffled her feet towards the dance floor.

"Why do you always do this?" Elise hissed. "Why don't you ask Mitch?"

"Mitch is too busy sulking in the corner." Darcie glanced back at the table before adjusting where they were standing. "There. Vaughn can see us perfectly from here. Start dancing!"

"You know, I don't like this side of you too much." Elise chuckled. "I don't know if I've ever seen you so bossy and desperate." When Darcie's smile faltered, Elise quickly added that she was joking.

I need to watch it. There's no need to rile her up even more.

The two shared a laugh before clapping in rhythm with the beat of the song. Initially scared about not knowing steps or sticking out, Elise was put at ease when the dancers stood in a circle to watch brave souls take turns in the center—that is, until Elise realized everyone was done and now all eyes looked at her.

"Come on, we'll go together," Darcie said, pulling Elise's arm again.

Laughing in spite of herself, Elise linked elbows with Darcie before spinning and bouncing along to the jig amidst cheers. She was surprised to realize that she was *actually* having fun. During one of their rotations, Elise caught sight of their table. Mitch was still scowling in the corner seat—although he had apparently changed his mind about having an ale—but it was Vaughn who caught her attention wearing an unreadable expression.

He had scooted away from the table to face them. Slouched against the back of his seat, resting his drink on his knee, he watched them with a heavy-lidded gaze. Getting back in the circle to give the next person a turn, Elise leaned in close to Darcie's ear.

"Your efforts are paying off, after all. He's watching you!" she yelled over the music. Glancing over their shoulders, both girls broke into giggles when Vaughn held up his drink to toast their dancing from across the room.

"Gosh, isn't he dreamy?" Darcie gushed. "So, you think he likes me?"

"Darcie, look at how he's looking at you. It's almost primal. If that's not desire, then I don't know what is." Elise wasn't joking. Vaughn's undivided attention on her friend dancing even sent something stirring in the pit of Elise's stomach. "Go make a move!"

As the song ended, and part of the crowd returned to their seats, a tall gentleman interrupted them to ask Darcie for a dance. Momentarily conflicted, Darcie accepted.

"Go keep Vaughn busy while I dance with this guy. Maybe I can get Vaughn on the dance floor if I show him what he's missing."

"Darcie, I'm not good at these games like you. Just go dance and have fun. Vaughn'll be waiting when you get done."

Approaching the table, she noticed Mitch's sour, pale complexion.

"You okay?"

"He's just exhausted," said Vaughn, gesturing for Elise to have a seat. "It's been a long night. Anyway, I noticed you didn't have any pie earlier. I took the liberty of ordering you a slice."

Elise looked down as he pushed the plate towards her. While dancing had helped alleviate the ache in her overfed belly, she still wasn't in the mood for anything sweet.

"Thanks, but I'm not hungry. Mitch, do you want it?" Mitch continued to stare a hole in the table, his face taking on a queasy shade of green for the second time that night. "Are you sure he's okay?"

"He's fine. It happens to all of us, although he seems a bit old for this to be his first night drinking."

"We have different laws where we're from," Elise explained, watching her friend in case he fell out of his chair.

"Sounds awful." Vaughn picked up the spare fork on the table and cut a bite, holding it out for her. "Here. Take a bite."

Elise leaned away with a chuckle. "I'm really not hungry. Don't worry about me. Why don't you go cut in with Darcie? I know she'd love it."

Shoving himself away from the table, Mitch stormed off without a word. Elise looked down at his fallen chair.

"Where's he going? What happened?"

What's gotten into Mitch? I'm worried about him.

"Probably has to get that ale off his stomach again. He'll recover." Sparing a momentary glance in Darcie's direction, Vaughn returned his attention to Elise before inching the fork closer. "I insist."

Elise's smile faltered as all hints of humor disappeared from his expression. Vaughn's tone was different too–soft, almost melodic. Her eyes traveled between his smirk and outstretched hand. This man wasn't used to being told no. Acutely aware of the returning butterflies in her gut, she tried to play it cool.

I don't want to look stupid, she thought. *What would Darcie do?*

Feigning what she hoped passed as a confident smile, Elise eased closer.

"If I take the bite, will you drop it?"

"You have my word." His gaze lingered on the fork as it disappeared between her lips. Dark shadows danced across his face in the flickering candlelight, sending a shiver down Elise's spine.

This is wrong. Stop!

Swallowing the bite, she thanked him before excusing herself to go check on Mitch.

What was that? What is wrong with me?

Her mind kept repeating—screaming was more like it—the same questions at her. Nothing happened, so why was she filled with guilt? Elise told herself she was looking into it too much. She always overthought everything. This was just another example. That's all.

Through one of the front windows, she saw Mitch standing outside. Walking out to join him, she bit her lip as she wondered what to say. Before she could speak, however, Mitch bent over one of the full horse troughs to scoop water onto his face. He did so three or four times before resting both hands against the wooden edge. His soaked red hair was plastered against his forehead while drops of water streamed down his face and dripped off his chin. The front of his drenched shirt clung to his skin.

"Feel better?" Chuckling at his odd behavior, she stopped when Mitch looked over his shoulder at her. His cold, hard glare pierced through her like a knife. His brows furrowed, and his chest heaved with every breath. Normally keen on not attracting attention,

Mitch didn't seem to notice or care about the whispers and stares from a handful of others standing outside. Elise had never seen him this agitated. "Seriously, Mitch, what's *wrong* with you? Did Vaughn say something?"

Mitch wiped his face with his sleeve. "It's not what he said."

"Well, *what* then? Maybe you need to lay down if you're drunk."

"I'm not drunk, and it's not what he said," Mitch repeated. "I don't like the guy."

"So, you stomp out and dunk your head in water a bunch of times? Am I missing something?" Elise asked. "What is making you so snippy with everybody?"

Rather than answer, Mitch glanced back into the dining room. She followed his gaze through the window and saw that Darcie had returned to the table. She was laughing at something Vaughn said as she finished the rest of Elise's slice of pie. Elise watched for Mitch's reaction, but he was careful this time not to give one. Why couldn't Darcie see what she was doing to him? It was so painfully obvious that Mitch wanted her.

"Why don't you just tell her how you feel?" Elise asked.

His answering glare made her instantly regret meddling. She would leave that to Darcie from now on. In his soaked, bothered state, Mitch looked dangerous. While the look certainly suited him, Elise pulled her lips into a thin line and stayed quiet.

"You think that's what's bothering me?" he asked, pointing over his shoulder. "I don't care what she does. She's free to do whatever she wants." Elise knew her confusion showed on her face. He rolled his eyes with a scoff, further making Elise feel like she was missing something. "We need to go look for Gavin by ourselves."

"But Vaughn knows the way," she said.

"Then we'll ask for directions," he argued. Elise kept her joke about men never asking for directions to herself. Mitch wasn't in a playful mood, and it would probably make things worse. When she failed to reply, he shook his head again as he stepped around her. "Forget it."

Fed up with his stubbornness, Elise whirled around and called out to his retreating figure. He paused in the doorway. "Instead of storming off, why don't you just tell me what's wrong? If you're not drunk, and it's not Darcie throwing herself at Vaughn, then why do you hate him so much?"

"Just drop it. I'm going to bed."

"No!" She moved to stand between him and the entrance. "I'm sick of watching you sulk around and feel sorry for yourself. Either cut it out or tell me what's wrong with you!"

"What's wrong with *me*?" He cocked his head, towering over her. Although intimidated, she held her ground. Elise knew it'd be better for Mitch if she were the one to get it out of him than let Darcie's temper do it. "*I'm* the only one who's not drooling all over that guy. You think that little display on the dance floor meant nothing? I've got to stick up for Gavin. It's what friends do."

If Elise was confused before, she was completely lost now. Maybe Mitch had had more to drink than he realized? He wasn't making any sense.

"What does Gavin have to do with Vaughn watching Darcie dance? She wanted him to see—"

"He wasn't watching her."

"What? Mitch, I saw him looking—"

"He wasn't watching her," he said through gritted teeth. Raking his fingers through his hair, he looked at her as if to ask if she could really be that stupid. "He was watching *you*."

CHAPTER 9

For the fifth consecutive time, Gavin was disarmed within seconds. Frustrated, he growled as he picked up his sword before waving it around to get a good feel for the next round.

"You're still doing it wrong," Tristan called out. "And quit swishing it around like that. You look like an idiot." Tristan stomped over to where Gavin stood before clapping him on the back. "Quit slouching. You've got to strengthen your core. Put your weight on your dominant leg." Gavin had no choice but to comply. He was sick of getting his butt kicked, but Tristan knew what he was talking about. Gavin adjusted his hands to the correct placement. "Better. Now, your first concern is to not be hit." Gavin thought that was a given, but he didn't say anything. "Beginners get hit often because they're too busy trying to slash, attack, and react. You want to counter and defend yourself simultaneously. Keep your hands and wrists protected."

"How am I supposed to remember all of this when a sword is coming at me?"

Tristan shrugged. "Be quicker than your opponent." Gavin scowled at him. "Let's go again," Tristan continued. "Keep the sword vertical above your shoulder. Throw the blade out as you step to the side." Gavin followed Tristan's lead as the instructions were given. He felt the motion from his shoulders all the way down his back. "Let the blade do the work as you step forward and follow through." Gavin did as he was told. Tristan sighed. "You're using your arms too much."

"What! How? I'm doing *exactly* what you're doing!" Gavin snapped.

"Control your temper. If *you're* not in control, they are. You'll eventually get the timing right. Do it again. Chest out. Sword vertical. No, loosen your grip a bit. Keep your hold fluid or you're going to exhaust yourself too quickly."

Once their blades met in midair, Gavin strained against the force. Although the drill lasted longer than before, Tristan gained the advantage and held Gavin's sword in his other hand moments later. Gavin stared at his own blade aimed mere inches from his chest.

"You were gripping too tightly," Tristan said. "When you go in swinging too heavily, you're sure to fail. The moment the blades meet is crucial. It takes the right pose and balance to decide control."

Every time he turned around, Gavin felt like there was another rule to remember. The guys in the movies made it look so easy. They just waved the swords around and stabbed each other. This was different. It was an art form, and it was one that Tristan was fastidious about. He glanced over at his group of similarly skilled—or unskilled—recruits. While also lacking in ability, Gavin noticed that the others weren't nearly as sweaty and worn out as he was. Was he really that out of shape? He sighed in relief when the whistle sounded, signaling a break.

"Let's go again." Gavin turned to see Tristan in his starting position once more. "What is it?"

"It's time for a break," Gavin said.

"For *them*. You asked for my help. Pick up your weapon."

Gavin had had just about enough.

"Why are you being so hard on me?" Gavin was too busy watching enviously at the other boys guzzling from their canteens and splashing their faces in the river that he didn't hear Tristan's footsteps. It was only when he saw an approaching shadow that he looked up.

Tristan stared down at him with a hardened expression.

"They see you as you are—weak. You want to prove them right? By all means, rest." He tossed Gavin's sword at his feet. "But Rona's taken an interest in you, and as the only other one here who knows what that means, I suggest you quit whining and pick up your weapon."

"Don't you think he's had enough, Tristan?" Both boys looked over as Everett approached with Erick. "He deserves a break like the rest of us." Tristan responded by turning on his heel and crossing the field towards his tent. Everett sighed. "He'll be back."

"He's right though," Gavin said. "I asked for his help. Whatever is going to help me get us all out of here is worth it."

Everett and Erick exchanged anxious glances.

"All of us?" Erick asked.

"Don't let anyone else hear you say that," Everett added. "If they think there's a chance of an uprising, you're looking for an even worse punishment than before. Best to focus on yourself and forget the rest of us. We've accepted our fates."

"Given up, you mean?" Gavin asked.

Erick frowned. "We'll most likely die in battle or by Rona herself. Even if we found a way out, she has spies everywhere."

Before Gavin could reply, Isaac blew the whistle, signaling the start of the next activity.

Archery sounds a lot better than picking up that sword again, Gavin thought. *How hard could it be?*

He had seen enough shows to know how to shoot an arrow. Once the targets were set up, the soldiers were placed back into their skill groups and instructed to take turns shooting. The line moved quicker than Gavin would've liked, and before long it was his turn. Glancing to his left, he saw Tristan stepping up to the front of his own line. Gavin watched him lift the bow with ease before pulling back and releasing the arrow with effortless precision.

Show off, Gavin thought. Mimicking what he saw, he lifted the bow and quickly released the arrow. Rather than shoot straight through the air, the arrow landed only a couple of feet in front of him. Trying to ignore the chuckles he heard behind him, he picked up another arrow and shot again. And again. By now the snickers and taunting were making Gavin's blood boil. Tightening his jaw, he pulled the last arrow back so tight he thought he might just break the string before releasing it with a flood of adrenaline. This time, the arrow traveled the entire distance, but shot into the outer edge of the target next to his.

Gavin squeezed the bow until his knuckles were white. He had half a thought to strangle the boys behind him who were in hysterics by this point.

"I can honestly say I've never seen that before," Tristan said when Gavin took his spot at the back of the line again.

"Why're you even over here?" Gavin grumbled.

"I'm on my way to rest. I have sentry duty in a couple of hours. Thought I'd stop and see how you were doing. Are you glad you took a break?"

"Leave me alone, man."

"I tried to tell you," Tristan continued. "Too bad Isaac wasn't here to see your little tantrum. I dare say the enemy better watch out. With skills like yours, their boots will get scuffed by your arrows for sure."

Gavin stepped out of line and grabbed the front of Tristan's tunic. Murmurs and whispers rang out around them as the others expected another fight.

"Careful, Striess," Tristan whispered. "Pick your battles wisely. If you're not in control, they are."

Feeling his adrenaline building, Gavin wanted nothing more than to punch the smirk right off Tristan's face. Locking his jaw, he took a steadying breath as the other boy's words sank in. Tristan was right. Even if Gavin got a shot in, Tristan was an advanced fighter. Despite his pale and sickly frame, Gavin knew Tristan had the strength training to take him down. Releasing Tristan's tunic, Gavin turned to join the back of his line again. Tristan made his way to his tent and the training resumed as normal for the next couple of hours.

"Striess," Isaac called as the recruits dispersed from the training area. "I want you to stand guard overnight."

"With Tristan? Forget it."

"Are you *willfully* defying me, Boy?"

Hearing Isaac's tone, Gavin instantly regretted his outburst. "No, sir."

"Good. If you want to be the best, you train with the best." When Gavin argued that Tristan got to rest beforehand, Isaac laughed. "It still amazes me how spoiled you are. When your rotation is finished, the entire group will hike back to the mountain in the morning. I want no issues from you. Understood?"

"Yes, sir." Gavin glared at Isaac's retreating figure. The only good thing that came from standing guard was that it allowed his body a break from any more physical exertion.

Sentry duty passed uneventfully, which Gavin figured he should be thankful about. At least that meant there were no threats around them. Standing this long on his feet, however, gave him a new appreciation for the guards he had bypassed in Haighdlen without a second thought. Gazing up at the early morning sky, Gavin's surroundings began to blur as his eyelids fought to close.

"Wake up already!" Tristan hissed, elbowing Gavin in the arm. "I overheard the officers talking. Rona's coming to visit today, and I don't want you getting us into any more trouble."

Gavin groaned.

"Why is she coming back so soon?"

"Does it matter?" Tristan had a point. Rona didn't need a reason to do any of the horrible things she did. "As soon as our replacements arrive, we'll pack up our gear and—"

When he didn't finish his sentence, Gavin turned to see a look of horror on Tristan's face. He had somehow grown even paler as he pointed at Gavin's shoulder.

"D-don't move," he stammered, pulling his sword out as quietly as possible.

Gavin shivered, bracing himself for an enormous bug or snake-like creature. Moving only his eyes, he saw a ball of light hovering next to him. When the light vanished, Gavin's curiosity got the better of him. Glancing to his right, he recognized the fairy standing on his shoulder.

"Hey, it's you!" His shoulders sagged with relief when he saw Sage. A sliver of hope swelled in his chest. "Are the others here too?"

"You know a fairy?" Tristan asked, hesitant to sheath his sword. He squeezed the hilt of it when two more balls of light bounced forward towards them. Tristan took a step back. "I'll alert the others."

"No, wait!" Gavin grabbed the fabric of Tristan's sleeve to stop him. "They won't hurt us."

"Says *you*," Hemlock scoffed. Tristan jerked his arm away from Gavin's hold. Turning sharply on his heel to warn the others, he was hit in the face by a cloud of dust. "Good shot, Thicket!"

Gavin heard Thicket's twinkling laughter between Tristan's spluttering coughs. Wiping his blood-shot eyes, Tristan blinked rapidly as he stared at the insidious creatures on Gavin's shoulders.

"Is *anything* normal about you?" Tristan rubbed more dust out of his eyes.

Ignoring the question, Gavin turned his head back and forth to address all three fairies.

"How did you guys find me? Do you know where the others are? Are they okay?"

"Ugh, Sage, shut him up and get this over with," Thicket said, rolling her eyes.

Gavin turned expectantly towards the youngest fairy, who hadn't taken his eyes off Tristan. Assuring Sage that Tristan wasn't going to hurt them, Sage looked back at Gavin.

"Elise and the others are safe. She wanted me to tell you they are coming to save you."

Gavin felt elated.

Thank God! Maybe I'll get out of here and see my friends after all. I'll see Elise again.

"There. Message received. Let's get out of here," Thicket snapped.

"Wait!" Gavin called out before they could fly away.

Hemlock rolled his eyes.

"I keep telling you, Sage. Humans are spoiled and greedy. They only know how to take and ask for more. Don't listen to a word he says."

"You're completely obsessed with these humans," Thicket chimed in, shaking her head in disapproval at the smaller fairy.

"Just one more thing. I promise," Gavin said. "Let me have some fairy magic to get me and these guys out of here."

As expected, Hemlock and Thicket burst into fits of laughter.

"It's too much," Thicket said as she fanned herself with her tiny hand. "It hurts." She and Hemlock continued howling at Gavin's request.

"I want to, but I can't do it alone," Sage replied, watching the other two until they recovered.

"Sage, don't you dare," Hemlock warned. "It's our fault for letting it go this long, but this time, Thicket and I won't allow it."

"Yeah, and they have that charming guide leading them. They'll be fine without us meddling," Thicket replied.

A charming tour guide? Gavin didn't think he liked the sound of that, but there wasn't time to learn more.

"I can't leave these guys here. They're in just as much danger as I am. Rona will kill them if I don't."

"That's their problem," Hemlock replied, crossing his arms. "Right, Thicket?" When Thicket didn't immediately agree, Gavin took advantage of her hesitation.

"Please," he pleaded. "They're kids. Help me get them home. I won't ask you for anything else. I promise."

Before Thicket could respond, Hemlock flew to hover in front of Gavin's face.

"I thought the girl was the worst of the lot, but it's this one. Don't you two lift a finger to help them. They're nothing but trouble."

"They've paid, as we've requested, for every favor," Sage reminded him.

"I hate humans," Thicket said, looking between Gavin and Tristan, "but I hate that tyrannical sorceress more. If we help them, we hurt her."

"So, either way, someone suffers?" Hemlock drummed his fingers together, considering his options, before nodding. "Deal. Pay up then."

Knowing he didn't have anything to offer, Gavin tried stalling by searching his pockets, but was saved when Isaac called out his and Tristan's names to move out.

"Get on my back and hide out in my bag until we get back to the mountain, so they don't see you," Gavin said. Scowling at the orders, the fairies reluctantly followed the instructions to stay hidden.

"You're not seriously taking them back with us, are you?" Tristan hissed.

"It's the only chance we have," Gavin said.

"You're stupider than I thought," Tristan muttered before shaking his head and storming off.

Gavin spent the entirety of the hike trying to come up with a plan to pay them. He had nothing valuable on him, and he doubted they'd be interested in a human-sized weapon.

Maybe Everett or Erick can help, he wondered.

"Can you guys keep a secret?" he whispered once their unit was back in the damp, guarded holding room. Everett and Erick nodded, scooting closer so they wouldn't be overheard by the patrolling officers. Gavin reached behind him before lifting Sage up on his hand. His two friends looked as if they were going to scream although no sound came out.

"That's more like it," Hemlock said, climbing Gavin's shirt before standing on his shoulder. "At least everyone else knows how to properly greet a fairy."

"There's two of them?" The blood drained from Erick's face as he gazed in amazement only to jump a moment later when Thicket popped up on Gavin's other shoulder.

"You're either really brave or really foolish, Gavin," Everett said, shaking his head. "Never make deals with fairies."

"Oh, he didn't tell you?" Thicket asked. "He's made several already. Wants to make another one."

Both boys looked up at Gavin.

"They're going to help us get out of here," Gavin said. Everett and Erick stared at him with blank expressions. "What?"

"Have you lost your mind?" Everett asked. "Making deals with fairies? You might as well sell your soul to the devil himself."

Gavin looked down at the three fairies, who didn't respond. They had been harmless up until now except hollow threats.

Why is everyone always afraid of them? What could they possibly do that's so bad?

"My great-uncle met a fairy once," Erick whispered with a shiver. "To this day, he thinks he's a Labrador." Gavin and Everett tried to stifle their laughter. Erick cracked a smile. "Sure, it was fun watching him fetch sticks for a while, but he only relieves himself outside as well."

Thicket and Hemlock erupted into such hard laughter that they didn't realize they were hovering until they were surrounded by light.

"What's going on over there?" an officer called.

Gavin yanked the two into his lap next to Sage. He held his breath until the officer moved on to another group of boys.

"That was close," he whispered.

"What're you all talking about?" All three boys jumped when Tristan crawled over to sit next to them. When he saw Sage, Thicket, and Hemlock, he growled in the back of his throat. "You brought them back *here*?" He looked as if the fairies were going to spit fire any moment.

"These three are different," Gavin explained. "They want to help us." Hearing Hemlock clear his throat, Gavin scoffed. "They're *willing* to help us. . .for a price." Everett and Erick looked at each other. "Please," said Gavin. "This is our chance to beat Rona and get home. If anyone can get us out of here, it's them."

When none of them offered anything, Gavin frowned. Without payment, the three fairies would fly away without a second thought. The hope building up in his chest started to fade away, along with any plans of seeing Elise and the others again.

What chance do my friends have of finding me here? If I can't find something these fairies want, it's useless.

"Will you take this?"

Gavin looked up to see Tristan holding his medallion.

"What're you doing?" Gavin asked. "That belonged to your dad. It's special."

"All the more reason to use it," Tristan replied, rolling the medallion between his fingers. "If they can help us get these kids to freedom, it will have been worth it."

I underestimated him, Gavin thought.

"We accept," Hemlock said, watching as Thicket and Sage took the medallion from Tristan's hand to a hidden crevice in the wall. "Payment has been received, but you're not getting our magic."

"What?" Gavin hissed. "But that was the deal! Tristan paid fair and square."

"And yet," replied Hemlock, rocking back and forth on his heels, "the last I checked, fair and square wasn't the way fairies operated. Not a word, Sage."

Sage closed his mouth rather than argue.

"Typical fairy," Tristan growled, crouching down to Hemlock's level. "Listen, you little gnat, if you're not going to help free us, then I want my medallion back."

"Not so fast." Hemlock leaped out of the way as Tristan attempted to grab him. "I said we weren't going to give you magic. I didn't say we weren't going to help get you out. If we cause any mischief, it will be of our own choosing. I'm done taking requests from humans. Come on, Thicket."

The boys watched as the two plotting fairies crept along the edge of room, careful not to fly and expose their lights. In the dimly-lit room, Gavin lost sight of them quickly. Five minutes went by with no sign of either fairy. Gavin noticed how focused Sage was on the other side of the room and assumed he could see the other two. He started to ask Sage what was going on, but the small fairy remained silent. Exchanging a glance with Tristan, Everett, and Erick, Gavin perked up as one of the officers inquired about a sound coming from the far side of the room.

"Do you see anything?" asked the officer.

"No, but I definitely hear something," said a second, pressing his ear against the wall. Both officers jumped as a third guard by the door let out a loud sneeze and moan before stumbling forward. A flash of gold dust floating around the man's face indicated he had been hit with a bout of fairy dust.

"It's an ambush!" cried the first officer. "Alert the commander!"

Before either could take a step, one of the lit torches on the wall separated from its sconce. As the torch bounced and landed on the ground, its flames engulfed one of the brown sleeping mats.

Within seconds, the flames spread from mat to mat until half of the room was consumed in the strengthening fire. All that could be heard were the screams, cries, and footsteps of the officers and recruits as everyone charged towards the only exit. The guard at the door struggled to find the correct key and was almost crushed by the fleeing crowd when the door finally opened. Gavin and his friends leapt to their feet as the fire intensified. Above the chaotic scene, two balls of light bounced with glee.

Sage hovered near Gavin's face. "Why must it always be destruction with those two?"

"We got to get out of here," Gavin said with a cough.

"Wait!" Tristan called, pulling on Gavin's sleeve. "I hear something. I think someone's trapped!"

Sure enough, Gavin could hear coughing and cries for help coming from the back of the room. He turned towards Sage.

"Get Everett and Erick out safely. We'll find out who's trapped and meet you all outside." Everett hesitated as Erick followed Sage. "Go! When you get out, don't stop running."

Everett ran out.

At least they're safe, Gavin thought as his eyes began to water from the smoke. *Now to find whoever is stuck and get out of here while we still can.*

Tristan had already run towards the cries and Gavin struggled to see through the flames. The smoke thickened around him, and he was acutely aware of the heat. He struggled to breathe. Covering his nose with the collar of his tunic, he inched towards the sounds of coughing.

Where are they? Gavin couldn't see any sign of officers or Isaac attempting to save anyone. *And they call* me *the coward.*

"What are you doing?" Thicket's voice squeaked in his ear. "You wanted to escape. Go!"

"I'm not leaving people trapped in here. I have to make sure everyone's out!" Gavin cried, shielding his face from the flying embers.

"Never grateful. Never satisfied," Hemlock complained.

"Can you both shut up and help me find Tristan?"

The balls of light zipped around the room until Thicket claimed to see him. She and Hemlock used their magic to create a path through the fire so that Gavin could reach Tristan. He was crouched over two crying boys.

"I couldn't find a way through." Tristan's voice was hoarse from the smoke and his face was smudged with sweat and ash. "Will they hold that open for us?" He cocked his head towards the path.

They better, Gavin thought.

"Let's get out of here!" he shouted, lifting one of the boys over his shoulder as Tristan did the same with the second. Saying a prayer, Gavin locked eyes with the exit across the room. So far, Thicket and Hemlock were holding the tunnel of fire open for them. But did he trust them?

We don't have a choice. We'll have to make a run for it.

Licking his lips, and taking a deep breath, he stumbled through the narrow path. He was losing his energy fast, and the boy's weight on his back was slowing him down even further. Gavin dragged his feet as fast as he could, but it was more of a limp than a sprint. As he neared the exit, he felt his lungs fill with more smoke and was overwhelmed by the need to cough. Not wanting to stop, he tried to hold his breath, but it only made things worse. As his chest tightened, he lurched forward as his knees wobbled beneath him.

"Almost there!" he heard Tristan cry behind him, urging him along.

Suffocating and overheated, Gavin staggered towards the deserted exit. The boy he was carrying had tightened his hold around Gavin's neck and his cries sounded amplified. All Gavin could do was focus on the door. The need to get out. The need to survive. Nothing else mattered. If he didn't go faster, the flames would block their way out. Panic flooded through him as he watched both balls of light above them fly out and join a third. Between them, they carried the medallion.

The realization of their retreat hit Gavin hard, and he looked over his shoulder to see the tunnel closing up behind them.

"Almost there. Run!" he cried, urging his legs to go faster despite the weight and fatigue.

The all-encompassing heat was growing, and he could hear heavy breathing behind him. As Gavin reached the doorway, he felt

Tristan's hand push him hard outside. Fresh air filled his lungs. The boys stepped out onto the mountainside walkway, but they didn't stop. The smell of fish and smoke filled the air as the ocean spray cooled their faces. Only when they reached the winding staircase through the doorway on the other side of the mountain did Gavin lower the boy on his back. Throwing the boy's arm around his neck, Gavin wrapped an arm around his waist to walk alongside him as Tristan did the same.

Down, down, down they hobbled around the multiple flights of steps until, at last, they entered the circular entrance room.

"Almost there," Gavin panted, wiping the sweat from his brow. Ducking under the low archway, the boys exited outside onto the sand. Seashells and rocks crunched beneath their feet. Crashing waves and seagull cries were music to their ears.

We made it!

Gavin's celebratory thoughts were short-lived, however, as they walked along the shore. With each step around the edge of the mountain, something didn't feel right. There were no sights or sounds of people—officer or kids—through the thick fog.

"Where is everybody?" Tristan asked.

As soon as the words left his lips, the question was answered. In front of them, hovering in the sky, were all the boys. Each one was frozen in place, unable to blink or speak, all wearing expressions of horror and shock. Gavin's eyes lowered to see Isaac and the other officers standing at attention, and ahead of the line was none other than Rona herself.

CHAPTER 10

Despite the amount of ale he consumed the night before, Vaughn was the first one ready to leave the following morning. By the time the other three made their way downstairs, he had arranged breakfast and convinced the innkeeper's wife to pack extra food for the journey.

"Eat quickly. We need to make good time today," he told them.

The other two obeyed, but Elise didn't have much of an appetite. Her stomach was in knots, having spent the entire night in denial. Not twelve hours earlier, Mitch revealed that Vaughn had been watching *her* dance instead of Darcie.

Guys go after Darcie. Not me, she reminded herself. *It's always been that way.*

Rather than return to the dining room, Elise had left Mitch to go to bed. Darcie didn't come up for another couple of hours. That had to mean something. When Darcie chose a target, she seldom missed. Mitch was mistaken.

Are you sure? Gavin went for you, her thoughts countered. While true, that was different, and she wasn't going to drive herself further insane by listing the ways.

"What is with you today?" Darcie finally asked after they had walked what felt like five or six hours with minimal conversation. While part of it was Elise avoiding confrontation, the other half of it was her trying not to show how out of shape she was. "Why're you so quiet?"

"I'm not," she replied, panting. That was the wrong thing to say. Darcie always knew when she was lying. "I'm worried about Gavin. That's all."

There, that's not a lie.

It was also enough to stop Darcie's questions. . .for now. Forcing herself to look at anything other than her best friend, Elise saw the sunlight glistening across some water way ahead of them through the trees.

"What is that?"

Please be some water I can cool off in.

"Lake Laulie," said Vaughn. He was in better physical shape than all of them combined, but Elise could hear the exertion of the trip taking its toll in his voice.

"What?" Elise didn't hide her shock. "How can that be Lake Laulie? We've been to it before and it's closer to Clara than we are now."

"Lake Laulie is a vast magical lake, but it's not near Clara."

But we've been traveling for almost a day and a half! How can we not be past the lake yet?

Sensing her confusion, Vaughn pointed towards the direction of the water. "Its magical properties also cause illusions. You probably thought you could see across it when you visited. Most inhabited lakes have the same protection. Things are not always what they seem here."

That's the truth. You'd think I'd know that by now.

"But when we followed the princess the other night, we saw the lake when we crossed through Clara," said Mitch.

"Impossible," Vaughn said. "If you were on foot, what you saw wasn't Lake Laulie."

"Then what *did* we see?" Elise asked.

"You might have seen the edge of The Bedeviled Swamp. Its size is also uncertain as it can change locations."

"Of course, it can," Mitch grumbled.

"But the king took us to Lake Laulie when we first came here," Darcie argued. "And we made it to the castle within hours on foot."

"The king has magic, doesn't he? I bet you made it back from Clara in record time as well." His raised eyebrow provided them with the answer.

Mom must've had a little fairy magic we didn't know about when she first left the castle. It would make sense that she'd save some to make the trip easier. We should've known it was too easy for her, especially in her condition.

Elise realized that every time they had traveled away from the castle before, they were in the presence of someone possessing magic. That would explain why Ruby needed Ian's magic with their carriage and all the other quick, easy distances before that didn't add up until now. Magic was funny like that. She wished Vaughn had magic. Maybe they'd be further, and her feet wouldn't hurt as much as they did.

"It sounds like you've been fortunate in the past to see so much of Haighdlen with such little effort. Most of us can't boast the same experience," Vaughn said.

Elise recalled looking at the map in the castle library. All four kingdoms seemed small enough when mounted on the wall, but now she felt stupid for assuming they could cross Haighdlen in a day.

"So, where are we then?" Darcie asked.

Vaughn stopped walking to search their surroundings. Seeing a clearing in the trees, he beckoned them forward. To their left, he pointed towards large rolling hills in the distance across the portion of Lake Laulie they could see. "Those are the Laurille Oak Hills."

The reference did little to help Elise's understanding, but she listened, nonetheless. All she cared about was getting to Gavin as fast as possible. Tugging on the chain around her neck, she retrieved the bottle hidden under the front of her gown.

"What are you doing?" Darcie asked.

"What's it look like? He just said magic can make us go faster. We were going to use it to travel before anyway."

"Yeah, but that was when we were going home," Darcie argued.

"Put that away!" Vaughn hissed. After checking their surroundings, he chastised Elise for holding the magic out in the open.

He waited until she hid the necklace. "I don't know what you had to do to possess fairy magic, but I told you last night that it was a mistake to trust fairies."

"*This* is how we get to Gavin faster." Elise didn't back down from his disapproving stare despite her knees feeling like they would buckle at any moment. "I feel stupid enough for not using it before. We're nowhere near the next kingdom, and you said we'd need to take a boat after that. Meanwhile, Gavin's in danger."

"I have half a mind to throw that necklace in the lake. Keep it hidden."

Elise knew Vaughn meant it. Why was he so against magic? The fairies had only helped them. She didn't have a reason not to trust them. She mentally corrected herself that Sage was the only one she could really trust. The other two validated Vaughn's opinion of fairies.

"Do what he says, Elise," Mitch said.

Now Mitch is taking his side? She thought Mitch of all people would support her choice to use the magic. Tightening her mouth into a thin line, she stared at the ground as she spoke.

"How much further can we get today without magic?" She gestured towards the tall mountain peaks visible above the trees ahead of them. "Let me guess. We have to go through those?"

"Certainly not," Vaughn replied. "Continuing eastward towards those mountains would add several days and unnecessary obstacles to delay us." He pointed off to his right. "We'll take the southern route. If we push hard enough, we could make it to the shore and take a small boat over to Laurishire." Mitch, Darcie, and Elise exchanged uncertain glances. "It's another town, located near where the Spryte River empties into Allegiance Gulf." He shook his head at their lost expressions and began walking again. "Just trust me that I know where I'm going. I'm surprised at your lack of foresight to carry a map. Let us pray we are able to find a boat quickly and get to the town. From there, we'll go on foot to the border."

Elise remembered from the map that Haighdlen and Vynchia were connected while the other two kingdoms were isolated.

"If we're taking a boat anyway, why not take it straight to Vynchia? Why get out and walk?"

"Trying to cross the entire gulf will be too risky, given the hazardous waters, so we will stay in the shallower parts to reach the other side. Going the rest of the way on land will be safer."

"And longer," Elise pointed out. She watched his shoulders tense as he took a deep breath.

"I am to guide you there, am I not?" When she didn't reply, he continued. "Trust that I will steer you clear of as many dangers as I can. Not many shortcuts exist. Should you attempt to use any," he said, lifting his chin towards her necklace. "I will not be joining you. Do you have a plan to save your precious Gavin or defeat Rona on your own?"

Smirking at her answering glare, he turned on his heel to continue leading them. She let Darcie pass her and walked next to Mitch.

"Last night you were ready to punch him, and now you're blindly following? I thought you wanted to find Gavin fast!"

"I do," he grumbled, staring a hole into Vaughn's back. His eyes flickered over to Darcie, who jogged to walk by their guide's side. "Some things just aren't worth killing yourself over. If he says he'll get us to Gavin, let's do it his way."

"I know you don't believe that. Come on, Mitch, *this* will get us there now!" She grabbed the chain of her necklace and shook it.

"But what if we need to use it once we get to Gavin?"

Her mouth opened, but no words came out. As much as she hated to admit it, he was right.

"*Fine.*" She huffed, crunching the leaves beneath her feet harder than she needed to. "But as soon as we reach Gavin, we use it."

"Ah, we're in luck!" Vaughn pointed behind them towards a horse and cart heading their way. He held up his hand, prompting the man driving the cart to slow the horse down. "Wait here."

The three watched as Vaughn jogged up to the cart. He was too far away to hear any words, but they could tell by his gestures that he was asking for a ride. Skeptical at first, Elise and the others were surprised when the stranger nodded and beckoned them to him. Vaughn helped hoist the ladies up before following Mitch onto the back of the cart. Crates of vegetables and grain took up most of the space, but given how painful their feet were, the four travelers had no problems adjusting to their new transportation.

As they set off, Elise didn't know how much time passed before her anger finally dissipated. She was too tired to argue anymore, yet the jarring ride made it impossible to nap.

It beats the alternative, she reminded herself. The bumpy cart ride was a dream compared to any more walking. Vaughn passed around some of the food from his satchel. Taking a sip of water from his canteen, he pointed to the driver.

"He's delivering these crates to a market near Cloakglynn. He says he can drop us off about a mile from the coast."

Another mile of walking, Elise thought with a groan. *If they'd trust me, we could use this magic and be home in five seconds.*

She didn't know what irritated her more; Vaughn being able to fall asleep within five minutes of finishing his sandwich or Darcie watching him sleep.

"Are you sure about last night?" Elise whispered so only Mitch could hear her. "It looks like Darcie's made up her mind about him, and we all know what that means."

Darcie gets what she wants, Elise thought. *Period.*

"I know what I saw." Mitch huffed, picking up an onion from a nearby crate. He idly rolled it around in his hands before tossing it onto Darcie's lap. She jumped in surprise and looked over at them. "Would you knock it off already?" he asked her. "You're just making yourself look desperate and sad."

"Shut up, Mitch! Go to sleep." Chucking the onion back at him, Darcie glared when Mitch caught it in midair with a smile. She crossed her arms before leaning on Vaughn's shoulder. Mitch's scowl returned as he dropped the onion back into the crate.

Elise closed her eyes, hoping the tension would clear itself. When would they both stop torturing each other? If Gavin were here, he would know how to tell Mitch to let it go. At long last, her feigned dozing paid off as she felt exhaustion winning despite her stiff resting position.

It was unclear how much time passed while she jerked in and out of sleep. When her brain gave up trying, Elise opened her eyes to a tranquil twilight sky. Deep red and orange clouds swirled against a darkening blue sky as the sun refused to give in to the night just yet. The first fireflies of the evening twinkled against the thick wall of trees on either side of the path. The sound of leaves and twigs crunching beneath the wheels and horse's hooves was only broken up by Mitch's periodic snores. Shivering at the evening chill, Elise was brought back to reality when she noticed Vaughn watching her.

How long has he been awake?

Maybe she was imagining things. She doubted her paranoia would be this high if it weren't for Mitch. Elise checked the other two who were still fast asleep. Darcie would be horrified if she knew about the trail of drool on Vaughn's shoulder. If it bothered him, he didn't show it. He was slouched with her friend's head draped across his left side, yet his eyes continued to stare in Elise's direction. Feeling her cheeks start to burn, Elise licked her lips and began attempting to stare a hole through the vegetable crates. Curiosity got the better of her, however, until she checked to see if he was still looking.

He smiled this time when they made eye contact. Elise found it hard to look away. Why did he keep staring? Maybe he overheard Mitch and was trying to play some trick. Feeling her anxiety rising, she gasped when the wheels of the cart rolled over an area of large pebbles. The bumps were enough to lift her bottom off her seat while also causing the other two to wake up.

"Sorry about that," the driver apologized once the cart slowed to a halt. Darcie blushed with a chuckle as she scooted away from Vaughn and wiped her mouth. "This is where I leave you."

Mitch hopped off the side to come help them out before Vaughn could. Elise's heart fell when Darcie declined his help, choosing instead to jump alone. Wanting to avoid Vaughn's help, as well as save Mitch's dignity, Elise reached out and accepted his hand. Once Vaughn joined them, the cart set off down the path towards the mountains.

"Didn't you say it was dangerous that way?" Darcie asked. "Should he be doing that at night?"

"He'll manage." Vaughn shrugged, not looking too concerned, as he adjusted the strap of his satchel across his chest. "Shall we?"

Thanks to the nap and break off their feet, the mile walk passed by uneventfully, and Elise's heart lifted when she saw the approaching shore. It was nightfall by the time the four of them reached the river.

"There won't be any boatmen until morning, so we'll sleep here."

"*Here*?" Mitch asked Vaughn. "Out in the open like this?"

"Is it safe?" Elise asked. "Shouldn't we try to find a cave or something?"

"Be my guest," Vaughn replied, already busy bending down to pick up sticks. "I'm going to build a fire and catch a couple of fish for dinner. You let me know how that works out for you."

"Come on, guys," said Darcie, joining in to collect firewood. "Vaughn knows what he's doing, and it's a clear night. If he says it's safe, then it's safe. We have to rough it a bit, that's all."

"Should we help him too?" Elise asked Mitch.

"Looks like he has all the help he needs."

This is going to be a long night, Elise thought with a heavy sigh.

Like Mitch, she wasn't a fan of watching Darcie fawn all over their guide, but Elise had to admit that they wouldn't have made it this far on their own. Not only did he have strength and charm, but he had survival skills. Elise could see why Mitch felt threatened, though he would never admit to it. He ate his dinner without a word and went to sleep early.

"I'm sorry about Mitch," Darcie said. "He should be more grateful."

"He's dealing with a lot," Elise said in his defense. "His best friend is missing."

"Yeah, well Gavin's *your* boyfriend, and I don't see you pouting off by yourself. The least he could do is try to be helpful."

"Leave him alone, Darcie," Elise said, growing impatient with her friend. Ever since Vaughn had entered the picture, Darcie was becoming more and more unrecognizable. Elise was ready for her friend to throw herself all over Vaughn and be done with it. Watching what it was doing to Mitch was pitiful, and Elise was about ready to pull her hair out.

"We need to go to bed," Darcie said. Elise scoffed. Whenever Darcie felt belittled or embarrassed, she was quick to boss everyone around.

I guess there's one part of her I still recognize after all.

"Let us count our blessings that it is a warm, rainless night," said Vaughn. "I'm quite a fan of sleeping beneath the stars like this."

"Elise, you coming?" Darcie asked.

"In a minute." Elise wanted to wait until both Mitch *and* Darcie were asleep so she wouldn't have to witness any more petty power games between them. While drowsy, she didn't feel like she could fall asleep yet. Pulling her cloak around her, she stared into the dancing flames before it dawned on her she had chosen to be alone with Vaughn. To make the situation worse, he stood up only to come sit by her. Again, she felt the heat return to her cheeks.

It's just the fire, she told herself.

Neither of them said anything. If not for the sporadic, popping sounds of the fire and the chirping choir of crickets nearby, they would've been sitting in a dead silence.

"You've been quiet today," he finally said, draping his arms across his knees. "Everything all right?"

"Yep."

"Are you sure?"

"Uh-huh."

Maybe he'll get the hint and leave me alone. I don't know what to say or do like Darcie does.

"I'm sorry if I'm causing a rift between you and your friends." His apology caught Elise off guard, causing her to look up at him, which was a mistake. The roaring firelight danced across his face the same way it had the previous night. His eyes, again heavy-lidded, appeared soft and genuine. She could see herself reflected in them.

How can this man look this good after trekking through the forest all day?

It only made her more self-conscious about her own appearance.

"You're not," Elise said. *Well, not completely*, she finished in her head. "There's just a lot on our minds."

"What's on *your* mind?"

The huskiness of his tone radiated throughout her body. This was quite a romantic situation. . .but it wasn't with Gavin. It was wrong. Everything about this—where she was, what she felt—was wrong. The voice in her brain reminded her that he was waiting for an answer. Elise looked around for something safe to talk about. She settled on the small flickering lights in the distance. Since everything around them was pitch black, they appeared to be floating in the dark.

"I'm wondering what those lights are way over there."

"That's the town of Laurishire," he replied with a hint of disappointment. "It's where we're headed tomorrow."

She made a noncommittal noise in the back of her throat before another long silence passed between them.

"Are you in love with him?"

"What?" Gasping, Elise inhaled too much smoke and choked. Shaking his head, Vaughn chuckled.

Some hero, laughing at me choking. I must look irresistible to him now, she thought.

"With Gavin?" she managed to say once she could catch her breath. "I wouldn't say. . .we haven't, I mean we just started to. . ."

Why is he asking me this? It's none of his business! Why is he smiling again?

"You're completely smitten." So, what if she liked Gavin a lot? It didn't give him a right to make fun of her for it. "Time to sleep."

It wasn't a question. Standing up, Vaughn made sure the fire was completely out before he helped Elise roll up her cloak into a makeshift pillow. His movements were tense, focused, and he said very little before resting his head on his satchel with his back to her. Elise's brow furrowed as she replayed their previous conversation through her mind again.

Did I say something wrong?

CHAPTER 11

Gavin's heart pounded. His blood pulsed, matching the deafening throbbing sensation in both ears. Despite having just escaped a fiery cave, the sight of Rona and the officers made him feel like he had fallen into a pool of ice water. Although a drop of rain fell onto Gavin's nose, it was only when he felt the boy beside him tug at his sleeve that Gavin realized how fast the weather was starting to turn. He wondered if it was happening naturally or if Rona was controlling it.

Rocks crunched beneath Rona's shoes as she stepped towards them. Frozen with fear, Gavin could hear seagulls crying in the distance along with the roaring waters crashing against the cliffs and boulders. The smell of fish mixed with rain and salt wafted through the chilled air that stung Gavin's chest after inhaling so much smoke. Before he could warn the others, Rona swiped her fingers to send the two younger boys up to join the others above them, leaving only Gavin and Tristan on the ground. Surprisingly, she spoke not a word, and side-stepped them to place her hand against the rockface.

What is she doing?

"Fairies have been here."

Gavin gulped.

Her calm, controlled tone unnerved him. He would've preferred her to lash out. Scream. Anything else. The uncertainty of what she would say or do next was what made Rona so threatening.

An amused smirk spread across her deep, red lips.

"I don't know whether to praise your cleverness or admonish you for such a foolish, untrustworthy collaboration."

"They should be killed for treason, Your Majesty!" Isaac spat. "I've never seen such insolence or blatant disrespect in my life. Would you like me to do it now?" The hungry, bloodthirsty look in Isaac's eyes as he gripped his sword was enough to make Gavin's blood run cold.

"Careful not to judge too hastily, Isaac. You forget your place."

"Forgive me, Your Majesty." Isaac reluctantly released his weapon, bowing his head along with the other men.

"Seeing as you are their commanding officer, any accountability or punishment must fall squarely on *your* shoulders. Do you still agree with a death sentence?" Isaac remained silent. "I thought not. No, Isaac, I will take care of this. . . *unique* situation." She held a finger up to Tristan's lips before trailing it down to his chest. "Fairies shouldn't get to have all the fun."

In a swift, fluid motion—taking Gavin by surprise—Tristan pulled a dagger from his boot before slashing the queen's hand. As she cried out, the officers immediately lunged forward with their swords before they were also suspended in the air with the adolescent recruits.

Rona's gasps were replaced with breathless chuckles as she inspected her sliced skin. Trickling down her palm, the blood created a thickening puddle on the sand.

Steadying her breath, the sorceress closed her fingers over the injury, creating a fist. Gavin watched with amazement as the blood slowly began to evaporate from the grains of sand, one drop at a time, until there were no signs of it at all. When Rona opened her hand again, Gavin saw that it was fully recovered, though the same couldn't be said for Tristan, who looked as if he had just swallowed poison.

"Ever the wild stallion." Rona sighed with disappointment. Reaching up, she gripped a handful of Tristan's hair before pushing him down to his knees. All hints of mischief and humor vanished from her face as she yanked his head back. "One day you will learn." Her lips grazed against his ear as she spoke. "Every creature I've ever chosen has been broken sooner or later. *You* will be broken too."

Lightning flashed and a clap of thunder roared across the sky, affirming her threat.

Releasing her hold on Tristan, Rona turned around and lowered her captives to the ground. No longer frozen, the boys and officers gained their bearings. Various groans, coughs, and splutters were heard throughout the crowd. A few boys bowed, quivering in fear that they would be tormented next. Lifting her chin, Rona looked down her nose at the groveling display. She placed a delicate hand over her heart. "Words cannot express the hurt and utter shame you all have caused by attempting to abandon me. After everything I've done for you, this is how you repay me. . .with treason."

"They didn't do this!" Tristan hissed, clamoring to his feet. "Do what you will with me, but those boys are innocent. They had no knowledge of this plan."

Two officers came over to seize Tristan. Despite his struggles, he was left with no choice but to fall silent.

"Be that as it may," she replied, "Naughty children go to bed without supper." Whimpers and cries trickled through the crowd until Rona held up her hand for the noises to cease. Gavin wanted to say something. He wanted to stand up for the kids, whose stomachs were probably growling already.

"Will there be anything else, Your Majesty?" Isaac asked.

"Yes," she purred, brushing the back of her knuckles down Tristan's cheek. He tilted his head away from the touch. "We must make an example of what happens when you try to stand up against me."

She ordered for Tristan to be seized, gagged, and tied against the nearest boulder for the night. Gavin watched as his friend was dragged through the sand to his punishment.

Sensing Gavin's urge to act, Rona called over her shoulder to Isaac. "Better add in extra drills this evening as well. Feel free to whip any who try anything else. I'll handle Striess."

"You heard your queen. Move out!" Isaac replied, joining the officers in moving the group of confused, pitiful—and now hungry—group of boys away towards the shore.

Rona waited for the group to be out of earshot before she regarded Gavin again. "And now to deal with the rebellious leader."

Gavin winced. Perhaps he would be strapped to the same boulder as Tristan. Maybe even lashed again. He wished the fairies would show up to create another distraction, but he knew better than to expect those three to hang around. At least he had received Elise's message before all of this happened. He was brought out of his wandering thoughts when Rona caressed his cheek the same way she had Tristan's.

"You have a passionate spirit." She spoke so softly that Gavin struggled to hear her over the strengthening wind and crashing waves. "Such a stupid, stubborn sense of arrogance, yet passionate, nonetheless. Quite admirable. If only you would realize how useless your struggle is and put that fire in your heart to better use. I can help with that."

"Whatever she's saying, don't listen to her! Don't let her in!" Tristan cried out as he was being bound to the boulder in the distance. Gavin winced as an officer struck Tristan in the face before placing the gag across the boy's mouth, but not before Tristan spit in his eye.

Rona turned Gavin's face so he could see his reflection in her eyes. "Don't waste your potential like Tristan has," she said. Her fingers were soft against his cheek, and for a moment, he felt himself lean into her touch before jerking away.

Stay focused. Don't let her play any mind tricks on you.

This woman was alluring, and she knew how to use it to her advantage. Gavin lowered his eyes to the ground, reminding himself just how sick this woman really was. She forced boys and young men into an involuntary army. They were ordered to train in treacherous conditions with little nourishment or hygiene, and every time someone had so much as a thought against her, they were met with punishment. Did she really think starving and oppressing these boys would make them more loyal?

A footman that Gavin hadn't noticed walked up to them followed by two guards.

"Should we get going, Your Majesty?" he called out. "The storm is getting stronger."

Rona nodded. The wind howled around them as the rain mixed with the ocean spray in the air. Motioning for the guards to come closer, Rona ordered for Gavin to be brought along as well.

There was no use in fighting, he knew, yet Gavin wanted to stay. If those boys had to ride out the storm, then he wanted to be with them. They were in this mess because of him, and the guilt gnawed at his conscience.

Once pushed into the carriage, Gavin was surprised that he wasn't handcuffed or flanked by the guards, who all remained outside. Rona sat opposite of him before directing the driver to take them back to her castle. As they lurched forward, the wind beat against the sides of the carriage.

Rona retrieved a compact mirror from a purse that sat on the seat next to her. She smoothed her hair back into place and ran a pale finger along her bottom lip to adjust some smudged lipstick. Her gaze flickered over to Gavin.

"You look ghastly. Here," she said. Tucking the mirror away, she conjured a canteen of water before holding it out for him. When Gavin didn't immediately reach for it, she shook it. "Take it."

That would taste so good right now. I'm so thirsty.

He couldn't, but he desperately wanted it. He yearned to feel something cool and refreshing in his dry mouth.

What kind of guy would I be if I got to drink cold water and be out of the storm, while the others are stuck out in it because of me? I can go without it.

As if sensing his inner monologue, Rona smirked at him before making the canteen disappear.

When Gavin couldn't bear the silence any longer, he slouched against the seat and stared at his beautiful captor.

"What are you going to do to me?"

"All in good time," she replied. "Let's try to enjoy ourselves. I'd like to get to know you a little better."

Gavin didn't like the sound of that. He also didn't like where his thoughts went after considering the meaning of her words.

How had things gone so wrong? He had truly held out hope when the fairies shared the message, even more so after they started the fire. Would Elise and his friends even be able to find him at Rona's castle? How would he escape once he was there?

What if we can't find each other?

"They're not coming." Rona's voice interrupted his never-ending cycle of questions. When he didn't respond, she continued. "I know you think they are, but it is impossible."

"What have you done?" Gavin asked. "Did you hurt them?"

"I haven't touched them," she replied, holding her hands up with an innocent smile that Gavin saw right through. "Though I daresay you're growing quite far from their minds."

What does that even mean?

He knew she'd never come out and say exactly what she meant. Despite telling himself not to let Rona get into his head, deep down Gavin knew she already had. He jumped as a flash of lightning startled him. The responding rumble of thunder carried his thoughts back to the ocean's edge where his new friends were stranded. He could picture their tortured faces in his mind, but one particular face haunted him the most. Tristan had risked everything, including his most prized possession, to free them. Gavin didn't have a plan, but he made a promise that he intended to keep.

I will save them.

Gavin didn't know what awaited him, but judging by the punishments she had already handed out, he knew Rona would ensure that they all had a truly awful night ahead of them.

CHAPTER 12

Elise was sure of two things. One, Vaughn stole produce from the cart the previous day to barter for a boat rental to Laurishire. While it made her extremely uncomfortable, Vaughn played it off as him being resourceful. Two, the Spryte River was wider than she anticipated. She was already irritable from not sleeping well, and now the choppy water rolling beneath them was making her nauseated.

"You're moving in the wrong direction," Vaughn said to Mitch, who was helping him row on the opposite end.

"I'm doing what you're doing," Mitch argued.

"Elise, are you okay?" Darcie asked. She placed a hand on Elise's knee. "You don't look so good."

Great, now I look sick, too.

It wasn't only the seasickness that made her miserable. Elise had had an uncomfortable dream. At any other time, she'd be eager to share it with Darcie, but given the topic, she wasn't sure it was a smart idea. Giving her friend a half-hearted attempt at a smile, Elise assured Darcie that she was fine. While there was no chance that Darcie believed her, the subject was dropped for the time being.

Elise stared across the river, hoping that they would reach the shore before she vomited in front of everyone. As if watching a reel from a film, the dream played back through Elise's memory.

She and Gavin sat together on the edge of Lake Laulie. The sunlight sparkled off the water's surface. In all other directions they were surrounded by dense trees that made it feel like a private, secluded hideout.

"How did you get away?" Elise asked.

"The fairies you sent brought me back." His smile made her heart swell as he interlocked their fingers together. "I missed you."

"I missed you too." *We can go home now*, she remembered thinking. Reaching up, Elise touched his face as they met in a kiss.

The dream was so vivid, Elise swore she could feel the warmth of Gavin's body against hers, but then everything changed. Expecting to feel his soft, tender lips, Elise was surprised when the kiss deepened. Desire coursed through her body as her fingers raked through his hair. Soliciting a moan from Gavin, her confidence soared. Without breaking the kiss, Elise rolled over until she straddled him. One of his hands stroked her back while the other tangled in her hair.

Everything was finally perfect. She never wanted to leave or let this moment end. When she did pull away to look at him, however, it was no longer Gavin under her. Staring back with the same desperate need was *Vaughn*.

To Elise's horror, the dream hadn't stopped there. It went *much* further than she cared to admit, and for some reason, her brain was determined to replay every sensual detail.

It was just a dream. You didn't do anything wrong. If that were true, why hadn't she been able to look Vaughn in the eye all day? *Stop it, Elise. This is only because Mitch said the guy was looking at you instead of Darcie. You have obsessed about it since then. Even if he did like you, it doesn't mean you feel the same.*

While Mitch's revelation about Vaughn still unnerved her, Elise clung onto the possibility that he was wrong. Even if she were single, Vaughn was off limits. Darcie had all but claimed him as her territory, and there was an unspoken rule that prevented any connection with a friend's crush.

It's not a crush! Elise almost screamed the words to get them out of her head. She was brought back to reality when the water calmed near the shore.

"Okay, spill it," Darcie demanded once they were on dry land.

"What?" Elise asked.

"You're hiding something." Not believing Elise for one second, Darcie continued, "I know you're keeping a secret because you're bad at it. Now, what is it?"

"I got a little seasick. That's all." Elise shrugged, thankful when Mitch stepped out of the boat and walked up to them.

Tossing the oar on the ground, he rotated his shoulders.

"I feel like my arms are going to fall off." Mitch stretched his back before turning to look at Vaughn. "Do we really have to keep going on foot? I'm exhausted."

While Elise hadn't helped to row, she also wished there were a faster way to the border. Instinctively, her fingers found the bottle necklace.

We might not have to use the whole thing to make a quick trip. Maybe just a drop could get us to the border.

"Don't even think about it." Vaughn's warning brought Elise out of her reverie. His brows furrowed as he glared down at the fairy magic resting against her chest. Clearing his throat, he turned to address Mitch. "We'll spend the day here. It's a good time to get a proper meal and wash up."

"The *whole* day?" Elise exclaimed. "Why would we spend an entire day here? We can keep going. It's still early enough that we can make progress."

"Yeah, why would we wait until almost sunset to keep traveling? That sounds dangerous," Darcie added.

Closing his eyes, Vaughn took a deep steadying breath. Elise had paid enough attention to know that he did this when he was trying to remain calm. "Beyond Laurishire lies many dangers."

"That you want to face after dark?" Mitch asked. "I'm with the girls. Let's keep going while it's daylight."

"We have very little provisions," Vaughn countered. "We need proper nourishment and rest to continue. Otherwise, we are setting ourselves up for exhaustion and hunger in harsh conditions."

This is doing nothing but slowing us down! I don't want to spend the whole day sitting around some stupid town. I want to save Gavin!

"Why does it have to take so long?" she cried out, unable to control her temper. Struggling to find the right words, she gestured towards Vaughn's body with her hands. "Can't you just do what you normally do and seduce some person into giving us what we need?"

"You flatter me." Despite Elise's agitated state, Vaughn failed to suppress an amused smirk. "But that's not going to happen here."

"Why not?" Mitch argued. "There's bound to be a ton of girls over there who will fight Darcie for you." Darcie punched Mitch in the shoulder. "What? Am I wrong?"

He's got you there, Darcie. Elise chuckled.

"There is something I probably should've mentioned before," Vaughn added. His cautious tone made Elise tense again. It was the first time she had ever heard him sound uncertain. He looked to be considering his next words carefully. "Laurishire is a close-knit community. It's much smaller than Clara."

What's wrong with that? Why does he look so uncomfortable?

"They're very. . .*traditional*," he continued. When the other three still didn't get his meaning, Vaughn sighed. "The best way to receive any help for free is to pretend that we're married couples."

What!

A long silence passed before Mitch groaned.

"Elise, use the magic already. I'm done."

At any other time, his reaction would've made her laugh, but Elise was still in shock over Vaughn's idea. Her ever-present sidekick, anxiety, chose this precise moment to join in the conversation.

Married? You can't pretend to be married. No one would believe you. How awkward is that going to be if we get a room?

"Wait," Elise said, both to Vaughn and her inner voice, "how does us appearing married help? Let's say we do get a room to rest. If Darcie and I share a room, and you guys share a room, like we did at the inn, isn't that even *more* traditional?"

Mitch and Darcie were quick to agree.

"It's the appearance of arriving together," Vaughn explained. "They won't take warmly to unmarried people of our ages traveling unchaperoned."

"But traveling together doesn't mean we're. . .*together* together," said Darcie.

"It doesn't matter." Vaughn shrugged. "If you're not up for it, then we need to start walking, but crossing through the town is our quickest route."

"This is screwed up, for real," Mitch said. "They think we're out here acting like animals just because we're young?"

"I can only tell you from my experience with these people," Vaughn replied.

Elise had a mental image of Vaughn being chased out of town by an angry mob after meddling with too many daughters.

"But we can leave before we'd be expected to spend the night, in case sharing beds is your issue," Vaughn added.

"This whole trip is my issue, man," Mitch grunted, kicking the tree closest to him. "What do you have against this fairy magic? Elise can pour a little, we'll get Gavin, and we can all go home. I'm so sick of these pit stops!"

Elise couldn't help but agree. It sounded like all of them were stressed out and frustrated with how long this was taking. If they didn't reach Gavin soon, Rona might kill him. Elise had to stop her thoughts from wondering if Rona already had. Finding Gavin was the only goal keeping her sane. Letting go of that hope would invite all the wrong thoughts and fears into her already anxious mind.

"We're not using the fairy magic."

It wasn't a question. Vaughn often decided things before any discussions or votes could take place.

"It sounds like we have no choice," Darcie said with a sigh. "I'm hungry, and I could use a bath."

Me too. I feel disgusting.

Pretending to be married for a few hours sounded like a small price to pay for a hot meal, bath, and restful sleep. Weighing her options, as well as remembering her dream, Elise knew one thing for certain.

I can't act married to Vaughn.

Not only would she be unable to hide her awkwardness, but Elise knew that Darcie would probably want dibs for the opportunity to be that close to their guide. Accepting the absurd option set before them, Elise blew a loose strand of frizzy hair out of her eyes and stepped in front of Mitch.

"Mitch," she said. Incapable of keeping a straight face, Elise looked up into her friend's confused hazel eyes. "Will you marry me?"

Mitch, who was also unable to hide the humor from his face, smirked and shook his head. "Wait, you're not going to get down on one knee?"

They all shared a laugh before Mitch accepted.

I hope choosing Mitch doesn't upset Darcie. Her best friend could deny it all she wanted, but Elise knew that Darcie and Mitch were hot for each other. Why they chose to act otherwise was beyond her. If Elise's choice did bother them, neither showed it.

Instead, Darcie shrugged with a smile.

"I guess that makes me Mrs. Darcie. . ." She trailed off, looking at Vaughn to reveal his last name.

"Garthorne" he replied.

Darcie repeated her new name before nodding with approval.

"It sounds noble."

"It sounds *fake*," Mitch mumbled so only Elise could hear.

"All right, it sounds like we are good to go," Vaughn announced. "We are about three or so miles from the town. I suggest we use that time to get to know one another in case we're tested."

Vaughn offered his arm to Darcie. She linked hers with his, and they led the way towards Laurishire.

Mitch and Elise waited for the other two to gain some distance before following behind.

"Where do we start?" he asked.

Elise shrugged.

"What do married couples know about each other?" She considered her own upbringing. "I've had a single mom my whole life."

"I'm not much better," Mitch said. "My parents divorced when I was four, so I can't really say I know what a good marriage looks like either."

"I'm sorry to hear that."

"Nah, don't be. Let's start with basics, I guess."

Their conversation reminded Elise of the walk she and Gavin had taken before they all first met the fairies. Favorite colors, foods, and hobbies were discussed. They memorized each other's birthdays, and Mitch had the brilliant idea to create a fake anniversary date.

"How should we say the two of us met?" Elise asked.

"Hmm, using the truth won't help. A traditional town won't like a girl who marries her boyfriend's best friend."

Elise laughed and slapped his shoulder. It felt good to laugh. So much of her thoughts had been consumed with missing Gavin.

I should probably feel bad for having a good time.

She tried to quit being so hard on herself. All of this was in pursuit of Gavin. The sooner they could get through this town, the closer they'd be to the Vynchian border.

How much longer could it really be? Vaughn's taking us the quickest route, so why should I feel guilty?

"How about we met in Clara," Elise said. "Maybe you work in a shop there?"

"And you stay home with our six children."

"*Six* kids?" Elise spluttered. "When did I have the first one? When I was ten? How old do I look?"

He chuckled. "Okay, three kids."

"I'll say no kids yet, but we plan on a big family."

"Deal."

What a bizarre conversation. This is more fun than it should be. Something tells me meeting the townspeople won't be though.

Elise hated lying. Not only was she not good at it, but it made her nervous.

What doesn't make you nervous?

Despite her best of efforts, Elise had yet to learn how to hide her anxiety.

"What do you think *they've* worked out?" Mitch nodded towards the couple in front of them.

"I think Mr. and Mrs. Garthorne come from money," Elise replied, tilting her chin up. "Maybe a cottage by the sea?"

Mitch scoffed. "Well, they better be able to explain our dirty clothes and lack of wedding rings."

Oh crap. She looked down at her left hand. *I didn't even think about that.*

"If they don't come up with anything better, I'll just say we were robbed," Mitch said. "Talk me up though. If anyone asks, tell them I put up a good fight."

Elise laughed. "Do you really hate him that much?"

"Pretty much."

Wow. At least he's honest.

She looked over to see Mitch staring at Vaughn's back. Elise wondered what was going through his head. Was it a simple case of jealousy or was it more than that?

Darcie, you're so blind.

Upon exiting the forest an hour later, Elise saw miles of green pastures and farmland. She could see a white fence surrounding a small wooden house and barn ahead of them. Given the vast, fertile landscape, Elise imagined there were quite a few farmers in Laurishire.

It's peaceful. . .like a painting.

"Ugh, this place stinks." Mitch tucked his nose under his shirt collar.

He's right.

Elise wrinkled her nose up as the mixed aromas of manure and hay wafted through the air.

On the other side of the white fence, a herd of cows grazed and rested.

Darcie pointed out a small calf resting next to its mother. "Isn't he just the cutest thing?" she asked. Turning her head, she noticed a sign on the path pointing towards the town square. "Is that our destination?"

Vaughn shook his head.

"We don't have money for an inn. Only these." He gestured to his satchel and sword. "We'll have a better chance seeking hospitality in someone's home."

Someone's home? Whether we're married or not, who's going to let us into their home off the street? That's going to be awkward to ask for.

"Look at us," Mitch said to Vaughn. "Would you let us into *your* home?"

"It's our only option," Vaughn replied.

Mitch stepped in front of him.

"No, it's the *craziest* option. What do you have against Elise's fairy magic? We saw Ruby use it. If we just picture finding Gavin, it might take us right to him."

"And if it doesn't?" Vaughn arched an eyebrow.

Mitch opened his mouth, closed it, and gritted his teeth as he stepped aside.

Vaughn held up a hand to stop them. Blocking their path, he stared at Elise, Mitch, and Darcie with a stern expression.

"If I am to remain your guide, do not mention that magic again." His eyes settled on Elise. "I mean it. If it's brought up again, I *will* destroy it. Is that understood?"

Something fluttered in Elise's chest. She felt like a thousand pins and needles were pricking her skin. Feeling like a child being punished, she looked at her friends.

Darcie crossed her arms and nodded.

Mitch's flushed cheeks made his face look splotchy, and his shoulders were tense.

They couldn't afford to lose Vaughn or the magic. Accepting their silence as compliance, Vaughn turned around and led them forward.

Approaching the first farmhouse, the four travelers stepped up onto the porch. Elise held her breath as Vaughn knocked on the door.

This is crazy. It isn't going to work. We'll be arrested before anyone will help us. Maybe nobody's home. Please don't answer. Please don't be home.

Elise's heart sank as the door creaked open a moment later.

CHAPTER 13

Back at the Lockesbarrian castle, Gavin was forced into a chair at the end of a long formal dining table. Seeing a guard twice his size stand at attention behind him, Gavin gave up any thought of fighting back as Rona took her seat on the opposite side.

Sheets of rain slammed hard against the floor-to-ceiling windows, blocking all visibility through them. Despite light emanating from the dangling crystal chandelier and tabletop candelabras, the far corners of the room were cast in darkness except when lightning flickered through the gray, clouded sky. One particularly bright flash caused Gavin to jump before a clap of thunder boomed. He felt the sound reverberate in his chest as his thoughts wandered to Tristan stranded out in this treacherous storm.

This is all my fault.

It was his idea to use the fairies. If he had waited, Elise and his friends might have made it to him at the training camp. The fairies wouldn't know to lead them to Rona's castle. Because of his impulsive decisions, he had let everyone down.

Guilt ate away at his conscience as servants bustled around the room serving dinner. Platters of scrumptious-looking food were placed between himself and Rona before their individual place settings were arranged.

He looked at the elegant china and silverware as red wine was poured into a delicate glass.

Another servant promptly filled Gavin's plate with the first course before joining the rest of the waiting staff against the wall.

A low churning, gargling sound erupted from Gavin's stomach that he feared could be heard over the storm. He suppressed the urge to bury his face into the food like an animal. Gavin had never felt such hunger. Averting his eyes away from the meal, he watched Rona cut a tender piece of steak before slowly lifting it to her mouth.

Rona's crimson lips closed around the fork as she met his gaze. Even from a distance, her exotic eyes pierced through him, cracking his resolve, causing Gavin's body to react.

She sensed this, of course. He could tell by the way her mouth smirked against the glass as she took a sip. The muscles in Rona's neck quivered as the wine went down, eliciting an appreciative moan from her.

She's doing this on purpose. Don't fall for it. Don't look at her.

The problem with listening to himself was that his eyes returned to the tempting hot meal in front of him, which he also couldn't have.

You're so hungry. Gavin felt saliva form in his mouth as he took in the juicy cut of steak. *The fork and knife are right there. Take a bite.*

The silence was only broken after Rona requested that her glass be refilled.

"Are you trying to bait me with your stubbornness?" Nodding towards Gavin's untouched plate, she slumped back in her chair and swirled her wine. "You've been bathed and provided a hot meal. It's highly offensive to turn your nose up to such hospitality. Especially when the sounds of your hunger are so deafening."

Gavin looked down at the succulent steak, cooked to perfection. He could imagine the satisfaction of biting into any of the options laid out before him.

"Eat."

Rona's stern command made Gavin feel like a four-year-old refusing to eat his carrots at the dinner table. He doubted Rona was going to have the same level of patience as his parents.

"You're really going to defy me?"

The calm steadiness of her tone unnerved him, and Gavin fought the urge to run.

I wouldn't get far anyway.

"I can't." Gavin pushed the plate away from him.

Powerful gusts swirled outside the window, whistling against the glass panes, as another flash of lightning lit the room. After the following rumble of thunder came and dwindled, Gavin found his voice again.

"My friends don't get to eat tonight, so I shouldn't either."

I can't eat knowing those boys are suffering because of me. I should be tied to that boulder. Not Tristan.

"How valiant." Taking another bite of her dinner, Rona sighed. "You remind me of an old lover of mine."

Uncertain how to respond and growing uncomfortable, Gavin shifted in his seat.

"Your loyalty is commendable," Rona said, twirling her fork between her fingers. "I find both duty and honor to be incredibly appealing traits."

Gavin didn't know when he had acquired these traits. Maybe it was because his dad was in the military. He had grown to admire the courage it took to defend a country, but he still had his own doubts about joining himself. Being forced into Rona's army had done little to convince him, but Gavin wondered if his dad would be proud of his choices if he could see him now.

I've disappointed him so many times. I doubt he'd ever expect me to stand up for an entire camp of soldiers. I guess he's rubbing off on me.

"Now all that's left is to shift where your loyalty lies." Rona turned her head towards the line of servants waiting against the wall. "Leave us."

A shiver trickled down Gavin's spine as the servants vacated the room, including the guard who had stood behind him.

I'm more scared of being alone with her than with having other people around.

He figured Rona counted on that. Once the door was shut, the room felt colder. Dangerous.

What is she going to do to me?

The lack of eye contact fueled Gavin's growing anxiety. The hairs stood on the back of his neck, and despite the chill in the air, he felt a layer of sweat coat his palms. With no one else in the room, he could do nothing but stare at the mesmerizing sorceress.

If you're going to beat or kill me, just do it already. This is torture.

Something told Gavin he didn't grasp the true meaning of that word. Nevertheless, he found his thoughts wandering to unwanted scenarios. He tried to excuse it away as hormones, stress, or even fear. Maybe Rona was controlling his weak, deprived mind.

With every passing minute, Gavin grew more aware of her curves, the way she moved, and more noticeably, how she made his body feel.

Stop it. He commanded his brain to look anywhere else, but Gavin's eyes only managed to be drawn to her more. *She wants you to be distracted. This is what she does to people. Fight it, Gavin. Fight it. Be strong.*

Rona didn't address him until her plate was finished. Dabbing the corners of her mouth with a cloth napkin, she rose from her chair and walked towards him.

Gavin closed his eyes to avoid staring at the way her hips swayed as she closed the distance between them. Locking his jaw, he clenched his hands into fists and tried not to pay attention to the sound of Rona's heels coming nearer.

What is wrong with me? I've been able to control myself and talk to her before. Why is it so hard now? Is she making this happen?

Turning towards another flash of lightning, Gavin regretted opening his eyes.

Rona's waist was mere inches from his face. Draping one arm behind Gavin's head across the back of the chair, she lifted his chin up with her other hand.

As her thumb brushed across his bottom lip, Gavin's fingernails dug into the wooden armrests. His heartbeat quickened as she caressed his cheek.

"Now that I have your attention," she whispered, "I'm going to ask you again." In one swift motion, Rona reached out and the diary appeared in her hand.

Take it! Open it. Get out of here now! Deal with the consequences later.

If he didn't think she could break his neck with the snap of her fingers, Gavin might've listened to the screaming voice inside his head. He watched as she placed the purple book on the table in front of him.

"Open it."

Do what she says. You can wake up at home. Who cares if some things are changed? You'll be home with Elise and your friends. You'll get to see your family. Flip the cover open before she can get her hands back on it. By that point, you'll be long gone. Let her do whatever she wants after that.

The old Gavin would've done that. Up until that point, he hadn't cared much for anyone other than himself. Now he could only think of Elise, the boys he had let down, and his friends. He wanted to be better for all of them. If that meant waiting here a little longer, then so be it.

He winced as Rona grabbed a handful of his hair and forced his head down until his nose touched the cover.

"Open it!" Rona growled before backing up against the wall.

Gavin thought back to the last time he opened the diary. Mistaking Elise's communication with Derek for the signal to use its magic, he had accidentally sent them through the portal before she was ready.

What if my friends get left behind? What if the boys die in battle? Rising doubt began to replace the previous urgent and insistent pleas to obey Rona.

"I can't."

Bracing for the pain that was sure to follow, Gavin tensed against the table.

Nothing happened.

A distant rumble of thunder indicated that the storm was passing. The rain had lightened and was now only spraying against the windows. All was still.

Gavin peeked over his shoulder to see Rona watching him.

"I've underestimated you," she said. The malice was gone from her voice. When he didn't reply, she pushed herself away from the wall to stand behind him.

Gavin froze when her hands slid over his shoulders. Expecting Rona to start choking him, he was surprised when her fingers began massaging the sore muscles in his neck and upper back.

No, don't. Stop. He tried leaning away, but when her thumbs found a sensitive area at the base of his skull, Gavin relaxed against Rona's touch.

That feels awesome, but I know it shouldn't. She's too good at this.

He felt at war with himself. His thoughts argued back and forth like an angel and demon.

Move. Get away from her, cried one part of him.

Just one more minute. At least she's not trying to kill you yet, argued the other.

At last, the moral side of him prevailed and he leaped from the chair.

"No, stop," he said. Turning around to face her, Gavin stepped backwards until he bumped against the door at the other end of the room. Whirling around, he located the handle and tried opening the door.

Locked? But those other guys just left. Why would they lock us in here? Unless it wasn't them.

Beads of sweat formed along his brow as he met Rona's eyes again.

She hadn't moved from behind the now empty chair, but Gavin knew she was to blame for him being trapped. After a moment of silence, Rona picked up the diary and crossed the room to join him. Forcing the book into his hands, she pulled Gavin away from the wall to stand behind him.

Whatever you do, don't let it open.

Gavin tightened his grip around the front and back covers. He felt Rona's arms wrap around him until her breasts pressed against his back.

Though she was shorter in stature, Rona managed to curl her fingers around his wrists.

"You're in control of what happens next," Rona whispered against the nape of Gavin's neck.

I don't like the sound of that.

"Tell me what this diary does, and you'll be rewarded." She placed a teasing kiss under his ear. "Refuse, and you'll be punished."

Inhaling the intoxicating scent of her perfume, Gavin closed his eyes as Rona's breath tickled his neck. He knew right from wrong, but it still didn't lessen the temptation.

Releasing her hold on him, Rona took a step back. "So, what will it be?"

Gavin lowered his gaze to Joranna's diary. It struck him as odd how much power one book could hold. His brain continued instructing him to hold it closed as long as he could while other parts of his body screamed out to take Rona up on her offer. Every time he had heard her name since arriving with his friends, Gavin would never have assumed she'd be so brazen and manipulative. Part of him worried if he *didn't* take her offer that she would hurt his friends or family. Only an idiot would turn her down. Weighing his options, Gavin considered the outcome of each choice before sighing.

I guess I'm an idiot then.

He'd have to say no. Despite Rona's tantalizing proposition, Gavin knew he couldn't do that to Elise. He had grown to care a lot about her and hurting her like that was the last thing he wanted to do. They had gone through so much together, and the next time he even *thought* about opening the diary, he wanted her by his side.

"No way," Gavin said, stepping away to gain distance from Rona. Holding the diary against him, he shook his head. "Forget it."

Rather than erupt in a fit of rage as Gavin expected, Rona only smiled.

I hate when she does that. Why isn't she angry? This lady is dangerous for sure.

"The dungeon isn't quite as comfortable as my bedchamber." She snapped her fingers.

The diary vanished from his hands, and after searching all around him, Gavin noticed that Rona was holding it again.

"But if you're certain, so be it." Rona shrugged. "I do love a good chase."

The sorceress called out for a guard, who appeared moments later through the now unlocked door.

"Mr. Striess has requested your finest cell. Please don't disappoint him," she said.

As he was handcuffed, Gavin's stomach growled while the rest of his body struggled with suppressed need. He knew he had made the right choice, but he also knew Rona wouldn't stop until she had broken him—mentally and physically.

Hurry, you guys.

CHAPTER 14

At least an hour had passed, and Vaughn was still unable to find someone willing to offer them shelter. The houses were far apart from each other, and every door they knocked on ended up getting closed in their faces. As Vaughn knocked on another door, Elise changed her mental plea.

She was no longer afraid of someone opening the door. Her legs and feet ached, and she wanted nothing more than to eat and sleep. Looking at the other three, she noticed that their worn expressions matched her own.

The sun was now directly over them, and they had gotten used to the once offensive stench of livestock.

Wiping the sweat from her forehead, Elise heard a dog barking and a crying child as footsteps approached.

As the door creaked open, Elise lowered her gaze to see a panting yellow Labrador, whose barks had turned into whines as it tried to fit its entire body outside to greet them.

A woman peeked around the door and used her leg to block the dog from pushing it open further.

"Chauncey, no. Stop that!" Blocking the dog's view, the woman looked up at them. On her hip, she bounced a small toddler, who tugged at the woman's lopsided blonde bun. Leaning away from her daughter's small hands, she blew a loose strand of hair from her face and regarded them again as Chauncey resumed barking. The woman's haggard appearance made Elise regret bothering her. "Can I help you?"

"I'm sorry to disturb you, madam," Vaughn called over the dog's incessant whining. He was once again interrupted as multiple children shouted from inside the house.

Growing impatient, the woman checked over her shoulder before turning back and raising her brows expectantly at Vaughn, awaiting his request.

Let's just go. This lady is swamped. There's no way she's going to let us in. Not with all that noise.

"Who are you?" Her brows furrowed as she took in the state of their clothing. "What do you want?"

"My name is Vaughn Garthorne, and this is my lovely wife, Darcie." He gestured towards Darcie, who cracked an uneasy smile as she tried to look presentable next to her fake husband. Vaughn peeked around her to Mitch and Elise. "This is Mitchell and Elise Peterson, friends of ours."

Elise felt odd hearing him refer to her with Mitch's last name. Although they had rehearsed, there was something about hearing it said out loud that made this ridiculous plan sound even more absurd. There was no way they would get away with this façade.

"We're weary from our journey and don't have enough money for an inn," said Vaughn.

"I don't have any money to give you," she replied.

"I'm surprised she hasn't slammed the door in his face like that lady from the third house we tried," Mitch whispered to Elise as Vaughn continued explaining their situation.

Elise nodded in agreement.

"And so, you see, we'll be on our way by sunset so as not to inconvenience you and your family overnight." Vaughn concluded his speech as the woman lowered her fidgeting daughter to the floor.

Once the child was out of sight, the woman shook her head and bent to scratch Chauncey behind his ears.

"I'm very sorry, sir, but I haven't got the room. The children, you see—"

Surprising herself, but overcome with fatigue, Elise stepped in front of Vaughn and Darcie.

"Please, ma'am," she begged. "We won't take up much room. If we could just get something to eat and rest, we'll leave you alone. It sounds like you're busy, but no one else will help us."

Please. Please say yes. I'm begging you to say yes. I don't care if we have to sleep on the floor. I'm so tired. Please help us.

Elise wished with everything in her entire body for the woman to understand and take pity on them.

I don't know what we'll do if she says no. I'm about to collapse. Come on, lady. We're desperate!

Mixed emotions played across the woman's face that ranged from distrust to confusion. Wiping her hands with her apron, the woman sighed and took in their appearances.

"You *do* look like you've been through a great deal."

Elise's heart fluttered inside her chest.

Is she going to say yes? Are we going to get to stay?

Biting her lip, the woman hesitated before nodding.

Elise could tell the mother wasn't at peace with her decision by the way she shifted back and forth and rubbed the back of her neck.

"I-I should have enough to feed everyone. I'm afraid there aren't any extra beds, but you're welcome to rest in the barn." She tilted her chin towards the farm behind them. "The boys are out working, but you shouldn't be in their way. My husband should be back from town shortly."

Mitch grimaced.

Vaughn put his hand out before the redhead could complain. Turning back to the woman, he bowed with a smile.

"Your generosity is most appreciated."

Elise, Mitch, and Darcie thanked her as well, but their replies were drowned out by Chauncey growling to get out.

Calling to someone inside the house to keep an eye on the baby, the woman closed the door and stepped off the porch.

She introduced herself as Valerie Dolluff and led the two couples across the property to a large wooden barn in the distance.

I don't see how taking a nap in a barn would be inappropriate if we weren't all married to each other.

Elise knew that it wasn't a big deal to keep pretending. She'd only have to be married to Mitch a few more hours and then they could be on their way. Trying to appear grateful—because, deep down, she really was—Elise trudged through the mud behind her friends past the hay and water troughs to the barn entrance.

To one side was a long line of animal stalls. Loose, rusty nails stuck out of the cracked, wooden rails and boards. Above them, Elise saw a stocked hayloft, which explained the overwhelming smell of hay and dust. She swatted at a couple of flies as Mrs. Dolluff led them past a row of various shovels and pitchforks.

"Love what they've done with the place." Mitch ducked under a spider web hanging from a beam. He groaned as they were hit with the overwhelming stench of manure.

"Yes, it takes a bit of getting to," Mrs. Dolluff said, nodding her head towards the pigpen. "My son has to come clean it out."

Elise held her breath as they continued to the back of the barn where more hay was stacked.

"Feel free to rest here. I'm sorry I can't give you something more comfortable." Mrs. Dolluff spread the hay out as best she could to give them something to sleep on. "Hopefully, this will do. I'll call for you when dinner is ready this evening."

The four of them thanked her and waited until she left before spreading out amongst the makeshift beds.

Lifting the satchel over his head, Vaughn placed it on the ground. "I can't stress how fortunate we've been. It's going to be a long night ahead of us, so get some rest." Adjusting his spot by the back door, Vaughn invited Darcie to lay next to him. When he caught Elise and Mitch staring, he rolled his eyes. "If she returns before we wake up, and we're all spread apart, it doesn't support our marriage story."

Do I have to sleep so close to Mitch?

Elise had come to view Mitch like a brother, and the thought of sleeping so close together—coupled with the fact that he was Gavin's best friend—didn't feel right. When they had followed Ruby to the portal, it felt natural to rest on Gavin while they waited. Their current situation was anything but natural.

The current arrangements didn't appear to faze Darcie at all. She shifted her body until it was against Vaughn's back.

Within ten minutes, the two of them fell asleep.

"Well, this sucks." Clicking his tongue, Mitch shook his head at the other couple.

"Yep," Elise replied.

Leaving at least two feet between themselves, Elise and Mitch stared up at the ceiling, unable to sleep.

Mitch drummed his fingers together before releasing a heavy sigh.

"I swear if he starts snoring, I'm punching him right in the face."

Elise snorted, covering her nose and mouth with both hands. Her shoulders shook with suppressed laughter.

"Oh, *that's* sexy, Mrs. Peterson." Mitch winked at her.

"Don't call me that." Chuckling, she slapped him on the arm.

I can always count on Mitch to make me laugh. That's for sure.

Darcie fidgeted, causing them to quiet down again.

I don't know if I can sleep on this hay. I itch like crazy, and the floor is too hard. I want my phone. She reminded herself they were lucky enough to have any shelter at all. *Close your eyes. Try to relax.*

Visualizing herself sleeping, Elise hoped it would convince her pessimistic thoughts to shut off. She wrinkled her nose around as an itch creeped up inside her nostrils. Using her sleeve to satisfy the itch, Elise blew out some of the trapped dust and sent a bit of hay sliding across the floor in the process.

Warm streaks of sunlight poured in, illuminating specs of floating debris. Sporadic shadows flickered throughout the room as birds swooped past the windows.

Go to sleep. You're so tired. Fall asleep already. You'll hate yourself if you don't.

Turning over, Elise fidgeted as pieces of hay poked through her sleeve and against her cheek.

I can't imagine how my hair is going to look when I get up.

At last growing accustomed to the animals' grunts and snorts, Elise began to feel the familiar weight of sleep coming over her. The sweet aroma of hay was a comfort as opposed to the stench of urine and manure upon entering the barn. With one last fleeting thought about whether Mitch had fallen asleep yet, Elise closed her eyes and relaxed with a sigh. Dangling on the precipice of sleep, Elise jumped as a loud snore escaped Vaughn's mouth.

All was still until Mitch sat up.

"That's it. I'm doing it."

Elise chuckled as she pulled Mitch back down again.

They both shared another laugh, as the snoring continued, until Darcie awoke only long enough to shush them.

This time, Elise succumbed to her exhaustion.

She didn't know how long she napped, but there was a renewed energy within her upon waking. The heaviness behind her eyelids was gone. Bits of hay slid back and forth beneath her as she stretched. Yawning, Elise sat up and looked around.

The sun had yet to set. Rich oranges and reds swirled across the part of the sky visible through the window.

I slept so hard. I must've really needed it.

Elise was also glad her nap hadn't been haunted by any more unwanted dreams. Memories of the last one flashed through her mind before Elise realized that Vaughn was no longer in the barn.

Darcie, who was already awake, waved at her.

Trying not to wake Mitch, Elise crawled over to Darcie on her hands and knees. She wiped the hay and dust from her hands with her dress.

"Hey," Elise whispered. "How long have you been awake? Where's Vaughn?"

"Hey. Not long," said Darcie, pulling some hay off her skirt. "Vaughn woke up with a bad headache. He offered to help as a farmhand since he already has experience."

"That was nice of him. I hate his head hurts so often."

"Yeah, I thought it was a migraine, but he was able to get up and work, so I don't know."

"And you didn't want to go with him?" Elise smiled at her friend.

"Ew, no." A small smile crept across Darcie's lips before she grew serious again. "I'm sorry about how I've been acting. I've been so stupid."

"No, you haven't—"

"*Yes*, I have."

Elise wasn't sure if there were dust particles or tears in Darcie's eyes, but she suspected it was the latter. She looked away so Darcie wouldn't feel embarrassed.

"I keep throwing myself at Vaughn, but he's clearly not interested," said Darcie with a sniff.

Elise fidgeted with her fingers.

I shouldn't tell her what Mitch told me at the inn. It would only make her upset. I'm still not convinced it's even true.

It had been hard keeping the secret from Darcie, because Elise was used to telling her best friend everything.

"I haven't been a good friend," Darcie confessed, wrapping an arm around Elise's shoulders. "I'm really sorry."

It's nice to have you back, Darcie. Elise hugged her. *I missed you.*

The two girls pulled apart as the barn door creaked opened, causing Mitch to jump awake.

"What's wrong?" he asked, squinting his eyes at Elise and Darcie. Bits of hay stuck to his collar and reddened face.

Both girls hid their smiles as they turned towards the entrance. Expecting Vaughn, all three were surprised when a teenaged girl approached.

"Oh, good, you're awake." Shifting from one foot to the other, the girl tugged at her braid before looking away when she met Mitch's eyes. "My mother sent me to tell you that dinner will be ready soon. You can wash up outside."

After they thanked her, she blushed and turned on her heel to return home.

"Looks like someone has a crush on you, Mitch," Darcie said with a wink. "Want me to work some magic?"

"No, thanks," he grumbled, stretching his long limbs upon standing. "You already have your hands full with your *own* situation. Leave me out of it."

He didn't hear Darcie's apology.

Mitch exited the barn first—which was best, Elise mused—because he missed the way Darcie's face wilted.

"Hey, don't mind him," Elise said, dusting off Darcie's back. "We've all been dealing with a lot. Come on, let's go clean up."

While she didn't get her desired bath, Elise felt better getting to wash her hands and face in one of the troughs outside.

I could use some perfume or something.

The back door of the house swung open as Mrs. Dolluff called everyone inside.

Elise, Mitch, and Darcie were already seated at the extra-long table with all eight of the Dolluff children before they heard the door slam. Three men entered and greeted everyone before taking their seats.

As Vaughn entered behind them, he jumped back as Chauncey rushed up to him, growling.

"Chauncey!" Mrs. Dolluff scolded the dog, who snarled and continued to resist and bark until he was forced outside. The muffled barks continued, causing Mrs. Dolluff to shake her head and scoff. "I apologize, sir. He's usually so friendly."

"It's all right," Vaughn sighed, taking his seat next to Darcie and examining the food spread out across the table. "Everything smells amazing."

"Thank you. Please help yourselves." Once everyone had prepared their plates, Mrs. Dolluff began introducing everyone.

First was her husband, Maksen Dolluff, whose dark beard, and muscular build, reminded Elise more of a lumberjack than a farmer. Next were their two equally handsome cousins, Cole and Arlo, who waved and grunted through mouthfuls of chicken. All three men, along with Mrs. Dolluff, appeared to be in their mid-to-late thirties.

The children were all introduced by order of birth. Knowing she wouldn't remember all their names, Elise listened politely as Mrs. Dolluff pointed to Lorelei, the girl who had come to wake them, followed by Treyton, Isla, Callan, and Willow. On the opposite side of the table sat Moirah, Ronan, and finally, the toddler they had met at the door, Briella.

Eight children. . .wow. Mrs. Dolluff has a great figure. I couldn't imagine having so many kids.

"So," Mr. Dolluff said, taking a bite of his dinner, "Valerie tells me you've fallen on hard times."

"Yes, sir," Vaughn replied when Elise and her friends remained silent. "We're on our way to Lockesbarrow. We hope to take a ship on the Vynchian side of the border."

"What on earth could be taking you there?" Mrs. Dolluff asked. "Dreadful place."

"Now, Val," said Mr. Dolluff before apologizing. "The King's proclamation has us all a little paranoid."

"What proclamation?" Elise asked.

I haven't heard about Derek issuing anything. Is he sending out guards to catch us?

"His Majesty is recruiting more troops. There's a tent set up in town for more volunteers to enlist." Mr. Dolluff avoided his wife's gaze. "I thought about signing it myself this afternoon."

"Maks, you can't!" his wife exclaimed. "Think of our children. Think of the farm."

"Let's have that discussion when we no longer have company," he said, "but you and the children are exactly *why* I'm considering joining."

"I signed up yesterday," said Cole.

"And I," replied Arlo.

Mrs. Dolluff scoffed before placing more food on Briella's plate.

"I heard King Derek's blocked all trade to and from Lockesbarrow." Cole shrugged. "Makes sense, I suppose."

"Do you think any other kingdoms will do the same?" Callan asked.

"I hardly think our nine-year-old needs to be part of this conversation," said Mrs. Dolluff.

"Agreed," said Mr. Dolluff before clearing his throat. "Don't trouble yourself with such thoughts, Cal. It'll all turn out right in the end. King Derek will see to that."

"Vynchia might join the trade block, but Leafbrooke won't," said Arlo, wiping his chin. "The Elves will keep their trades open for sure."

"Agreed," said Cole. "We get our best arrows from them, but knowing their secretive nature, they're probably issuing the best bows to the Lockesbarrian army."

"I wouldn't doubt it," said Mrs. Dolluff. "There's not enough at risk for the Elves to block off trade to an entire kingdom."

"Very true, my dear," said Mr. Dolluff. "Leafbrooke will prosper from a war before joining one."

I don't like the sound of all this.

"Will you men join too?" Lorelei asked Mitch and Vaughn.

Vaughn offered her a gentle smile while Mitch shifted under her gaze.

"Lora, that is hardly an appropriate question for our guests. I do apologize," Mrs. Dolluff said, picking up some pieces of bread that Briella had dropped onto the floor.

"I wish I could join and fight with you, Father," Treyton chimed in. He was most likely thirteen or fourteen, and there was an unmistakable hunger in his eyes at the thought.

"Treyton Dolluff, don't you even *joke* about a thing like that." At her wits end, Mrs. Doluff turned to also scold Moirah and Ronan, who had started playing with each other's food at the end of the table. Turning back to her eldest son, she huffed and wiped a strand of hair out of her eyes. "This is not a game, Son."

"I know it's not," he argued. "Reed Winslow signed up yesterday, and I'm six months older than him!"

"I don't care what that reckless boy did. It's *out* of the question," she replied. "I don't know what his mother is thinking, letting him enlist for the war when her own nephew was one of the ones kidnapped last year."

One of the ones who were kidnapped? I wonder if her nephew is in the same place as Gavin.

"I'm full. Can I leave the table?" Willow whined, swinging her legs until her feet kicked the bottom of the table in a steady rhythm.

"Yes, I believe that is best." Mrs. Dolluff stood. "I better get the little ones off to bed. Please excuse me."

Fighting Briella, who had begun kicking and screaming about going to bed, Mrs. Dolluff escorted the five youngest out of the room.

Mr. Dolluff chuckled. "There goes the very best of women. The heart and patience of a saint, she has. I couldn't love another woman, and that Bri has a strong set of lungs in her, does she not?"

Everyone around the table smiled in silent agreement.

Setting his fork down, Treyton groaned and rolled his eyes.

"*You'll* let me join. Won't you, Father?"

Mr. Dolluff chuckled around a bite of potatoes as he regarded his eager son.

"You'd make a fine soldier, Trey." He winked at his boy. "But I'm afraid I have to side with your mother, or neither of us will live long enough to make it to a battlefield."

Everyone, except Treyton, shared a laugh and finished their dinners as the subject was closed for further discussion.

"Val said you were planning on leaving soon," Mr. Dolluff said. "Why such a hurry? You're welcome to stay the night."

"You're too kind," Vaughn said, "but we mustn't trespass on your hospitality any longer than necessary. You and your family have already been generous enough."

Leaning back in his chair, he took in their clothes and shook his head. "At least let us offer you new clothes. Loralei, fetch these boys a couple of my shirts. See if you have a dress or two you can spare for these ladies. There won't be time to clean their own before they leave."

Loralei nodded and excused herself.

Mr. Dolluff also asked Treyton and Isla to clear the table. As his oldest children got to work, he looked at Elise.

"You bear a striking resemblance to Queen Joranna. You could almost pass off as a relative," he joked.

Feeling her anxiety growing, Elise let out an uncomfortable laugh. Her knee bounced under the table as she prayed Vaughn would say it was time to leave.

"If you don't mind me asking, why are you in such a hurry?" Mr. Dolluff asked.

Before any of them could answer, Lorelei returned with a pile of clothing in her arms. She passed out two dresses to the ladies, gave Vaughn his shirt, and looked down at the floor as she held out Mitch's shirt. Even in the dim candlelight, her face burned a bright red that disappeared into her hairline.

"You better watch out, Father," Treyton called out, leaning over to examine his sister. "You're about to lose your daughter to a married man." To add insult to injury—and in true little brother fashion—Treyton tugged on Lorelei's braid until she cried out and punched him in the arm.

"All right, that's enough. Settle down," said their father with a poorly concealed smile.

Lorelei's eyes welled up as she excused herself from the room. Isla glared at Treyton before following her sister out.

"What? She's fine," he said with a shrug.

"Well, you just earned yourself another half hour of chores," said his father.

"But, Father—"

"I don't want to hear it. If you have enough energy to show off in front of our guests, then you can work. There's still daylight left, and the stalls need sweeping."

Elise tried to hide her smile at the sight of the boy's pout as he shuffled his feet and walked outside.

"We better get out there too and finish up," Cole said, slapping Arlo on the back.

"Oh, I'm sure you'll want payment for working with us today," Mr. Dolluff said to Vaughn.

"That won't be necessary, sir."

"No, I won't hear any arguments. I insist you accept payment."

Vaughn looked at Elise, Darcie, and Mitch before licking his lips.

"Perhaps just enough to rent a cart then, but nothing more."

Mr. Dolluff stroked his beard as he considered the offer.

"I'll do you one better. I'll arrange your transportation myself. It's hard to trust many people these days," he said to Vaughn before turning to look at Cole and Arlo. "Do you two know of anyone who could give these travelers a ride down to the coast tonight on short notice?"

"I'll go." Arlo raised his hand.

"What's all this about?" Mrs. Dolluff returned and glanced down at the borrowed clothes Elise and her friends held. "What did I miss?"

"Since they have to leave, I offered some clean clothes and a ride as proper payment for a day's work. Arlo volunteered to take them where they need to go."

"Arlo, you've been out in the field all day. You need your rest," Mrs. Dolluff argued.

Her cousin shrugged.

"All this war talk has me fired up anyway. I'll take the spare cart if that's good with you, Maks."

Mr. Dolluff nodded.

"Come to think of it, I'll go too," Cole said. "He's a horrible driver."

"I am not!"

"Tell that to the cart we pulled from the pond last winter." Cole winked at the four visitors. "We'll meet you all outside shortly. Thanks for dinner, Val."

"It's decided then," Mr. Dolluff said, the humor returning to his eyes. "Get changed and my cousins will see you as far as the lake's edge."

Elise didn't know the distance to the lake, but Vaughn's shocked expression told her that it was an impressive offer.

"I'll give you the day off tomorrow to rest. It'll be midnight before you reach the lake as it is," Mr. Dolluff told his cousins. The three discussed who could fill in for the following day.

"Let me change first, and I'll help load up the cart," Vaughn said, leaving the table with the clean shirt folded across his arm.

Once the details of their departure were finalized, Mr. Dolluff looked surprised to see Elise and her friends still sitting at the table.

"You can take turns changing in Lorelei's room." He pointed towards the hall.

They thanked him and exited the room.

"Now what?" Mitch asked as they stared down a narrow hallway of closed doors. "If we pick the wrong one, we might wake up a kid."

Before her anxiety could escalate, Elise breathed a sigh of relief as one of the children came out of a bedroom.

"Hey there." Elise bit her lip, unable to remember his name. "Can you tell us where Lorelei's room is?"

Yawning, the little boy pointed two doors down before passing them to find his parents.

"I'll go first," she told Darcie and Mitch before entering and closing the door behind her.

Using what little light came through the small window, Elise walked over to sit down on the bed as she began to unbutton her dress.

"Elise?"

Jumping off the bed—a hand over her startled heart—she whirled around to see Vaughn standing shirtless in the corner. Caught off guard, embarrassed, Elise backed up against the wall and grabbed the loosened fabric of her dress before it slipped.

"I-I'm so sorry," she stammered as he took a step closer. "I didn't know you were in here." Fumbling along the wall for the way out, Elise closed her hand around the doorknob.

Get out. Get out. GET OUT.

Desperate for an escape from this nightmare, she gasped when he placed a hand against the door, preventing her from opening it.

What's he doing? This can't be happening right now. I'm so humiliated. Now he's going to see me have a panic attack.

Elise didn't know why she still pulled on the doorknob a couple of times. It was useless against Vaughn's strength.

"I'm so sorry. I didn't mean to. I'll leave."

"Elise, relax. I can't let you go out there in your present state."

Shaking her head, she kept apologizing as she tried to step around him.

Mitch and Darcie might think something is up. They can probably hear us unless they went back to the dining room.

"You must calm your nerves. You did nothing wrong."

The gentleness of his voice, at last, broke through her chaotic train of thought, and she allowed herself to breathe.

He was so close that Elise could feel his breath against her face. Stunned by the turn of events, she waited for the inevitable panic attack to present itself. When he didn't step away, and her head remained silent, Elise began to process what was really happening.

In all the romance books she'd read, this type of scenario was always her favorite part. It was the chapter that got Elise's heart racing, but now that she was experiencing it, her internal voice began screaming for her to get out. . . until she looked into his eyes.

Stay.

Had her thoughts really changed course that fast? She didn't recognize this part of herself. An internal battle raged on as Vaughn pulled her hand off the doorknob and into his own.

Leaning his shoulder against the door, he circled the back of her hand with his thumb.

"Don't be afraid of me."

I'm not afraid.

Again, where did *this* side of her come from? A mere second ago, she was trying to give him his privacy, and now they were much too close to each other.

Vaughn's eyes scanned her face as she glanced between his eyes and mouth.

Elise's heart drummed inside her ears and she expected to hyperventilate. Although it wasn't altogether pleasant, the scent of his sweat—coupled with her proximity to him—made Elise feel lightheaded.

Sensing this, Vaughn brought his free hand up to steady her. Only he didn't remove it.

What is happening? What if someone walks in right now? Why can't I move? Why don't I want to move?

Vaughn's finger traced along Elise's collarbone and slid under the fabric of her gown until the loose garment draped from her shoulder. Releasing her hand to grab Elise by the waist, Vaughn gauged her reaction—or lack of a reaction, really— before lowering his lips to the newly exposed skin.

What are you doing? We can't do this. It's wrong. You're not Gavin. I need to get out of here. Why won't my feet move? Why does this feel so good?

All she could hear was her own heavy breathing. Elise's body went limp against the door as he turned her. Her skin burned beneath his touch despite the internal pleas to run. Tilting her head back, Elise arched her body against Vaughn's strong chiseled frame. Her one last attempt to stop him only managed to escape as a moan. Elise's thighs quivered as she felt his own body react. She envisioned herself leaving, yet her feet were glued to the floor as his lips moved up to her neck.

What is he doing to me? Why do I like it? Her head swam with desire. *This isn't me. It's not real. It's one of my dreams again. Wake up, Elise. This isn't what you want. . .oh, but it is. I. . .we. . .have to stop.*

As Vaughn's breath tickled her ear, Elise thought she felt him tug at the skirt of her dress just as the door opened and pushed them both.

"Elise?" Darcie's voice called from the other side.

Vaughn stepped back as Elise pulled her sleeve back up. All hints of her previous trance vanished, and she was hit with an ice-cold slap of reality.

"Aren't you ready yet? It's been—"

Crap! This isn't happening. This is NOT happening.

Spotting the two of them, Darcie gasped, and Elise's cheeks flushed as she avoided her best friend's discerning expression.

Expecting Vaughn to throw out a savvy or sarcastic comment to get them out of this predicament, Elise was baffled when he simply crossed the room to get his shirt and left without a word. As the door shut behind him, Elise mustered up the courage to meet Darcie's eyes.

What did I just do?

CHAPTER 15

Crying out, Gavin awakened for what felt like the third or fourth time. Unable to discern what time it was from the lack of windows or light, he closed his eyes to try falling asleep again.

It's no use. I'm too hungry to sleep.

His stomach grumbled in response. Gritting his teeth, Gavin clenched both hands into fists and fought the urge to take Rona up on her offer.

It'd be a hot meal and a warm bed for the night. . .

He shook his head, ridding his mind of the thought almost as quickly as it had formed.

No, stop it. I'm not doing that. I don't care what Rona says. I'm not doing that to Elise. My friends are coming.

The thought of his friends shifted Gavin's focus to the new ones he had made. Again, he wondered if Tristan and the others were okay. Was it morning yet? Had Tristan been released?

What if I die in here and can't save them? What will happen to them?

Hearing a rustling sound nearby, Gavin froze.

What was that? Is someone in here with me?

"Hello?" he called out.

The sound stopped. There was no reply.

Gavin steadied his breathing once more. When the sound resumed, less than a minute passed before Gavin felt something crawl across his feet.

He yelped, kicking at whatever was in his cell. There was a squeak, followed by the sound of it hitting the wall.

What is that! Was it a rat?

Gavin scooted back against the wall, bringing both knees up to his chest. Rocking back and forth—feeling more paranoid by the minute—he was only able to pay attention to his own erratic breathing.

This is a nightmare. I hate rats!

There wasn't much difference between this cell and the one in Haighdlen, but this was worse. Not only was he without the others, but now he had to worry about what might crawl on him if he tried to sleep.

Yeah, that's not happening now.

"Is someone there?" a voice called.

Gavin's breath caught in his chest. Not responding at first, he waited until the other person asked again. It sounded like an older man across from him, but it was too dark to make out anything for certain.

"Hello?" Gavin repeated.

"Ah, I was right. I was. . .asleep, so I didn't know. . .if I'd dreamt about someone. . .talking to me."

The man's words came in short bursts, sounding as if he were struggling to form them.

"Do you. . .have a name, son?" he asked Gavin, who answered before returning the same question. "I *do* have a name." He scoffed before Gavin heard a chuckle. "Can't be sure. . .at the moment. I do hope it was. . .a nice one, though."

Something's not right. A sense of unease came over Gavin. *Is he okay?*

Licking his dry lips, Gavin raked both hands through his hair.

I've got to get out of here. Maybe if I scream loud enough, someone will come. This would sure be a good time for one of those fairies to show up.

The other prisoner began muttering to himself, listing off possible names before Gavin heard a frustrated grunt from another cell nearby.

"Are you going to be talking much longer? The rest of us are trying to sleep!"

This voice sounded younger. Closer to Gavin's age, if he had to guess.

"Howard?" the older prisoner suggested before giggling to himself. "No, no. . .definitely not. I much prefer. . .Jeremy."

"Your name is Horace!" the boy snapped. "Now, go to sleep."

"Horace?" The older man grew quiet as he considered the name. "Yes, that'll do. I like that name."

Gavin bit his lip before calling out in the direction he had heard the younger man speak from.

"Who are you?"

"Horace!"

"He's talking to *me*, old man!" the other boy said, cursing under his breath. "Honestly, he's going to make me as batty as him one day. I'm Rory."

"What happened to *him*?" Gavin asked, nodding towards Horace even though he knew Rory couldn't see him.

"Couldn't keep his mouth shut," Rory said. "He was once the town storyteller, weren't you, Horace? I even went to listen to him a few times when I was a boy." He paused before continuing. "Loyal to the previous queen, he was. Horace told everyone who'd listen about Queen Prisha. Didn't sit right with Queen Rona, of course. When Horace tried to tell the new queen's story, he disappeared. I didn't know what had happened to him until I got thrown in here as well."

Gavin relaxed his legs in front of him, unsure if he wanted to know more. Unable to suppress his curiosity, he asked what Rory had been arrested for.

"Assaulting a guard." Rory's tone suggested that this was a minor offense. "A troop showed up at my house and tried to take my little brother for the queen's new army."

"Why not you?" Gavin asked.

"Can't see it in here, mate, but I've only got one leg. Smashed it up nice when I was little, and the doctor had to stop an infection. Pretty useless to an army."

"I'm sorry."

"Eh, it is what it is. But watching my mother get thrown into hysterics and hearing my brother screaming while the soldiers carried him off snapped something in me." Rory's voice cracked at the end of his sentence, causing him to fall silent until he was in control of himself. "I did all I could, of course. I hobbled across the room and punched at whoever I could reach, but I was no match for them. They beat and carried me off for a different sentence, and I haven't seen my family since."

Geez, what kind of place is this? I don't have any real problems compared to these people!

Gavin thought about Rory's mom and where she was today.

Losing two sons in one day. . .

His growing guilt felt like an anchor in his chest, and for the hundredth time since arriving in Lockesbarrow, he wanted nothing more than to call his parents and apologize for his past spoiled, entitled behavior.

"Why is she doing all of this?" Gavin asked. "What made Rona so power crazy?"

"You'll have to ask Horace," Rory said.

At first, Gavin thought he was joking, given Horace's mental state, but then the other boy elaborated.

"His mind isn't all gone. Rona cursed him. He told me about it one night. The memories come and go. It's a favorite punishment of Rona's, I've been told. You have to catch him in a lucid state."

"When will that be?"

"Could be a few minutes or hours. It varies," Rory replied. "When he's in his right mind, he's decent company."

Sounds terrible. She's even worse than I thought. No wonder everyone is so afraid of her.

Gavin became aware of how silent the rest of the prison was.

"Are we the only three in here?" Gavin asked.

"There are others. Probably sleeping. Can't judge time in this place, but I'd imagine it's early morning."

As if on cue, Gavin heard someone cough in the distance. A full dungeon of prisoners would explain the overwhelming stench of body odor that had attacked his nostrils since he arrived.

"And you sit here in complete darkness all day and night?"

"The guards carry torches. Two meals are delivered a day—one in the morning and one in the evening," said Rory.

"Do you know how long you've been down here?" Gavin asked, shocked by Rory's indifference towards his fate.

"At least a year. Lost count recently."

Rory's answers became more dismissive with every question that followed about his capture.

Gavin took the hint and the two fell silent. He dozed in and out of a troubled sleep that was only broken by the sound of a door creaking open.

Filled with both dread and anticipation, Gavin scrambled to his feet when he heard approaching footsteps.

The pitch-black dungeon began taking new forms as the torchlight grew closer. Shadows danced across the newly exposed stone walls.

The other prisoners—silent and invisible up until now—awakened to beg for food and freedom. Their cries and pleas pierced through Gavin's heart, but it appeared that is where the mercy ended.

The guards took no notice of anyone but simply pushed trays into each cell without a word.

At this point, Gavin would welcome anything edible to fill his stomach.

When the guards reached his cell, Gavin backed away. He watched as a small section of the bars was pushed inward to allow the tray to pass through before it was promptly slammed shut and locked again.

"You there," one guard barked, "the queen wants to see you in an hour. We'll be back."

"That can't be good," said Rory.

It took Gavin a moment to realize Rory was talking to him. Now that the trays had been delivered, there was a constant wave of noise that made it difficult to hear the boy across from him. As unsettling as a quiet prison had been in the darkness, hearing the range of sounds coming from the awakened, faceless inmates made the hairs on the nape of Gavin's neck stand on end.

"What can't be good?" Gavin asked.

A bead of sweat rolled down his temple. Unable to see anything, Gavin stepped closer to where the tray was dropped before lowering to his knees. Extending both arms out, his tremoring hands felt around for any hint of food until his fingers wrapped around something soft. He lifted it to his lips, inhaling the sweet scent of bread before cramming the entire roll into his mouth. It was only after he had swallowed it that his brain registered its staleness.

"The queen wants to see you. Sounds like you're the next chosen one," Rory replied.

"Chosen one for what?"

I don't like that. I don't want to be chosen for anything.

"To be Rona's swain," Horace said.

Gavin was even more confused.

"Her what?"

"Her lover," Rory said.

The blood drained from Gavin's face. Feeling his knees lock, Gavin wondered in the back of his mind if he was going to fall over. This couldn't be happening. Everything kept getting worse and worse. Sure, Rona had flirted with him, but Gavin never expected to be *chosen* for anything. Especially something like that.

"I'm not doing that," Gavin said.

"You're not the first. . .to declare that," Horace said with a chuckle. "But you'll succumb. They all do."

All?

"It sounds like the old man has his wits about him!" Rory exclaimed. "You may want to ask him your questions. He may only be with us a few minutes."

"Ask me what? What do. . .you mean?" the older prisoner asked.

Here's my chance, I guess. Let's hope he cooperates.

"Why is Rona doing all of this?"

Horace did not answer right away. A long moment passed in which Gavin feared the man's memory had lapsed once more. At last, he answered.

"Some days. . .it feels like a lifetime ago, yet there are other times. . .like now, where it seems only yesterday," Horace said.

"You're in for quite a story," Rory replied.

Although Gavin knew Horace couldn't help his speech, the constant pauses unnerved him. While eagerly awaiting Horace's story to progress, Gavin located the rest of the food near the tray and began eating as he listened.

Horace spoke only above a whisper, making it more frustrating for Gavin to hear over the raucous of the prison.

"There once. . .was a young girl," Horace began, "who loved her brother. . .so very deeply." He coughed before clearing his throat with an apology. "The pair of them worked here. . .in the castle. He a cook, she a maid."

Rona, a maid? There's no way.

"They were hired one summer. . .while the royal family was away," Horace continued. "When the season ended. . .the family returned, and Queen Rona's brother. . .fell in love with Princess Prisha."

The king and queen probably freaked out. Either them or Rona.

"Careful, Horace!" hissed a raspy voice from a nearby cell. "Don't go saying that name around these parts. Her Majesty will have your tongue cut out. It's hard to tell stories if you're mute."

Gavin shivered, feeling a chill run down his already sweat-coated back.

Rory encouraged the storyteller to continue.

"Rumor has it. . .the young princess returned the boy's love." Horace coughed again. "But when the king and queen were found murdered. . ."

Murdered! Did Rona murder them?

"Queen Rona's brother was accused. . .and sentenced to death." Horace fell silent.

Wait. That can't be it. There has to be more!

Gavin wasn't ready for the story to end. He threw out more questions for Horace to answer.

"And after that? If the Princess loved him back, why didn't she save him? What happened to her?"

"Go easy on him," Rory said. "It wears him out to relive it all again."

Gavin paused waiting for Horace to continue. This was the most he had heard about Rona up until now, and he knew that he was against the clock before Horace's curse would take over again.

"That was almost. . .let's see, almost thirty years ago. My, my, my." Horace chuckled to himself. "Isn't that something?"

Rona must have spelled herself to stay youthful. That's not surprising.

"When her brother was not spared, Queen Rona. . .vowed to have her revenge and. . .one day rule Lockesbarrow."

"So, she just took over?" Gavin asked. "Why didn't she stop them from killing her brother?"

"She didn't take over right away," Rory said. "It took years of fear mongering and planning on her part. Built a name for herself and spread the threat of what was to come for the other kingdoms. As for her brother's fate, she wasn't as skilled as she is now. Queen Rona brushed up on her magic and officially captured the throne when she had enough power and spies."

Gavin thought of Brahm. He and his friends had been convinced it was Derek's steward, Ballard, who was the spy until catching Brahm in the library stealing the king's documents. It was hard to believe that was only a handful of days ago.

Gavin felt like his head was spinning. Pieces of the puzzle were finally connecting, yet there were still so many missing.

"But what does she want with *me*?" Gavin asked. "She has her army. She has the—" He was about the say diary but cut himself off. "Weapons she needs."

Rory scoffed. "She has other needs than power, mate."

The chuckles and whistles from the other cells made Gavin feel sick to his stomach. Sliding his back down the wall, he landed hard on the floor and stared out into the nothingness in front of him.

I can't do that. I won't do that. She can find somebody else.

After voicing these thoughts, more laughter ensued. Despite his serious declaration, Gavin felt the familiar heat of embarrassment rush to his face.

"You heard Horace," Rory said, "you'll eventually give in. They all do. No one has control over who she chooses."

"That is true," said the same voice who had chastised Horace earlier for speaking Prisha's name. "One time, she even chose one who had fled the kingdom entirely. Found him all the way in Haighdlen. Some claimed he got away, but not before she convinced him to work for her. He eventually gave into her desires, of course. Nothing stops Queen Rona from getting what she wants."

"I've turned her down once." Gavin shrugged. "I'll just do it again."

"*Encourage* her again, you mean," said Rory. "The sick woman thinks it's a game."

"There has to be something I can do when the soldiers come back to get me," said Gavin. "Horace, do you know of anything she doesn't like that I can do to change her mind?"

"Who?" asked Horace.

"The queen!" Losing what little patience he had left, Gavin growled and spoke louder. "What kinds of things will make her leave me alone?"

"We're all alone." Horace chuckled. "All alone." He began to sing the words, repeating the phrase many times.

No! Did he lose his memory again? I need to know more. I need to know what to do!

It was no use. The real Horace was gone, along with any hope Gavin had of learning anything else.

Clenching his jaw, Gavin turned around and slammed his fist against the wall. He lost count how many times he punched and was most likely going to suffer from his injuries later. For the time being, however, every connection with the stone barrier released a fraction of his rage and adrenaline. The pain felt good.

At last, clear thoughts returned to his now exhausted mind. Gavin panted and rested his forehead against the wall. Sweat rolled down his back and chest. With his energy spent, he no longer found pleasure in the pain that was now excruciating.

The others quieted in response to his tantrum. Gavin didn't care what they thought about him. They weren't the ones Rona wanted for one reason or the other.

The normal buzz of voices and crying resumed throughout the dungeon, though Gavin paid it little attention. His mind was elsewhere.

Rona was going to try seducing him. It had been difficult to turn her away the first time, and there was a part of Gavin that feared the other prisoners were right.

What if I'm not strong enough? What if I give in?

He could only think of Elise. His heart pounded with every passing moment. Gavin's thoughts played out each scenario, all ending with breaking Elise's heart.

He wanted to be strong for her. He *needed* to be strong for her.

How long has my leg been bouncing like that?

Coming out of his daydream, Gavin stopped the unconscious movement and tried to gain control of his rising fear. His insides quivered as his mind played tricks on him, creating false shapes in the darkness. Anticipating the guards any minute, he jumped at any sudden, loud noise.

When he couldn't control himself, the rage and guilt returned. The sheer fury about his predicament made him want to rip his cell apart, while the shame was heavy enough to convince him he was somehow to blame.

Despite his stillness, Gavin's heart throbbed rapidly. Closing his eyes, he swallowed for the hundredth time in spite of its dryness.

Gavin grimaced when he heard the familiar sound of the dungeon door creaking open.

They're here.

CHAPTER 16

It would have been easier if Mr. Dolluff had lent Elise and her friends a cart rather than send Cole and Arlo to guide them. While this option was safer—especially traveling at night—their presence only managed to amplify the unspoken tension lingering beneath the surface.

Despite their guides' playful banter, Elise couldn't bring herself to feel any sort of merriment.

Getting caught with Vaughn in Lorelei's bedroom hours earlier set off a string of unfortunate events that threatened to not only ruin Elise's friendships, but the remainder of the journey to save Gavin as well.

Darcie had left the room immediately, and by the time Elise caught up with her, Mitch was informed of the entire situation. It was decided that they wouldn't speak of what happened until they were alone in case the Dolluffs changed their minds about helping them. What followed was an endless cycle of cold shoulders, shaking of heads, and judgmental stares from her two friends. The final, crushing blow came when Mitch and Darcie spent the better part of the ride whispering in hushed voices, resulting in Elise's insides being drenched with paranoia.

She couldn't blame them. Mitch was hurt for Gavin, and Darcie's eyes betrayed both heartache and jealousy. They didn't want to listen to Elise's reasons or excuses. As much as she tried to tell them that nothing happened, it was no use. Elise was forced to resign her arguments and spent the ride huddled towards the back of the cart with Vaughn, who didn't even make eye contact with her once.

As Mr. Dolluff predicted, the group reached a clearing in the woods that Cole and Arlo deemed safe shortly after midnight.

Grabbing one of the blankets Mrs. Dolluff had packed for each of them, Elise settled down by herself next to an overturned tree. While her thoughts when sleeping outside tended to revolve around avoiding bugs and snakes, tonight Elise's mind focused elsewhere. Glancing over, Elise watched Mitch and Darcie spread out next to Cole and Arlo with their backs towards her.

At least Cole and Arlo are acting like they don't know anything. Let's hope it stays that way.

She noticed Vaughn also chose a secluded spot like her on the opposite side of the party.

I guess it's no longer important to look like we're married.

It was hard to think they had tried to pass themselves off as couples earlier that day. The rate in which everything fell apart made Elise's head spin. She supposed she should be thankful Darcie didn't make a scene at the house.

This is so messed up. Why am I the bad guy? No one is even acting mad at Vaughn! And why isn't he talking to me either? I don't know what happened in that room, but that wasn't the real me. I would never do that to Gavin. My friends should know that. As soon as Cole and Arlo leave, I'm going to tell them everything whether they want to listen or not.

Overcome with fatigue, regret, and—she hated to admit it—embarrassment, Elise tucked her face under the blanket and released the cry she had been holding all evening. She hoped the collective noises of chirping crickets and Vaughn snoring were enough to mask the sound of her sobbing. As good as the release felt, Elise's eyes burned with every new arrival of tears that erupted in waves down her face.

I don't see a way out of this. I wish Gavin were here right now. He'd believe me, wouldn't he? Why. . .why wasn't I able to leave the room? What would have happened if Darcie hadn't walked in?

Elise silenced her mind before it went down a road she wasn't ready to face. As good as Vaughn had made her feel during those intimate moments, Elise couldn't shake the feeling she had not been in full control of her own actions. It didn't add up, because she knew that Vaughn didn't have magic, so what possessed her to receive his attentions without fighting back more?

She didn't want Vaughn. There was no future with him, and she wasn't the type of girl he went after anyway. Nothing about this scenario made any sense, which complicated the explanation she formed in her head to share with the others when the time came.

Elise wasn't sure she even slept by the time everyone started to stir at the first signs of dawn.

After eating the breakfast packed for them, it was time for Cole and Arlo to head back to Laurishire.

Finally!

After remaining quiet for so long, afraid she would lose her sanity, Elise mustered up enough courage to ask Mitch, Darcie, and Vaughn to sit.

Feeling a growing lump in her dry throat, Elise's voice was hoarse from crying most of the night. Knowing her eyes must be blood-shot as well, she stared at the ground while trying to repeat the internal words that needed to be said aloud.

With all eyes watching, Elise felt like her knees would buckle at any moment. Looking at Vaughn, she waited in case he wanted to say anything.

He didn't.

Great. Just me then. Thanks.

Elise licked her lips and picked a spot above Darcie's shoulder to focus on so she wouldn't lose the nerve to do this. Fidgeting with her fingers, she took a deep breath.

"I know you don't want to hear this, but it's the truth. Nothing happened."

"That's not what I saw." Darcie rolled her eyes. "It looked like a whole lot of something."

Mitch narrowed his gaze. Shifting on the rough bark beneath him, he crossed his arms and sneered at her.

Geez, I would think he'd be relieved it wasn't Darcie.

"I can't explain it," Elise said, refocusing on the spot between Mitch and Darcie rather than meet their eyes, "When I saw Vaughn in the room already, I tried to leave, but I couldn't."

It was Mitch's turn to roll his eyes.

"I really did! But then something happened." Furrowing her brows together, Elise relived the moments leading up to Darcie coming in. "It was as if another force was in control of my body. My brain screamed to walk away—"

"I don't think your brain was involved at all," Mitch muttered.

Elise scowled as heat rushed to her face.

"Oh really? Why don't you ask *him*?" she screamed, pointing a finger in Vaughn's direction. "Because the last I checked, Darcie saw the *two* of us together, but all you both can do is judge me. What about him?"

"I've always judged Vaughn." Mitch shrugged, nodding towards the other man. "I expect this crap from him, but something must've encouraged him to stay in the room."

"Something did," Vaughn said, speaking for the first time. He kept his gaze on Elise. "I saw that she was in distress, overtaken by her nerves, and I was merely trying to calm her. Nothing untoward occurred."

Why didn't he say that in the first place? Ugh, I could strangle him right now!

Why did he put her through all this torture if he planned to help after all?

"Well, I know what I saw—"

"You saw nothing!" Vaughn snapped at Darcie, startling her, before lowering his voice, "because *nothing* happened."

Pushing on his knees, Vaughn stood with a huff before looking down at Elise's friends.

"We need to move past this. Continuing to vilify her, or both of us, will only manage to slow our progress down further. Your friend, Gavin, may not have much time left."

A silence fell among them as the weight of Vaughn's words sank in.

Despite her gratitude for his support, Elise wasn't ready to thank Vaughn yet. Not after what he put her through in the last twelve hours. And yet there was still a part of Elise's stomach that flipped when he looked at her the way he did at that moment.

What is that? It's almost magnetic. . .

Elise pushed the confusing feelings aside. It appeared that Darcie and Mitch were convinced for the time being.

I've got to be careful around him. If that weird feeling comes over me again, I don't know if I'll be so lucky.

Vaughn secured his satchel and sword before stepping around them to lead the way without another word on the subject.

"Was he really just there calming you down?" Darcie whispered when Vaughn had gained enough distance ahead of them. "What were you even panicking about?"

Elise could tell by the way Mitch tilted his head that he was eavesdropping, which caused a sinking dread to fill her stomach. She felt like a thousand small needles were prickling the sides of her arms and face.

"It's me," Elise replied with a shrug and hollow laugh, which she hoped would sound convincing. "When am I not panicking, am I right?" When they didn't join in, she cleared her throat.

I need to tell the truth while still covering up what could have happened.

"I freaked out when I saw him in there, and when I tried to leave, he saw me getting nervous about being seen together. He didn't want me to go out looking like that to draw attention, so he tried to calm me down."

"With his tongue?" asked Darcie.

Elise glared at her.

"What're you going to tell Gavin?" Mitch asked.

"I'm not telling him anything, because there's nothing to tell!" Elise hissed. "I didn't kiss Vaughn. Nothing happened. Please drop it!"

"It's a good thing I came in when I did then," Darcie muttered.

Digging all ten fingernails into her thighs, Elise bit the inside of her cheek and fought the urge to pull Darcie's hair.

How can she come off so high and mighty? The things Darcie has admitted to me over the past couple of years. . .this is nothing compared to those. This is all because it's Vaughn.

Unfortunately, ignoring Darcie was the best option until Elise could calm herself down. Throwing shade back and forth at one another was only going to make things worse. Attempting to distract herself, Elise looked around and noticed a lake off to the left.

"A lake!" she cried out. "We need to stop here."

Mr. Dolluff kept his promise to get us to a lake. Now I can finally bathe!

"Not yet, Elise," Vaughn said.

I hate when he talks like he's my dad or something. He can't stop me. I'm filthy.

"I'll only be a minute."

Leaving the forest path, Elise made a beeline for the lake until Vaughn jogged ahead and blocked her from getting closer.

"You're not going over there."

Towering over her, he swayed side to side every time she tried passing him.

Elise stomped her foot, glaring back with the same exasperated expression Vaughn wore.

"I want to take a bath. Why is it such a big deal?"

"You can," he said, blocking her again, "but not this lake."

"Why not?"

"Because this is Lake Mirage. It's not safe to even be this close to it. If you'd follow me a little further, we'll see the ocean, and you can bathe however long you want in those waters. I promise."

Elise quit struggling and sighed.

Lake Mirage. Derek said something about Lake Mirage once. What was it?

"Where have we heard that name before?" Darcie asked.

"That's what I was just wondering," Elise said. "Didn't Derek tell us about it?"

"Wasn't it about some evil merpeople or something?" Mitch lifted a hand to his forehead to block the sun as he gazed out at the lake. He shrugged. "Doesn't look that scary from here."

"Take a step closer, and I assure you, you'll think differently," Vaughn warned. "Please return to the path with me, and I will guide you to a safer area to wash."

Elise might have argued more if she had known he meant two more hours of walking. To her amusement, she was saved the hassle since Mitch made sure Vaughn got an earful the entire time.

When her restlessness reached its peak, Elise noticed that the trees had thinned out around them and there was a cool breeze in the air. Through the gaps on either side of her, Elise saw water and could hear laughter in the distance.

Which one is the lake?

Looking down at her feet, she realized that there were fewer leaves and brush to step over as the land narrowed ahead of them. The path they walked on became more populated, and Elise counted no less than four carriages and three horsemen traveling back and forth on the road.

Why are there so many people here?

Glancing to her left, Elise only saw shallow marshes overrun with long, untamed, cordgrass. It was deserted.

More laughter and voices caught her attention, and Elise looked over to the other side where an endless and inviting shoreline greeted them.

Now, that's more like it! What a beautiful ocean.

Families were scattered along the calm water's edge. Children chased and splashed each other while men and women rested on the sand. Seagulls squawked above them and there was a taste of salt in the air. Sunlight glittered off the blue-green water like diamonds between the distant whitecaps, and for a moment, Elise forgot she was still in Haighdlen.

"I definitely prefer *this* place." Darcie's voice was filled with awe. "I'm so sick of the forest scene. Can we stay here? It seems safe enough."

Mitch nodded and repeated Darcie's question.

Elise whirled around when Vaughn agreed they could go down to the beach now.

"We can't stop here." Feeling everyone's eyes on her, Elise rolled her own and nodded towards the people. "I can't wash in front of *them*." She looked further down the beach where there were less people, but it was still occupied by people horseback riding through the shallow parts of the water. As breathtaking as this place was, Elise couldn't see a single area where she'd be hidden.

"The grass is pretty tall over there," Mitch said, nodding towards the marshy areas. "Just go squat down and throw some water on your face if you don't want people watching."

"That is forbidden," Vaughn said. "Everything to that side is too close to Lake Mirage, which is why it's deserted. King's orders."

"Since when do you follow orders?"

Vaughn ignored Mitch's question and led the way down towards the sandy shore.

CHAPTER 17

Although physically removed from the dungeon, Gavin feared it was only the beginning of his punishment.

After receiving another bath, Gavin was dressed in clean clothes once more before a group of six guards proceeded to lead him to Rona.

Gavin didn't know what he was walking into, but if Horace and Rory were correct about the temptation ahead, a decision was going to have to be made.

If I give Rona what she wants, I don't know if I can ever look Elise in the eyes again. The thought alone scared him. *But if I don't, she might punish the other boys because of me.* That almost scared him more.

Deep down, Gavin knew what really frightened him was the possibility of him giving in for his own sake. He could argue back and forth about the morality of his choice, but at the end of the day, Rona was a strong, attractive woman who didn't know the meaning of the word no.

Would she kill me if I refused her? If so, am I willing to die *over that? It'd be easier to ask for forgiveness than get myself killed.*

When presented at that angle, giving Rona what she wanted might buy his friends more time to arrive. Perhaps they would understand that the ends justified the means. . .but could he live with himself?

I'm assuming what Horace and Rory said is true, but I could have it all wrong. Sure, she's flirted a little, but Rona hasn't come out and said she actually wanted me or anything. Maybe I'm making it all up in my head.

He hoped rather than believed it to be true.

If she didn't want anything, she would've left me in the dungeon. I certainly wouldn't have had another bath.

That much he did know. Gavin's thoughts traveled back to the prison. In the torchlight, he had seen Horace's bemused expression and Rory's pitying glances before being led out by guards.

"...you'll eventually give in. They all do. No one has control over who she chooses."

Rory's words echoed through Gavin's mind as he entered the massive throne room. Expecting to meet Rona, he was surprised when the guards escorting him crossed through the room without stopping.

Walking down the adjoining corridor, Gavin's curiosity grew. This wasn't the way he was taken to the dining room either.

Where are we going?

After passing by what felt like twenty closed doors, the lead guard paused outside of one before turning to address Gavin.

"You will only speak when spoken to. No harm is to come to the queen. If any threat is detected, you will not make it out of this room alive. Is that clear?"

Gavin nodded, feeling as if his tongue had become glued to the roof of his already dry mouth.

Why is this visit scarier than the others?

Gavin's breath hitched as he stepped into what appeared to be some sort of drawing room or parlor.

Whatever it was called, Rona had certainly decorated it to fit her tastes. Gavin couldn't imagine the previous queen favoring such dark and sinister furnishings.

All five of the tall windows, which would have allowed ample amounts of sunlight to pour in, were concealed behind heavy, velvet purple drapes. The only light came from two oversized chandeliers adorned with hanging crystals and an ornate fireplace trimmed with black marble. A couch and two armchairs faced the fire, but Gavin's eyes were drawn to the figure sprawled out across a lush white chaise lounge in the center of the room.

"Leave us."

Unable to sense Rona's mood from her words alone, Gavin avoided eye contact, choosing instead to focus on the decorative carpet as the guards left one by one. Knowing they'd wait outside the door, he needed to be careful not to cause them any reason to return.

"Come to me," she said.

Gavin's feet felt as if they had taken on a life of their own. Although his brain screamed to run in the opposite direction, each step brought him closer until he stood in front of her.

She was breathtaking to behold. Dressed in a form-fitting powder blue gown, Rona balanced the diary in one hand while leafing through its empty pages with another. A heavy sigh escaped her lips.

"I must confess I've never disliked a book more."

Grab it. Do it now. You can get out of here before she tries anything.

Gavin's impulsive thoughts came faster than he could process them. Flexing his hands on either side of him, he watched Rona examine the book.

"How did you find your cell?" Rona peeked up at him through heavy lashes.

"Fine." Gavin wasn't going to cave to her flirting. Not yet, anyway. "Never slept better."

Rona's lips spread into a wicked smile as she pushed up into a sitting position and closed the book. It fell, forgotten, as Rona grabbed a fistful of Gavin's shirt and pulled him to her.

Gavin stumbled before regaining his balance. He heard his rapid heartbeat ringing in both ears as her knees pressed against his thighs. Gavin knew he should back away, but her grip prevented it.

"This color suits you." She caressed the burgundy fabric of his shirt with her free hand. When she glanced up at him again, Gavin was reminded of a skilled lioness sizing up her prey.

The look alone was almost enough to undo him. An involuntary shiver ran down his spine as she grazed her fingers along Gavin's rib cage. When Rona released her hold on him, he was surprised to notice he didn't make an attempt to move away.

"What do we have here?" she purred, cradling Gavin's right hand between both of hers.

In the candlelight, Gavin was able to see how swollen and bruised his knuckles were from punching the dungeons wall. It had released his aggression in the moment, but Gavin winced when Rona stroked the sensitive skin with her fingers.

"The rage you carry within your heart is really something." She clicked her tongue before placing a kiss across the darkest area of his hand.

Gavin stared at the imprint that her lipstick left behind but said nothing. He didn't want to admit how soothing it felt.

If Rona did notice, she didn't say anything as she ran her delicate fingers in small circles across the bruises. With each delicate caress, the scratches and bruises were erased until his hand was unblemished except the smeared lipstick she left behind. Locking her eyes with his, Rona lifted Gavin's hand and placed his palm against her cheek.

"You mustn't do that to yourself, love."

Multiple scenarios flashed through Gavin's mind of what could happen next. He was ashamed to admit that backing away from Rona was the last one. Had there ever been a time where he was *this* tempted before? As much as he struggled, his body was taking over by the second, which he knew Rona was counting on.

The firelight danced across her beautiful pale features as she stood up. Gavin wondered in the back of his mind why she always chose such angelic, pastel colors that contradicted her brazen personality. Given the account of her by Horace and Rory, perhaps he should've been surprised she was wearing clothes at all. Gavin stopped his dangerous train of thought there.

"Do you know why I summoned you here?" she whispered.

She spoke so softly that it was difficult for Gavin to hear her over the crackling fire.

"You want me to make the diary work." Keeping the emotion out of his voice, Gavin focused on a statue behind Rona to avoid gazing into her mesmerizing eyes.

"Precisely."

Not about to be ignored, Rona trailed her fingers up to Gavin's shoulder before snaking a hand around his neck.

What is happening to me? She didn't affect me this much back at camp. Why now?

He didn't know the answer—and doubted he ever would—but it didn't matter. Gavin knew he had to fight his urges. He looked around the room for a distraction.

At first, he saw the diary on the floor. He could pick it up, maybe even trick her into thinking he'd open it, but would that work? She was probably expecting that.

Scanning the room, Gavin's eyes fixated on a painting he hadn't noticed before above the fireplace.

I can ruin the mood at least.

"Who's that?"

Pulling away from him, Rona followed Gavin's gaze to the painting.

"My brother, Dmitri." Her terse response signaled the end of the conversation as she turned back to face him.

Not if I can help it.

If Gavin could keep her mind otherwise occupied, she might give up on her pursuit. "Is he a king or something?"

"He should've been." Rona turned a cold shoulder to him.

Feeling the heightened tension ease between them, Gavin relaxed his shoulders and allowed himself to hope his plan would work.

Just keep her talking.

"What happened to him?"

"He died."

Lowering herself onto the chaise lounge again, Rona draped an arm over her head with an exasperated sigh and stared at her brother's portrait.

The once confident and seductive glint in Rona's eyes was replaced by an empty, forlorn stare. If not for the subtle rise and fall of her chest from breathing, someone might assume she was lifeless.

Unable to stand the silence any longer, Gavin cleared his throat and bounced on the balls of his feet.

"How did he die?"

"I know what you are doing." Even Rona's voice sounded hollow as she called out to him. "You mean to distract me, throw me off the scent. . .make me relive the most tragic day of my life before you strike."

"No, I don't." Gavin bit the inside of his cheek.

Rona scoffed. "You lie as badly as you fight." She paused another moment to examine the portrait of Dmitri before waving towards the door. "My mood has officially soured, and I'm expecting another visitor soon. I suppose I have no use for you after all. You'll be returned to the camp tomorrow."

An odd sensation came over Gavin at the idea of returning to the camp. While he wanted to assure the safety of Tristan and the others, he was surprised to realize that he wanted to stay in the room with Rona.

I must be crazy. Maybe she's put a spell on me.

For the first time since arriving, Gavin witnessed a vulnerability in Rona that called out to him. Did he feel sorry for her? Was she a victim too? Gavin shook his head to come out of his thoughts. No matter how much humanity Rona chose or didn't choose to show, her present behavior couldn't undo the horrific crimes she had committed.

Now I'm *the one getting distracted. Quick, say something!*

"I'm sorry he's gone, but would he want you to do all this?" Gavin nodded towards the painting. "Kidnapping those boys and killing people won't bring him back."

Gavin immediately regretted his words.

In one swift motion, Rona stood and crossed the room until she stood in front of him again. All hints of anguish faded as she poked a long finger against his chest.

"*Don't* mistake my past suffering for weakness. You are not here to befriend me." She continued before Gavin could argue back. "I will not tolerate an ounce of pity, nor humor any attempts to trifle with me, especially from the likes of *you*."

Expecting her to call the guards, Gavin stiffened when Rona hiked up one side of her skirt to retrieve a hidden dagger. He watched as the firelight flitted across the lethal blade. Feeling his heart pound within him, Gavin's eyes darted around the room looking for an escape.

Would Rona really stab me right here like this? One minute she wants me, and now she's threatening to kill me. She's psychotic!

Rona held the dagger in one hand while twisting the tip of the blade against her fingertip, much like Gavin had seen Brahm do in the carriage on his first day in Lockesbarrow.

Various scenarios swept rapidly through Gavin's mind as his anxiety grew. What would he do if she tried striking him? Would he grab her wrist? Attempt to take the dagger? What then?

Rona met his gaze and Gavin saw the calm, alluring heat return to her eyes.

She's all over the place. I can't keep up with her mood swings. I need to get out of here before she kills me.

Gavin looked between the discarded diary and his exit. If he took off at a run, would he even stand a chance?

He was back where he started. At the end of the day, Horace and Rory were right. There wasn't anything powerful enough to distract Rona from what she wanted.

As if sensing his train of thought, Rona placed the dagger in Gavin's sweaty hand. She responded to his confounded expression with a breathy chuckle that stirred something in his stomach.

"There you go. Kill me."

What? What is she trying to do?

Gavin stared at the dagger before making the mistake of looking back at Rona.

"If you're so high and mighty like you act, then take charge," she said. "You're brave enough to question my motives. Go on. Do it."

When he didn't move, Rona reached out to wrap her fingers around his hand, pressing the blade to her throat.

Mesmerized, Gavin watched the sensitive skin of her neck quiver before him. He wanted to run, but his feet remained frozen. Once again, he found himself unable to speak.

How did we get here? Why is she doing this? I can't kill her.

Rona's fingers slid around Gavin's wrist and guided the blade lower across her skin.

Gavin's eyes followed the tip of the blade as it trailed down and across the curve of her barely concealed bosom. He felt flustered as Rona's other hand tugged the fabric of her gown down, exposing a smooth pale shoulder. He wanted to pull it the rest of the way.

Gavin might've shown more resolve had she not been locking eyes with him the entire time.

Rona's brazen nature was attractive, and she knew it. For someone with a dagger against her chest, Rona appeared calm—perhaps even encouraged by Gavin's lack of struggle.

"You could end all of this here right now, you know. No one else would get hurt," she purred.

Except me. The guards outside would take him down before her body hit the ground. *They'd kill me the instant anything happened to Rona.*

"There'd be no war, no suffering," she continued. Rona lifted her other hand to stroke his hair. "You would be the hero."

Gavin knew she was playing mind tricks on him, yet he couldn't stop his heart from swelling at the prospect of being a hero like he always viewed his dad had been. All it would take would be one good plunge of the dagger into Rona's heart, and yet, here he stood, weakened by the beauty in front of him.

The crackling fire was the only sound around them as she baited him to make the next move. When he didn't, she chuckled.

"It's just as I told you. You don't have it in you. You're not a fighter. . .but I can change that." Releasing his hand, she ran both of her hands down Gavin's arms. She leaned up and placed a kiss behind his ear.

A shiver ran down his spine. Gavin didn't want to admit how much he wanted to reach out and grab her. He was losing control of himself by the second.

Moving her hand up his chest, she unfastened the first three buttons of Gavin's shirt.

She wants this as much as you do. Kiss her already! Deal with the rest later.

Rona placed a finger across his lips. "There's so much I can teach you. . .if you'd let me."

When her breath tickled his skin, he was almost undone.

Stop her. Take the dagger, even if you can't kill her. Threaten her, grab the diary and run. Run. Get out now. Why can't you run?

Looking down into her eyes, he knew she had won. He felt his control snap and his lust for her grew. All he could think about was removing the rest of her clothing. The dagger dropped to the floor as Gavin wrapped a trembling hand around her waist.

Rona lifted her chin up towards him. He fought the need within him until he no longer could. Tilting his head, Gavin inched his face closer to hers.

I'm sorry, Elise.

Before his mouth could meet Rona's, however, a knock at the door cut through the aroused silence.

CHAPTER 18

Vaughn found a spacious area for their party to rest about a half a mile down the beach. Given the large crowd, he suggested that they rest until most of the families left before anyone tried to bathe.

"Why does everything end with resting or stalling?" Mitch asked. "Let's keep moving."

"Elise would like to bathe, and this is the best place for her to do so," Vaughn said. "We just have to wait for it to be more secluded."

"Well, then let's go to a secluded part of the beach."

Vaughn shook his head at Mitch's suggestion.

"Have patience, Mitchell. These families won't be here all day. As the sun sets, they'll start to depart and then—"

"Whoa, hold on. We have to stay here until *sunset*?" Mitch turned towards Elise. "This is crazy. Elise, look, I know you want to take a bath. We all want to clean up, but is it worth losing an entire day over? And one more thing," he said, facing Vaughn again. "What happened to the guy who said that Gavin may not have much time left? You keep switching when we're in a hurry or not. What's that about?"

"Mitch, leave him alone," Darcie said, holding a hand to her mouth to stifle a yawn. "Let's get a nap, take a bath, and make up time tonight. You're getting yourself all worked up, and it's not going to help."

"Honestly, it pisses me off that I'm the *only* one getting worked up! Am I also the only one who cares about saving Gavin?" Mitch looked over at Elise, awaiting a response.

"Mitchell, it has been an exhausting day already," Vaughn interrupted. "Sleep, or don't sleep, but trying to engage us in an argument isn't going to help matters."

Heat rushed to Mitch's face, and for a moment, it looked as if he might explode. His hands curled into fists as he kicked at the sand before plopping down beside Darcie.

He knows I want to save Gavin more than anything. No, I don't want to keep stopping, but I can't get naked in front of all these people.

Rather than try to reason with Mitch in his current state, Elise resolved to talk to him later as she removed her traveling cloak. Rolling it into a makeshift pillow once again, she nuzzled her face against the soft fabric. Although she hadn't spoken a word, somehow pieces of sand had already gotten into her mouth. Using her sand-covered hand was useless, so she hunched over to spit the offending sand out next to her.

Although the cool air sent a shiver down her arms, the sound of the soft, rolling waves made up for it. Within ten minutes, Elise had relaxed more than she had in days. There was something about a beach that could do that to her. As she drifted, however, she was filled with a worrisome thought.

I don't want to fall asleep. What if I dream about Vaughn again?

Elise cleared her throat, adjusted her position, and forced her mind to only listen to the ocean.

Block everything out except thoughts about Gavin. Think of only Gavin. Please let me dream about Gavin.

And there he was, smiling at her. Gosh, she missed his smile. Though she was somewhat aware that this was a dream, Elise didn't care. She would take any alone time she could get with him, real or fantasy.

She raked her fingers through Gavin's tousled hair and caressed his face.

"Stay with me." She kept her hand on his face, afraid he'd disappear if she let go. "Don't leave."

I don't want you to turn into anyone else. Stay here.

He leaned into Elise's touch, turning his face to kiss her palm.

"It's too late." Wrapping his fingers around her wrist, he lowered Elise's hand away from him. "You've given up on me."

A numbness spread throughout Elise's limbs, and she spluttered in disbelief.

"N-No, I didn't—"

"You chose someone else and forgot about me."

"Gavin, that's crazy! I haven't forgotten about you. You have to listen to me!"

When she reached for his arm this time, her hand went right through him. Pulling it back, Elise glanced up at Gavin's sullen expression.

What is he talking about? I haven't given up!

"Goodbye, Elise."

The next thing she knew, Gavin was walking down the beach away from her. Although she ran as fast as she could—yet simultaneously as if in slow motion—Gavin continued getting further and further away until he disappeared altogether.

Elise screamed his name, but it was lost in the wind. Pausing to catch her breath, Elise felt two arms wrap around her from behind in a warm embrace.

Oh, good, you changed your mind!

As she turned around to thank Gavin, the surrounding beach area cracked like a thousand shards of broken glass.

"You've given up on me," Gavin's voice echoed. "You chose someone else. . ."

Knowing whose face she'd see instead of Gavin's, Elise clenched her eyes shut.

Wake up. Wake up, Elise! Control it. Try to control your dream. Bring Gavin back. Don't look at Vaughn.

"Elise?"

No, don't open your eyes. Don't look at him.

"Elise, wake up!"

When Elise awoke, the first thing she saw was Vaughn's face peering down at her.

"Were you having a bad dream?"

Bolting upright, a frustrated, guttural, cry escaped Elise's lips as she kicked at the sand in front of her.

"Elise, wait. What's wrong?" Vaughn reached for her hand, but Elise yanked it away.

"Don't touch me!" she said. Her outburst was loud enough to wake Mitch and Darcie, who also asked if everything was okay. Ignoring them, Elise kicked off her shoes and stomped away down the beach.

Although her dream felt like it only lasted five minutes, the small sliver of sunlight left indicated that hours had passed. All except a handful of people were already gone. That was enough of an invitation for Elise to bathe now. Anything to stay away from Vaughn.

The ocean breeze chilled her tear-streaked face, making Elise shiver as she made her way to the water's edge. The fabric of Elise's skirt hugged against both sand-covered legs as she let the approaching tide cover her bare feet.

Geez, that's cold! How am I going to put my whole body in there?

Using one of the isolated boulders positioned down the beach, Elise hid herself from view and unbuttoned the dress until it fell in a heap on the sand.

Panic flooded her exposed body.

You've got to do this. You whined and complained about needing a bath. Well, here you go. This is it. Now, hurry before someone catches you. Get deep enough to hide yourself.

Using her hands for cover, Elise jogged forward into the awaiting ocean. She shrieked as her body was stabbed by what felt like a million ice-covered knives.

Why does it have to be so freezing?

Elise writhed and kicked, praying for relief as she pressed forward.

Once I get my whole body in, I'll adjust. I'll adjust. Please let me adjust. This is torture. I probably should've waited.

Knowing it was too late to turn back now, Elise got deep enough to lean forward and swim until the water reached her shoulders. She blew out a deep breath and leaned back to soak her hair. The bottle necklace, which she had chosen not to remove, floated in front of her.

Elise was deep enough that the waves rolled past her before breaking closer to the shore. Now that the water no longer felt like it was killing her, she was able to relax and have fun bouncing up and down in the billowing ocean.

I want soap, but I'll take what I can get. Anything is better than nothing.

Elise scrubbed every inch of her body with both hands, removing as much dirt, sweat, and sand as she could. Looking out at the horizon, she inhaled the sweet salty air. As awkward as she had always been, there was something dangerously freeing about swimming naked in the ocean. For the first time that day, her mind was quiet. All of Elise's stress and worries were miles away.

If only it would stay like this. . .

"Feeling better?"

Elise screamed and covered herself as Darcie swam into view.

Darcie chuckled as her teeth chattered from the cold.

"Relax, it's me." When Elise didn't lower her arms from her chest, Darcie rolled her eyes. "We've been through enough sleepovers and gym classes together. I've seen you already. Calm down."

Elise made sure the water came up over her collarbone.

Darcie kept a safe distance anyway as she washed herself.

"I needed this." Scrubbing her scalp, Darcie finished rinsing while floating over the oncoming waves with Elise. "That feels so much better."

A short silence followed after Elise agreed, and she wondered if Darcie was going to bring up their recent argument.

Please don't. Let's forget it ever happened.

"Now that's it's only us," Darcie began, "you can tell me the truth. Did you kiss Vaughn?"

Or not.

"No."

It wasn't a lie. He had kissed Elise's shoulder and neck, but she kept *her* lips to herself. . .something she was thankful of now that the moment had passed.

"Okay, I believe you."

No, you don't.

"There's still something you're not telling me though. Spill it." Darcie's playful smirk returned as she stared at Elise without blinking.

"Fine." Elise looked down into the water as she spoke. "I've been having dreams lately. Weird ones."

"About what?"

"Vaughn."

Elise expected her best friend to get upset or jealous, but Darcie only swam closer.

"Tell me *everything*."

Elise rolled her eyes with a breathy chuckle.

"You're hopeless. You know that?"

One second she's angry and now she wants details? She's crazy.

"Yeah, well you're the one who fooled around with my pretend husband." Darcie grinned with a playful shrug. "Now spill. Don't leave anything out!"

With the initial tension out of the way, Elise was finally able to relax. It felt good to share with Darcie like this again. For the last week, Elise was worried she was losing her best friend. Watching Darcie's dramatic expressions as she relayed the more lurid details of her dreams brought back a sense of normalcy that Elise desperately missed.

I needed this.

"I wouldn't have wanted to wake up." Darcie laughed as she combed a lock of wet hair out of her eyes. "This is a different side of you, that's for sure. I didn't know you had it in you."

The two shared a laugh until a guttural cry pierced the air followed by sounds of men arguing.

"Is that Mitch?" Darcie asked.

Elise craned her neck, but it was difficult to see around the boulders on the beach. There was a physical struggle going on, but it wasn't apparent what was happening until Mitch and Vaughn came into view.

Mitch had two fistfuls of Vaughn's shirt as he slammed the latter man against the nearest boulder.

"We need to get up there," Darcie said.

Although Elise swam as quickly as she could, it felt like they would never reach the beach.

"Don't come out yet!" Mitch called over his shoulder to them. "He's seen enough of you two."

"What are you talking about?" Elise shouted back.

"I caught him spying on y'all out there."

Did he see us naked?

"Mitchell, let them come to shore and dress. We can go somewhere private and handle this," Vaughn replied. "You must calm yourself."

"*Don't* tell me what to do, man. You're sick. I should punch you out right here."

"You will only draw more attention to us, Mitchell," Vaughn said. His calm demeanor only managed to fuel Mitch's rage as the redhead's hand cupped Vaughn's neck.

"Mitch, stop it!" Darcie cried. "Everybody, hang on. Let us get dressed!"

Mitch released his hold and backed away. He and Vaughn turned away so that Elise and Darcie could dress in private behind another boulder.

Elise didn't think she had ever dressed so fast. Heat rushed through her face, and she didn't know if she wanted to laugh or cry from humiliation.

Tugging at the fabric of her dress, which clung to her wet body, made it even more difficult to adjust. Elise bent down to pick up her mother's drawing she had hidden beneath her dress while she swam. Fearful it would be damaged if she tucked it against her moist skin, she held it by her side for the time being.

This dress is stuck to me. I doubt it's hiding very much at this point. They will probably still get an eyeful.

Her suspicions were confirmed when she noticed how little Darcie's dress concealed anything while soaked. Unhappy with her own exposed state, Elise crossed her arms.

"Are you both good now?" Mitch asked.

"Yeah," Darcie replied when she noticed that Elise hadn't found her voice yet. "So, what's going on?"

It was obvious to Elise that Mitch was trying to do the honorable thing by looking up while he spoke about what he saw, but she noticed his eyes lower a couple of times when Darcie stepped closer.

"He was. . .watching you guys." Mitch shifted from one foot to the other, raking a hand through his hair. The red splotches returned to his cheeks as they often did when he was irate about something. "Who knows what else he might do?"

"You're overreacting," the other man replied, looking over at Elise and Darcie. With a softened tone, Vaughn raised his hand. "I never claimed to be a gentleman. I'm afraid I'm weak at the sight of such beautiful women. I sincerely apologize, but I can assure you the invasion of privacy ends there."

It still doesn't make it okay. He's seen me naked. How am I supposed to act around him now?

Elise didn't know what to say, and judging by Darcie's rare silence, neither did she.

When neither Elise nor Darcie answered fast enough, Mitch scoffed and turned on his heel.

"Why're *you* so mad?" Darcie asked. "It's not like he was watching you."

Mitch's shoulders tensed as he stopped. His hands curled into fists and his jaw locked as he turned back to face them.

I don't know if I've ever seen him get this mad. He looks like he's going to blow up any minute.

Mitch's face twisted, and the reddish hue spreading across his skin looked like it was turning purple. Gaping at Darcie, Mitch struggled to speak as a visible vein throbbed above his raised eyebrows. His mouth opened and shut five or six times before a proper syllable came out.

"B-because, i-it's. . .it's wrong!"

He's right. All of this is wrong. I'm glad Mitch is standing up for us.

Elise started to thank him, but her words came too late as Mitch had grown impatient by their lack of responses.

"I'm out of here. If you two are going to be stupid enough to listen to his crap, fend for yourselves. I'm tired of trying."

"Mitch—"

Mitch raised a hand to cut Elise off. He then pointed to the bottle hanging around her neck.

"Give me the fairy magic, *now*. If Ruby can figure out how to use it without having magic, then so can I. I'm going to get Gavin and go home. You can continue this nightmare camping trip without me."

"*Don't* give it to him," Vaughn ordered. "Mitchell, I'll gladly let you hit me if that is what you need to do, but you're not going to use any magic and that's final."

"I told you don't tell me what to do," Mitch growled. Gritting his teeth, he closed the distance between himself and Vaughn. "And if hitting you is what you want me to do then—"

"Both of you stop!" Darcie looked over her shoulder at Elise before tilting her head towards the two men. "Elise, help me out here."

Elise felt conflicted once more where Vaughn was concerned. She sided with Mitch. Vaughn had no right to watch them swimming naked in the ocean, but they had also chosen to wash there where anybody could've seen them despite trying to find a less populated area. On the one hand, she could choose to be flattered that he found her attractive, but this went well beyond that. All of this was wrong, like everything else she felt when Vaughn was around. It was unclear what side Darcie was taking, but as Elise processed what happened, her mind cleared the way for the hurt and betrayal Vaughn had once again caused.

It's not just seeing me naked. I feel violated. How can I keep trusting him? I don't know if I ever trusted him, but I don't know what I feel now.

"Don't bother," Mitch said before Elise could reply, "I'll make it really easy for y'all."

Ignoring their calls, Mitch stomped through the thick sand in the opposite direction towards the marshy grounds.

Where is he going?

"Go get him!" Elise said to Vaughn when it was clear their friend wasn't coming back.

"Why should I?"

Darcie interrupted before Elise could answer.

"Because it's *your* fault he's gone!"

"I take no responsibility for his unstable temper," Vaughn replied. "He'll be back. He has no magic to leave, and if you're smart," he added to Elise, nodding towards her necklace, "you'll keep that magic far away from him."

"Mitch was just protecting us," Darcie said.

I'm glad she saw it like that too. I get why Mitch is mad. Vaughn can't charm his way out of this one.

"That's an exaggeration to say the least. You were never in need of protection."

"It was still wrong," Elise said, glaring at the intimidating, yet attractive, man in front of her. She swallowed hard and squashed the rising nerves that threatened to break through the surface. "You knew what we were doing, and you went out of your way to watch us. How do you think that makes us feel?"

"You're free to feel however you like," Vaughn said. "I meant it as nothing more than a compliment."

"So what? We should say thank you?" With crossed arms, Darcie scoffed and rolled her eyes. "I should punch you myself."

"I won't stop you. I violated your privacy and trust, and for that, I am once again exceedingly sorry."

He doesn't mean it. He'd do it again if he could.

"Wait, where did Mitch go?" Elise asked, unable to see him any longer on the beach.

Vaughn rested a hand against his forehead to shield against the sunlight as he searched for their friend.

"He wouldn't be so reckless. . ."

"About what?" asked Darcie.

"The other side of that area is Lake Mirage," he said.

Elise looked between Vaughn and the marsh covered land in the distance.

"But you told us not to go over there."

"Yes, and Mitchell has done such a *wonderful* job of following my orders so far."

He has a point. What is Mitch thinking? Why didn't he turn back?

Elise didn't have a good feeling about any of this. Mitch was too angry to think rationally right now. He wouldn't know he was in danger until it was too late.

"We have to catch up to him," Darcie said, echoing Elise's thoughts, before both ladies started running towards the lake.

"You're going to get yourselves killed!" Vaughn growled, catching up to them with little effort. His taut body created a barrier that they didn't dare try to pass, and his hair blew wild in the sea air as he glowered at them.

Elise shivered and found herself afraid of him.

"I said *not* to go over there!" He spoke as if he were disciplining children. "Eugena banished that tribe for a reason."

"Well, then you better get over there first and keep him safe!" Darcie argued, not sounding intimidated by Vaughn's temper in the slightest. "What if he needs us?"

"You can do nothing for him," he said, towering over the indignant brunette. "*I* will. Stay here." When both girls tried following him anyway, Vaughn growled again and put his arm out with an exasperated sigh. "Just *please* do what you're told for once!"

There's no way Darcie's going to listen to him.

In true Darcie fashion, Elise's best friend simply waited for Vaughn to be out of sight before trudging through the sand, beckoning Elise to follow her.

Elise tucked her mother's drawing into the front of her dress and chased after Darcie. She knew Vaughn would be furious with them, but Mitch was worth it. They could suffer through a lecture later.

Pausing to catch their breaths once they reached the path again, Elise and Darcie spotted the men near the lake's edge.

Elise couldn't make out what they were saying, but given the way Mitch paced and shook his head, little had been done to calm him down.

Vaughn tried coaxing him away from the water, but Mitch only waved him off as he stepped near the lake's edge.

"Why is he being so stupid?" Darcie asked. "He knows better than to get that close!"

Maybe he doesn't realize how close he is.

As if in slow motion, the girls watched in horror as two sets of hands reached out of the water and grabbed Mitch by the ankles.

Mitch landed hard on his stomach as his legs were pulled out from under him. Panic-stricken, he cried out and attempted to grasp anything as his body slid backwards.

Darcie's shrill, frantic scream cut through the air as she cried out Mitch's name.

Mitch's hands spread out on either side of him, his fingernails collecting sand and dirt as they scraped the ground for traction.

Reaching Mitch first, Vaughn gripped the younger man's wrist. The force with which Mitch was being pulled was no match for Vaughn's strength alone.

Elise felt anxiety penetrate her thoughts as her limbs grew numb. Her nerves were freshly raw from Darcie's earsplitting cry, and Darcie was halfway to the lake before Elise felt strong enough to follow.

Throwing caution to the wind as she arrived, Darcie threw her arms around Vaughn's waist and bent her knees for balance.

Elise gripped Darcie around the waist in return as all three became entangled in a game of tug-of-war against the aquatic creatures.

As intense as her focus was about rescuing Mitch, a sinking dread filled Elise as she felt them being pulled closer to the water.

"It's no use." Vaughn panted. "Let go."

"We aren't giving up!" Darcie cried out, her face soaked with tears. "Hold on, Mitch! You'll be okay!"

"We have to release him," said Vaughn. "He's theirs now."

"Don't you *dare* let go!" Darcie snarled. She hunkered down further as beads of sweat formed along her forehead.

Elise wiped her own face against Darcie's back as she continued to pull. "Is there anything else we can grab onto?"

"I have a rope," Vaughn said. He grunted against the force before continuing. "We can tie it around him if he goes completely under, but there's no guarantee. They've set their sights on him. If we don't release him soon, we'll be taken under as well."

This can't be happening. This can't be happening!

Mitch whimpered, pleading for them not to let him go. Tears streaked down his cheeks as he struggled to hold onto Vaughn.

Drops of water splashed against Elise's face as Mitch thrashed and kicked his feet against the hands pulling him.

Half of his body was already underwater, and with every passing second, Elise's panic grew as they were also sliding closer to the lake's edge.

"We have to try. Where is the rope?" Darcie cried.

"It's in my satchel on the beach." Vaughn's words were strained. The skin of his forearms was scratched from Mitch's fingernails. "You'll never return in time."

"It's all we've got," Darcie said, struggling to stay on her feet. "Elise, go! Go get it! We'll try to hold them off."

However reluctant she felt about letting go, Elise didn't need to be told twice. Releasing her hold, she took off running.

Vaughn's voice echoed through Elise's mind.

You'll never return in time.

She had to fight the intrusive thoughts. There was no other choice but to make it back in time.

Her legs felt sluggish from fatigue, but she tried to run nonetheless, ignoring the cramping pain in her chest. It was as if she was having an out-of-body experience. She could see herself running along the beach up ahead. Yet it felt like it took twice as long to even reach the path.

By the time the beach came into view, Elise worried she had lost too much time. She couldn't see the satchel from this distance, and it looked like everyone else had left whom she might've asked for help.

I don't see it. It could be anywhere.
Elise searched in every direction as she began running down the hill. Feeling her heart pounding, she rested a hand against her chest before her fingers closed around the bottle necklace.

Open it.
Elise hesitated. On the one hand, there was no guarantee a rope would work, but there was an even smaller chance that Elise would make it back in time to use it. With each passing second, Mitch was inching closer and closer to being captured.

Open it now!
Vaughn would be furious. Perhaps even punish them in some way for deliberately disobeying him, but this was Mitch's life on the line, and Elise wasn't going to let him die.

Is this all really happening right now?
Turning on her heel, Elise raced back up the hill while uncorking the bottle. As soon as she reached the top, Elise was overcome with terror as Mitch's fingers slipped beneath the surface.

Vaughn grabbed Darcie, who tried jumping in after him. Her cries and hysterics only convinced Elise she was doing the right thing. She had mere seconds for this to work. It may have already been too late.

I don't know what I'm doing. What did Mom do?
Careful to save half for their future trip home once Gavin was retrieved, Elise poured a small amount of the blue fairy magic into her hand. She closed her eyes and concentrated on what she wanted the magic to do.

We can use the rest later. Save Mitch. Bring him back. Please.
Nothing happened.

What am I doing wrong?
It was hard to think clearly during a panic attack, which ravaged through her body without remorse.

Mitch is dying. I have to figure this out. He'll drown!

Elise's tears poured down her face. She couldn't breathe. Glancing down at the oozing magic in her palm, she tried to remember what her mother had done.

Ruby used the magic to create a traveling portal by touching a tree. Did she need to touch something to make the magic work?

No, the fairies would've told me if I needed to do that.

She knew that wasn't necessarily true, but regardless, she had to try a different approach.

I need to focus on what exactly I want the magic to do.

Then an idea struck her.

Vaughn had told them they were going to Vynchia. She could take them there now and save Mitch at the same time.

While I'm at it, I could just take us all straight to Lockesbarrow where he thinks Gavin is.

While true, there was a reason Vaughn was adamant about going through Vynchia, so maybe it was best to follow his plan.

Closing her fist, Elise squeezed the magic between her fingers and shut her eyes. It was hard to concentrate through Darcie's desperate cries, but Elise pressed on.

Take us to Vynchia. No, Lockesbarrow. Vynchia? Take us to—

"What are you doing?" Vaughn cried out.

Elise opened her eyes and saw a look of horror on his face. She looked down at her hand. The blue magic dripped on the sand at her feet with no way to hide it.

"What have you done?" Vaughn's guttural, animalistic cry made Elise freeze as he made his way towards her. Ice cold terror flooded her body.

Take all of us to Vynchia now!

Expecting the same dizzying feeling as when traveling through the diary, Elise was surprised when it felt like she had the wind knocked out of her. It lasted only a moment, and when she felt her breath return, the surrounding beach began to blur and swirl around her.

Is it working?

There was no indication that she was moving anywhere, and Elise had no way of knowing if her friends were nearby. A whooshing sound grew louder and louder until it reached a deafening pitch and somewhere in the back of her mind, Elise thought she heard screaming.

That's me.

Expecting the familiar darkness to come across her, all at once, the swirling tornado-like wind calmed, and everything fell silent.

CHAPTER 19

Gavin lurched himself away from Rona as another knock sounded against the door.

"You have a visitor, Your Majesty," said one of the guards from the hallway.

Rona said something in reply, but Gavin wasn't paying attention to the words being exchanged. His mind was still in shock at what was about to happen before being interrupted. How far would he have gone? The heaviness of the moment hit him like a punch to the gut.

"Your Majesty, may I please come in?" asked a familiar voice. *Brahm?*

Rolling her eyes with a groan, Rona picked the dagger up off the floor before replacing it back under her dress as Gavin buttoned his shirt. After readjusting herself, she allowed Brahm to enter.

"Your Highness, I must—" Brahm stopped dead in his tracks when he noticed Gavin. "What is *he* doing here?" When his question went unanswered, Brahm glared at Gavin's disheveled appearance. "You're choosing *him* now?"

Rona gave a coy smile as she returned to the chaise lounge and addressed Gavin.

"I still love that he gets jealous." She cocked her head in Brahm's direction. "Thaddy's never been fond of sharing."

Wrinkling his nose, Gavin felt a twisting sensation in the pit of his stomach. The mental image of Rona and Brahm together ruined any mood Gavin might've found himself in moments earlier.

Why is Brahm here? If Rona planned to bring me here, why would she have invited him at the same time?

Something wasn't adding up, and with each passing moment, Gavin's uneasiness grew until he was covered in a cold sweat.

"Have you figured it out yet?" Brahm nodded towards the diary still lying on the floor.

Without getting up, Rona reached over and grabbed the diary before opening it to reveal its empty pages.

"There's power in this diary unlike anything I've ever seen," she said. "It pulses through my fingers when I touch the pages, yet nothing reveals itself. Mr. Striess here remains silent on the subject."

"Still being defiant, is he?" Brahm asked. His brows furrowed with disappointment.

Doesn't bother me, man. I've seen that look on my dad's face too many times.

"We were just discussing my brother." Rona rested the book flat against her chest before nodding towards Dmitri's portrait.

"He was a good man."

"Don't be such a sycophant, Thaddy." Rona shook her head with a chuckle. "You never knew him."

An awkward silence passed between all three of them before Brahm cleared his throat.

"May I ask why you sent for me?"

"How is your sister doing?" Rona asked, ignoring his question.

Brahm's lips tightened into a thin line, fighting back his irritation at her unwillingness to answer.

Gavin had a feeling she was the only one Brahm allowed to treat him this way.

"Ingrid is well and safe. She was able to reach Lockesbarrow with her daughter."

"That's good to hear. I shall invite them to court. I've always enjoyed Ingrid's company," Rona replied before looking back at Gavin. "Up until you arrived, Brahm, I was quite enjoying Mr. Striess's company as well."

Puffing out his chest, Brahm's shoulders and jaw tightened, giving Gavin the impression that the other man was holding his breath.

"I love making him angry," Rona said. "He's so fun to tease."
I doubt he thinks so.

Rona circled Brahm like a shark closing in on its prey. She paused to kiss his ear, much like she had done to Gavin.

"Unlike *you*," she said to Gavin, "Brahm here insures I always get whatever I want without question." She ran a hand up Brahm's chest with a predatory glance. "Or else."

Or else what?

As if sensing Gavin's unspoken question, Rona traced her finger down the length of the scar that split Brahm's face. Gavin had first noticed it when he and his friends were in the Haighdlen dungeon, but no one ever explained where it had come from.

"Are you ready to tell me how this diary works?" Rona held the diary up next to her face. "Or do you also need some *persuading*?"

Gavin winced as he considered the same fate. When he made eye contact with Brahm, the latter nodded for him to do what the queen asked.

Brahm is so brainwashed. He'll do anything Rona says no matter how much she hurts him. He's just as crazy as she is. I don't want to end up like that.

The diary obviously didn't work for Rona or Brahm, but if *he* opened it, Gavin was sure it would open the portal. Would it only take him? Would it somehow find Elise and the others and reunite them? At this point, Gavin was growing closer to risking it.

But what if Rona's cursed it somehow? What if it takes her too? Then Elise, Mitch, and Darcie are in danger. I don't know what to do! I wish we'd never came through this stupid book!

"If I help you," said Gavin, once he found his voice, "will you send my friends back to their families?"

"Which friends might these be?" she asked.

"The boys back at the camp."

Their stunned expressions broke when Rona and Brahm burst into laughter while heat rushed to Gavin's ears.

Keep your cool, man. Control your temper. Remember what Tristan said. If you're not in control, they are.

"I'm very much interested in this diary's power," Rona said between breaths, "but I hardly think it's worth releasing an entire army over." Placing a hand across her stomach to compose herself, Rona wiped away a smudge of mascara and regarded him with a warm smile. "It must be exhausting carrying that adorable, loyal heart around wherever you go."

The patronizing compliment made Gavin feel as if he were back in elementary school. Gavin couldn't see how his request was so unreasonable. If they wanted the diary so badly, he wanted to know he did it for the greater good.

"What do you even want it for?" Gavin looked between Rona and Brahm to see if either were willing to answer.

If Rona didn't even know what Joranna's diary did, then why was she so adamant about him giving away its secrets?

What would she do if I showed her? What would happen to me?

Rona closed the distance between them until her chest pressed against his. Leaning forward, she brushed her lips against his ear. She prevented Gavin from stepping away by grabbing his shirt.

"Is this the part where I divulge my grand scheme to you?" She traced the curve of his ear with the tip of her nose. "Is that what you're waiting for?"

Gavin was surprised to realize he *was* waiting for her to tell him her plans.

I guess I've watched too many movies. She isn't going to stand here and give a long speech about what she's up to. I'll have to find out another way.

The rest of his thoughts trailed off as her breath tickled the sensitive place behind his ear. He tensed as she placed a kiss there. Gavin felt a chill trickle down his body.

The growing fog in Gavin's brain faded when Brahm cleared his throat.

Gavin was thrust back to reality when Rona released her hold on him.

How does she keep doing that?

"You know, Thaddy," she said to the other gentleman, "I've always been drawn to bad boys, but it looks like I may have come across a good one worth my time."

Gavin could feel Brahm's eyes on him. Was it possible to feel someone's hatred from across a room?

Rona brushed a strand of loose hair from Gavin's forehead. "There's only ever been one good man to ever have my respect."

She didn't say her brother's name, but Gavin followed Brahm's line of vision to the portrait.

"Your unwavering devotion reminds me of him."

Gavin didn't know how to feel about the comparison, but he knew the similarities ended there. While Rona's affection for her brother was innocent, the way she looked at Gavin was something entirely different. His mind drifted back to when he almost lost control with her moments ago, but he had to end those thoughts before his body deceived him.

The corners of Rona's mouth lifted into a knowing smile as she took another daring step towards Gavin.

This time, he didn't move away, despite his indecisive thoughts urging him to do so.

"Can I give you some advice about devotion?" Rona shifted Gavin so that he was forced to look at Brahm over her shoulder while she straightened his collar. "It always comes with a price."

Gavin stared at the sliced skin across Brahm's face as Rona continued whispering into his ear.

"What you have to ask yourself is whether or not those closest to you would pay the same price."

Gavin gasped as she grabbed a fistful of hair at the base of his neck before jerking his head back.

An image of a man flashed behind his clenched eyes. It came and vanished so fast, Gavin wasn't sure if he imagined it or not.

"Did you see something?" Rona purred without loosening her grip on him. "Let me show you the last time *I* felt devotion."

Gavin didn't know if his eyes were closed, or if Rona's magic was playing a memory in front of him, but he felt as if he were standing in the same dining hall where Rona had summoned him the night before. Only this time, Rona was clearing the table. Her smudged young face and plain brown dress indicated her low status as she pulled a cloth from her apron pocket. Wiping the table, she didn't appear to notice Gavin watching.

Did I travel back in time, or is this a memory?

He couldn't be sure. It all looked and felt so real. Would Rona hear him if he called out to her?

The door swung open as the same man Gavin had seen flash through his mind entered.

It was Rona's brother, Dmitri. Given a longer look at him, Gavin recognized the other man from the portrait.

Dmitri didn't look older than twenty, yet the lines on his forehead suggested he carried a massive amount of responsibility on his shoulders. Upon spotting Rona, he grabbed her by the wrist and tugged his sister to the nearest closet.

As the door slammed shut, Gavin felt himself lunge forward as if pulled by an invisible rope. In an instant, he was also in the closet with the siblings.

The only light came from under the doorway, and Rona was shushed when she asked Dmitri if he was insane. He cut her off again before she could ask what he wanted.

"Rona, what happened?" Though Gavin couldn't see him, the fearful urgency in Dmitri's voice was palpable. "What have you *done*?"

"Honestly, Mimi, calm yourself!" she hissed. "Why do you think I've done anything?"

"The king and queen are *dead*!" A silence followed. "Please tell me you had nothing to do with it. Please."

Gavin heard Rona release a heavy sigh.

"It was for the best." She ignored her brother's groan. "I don't know why you sound so surprised. You heard the whispers. The endless mocking. They knew Granny was right about our family belonging on the throne, yet they chose to rub her death in our faces and subject us to this monotonous servitude!"

"That kind of talk is going to get you hanged."

"*This* kind of talk is going to get our family on the throne someday. I promise."

"Your stupid, impulsive tantrum has just created a crippling wave of panic throughout an entire kingdom!" Dmitri argued. "You're too young to understand the political crimes and damages you just caused."

"I did it for you!" Rona's indignant response made Gavin think she was on the verge of tears. "It's all been for you. For us. You should be king of—"

"*Enough*, Rona!" he roared.

Gavin jumped at Dmitri's outburst and wondered if Rona had done the same.

Another long silence passed between them.

"What am I supposed to tell the princess?" he asked in a voice barely above a whisper. "Did you ever consider what came next? How did you even manage it with all of their protection?"

When Rona spoke again, her once confident voice now cracked under the weight of Dmitri's disapproval.

"Granny taught me a f-few spells."

Dmitri cursed under his breath.

"She was teaching me magic until she fell ill," Rona continued. "I'm not too strong yet, but I'll get there. I promise!"

"Don't you see that it's too late for any of that," Dmitri said. "We had a better chance of me marrying into the throne."

Rona scoffed.

"Mimi, there's no way she would've agreed to marry you. Whatever the two of you have—"

"*Had.*"

"If you want to be dramatic about it like that," Rona murmured. "Whatever you think the two of you *had*, it was never going to lead to matrimony. I did what was necessary."

"Do you hear yourself right now? This is insanity!" he hissed.

Gavin felt his heart pounding against his chest. He felt out of place, and a little claustrophobic.

I need to get out of here. This is too heavy.

As if the universe heard his wish, the door was yanked open, and Dmitri was seized by faceless guards.

Gavin shielded his eyes from the sudden harshness of light that burst into the closet. He caught a brief glimpse of Rona hiding behind a stack of brooms, mops, and buckets before the door slammed shut and all was darkness.

In the blink of an eye, Gavin now stood in the throne room where he first met Rona. The ornate room was filled with countless courtiers that made Gavin question if he had traveled back to that exact day. Craning his neck, he got his answer when the horn players lifted their instruments to announce a royal entrance.

Instead of Rona, another young woman walked towards the massive seat at the head of the room.

"All hail, Queen Prisha!" cried the occupants of the room.

Prisha was dolled up like Gavin would expect a queen to be. She had the embellished gown and overly made-up face, yet her eyes were heavy-lidded and bloodshot. Taking a seat, she gestured for the same announcer to carry on with business.

"A former member of your staff requests an audience with Your Majesty," said the voice, yet Gavin couldn't see who was speaking.

He was distracted, along with everyone else, by the sound of another door opening near the back of the room. Two guards carried Rona forward by the arms before tossing her to the floor in front of the young queen. The hem of her dress was ragged, and her bare feet and cheeks were dirty, leading Gavin to speculate if she had spent time in the dungeon.

"Well?" Prisha asked, without a trace of emotion.

"Majesty," Rona said, pushing herself up to her knees before bowing her head. "I come to negotiate the terms of my brother's sentence and beg Your Majesty to pardon him."

Queen Prisha made no reply, yet the room began to come alive with hisses and judgmental whispers.

Rona ignored them all.

She looks so broken.

Knowing what Rona was like now, it was hard to imagine there was ever a day where she looked so frightened and helpless.

The future sorceress hugged herself as she continued.

"He's innocent. He played no part in the late king and queen's deaths."

Prisha pursed her lips before glaring down at Rona's disheveled appearance.

"You possess a rather firm opinion on the matter," she said. "Do you have any confessions of your own, for your brother has confessed to the crime in question."

"He lied!" Rona sobbed, her voice echoing throughout the chamber. She crawled closer before a guard stepped in front of her. Rona leaned to peer around him. "Please. He's all I have. We're orphans, you see. Please, Your Majesty. I know you care for him too!"

A collective wave of gasps and outbursts erupted throughout the throne room until Prisha held up her hand to silence everyone.

"You insult me," the queen said with a bite to her tone. It was the first emotional reaction Gavin had seen the monarch display, yet the pain in her eyes made him question if she meant what she said. "Not only do you request an audience while I am still in mourning, but you have the nerve to look me in the eye and claim I had a dalliance with one of my disgraced servants."

"I know the truth," said Rona, lifting her head from its bowed position. Her hair looked greasy and matted, while her pale frame appeared malnourished. "I know *everything*."

A muscle in Prisha's cheek pulsed as her eyes flashed down at Rona.

"I see you have not been punished enough by simple association with a murderer." Prisha's eerily calm voice sent a cold shiver down Gavin's spine as he watched from the back of the room. Gripping both armrests, she straightened her posture while the rest of the room waited with bated breaths for her next words. "So, along with your brother's pardon, I take it you're also here to request your position back?"

"Never," Rona replied as she stood up. "I intend to have *yours*."

Shouts of "treason!" and "hang her!" rang out with such a riotous thunder that Gavin feared they would trample over Rona before Prisha could respond.

Prisha stood as the same guards seized Rona once again. The room fell silent as Queen Prisha stepped forward until she was mere inches from Rona.

"You hold that neck of yours a little *too* high, my dear," she whispered. "One day you might find yourself without one."

The courtiers reacted with approval, yet Gavin watched in amazement as Rona only gained momentum from the threat.

"This may be the only time I get this chance," said Rona, lowering her gaze to the floor before making a concentrated effort to lift it. "Release my brother, or your kingdom will be overthrown."

It may not have been the reaction that Rona wanted, but it certainly was the one Gavin expected.

The queen, joined by the rest of the room, broke into such a loud burst of laughter that it caused a ringing in Gavin's ears.

"You do put on a good show," Prisha answered with a chuckle.

"And *you* put on a good charade," Rona replied, causing Prisha's smile to fall. "You love him. I know you do. Release him before his hanging, and this can all be a bad dream."

"Guards, remove this woman. Arrest her for treason," Prisha replied as she walked back to the throne. "And as for your brother's sentence," she called before Rona was carried off. Her empty eyes stared into Rona's before she pursed her lips again. Swallowing a cry, the queen fell into her seat. "It's already done."

Gavin didn't know it was possible to hear someone's heart breaking, but in that moment, he sensed that Rona's shattered into a thousand pieces as if made of glass.

The raw, guttural cry that ripped through her body echoed off the walls, piercing through Gavin's own resolve.

Yes, she was evil. Yes, she had done terrible things. But in that moment, she was a sister who had lost her brother.

"Enough, Your Majesty!" cried a distant, familiar voice. "Don't do this to yourself!"

Gavin's head felt like he was swimming, and the room melted around him like wet paint until he found himself back in the lounge with Rona and Brahm. Only when Rona released her hold on him did Gavin notice Rona's tear-stained cheeks.

"It pains me to see you do this to yourself. This pathetic piece of scum isn't worth reliving such painful memories."

"Oh, but he is," said Rona. She wiped a hand across her face until magic restored its flawless appearance. "He needs to know *why* I need him."

"Then let me tell him," Brahm offered, bending down on one knee to take Rona's hand. He placed a kiss against her knuckles. "Or show him instead."

Show me what?

Gavin didn't like the sound of that, but something else bothered him more.

Why does she need me?

CHAPTER 20

Once the wind calmed, Elise gained the courage to open her eyes. Relief washed over her when she saw Vaughn and her friends. . . until Elise realized Mitch wasn't moving.

Upon finding his unconscious body, Darcie draped herself across him.

"Mitch? *Mitch*, wake up!" Smacking his face, Darcie cried out his name with more fervor, urging him to look at her. She paused to rest her ear against his chest. "I don't hear anything. Vaughn, can you help him? Does anybody know CPR?" Without waiting for an answer, she stacked her hands on top of one another and made her own attempt to revive him. "I don't know if this is right! Somebody help!"

Elise fell to her knees across from Darcie and examined Mitch. *He looks terrible. I hope we're not too late. . .*

Drenched and unresponsive, Mitch was losing his color fast.

"Try breathing into his mouth," Darcie told her. "Pinch his nose first."

Fighting an approaching panic attack, Elise did as she was told. Mimicking what she had seen on television and movies, she pinched Mitch's nose and leaned down when Darcie paused her chest compressions. She blew a soft breath into his mouth.

Nothing happened.

"Harder!"

Elise jumped at Vaughn's order. In all the commotion, she had forgotten he was there.

"You need to make his chest move," he said.

If you know what to do, then why aren't you doing it?

Elise knew better than to argue at that moment, instead choosing to follow his instructions. She took a deep breath and blew into Mitch's mouth until she saw his chest rise out of the corner of her eyes.

"Again." He overlooked their progress. "Okay, wait. Darcie, you need to push faster this time." When it was apparent Darcie was tiring, Vaughn traded places and took over.

"What can I do?" Elise asked.

"You've done enough." Panting, he lowered his head to continue pressing against Mitch's chest. Vaughn jerked his head back to move unwanted hair from his face before scowling at her. "Move out of the way!"

His scathing tone took Elise by surprise. She moved to stand beside Darcie, who had turned away from them.

Vaughn called out Mitch's name with no answer.

Elise hugged Darcie, who began sobbing into her shoulder.

Please, please save him. Please let him be okay. Let him live.

She felt a fresh batch of tears escape down her cheeks. Squeezing Darcie, Elise continued to pray that Mitch wouldn't die.

Please. Don't let him die like this.

Elise's fears and prayers spun so fast out of control within her mind that, for a moment, she thought she might've only imagined a choking sound cutting through hers and Darcie's tears.

Pulling away, both girls looked down to see Mitch rolled onto his side, gurgling, and spitting up water next to Vaughn.

He's alive! He's alive, I can't believe it!

Shivers coursed down Elise's arms as Vaughn stepped back to allow Darcie to kneel by Mitch's side again.

"I'm so glad you're okay!" Darcie wrapped her arms around Mitch's neck. Her shoulders shook with uncontrollable sobs.

Elise smiled when Mitch wrapped an arm around her best friend in return. Saying a thankful prayer, Elise felt her nerves settle down. While grateful for Mitch's safety, Elise imagined it would be a long time before she forgot just how close they had come to losing him.

I don't know what we would've done.

Realizing Vaughn was standing beside her, Elise tried to ease the tension mounting between them.

"Thank you," she said. "I don't know what we would've done without—"

Vaughn turned and walked away.

Is he really that upset because I used the magic?

After checking to make sure Mitch and Darcie were okay without her, Elise took a deep breath and followed him.

It's okay, Elise. You didn't do anything wrong. Stand up to him. Don't be afraid. Don't be afraid. You can do this.

"What's your problem?" Elise called out to his retreating figure. "Hey, answer me!"

Vaughn turned abruptly to face her.

The intensity of his gaze made Elise choke on her next words, and for a moment, she could only stare back at him. Vaughn's long, damp hair fell in waves around his face, and she tried ignoring her thoughts about what it would feel like to run her fingers through it.

What is wrong with me? I shouldn't be thinking this! Focus, Elise. Don't let him win.

Vaughn's forehead creased between his furrowed brows as he walked back in her direction.

Elise's thighs quivered as she looked up at his face. Her mind traveled back to the previous night in the Dolluff's small bedroom. Given the menacing way he towered over her now, Elise imagined Vaughn's urges were long gone. She had never felt more despised in her entire life as she watched his hands flex by his sides.

A muscle twitched above his locked jaw, and Elise watched Vaughn's shoulders tense beneath the damp white fabric of his shirt.

Look him in the eye, Elise. Don't be intimidated. Show him you're not afraid.

But she *was* afraid. How could she not be? Was she supposed to be able to hide it?

Be brave. Stand up to him!

Elise tried to ignore the rising nausea in the pit of her stomach.

"Why are *you* so angry?" She sounded more confident than she felt. That was good. Crossing her arms, Elise tried to make herself look taller.

How does Mom do it? She always looks so tough.

Imitating her mother, Elise locked both feet in place and tipped her chin upward. "Are you *seriously* pouting about me using the magic?"

One of his brows lifted as the corner of his mouth curved up in amusement.

What's so funny? Ugh, he can see right through me.

"First off," he said, poking a finger against his chest, "I don't pout."

It sure looks like it.

Stepping back, Vaughn ran a hand through his hair and regarded her.

Elise struggled to remain still under his scrutiny.

What is he looking at? Is he trying to distract me?

"Secondly, I'm not the one who put us all in grave danger, so don't question *my* anger about—"

"Grave danger?" Elise shrieked. "I saved us all!"

He scoffed.

"What's going on?" Darcie asked. "What's wrong?"

Darcie had managed to help Mitch stand and had his arm draped around her shoulders for support.

His color was returning, but he still looked weak.

"He's mad because I used the fairy magic," Elise answered.

"Is that what that was?" Darcie asked. "I wondered what happened."

Elise nodded.

"How did you learn to use it?" Mitch asked, his voice hoarse and weak.

"I kept thinking I wanted it to take us to Vynchia. That's where Vaughn said we had to go anyway, so I sped up the trip while also saving Mitch. Yet, somehow," she said, jerking her head in Vaughn's direction, "I've put us all in 'grave danger'." She traced the chain around her neck until she held the bottle necklace up for them. "But don't worry. I left a little bit. I'm hoping it will be enough to send us home like we planned once we save Gavin."

Hearing Vaughn's hollow chuckle behind her made Elise's skin burn. Turning to face him, she felt her temper soar.

"*What's* so funny?" she spat.

"I'm just in disbelief at your ignorance." He nodded towards her necklace. "You didn't even use it all. No wonder it didn't take us to the right place."

"How do you know this isn't the right place?" she asked heatedly.

"Because this *isn't* Vynchia. We're half a mile from the border." He pointed to a sign twenty feet away on their left that validated his claim.

Why didn't it work? What've I done?

Elise's shoulders slumped as her knees threatened to buckle beneath her.

"Why didn't you use it all, Elise?" Darcie asked.

"Yeah," Mitch agreed. "The fairies said it was only good for one trip."

Her mind filled with the memory of the night they received the magic from Thicket, Hemlock, and Sage while following her mother through the forest.

I forgot they said that. . . that's been our plan all along. Why didn't I remember? We kept saying it was for only one trip. What's wrong with me?

"I was trying to save a little to get us home," she said. "I didn't know—"

"No, you didn't *listen*," Vaughn interrupted. He buried his face into his palm. "I don't know why I'm surprised at your stubbornness."

Elise felt deflated. All hopes of standing up to Vaughn vanished.

I'm an idiot. How could I forget that?

In those frantic moments by Lake Mirage, Elise had been so preoccupied with saving Mitch, she hadn't thought about the repercussions. She assumed there'd be enough magic later.

"This is not what I signed up for," Vaughn grumbled.

Elise's humiliation peaked as she stomped up to him once more.

I've already made myself look stupid. I don't even care what he thinks about me at this point.

"So, what, you're quitting?" Elise used every ounce of strength she had to keep her threatening tears from falling. "Ruby trusted you to lead us, but if you're too weak to—"

"Your mind is weak!" he roared. "You don't possess the ability to use *that* properly." He pointed to the bottle necklace.

Elise wrapped her fingers around it. There was a quarter amount of magic left.

"It could still work." Even she could hear her own doubt.

Vaughn shook his head as he scoffed again.

"I knew you were naïve, but I never thought you'd be so stupid."

"I got us out of there. You should be thanking me!" she cried out.

Elise flinched as his hand clutched the chain and yanked it from around her neck. The clasp separated as if made of paper under his forceful grip, and Elise watched in shock as the bottle disappeared into Vaughn's pocket before lunging for it.

Did he really just do that?

Ignoring her friends' cries to calm down, she fought against Vaughn's hold on her arms.

"Elise, stop!" Vaughn shouted over her struggle, preventing her from reaching the necklace despite Elise's flailing about. "It's for your own good!"

Who does he think he is?

"My own good? How is any of this for my own good?" she screamed. Elise's cheeks were soaked within seconds as a sob escaped her lips. Her fingertips grazed a piece of chain hanging out of Vaughn's pocket before he pushed her off. She stumbled for a moment before gaining her balance with a huff. Glaring daggers at him, Elise growled. "Mitch almost died, Gavin might be *dead*, and every time we get a little bit ahead, there's something else wrong! I'm sick of it! I'm sick of all of it."

Mitch has been right all this time. We aren't getting anywhere.

Falling to her knees, she collected herself and nodded towards Vaughn's pocket, her voice barely a whisper. "Please, give it back."

It's my mom's. . .

"Absolutely not," Vaughn replied. "I've got enough to worry about thanks to your little misguided rescue. My satchel is back at the beach along with the safe passage letters. Now we're caught in the middle of nowhere. It's one more mess of yours for me to clean up."

I thought I was doing the right thing. . .I'm sorry.

Vaughn pushed the dangling chain into his pocket and walked over to assess Mitch.

Elise met Darcie's gaze and mouthed an apology, but her friend waved it off.

At least she's not angry with me.

"You're lucky to be alive, Mitchell." Vaughn helped Darcie steer him toward the nearest tree before lowering him to sit down at its base. "But you still need rest before we continue to Vynchia."

Elise waited until Vaughn left in search of firewood before she spoke again. She didn't want to give him any more excuses to rip her apart.

"Hey," Darcie said once Elise sat down on Mitch's other side, "don't let Vaughn get to you. He's just stressed."

"Yeah, but he's right. I was only trying to help. I knew I wouldn't be fast enough to get the satchel back in time."

"Don't worry about it," said Mitch. "Whatever he says, you saved me, Elise. Thank you."

Mitch's words eased her guilt, and she felt a weight lift from her shoulders. She could deal with Vaughn's disappointment but couldn't handle it from her friends.

"Mitch was telling me what happened when he was taken under the water," said Darcie.

All concern for Vaughn vanished as Elise's attention switched to Mitch.

I want to hear everything!

"All I said was that it happened so fast. One minute, I was walking to calm down, and the next. . ." Mitch's eyes became unfocused as he relived the memory. Staring into the distance, Mitch trailed off as if even he couldn't believe his words. Shaking his head, he apologized. "I don't. . .know if I can explain it."

"Try," Darcie pleaded. "Keep going."

Elise remembered Mitch making a joke about being tortured by attractive mermaids during their first visit to Lake Laulie, but she imagined this latest encounter in Lake Mirage made him regret it.

"What made you go that far over there?" Elise asked, hoping to encourage her friend to explain more.

Mitch gained control of himself and started again.

"I don't know. . .I remember being pissed off he was watching y'all, and then it was like it didn't matter what he did anymore. If Gavin had been here. . ." His eyes shifted to Elise before he continued. "Anyway, Vaughn went too far. He knew it. I had to walk away." Mitch cleared his throat and coughed before continuing. "It wasn't like I went that far on purpose. By the time I calmed down enough to realize where I was, I couldn't turn around."

Mitch shook his head as his body shivered.

"Why not?" Elise asked, mirroring the same look of concern as Darcie.

Is he okay?

"That's j-just it." Mitch's uneven breaths made him difficult to understand as his teeth chattered. "I-I don't remember. I heard a s-splash and when I-looked up. . ."

What's going on?

"Mitch, you're not making any sense. Are you okay?" Elise asked.

"What's wrong? Mitch? Mitchell, look at me!" Darcie shook Mitch's shoulders, but his eyes rolled back into his head. She screamed. "Mitch!"

"He can't hear you," Vaughn quipped, walking back up to them with a small pile of branches and brush. "The lake's magic is still in his body. It's nothing short of hypnotism, really."

"Help him!" Elise cried out, watching Mitch's head fall limp onto Darcie's shoulder.

"There's nothing to be done. He got too close to them is all. It'll pass."

There has to be something we can try. Why isn't Vaughn freaking out?

"But why didn't it happen to any of us when we went down there?" Darcie asked Vaughn. "You and I were right there with him."

"We weren't their target."

"So. . .beautiful." A dreamy expression washed across Mitch's face as he jerked his head back against the tree trunk behind him. Beads of water still clung to his forehead and mixed with his sweat as he closed his eyes.

"The mermaids are known for their exotic, ethereal beauty," Vaughn informed the girls, "but it's only a facade."

Mitch made an attempt to say something but nothing came out.

"What is it, Mitch? Tell me," Darcie coaxed. She caressed one of his cheeks in her hand.

"C-cold," Mitch whispered, staring over her shoulder.

Before anyone could react, Darcie began running her hands up and down the sides of his arms, trying to warm him up.

"It won't help," said Vaughn. "He's imagining it. It isn't real."

Mitch chuckled to himself. "They touched me."

"Are you sure he's going to be okay?" Darcie asked, drying Mitch's brow with her sleeve.

"Yeah, he seems so out of it," Elise said.

Vaughn crouched down to observe Mitch. When he didn't answer fast enough, Darcie groaned.

"He was acting just fine until he started talking about it!"

"It's only remnants of their spell—I've heard it can be a terrible shock to the mind if one can make it out alive." Vaughn began adjusting the wood for the fire. "He should be more lucid in the next couple of hours."

Elise and Darcie jumped as Mitch's scream broke through the silence.

Flailing his arms and legs, Mitch scrambled up until he stood against the tree with a look of terror.

"Mitch? Mitch, what is it?" Standing up, Darcie waved her hand in front of his face, but he stared above her head at something they couldn't see. "Mitch, you're scaring me. What's wrong?"

Elise fumed when Vaughn didn't even glance behind him.

"No!" Mitch cried out, drawing an arm out to shield himself. The heels of his shoes scraped off pieces of bark when he couldn't create any more distance. "No, please. Don't. Don't do that!" Mitch swung both arms around before hiding his face again.

"Back away. He's not talking to you," Vaughn said, pulling Darcie out of harm's way. He inched closer to Mitch until he could safely lower the redhead's arms.

Mitch flinched at the contact before cowering in a ball on the ground. Trembling, he whimpered and clenched his eyes shut.

This is freaking me out. What's wrong with him? We need to do something!

"Mitch? Can you hear me?" Darcie asked, kneeling by his side again. "Mitch, answer me!"

"Don't, don't d-do that. Stop. Stop it!" Mitch covered his ears and let out a torturous wail.

"Vaughn, you have to help him!" Elise shouted over her friend with a shiver. "He's in pain!"

I don't like this. I really don't like this. Somebody make him stop!

"I told you, it's an illusion," Vaughn answered with a hint of annoyance. "He's reliving what they showed him."

"What do you mean what they showed him?" Elise asked. "He was only down there for a few seconds!"

"To *us*, it was seconds." Vaughn helped Darcie stand again before they all looked down at Mitch's writhing body.

Elise glanced up at Darcie's pale, alarmed expression. She had never seen someone look so lost and afraid.

"We need to find a doctor or something," Elise said, whirling around in desperation.

"You need to listen for once and leave him alone," Vaughn growled.

Elise scowled.

"Then what can we do?" Darcie asked. "*Please*, give me something to do. I can't do nothing."

Vaughn softened at the raw emotion in Darcie's voice. "Make him comfortable. Keep calm until he comes out of it."

Sounds easy enough.

Elise and Darcie crept closer to Mitch without startling him.

Darcie situated herself on the ground while Vaughn and Elise guided Mitch into a resting position and propped his head on the brunette's lap.

"We should all rest," Vaughn suggested, patting the ground beside him for Elise to join them.

She wasn't particularly tired, but given how the morning had played out so far, Elise knew to do as she was told.

CHAPTER 21

The clock in the hall chimed twelve times. Gavin's stomach gurgled in reply. He was past the point of simple hunger and shook his head to rid himself of an approaching headache.

I need lunch. I can't remember the last time I ate.

Brahm was still on one knee, urging Rona to allow him to take over.

"Very well, Brahm," she replied, composing herself before she looked over at Gavin. "But let it wait. I can hear his poor stomach from here."

"I can have something sent down to his cell."

"Hold your tongue, Thaddy," she said, her playful wit restored. "Although he was incredibly rude to me at dinner last night, he is my guest and I imagine with proper nourishment, he will reconsider my offer."

Gavin's rumbling stomach answered for him.

"That's what I thought. Let's proceed to the dining hall." She left Brahm on the floor and winked at Gavin as she led the way out.

One of Brahm's knees popped as he stood and stretched before following the queen.

"I hope you know what you're getting into," Brahm mumbled as he bumped his shoulder against Gavin's as he left.

But that was just it. Gavin *didn't* know what he had gotten into. Rona's moods were all over the place. One minute she was seducing him, the next she was threatening to kill him. It was enough to give him emotional whiplash, and he still didn't have a way to escape.

He mulled over his options as he was led to the dining hall. Only Brahm was present at the large table.

Where's Rona? She left first.

Gavin was shown to his seat across from Brahm while a plate was prepared for him. Once served, it took every ounce of strength he had not to attack the food like an animal. Brahm hadn't touched his food yet, making Gavin assume they had to wait for the queen.

He squinted his eyes against the harsh midday sunlight pouring in through the large windows. All the rooms he had been in so far were darkened to Rona's liking, and he felt like he hadn't seen the sun in days.

If this meal is another attempt to persuade me, it won't work. I have to get out of here somehow. Even if it means going back to camp. Tristan and I can come up with another plan, I'm sure.

"I can't help you," Gavin said, breaking the awkward silence between them. "You have to tell her to let me go."

Brahm chuckled into his wine glass.

"I'm serious," Gavin pressed. "It's not my diary. I don't know how it works, and I'm a terrible soldier. I can't give her anything she wants."

Brahm lifted a brow as if to say that wasn't all she wanted, and he knew it.

"Okay, I'm *not* giving her what she wants."

"I certainly didn't know what I was getting myself into when I brought you here," said Brahm, "but you have certainly provided me with endless entertainment. Please allow me to be present when you defy Her Majesty."

Gavin leaned forward to argue but regretted it when his nostrils filled with the strong aroma of steak, potatoes, and freshly baked bread in front of him.

"She's crazy," Gavin whispered. "I can't give her—"

He jumped as the door was opened for Rona.

"Forgive me, gentlemen. I had a bit of *business* to attend to."

I don't like the sound of that. What is she up to now?

Taking her seat at the head of the table, she regarded both men with a pleasant smile before inviting them to start eating.

Brahm dug in immediately, and Rona chuckled when Gavin didn't lift his fork.

"You can stop with the heroic act. Your pathetic friends will have eaten by now."

Knowing the boys back at camp were no longer being starved, Gavin allowed himself to cut into the steak. It was cooked to perfection and melted in his mouth. He fought not to moan before devouring a second bite.

She would like that too much.

"Getting along at last?" Rona looked between the two men.

"Hardly," Brahm quipped around a mouthful of potatoes before pointing his fork at Gavin. "The little coward still wants to leave."

Feigning a dramatic pout, Rona rested a hand across her chest.

"Hot baths, fresh meals, and even an invitation to my bedchamber." She clicked her tongue before taking a drink. "What are we going to do with him, Thaddy?"

"*Please*, Majesty." Brahm's gaze darted to the servants lined up listening against the wall. "Please, not in here."

"You're so sensitive." She rolled her eyes before cutting a piece of steak. "What do you think makes him so ungrateful, Brahm?"

Gavin's ears grew hot as he felt both sets of eyes on him.

"The kidnapping could have something to do with it," Gavin mumbled, keeping his eyes on the table.

"Oh, that was all Thaddy—Excuse me, *Brahm*." She smirked at the former captain before turning back to Gavin. "And I've done nothing but care for you since. If only you'd be a good soldier and do what you're told."

"I'm *not* a soldier." Gavin huffed as he swallowed a large bite. "I'm not a soldier, a spy, or anything!" He quickened his intake, fearing they might take his food away.

With a delicate sigh, Rona set her knife and fork down beside her plate.

What is she going to do? I hate when she's calm like this. Something bad always happens.

"You've had more chances to comply than most can boast." Rona was careful to keep her tone soft as she dabbed the sides of her mouth with a cloth napkin. "If you'd prefer torture, that can be arranged."

Gavin met Brahm's gaze across the table and could only imagine the other man would love nothing more than to be the torturer.

I need to get out of here. They're both sick freaks.

"If formalities and hospitality fail to persuade you, how's this?"

In one smooth motion, Gavin's chair slid out from under him before crashing against the wall as his body hit the floor.

Landing on his tailbone, Gavin winced and used the table to prop himself up to his knees.

Before he could stand, however, Rona was by his side and gripped him by the collar. He could feel her breath against his cheek.

"Listen here, you arrogant piece of *filth*," she hissed, "Brahm heard you confess to Derek and Joranna that you use that diary to time travel."

Gavin thought back to the day he and his friends had spent in the Haighdlen dungeon. Brahm had insisted they confess to him, but they were adamant they would only talk to Derek.

"Now, I've given you all this time to tell me what I already know, so there's little to gain from any more insufferable antics. Tell me how to use it this instant!"

Why does she care so much about this stupid diary? She's already queen! What would she need to go back—

Then it dawned on him.

"You want to go back and save him." When Rona didn't answer, he continued. "That's it, isn't it? You want to save your brother."

He looked between Rona and Brahm for any hint of an answer.

There has to be more to it than that though. What else is she planning?

She softened before him.

"Clever boy," she replied at last, loosening her grip so he could stand. "You've figured it out. Come."

There's something she's not telling me.

Gavin felt the hairs on the back of his neck stand as she beckoned him and Brahm to follow her down the hall.

Once they were back in the drawing room, Rona led Brahm over to sit upright on the chaise lounge. Standing behind him, she raked her fingers through his hair in a similar manner as she had with Gavin.

Brahm tipped his head back as she massaged his neck. He moaned at her touch.

He's so desperate. For a tough guy, he sure is a lap dog with her. How much has she hurt him already? Why does he keep coming back?

The same questions kept coming up as he watched Brahm relax against Rona.

She unbuttoned the top two buttons of his shirt, exposing the hair underneath, before reaching in to caress his chest. When his shoulders slumped, her fingers returned to Brahm's scalp. Raking her nails through his oil-covered hair, she pressed against his temples.

Brahm cried out but didn't pull away. Clenching his teeth, the former captain gripped the edge of the chaise lounge. His legs stiffened as he arched his back, but Rona showed him no mercy.

"Come here," she said to Gavin. "Don't be frightened."

It's hard not to be.

Shuffling his feet forward, Gavin stepped around the chaise lounge until he was beside Rona.

Staring down at Brahm, Gavin could see the other man trembling.

"What are you doing to him?"

"Viewing memories," she replied with her eyes shut. When she opened them, Gavin noticed they were glowing.

He took a step back.

"Would you like to see?"

No way.

Brahm was starting to mutter and whimper beneath her touch.

Gavin didn't want any part of it. He realized that he had no choice in the matter when Rona held up one hand in front of her. Following her line of vision, Gavin watched Dmitri's painting ripple as if made of water until it resembled a mirror. Rather than their reflections, however, he saw a distant version of himself at the training camp.

Viewing the memory like a movie from Brahm's point of view, Gavin watched as he punched the officer outside of his tent instead of Tristan. He could make out Everett and Erick standing nearby with looks of terror before the vision faded. Gavin thought Brahm had already left that night, but it was clear he had seen it all happen.

That was a bad night.

"If only you could put that aggression to better use," Rona said. "Ahh, here's my favorite."

Gavin's eyes widened as he looked up to see Elise within the frame. As if watching through Brahm's eyes, Gavin saw a hand wrap around Elise's neck and realized this was from the library the night Brahm was arrested. Although he had been in the same room, it was a different kind of pain to relive it from this perspective.

He had almost lost her that day.

"We both have something precious worth fighting for," Rona said. "Just show me how the diary works, and this will never have to happen to her again."

Gavin stared at Elise's twisted, tortured expression before it faded again.

Rona pushed Brahm off the chaise lounge onto the floor before taking his place. She held out her hand to summon the diary.

It shot across the room and fell open, hovering in front of Gavin.

He stared at the blank page, wondering what had been written there before being concealed. Gavin felt a lump form in his throat.

"What will you do if I can make it work?"

"You'll be reunited with your friends, and this all becomes a bad dream," she said.

Well, at least that means my friends are still alive.

"And if I don't?"

"Do I really need to revisit the last memory?"

A bead of sweat rolled down Gavin's back as he pictured Brahm's fingers around Elise's neck.

It's never going to end, is it? She's never going to give up. Elise will die if I don't. I'd rather risk the book working and give in to any other of Rona's demands to keep Elise and the others alive.

Elise would understand, right? Gavin wasn't sure. He was doing all of this for her though. Rona would corner him no matter how many times he tried escaping her.

"What if it doesn't work?" he asked.

"But what if it does?" she countered.

Gavin mustered up what little courage he had left to make a demand of his own.

"Let me see Elise."

"I beg your pardon?" Brahm asked. "Majesty, are you really going to let him—"

Rona held out a hand to silence him.

Gavin cleared his throat.

"I need to know she's safe before I agree to help you."

A moan escaped Rona's lips as she looked him up and down.

"I love when a man takes charge." She considered his offer before Gavin saw the familiar glint of mischief flash behind her eyes. "Very well."

He flinched as the diary shut mere inches from his face before falling to the ground.

"Goodbye, Brahm," she said.

"What? Your Majesty, you can't be serious." Brahm wiped the sweat off his forehead with a handkerchief from the queen's recent memory sweep.

Walking over to a table against the wall, Rona picked up a small velvet-lined box Gavin hadn't noticed earlier. She smiled at his curious stare before opening the lid to pull out a lock of light brown hair. "I'm afraid all you can provide me with are *memories* of his precious Elise, Thaddy, but there is someone better who can help me."

CHAPTER 22

Picking up a fallen brown leaf, Elise waved away a persistent fly before using it as a fan to cool her face. She was so preoccupied with saving Mitch before, that she hadn't realized how dry this area was. The fire had mostly died down, but the heat from it was still enough to make Elise sweat beneath her clothes.

I should be napping like the others.

Vaughn's incessant, offensive snoring would insure *that* wouldn't happen anytime soon.

At least he couldn't yell at her anymore while he was asleep. While Elise knew she shouldn't care what he thought about her, knowing she had disappointed him nagged at her brain. She didn't like it when anyone was upset with her.

I still don't think I did anything wrong. I got us out of there.

Elise didn't want to think about what the alternative scenario would've been if she hadn't reached the beach in time. Turning her head, she saw Darcie leaned against the only tree around them. Her eyes were closed but she fidgeted in discomfort. Mitch's head still rested on her lap, his shoulders lifting and falling in a sound sleep. The shivers and outbursts had finally ceased in the last hour, and Elise remained hopeful Mitch would wake up recovered.

In the meantime, she twirled the stem between her fingers, pulling the pointed crunchy ends of the leaf apart bit by bit. Sweeping the discarded pieces off her dress, Elise's eyes closed when a welcome breeze blew past them.

"Psst."

She glanced back and saw Darcie watching her.

Darcie gave her a small smile that Elise returned with a wave. The brunette looked down at Mitch and chuckled.

"My leg is asleep," she whispered.

The two girls shared another chuckle before Darcie ran her fingers through Mitch's hair.

I wish I had a camera.

When Darcie lifted her head up, she nodded towards something over Elise's shoulder.

Elise turned around and felt the breath catch in her chest.

She didn't often pause to admire the sky, but on evenings like this, it was difficult *not* to stare in awe at the dramatic sunset.

With only moments left to shine, at the peak of its beauty, the sun boasted streaks of the most vibrant oranges and yellows that swept amongst the clouds like brush strokes.

I've never seen a sunset like that back home.

A flock of birds soared over their heads, the rays highlighting the tips of their wings, as they chirped and raced towards the horizon.

I wish Gavin were here to see this.

Her face fell.

What if we don't find him in time? What if we're too late?

Her incoming panic attack was cut short before it could escalate as Vaughn snorted and woke up from his own snore.

Well, that's attractive.

Taking a deep breath, Elise released it slowly as she drummed her fingers against her thighs.

I need to stop thinking like that. This might be a setback, but we're going to find Gavin. He's okay. He has to be okay.

Wiping the sides of his mouth, Vaughn sat up and dusted himself off. He cocked his head towards Mitch.

"How is he?"

"I think he's over it," Darcie said. "He's been pretty calm for a while."

"That's good." Vaughn stood up and began stomping out the remaining embers. "We'll get going when he feels up for it."

Less than ten minutes passed before Mitch stirred and sat up. Despite having slept most of the day, his eyes were puffy and red. Hair stuck up near the back of his head from where Darcie had run her fingers through it.

"When did we get here?" His voice was still hoarse. Mitch raked a hand through his hair and stretched with a yawn.

"You don't remember?" Darcie asked.

"The last thing I remember was being pulled into the lake." He squinted as he tried to recall more without success.

Careful! The last time he talked about it he went crazy. Hopefully it's out of his system.

"Well, you're safe now," said Darcie, who exchanged a worried glance with Elise.

She's worried about it happening again too.

"Vaughn said we'll keep moving when you feel better," Elise told him.

Mitch was able to stand while supporting himself against the tree, but Elise watched as Darcie hovered nearby just in case.

"How do you feel?" the brunette asked.

Stretching his neck from side to side, Mitch massaged both shoulders.

"Good, I guess, but really sore. My throat hurts."

"Swallowing a lot of water and nearly getting murdered by sirens will do that to you," Vaughn said as he finished putting out the fire. "The worst seems to be over, though. I'd say you're a lucky man, Mitchell."

"We're only a half mile from Vynchia." Stretching both legs, Darcie wiggled her feet to wake them up. "When we get there, you can rest, and we can get something to eat."

"*If* we can get across the border," Vaughn mumbled.

"Why wouldn't we?" Mitch asked, looking between the other three. "We have the safe passage letters from Ruby, right?"

"Not anymore." Sitting on a nearby rock, Vaughn removed the sword from its hilt and cleaned it with the bottom of his shirt. "You can thank Elise for that."

Watching Mitch's eyes shift, Elise's breath hitched again, and she rubbed the fabric of her skirt in tiny circles to release tension. When had her hands gotten so sweaty?

"Elise saved us," Darcie said.

Vaughn scoffed, inspecting his blade.

"How?" Mitch asked.

"With the fairy magic," Elise replied. "It was the only way to get us out of there in time."

Mitch was quiet for a moment as he processed everything.

"Wow. Elise, thank you." He looked up at the now twilight sky. Rubbing the back of his neck, Mitch walked around the tree, deep in thought. "If the magic is gone, though, how are we going to get home?"

"You probably won't."

Elise glared at Vaughn.

He is not helping.

"What about Gavin?" Mitch asked. "How do we get to him without the letters?"

"We're going to figure it out, and we're going to save him. Right, Elise?" Darcie smiled at her.

Elise smiled back, but it didn't reach her eyes. She wanted to be optimistic like Darcie, but Vaughn's constant judging and Mitch's uncertain expressions made her doubt everything.

Ever the meddler, Darcie pulled Vaughn up to stand before issuing orders for everyone to quit feeling sorry for themselves.

"Mitch, I need you to try pushing yourself for this last bit of the walk. Elise, at the end of the day, you saved Mitch. We can figure out what that means for us getting home later." She turned to Vaughn. "Yes, your satchel is gone. I'm sorry. It looks like that sword is all we have, but it's all we need. Now, where exactly are we? Do you know?"

Vaughn raised an eyebrow and regarded Darcie with a bemused expression before pointing ahead of them.

He's not used to bossy Darcie.

"If Vynchia is half a mile *that* way, then we're probably near Klaren Lake."

"No." Mitch shook his head. "No more lakes."

Vaughn chuckled.

"There aren't any mermaids in that lake, but don't worry. We won't need to go that direction."

Mitch sighed in relief.

"Well, that's good because—"

Vaughn put a finger to his lips to silence Mitch. Taking several steps backwards, he scanned the area before wrapping a hand around the hilt of his sword.

The hairs on the back of Elise's neck stood on end as she looked around.

I don't see anything. What's wrong?

Vaughn removed his sword and stepped around them as he examined the terrain. He sniffed the air.

Mitch and Darcie shrugged, not finding anything either.

Before Elise could ask Vaughn what he heard, she screamed as a large animal leaped out from behind a secluded area of tall grass and tackled him to the ground.

"Vaughn!" she cried out, watching the sword slide out of his reach.

Where did that thing come from? How did we not see it?

The rest of the surrounding area was open and deserted. How had it managed to hide and creep up on them so well?

Elise's heart pounded as she watched Vaughn wrestle with the beast as it tried biting at his throat.

We have to help him!

She didn't know how, and found herself frozen in shock, unable to look away.

Elise couldn't identify exactly what it was, but it looked like a mix between a wolf and a lion, but it didn't appear to be in a pack.

Vaughn used one of his hands to protect his throat, and the other to push against the animal's weight. When that didn't work, he clawed and pulled at the back of its neck. Bringing up one of his feet, Vaughn was able to kick it off of him. Before he could get away, however, the wolf-like creature grabbed his arm and yanked him back to the ground before attacking his leg. Vaughn groaned in pain as he struggled to free himself from the beast's mouth.

The bottom part of Vaughn's pant leg ripped, dangling from the persistent predator's teeth.

"Get my sword!"

Mitch, Darcie, and Elise scrambled, momentarily in shock, until the latter managed to scoop up the sword.

How do I get it to him?

"Hurry, Elise!" Darcie cried out.

"Throw it to him!" Mitch said.

"Stab it!" Vaughn roared. His voice was strained as the wolf tackled him again.

Elise saw streaks of blood staining Vaughn's shirt as panic flooded her body.

He's going to die. It's going to kill him. We're going to be stranded or get killed too!

"Do it!"

I can't kill it. It'll kill me first. I can't. I can't.

The familiar rush of her crushing thoughts made her immobile as she stared in utter disbelief and terror.

"Elise, you've got to do this!" Darcie cried.

She's right. I can do this.

Tightening her grip on the hilt, Elise inched closer to the altercation. With the wolf's back to her, Elise held up the sword, ready to strike when she heard a gruesome, gut-wrenching cry pierce the air.

The animal's teeth had sunken into Vaughn's ribs and wouldn't let go. It jerked its head, sinking its teeth deeper into his skin.

Elise grimaced.

I'm too late. I'm too late. He's going to die. It's all my fault.

She held out the blade and nudged it towards the wolf's head. It released its hold on Vaughn, baring its blood-soaked teeth at Elise. The skin above its nose wrinkled as it snapped at the sword.

Hearing movement behind her, Elise turned to see Mitch and Darcie running up with a torn branch from the tree and rocks.

Outnumbered, the solitary animal backed away, eyeing all three with a growl. Blood dripped from its chin as it crouched lower. The fur along the wolf's spine stood up as it flexed its claws.

We're going to die. We're no match for it.

"On the count of three," Darcie whispered. "Okay?"

Neither Mitch nor Elise answered but looked down at Vaughn, whose wound had bled so heavily that he had lost consciousness.

"One," Darcie said.

The wolf took a step closer to them.

"Two," she said a little louder, a tremble in her voice.

The beast barked at them, shooting out a string of saliva that landed on Vaughn's leg.

The blood pounded in Elise's ears.

"Three!"

At Darcie's signal, Mitch swung the tree branch before stabbing it in the wolf's direction.

Darcie tossed pebbles left and right at its head, and Elise jabbed the blade again towards its face until, finally, the beast lowered its ears and ran off.

"What *was* that thing?" Darcie asked.

"I don't know." Mitch panted as he dropped the branch. What little energy he had gained back appeared to be gone. "But we're lucky it was just one. Right, Elise?"

Elise's attention had already moved to Vaughn, who lay motionless at their feet. She fell on her knees by his side and began examining the damage.

"Vaughn?" she asked.

Please don't die. Please.

First Mitch. Now possibly Vaughn. This day kept getting worse and worse. Shaking his shoulders, she watched his head jolt back and forth from her force before falling limp.

"How bad is it?" Darcie asked.

Elise reached towards Vaughn's wound before curling her fingers inward. Grimacing at his shredded clothing, she wrinkled her nose as the smell of blood attacked her nostrils.

I can't. I don't want to look. I can't handle this.

"Maybe we can stop the bleeding," Darcie said. "Mitch, you sit there and rest. We might be able to wrap something around it."

Elise watched her best friend sit on his other side, immediately feeling déjà vu from earlier that day.

Darcie is so brave. I wish I could take charge like her.

All three turned their heads away as Darcie peeled off Vaughn's shirt. The discarded rags of fabric lay soaked by his sides, and Elise felt her stomach churn with nausea at the sight of the open wound.

"Guys, what do we do?" Darcie held a hand over her nose with a gag. "There's too much. He's going to bleed out before we could make it anywhere."

"Is anybody out there?" Mitch screamed out. He turned in circles, repeating the question.

"It's no use," Elise said through fresh tears. "Nobody's going to hear us. We've been out here all day."

"It's our only chance though. We need help." Darcie stood up to join Mitch. Taking a deep breath, she called out into the wide-open space. "Somebody help! Please help us!"

The vial. . .no, I can't. Vaughn was so angry last time, and if I use the rest of it, there will be no hope of getting home once we find Gavin. But we need to save him. What do I do? There might be enough anyway.

"Vaughn, can you hear me?" Elise touched a finger to a gash across his cheek. She placed her ear against his chest. There was still a faint heartbeat. "Stay with us. . .stay with me."

As Mitch's and Darcie's cries for help radiated around them, Elise burrowed her face into Vaughn's neck. She snaked a hand through his hair and cradled his head.

"You can't die. Don't die, please." Her shoulders shook with sobs. "We can't do this without you."

I need him to be okay. I want him alive. Wake up, Vaughn. Please, wake up. Let someone come. I need him to wake up.

Elise's eyes burned. Her heart felt like it would burst as she held on to Vaughn. Grief-stricken tears streamed down her face with no sign of stopping.

I need you, Vaughn.

Knowing what she had to do, Elise sniffled and reached towards his pocket.

"What're you doing?" Darcie shrieked.

Elise looked up at her friends' matching expressions. They looked as if she had grown a tail.

"I'm getting the magic."

Is it the blood on my hands? Why are they staring like that?

"No, what's happening to *him*?" Mitch pointed at Vaughn's wound.

Looking back down, Elise gasped.

What is that?

Something terrifying was going on with Vaughn's body. Dozens of thin flesh-colored strings began growing from the sides of his wound. They reminded Elise of spaghetti noodles as they twisted over one another across the open gash.

Leaning her head closer, Elise realized they were more like threads being sewn. Sure enough, the edges of the bite marks began to stitch together.

"He's. . .healing!" Elise chuckled in disbelief. How could this be happening? She let go of Vaughn and stood up next to Darcie and Mitch.

The threads froze in midair before falling across Vaughn's ribcage.

A jolt of panic flooded Elise's brain.

"Why did they stop? What's going on?"

While Mitch continued to call out for help, Darcie's forehead creased in concentration as she stared at the lifeless strings. She opened her mouth twice before she finally asked Elise to touch Vaughn.

"What? Why?" Elise asked.

"Just do it."

Unsure what her friend was up to, Elise lowered herself down before touching Vaughn's stomach.

All at once, the threads came to life again before continuing to sew Vaughn's skin back together.

Elise pulled her hand away with a squeal.

Again, the threads fell by his side.

"Elise. . ." Darcie's eyes widened as a hollow chuckle escaped her lips. "*You* have magic!"

No, I don't. That can't be what this is. Maybe it's Vaughn doing it. It has to be.

Before she could argue with Darcie, the sound of approaching footsteps cut her off.

CHAPTER 23

Gavin remained silent as Brahm stormed out of the drawing room. If the former captain hadn't put him through all of this, Gavin might've felt sorry for the older man. For now, though, he kept all his attention on Rona, who still held the locks of hair between her fingers.

Whose hair is that? What is she going to do with it?

"Let's check in on your little Elise, shall we?" Holding the hair up to her lips, Rona whispered an incantation until the pieces started to glow. When Gavin tried asking Rona what was going on, she placed a finger to her lips and nodded towards the painting.

Dimitri's portrait rippled in the same fashion as before, but instead of a memory playing in front of him, Gavin only saw an arched ceiling.

Why isn't anything happening?

"Where are you?" Rona's eyes didn't leave the frame.

At first, Gavin thought the image was flickering, but as it swam left and right, he realized it was someone blinking.

They were seeing through someone else's point of view. With a sinking sense of dread, Gavin suspected it was the owner of the hair.

"I don't know."

Gavin clasped both hands over his ears as a deep, deafening voice echoed throughout the drawing room.

"What's wrong?" Rona was not at all affected by the volume. "Answer me."

"I'm wounded."

Even with his ears muffled, Gavin could make out the other man's strained words clearly.

"*We were attacked.*" Releasing a groan, the speaker covered his eyes and the frame went pitch-black.

We'll only see what he sees, but what does any of this have to do with finding Elise?

"Open your eyes. Let me see!" Rona commanded.

"*It hurts. You know it kills my head when you do this. Leave me alone.*"

Gavin lowered his hands and could make out whispers coming from somewhere out of view. The voices were close but none of them acknowledged the present conversation.

Are we only hearing his thoughts? This is crazy. She can get into people's heads now, too? What can't *she do? Nobody's safe around her.*

"Guys, he's waking up!"

Gavin perked up.

Is that Darcie? Are they all there? Is Elise and Mitch with her too?

His heart skipped a beat as Elise's blurry face came into view. She went in and out as the person lying down blinked a handful of times to focus.

Gavin's chest tightened at the sight of her. Behind Elise, he could make out Mitch and Darcie also peering down at whoever was giving Rona access.

"Another headache, huh?" Darcie asked. "I'm so sorry. After everything you've been through. . ."

"Rest up, man," Mitch said. "We've got time."

None of them were afraid. They talked as if this stranger was a friend.

"What happened? Where are we?" The man's actual voice was soft, yet hoarse. As he glanced around the room, Gavin and Rona were able to make out a well-furnished bedroom, which included a dresser and full-length mirror.

Go stand in front of it. Gavin wanted to see what this traitor looked like. His friends were in danger and didn't know it. *If I ever meet him face-to-face. . .*

"We're at the Vynchian palace," Darcie replied. "Some guards patrolling the border heard us yelling for help."

"Vynchia?" Rona cursed under her breath. "You weren't supposed to be that far yet, you idiot! How could you let this happen?"

There was no reply.

"We almost lost you." Elise's reddened eyes made Gavin suspect she had been crying.

"There was so much blood," said Mitch. "It was scary."

As the man looked down, Gavin could see large blood-stained bandages wrapped around his abdomen.

Rona clicked her tongue. "My poor angel."

"How did we escape?" the faceless man asked.

Darcie leaned in with a smile. "We found out Elise has magic." *What? Since when?*

How was that possible? Gavin had never seen her use magic before.

"Well, well, well." Rona winked at Gavin before looking back up at the frame. "What a delicious development. We must know more. Ask her about it, Vaughn."

Vaughn?

So, that was her minion's name.

"*Please leave her out of this,*" Vaughn's mind replied. "*I-I can't do this anymore.*"

Do what, exactly? What did Rona tell him to do?

Gavin dried his sweat-covered palms against his pants. Something was going on, and judging by the way his friends treated this person, it had been going on for some time.

Rona gritted her teeth.

"What's wrong with you? Don't you *dare* go soft on me now. Do it!"

Hearing the man sigh, Gavin took a step closer to the frame as Elise stepped closer.

Don't you dare hurt her. If you even lay a hand on her. . .

"You saved me?" Vaughn asked.

Pressing her lips into a flat line, Elise nodded.

The rest of the room came into view as Vaughn sat up in bed. Mitch and Darcie hurried to help him adjust without causing too much pain. Once he was situated, Vaughn patted the bed beside him for Elise to sit down.

Oh, you can forget it, pal. There's no way she's going to—

Gavin's hands, curled into fists by his sides, froze when Elise sat down and reached out to caress Vaughn's face.

"You're pretty scratched up still. How's your headache?"

Why is she touching him?

"I'm used to it. It'll pass." Vaughn reached out to grab her hand. "Thank you for saving me."

Caught off guard by their intimacy, it took Gavin a moment to realize she had handcuffs on.

"Don't thank me," Elise said as Vaughn inspected her wrists. "We're not quite out of trouble yet."

"Yeah, we've all got matching sets." Mitch scoffed, holding up his own chained wrists.

"Why were we not thrown in the dungeon?" Vaughn asked, echoing Gavin's own thoughts.

Darcie shrugged, running a thumb across the chain linking her hands together. "When we told them how we got here, and that we knew Derek, they summoned for their queen."

"Ah, Arymei," Rona whispered, breaking Gavin's focus. "The plot thickens. This just keeps getting better and better."

As fate would have it, the door opened at that precise moment. Four guards entered and—much to Gavin's surprise—so did Derek, followed by a woman he assumed was the queen.

With widened eyes and frozen expressions, Gavin's friends appeared as shocked as he was by Derek's presence.

"The handcuffs are a bit much, don't you think, Ary?" Derek asked.

"Security measures must be taken." Arymei's piercing gaze penetrated through Gavin's soul. "The wounded one shall be fitted for a set when he's healed enough for questioning."

"Why are you here?" Elise asked Derek. When he didn't answer right away, she sighed. "You talked to Ruby, huh?"

Gavin detected a hint of guilt in her tone.

"I confess she happened upon me shortly after reading your letter," he replied. His eyes flickered towards Vaughn. "Arymei, I'd like to speak to Elise in private if that's all right."

What does he want to say to her? Does he know something?

Did Derek know that Vaughn was working for Rona? Was he about to unveil it to her?

Get him away from Elise. Get everyone away from him.

"I'm afraid that will have to wait." Arymei swiped a lock of fallen hair back in place as she regarded her reflection in the mirror. "We need to finalize our plans."

"Ask her about the plans," Rona pressed, making Gavin jump.

Engrossed in what was happening, he had forgotten she was even in the room.

"As you wish," the king said to Arymei. Derek sent another glance Vaughn's way before standing.

Arymei assigned one of the four accompanying guards to stay behind with the others before leading Derek out.

"You fool!" Rona spat. "We've lost our chance. Imbecile!" Rona looked like she had swallowed a mouthful of sour grapes.

"It doesn't matter anymore."

By this point, Gavin had adjusted to Vaughn's thoughts echoing throughout the room. He only wished he were allowed to make his own demands.

"Oh, really? And why is that?" Rona asked.

"Please, Majesty. . .Don't make me keep doing this."

Do what? What is he supposed to do?

Gavin's heart pounded within his chest. Struggling to control himself, he wanted Rona to tell him everything.

"What was that about?" Elise asked, catching Gavin's attention again. He watched her walk over to stand in front of the mirror. "What do y'all think he wanted to tell me?"

Gavin watched Elise fiddle with her hair. The chain between her cuffs rattled as she tried getting the frizz to lay down before giving up.

She looks beautiful. I wish I was there with her.

Gavin's stomach hardened as the ache in his chest grew. He had never missed anyone the way he missed her now. There was nothing he wanted more than to be in that room with all three of them.

If Vaughn hurts any of them, I swear I'll—

Gavin's thoughts were cut short as Derek returned.

"Good news, everyone. I have convinced the queen of your innocence, and she's even offered to schedule a tour of the local town for you tonight. You must be eager to see a different kingdom, right?"

Just like that? What exactly did he tell her?

His friends stared at Derek as if he had spouted wings. If it were under lighter circumstances, Gavin might have burst out laughing.

Something is going on. He's not acting right. This is all too fast. He knows something's wrong with this guy.

"Except. . .your friend, of course." Derek nodded towards Vaughn. "He will still need to be questioned, and the doctor says he will need to remain here to complete his healing."

"How convenient." Rona stomped her foot with a groan. "They're onto you. *Don't* blow this. Go with it for now. He'll reveal what they're up to soon enough."

Vaughn nodded.

"And these?" Mitch held out his hands.

"They'll be removed before you go." Derek chuckled as he looked over at Darcie and Elise. "So, shall we?"

"What? Right now? Really?" Darcie's eyes lit up as she grinned from ear to ear.

"Well, it beats sitting around waiting for the next few hours like prisoners." Derek didn't meet Vaughn's gaze, but Gavin picked up on the slight.

"I can't leave Vaughn," said Elise. "He gets these really bad headaches and shouldn't be alone. You guys go ahead."

Why does she care so much? She left me to go tour Haighdlen.

Gavin knew it wasn't fair to judge her considering he had pressured Elise to leave him when he was healing. It still didn't stop the punch to the gut he felt.

"I assure you, Elise, he is taken care of. The doctor will be in to check on him," Derek said.

"Elise, come on," Darcie whined. "Vaughn understands. Don't you, Vaughn?"

Elise's concerned expression came into view again as Vaughn looked over at her.

"Go," he said.

"This way." Derek led the way out.

Mitch followed first while Darcie pulled Elise towards the door as best as she could with handcuffs on.

"Oh, Elise, one more thing," Vaughn called out.

What's he doing now?

Elise sent Darcie ahead with a promise to follow in a minute before walking back to the bed.

"What is it?" she asked. "Is it your head?"

Vaughn shook his head. Looking down, he rummaged in his pocket before pulling out something connected to a chain that Gavin couldn't see before placing it in her hand. It was clear from the way Elise clutched it to her chest that it was significant.

"Elise!" Darcie's voice called from the hallway. "Come on!"

Crossing the room, Elise paused to smile at Vaughn from the doorway.

"Thank you. Feel better."

Gavin's jaw tightened, along with his shoulders, as every part of his body felt on fire.

He knew that smile. Gavin had seen that smile all year when Elise thought he wasn't looking. It was always meant for *him*. . . His blood boiled as he watched her walk out before the painting returned to its original state.

Does she have feelings for this guy?

"Ooh, that was too much fun. I love a good love story." Her taunting chuckle irked Gavin more as she closed the lock of hair back in the box. "Vaughn will be able to find out those plans for us, so we can be ready. I'm so glad you suggested that we check in on Elise. It really helped. Don't they look well together?"

This wasn't what Gavin wanted. He didn't mean to put them all in *more* danger, and he wasn't sure what Vaughn was capable of.

What have I done?

CHAPTER 24

Elise managed to tuck the bottle necklace down the front of her dress, despite the awkwardness of handcuffs. While it was a risk, she doubted the queen would allow her to keep it if it were found.

I wonder what made Vaughn give it back?

Her smile faded under Darcie's scrutinous stare after she joined the rest of the party in the hall. Ignoring her, Elise asked when they could have their handcuffs removed.

"Allow me." Derek requested a key from one of the guards. Keeping his back to the others, he approached Elise.

Shouldn't he be letting the guard do it?

Derek's forehead creased with concern. Without making a sound, he asked if she was all right.

It took Elise a moment to read his lips.

Why is he acting so weird? And why did he want to get us out of the room so fast?

When she nodded, Derek reached out to take her wrist.

Both jumped as an electrical energy surged between them.

Derek flexed his hand, careful to remain discreet in front of Arymei.

I forgot about that.

Judging by Derek's wary expression, he had too.

Elise recalled the same reaction occurring when she had touched Derek's painting and danced with him during their waltz lesson.

Why does that keep happening? And why only him?

Bracing himself, Derek locked his jaw and proceeded to uncuff her.

Elise bit her tongue to keep from whimpering, praying he would be done quickly. She tried mouthing an apology, but he shook his head before moving onto Mitch and Darcie.

I hope I didn't hurt him.

A burning sensation coursed up her arm. Massaging the tender skin, Elise played it off when Darcie asked if she was okay.

After all, Derek was still within earshot.

I don't want him regretting helping us.

"Good fortune follows you, I'm told." Sizing up the three teenagers, Arymei's eyes shifted between them. "I'm inclined to believe it, since I never allow prisoners to be released so soon." When no one replied, she turned her attention to their appearance. "Do you often keep such disheveled—and, dare I say it—*pungent* company, Derek?" She grimaced.

Elise's cheeks burned under the queen's discernment. Did they all really smell *that* bad? She fought the urge to check herself closer.

We washed in the ocean. It's all we had!

When compared to the monarch's extravagant gown and jewelry, Elise couldn't blame Arymei for judging them.

Chuckling, Derek returned the key to the guard before flexing his hand again behind him.

I hope his hand isn't blistered. Mine feels like it's on fire!

"They're rather enjoyable once they are washed and fed. I assure you."

Arymei hummed in disbelief before walking away towards the throne room.

Derek waited until she was out of earshot before speaking again.

"Joranna and I have been so worried." Dropping the cheerful façade, he appeared to be himself again.

"How did you know where we'd be?" Elise asked. "Is it safe for you to leave Haighdlen?"

"Don't worry about me," Derek said. "Normally, I'd send an ambassador for such a task, but it's getting more difficult to know who

I can trust. After Brahm…well, I'm just glad I was able to arrive in time. I was beginning to fear the guards wouldn't find you at all. Why *did* you three rush off like that?"

Elise's stomach knotted with guilt.

"We went to find Gavin." When Derek opened his mouth, Elise continued before he could interrupt her. "We know you had people out looking, but we couldn't just sit around and wait. At least *I* couldn't, and Ruby was able to help."

"She gave us safe passage letters," Darcie said.

"But we lost them," Mitch added. "So, it helps that you showed up."

"I hope we didn't get her into trouble." Avoiding Derek's eyes, Elise fidgeted with her fingers.

Shaking his head, Derek stiffened at the sound of approaching footsteps. He continued in a hurried whisper. "The thing is, Elise, Ruby said that she never received—"

"Derek?" Arymei called.

Mitch cursed under his breath.

"We need to get on with matters. I've arranged for new attire and a tour with my steward to pass the time, so there's no need to hover over them like this. You and I have business to discuss."

Derek waited until the other three thanked Arymei before responding.

"That's generous of you, Ary. I'll join you directly." Derek turned back to Elise, Mitch, and Darcie with a bemused expression. "What was I saying?" He looked between them before sighing. "I don't recall now."

Four maids approached less than a minute later.

"Ah, there we are. You're in good hands. They'll get you cleaned up and refreshed for your tour." Derek held his arm out for Elise to lead the way.

"I-I can't," she stammered, looking back at the closed door behind her. "I can't leave Vaughn here. Look what happened when I left Gavin."

"Who exactly is that gentleman?" Derek asked.

"The princess hired him to help us," Mitch said.

Derek cleared his throat with a sudden urgency to his movements.

"We need to talk more, but now is not the time." Derek peered over Elise's head at the same door. With a nod, he shared a silent exchange with the guard standing watch.

What's going on? Why're they treating Vaughn like this?

"Is everything all right, Your Majesty?"

Everyone turned to see a well-dressed gentleman standing next to the maids.

When did he get here? Elise looked closer. *Wait, I think know him. Is that. . .*

"Dalton!" Derek clapped the other man on the back. "You're just in time. How are things with you?"

"I can't complain, Your Majesty." Dalton had the same easy-going smile and smooth voice that Elise still admired. While it had been over twenty years in Dalton's lifetime, to Elise, it had been only a few days since he had rescued her on the dance floor at Derek's and Joranna's engagement ball. "Queen Arymei tells me I am to give a tour to some guests of yours."

Elise's gaze lowered to the floor until she was sure the steward wasn't looking at her.

Time had been kind to Dalton, who only seemed to have grown handsomer with age. Though he had matured, particularly around his eyes and smile, Dalton's smooth brown skin didn't sport a single wrinkle or blemish.

He probably doesn't remember us.

Derek took his leave with a promise to speak again soon, before Dalton led them up the nearest staircase.

Elise felt rejuvenated after a proper bath. The hot water had been a welcome treatment for her sore muscles, but she couldn't ignore the merciless pangs of hunger. Initially anxious when Dalton declined dinner, Elise grew hopeful when he promised them an exquisite meal in town.

Yes, but how long do we have to wait to get it? I'm starving!

Fortunately for the weary travelers, their carriage arrived outside of Audney's marketplace in less than half an hour.

Dalton instructed the two accompanying guards to stay close and asked the coachman to wait for them by the stables.

"You're in luck," he announced as they stepped out onto the street. "You have the honor of visiting Vynchia during the Blooming Festival. Audney hosts the most spectacular events."

"What's the big deal about it?" Mitch asked. "Do they just plant a lot of flowers or something?"

Dalton chuckled.

"Not quite." He led them through the arched entryway. Similar to Clara, the countless shops were built close together with pointed roofs, creating the illusion that the street was made up of one continuous structure on both sides.

I thought Clara was busy!

Despite the incredibly late hour, there was little room to stand as a sea of diverse-looking people bustled back and forth between shops, carts, and isolated tents. The overlapping conversations ranged from casual greetings to intense negotiations.

Elise was unable to catch more than three or four words at a time before becoming distracted by a louder vendor, crying child, or grunting animal being led through the square. Shuffling her feet, Elise's eyes darted back and forth. She tucked both arms by her side and stayed close to Dalton.

Darcie had already tried telling her something twice, but both times Elise motioned with her hand to her ear that she couldn't understand.

Dalton, on the other hand, navigated through the sea of townspeople with an ease Elise couldn't believe. Nodding here and smiling there, he led the way towards a tavern to their left. The opening was small, and had Dalton not been there, Elise doubted she would've noticed it.

Careful to stay within the path Dalton created, Elise paused as her senses were attacked by the most delicious smells emanating from inside. The intoxicating aroma made Elise think of her favorite steakhouse back home.

What is *that?*

"Let me arrange for a table!" Dalton shouted as he pointed towards the tavern before disappearing inside.

"This place is nuts!" Mitch plugged a finger into one of his ears. "I think we should've just eaten back at the castle!"

Forty-five minutes later, however, had Mitch singing a different tune.

Being escorted by the queen's steward came with its own privileges, including a private dining room in the back of the tavern.

It was larger on the inside than its exterior suggested, and the secluded dining space alone had room to fit six or seven tables, yet it only contained three.

The noise from the main dining area had been reduced to a dull roar on the other side of the walls. Besides the sound of a glass or two shattering here and there, it was the ideal location.

At least I can hear my own thoughts.

Dalton and the teenagers were seated at an oversized round table in the center of the room while the accompanying guards sat at one of the smaller tables.

Once they were settled, the staff brought bowls of water to rinse their fingers. Fine china and silverware were placed in front of everyone at the same time a waiter walked around to fill glasses.

Given their hunger, Elise and her friends said very little as they inhaled the bread and salads placed in front of them.

I don't even care if I'm using the right fork at this point.

After the first course had been consumed and cleared, Dalton held up his glass.

"A toast," he said, "to a happy reunion."

Elise and Darcie exchanged shocked expressions.

"Wait," Darcie said. "You remember us?"

"Of course." His smooth, confident smile returned. "You all look as if a day hasn't gone by. It was hard to mistake you." Taking a long sip, he drained his glass. "You'll need to give me your secret to appearing so youthful."

An awkward chuckle traveled around the table. That particular subject of conversation did not progress any further once the second course arrived.

Thank goodness. I don't know what to tell him. I still can't believe he recognized us!

Having already stuffed herself with the first course, Elise was surprised how hungry she still felt as an exquisite piece of steak was placed in front of her. Plopping a piece of the boiled potato into her mouth, she busied herself by looking around the room.

An oversized map on the wall caught her attention.

It was a larger version of the one Elise saw hanging in Haighdlen's castle library. Her eyes followed the distance they had traveled since leaving Ruby.

"It's crazy, isn't it?" Darcie asked, nodding towards the same map. "To think we've come all this way?"

"We still wouldn't be here if it weren't for you, Elise," Mitch said around a mouthful of roasted green beans. "I could even still be in Lake Mirage."

"Lake Mirage?" Dalton asked. "Whatever would you be doing all the way over there?"

Elise, Mitch, and Darcie looked at one another.

"Our guide told us it was the best way here," Darcie replied.

"Only if you like torture." Dalton sliced into his steak. "With a bout of fairy magic, you should've transported yourselves directly here from the start." With a shrug, he added, "Or hired a boat in the town of Majestic Oak." Pointing his fork at the wall, he drew their attention to the map once more. "It could've taken you right to our main port here in half the time."

What! I know he didn't trust the magic, but why didn't Vaughn say anything about Majestic Oak? We could've already reached Gavin and . . .Wait. . .

"How did you know about the magic?" Elise rested a hand against the fabric of her dress hiding the bottle necklace.

Dalton didn't appear surprised by her question, but he waited until he swallowed the bite he was chewing.

"I've worked closely with two prominent, and *magical*, royal families. I'm experienced enough to detect gifted energies." A coy smile spread across his face. "Not to mention you have checked on it no less than eight times during dinner alone."

This guy's good.

Elise shifted, suddenly aware of her every move. Everything in her wanted to check again to make sure it was still there with her mother's drawing, but she resisted the urge.

"You all took perhaps the longest route here." Dalton chuckled as he grabbed another roll from the center of the table. "You'll want a better guide next time."

Elise's stomach lurched.

Mitch looked as if he had been punched in the gut, and Darcie's gaze shifted in alarm between Elise and Mitch. All three looked ready to erupt.

Sensing the change of mood, Dalton's smile faded.

"I'm sorry if I have offended you. I meant no harm."

"No, it's not that," Elise said. There was no point diving too far into detail, so she settled for, "We're just in a hurry to get to Lockesbarrow."

Dalton hummed in the back of his throat.

"I might advise against that." Dabbing his mouth with a cloth napkin, he grew serious for the first time. "It's not even safe to be traveling here right now, if I'm being honest, but Lockesbarrow is in a terrible state at present."

"What do you mean?" Elise asked.

Dalton waited for a waiter to leave the room before he answered.

"Their queen has all but declared war on Haighdlen and Vynchia."

Elise didn't know how much had been disclosed to Dalton already, so she kept her knowledge of Derek's own plans to herself.

"The rumors are growing of an impending attack, and ports will start closing if the threat continues. I'd hate for you to become stranded. It's not worth it," Dalton added.

"We don't have a choice," Elise said. "We have to save Gavin. He's been taken there."

"Then he's lost by now, I'm afraid," Dalton said. "I don't wish to upset you, but it's very unlikely he could escape such a terrible fate."

Elise regretted eating so fast as it now threatened to come back up. She took a sip of water to ease the nausea.

He's wrong. He has to be wrong.

"Well, we're not giving up," Mitch quipped. "We've come this far."

"As soon as Vaughn feels better, we're going to—"

"We can leave him here for all I care," Mitch said, interrupting Darcie. "It's obvious, isn't it? He played us."

"We don't know that," Darcie argued. "He could've taken us the best way he knew, so that—"

"Ugh, don't be stupid. Stop defending him!" Mitch snarled.

Elise and Darcie jumped as his fist slammed against the table, scattering silverware everywhere.

The guards made to stand, but Dalton held out his hand.

"Perhaps we had better finish dinner and get some fresh air," Dalton suggested.

Mitch fumed but said nothing.

Pursing her lips, Darcie stared a hole into the table.

Dessert was served without a single word from anyone.

Elise tasted the decadent chocolate cake, but she listened to the inner voice that told her to stop.

Though the tense silence between Mitch and Darcie was palpable and continued long after dinner concluded, Elise admired Dalton's ability to carry on with the tour.

"So, the Blooming Festival honors the great King Alaric and his wife, Queen Roseia. A curse was cast on the queen's family, and these festivities honor that curse being broken."

"What kind of curse was it?" Elise asked.

"No one really knows for sure. Legend has it that the queen was eager for an estranged marriage to prevent the curse from spreading to any heirs," Dalton said.

"But she married a prince." Mitch's puzzled expression mirrored Elise's own train of thought. "Isn't their whole job to marry and have kids?"

"Precisely," Dalton said. "It was a quite a scandal for that time, and the story of their whirlwind romance continues to be shared today."

I'd love to hear that story one day.

As the group continued walking, a fountain in the middle of the square caught Elise's eye.

"Hey, wait. I've seen that before."

The whole party stopped when she pointed to it. A handful of people stood around tossing coins into it.

That's the fountain that I saw in Haighdlen.

The towering statue of a woman on top was identical to the one Elise had seen throughout their search for Brahm and when they followed Ruby earlier that week. She had the same sculpted wavy hair, full figure, and coins in her hand.

"In the royal garden, yes," Dalton replied. "All of the Four Great Kingdoms have one. The symbolic design displays strengths from each one." Sensing their next question, he continued. "There was a time of great peace under the reigns of King Claramond of Haighdlen and King Alaric of Vynchia. Together they worked with the leaders of Lockesbarrow and Leafbrooke. The fountains were created as a sign of unity throughout the lands. Sadly, the fountains are the only reminder left of that alliance."

He pointed towards the stone woman's head.

"Her crown is made of oak leaves, symbolizing Haighdlen's nobility, strength, and loyalty. In her left hand, she holds coins to represent Vynchia's wealth and prosperity. In the other, she holds a map to explain Lockesbarrow's nautical pursuits."

"What's the fourth one then?" Mitch asked.

"The tranquil expression she wears displays the poise and wisdom of the Elves."

I wouldn't have guessed one statue could mean so much.

"That's enough of a history lesson for now. It's time for you to enjoy the town a bit. Here." Dalton pulled three small pouches from his pocket and handed one to each of them. "It's only a few coins, but it should allow you to have some fun."

Elise was still mesmerized by the water. Something about seeing it as an attraction in the middle of a busy town made it look more historic and powerful than in the garden.

Dalton followed her line of vision to two children who walked up to throw a coin into the fountain before returning to their mother.

"The water is said to have magical qualities," he added.

"Sure, it does." Mitch rolled his eyes. "I'm about done with anymore magical qualities. I'm going to go find something else to do." He muttered a quick thanks to Dalton for the coins before calling over his shoulder to Darcie. "You coming?"

Darcie, who hadn't spoken since the tavern, looked taken aback by Mitch's question, or even his attention. Her eyes darted between Dalton and Elise before she followed his retreating figure into the crowd.

That's probably for the best. Who knows what trouble he'd get himself into if he were alone? Maybe they'll get a chance to talk if they're alone.

"Many people believe in its powers." Dalton nodded towards Elise's pouch, bringing her attention back to him. "Why don't you try it? Go on. Make a wish."

Elise poured the coins out into her hand before stepping up to the pool of water. Looking up into the woman's tranquil eyes, she concentrated on what she wanted most.

This reminded her of the trips to the mall with her mother as a child. Ruby had never allowed Elise to throw in pennies like the other children, but she never understood why. Had she thought there was a chance of magic existing in their world too?

Even if there is no real magic, it can't hurt.

Feeling Dalton's eyes on her, she shrugged and tossed a coin into the water.

I wish for Gavin to be found alive.

Goosebumps spread across her arms, and she was filled with a frightening sense of self-awareness. Despite knowing no one could hear her thoughts, the idea of her wish not being granted made Elise feel defeated. She chanced a look over at Dalton, who was watching a group of musicians play a lively tune. Near them, six or seven couples danced in the only open area not occupied by shoppers. Craning her neck, Elise sighed. She couldn't see Mitch or Darcie anywhere.

"Shall we join the next one?"

The next one?

Elise peered down at Dalton's offered hand before taking a step back.

"Oh, no, thank you. You go ahead."

Heat rushed to her face when he insisted that she join him.

No, I can't. Not in front of all these people. That night at the engagement ball was bad enough!

"I can't. I-I don't know how."

Dalton took her hand.

"Of course, you do." He gave her a wink of encouragement as a wry smile spread across his handsome features. Stepping backwards, he pulled her towards the other dancers. "You learned from the best."

Elise failed to contain a smile of her own as a new song began. She was overcome with déjà vu as her mind traveled back to the night Dalton rescued her from embarrassment at Derek and Joranna's engagement ball after Gavin had gotten cold feet.

Although her mind screamed that she couldn't remember the steps or the lesson, Dalton moved with such ease and control that she soon fell in step with him.

I can't believe it. I'm actually doing it! Wait. I don't know what step we're on. Don't trip, Elise. Don't fall.

"Relax. Look at me."

She looked up at the older gentleman and felt her anxiety wilt.

"You're doing fine. Just follow me."

Once again, Dalton kept Elise from getting too caught up in her head. As the music swelled, she was filled with a confidence she didn't recognize. She wasn't afraid, and she didn't trip over her own feet. It wasn't until the final notes sounded that Elise realized how clear her mind had become in the last five minutes. She wondered if Dalton was aware of how much she welcomed the distraction.

Before she could thank him, however, Darcie came running up to them.

"Elise, you've got to come see this!"

Elise had enough time to mouth a quick apology before Darcie pulled her towards the other side of the square.

CHAPTER 25

Despite Rona's second offer to spend the night with her, Gavin opted for a cell. Though placed in a different one away from Horace and Rory, Gavin didn't regret the decision until the early morning hours when he was awakened by a swift kick to the stomach.

"Get up," said an armed guard.

Gavin groaned. *Geez. What is with everybody here? I can't breathe.*

Doubled over, he cradled his stomach with both hands. His insides were on fire, but before Gavin could gain his bearings, he was lifted and dragged back to the same drawing room.

Upon entering, Gavin was surprised to find that Rona was not there. However, he rolled his eyes when he caught a glimpse of Brahm standing by the fireplace.

"Yes, the feeling is mutual." Brahm tucked his hands behind him and walked closer to inspect Gavin. The disgraced captain's face scrunched up as he took in the younger man's appearance before addressing the guard. "Did Her Majesty not give *explicit* instructions for him to be cleansed every time he leaves the dungeon?"

"But Queen Rona said to bring the prisoner right away, and—"

"Get him out of here!" Brahm barked. "Now!"

Gavin turned his head away as spit spewed from Brahm's mouth. It was then he caught a whiff of Rona's perfume. He sensed her presence before she even spoke. Memories of the previous night flooded through his mind before he could control himself.

"Haven't I told you to play nice, Thaddy?"

Gavin didn't hear Brahm's spluttered response. He was too occupied by how tight Rona's gown fit her.

How did she even get that on? It looks like someone sewed her into it.

The cerulean fabric hugged her curves in all the right places, and Gavin couldn't help but think it'd look better on the floor.

Stop it. That's what she wants you to think.

One of her soft hands tucked under Gavin's chin, bringing his face up to hers.

"I'll do the honors."

What? No way was she going to give him a bath. There was only so much he could handle. Gavin knew he could get punched, screamed at, and thrown in prison, but this would break him for good.

He was halfway down the corridor when he realized the guard was steering him towards the bathroom.

No, please no. I can't get naked in front of her. What if I embarrass myself? What if I give in to her? This has to be a joke.

His thoughts came rushing so quickly, one after the other, he eventually couldn't tell where one started and another ended. No matter how much he struggled or dragged his feet, it was no use. The familiar door grew closer. Gavin threw out one last wish that this wasn't really happening—that he'd wake up in his cell—but as the guard pushed open the door, he saw that Rona was already in the room.

How did she get in here so fast? He rolled his eyes as soon as the thought formed. *Magic. Of course. I'm an idiot.*

A passing maid paused behind Gavin and the guard. Seeing Rona filling the tub, she bowed when the queen looked up at her.

"Shall I bathe him for you, Your Majesty?"

Gavin nodded.

Yes, please. Anybody else.

"That won't be necessary," Rona replied. "Leave us."

The guard shoved Gavin over the threshold before closing the door.

Gavin's eyes immediately looked down at his feet.

*I should've opened that stupid book. Why. . .why. . .why didn't
I just open it?*

If he were being honest with himself, he also wondered if it
would've been easier to give her what she wanted. Perhaps if she had
her way with him, he'd be free by now.

*Would it really be the end of the world for her to go back and
save her brother?*

"Get in."

Gavin didn't move. He couldn't. Getting in meant giving into
her. As tempting as it was, he didn't want to do that to Elise. He had to
hold onto his resolve for as long as he could.

"Brahm's waiting," Gavin said. "He'll be mad."

"He will get over it."

Gavin was out of ideas to stall her. He wouldn't be surprised if
she spelled him into the tub at this point.

"Can we please do something else?" *Anything else?*

"I could always drown you."

Gavin's mouth parted as he lifted his eyes. He didn't know
why her answer shocked him. For a moment, all he could do was stare
as if waiting for her to reveal a joke. But he knew better. He knew *her*
better. She was certainly capable, but it was the playful way Rona said
the words that terrified him.

After another moment of silence passed between them, Rona
pinched her nose with a sigh.

It's working.

When she spoke again, there was a bite to her tone as she
pointed to the tub. "As much as I find your obstinance titillating, I'm
afraid I can't play today."

Swallowing the lump in his throat, Gavin straightened his spine
and met her gaze. Steam swelled between them until his view of her
was clouded, yet he held his ground.

"If you're so busy, why are we here? What're you going to
do?"

Gavin wished he hadn't asked, because in an instant, she
vanished and reappeared behind him before ripping his shirt off in one
swift motion. The discarded fabric lay in shreds at his feet as she

shoved him forward. Before she had a chance to reach for his pants, Gavin hurried to remove them and lowered himself into the water.

"That's better," she purred.

Gavin scooped as many bubbles around him as possible. He clenched his eyes shut as she kneeled beside the tub. It was a wonder her dress didn't rip when she sat, but he couldn't think about that right now.

This isn't happening. If I don't do something, I won't be able to pretend anymore. She'll know what she's doing to me.

"Look at me, Gavin."

Again, he didn't move.

Rona clicked her tongue. "After all those times I healed and protected you, you won't even look at me? Am I *that* repulsive?" She leaned over the edge and lowered a hand into the water.

Gavin recoiled from the unwanted advance. If anything, this only amused her more.

"Very well then," she said.

Gavin's eyes shot open when something brushed against his leg. He watched, frozen, as Rona lowered herself into the tub with him, gown and all. The water sloshed and spilled over the sides into the floor. She didn't appear bothered by her soaked clothes. In fact, Gavin thought he even saw a smirk cross her lips when he looked up from where he had been staring. With no escape, Gavin's back pressed against the porcelain as she sat opposite of him.

"I was wrong," she said, arching an eyebrow. "Perhaps I *do* have time for one little game." Rona held out a bar of soap for him to take.

She's insane. She's never going to give up.

Gavin gulped and complied, watching her gaze follow the soap's path across his skin. Feeling his own body respond to the attention, he quickened his motions and threw the soap across the room.

"There, I'm clean. Let's go."

She chuckled.

He hated when she chuckled, because of what it did to him. What he wouldn't give for an interruption at that moment.

"You missed a spot."

Before Gavin's brain could process what was happening, Rona lunged across the tub and pinned him underneath her. More water escaped onto the floor as Gavin turned his head away.

He gasped as Rona's lips touched the exposed skin of his neck. Stretching his arms out on either side, Gavin gripped the porcelain until his knuckles were white. Pressing his toes against the other end of the tub, Gavin groaned as the seductive queen sank down to sit on his lap. It was impossible to ignore his body's reaction.

Much like the encircling steam, Gavin's brain grew foggier with every kiss that Rona trailed up his neck.

Pausing behind his ear, she waited for him to look at her. Rona's eyes flickered between Gavin's mouth and eyes as she placed a hand across his bare chest.

"I. . .I can't." Gavin's moan betrayed his words. It was getting harder to resist as her hand wandered.

His thoughts swam as she leaned back to unbutton the back of her dress. Her scent was intoxicating. *She* was intoxicating.

I can't fight much longer. She's driving me crazy. I want her so bad. . . No! Stop it, Gav. You can't do this. Look anywhere else. Do anything else!

Rona peeled one sleeve down while her free hand squeezed Gavin's thigh.

"I'll. . .I'll do it." The words only managed to come out as a whisper. Seeing her reach for the second sleeve, Gavin tensed beneath her. "I'll open the diary!"

Rona paused with a triumphant smile before snapping her fingers.

In the blink of an eye, Gavin found himself sitting completely dried and dressed beside Brahm in the drawing room while Rona opened the box containing Vaughn's hair.

She looks back to normal too.

Gavin sat—dumbfounded and unwilling to move—as he studied the couple.

The former captain didn't act surprised by their sudden appearance, but that didn't stop Gavin's own paranoia.

Does he know what just happened? Why does he keep looking at me like that?

Gavin didn't know how Brahm could possibly know, but watching Rona hum to herself and pace in front of the fire, made him question if the bathing incident even happened at all or if he was losing his mind.

This is it. This is how it's going to happen. She's going to make me go insane. I'll end up like Horace for sure.

"Everything is ready!" Rona exclaimed, bringing Gavin out of his thoughts. She whispered the same incantation until the locks of hair began to glow. Just as before, the portrait of Rona's brother rippled until Vaughn's surroundings came into view. It looked like the queen's minion was still in the same guest room at the Vynchian palace.

Gavin's heart leapt when he saw Elise, Darcie, and Mitch sitting at the foot of Vaughn's bed.

"Something has to be done about these headaches," Darcie said. She leaned forward to place a hand on his forehead.

From Gavin's point of view, it looked like Darcie was looking directly at him through the frame.

"Are you sure you feel okay?" she asked.

"I'll be all right. Thank you," said Vaughn. "Please, continue what you were saying."

Darcie didn't need to be told twice and promptly resumed her animated account of their tour the previous evening.

"Dalton was nice enough to give us some coins. I couldn't decide what I was going to get. I didn't want to waste them in a fountain like Elise did, but then—oh, crap!" Her high-pitched shriek made Gavin flinch. Darcie ran a hand across her wrist. "Where is my new bracelet? I must've left it in the carriage! I'll be right back." Before anyone could respond, she raced out of the room.

"Wait up!" Mitch called out as he walked to the door. "I don't want her going alone. Elise, you coming?" He looked back at his friend sitting on the bed.

"In a minute," Elise replied.

Mitch looked torn on whether to leave or not.

Don't leave Elise alone with her, Mitch. She's in danger. Be a good friend.

Gavin sighed as he watched his best friend run after Darcie.

"Now's your chance," Rona said. "I am ready with the diary at last." She cast a look over her shoulder at Gavin as she spoke. "Find out where Derek and Arymei are. Detour them to the shore here. I will be waiting for you all there."

The blood rushed from Gavin's face. Was she going to ambush them?

"Look at her, Majesty," Vaughn's voice echoed throughout the chamber. *"I want no part in this."*

"Save your weak sentiments and do it!" Rona growled. "Distract her, tempt her, whatever you have to do to stall until you have convinced Derek. *He's* your target. Bring him to me."

What! What is she planning to do?

Gavin's heart raced as he put the pieces together in his head. Derek was going to be led into a trap. And what about his friends? What was going to happen to them?

Another moment passed before Vaughn broke the silence.

"Darcie is certainly a storyteller."

Elise chuckled. "You should've seen her in our public speaking class. She actually lost points for poor time management."

When her smile faded, Vaughn was quick to jump in and change the subject.

"While we're alone, there was something I wanted to ask." The image bounced unsteadily as Vaughn scooted closer to Elise.

When she made no attempt to move, Gavin sat on the edge of his seat, determined not to miss a word between the two in the frame.

"Did you really use magic to save me?" he asked.

Gavin watched a crease form along Elise's forehead before she began twisting her fingers together on her lap.

She's anxious. Why is she nervous around him?

"I think so," she replied. "Mitch and Darcie think I did anyway."

Gavin's anger eased as he got a closer look at Elise's wilted demeanor. Her normal pale complexion had darkened with a sunburn that highlighted more freckles than he had noticed before. The bags beneath her sunken eyes exposed Elise's exhaustion, and he wanted nothing more than to break through the frame to be by her side.

"*You* don't believe it?" Vaughn's voice rang out through the drawing room.

"I don't know what to believe anymore." Elise scoffed and picked a piece of lint off her skirt. Leaning back on her hands, she gazed at the ceiling.

A long silence passed between them.

"Thank you for saving my life." Vaughn placed his hand on top of hers.

Rather than pull her hand away, Elise stared down at Vaughn's.

Gavin wished he knew what she was thinking. Watching this was torture. If only she knew what it meant for him to be able to see her. A nagging voice within his mind reminded Gavin that he wasn't at the center of Elise's thoughts anymore. He tried to tell himself it wasn't true. . .but then Elise smiled again. And once more, it wasn't for him. If only she knew how much that killed him inside. After all, she was the only reason he was still breathing. The thought of seeing Elise again had kept him fighting. Yet seeing her like this. . .made him wonder if it had all been a waste.

It was at that moment he gave up any lingering hope that she would look at him the same again.

"Get *on* with it!" Rona ordered. "Ask her about Derek already."

Gavin's view of Elise was blocked as Vaughn massaged the bridge of his nose.

"Let me get the doctor." Elise stood, but Vaughn didn't release her hand.

Guiding her back down on the bed, he tucked a loose strand of hair behind Elise's ear. "I don't want a doctor. I need to tell you something."

Gavin's heart skipped a beat as he gauged Rona's reaction. Was he going to tell Elise the truth?

If Rona was worried, she didn't show it, but that didn't stop Brahm from crossing the room to put distance between them.

Why is Brahm still here, anyway?

Nevertheless, Gavin followed his lead and took a step back.

"How did you save me?" He raked his fingers through her hair. "Why did you do it?"

Elise followed the trail of his hand until it came back to rest on top of hers again. Licking her lips, she glanced back at the door. "I don't really know how I did it." She paused, and Gavin watched her eyes become distant as she relived the memory. When Elise spoke again, her voice was small. "There was so much blood. You weren't moving. I kept calling your name, but you. . .you couldn't answer. Everything in me panicked. I didn't know what I'd do if—" She caught her words, but tears welled up in Elise's eyes.

If what? Is she that *hung up on this guy?*

Gavin's rage pulsed within his veins as Vaughn scooted closer to hug his girlfriend.

As the two pulled apart, Vaughn raised his hand to cup Elise's cheek and swiped his thumb across a tear falling down Elise's cheek.

Why isn't she walking away? Gavin gritted his teeth and curled his hands into fists beside him. Clenching his eyes shut, he reminded himself how hard it was to fight Rona's charms. It didn't lessen how he felt about Elise. Despite the coincidence, Gavin felt betrayed. Perhaps he didn't have a right to feel that way, but his blood ran cold when Elise's gaze lowered to the bottom of the frame as she looked at Vaughn's lips.

Elise, don't. Please don't.

"Tell me," Vaughn purred. "Say it."

Gavin looked up at the frame again. Even from where he stood, he could feel the heat between the other two. It didn't matter if Vaughn was faking or genuine. What mattered was Elise's wet, heavy-lidded eyes that desired another man besides him.

Vaughn's thumb slid from Elise's cheek to her bottom lip, caressing it.

Gavin's mind spiraled when she leaned her face closer. . .

He jumped at the sound of the door opening. The view switched from Elise to a maid standing in the doorway. Just outside, Gavin could see a guard on duty. He hoped, rather than believed, that Elise was safe.

The young woman looked between Vaughn and Elise with an unreadable expression before clearing her throat with a curtsy.

"Queen Arymei and King Derek wish to meet with you in the throne room."

"Thaddy!" Rona snapped over her shoulder. "It's time. Prepare the others."

Gavin watched as Brahm left the room.

Time for what? What is she going to do?

When Vaughn made to follow Elise, the young woman bit her lip and stammered. "Y-you'll need to w-wait here, sir. Per their orders."

A wave of relief washed over Gavin.

Good. They're onto him.

"Get yourself to that meeting in whatever way you can," Rona commanded to Vaughn.

"What are you going to do?" Gavin asked her, finally finding his voice. Was she really going to teleport to Elise? What means would Vaughn go through to make sure he also made it to the royal summons? Panic flooded through Gavin as his eyes shifted from Rona to the open box on her palm.

I have to break the connection.

He sprinted across the room and lunged for the box, but Rona was faster.

Whirling around, she held out her other hand, freezing him in place.

Gavin felt invisible fingers close around his neck as he was shoved up against the wall.

"All in good time, my love." Rona stepped up to him. "You have proven to be a much-needed distraction while I waited for Derek to act." She caressed his cheek as Vaughn had done to Elise. "But don't worry. Your part isn't over yet."

That's what I'm afraid of.

CHAPTER 26

"Y-you'll need to w-wait here, sir. Per their orders," said the maid.

Elise scowled. "We wouldn't be here without Vaughn. He needs to come too."

Whether we took the longest route or not, he doesn't deserve to be cast aside.

Elise was surprised by her bold statement. Normally, she wouldn't dream of going against a direct order, but she also didn't know what was going on with her lately. She was reminded of a conversation with Darcie the night before after dancing with Dalton.

"What's got you so distracted?" Darcie had asked her. Taking Elise by surprise, she added, "Gavin or Vaughn?"

The truth was. . .she wasn't sure. Elise felt like she had one cohesive thought since Gavin first went missing. Her goal had been to find Gavin. It was all she wanted. . .except the last few days when new feelings stirred within her. The problem was she couldn't explain the feelings. They didn't feel the same. With Gavin, Elise knew with her whole heart that she wanted to be with him. When it came to Vaughn, the feelings seemed. . .forced. She had tried conveying her confusing situation to Darcie without any luck.

"It's not like you've done anything with Vaughn. You didn't do anything wrong," said Darcie. With a mischievous chuckle, Darcie went on to joke she was jealous that Vaughn appeared to feel the same way towards Elise.

She wasn't joking, but at least she's not mad at me for it.

While Elise's thoughts and urges bordered on pure lust when it came to Vaughn, it was still hard to shake the odd energy between them. When she was alone with him, she wasn't herself. She didn't recognize herself or her actions. She had almost kissed him just now.

I'm glad the maid came when she did. What if Mitch or Darcie would've seen?

Elise jumped when Vaughn placed a hand on her shoulder.

"Perhaps, I should stay here," he offered.

An irrational wave of emotion flooded Elise's system. She glared daggers at the maid and guard.

"You can tell your queen and King Derek that Vaughn will be joining us or there won't be any meeting."

Whoa, where did that come from?

The maid and guard exchanged a look before the young woman conceded and led the way out.

Taking a deep steadying breath, Elise calmed when Vaughn took a step back and gestured for her to go first. Feeling her anxiety soaring, she hurried past the guard without looking up at him.

The man on duty followed behind them as they made their way to the throne room.

Great. I've scared that poor girl and the other guy thinks we're criminals. What is wrong with me? Seriously? One minute, I'm a raging monster, and the next I'm making demands? I'm normally afraid of my own shadow. She held out her palms in front of her as she walked. *I don't feel right. Something's wrong, but I don't know what it is. I want to cry, hide, and scream all at once.* She felt like her body couldn't contain all that was going on inside her.

Entering the spacious, elegant throne room, Elise saw her two friends had already been escorted in. She looked down at Darcie's wrist and noticed the recovered bracelet. Elise gave her friends a brief smile before Derek interrupted from where he stood next to Arymei.

"I asked only for the three," he told the maid.

The young woman's face paled under the king and queen's scrutiny. Her lips parted, but only a strained, choking sound came out.

"She wouldn't come without him," the guard quipped.

The maid nodded.

"Is that so?" Arymei huffed, sizing Elise up and down.

Elise didn't know where her burst of confidence had come from earlier, but judging by the goosebumps that sprang up along her arms and neck under Arymei's disapproving stare, it was long gone. A layer of sweat formed along Elise's forehead and palms. Her knees felt weak.

I think I'm going to pass out.

Derek looked over Elise's shoulder at Vaughn. "You seem to have recovered well enough."

Vaughn bowed his head. "I have, Your Majesty. I cannot thank both of you enough for such attentive care. I hope you don't find my presence obtrusive."

Neither ruler responded.

"We also wanted to say thank you for last night," said Mitch in an attempt to ease the tension. "Apart from a crazy fortune reading, we had a good time."

"Vynchia is beautiful," Darcie added.

Arymei's severe expression softened. "Dalton had nothing but positive things to say about you all. I am glad to hear you appreciated it."

When another silence followed, Elise regretted inviting Vaughn to come with her. He was the elephant in the room, and she wondered how Arymei and Derek were making him feel.

"Perhaps we had better get right to the point," Derek offered before pausing. Rather than continue right away, he tensed. Looking at Elise, Darcie and Mitch, he sighed. "I have arranged to send you three back to Haighdlen. You leave within the hour."

What! We can't do that!

"But we haven't found Gavin yet!" Elise cried.

"We've come all this way!" Mitch argued.

"Please. You can't send us back yet," Darcie added.

All three began to speak over one another until Arymei held up her hand to silence them. "That is quite enough. Honestly, children, contain yourselves. The plan is incredibly dangerous enough without having too many moving parts."

Plan? What plan?

Elise bit her lip and looked at Derek. For a moment, he didn't resemble the kind, just ruler and grandfather she had come to know. He looked tired and stress lines surrounded his eyes and mouth.

Derek frowned. "Indeed. We're arranging to have Queen Rona visit Vynchia in hopes of discussing peace treaty options."

He's lying. He already told the family they're declaring war. Why is he lying to Vaughn?

"May I speak plainly, Your Majesty?" Vaughn asked. Stepping forward, he cleared his throat. "Any sort of travel is a risk at the moment. We've been fortunate up until now, but we can't expect it to continue."

"Thank you, but we will rely on our respective councils regarding kingdom securities," Derek replied.

"But can you be sure they haven't been compromised?" Vaughn questioned. When neither ruler responded, he stepped closer. "I believe I have a way for everyone to get what they desire."

What is he doing? They're never going to go for any of his ideas.

For someone who nearly died the night before, Vaughn showed no hesitation while addressing the two people in charge of his fate.

"I took a vow to guide these travelers to Lockesbarrow," Vaughn continued. "With all due respect, I wouldn't be a man of my word if I wasn't allowed to complete my mission. Your Majesties wish to speak with Queen Rona before any blood is shed, but it's well-known she never leaves her own kingdom. I grew up there, and I advise Your Majesties to take us with you and go to Lockesbarrow yourselves."

There's no way Derek would do that. If Joranna even thought he was considering it for a minute, she'd be furious! Elise failed to hide her anxiety as she met Darcie's gaze. Mitch looked ready to throw up as well. There wasn't going to be a plan that everyone agreed on. *Derek needs to be home with the family. We need to try and get Gavin and the diary. Anything else is just going to make everything worse.*

"I question your eagerness to return," Arymei said at long last. "In any case, if we were to seek Rona out, one of us should stay behind. It isn't wise to leave both kingdoms in pursuit of one ruler."

"I am of the same mindset," Derek said. With a heavy sigh, he nodded. "I will accompany them." When Arymei tried to argue his decision, he shook his head. "If all goes according to plan, we can spell our way back by nightfall. If fate is not on my side, Haighdlen's throne is perfectly secured with plenty of heirs. With no children of your own, Vynchia is not so fortunate, Ary. Besides peace, our ultimate goal is to restore the Lockesbarrian throne to its rightful ruler."

And to find Gavin.

"Do you really think Prisha is alive?" Arymei asked with an incredulous expression.

"I do." Derek looked back at Vaughn. "In the unfortunate case that she's not, anyone will do besides Rona. The hardest part is going to be locating a safe place to land without her knowing."

Vaughn grimaced.

"Another headache?" Darcie whispered.

He nodded before addressing the king. "I have many happy memories there. The shore near the Whistpore Mountains is a safe location to transport to undetected. From there you can prepare to arrange a meeting."

"He knows too much," said the queen. "Perhaps we arrest him for treason?

Elise's blood boiled at the other woman's arrogance. *Why can't they see that Vaughn's only trying to help?* Even Dalton had questioned him as a guide. Sure, there were things about him that hadn't always sat right with her, but when it mattered, he'd been there for them.

"I think we can trust him," said Mitch.

Elise looked over to him in shock. Had Mitch really just stood up for Vaughn? His support encouraged Darcie to speak up as well.

"He's risked his life so many times for us already," Darcie said. "He's telling the truth."

Derek and Arymei looked at Elise.

Their expectant stares made her mouth grow dry. She wanted to show her support without betraying any confusing feelings she had for him. Elise made the mistake of looking up into his eyes. She saw a tortured soul who was trying to do the right thing.

His expression softened, pleading for her to speak up on his behalf.

"Vaughn has been nothing but honest since we've met him," she said. "He's guided us all the way here and kept us safe. Like Darcie said, he's almost died protecting us, but he's still here. I feel like that says something. You can trust him."

Seeing the looks of doubt being cast down at them, Elise shifted her focus to magic. Instead of speaking anymore, she turned her attention to what she wanted. If she did have magic, this would certainly be the time to use it. They were this close to saving Gavin, and she wasn't about to be sent back to the beginning without him. As Vaughn made one last plea, Elise closed her eyes.

Please trust Vaughn. You can trust him. Take us to Lockesbarrow. Let's find Gavin and get the diary. You can talk peace once you're there if you want or attack if you want, but we need to go. Take us there. Take us now.

"They're certainly willing to vouch for his character," Arymei said, making Elise open her eyes again.

"Indeed," replied Derek. His studious expression bore into Vaughn.

Take us, please. Believe him, Derek. He's a good man. He's a good man.

"They've made him out to be a good man, but do we act on it? Should we summon the councils again?"

No, no more councils! Enough meetings! They aren't solving anything. Make a decision and go. Take us to Lockesbarrow. Please. Please. Please.

"We already know where they stand on the issues, but I'm afraid the matter inevitably falls in our hands," said Arymei. "If we do this correctly, we can extinguish any threat before a drop of blood is spilled. Prisha could be back on the throne by next week if she were to come out of hiding."

Yes! Let's go. Let's leave now.

"I will reach out to Joranna and explain everything. When can you have men prepared?" Derek asked.

Now. We want to go now.

"Within an hour," the queen answered. "Our magic joined together should give you enough power to send everyone at once. However, I want them all under a guard's watch in the meantime."

Yes! I'm going to get to see Gavin. I need to see him.

"It's settled then," Derek said.

Arymei ordered for the guard to take them back to the same room Vaughn had healed in, but Elise ran up to Derek before another guard nearby stopped her.

"Your Highness!" she called out.

Derek waited for Arymei to leave the room before he walked back over to her.

"Thank you," Elise whispered. "You won't regret this. Vaughn's a really great guy. We can trust him. I know he's going to take us to Gavin."

Derek lowered his gaze and smiled, but it didn't reach his eyes. "I'll only say this, Elise. It's the ones we truly believe in who can hurt us most. I'll see you in an hour."

What does that mean?

"Tell the family I said hi," she called to his retreating figure.

He paused in the doorway and nodded before proceeding down the hall.

Why do I feel like I've disappointed him?

Elise couldn't explain the building guilt in the pit of her stomach. While she shouldn't have used her magic, she had grown fed up with delaying her chance to see Gavin any longer. The hour Derek needed to prepare felt like days to Elise. She questioned what he could possibly need so much time for.

"Give him a break, Elise," Darcie said when Elise had voiced her impatient opinion. "The man's about to leave his family."

"Yeah, but he's going to be fine," Elise said. "Once we have Gavin and the diary, he can make a quick escape for us."

"He said he wants to have a peace talk," said Mitch.

Elise scoffed. "He didn't mean that crap. That's the last thing he wants to do. I don't know who he's fooling."

"Why is he going?" Mitch asked. "Don't kings have ambassadors to do this kind of stuff for them?"

Good point.

"It'll be easier and faster if he uses his magic," Vaughn said. "And they know Rona won't waste time on an ambassador. She's not one to play by the rules."

"Are you nervous about seeing her again?" Elise asked him.

"Of course," he said. "I'm terrified, but I meant what I said on the night we first met. For you, I'd brave a thousand Ronas."

There was a sweet sentiment when he said it this time. All hints of fun and flirting were gone.

Elise felt her heart swell as they locked eyes once again. There was something magnetic about his stare that she had yet to understand. Fortunately, she was spared the hassle as Derek and Arymei summoned them back into the throne room.

Arymei grouped everyone who was traveling, including a handful of soldiers, in the center of the room. As she started waving her hands around, a bright light emitted from the queen's fingertips.

Derek held up his hand and joined in.

Elise was careful to keep a distance from him in case a shock jolted between them again.

Once the two rulers' magical energies combined, Elise felt wind rushing in her ears. It was an altogether different sensation than traveling through the diary. Rather than a suffocating pressure, she felt weightless. The throne room began to blur, and the next thing she knew, Elise could smell the overwhelming scent of salty water. In the distance, she could hear the cry of seagulls.

Vaughn reached over and intertwined their fingers together.

Elise joined her other hand with Darcie who also grabbed a hold of Mitch.

She closed her eyes and took a deep breath. Elise imagined her heart would burst from anticipation.

I'm coming, Gavin.

This was it. . .the moment she had waited for since leaving Haighdlen. A smile spread across her face as Vaughn squeezed her hand. She squeezed his hand back.

And then everything stopped.

CHAPTER 27

Gavin had imagined countless scenarios of what the moment would be like when he saw Elise again. Would she smile? Would she cry? In every instance, however, the overall outcome was happiness.

He wasn't prepared for the look of devastation and confusion that crossed her features when their group came face to face with his captors.

Rona waited by the water's edge with Gavin to her left and Brahm on the right. A dozen or more guards flanked them on either side.

Derek whispered something to his group that Gavin couldn't make out, but that he assumed was an inspirational pep talk. If that were the case, it wasn't very effective since no one on their side of the beach looked inspired. There was a collective expression of shock and fear among the new arrivals.

Regardless of the grave situation, Gavin's heart skipped a beat when he saw his friends. He fought the urge to run to them, knowing Rona wouldn't let him get far. He kept his feet in place while every fiber in his body lunged to be where he belonged.

When Elise saw him, Gavin's breath hitched, and he couldn't look away. With tear-stained cheeks and the ocean breeze blowing through her hair, she was breathtaking. He was afraid to blink in case this was all a dream or spell. In that moment, the two of them shared multiple silent exchanges with their eyes, both saying more than they ever could with actual words.

And then Gavin noticed Vaughn near one of Derek's guards. His elation came crashing to a halt as he locked eyes with the other man across the beach.

I could kill you for what you've done.

After all, it was Vaughn's fault Elise had been tricked and brought here under false pretenses. He was the reason Gavin couldn't be sure of Elise's true feelings anymore. There was enough anger and hate in Gavin's body to do something stupid, but the fear of Rona's power kept him still.

Derek took the first step towards Gavin's group.

"I never thought I'd see the day when King Derek would step on Lockesbarrian ground," Rona announced. A gleeful smile spread across her face. "Surprised to see me?"

The king stared at her but made no reply.

"How do you like my little welcome party?" Rona gestured around her. "A reigning king should have the royal carpet treatment after all."

"Release the boy, Rona," Derek said. His stoicism was commendable given how terrified Gavin felt witnessing the exchange.

"My, my, skipping the pleasantries I see." Rona smiled at Gavin before facing Derek again. "You also have something that belongs to me."

If Derek knew what she was hinting at, he didn't show it. Gasps and whispers spread through the group of onlookers behind him as Vaughn stepped out from among them and crossed the beach.

As he approached, Gavin kept his gaze on his friends. Mitch looked ready to pounce, much like Gavin, while Darcie stood frozen with her mouth open. It was Elise's reaction that broke Gavin's heart. He had never seen someone look so heartbroken and betrayed. Fresh bouts of tears fell down her cheeks and she kept shaking her head, mouthing something to Darcie that he couldn't make out.

As Vaughn approached, he kneeled before Rona until she signaled for him to stand near Brahm.

Derek beckoned Gavin forward, but as he stepped closer to the king, Rona held out her hand to stop him.

"Not so fast. A promise is a promise." She pulled out the diary and handed it to Gavin.

Gavin made eye contact with his friends again. All three of them craned their necks to see the infamous diary.

Everyone was still during the book exchange.

The only sounds came from the crashing waves and passing gulls.

Using his sleeve to wipe away the sea spray from his face, Gavin gauged his friends' reactions.

Mitch nodded for him to open it. Darcie mouthed the words, encouraging him to do the same. Elise, however, stared at the diary as if she wished it would catch on fire. Her entire demeanor had wilted the moment Vaughn walked the length of the beach. She looked so deflated by the whole encounter, Gavin questioned if she was even happy to see him.

"Be careful, Gavin," Derek warned.

"Nice try, Derek, but a deal is a deal," Rona argued. "He said he'd do it, and now he will."

Gavin stared down at the cover. How many times had Rona put him in this predicament? His hands shook as he gripped the sides. He dug the toes of his boots into the sand to ground himself from his growing anxiety. Again, he made the same argument in his head that had occurred before.

I don't know if this will take us home. I haven't helped free the other boys yet. I don't even know where they are.

Feeling the weight of everyone's eyes on him, Gavin stuck the tip of one finger between the pages.

"Don't do it!" cried Elise. She separated herself from the crowd and stepped up behind Derek. She ignored his suggestion to step back with the others and only spoke to Gavin. "This is what she wants, Gavin. You can't do it. We can get home another way."

He felt torn in both directions. "How?"

"I have a little power," Elise confessed, not knowing he was already aware. "But we still have some—" She tucked a hand down the front of her gown and felt up and down the bodice of her gown.

"Looking for this?" Vaughn asked, holding up the bottle necklace by its chain.

"What?" Elise's words came out in a breathless hiss. "But you gave it back to me. How did you get it?"

"It must've been while he was consoling you, dearest," Rona said as she held her hand out.

Gavin watched Elise's eyes widen as Vaughn handed over the fairy magic.

"Rare magic, indeed. So hard to come by, and almost certain to get you home." Rona shook the bottle back and forth, watching the contents swirl around before opening it. Looking down at Elise, Rona flipped it upside down without warning.

Gavin's heart shattered as Elise's guttural cry pierced the air. He watched her fall to her knees and stare in utter disbelief at what had just happened.

The magic illuminated the area it fell on momentarily before seeping into the ground.

Gavin tried to get to her, but Rona slapped a hand across his chest.

"Don't even think about it," she warned. "She's not your concern."

But she is *my concern!*

Darcie and Mitch ran up to join Elise. Darcie wrapped Elise in her arms and whispered in her ear. Although Elise's eyes were hidden by her hair, Gavin could hear her gut-wrenching sobs.

I'm opening the stupid book. This has gone on too long. Rona can do whatever she wants. I'm done. All I want is to go home with my friends.

"Rona, this ends today," Derek said. "You will not have any other kingdom, and this one is not yours either. Surrender." When Rona merely laughed, Derek hardened his tone and reached for his sword. Unsheathing it, he held the blade out towards her. "Surrender, witch! Or do you choose suffering?"

Rona chuckled.

I can't let Derek get hurt. I have to protect Elise's family and end this now.

Before she could respond to Derek, Gavin ripped open the book.

"Gavin, no!" Derek screamed, lunging for him, but it was too late.

Glancing down, Gavin saw the blank pages flipping rapidly in a rush of wind before getting distracted by the familiar choking sensation that accompanied a trip through the diary. Sand and sea foam began to stir up and swirl all around them. Gavin tried to run to Elise one last time, but Rona ripped the book out of his hand and pushed him down to the ground. As his vision swam, the last thing Gavin saw was Rona's magic shoot out from her hand in a bright flash that hit Derek square in the chest. He tried to process the screams and cries around him, but everything faded to black right as Derek's body hit the ground.

CHAPTER 28

Elise awoke on a hard wood floor that creaked beneath her as she sat up. Recognizing Joranna's house, Elise scrambled to her feet and realized she was the first to wake up.

"Hello? Nana?" she called out. There was no answer.

After shaking Darcie and Mitch until they stirred, Elise fell to her knees and leaned over Gavin. For a moment, she could only stare at him. It was so surreal to be this close to him that Elise had to convince herself she wasn't dreaming.

He's alive. . .and he's really here. We're together again!

Caressing his cheek, she whispered Gavin's name until he stretched with a groan. When he did wake and sit up, Elise practically knocked him over again when she threw her arms around his neck.

I can't believe I'm holding him. We did it!

Fresh tears spilled down her cheeks when she felt his arms wrap around her. The two sat together on the floor in a tight embrace for several minutes.

When they pulled apart to stand up, Gavin hugged Darcie before turning towards Mitch. He held out his arms and could see his best friend struggling to contain his emotions.

"It's okay to cry, Mitch," Gavin assured him.

Mitch sniffed and buried his face into Gavin's neck as he wrapped him in a fierce hug that was reciprocated.

The guys are together again. I was so afraid we'd never find him.

Overcome with emotion, Elise wiped her burning eyes with part of her sleeve as the reunion concluded. Everything was perfect. . . until Elise remembered what had just occurred back in Lockesbarrow.

"Oh my gosh, Derek!" she cried. "I've got to get back there and make sure he's okay!"

"Whoa, whoa, whoa." Gavin grabbed the sides of Elise's arms to calm her. "We don't know what exactly happened."

Elise knew deep down that Gavin had the same fears she did, but it frustrated her how calm he acted about it.

"Yeah, she could've killed him," Mitch said.

Elise didn't want to hear that. She couldn't accept that anything bad had happened to him. All she could focus on was getting back to see for herself. Despite her friends' pleas to sit down and relax, Elise knew she had to keep moving to keep her adrenaline from skyrocketing. Now that Gavin was safe, her anxiety transferred to Derek's wellbeing. Elise's mind kept replaying the memory of her grandfather falling to the ground from a blast of Rona's magic.

What about Joranna? Has anyone contacted her yet? I need to get back there!

"Elise!" Darcie's voice cried from the living room as Elise ran up the stairs. "Elise, the diary isn't here. You can't go back."

Shoot. She's right. There has to be somebody here who can help.

Elise began calling out her relatives' names one by one. When it was clear no one was home, she came down the stairs at a slower pace.

"No one's home and the diary's missing." Elise ran a hand through her hair. "How're we supposed to get back?"

"Why did it bring us here if no one's home?" Darcie asked, walking around the downstairs to double check they were the only ones there. "Are there any other cars out front?"

Gavin peeked out the window. "Only Mitch's."

"Thank God," Mitch replied as he stood up from the couch. "Let's get out of here."

He and Gavin made their way towards the front door. When Elise and Darcie didn't follow, they paused. "Y'all coming?"

Elise looked at them as if they were crazy and scoffed.

How am I supposed to leave? Nothing is fixed yet. I don't know why it brought us here, but we're not done. I have to get back and save Derek.

"I can't go home," she said. "You guys go."

"Sounds good. Come on, Gav," said Mitch.

Darcie pulled Mitch away from the door. "Guys, we can't leave Elise here alone."

There was a brief, awkward silence between the four of them as their initial joy and excitement faded.

When neither boy replied, Elise shook her head. "I can't believe you two are trying to leave."

She jumped when her phone started ringing from somewhere in the kitchen.

Darcie offered to get it and disappeared into the other room. When she returned, she held the phone out to Elise.

"You have two missed calls from your mom," she said, tucking her lips into a thin line.

Crap! She's probably on her way now. I'm running out of time.

"All the more reason to go home," Mitch said. "Let's go."

"You guys go. I have to figure out a way to get back." Elise examined Joranna's other books for any clues or helpful titles. "This would be a lot easier if we could just open the diary."

"Not necessarily," Gavin said. "When I opened it, it was blank."

"Blank?" Elise asked. "I thought it was only blank when someone other than one of us opens it."

"Me too," said Gavin. "But it was blank."

"What does that mean?" Mitch asked.

Elise sat down on the floor and cradled her head in her hands.

Why was it blank? It's always shown the entries when we've opened it. It worked for me, and it worked for Gavin that time he used it in Haighdlen. Is something wrong with the magic? Is that why nobody's here right now?

Elise steadied her breathing as she tried calming herself.

"Maybe it's a sign," Darcie chimed in. When the other three looked up in confusion, she grew animated and paced around the room. "Think about it. We've changed stuff in the past so much already, right? Maybe it's affecting what happened later."

That does make sense.

"So, you're saying, the rest of Haighdlen's future hasn't been decided yet?" Mitch asked.

"Exactly!" Darcie said.

"We've got to find a way to get back *now*," Elise replied as she began searching Joranna's cabinets.

"Good luck," Gavin called out. "Call us when you need a ride home."

Elise paused what she was doing and watched Gavin and Mitch walk out the front door. Crossing the room, she followed them out onto the moonlit porch. She watched helplessly as they approached the car.

Mitch opened the driver's side door and pulled his keys out from under the floor mat.

"Fine!" she called out before they sat down and closed the doors. Heat rushed to her cheeks. "Leave! Take the easy way out!"

The passenger door opened and Gavin got back out. A shiver ran down Elise's spine as he slammed the door shut and stomped back up to the porch.

Elise tilted her head back to look at his towering stature.

"The easy way?" he panted. He had never been this angry with her before. "You think I'm taking the easy way out? No, Elise, I'm taking the smart way out."

"I only meant—"

"No, you meant exactly what you said," he argued. "You have *no* idea what I've been through."

She could feel his breath on her face and for a moment, they only stared at each other. This was a side of him she wasn't used to seeing aimed at her.

He's right. I don't know what he's been through.

"Hey, guys, let's focus," Darcie said as she stepped outside as well. She waved for Mitch to exit the car and waited for him to sulk back up to the porch. "Let's go inside and figure out a plan. You guys can't leave yet."

It seemed that neither boy wanted to argue with Darcie and followed her back into the living room.

"We need a new plan. That's all," she said once everyone was situated. "Let's brainstorm some ideas."

"There's nothing to come up with," Mitch said. "There's no diary and none of Elise's relatives are here to send us back."

"He's right," Gavin said. "And Rona's probably already used the diary to go back in time."

"Why would she want to do that?" Darcie asked.

"And how could she?" Elise asked. "It's blank for anyone who wasn't sent back originally."

Gavin shrugged. "I'm just telling you what I know. She wants to go back and save her brother from being killed, and she grabbed it out of my hands while it was sending us. Maybe it let her use it too."

"I thought she wanted to gain power and take over the other kingdoms," Darcie said.

"She wants that too," Gavin replied.

There was a heavy silence as they all considered the possibility.

"This is all my fault," Elise said, lowering her head. "I used my magic to convince Derek to take us all to the beach. I was so desperate to save Gavin and get the diary, I didn't think about anything or anyone else."

"It wasn't just you, Elise," said Darcie, cradling her face with both hands. "We should've been smarter about Vaughn."

"I kept trying to tell you," Mitch offered. "I never trusted him."

Darcie rolled her eyes. "Not helping, Mitch."

"It all makes sense now, though," Elise added. "The long route, the broken wheel, all the thought manipulation and headaches. . .ugh, we were such idiots."

"He wasn't the only one manipulating people," Gavin said.

"Did she hurt you?" Elise whispered.

"It's done and over with. Let's keeping looking for clues to help you out, Elise."

"To help me?" she asked. "You're really not coming back with me?"

"Why, so you can flirt in front of my face this time?" he challenged. "If you're going to fall for someone else, I'd rather not be around to see it."

"It wasn't my fault!" she cried. "I never wanted him. He kept using magic on me. Darcie wanted him. Not me."

"It's not what it looked like," Gavin muttered.

"What it looked like?" Elise asked. "When did you see—"

"Oh, I saw plenty. Rona has her ways," Gavin said.

Elise folded her arms and scoffed. "From what I gather, she has her way with a lot of people. Were you one of them?" When Gavin didn't respond, Elise continued. "So, you can get mad at me for being tempted, but it's okay for you to be? It doesn't work like that, Gavin!"

"Maybe this isn't working," he snapped. "This. Us. All of it. What was the point? What have we accomplished? Rona still managed to hurt your grandfather, your mom still got pregnant, and Rona is out there making everyone miserable. Why? Why would you want to go back? What will it solve?"

He stomped out of the room to use the bathroom. Once he was out of sight, Elise allowed her tears to fall. She hadn't wanted him to see how much his words had stung, but now that he was gone, she fell apart.

Darcie sat down next to her and cradled Elise in her arms.

"Don't listen to him, Elise. He's stressed out and still dealing with everything that's happened. We did help your family."

"B-but h-he's right," she sobbed, soaking Darcie's sleeve. "Was any of it worth it?"

Darcie patted her arm and rocked her back and forth.

"You want the truth?" Mitch asked. "I think you've helped more than you give yourself credit for. We've all been through traumatic crap this week."

Gavin walked back into the room but didn't speak right away.

Elise wiped her eyes and leaned away from Darcie. Once she composed herself, she stood again. Pushing a rising bout of anxiety down, she looked up at Gavin.

"I'm sorry," she said. "You're right. I don't know what you went through, and if you want to go home, I won't stop you." She took a steadying breath before looking into his eyes. "It's just not time for me to be done yet."

Rather than argue, Gavin cupped her cheek and kissed her. His lips were soft, and she fell into his arms. Deepening the kiss, she held onto him as if he might vanish at any moment.

He pulled away and looked down at her. His expression softened. "I'm sorry too," he whispered.

Darcie squealed and clapped her hands.

"Aww, you guys are the cutest! Now that that's settled, let's figure out how're we're going back."

"I can go alone if y'all want," Elise offered.

"Shut up," Gavin said with a chuckle. "Something tells me Mitch and I would've ended up turning back around anyway." He wrapped an arm around Darcie's and Mitch's shoulders before nodding his head for Elise to join in the group hug. "Let's finish this the right way and save your family."

"We'll need some other kind of magic," Elise said. She considered her mother's drawing, but given that Ruby didn't have any magic, she trashed that idea. Had her grandmother told her about anything else magical that could help them?

"I'm going to keep checking drawers and closets for anything that might help," Darcie said.

Elise's eyes widened.

That's it!

"Darcie, you're a genius!" Elise raced to the closet and pulled out the pink silken scarf Joranna had shown her during Elise's first visit. "Nana said this was sewn by some kind of fairy and given to her by a fairy king. Maybe we can use this!"

She held it out for them to see.

"But it's a scarf," Mitch said.

Elise groaned. "Yes, but it's a *magical* scarf."

"Use it then. Try it!" Darcie said.

Elise looked up at Gavin, who nodded. She cleared her throat and held the fabric out in front of her. "Take us to Haighdlen!"

She waited for a portal, a flash, or even a heavy feeling in her chest. . .but nothing happened.

"Why isn't it working?" she asked.

Mitch shrugged. "Maybe because it's just a scarf."

Elise growled and stomped her foot.

"Ignore him, Elise," Darcie said. "How did it work the last time you used your magic?"

"I don't know," Elise said honestly. "I thought about what I wanted most."

"Then focus on that. Hold it up again and this time, really focus on what you want it to do. It's made by fairies. What would the fairies tell you to do?"

"Pay," Mitch muttered.

"Mitch! Ugh, quit interrupting!" Darcie said. She continued rambling about how unreliable he was whenever they were in a serious situation.

The two began bickering back and forth.

Gavin smiled. "Well, it looks like some things haven't changed too much," he whispered to Elise.

She chuckled. "Yeah. It's nice to see them back to normal."

He nodded towards the scarf. "Go ahead and try it again."

Elise took a deep breath and tried to tune out her friends' arguing.

We need to get to Derek. Take us to Derek. Show us what we need to do. Please. Please.

"Elise, it's working!" Darcie cried out.

Elise opened her eyes and saw that the scarf was glowing.

"So, we'll head back and check on Derek," Mitch said. "Then what? What about Rona?"

Elise grew solemn as she finally accepted and shared what she had already known for some time.

"It's going to have to be me," she said. "I'm going to have to defeat Rona." She waved away their arguments. "Guys, stop. Just grab on and let's handle it when we get there."

The next part of their journey would not be easy, but everything they had encountered was worth it to have Gavin back safely. She was thankful to have him, Darcie and Mitch by her side. No matter what challenges awaited them, Elise knew she already had everything she needed.

The Final Entry

CHAPTER 1

Elise Laurille knew better than to gamble with fairy magic. If her limited experience had taught her anything, it was that the outcome would *always* be the opposite of what she anticipated.

Why should I expect anything different this time?

Because there was no other choice.

She had already spent the better part of a week time traveling with friends through a diary to uncover secrets about her family's past. However, the clock in her grandmother's present-day living room showed she was only gone mere hours.

How can that be?

Elise nearly died seeking the identity of the spy responsible for the future downfall of her family's kingdom, Haighdlen. Not long after, Elise's boyfriend Gavin was kidnapped by the same elusive spy and forced to join Queen Rona's army. The journey to rescue him alone came with its own risks and revelations, resulting in the loss of more precious fairy magic that could've helped them along with the diary.

The same one Rona now possessed.

To make matters worse, Elise's grandfather Derek Laurille was struck by Rona's curse right as they were sent home. Now Elise and her three friends were left fearing Derek's fate as well as Rona's looming plans.

Still, something else plagued Elise's mind about returning to Joranna's house. . .apart from Gavin, Mitch, Darcie, and herself, no one was home. Her family should've been there, and Elise had a growing suspicion it had something to do with the fact that Gavin saw only blank pages in the diary before it brought them back.

Without it, Elise needed another source of magic to help the Laurille family. Since the extent of her newly discovered powers was uncertain, Elise prayed Joranna's antique scarf was the answer.

She gripped the silken fabric tightly. Sewn by fairies and gifted to Joranna by their king, its magic was the only chance Elise and her friends had to make it back to Haighdlen.

The irony of their situation didn't escape Elise's notice. After days of wishing and praying to return home, here they stood seeking a way back through another magical item.

Hoping to summon the scarf's magical energy, Elise clenched her eyes shut and focused on what she wanted most. She hadn't received proper training like her extended family, yet with every unsuccessful passing moment, her desperation grew.

We need to get to Derek. Take us to Derek. Show us what we need to do. Please. Please. The image of her grandfather falling after being struck with Rona's magic was all she could think about. *What if we're too late? What if we're stuck here? No, I can't think like that. I need to think about the magic. Focus, Elise.*

"Elise, it's working!" her best friend Darcie cried.

Elise, Gavin, Darcie, and Mitch all stared in awe as the scarf began to glow before them.

Yes! I can't believe it's actually working!

"So, we'll head back and check on Derek," said Mitch with a shrug. "Then what? What about Rona?"

After a tense silence, Elise straightened her shoulders and replied what she had already accepted in her heart. "It's going to have to be me. I'm going to have to defeat Rona."

Gavin, Mitch, and Darcie began to argue against her declaration, causing Elise to lose focus on the magic. As the illuminated garment flickered, she waved away their overlapping interruptions.

"Guys, stop. Just grab on, and let's handle it when we get there."

I don't expect them to understand. Not yet anyway.

A swell of energy coursed through Elise's fingertips once all the noise ceased, and she concentrated again.

Take us where we need to go. Please work. We need to get back.

"I don't like this," Mitch said, glancing around the empty room as if he expected a ghost to materialize from the walls. "It's just a scarf. You can't expect something to do what you want just because it might have a *little* magic."

Darcie shushed him.

Block him out. If you don't believe this will work, you'll never get back.

Again, the light flickered before dying out.

Darcie stomped her foot. "Ugh, see what you did, Mitch? You made Elise lose her concentration! Do you want this to work or not?"

"He's right though." Gavin stared at the scarf in Elise's hands. "Sure, fairies made it, but how do we know it can be a portal? Maybe it's just something they expected Joranna to wear."

Elise wilted. Was it so ridiculous to hope for a way back without her family's help? They had come this far, and risked too much, to try forgetting it all now. She met Gavin's gaze.

The two had yet to talk about what transpired while Gavin was captured, but Elise felt an awkward, ugly amount of tension festering between them. As much as she wanted to hear every detail, Elise knew her family's safety needed to come first.

Elise focused on the carpet rather than at any one of her friends. "Fine. We can forget it. Y'all can go home after all."

"Oh no, you don't." Darcie's pestering, bossy tone that she was known for pulled Elise out of her thoughts. "You can have your pity party later. No one's leaving except through *that* scarf. Now everybody shut up and let her concentrate. Go on, Elise."

Knowing better than to argue, Gavin and Mitch watched Elise expectantly.

She cleared her throat before trying again. . .and again.

"What if you tried wearing it?" Darcie offered.

Elise felt ridiculous but took her friend's suggestion anyway. *We've tried everything else.*

For a moment, she felt nothing but embarrassment with everyone's eyes on her. Before she could remove the garment, however, it began to shine so brightly that all four teenagers had to shield their eyes from the flash. Only when it dimmed could Elise process that someone was whispering in her ear. She looked over her shoulder towards the voice but didn't see anyone.

"Do y'all hear that?"

"Hear what?" Darcie asked.

"That voice." Elise turned in a full circle without finding the speaker. The whispers were so faint she couldn't make out actual words.

"Nobody's talking," said Gavin.

I'm hearing things. I've gone crazy.

Elise's heart raced as she yanked the scarf from around her neck and threw it on the ground. The voices stopped. She backed away from the pile of fabric and began pacing to steady her breathing. Despite her best efforts, she was unable to calm down before becoming enveloped in a full-blown panic attack.

She saw her friends' mouths moving, but her brain couldn't process what they were saying. They couldn't possibly understand the paralyzing fear jolting through her veins like electric shocks. From a young age, Elise feared her anxiety would cause a nervous breakdown, and hearing voices no one else could triggered the nightmare within her. It felt real in a way she couldn't put into words.

Elise's shallow breaths came faster and faster until she thought she would pass out or throw up. Either outcome would be welcome. She hated this part. It didn't matter if it was the hundredth time or more, they all felt like the first one.

She started to leave the room, a common coping mechanism that usually helped, but froze when Gavin grabbed her hand. Elise's thoughts raced like a tornado as sweat coated both of her palms.

I'm crazy. I've finally gone crazy. I knew this would happen. I'm hearing things that aren't there. Nobody else heard it. That's not good. That's not good. Why did we ever come here? What are they thinking about me now? Gavin's going to leave me for sure. He knows I'm insane.

"Elise, calm down," Mitch said.

Tears welled up in Elise's eyes. She couldn't look at anyone. Through her mental fog, she caught pieces of her friends' conversation.

"Don't say that," Darcie snapped. "She hates that. Plus, it doesn't work. She has to come out of it on her own."

Elise stared down at her hand as Gavin squeezed it. Closing her eyes, she forced herself to exhale slowly. As her breathing relaxed, she thought back to when Gavin saw her panic for the first time while rowing on a lake. He had been so patient and helpful, much like he was at that moment.

All signs of irritation were gone now as he rubbed small circles on the back of Elise's hand while assuring her that she was safe. If Gavin noticed how clammy her skin was, he didn't show it.

At long last, the turbulent storm clouds of doubt and fear parted, and she could process everything again. Pulling away from Gavin, she wiped both palms dry on her skirt. Right on schedule, shameful tears stung the back of her eyes. "I'm sorry," she whispered.

This is so embarrassing. I don't want to be this way. I wish I could make it stop.

"Don't be," Gavin said. He hesitated before wrapping his arms around her.

As both stood in a silent embrace, the fabric of Gavin's collared shirt tickled her nose. Elise inhaled his familiar scent and felt her remaining tension vanish as she melted against him.

I missed you.

He kissed the top of her head. "I'm right here. You're safe."

She tightened her hold on him as if he were the source of her oxygen.

"What did you hear?" Mitch asked when Elise and Gavin pulled apart.

"I-I couldn't make it out, but I also didn't feel in control of myself, and that's always been a fear of mine." When no one responded, she felt the need to elaborate. "That one day I'm going to go crazy, and no one will want to be around me." She let out a dry, hollow chuckle, trying anything to lighten the mood and distract herself from more irrational thoughts. "I guess it. . .freaked me out. That's all. I'm sorry."

"Don't be and quit apologizing. That'd freak me out too," Darcie said. Giving her friend a hug, she looked down at the scarf. "But you know you have to put it back on, right?"

I was afraid she'd say that.

"You don't have to," Gavin said. "We can find another way."

"Like what?" Mitch argued. "It's the only other thing we know that has magic."

"A minute ago, you doubted this whole plan," Darcie pointed out. "What changed?"

"The scarf is talking to her." Mitch pointed at the garment. "*Something* was working. Put it on again."

When Elise hesitated, Gavin picked the scarf up and held it out towards Mitch, who flinched. "See? You're scared of it too. So, leave her alone, okay?"

"Hey, I almost died out there, man! Forgive me if I don't trust any of this crap."

Gavin glared at his best friend. "You're not the only one."

Elise felt a shiver course down her spine. She had so much to learn about Gavin's terrible endeavor in Lockesbarrow. The truth was, they had *all* struggled in one way or another, and if she didn't do everything she could to end this forever, what was the point of entering the diary in the first place?

Mustering what little courage she could, Elise took the scarf from Gavin and wrapped it around herself once more.

"Try to focus on what the voice is saying," Darcie insisted.

Elise nodded before closing her eyes.

At first, she could only hear her own uneven breathing. Then, following a familiar flash of light, the whispering resumed.

Goosebumps prickled her arms as her anxious thoughts screamed out to flee the situation. Elise's toes curled as she rocked back and forth, determined to stay put and hear the words. Ignoring

Darcie, who shushed Mitch again, Elise was surprised to realize that the voice was growing louder. . .

A beating heart in every stitch,
Doomed follies on the rise,
One need only summon truth,
To conquer grounded lies.

Elise's brows furrowed as the riddle repeated three more times.

What are 'grounded lies'? They're going to flip out when I tell them. It doesn't make any sense. I'll never get us back to Haighdlen at this rate.

Elise sighed as she removed the scarf from around her neck. Did she want to defeat Rona? Yes. Did she want to save Derek? Of course, but if she were being honest with herself, all of that seemed out of reach.

I can't tell them how I really feel. I put them all up to this. They're here because of me. How would they react if I admitted that I want to go home after all?

At that moment, the scarf flashed like a bolt of lightning, causing all four to jump back with cries of terror.

The light flickered before burning so brightly, Elise couldn't look directly at it.

Is this working? Is it finally going to take us to Derek?

Elise chuckled in disbelief before urging her friends to grab onto the silken garment.

Hearing the echoing riddle ringing in her ears—this time as an urgent chant—Elise watched as Darcie grabbed Mitch's wrist before stuffing a piece of scarf into his hand at the last second before all went dark.

CHAPTER 2

Elise moaned as her muscles spasmed. Struggling to stand, she felt as if her limbs were made of concrete. She took in the surrounding forest area. If the bright crisp gold and reddish orange foliage was anything to go by, it was autumn. Unable to discern if the scarf sent them all backwards or forward in time—or even to Haighdlen, for that matter—Elise felt her barely quenched anxiety resurface.

This isn't where we left before. Are we in Haighdlen? Where is everybody? Derek isn't here.

Dusting the dirt off her dress, Elise felt a sharp pain against both palms where splinters had pierced into her skin upon landing. She was able to pull three out on her own, but the remaining ones proved to be too deep. She then attempted to remove twigs that were tangled within her hair.

The sound of crunching leaves made her jump, but she visibly relaxed when she saw Gavin.

"A little scraped, but not too bad. You?" He chuckled as Elise's fingers got caught. "Here, let me help." Gavin removed the offending twig she had been after and tossed it onto the ground. After she thanked him, he shrugged with a small smile before the same awkward silence from before filled the air between them.

Elise broke eye contact first and glanced around. "Have you seen Darcie and Mitch?"

Gavin pointed over his shoulder. "Mitch is snoring away somewhere over there."

Elise's brief smile fell when he didn't continue. Her brows creased. "And Darcie?"

"I haven't seen her."

The color drained from Elise's face.

Did she not make it back with us? Is she still at Nana's?

Whirling around, Elise cried out Darcie's name before Gavin shushed her.

"Cut it out!" he hissed. "We don't know where we are or what's here!"

"How else are we going to find Darcie?" she argued.

"By staying alive long enough to look for her!"

Elise hated to admit he had a point, and perhaps screaming at the top of her lungs in a strange place probably *wasn't* the brightest idea.

"What're y'all fighting about?" Mitch stumbled through the piles of leaves and fallen branches. With an audible yawn and wearing a bemused expression, he rubbed the back of his neck. "Where's Darcie?"

When Elise informed him that she was missing, all traces of drowsiness vanished from his face. Instantly alert, Mitch's movements took on a frenzied, hectic state as he sidestepped the other two.

Elise and Gavin followed his lead. For the next half hour, the three scoured the surrounding woods looking for their friend.

"She's not here, guys," Gavin called out, waving the others over to him.

"We can't stop. We have to keep looking." Panting, Mitch continued to scan the area. A layer of sweat glistened along his furrowed brows. "She could be unconscious somewhere."

"Do we know if she made it here at all?" Gavin asked, echoing Elise's previous fear. "Maybe she's still at Joranna's house."

"This is great. Just great." Mitch raked a hand through his hair as he paced around the other two. "Let's head back and check. Where's the scarf?"

Crap. He's going to kill me.

"I-I don't have it," Elise confessed. She held out both palms. "It was missing when I woke up."

Mitch looked from Elise's empty hands to her face with a scowl.

Anticipating an outburst, Elise stepped closer to Gavin. "We'll find her. I promise." She could tell by the way his nostrils flared, coupled with the twitching muscle in his cheek, that Mitch wasn't convinced.

He hung his head. When he finally spoke, Mitch' voice sounded flat, defeated, and lifeless.

"How many times am I going to regret not getting in my car?" He clenched both fists by his sides before sucking in a breath through gritted teeth. "It's either prison, magic, or a near-death experience. Are we just supposed to keep blindly following you?"

His stare pierced through Elise's eyes, sending a cold chill down her spine.

"Mitch, I understand—"

"No, you don't understand," he snapped. "That's the problem. You don't understand anything that's going on. We keep getting by with dumb luck, but you're going to get us killed. If anything happens to her—"

"Hey! Ease up, man." Stepping between them, Gavin rested a hand on Mitch's chest.

"No, *you* ease up!" Mitch shoved Gavin away from him. "Aren't you tired of it? Gav, you got ripped away from home, kidnapped, and somehow made it back alive. We had the chance to go home. We could've avoided all of this! Derek was always going to die, so why do we care?"

Did he really just say that?

Mitch jerked his chin towards her. "How do we know she's not using her magic on us right now?"

Elise's chest fluttered as a fresh bout of anxiety did a somersault in her stomach.

"Mitch, go cool off," Gavin warned. "*Now.*"

"Or what?" Mitch argued.

Although Gavin was often the calmer of the two, Elise knew her boyfriend also possessed an untamed temper when provoked. Gavin's stiffened shoulders made Elise wonder if their altercation would turn physical.

I have to do something. This isn't going to help us find Darcie.

Someone was going to get hurt. She just got Gavin back, and Mitch had also recently suffered a near-fatal encounter in Lake Mirage. Tensions were high as it was. They didn't need to start turning on each other.

Elise touched Gavin's elbow before stepping in front of him. "Both of you need to stop. This isn't going to get Darcie back."

"We wouldn't have to if we had gone home in the first place," Mitch countered.

Heat rushed to Elise's cheeks as she glared at him. Deep down, she knew his anger spurned from worrying about Darcie, but that didn't give him any excuse to attack her. "Will you get over that already?" Elise snapped. "You're here now."

"Because of *you*!" He sneered at her. "All of this is because of you."

"Shut up, Mitch," Gavin said. "I swear, if you don't back off and—"

"It's *always* going to be something with her, Gav!" Mitch blurted out before Gavin pushed him to the ground.

Elise couldn't admit it out loud, but having Gavin stand up for her meant more than he would ever know. However, it was hard watching the two friends fight.

This is *all my fault.*

Ignoring Mitch's grumbling, Gavin turned back to look at Elise. "Can your magic help us? Or that voice you heard? What did it say?"

In all the excitement, Elise had forgotten about the voice. She closed her eyes and tried to remember the riddle. "Something about a beating heart, rising follies, finding truth, and grounded lies."

Gavin tilted his head as a line appeared between his brows. "What does that mean?"

"Nothing." Mitch dusted himself off as he got back up on his feet. "It doesn't mean anything. It's another distraction to throw us off."

I wish I had the scarf with me right now. How did that stupid riddle go? "'*A beating heart in every stitch,*'" she began, struggling to piece the puzzle together. "Doomed rising, no, '*doomed follies on the rise.*'"

Am I even making sense? Seeing Mitch roll his eyes, Elise supposed not. She wiped both hands along her skirt, immediately regretting it due to the splinters, and paced while collecting her thoughts. "One should find the truth. . .Um, '*one need only s-summon truth,* and. . .'"

Mitch growled as he turned and punched the nearest tree.

Elise flinched when she heard his painful grunts. "'*To conquer grounded lies.* That's it!" She repeated the entire riddle.

"I still don't—" Gavin paused, watching Mitch shake his injured hand. "I still don't know how that can help us."

"Me neither." Elise took a deep breath. Maybe it was time to tell him they landed there because she wished to go home, not knowing the scarf would follow its own path. "But I think I know why—"

She froze. Only when Mitch stopped grumbling could she hear it again. It was a familiar noise that sounded like. . .snickering. Her heart threatened to leap out of her chest. There was only one sort of creature she knew that snickered like that. . .

Fairies!

"Do y'all hear that?" she hissed, silencing the boys who had begun to argue again. For a moment there was only the surrounding sounds of nature—birds chirping, the wind whistling through the overlapping trees. . .and there it was again! Elise jerked her head upwards, convinced she had seen a small ball of light disappear into the thick coverage of leaves above them.

"Ugh, not again. Please, no." Mitch tilted his head back with a groan as he cradled his injured hand. "Not them."

"Hello?" Elise shouted up into the trees. She shielded her eyes against the harsh rays of sun that managed to penetrate the foliage. "Can you hear me?"

"Elise, what are you doing?" Mitch asked. "Don't get them involved!"

"Right now, they're our only chance to find Darcie," she snapped. When he didn't reply, she called out again.

"Maybe he's right, Elise," Gavin said, cutting off one of Elise's attempts. "Let's try something else."

This time, no less than six balls of light emerged and hovered over their heads.

Mitch backed away before shielding his eyes. "Cover your eyes guys. Their dust *really* stings."

Elise thought back to the night they followed her mom through the forest. Mitch was hit directly in the eyes with fairy dust. She couldn't blame his hesitation to get the mischievous creatures involved, but she had to try. Elise couldn't make out any of their faces from where she stood, but she made the attempt to look at each fairy as she spoke. "We used the scarf you gave Queen Joranna, but I think something went wrong."

"Of course, something went wrong!" a squeaky voice called down from one of the lights. "It wasn't yours to use, now, was it?"

"Typical human," said another, clicking its tongue. "Stealing whatever they want."

Don't fairies take whatever they want too?

"I say we kill them now and be done with it," suggested a third voice with a drawl of boredom.

A sickening sense of dread pooled into the pit of Elise's stomach as the other lights bounced in agreement.

"We're not afraid of you," said Gavin.

Elise shook her head as Mitch uncovered his eyes.

What is Gavin doing?

"Gav, shut up! What're you trying to do?" Mitch hissed. He ignored Gavin's attempt to shush him, and instead closed the distance between them. "We won't find Darcie if they put some stupid curse on us."

"Wise words coming from the foolish one," one of the lights called out before a ring of laughter spread again.

Mitch glared up at the taunting fairies. "Go ahead, Elise. Set them on fire or something."

Elise suppressed a smile at the idea she could control any type of magic with that kind of precision. Mitch hadn't been far off when he labeled their progress 'dumb luck'.

"Look. Can you help us or not?" Gavin asked the fairies.

"Now, that depends," said a deep, alluring voice to their right, "on whether or not you *want* to be helped."

All three teenagers jumped as a tall, mysterious man emerged from behind a tree.

Who is that? Has he been there the whole time? At first captivated by his regal robe dragging through the multicolored leaves, Elise's mouth dropped open when she noticed an impressive pair of wings.

"Bow to King Horanis!" shrieked one of the fairies before all of them landed on the nearest branch with a bow of their own.

Horanis? But he's so. . .can he really be a fairy? He's bigger than we are!

Elise felt Gavin tug on her sleeve. He and Mitch were already kneeled on either side of her, most likely feeling the same stunned, speechless terror she was. Following their lead, she hiked up her skirt while bending down.

"Hello, Elise," said the winged man.

Elise felt as if she swallowed a jagged icicle. She was frozen to the spot, unable to form a response. King Horanis was nothing like she expected, *if* she ever thought about him before. Both of her arms felt numb, and she made the mistake of looking directly at his face. Heat rushed to her cheeks. "H-how do you—"

"Oh, you're very well-known in *our* kingdom." Horanis circled around them, much like a predator would its prey, but kept his eyes on her.

Elise's heartbeat throbbed in her ears as she stared into his piercing gray eyes. Words poured from Horanis's mouth like warm honey, and his chiseled features were that of a man in his mid-to-late thirties, but she knew better than to judge a magical being by appearances only. Intimidated by the king's unwavering stare, Elise looked down at the ground where fallen twigs snapped beneath his feet as he walked. A pile of leaves dragged behind his garment.

"*Your* kingdom?" Gavin asked. "Aren't we in Haighdlen?"

Horanis paused in front of them. "You were. Now you're not. There are kingdoms *within* kingdoms."

Elise and the boys exchanged dubious glances.

"I don't get it," Mitch said. "We never left the forest."

Horanis smirked as he regarded him with menacing amusement. "And unless you return my scarf to me, your beautiful friend won't either."

CHAPTER 3

"Simply produce my scarf, and you may have her back." Horanis's already regal stance was amplified by his impressive wingspan as he studied them. Had he not just confessed to holding Darcie captive, Elise would've found him irresistible. He resembled the majestic, domineering creatures she had only read about in storybooks. There was a silky, seductive—no, *ethereal*—quality to the way Horanis moved and spoke that kept Elise on edge, anticipating what he would do next. In the back of her mind, she wondered if his appeal was purposefully controlled through his magic to lure people in.

Did he lure Darcie in? Is she hurt? Will he kill her?

"W-we don't have it," Elise said. "It disappeared when we landed here."

"Pity." Horanis shrugged as if he had only misplaced a common trinket before stroking his chin. "She will make a perfect wife for one of my lords."

Mitch leapt to his feet with startling speed. He tightened both fists until his knuckles turned white. However aggressive he may have wanted to come across, Mitch was meek compared to the fairy king.

Horanis chuckled. "She is already spoken for, I see." He sized Mitch up and down before his face split into an impish grin. "What is she worth to you?"

"Look around." Gavin spread his arms out on either side. "We don't have anything to give. Just free her already."

"I'm afraid that's not how this works." Though replying to Gavin, Horanis kept his eyes on Mitch while he spoke. "Make an offer."

Mitch relaxed both hands, but his skin remained splotched and heated.

Elise wondered if the king enjoyed getting her friend worked up. Given Horanis's perverse merriment, she assumed he must do this sort of thing all the time. She watched a multitude of emotions play across Mitch's face, ranging from calculating, fearful, to rage. His raw, unchecked vulnerability unnerved her.

Mitch is going to lose it any second now. He looks insane.

Elise jumped when Gavin squeezed her hand, luckily avoiding the sore skin. *He's scared too.*

Horanis, however, wasn't at all fazed by Mitch's temperament.

Mitch's shoulders fell as he hung his head. "Then what?" His voice was lifeless, resigned, and Elise hardly recognized him.

"We negotiate a trade." Horanis swiped a long lock of hair out of his eyes before he gestured towards the forest path. "Then you all go skipping about on your journey."

Don't do anything stupid, Mitch. We don't have anything to give them. There has to be another way. Elise waited with bated breath for one of the two men to speak. *And if we don't?* "What if we don't?" Elise asked, surprising herself by blurting the thought out loud.

The fairy king shrugged once more. "Then we have reached an impasse and I must kill you."

How can he be so calm about all this? You'd think he was discussing the weather!

"Mitch, let's go," Gavin said. "We'll try to find the castle. Maybe they can give us something to trade so we can—"

"No." Mitch shook his head but kept his eyes on Horanis as if expecting the king to spring a sneak attack.

"Gavin's right," said Elise. *That's a great idea. We can get what we need and come back for Darcie without anyone getting hurt.* "We can come right back—"

"I said *no!*" Mitch snapped.

Elise looked up at Gavin, who shook his head not to say anything. Both watched as Mitch and Horanis squared off, ready to make a deal. Horanis's anticipation was palpable, and his eyes glinted with mischief, reminding Elise of a crooked salesman. There was no way they could trust anything he said. *Mitch has to know this guy won't play fair. What's he doing? Why won't he listen?*

Another agonizing moment of silence passed. Taking one last look around the forest, Mitch took a deep breath and cleared his throat. "Let her go. Take me instead."

What!

The forest came alive as both the visible and hidden fairies chimed out their excitement. There were snickers, laughs, and jeers coming from all directions, all encouraging Horanis to take the offer while Gavin and Elise pleaded for Mitch to stop.

Elise watched as the trees shook violently, sending a flock of startled birds flying into the sky with wild chirps and squawks as well as autumn leaves fluttering to the ground.

"Ooh, take the deal!" said a twinkling voice louder than the rest. It belonged to a ball of light that bounced back and forth between Mitch and Horanis. After a couple of somersaults, it lowered onto Horanis's shoulder before dimming out to reveal a small fairy girl.

Hey, wait a minute. I know that fairy.

"Thicket?" Elise asked.

Thicket smiled, crinkling her freckled nose, before speaking into Horanis's ear. "Can I have him? Please?"

"No! You got the last two. It's *my* turn to torture!" said a gruff little voice.

Elise recognized the second voice as Hemlock, an irritable yet equally mischievous fairy. *There were always three of them together. Where's Sage?* She looked up into the trees, but didn't see the younger, wiser fairy who had always helped her.

Thicket and Hemlock argued until their mousy voices overlapped one another.

Elise winced against the ringing in her ears. *Ugh, I wish they'd stop. I'm getting a headache. What do they even want Mitch or Darcie for?*

Horanis massaged the bridge of his nose before commanding they be quiet. "You must forgive my children. They can be quite a nuisance."

Children! Horanis is their dad?

The startling confession rendered the three teenagers speechless. Elise stared between the fairies, while Gavin and Mitch gaped at each other. The latter looked as if he were attempting to solve an advanced calculus problem in his head.

"So. . .are they," Mitch asked Horanis, struggling to find the words as he pointed above his head, "are all of these your kids?"

The branches of the surrounding trees shook with howling laughter. Elise supposed there must have been at least a hundred more hidden fairies in the area.

Horanis struggled to hide his humor as he regarded the three travelers. The corners of his mouth curved upward into a wry smile. "These three are plenty, I assure you." He cleared his throat before continuing. "But enough of this nonsense. Where's Sage?"

"I'm here, Father."

Elise's heart fluttered when she saw the smallest blond fairy responsible for their past triumphs land on Horanis's other shoulder. Even in the presence of his father, the little fairy wore a solemn, stoic expression.

I'm so glad to see him! He'll help us for sure.

"Sage, there you are." Horanis held his hand out towards Mitch. "You remember our gallant young friend here. He's just offered himself to take the girl's place. What say you to this?"

"Why do you seek his advice?" Hemlock asked. "I'm older than him."

"Or me," Thicket pouted. "I'm the oldest!"

"Silence, you two!" Horanis hissed. "I've decided that since Sage has yet to receive a human, I'm giving him the choice of which one he'd like."

Thicket crossed her arms with a petulant scowl.

Hemlock, on the other hand, flew to hover in front of Horanis's face. "Father, no! Sage has done nothing but disgrace us in front of these humans. He's helped them multiple times despite our objections and doesn't deserve such a choice!"

"Hemlock's right, Father." Thicket pointed to Gavin. "We nearly died in a fire the last time we helped *that* one."

The blood drained from Elise's face. *What are they talking about? What fire?* She still had so much to learn about what really happened when Gavin was captured by Rona. Elise looked up at her boyfriend, but he shook his head to drop it.

"Is this true, Sage?" the fairy king asked. "Are you helping humans without charge?"

"I've always required payment," Sage replied, "but I have accepted less than most would with regards to *her*."

Elise gulped when Horanis and Sage looked at her. *What're they going to do?*

"You detected it as well?" Horanis asked.

Detected what?

Sage nodded. "I did."

What're they talking about?

"As I expressed to them before, she has a caged power within her," Sage added. "A purity that Rona both craves and fears."

Horanis hummed. "Let us hope you are right. However, there's still the choice between our hero here and the maiden. Which would you prefer to take?"

As pale as Sage was, Elise believed Mitch surpassed him. Her friend's face was as white as a ghost. Though he tried to harden his stance, Elise could see his hands shaking.

Thicket and Hemlock whispered their choices into Sage's ear, but he paid them no heed.

Elise bit her lip as he scanned the area. As much as she appreciated his help, Sage always took forever to speak or make decisions. Elise swallowed a groan and suppressed the urge to stomp her foot. Offending the *one* fairy who would most likely help them wasn't the smartest plan.

At long last, the smallest fairy answered. "I desire neither."

"What a waste, as usual." Thicket clicked her tongue. "Can we not banish him already, Father?"

"I'd never turn away such a prize," said Hemlock. "The girl is lovely, yet Sage turns his nose up at her. Nothing is ever good enough for him."

Horanis turned to face Sage with furrowed brows. "Why will you not choose?"

If Sage was intimidated by the discerning looks aimed at him, he didn't show it. "I don't possess the same visceral need for torture. I have no need of a human." He glanced over at Mitch. "His sacrifice for her release should be payment enough to let them both go."

Elise thought Thicket would explode. The fairy's face was an ugly shade of purple as her face contorted with rage. Hemlock wasn't any better, ripping at his hair as he paced on a nearby branch.

Horanis isn't going to like Sage's answer. Maybe I can make a deal with them instead.

Elise licked her lips as she mustered the courage to interrupt the fairies. "What if I made a deal of my own?"

Thicket, Hemlock, and Sage hovered in balls of light near Horanis's face as the fairy king studied her. The balls of light whispered into his ear, but she couldn't hear what they were saying. "Did you not say there is no scarf nor money? Please enlighten us as to why we should hear any offers."

"What are you doing?" Gavin whispered.

Elise felt her stomach do a somersault as her knees began to buckle. She took a deep steadying breath, willing the panic attack that was creeping up to go away. With a hopeless sense of dread, she looked down at her shoes as she addressed the family of fairies. *Here goes nothing.* "I would like for you to give us our friends back and send us to Haighdlen Castle."

Crossing his arms, Horanis scoffed. "Anything else?"

Elise made herself look up. She knew by the glint in his eyes that he was only humoring her, like an adult speaking to a child about Santa Claus. Beside her, Gavin rocked back and forth as if itching to add something. When he met her eyes, she nodded for him to add something.

"I also want my friend's medallion."

What friend is he talking about? I have way too many questions for him if we ever get out of here.

Hemlock spluttered. "What makes you think we have it?" Puffing out his small chest, he glared at Gavin, Mitch, and Elise.

"It's been months!" Thicket added.

"I know you're all greedy hoarders who will keep something as long as it hurts someone else," Gavin said.

He's going to get us killed! To Elise's surprise, Thicket beamed with pride as she landed on her father's shoulder.

"Indeed." Thicket gestured for the other two to land as well. "It's always worked out for you before. You could sound a *bit* more grateful."

"That's right," said Hemlock. "We've done nothing but save your foolish necks. It's never enough, is it? Look at you, making demands again. Let's take all four of them, Father. They've had more than enough chances."

"My disobedient children make a fine point," Horanis said. "But let me see if I've got this right. You wish for me to release your friends, send you all to the castle, *and* return a traded medallion. . .for nothing?"

It does sound stupid. No one in their right mind would make a deal like that. We're dead for sure. "I'm going to take care of Rona. If you help me, I can save everyone."

After a brief pause, the trees shook again as waves of laughter erupted from the colony of fairies. Horanis joined them.

Elise felt two inches tall, but she didn't want to let them know they had gotten to her. She couldn't blame them. There was nothing about her appearance or past that would suggest she could destroy an evil sorceress. "I know it sounds crazy, but—" as she pointed a finger at her chest, something crinkled against her skin. Elise pulled out the picture her mother had drawn during Ruby's fifth birthday party. As wrinkled and stained as the paper was, Elise could still make out herself and Ruby on a unicorn together. She ran her fingers across the page, remembering that fateful night. Not only had a fire been set in her bedroom, but it was also when she and Gavin kissed for the first time in the royal gazebo. Elise looked up at Gavin, who shook his head.

"Elise, don't. That means so much to you."

Elise sniffed and blinked back oncoming tears. *I don't see how they would use it, but it's all I have to give. We need Darcie and Mitch safe before we can go to the castle. I don't know what that medallion means, but it's obviously important to Gavin, so it's worth it.* Holding the drawing high in the air, she cleared her throat. "Would you accept this?"

Shaking his head, Horanis chuckled again. "Absolutely not. I cannot—"

"*I* accept it." All eyes turned to Sage on Horanis's right shoulder. "I will help you get to Haighdlen Castle and try retrieving the medallion."

"Sage, what has possessed this sort of behavior?" Horanis asked his son.

Before Sage could answer, Thicket tugged on a strand of Horanis's hair. "We've tried telling you this for years, Father. Ever since that girl showed up, he's done nothing but defy your rules."

"He's damaging our reputation, no, *your* reputation," Hemlock argued. "He's giving away everything for a filthy piece of paper. And what for?"

"*It* is valuable," Sage replied. "If you ceased your bickering a moment, you would sense its value to her. A sacrifice of this magnitude is worth a great deal. It is difficult for her to part with it." Sage's wings hung low behind him as he looked at Elise. "I take no pleasure in causing you pain, but I must take payment for such demanding favors."

I understand. Elise nodded while trying to keep tears from falling. She suspected that Sage sensed this too.

"No, you must take *more* payment!" Thicket hissed. "She asked for three favors—that's three transactions!"

"I don't wish to play this game any longer," Sage replied. "Father, please use the scarf and help them. Find other humans to play with, for these have important fates."

How does he know that? Wait, did he say scarf?

"Hold up," Mitch said. "What scarf?"

Sage ignored him. "She's given all she has, is the only one able to vanquish Rona, and stands the only chance of setting the timeline right."

Okay, Mitch heard him too. He said scarf. What timeline is he talking about? What's wrong with it?

Horanis looked between Mitch, Gavin, and Elise. Several moments passed as he assessed them individually.

Elise blushed under the king's stare, especially when he stopped to give her his undivided attention. She tried avoiding his eyes, but something pulled her gaze to him.

Please. Please let us go. I need my friends with me, and we need to get to my family. I can't wait much longer.

"Fascinating." Horanis hummed again before addressing the three travelers. "Very well. My son makes a compelling argument. I shall send you to Haighdlen Castle. On my terms, of course." He pulled the silk scarf from his sleeve and shook it out.

"Are you kidding me?" Mitch roared. "*You've* had it this whole time? And you were going to punish us?"

"But why?" Gavin asked.

"Because I could," Horanis said with a shrug. "It was a great game while it lasted, but Sage is right. If you're going to mend the timeline, you'd best be off."

Elise couldn't hold her curiosity in any longer. "What timeline are you talking about?"

"The one Rona created," Thicket said. "She's gone and altered time itself."

"Nothing is as it should be," Hemlock said. "You'll see."

"She has the diary," Elise said to Gavin. "Do you think she's changed anything about my family?"

"You need to go. Now," said Sage. He nodded towards Thicket and Hemlock, who flew over to collect the drawing in Elise's hand before giving it to Horanis. They both disappeared into the tallest tree behind them before everything grew still. Less than five minutes passed before they returned with a medallion dangling between them.

Gavin reached up and caught it in midair. He ran his thumb across it with an unreadable expression that pulled at Elise's heart.

Who does it belong to?

"Now, where's Darcie?" Mitch spun around as if Darcie would appear out of thin air. "I want to get out of here."

"All in good time," Horanis said, examining the drawing. "Such sentimental value." He turned to face his youngest son. "Does this satisfy you?" When Sage nodded, the fairy king continued. "Very well. Despite our interference, it appears my son is pleased with your deal."

"Great," Elise said. "Now, what can you tell me about this timeline problem?"

"Oh, I could tell you plenty," Horanis moaned. "But I won't."

"Figures," Mitch whispered under his breath.

"I will leave you with this," the fairy king added as the scarf began glowing in his hands. "It won't do any good to ask anyone else. They won't know anything other than their current reality."

"Then how can we fix it?" Gavin called out as the wind picked up.

Autumn leaves began swirling as the scarf burned brighter. Horanis smiled with a wink. When he spoke, his voice echoed around them as he shrunk down to the size of the other fairies inside a glowing orb of light. "Forget what you know."

What does that mean? Elise screamed when the scarf flashed like a firework. She shielded her eyes and clung onto Gavin. *What's happening?* The forest grew dark as the sound of Horanis's sinister laughter faded into the distance.

CHAPTER 4

Elise gasped as she was shaken awake. Gavin's hand rested on her shoulder, and it took a moment to realize where she was. Although covered in the same autumn blanket of leaves, there was no mistaking the manicured beauty of the royal garden. She smiled up at Gavin before memories of fairies came flooding back to her. Bolting upright, Elise scrambled to her feet. *Where's Darcie? Did she make it?*

Her breath hitched when she saw Mitch sitting next to Darcie's unconscious body. Mitch looked up at her with bloodshot eyes. He wiped his hand across them as Elise knelt across from him.

"She should be awake by now. I've tried everything." Mitch's shallow breath rattled in his chest as he shook Darcie's shoulder like Gavin had done to Elise. "Her breathing's not right either. Something's wrong."

Panic flooded Elise's body. "Are you sure?" She placed her ear against Darcie's chest. Elise could hear a faint heartbeat, but it certainly wasn't following a steady pattern. *Darcie, no. No, you can't do this. You can't.* She clasped her hands on top of one another like Vaughn taught her when they saved Mitch from deadly mermaids. Each attempt pushed the splinters deeper into her skin, but she ignored the pain. After twenty or thirty compressions, Elise paused again to listen for a stronger heartbeat. "Gavin, maybe you should try."

"I've tried all of it." Mitch's voice was lifeless as he looked down at Darcie. His features darkened as he clenched his jaw. "It would be like the fairies to kill her, anyway, wouldn't it?" he choked out. When Elise didn't answer, he spun around and doubled over as his body shook with broken sobs.

Gavin placed a hand on his best friend's shoulder, but Mitch pulled away. Shaking his head, Mitch could do nothing but cry her name into his hands.

Elise's chest tightened as she ran both hands through her hair. It was only then she realized how many leaves and twigs were trapped within her tangles. She would have to worry about that later. *This is a nightmare. It can't be real. I can't lose Darcie. I have to do something. Maybe my magic can help. If I could reach my Aunt Sarah, she could heal her quickly.*

Knowing she didn't have the time or ability to reach her aunt, Elise placed her hands on Darcie's cheeks and concentrated on what she wanted.

Wake up, Darcie. Don't die. Wake up. Stay alive. We need you. Please wake up now.

Elise opened her eyes but saw no change. Mitch's guttural cry tore through what resolve she had left, and Elise lost control of her own emotions. Hugging Darcie against her, Elise rocked back and forth, letting her tears fall into Darcie's hair. *Please, wake up. We can't do this without you.*

"Maybe there's another way," Gavin said. When Mitch and Elise looked up at him, he took a deep breath. "We're in a magical kingdom. If Elise's magic won't work, maybe another kind will."

"Like what?" Elise asked. She would try anything to help her best friend.

"Like a kiss."

Is he serious?

"Now's not the time for jokes, Gav." Mitch sniffed and used his shirt to wipe his face.

"Yeah, we really need to think this through. She's still breathing. It's not far to the castle. Maybe we *can* reach Sarah in time to—"

"Guys, I'm serious," said Gavin. "It works in the fairy tales. What about this place makes you think this isn't a fairy tale? We were *literally* just sent here by fairies."

He's got a point. Anything could work. "Yeah, but it has to be a true love's kiss or something like that," Elise pointed out. She and Gavin paused before looking at Mitch, who shook his head.

"No, forget it. It won't do any good anyway."

Elise rolled her eyes with a groan. *This is taking forever. We don't have time for this.* "But what if it does? We need to hurry before a guard hears us or something." She looked around for any eavesdroppers. "Come on, Mitch. Wouldn't you rather be wrong than not try?"

Mitch scowled before roaming his eyes across Darcie's sleeping figure. He mulled over his options before shaking his head as if to wake himself from a bad dream. "Guys, this is stupid. There's no way—"

"Just shut up and kiss her already!" Gavin snapped, attempting to keep his voice low.

Please. Elise pleaded with him to try whatever it took to wake Darcie up. Seeing Mitch hesitate again, she propped Darcie up into a sitting position against her.

He shook his head once more. "She'd punch me if she knew," he whispered with a grimace.

Poor Mitch. Elise reached out as best she could under Darcie's weight and placed her hand on his shoulder. "Not if it saves her." When he looked into her eyes, she watched his expression soften.

Mitch took a deep breath and braced himself for what he had to do. With a nod, he beckoned Elise to push Darcie closer.

Expecting him only to lean in, Elise was surprised when Mitch pulled Darcie into his arms completely. Sensing the awkward intimacy on Mitch's part, Elise backed away and stood by Gavin a few feet away. She intertwined her fingers with his.

Both watched as Mitch cradled Darcie's head against his arm. He caressed her cheek before whispering something into her ear.

What's he saying? This is driving me crazy! Come on, Darcie. Wake up. Please wake up. This just has to work.

Mitch sat back to gaze down at Darcie's slumbering face. With one last glance at Gavin and Elise, he closed his eyes and pressed his lips softly against Darcie's.

There were no immediate signs that the kiss worked. Fireworks didn't shoot off, fairy dust didn't burst into the sky, and the only sounds came from various birds above them.

Elise felt as if her heart jumped into her throat. *Why isn't anything happening?* She stomped one foot as fresh tears fell down her cheeks.

Mitch's own tear-stained face fell as he carefully lowered Darcie to the ground where she continued to lay motionless. He met Elise and Gavin's eyes before shaking his head.

Elise buried her face into Gavin's sleeve and sobbed until her chest ached. He wrapped one arm around her and the other around Mitch. All three shook, overcome with grief, and held one another while Elise's thoughts screamed in her head that none of this was real. *It can't be real. This isn't the way any of this was supposed to be.*

The sound of a groan brought Elise out of her despair. Peeking over Mitch's shoulder, she perked up when Darcie sat up and stretched out her arms. *Darcie! She's alive!* Without a word, Elise pushed past the boys and ran to her best friend, attacking her in a tight hug. She clutched her best friend so tightly there was a very good chance Darcie could be in pain, but that would only be more proof that she was alive.

Darcie squeezed her back as the boys approached.

"Elise, what's wrong?" Darcie asked when Elise pulled away. She looked warily between all her friends. "Why're y'all crying?"

"We. . .we thought we lost you," Elise said.

"Why would you think that?" she chuckled. "We just left your grandma's house. It looks like the scarf took us where we needed to go. Isn't that the gazebo over there?"

Gavin, Mitch, and Elise exchanged anxious glances.

"What? What aren't you telling me?" Darcie's eyes widened as she looked at all three. "Okay, seriously, someone say something. You're freaking me out."

Gavin spoke before Elise could find the right words. "You were taken by fairies. The king fairy, actually."

Darcie laughed as she stood. "Yeah, right. Come on, guys. We can play pranks later. We have to get to the castle and check on Derek."

"He's telling the truth," Elise called out as her best friend walked away. "If Mitch hadn't kissed you, then—"

"*What?*" Darcie spun on her heel. All traces of humor were gone as she glared at them before fixating on Mitch. "Excuse me?"

Elise gulped. "Darcie, it was the only way to save you!" She motioned for Gavin to chime in when Darcie began stomping back towards them.

The tips of Darcie's ears were red hot as she stopped in front of Mitch. Before Gavin could say anything, Darcie grabbed two fistfuls of Mitch's shirt and shook him. "*Why* would you do that? If I was asleep, why would you do that without me knowing? Ugh, I could just punch you!"

"Told you," Mitch said to Elise.

"Don't look at them. Look at *me*!" Darcie demanded, forcing his attention back on her as she jabbed a finger against his chest. "You had no right to do that. Do you hear me? *No* right!"

"Yeah, well, you don't have to worry about it happening again, all right?" Mitch yelled back at her. "Next time, it'll be because you asked me to."

"*Next* time?" she shrieked, ignoring her friends' attempts to shush her. "No, there won't be a next time, Mitch, because there shouldn't have been a *this* time. Ugh, what were you thinking?"

"I was thinking I'd lost you, okay?" he shouted. Closing his eyes, he took a deep breath and tried again. "We thought you were dead."

Darcie shook her head, still unconvinced. "We traveled like we always do. So, why would this time be—"

"You don't remember anything that happened?" Elise asked.

Darcie groaned in frustration. "The scarf just brought us here, and I took a little longer to wake up. Big deal. Don't try to excuse what Mitch did with a stupid story about—"

"No, Darcie," Gavin said, interrupting her. "No, we didn't just travel back. We've been here a while, but *you* weren't there when we woke up."

Darcie released Mitch's shirt but remained silent.

"We looked everywhere, but we couldn't find you," said Elise. "When the king said he wanted to keep you, the only way to save you was to pay them, but we didn't have the scarf he wanted back, so—" She gestured towards Mitch.

Darcie's brows furrowed in confusion.

"Mitch offered to take your place and stay with them," Gavin said.

A tense, awkward silence filled the space between them as Darcie processed everything. "Then, how did we *all* get away?"

"Turns out those three fairies we met before are the fairy king's kids and he had the scarf the whole time," Gavin said. "One of them took Elise's drawing as payment. He said there's some timeline for us to fix, and then they let us go."

"But when we got here, you were under some curse or whatever," Elise said. "We didn't know what else to try."

Mitch, Elise, and Gavin waited until the full realization dawned on Darcie's face.

Elise knew Darcie felt betrayed, but she hoped learning the truth would allow her friend to forgive them. Especially Mitch.

"And you," Darcie said to Mitch, "you offered to take my place?"

Mitch nodded.

Biting her lip, Darcie drew tiny circles in the dirt with the toe of her shoe while she pondered everything.

She has to know we're telling the truth. Elise held her breath.

When Darcie lifted her blushed face, she no longer appeared frustrated. Instead, she wore an expression of shame, embarrassment, and something else Elise couldn't decipher. Rather than speak right away, Darcie closed the distance between herself and Mitch. Upon reaching him, she searched his eyes in silence.

Elise didn't know what her friend was attempting to find, but she desperately hoped for Mitch's sake it wouldn't start another argument. *What is this going to do to him? Is she still mad?*

Mitch was at least a foot taller than Darcie. Yet even while towering over her, his tense shoulders and wide eyes gave him away.

He looks like he'd rather face Horanis again than make her upset.

Darcie waited until Mitch met her eyes. "Do it again," she whispered.

Elise and Gavin exchanged another anxious glance.

Failing to hide his confusion, Mitch tilted his head with a shrug. "Do what?"

"Kiss me."

Mitch looked as if someone was about to dump a bucket of ice water over his head. He glanced over at Gavin and Elise with a dumbfounded expression.

"You said the next time would be when I asked you to," Darcie reminded him. Taking his hand, she interlocked their fingers together. "I can't believe you sacrificed yourself like that for me."

Mitch grew serious as his eyes darkened. "Yeah, I couldn't just—"

Darcie pressed a finger against his mouth.

The two stared at one another, sharing more with silence than was possible with words. Standing on her toes, Darcie snaked a hand around Mitch's neck and pulled him lower until their lips crushed together.

Mitch's tense demeanor melted away as his arms wrapped around Darcie's waist.

Elise felt her heart swell. Seeing Mitch and Darcie finally give into their desires clouded all their problems for the time being. *About time!*

"Let's give them a minute," Gavin whispered, causing Elise to jump. When she nodded, he led her to another section of the garden.

Once they were alone, Elise was unable to contain her excitement. "Can you believe it? I'm so happy for them!"

They finally gave in to each other's stubbornness.

"Me too," he said, sitting down on a nearby bench. He patted the empty space next to him and waited for Elise to sit. "He's liked her for a really long time."

She rested her head against Gavin's shoulder. *I've missed this.* "That was a good idea you had about the kiss. I thought we'd lost her." Elise closed her eyes, relishing the feel of both the sun and cool autumn breeze against her face. In that moment, she and Gavin were the only two people in the world. *I just hope nobody finds us here.* The perfect moment was short-lived, however, as Elise winced when he pulled her hand towards him.

"What's wrong?" Gavin was suddenly upright—completely alert. After studying her open palms, and seeing the handful of splinters on either hand, he sighed with relief. "Why didn't you tell me earlier?"

"There was kind of a lot going on," she replied with a sheepish smile. Elise nodded when he offered to remove them and braced herself. Clenching both eyes shut, she bit her tongue so as not to cry out while he took each piercing splinter out. If the process hadn't been accompanied with pain, Elise would almost label it an intimate, romantic gesture. She exhaled slowly once he finally tossed the last one on the ground. "Thanks."

"You're welcome." He gave Elise a lopsided smile before removing a leaf from her hair. "Now, *this*, I can't help you with."

"What are you talking about?" Elise ran a hand through her hair and felt countless tiny broken twigs and crispy leaves tangled within her frizzy red locks. Unable to contain an embarrassed chuckle, Elise feigned a pout as she yanked a few unwanted pieces out. "Why didn't you say anything earlier?"

Gavin shrugged with a smirk. "There was kind of a lot going on." He laughed at her answering glare. "I wouldn't bother anyway. You'll never get it all out without a bath."

She leaned back into his embrace with a defeated sigh. "Let's hope we get one soon. At this point, I don't care how many maids try to help." It was a known obligation that the castle staff helped them bathe and dress, despite their own reluctancy.

Gavin kissed the top of Elise's head and caressed the side of her arm. Locating the gazebo nearby, he cocked his head towards it. "Feels like forever ago, doesn't it?"

She nodded with a contented yawn. *Our first kiss. It does feel like a long time ago. How has it only been a few days?* Elise tilted her head back to share a sweet kiss with him. It was still surreal to have Gavin back. There were countless moments on their journey to save him where Elise feared it would never happen. Her train of thought continued wandering, again speculating what all Gavin had experienced while they were separated. She felt the weight of Gavin's head increase as his breathing slipped into a steady pattern. *Is he asleep?* Chancing a peek, she noticed his eyes were closed. *He's exhausted.* It broke her heart to see how worn out he was.

"What did she do to you?" she whispered, caressing the back of his other hand. While Elise was merely thinking out loud to herself, it shocked her when he replied.

"Not here." Gavin sat up with an audible yawn as he stretched, causing Elise to scoot over. "Maybe later."

She frowned. *Why won't he tell me? Is he hiding something?* Elise opened her mouth to ask him but was distracted when Mitch and Darcie came into view holding hands.

"Are y'all good?" Gavin asked with a smile.

"We're good." Darcie beamed before giving Mitch's hand a squeeze.

I don't think I've ever seen her look so happy. Elise couldn't have been more thrilled for her friend. Nodding towards the castle, Elise suggested they find Joranna.

"Wait!" Gavin hissed, pulling her behind him. "Someone's coming."

Elise heard footsteps approaching. They would be found any minute now. *This isn't where I want them to find us.*

"Over here!" Mitch whispered, pointing to a section of hedges that would conceal them. He waved his arm until the others were crouched in safety before also hiding.

It took a moment to get adjusted where all four could properly see who was coming. *Who would be coming this deep into the garden in the middle of the afternoon?* No sooner had the thought left her mind than Ruby and Charles walked into the gazebo.

CHAPTER 5

While the autumn weather was one indication to time passing, Ruby's rounded stomach confirmed just how far Elise and her friends had traveled into the future.

"I thought they weren't allowed to see each other," Darcie whispered.

"Knowing my mom, they still aren't," Elise muttered.

Princess Ruby was known to break the rules for the fun of it, often causing problems for others, particularly Elise. Fortunately, for now, Ruby hadn't seen the four teenagers. She was more preoccupied with the gentleman accompanying her.

"I don't get it," Mitch said. "I thought you said she was getting married off because of the baby."

Elise shushed him when Ruby and Charles started talking. *He's right. She was supposed to get married. I wonder what happened. . .*

"We should be safe out here," Ruby whispered, scanning her eyes around the gazebo.

"Ruby, this isn't a good idea. We should head back," Charles replied.

"Not until you tell me everything you know. Richard has sworn the doctor to secrecy and Mother doesn't leave Father's side." When he didn't reply, she continued. "We're all going mad with worry. Sarah is in hysterics, Ian keeps to his room, and you're the *only* one I can depend on at present. Why all the secrecy?"

"It's for the best, Princess."

"Don't use that excuse," she spat. "You sound like one of them. You're better than that." A hush fell between the two. "Richard might believe what he's doing is for the best, but if Father's health is declining as rapidly as I fear, we have a right to know."

Charles frowned with a sigh.

Why is it being kept a secret?

Stepping closer to take his hand, Ruby pleaded with her eyes. "Charlie, it's *me*. Whatever it is, please share it. You're Richard's closest friend. Surely, you know *something*."

Avoiding her gaze, Charles pulled his hand away. "I can't. I'm sorry." He cleared his throat and stepped back. "Sunset is approaching. Allow me to escort you back to the courtyard and—"

"Don't bother." Ruby jerked the front of her skirt up with a huff. As she shoved passed him, Charles reached out and grabbed her arm.

"Quit pouting," he growled. His face was mere inches from hers, but there was no denying the unspoken restraint behind his tone. Charles' glare softened into a pleading stare of his own. "Just do what you're told, *please*."

"Are you sure your mom *never* mentioned this guy?" Darcie whispered.

Elise shook her head. "She never said anything about him, but he was clearly the love of her life." *I'm dying to know why she cut him out of her life.*

Pulling her arm out of his reach, Ruby turned away from Charles before stomping out of the gazebo.

Elise panicked, afraid the two would walk out of earshot. *Why can't he give her a straight answer? Is Derek okay or not?* She pressed herself against the hedge, desperate to catch any more of what her mother and Charles were saying. It looked as if the latter convinced Ruby to return since Elise saw her mother come back into view. Rather than here what was said, she heard a scuffle behind her followed by the sounds of crunching leaves and someone whimpering. She turned to see Mitch's hand across Darcie's mouth.

"What happened?" Elise asked.

"Mitch stepped on my foot!" Darcie hissed once she pulled Mitch's hand away from her mouth. "Ugh, seriously, why did you do that?"

"There was a bee! I'm sorry," he argued back when Darcie rolled her eyes.

"Good going, Mitch," Gavin whispered with a chuckle.

"The thing was massive! It kept flying around my head. How was I supposed to know her foot was there?"

Seeing Darcie open her mouth to respond, Elise shushed them before their argument could escalate anymore. Gritting her teeth, she took a deep breath. *Ugh, these two get on my nerves sometimes. What all am I missing? I can't hear a thing.*

"What do you mean you are not able to see me again? Since when has it mattered before? We have been secretly meeting for months!" Ruby snapped.

Elise didn't hear Charles' reply, but judging by the sneer on Ruby's face, it wasn't what the princess wanted to hear.

"You dare to blame me for that?" Elise heard her mother ask. She wasn't sure what Ruby was talking about, which only managed to irritate Elise more.

"I never said anything about blaming you," Charles replied. "The least you could do is listen without jumping to conclusions about matters you know little about!"

"I would know more if you would simply tell me! About us, about my father, or anything!" Ruby grabbed her skirt once more as she stepped up to him. "I am not a child anymore. Neither are Sarah and Ian. We deserve to know the truth without being left to Richard's will. You know as well as I do the power has corrupted his good sense."

"*Careful*," Charles warned, glancing around to insure no one was listening. "He may be your brother, but it could be thought treasonous to defame the man being crowned king in the coming days."

Ruby's face paled. All signs of anger wilted from her features as she froze. When she spoke, her voice was on the verge of breaking. "Days?"

Elise held her breath. *Oh no.*

"Possibly hours," Charles admitted. "Prince Richard has already ordered for the coronation preparations."

What!

Hesitating on the spot as Ruby broke into tears, Charles gave in and pulled her into his embrace. For a moment, the only sounds were the princess's muffled sobs against his shoulder until she pressed against his chest to gain distance.

"*Who* told you this? I demand you tell me this instant!" she sobbed, wiping her cheeks. When he didn't answer, she glared daggers at him and lunged forward, slapping her hands desperately against his chest. "Why will you not answer me?" Ruby shrieked in hysterics.

Charles remained stoic, allowing her to take her outrage out on him, even when Ruby screamed inches from his face before she finally tired herself out and leaned back against the gazebo railing.

Ruby's makeup smeared further across her face as she continued wiping oncoming tears away. Placing a hand under her rounded belly for support. Wincing, she held her other hand up to prevent Charles from approaching as she steadied her breathing. "How my mother did this four times is beyond me. Do *not* come any closer," Ruby commanded when Charles tried taking another step to assist. "I require *nothing* from you." With one last deep breath, she was able to correct her posture and continue. "That is how you want it. Is it not?"

"Ruby, this is for the best as we—"

"It is Your Highness or Princess to you," she corrected. "If our friendship cannot continue, then I suggest you address me properly before corrective action is taken. We both know you wish to remain Richard's little lapdog."

"I never wished for this to—"

"Yes, you did," Ruby argued. She paused to hold back more tears as she cleared her throat. "The night you kissed me. From the moment you declared your affections, you have been trying to recant them."

"Do you think it was easy for me?" Charles tensed his shoulders as his words spilled from his mouth like fire. "Do you think I rejoiced all those nights I helped you over the wall so you could carouse with strangers?" When she opened her mouth, he closed the distance between them. "No, *Princess,* you will stay and hear every word of this."

"How dare you—"

"Put up with your childish antics for so long?" he offered, ignoring her answering glare. "It was not without its challenges I can assure you." When she sidestepped him again, he backed up five or six steps to remain in front of her. "You will not treat me as you have done everyone else, because I have done what no one else would even against my better judgment. You do not like to be held accountable for your actions, but in a few months' time or less," he said, nodding towards her stomach, "it will be out of your hands. Now, I do love you. Every part of me longs to reach out and touch you, but I. . ." He closed his eyes, restraining himself. "I simply cannot."

"No, you *will not,* because you are choosing to run away from what we could become. You push me away, yet every time I leave, you follow. There are stolen touches, kisses, glances. . .just enough hints to betray your true desires before you retreat like the *coward* you are!" Ruby shook her head in disgust. "Maybe, if circumstances were different. . .if I were not a princess—"

"If the child were mine," Charles blurted at the same time.

Ruby froze once more, staring in shocked silence at the man across from her. Regaining her composure, she held her head high as she looked into his eyes with a solemn yet defiant expression. "You have said enough. This is the last time I shall bother you. Good day, Lord Fenton."

Charles hesitated.

Elise's heart broke watching the exchange. *Mom, I'm so sorry.* "We need to wait here before we follow them."

"I think we need to let her know we're here before we try sneaking in," Mitch said.

"Why? So, she can know we were listening?" Elise asked.

"I can't believe he said that to her," Darcie whispered. "Poor Ruby."

"Yeah, that was low," Gavin said. "She's going through enough, but Mitch is right. We should talk to her before we try going into the castle. I really don't want to end up back in a cell."

Elise sighed. "Okay, hang on. I'll get her attention. It doesn't sound like we can rely on anyone else right now."

There was a part of Elise that was scared to go back to the castle. It wasn't because she and her friends had just arrived. It was because Elise didn't know what to expect. If the fairies were right, and they usually were, then everything would be different. It sounded like Richard had grown even more conceited and corrupted than in their original timeline. Elise's mind traveled back to a conversation she had with her uncle at Joranna's kitchen table.

"Elise, I may be one of your biggest challenges later on. All of my life I have wanted to be my father. I have wanted to be what he stood for. I don't know how far into my mother's diary you are going to travel, but as I grow older, I will become arrogant. I will not fear anything, and that is dangerous. Do all that you can to convince me of my weaknesses. It is the only way I can get stronger. Convince me that I am not him."

Elise fidgeted with her hands. *How am I going to do that?* No matter how she approached the situation, it sounded like a death wish. Standing up to Rona was one thing, but standing up to her own uncle was another. A wave of panic coursed through Elise's veins as she pondered how far Rona's meddling went. *We also have to somehow get the diary back. Things are just getting worse and worse.*

Biting her lip, Elise kneeled to pick up a pebble. Saying a quick prayer, she tossed it towards Ruby. The pebble bounced a couple of times but fell short of its target. Elise tried again, but the second and third pebbles didn't travel far enough either.

"Move, let me do it," Mitch said, nudging his way past her.

"Mitch, I've got it," Elise argued.

"Clearly not. We're going to run out of rocks waiting for you."

Elise glared at him but allowed Mitch to take the lead. She watched him close one eye as the tip of his tongue stuck out while he aimed.

Rocking his hand back and forth near his ear as if about to throw a dart, he finally released. Mitch's pebble went further than all of Elise's attempts before hitting the ground with a couple of extra bounces. It landed near Ruby's foot, but the solemn princess didn't notice.

"Want me to try?" Gavin offered.

Mitch groaned, patting the ground until he found another pebble.

It's not as easy as it looks, is it? Elise got a sick satisfaction watching Mitch also struggle to reach their target. After two more failed attempts, he was able to toss a pebble far enough until it bounced off the gazebo railing next to where Ruby was standing.

The princess jerked her head towards the hedge. "Who's there? Show yourself!" Ruby tensed, shielding her stomach with both hands until Elise and the others stepped into view. Upon recognizing them, the princess relaxed her shoulders with a deep breath. "It's you! I thought I'd never see you again. When my friend returned claiming he had been robbed, and saw no sign of you, I feared the worst."

Elise realized she hadn't considered Ruby's reaction to Vaughn's interference. The princess had arranged a meeting with a friend with letters of safe passage to Vynchia. When Vaughn showed up in possession of the letters instead, they followed him believing he was Ruby's aid who would lead them to Gavin.

"We were tricked by the same guy," Darcie said.

"And your Elven bottle necklace is gone." Elise's mind traveled back to the soul-crushing moment when Rona dumped out the remaining fairy magic. Gavin saved them by activating the diary before she could even think about finding it. "I'm sorry."

"Never mind that. I am glad you are safe."

"We're sorry about Charles too." Gavin nodded in the direction Charles walked away.

Realization dawned on Ruby's flushed features as she shifted her gaze anywhere but theirs. "I-I don't suppose you heard us just now."

"We did," Darcie said.

"We're so sorry," Elise added.

"Yeah, he's a jerk," said Gavin. "Don't listen to him."

Ruby smiled with a heavy sigh. "I wish it were that easy." She drew small circles with her fingertip along her belly. "But he is right. No respectable man wants anything to do with me these days."

Elise's chest tightened as she felt her temper flare on Ruby's behalf. "Why? I thought you were supposed to marry someone before you started to show?"

Ruby chuckled. "I am not sure where you have all been these last months, but much has changed. Those plans were forgotten long ago."

I don't understand.

"So, you're stuck here?" Gavin asked.

Ruby nodded. "I am restricted to the grounds with an early evening curfew to be indoors."

"That sucks." Mitch shook his head. "They're treating you like a prisoner."

"It's just a baby!" Darcie gestured towards Ruby's stomach. "Why is your mom treating you like this?"

"It is not her," Ruby said. "I doubt she is fully aware of the measures in place to shield me." The princess stared off into space as her thoughts traveled far away from the garden.

A cold chill coursed through Elise. *She's completely isolated from everything. Why isn't Joranna helping her?* Elise ached to bring up the latest conversation between Ruby and Charles, but she thought it best to stay quiet on the subject. After all, they needed to focus on getting into the castle.

"Since we just got here, could we talk to the queen?" Elise asked. "We want to check on the king too."

Ruby returned her attention to the four travelers before shaking her head. "I can get you as far as the main hall. I am afraid Richard's study is the furthest you will get to Father."

Richard's study? He's already taken it over? Why is no one allowed to see Derek? Feeling her adrenaline build, Elise exhaled slowly. *Calm down. It's a step in the right direction. Maybe I can use my magic to get further.*

"That would be great." Elise plastered on a grateful smile.

"Could we get cleaned up before we see your brother?" Darcie nodded towards their soiled clothing.

"And get something to eat?" Mitch suggested.

Hesitating at first, Ruby nodded. "I can arrange that. Follow me."

A wave of anxiety sloshed around the pit of Elise's stomach as they approached the double French doors leading to the ballroom, but she reminded herself Ruby's reluctance wasn't a setback.

It'll be nice getting a hot bath and a meal before we try learning anything anyway. In anticipation, Elise's stomach growled so fiercely, she glanced around to see if anyone else noticed. If they did, no one said anything as the group crossed the ballroom towards the main hall.

Ruby made it halfway into the hall before jerking backwards with a gasp, causing the others to bump into her. Fumbling, Ruby pushed back against them and slammed her back against the wall of the ballroom.

"What's wrong?" Elise asked before Ruby shushed her.

The princess nodded her head towards the hall.

Elise inched close enough to the doorway to see Richard and Charles speaking in the hall. She mouthed to her friends what was going on. One by one, they all crowded around Elise within earshot of the two men.

"What did she want this time?" Richard's impatient tone struck a nerve in Elise.

"She simply wanted news on the king's health," Charles replied. Richard mumbled something under his breath before his friend continued. "I did not disclose anything."

Elise glanced over at her mother, whose eyes were clenched shut as she also listened in on the lie.

"Good. Why she felt the need to come to you is beyond me given my strict instructions about the matter." Richard cleared his throat. "Did you follow my instructions?"

"Yes, Your Highness."

"You broke her heart once and for all?" Richard asked. When Charles replied he had, the prince continued. "Excellent. Perhaps now she will stay in her place where she belongs until she delivers."

Elise was brought out of her own angered state by the sound of Ruby huffing. The princess wasn't known for being patient or putting up with such blatant bigotry. Ruby sucked her lips into a tight line as her forehead creased.

She wants to interrupt. Don't, Mom. Please stay quiet. It'll only make it worse.

"I'm about to flip," Darcie whispered in Elise's ear. "They're treating her like crap for this. We need to help her."

"Now's not the time," Gavin whispered above Elise's head. "If we walk up to them now looking and smelling like we do, we'll just make things harder on ourselves."

They waited until the men's voices faded enough for Ruby to feel comfortable leading them into the hall.

"Try to be quick," Ruby whispered. "I will have the maids prepare your rooms, clothes and bring you something to eat. Richard does not need to know you are here yet, but the council members will be arriving shortly for a meeting."

"We need to be at that meeting," Elise said.

"Do not be stupid," Ruby replied. "You will not get past the door. Once you are refreshed, we will meet outside his study to speak with him afterwards."

There was no use in arguing with the princess. *At least she's willing to help us.*

Over the next hour, all four were treated to a much-needed bath, change of clothes and snack in their own respective guestrooms. Given the last few days, Elise stayed silent when the maids stepped in to help with the process. On every other occasion, Elise often felt embarrassed, awkward, and reluctant for the assistance. Perhaps it was due to the familiarity of the process that she no longer felt his way. To her surprise, Elise was able to relax and even enjoy the treatment. Not only did the hot water soothe her aching muscles, but the fresh fruit and bread afterwards were extremely flavorful on an empty stomach.

As Elise finished the offered snack, one of the maids styled her hair. *Much better.* Richard could take her seriously now. There was still the issue of what all she would say, but Elise hoped inspiration would come when she spoke with the prince. It was critical they not only learn of Derek's condition, but also of all the changes she would need to fix. As she swallowed the last bite, Elise thanked the maid with a grateful smile. It was incredible how much a bath and snack improved her mood. Except for being mildly drowsy, she felt rejuvenated and ready to take on the world.

As planned, Elise, Gavin, Mitch, and Darcie met Ruby in the main hall.

"That is more like it." Ruby smiled at their appearances. "I have been told the council is about to conclude its meeting. It should only be a moment. Good day."

"Wait!" Elise called when Ruby turned to leave. "You're not coming in with us?"

"I believe you have seen and heard enough to know it is best I am not around during these types of meetings."

"Please," Darcie said. "We wouldn't have gotten this far without you."

"Yeah," said Gavin. "Since when do you care what they think?"

Mitch nodded. "Show them they can't treat you like that."

Ruby paused a moment before she smiled. "You know what? You are right. If Charles cannot help me, perhaps there will be strength in numbers when Richard is ready to talk." Stroking her belly, Ruby paced back and forth in front of the guarded door for the next ten minutes until it opened with a swift pull.

"Are you all right, Charles?" Richard asked as he paused in the study doorway. The guard stepped out of the way so Charles could join the prince. "All you did was scribble notes in there yet scarcely spoke three words together. Surely, you are not out of spirits concerning the matter with my sister. It is only Ruby."

I'm going to kill him! What does he mean 'only Ruby'? He doesn't know we're here or he wouldn't have said that. Elise stepped closer until her movement caught Charles' attention before he could reply. A sick satisfaction twisted deep in Elise's gut while watching both men acknowledge their entire party. She was proud of Ruby for maintaining her composure despite Charles' unwillingness to make eye contact.

"Prince Richard," Elise said with a curtsy, ignoring their shocked expressions. Attempting to be as subtle as possible, Elise stepped closer to the doorway where the king stood. "We're friends of your parents. Do you remember?"

What are you hiding? Why are you acting like this?

Richard stumbled over his words before forming a proper sentence. Regaining his formal composure, he signaled for Elise to stand. "Yes, of course, welcome. Forgive me. I was not made aware of your arrival." Realization dawned on his face as he located Ruby standing near Elise's friends. A silent, yet resentful exchange passed between the siblings before Richard returned his attention to Elise. "You appear to be doing well. I should like to speak later about the purpose of your visit, because as you can see, I am quite busy at present." Lifting an arm towards the study, Richard stepped side only enough to allow Elise a brief peek into the room.

Finally! Almost immediately, Elise's excitement was replaced by sheer terror. Sitting in a chair, speaking to another council member in a matching blue coat, was none other than Vaughn himself!

Trembling, unable to speak, Elise's chest tightened when he noticed her. *What is* he *doing here?*

CHAPTER 6

Elise backed away from the door until she accidentally bumped into Ruby. *I need to get away. I need to hide.* She hastily looked for an escape as intrusive waves of panic crashed into her thoughts. *We need to leave. Now.*

"What is the matter?" Ruby asked.

"Nothing. I'm fine." It was almost always her default reply when questioned about an approaching panic attack despite it being the furthest from the truth. *I don't want them to see me like this. What if he walks out here? What would I say?* As the anxious thoughts tormented her, another voice ushered in. *You were the one stupid enough to trust him while he was working for Rona. You should've known he wasn't really trying to help find Gavin.*

"Elise?" Gavin's voice sounded far away yet she sensed his presence.

Ugh, and poor Gavin was being tortured while you flirted with someone else. Vaughn even kissed your neck at that farmhouse while you just stood there and did nothing. Deep down, Elise knew the stampede of insults was filled with lies, but she was unable to overcome the mental beating of each one. *You don't deserve Gavin. He's too good for you. Look what all he's done and suffered through while you blindly followed a stranger. You tried ignoring it, but now Vaughn's here* and *he saw you! Gavin will probably leave you when he finds out.*

Then came the part she always dreaded. There was often a lingering effect on some panic attacks that included having an out of body experience. It was as if she could see herself in the hallway, watching everyone's concerned expressions, yet she couldn't speak. Immobilized by the false sense of fear, all she could do was stand there reliving the last few days. *Get a grip, Elise! This is crazy. Get yourself together. You can't do this now. Everyone's watching. Even Richard. He won't talk to you unless you snap out of it!*

"Should I fetch the doctor? You look ill," Richard said, bringing Elise back to reality.

"No, I'm okay." Tapping her hand against her thigh, Elise took a deep breath. *Fake it until it's true,* she reminded herself.

"What did you see?" Gavin whispered.

Before Elise could answer, Vaughn stepped out into the hall. "I believe everything is concluded, Sire. The others wish to know if they should return to their homes or stay to continue."

He didn't bother to look over his shoulders at the travelers, but that didn't stop Elise from glaring daggers into his back. Had she not followed him for so long, she might not have recognized him so quickly. Dressed in a tailored councilman's coat, with his long hair tied back from his muscular face, anyone could be fooled by Vaughn's false status. He had even adopted the classic haughty stance to match the other members who could be heard mingling inside the study.

While Elise's friends didn't suffer panic attacks, they were also unable to conceal their own shocked reactions.

Darcie made an odd squeaking sound as if she were trying to see how long she could go without breathing. Having been the first to fall for Vaughn's charms, she remained frozen except to peek up at Mitch.

Elise suspected her best friend felt foolish for how brazen she had acted on their journey. *Especially now she and Mitch just got together.*

Mitch's blotched skin betrayed his limited self-control. If Darcie wasn't holding his hand, Elise imagined it would've already connected with Vaughn's jaw.

The reaction that surprised her the most, however, was Gavin's. The Gavin she knew would've interrupted Vaughn and the prince, stirred up a scene, perhaps even thrown a punch since Mitch hadn't. Yet, he stood there. To everyone else, he might have looked indifferent, but Elise knew him better than that. She could tell by the way his eyes shifted between the two men, coupled with his tense shoulders, that he was holding himself back from doing something stupid.

Is he mad at me? Does he blame me for what happened? Does he even know everything that happened? Elise hadn't gotten the chance to really talk to him about what they both went through, but Gavin also silenced her when she tried. His hurtful words from Joranna's house before they traveled back rang in her ears again.

"Why, so you can flirt in front of my face this time? If you're going to fall for someone else, I'd rather not be around to see it." His verbal attack was soon followed by, *"Oh, I saw plenty. Rona has her ways"*.

Sure, he apologized after, but Elise knew the truth behind what Gavin said. As traumatic as it was for *her* to see Vaughn again in person, it must be equally hard to see him this close for the first time after Rona's mind games.

"Have them stay, Rodrick," Richard replied, nodding over Vaughn's shoulder towards Elise. *Rodrick?* "I shall have our friends here stand before the council to answer any question they may have. Let them adjourn and reconvene in two hours."

"As you wish, Sire." Vaughn bowed.

"No!" Darcie cried, causing Vaughn to turn around. "You can't let him stay."

"She's right," said Elise. "You can't trust him. He's working for Rona!"

Among the anticipated reactions from her uncle regarding the accusation, laughter wasn't one of them.

The prince spluttered, doing a poor job to conceal his amusement. Only when he and Vaughn managed to contain their chuckles did Richard try speaking again. "I wasn't prepared for that. Forgive me," he chortled. "Now, Elise—"

"It's the truth!" she exclaimed.

Darcie took a step closer. "His name is Vaughn Garthorne, and he's one of Rona's spies!"

Sharing an amused glance with the prince, Vaughn cleared his throat. "Ladies, if I may—"

"How's your head?" Elise quirked an eyebrow, relieved to have found her long-lost courage again. "Any more headaches?"

Throughout their journey, Vaughn had been afflicted by recurring headaches, which—apart from invoking sympathy—were later revealed to be Rona communicating with him.

"Perhaps you ought to call the doctor after all, Sire. Nevertheless, I shall give the council your message at once." Vaughn turned his attention to the travelers. "Until we meet again." His eyes lingered on Elise before he stepped back into the study.

And there it was, flooding through her veins. The power he still had over her. With one piercing glance, he awoke all her insecurities. Elise's lower stomach cramped as if she had swallowed a brick. She didn't like the way his eyes had just roamed her body, but it wasn't because it frightened her like Brahm's leering did. It was the opposite. What scared her was the way Vaughn manipulated her without a single word. Whether he used magic to achieve this or not— and she prayed he did—Elise was left to process his effect on her.

Bombarded with memories, Elise was transported back to the farmhouse they had visited. Upon walking in on Vaughn changing, he convinced her to stay before backing Elise into a corner. She could still feel his hot breath on her shoulder as his hair tickled her ear. If that weren't enough, the feeling of his firm, experienced hands on her waist had made it extremely hard to resist. There was still a part of Elise that wondered what would've happened if Darcie hadn't walked in on them. Not to mention when Elise used her magic to prolong his life until he could receive proper treatment after a vicious animal attack. Whatever conflicting feelings she had experience at the time, Elise knew her heart belonged to Gavin.

"You'll want to tread carefully around the other members when you stand before the council," Richard said to Elise and her friends. "We wouldn't want them getting the wrong impression. Isn't that right, Charles?"

Charles nodded, still unwilling to speak or look at the princess.

"I should like to be present when they're questioned," Ruby said.

Richard chuckled. "Whatever for?"

Elise sensed her mother's anger rising.

"There may need to be an investigation amongst your council, and I have connections with a possible victim—"

"Prince Richard!" called an urgent yet familiar voice.

Elise looked up to see Ballard approaching the group. As the castle steward, he had a talent for serving the royal family and putting his nose where it didn't belong. The only reason Elise didn't completely despise him was he saved their lives when Brahm and his sister were caught committing treason.

Ballard held up a sealed envelope. "This has just arrived from King Dmitri of Lockesbarrow."

"King Dmitri?" Gavin blurted out. His voice was laced with alarm and confusion. "Did you just say *King* Dmitri? Of *Lockesbarrow*?"

Ballard sniffed before looking down his nose at the teenagers. "I don't believe I stuttered."

"What correspondence could you possibly have with Lockesbarrow?" Ruby asked, looking at her brother as if she were meeting him for the first time. "Richard, surely you aren't—"

"It'll have to wait, Ruby. I'm afraid business calls." Richard spun on his heel.

Ruby scoffed at his retreating figure. "Then you dare commit treason against your *own* family?" She made sure to call out loud enough for the nearby servants to eavesdrop, causing him to halt and turn back.

Oh no. What's he going to do? Elise cowered before her uncle's fuming figure as he approached, but Ruby's chin only lifted higher as she squared her shoulders. *Mom, don't do anything stupid!*

"What have I told you about raising alarm within the castle?" Richard spoke through gritted teeth in a tone so low, Elise struggled to make out every word. "Your *foolish* spectacles only manage to stir up *meaningless* gossip. Now, I'm trying to—"

"Be Father," she quipped.

Clenching his eyes and mouth shut, Richard took a steadying breath. "Even if that were true, I would only be helping the kingdom."

"Does Mother know about this?" Ruby asked. "Or Sarah? Perhaps Ian? I should only be too delighted to fill them in on your latest developments without Father's knowledge *or* approval."

"I'm trying to be the leader Haighdlen *needs* right now." Catching stares from the surrounding staff, Richard lowered his voice. "Be patient and you'll see. I'll be just like him."

"That's impossible," Ruby replied coldly, ignoring Charles' poor attempts from behind the prince to caution her. Keeping a steady gaze on her brother, Ruby sneered. "You may have his looks, his temper even." She narrowed her eyes. "But you'll never have his heart."

A muscle twitched in Richard's cheek as he glared down at his little sister. "May I remind you who controls your curfew?"

"I'm not afraid of you," she replied.

I am.

"Perhaps you should be," Richard answered. "Perhaps you should even restrain yourself and let the adults handle this." When she stepped closer, he nodded towards her stomach. "Careful, Sister. You would not want to do anything *else* you will regret."

Gavin grabbed Elise's arm as Ballard snickered.

I'll kill him! I'll scratch that disgusting smile off his face. No one makes fun of my mom like that!

Rage pulsed through Elise's heated body. If looks could kill, she was sure hers would shoot fire at her uncle and the surrounding onlookers who maintained a tense silence. The argument between the two siblings threatened to continue until Charles stepped in front of the prince.

"Shall I escort them to the library until the meeting, Your Highness?"

"Thank you, Charles," Richard said, keeping his eyes on Ruby. "And Ballard? Would you please escort my sister to her room? Be sure she behaves herself this evening."

Ballard offered a hand, but Ruby stomped off without him. Rolling his eyes, Ballard tugged on his vest before turning to follow the defiant princess.

"This way," Charles said, ushering Elise, Gavin, Mitch, and Darcie towards the library.

Derek is dying, Charles broke her heart, Ballard snickered, Richard belittled her, and Joranna has shut herself away. No wonder Mom felt trapped. We've barely been here an hour, and it's clear she hasn't got a friend in the world.

Elise hung her head as she followed Charles in silence. Determined to defend her mother, she waited until he stepped into the room and closed the door.

"How could you just stand there and say nothing?" she shouted. "She *needed* you!"

"Please, do not shout." Charles held a finger to his lips. "It is not that simple."

"Not that simple?" Elise shrieked. "So, you'll only love her if it's *simple*!"

"That is not what I meant. It is because—"

"How could you do that to her?" Elise cried, pulling her hand away when Gavin tried to hold it. "And then to tell her you couldn't be with her because she's not pregnant with *your* kid? I could kill you!"

"Will you please listen?" he hissed, watching to make sure the door didn't open. When he deemed it safe, he reached into his coat pocket and removed a folded piece of paper. "Would you please give this to Ruby?"

"No way!" Mitch said. "We're not doing your dirty work."

"You've put her through enough, man," Gavin said in agreement.

"We could burn it for you though," Darcie offered.

Elise felt grateful to have her friends' support. Gaining control of her emotions, she continued in a requested whisper. "And why does Richard want us to talk to the council? We just got here."

Charles shrugged. "Probably because every time you ever visited with the king, information was shared or discovered."

"We don't have time for this," Elise said, pacing back and forth in front of the fireplace. "We need to see Derek."

"I am afraid that is not possible," Charles replied. "Please wait here until His Majesty summons you."

"What're we supposed to say in there?" Gavin asked. "What happens if we don't say the right stuff?"

"I don't want to go back to the dungeon," Mitch said.

"I am sure it will not come to that," Charles assured them. "Simply tell the truth, speak only when you're spoken to, and above all else be respectful."

I still don't know what to say, but at least Charles will be in there so it's someone we know.

Relaxing her crossed arms and stiff shoulders, Elise smirked. "I see why he won't allow Ruby in then," she teased. When Charles returned a knowing smile, Elise could see the sadness behind his eyes. She pursed her lips. "You really love her, don't you?"

"With my life."

Elise hesitated, rocking back and forth in thought, before guilt got the better of her. "Fine. Give me the letter."

Holding the letter out, Charles pulled it back as it grazed Elise's fingertips. "It is for the princess's eyes only."

Elise nodded.

Charles warily gauged everyone's reactions before handing it over and walking out.

Crossing the room, Darcie pressed her ear against the door. "Okay, he's gone. You can open it now!"

How can I? Elise felt torn. Every inch of her longed to unfold the paper and devour every word. *Is Charles about to break Mom's heart again? Is he going to propose?* If this letter was what he was writing during the council meeting, it could be important. She knew he wouldn't be so secretive if it weren't. "Do y'all think I really should?"

"Yes!" the other three cried in unison.

Elise bit her lip. *Mom hates when I go through her stuff. She's so private. If she knew I was even thinking about doing this, she'd flip.*

She looked up at Darcie. "You had a good idea. Let's burn it. Maybe it's for Mom's own good not to read it."

"Elise Charlotte Laurille, you better not burn that letter! If you don't open it *right* now, I'll—" Darcie paused. Her eyes widened before she covered her mouth. Bouncing up and down, she frantically fanned her face.

"What? What's wrong?" Mitch asked.

"Spit it out," said Gavin.

Elise's brows furrowed. Darcie only did this when she was over the moon about something or petrified. Given the wide grin that ate up her friend's entire face, Elise assumed it was the former.

"Your name!" Darcie breathed.

"What about my name?" Elise asked. "You've known it for years. You use it to fuss at me. What's the big deal?"

"Your. . .*middle*. . .name," Darcie panted, finally calming down as she glanced between the other three.

"Charlotte?" Elise asked.

Darcie nodded, waiting for one of her friends to catch on. "How did we not pick up on it the entire time we've been traveling through time?"

"Probably the same way we aren't picking up on it now," Mitch countered.

Darcie rolled her eyes. "Think about it. *Charlotte*."

She doesn't mean what I think she does, does she? Gavin and Mitch wore matching blank stares, but Elise's lit up as she reached the same conclusion. "Do you think?" she asked.

Darcie nodded before clapping her hands as she resumed bouncing. "Elise is named after Charles! That means they stay in love!"

"Is that what you were trying to say?" Mitch asked, looking at Gavin, who shrugged.

"Yes!" Darcie scoffed. "Charlotte is a female variation of Charles. Both could even be nicknamed Charlie."

A hush fell throughout the room as they considered the possibility.

"That's a stretch, don't you think?" Gavin asked, tilting his chin with narrow eyes before turning to Elise. "Did your mom ever tell you who or what you were named after?"

Elise shook her head. She couldn't remember ever asking Ruby specifically, but knowing her mom, she would not have gotten a straight answer anyway.

"I'm with Gav," said Mitch. "I think you're looking into it."

"Elise." Darcie's voice went up an octave the way it always did when she was ready to prove a point. Planting both hands on her hips, she proceeded with her argument. "Do you have any relatives named Charlotte?"

Elise tried to remember before shaking her head again. "I don't think so."

"Well, that doesn't mean anything," Mitch said.

"Yeah, she didn't know any family until after visiting Joranna," Gavin said. "There could a long-lost cousin or grandma somewhere."

"Okay, *fine*," Darcie snapped. "We're in the library. There's probably a genealogy book somewhere."

It was Mitch's turn to roll his eyes as he draped himself across an armchair. "I'm not searching for another dumb book. Besides, we don't know when they'll call us. We should work on what we're going to say instead."

"He's right," Gavin said.

"Then we agree Elise was named after Charles?" Darcie asked. When Mitch tried asking why she needed to be right all the time, she cut him off by repeating the question louder. "Say it," she demanded when no one answered the second time.

"Fine," Gavin said. "She's named after Charles."

Darcie glared until Mitch reluctantly nodded. With a triumphant grin, she nodded towards the letter in Elise's hand. "There. See? Ruby clearly names you after the guy when you're born, so whatever is in that letter can't be *all* bad."

She has a point. Elise peeled the corner open before freezing again. *I can't. It's not right. I need to keep it a secret. What if I read something I shouldn't know? It could mess up what we're trying to do here.*

"Drop it, Darcie," Mitch said. "She doesn't want to. Let's talk about the meeting."

"Elise!" Darcie groaned as she raked her fingers through her spiky brown hair. "You're driving me *crazy*."

Elise held the letter out of reach as Darcie lunged for it. "I want to, okay? But we can't! It's not right, and you know it."

"I don't care. Give it to me," Darcie pleaded as she tried catching Elise off guard. When she failed a third time, Darcie stomped her foot. "If Charles really wanted to keep it a secret, he would've delivered it himself. Open it. Then we can talk about the meeting."

Elise wanted to honor Charles' wishes. Her hand hovered over the exposed corner, feeling as if an angel and devil were perched on her shoulders. *This is wrong. I shouldn't. He didn't look like he wanted us to see what he wrote.* Then came the side of her that Darcie loved the most. *But what if it would help Mom? She needs to know someone out there loves her. Plus, if it* is *bad news, we can burn it and save her the heartache.*

She met Gavin's eyes, secretly wishing he'd make the choice for her. When it was clear he wouldn't, she shifted her attention to Mitch, who nodded eagerly. Elise took a shaky breath, feeling the weight of the princess's future on her shoulders. *I can't. . .No, I'll wait. It's the right thing to do. I'll give it to Ruby when I see her again.* She made the mistake of looking up at Darcie, whose eyes stared at the letter with the same intense hunger growing in Elise's gut. *Do it. They all know you want to. It wouldn't be the worst thing if you folded it back correctly. Read it.*

Knowing she'd possibly regret it, Elise unfolded the letter. Skimming the message at first, catching random words and phrases, she struggled to fully comprehend the message due to Darcie's persistent begging to let her read it as well.

"Ugh, fine. Here!" Elise snapped, slapping the letter down on a nearby table. "We'll *all* read it, okay? Just shut up already!"

"Thanks," Darcie beamed, unphased by Elise's outburst. "He has super fancy handwriting, doesn't he? That's so romantic."

Elise exhaled sharply to curve her annoyance. Darcie often got what she wanted by being bossy or whining until the other person cracked. *Don't make a big deal about it. It's how she is. Besides, we don't know when Richard will call us back to the study. There may not be another opportunity.*

All four hunched over the table to read Charles' words for themselves.

October 2, 1988

My Dearest Ruby,

Let it be known I am acutely aware of the inherent risks in writing this letter— particularly those surrounding my life and title— but I aim to ease your grievances by expressing my sincerest affections. It is doubtful we shall speak again before the events listed below transpire.

The first matter of importance concerns the king. Why Richard is choosing to process His Majesty's failing health with secrecy, I know not, but it is no excuse for the way I broke the news to you. Forgive me. The curse placed upon your father is a manifestation of true evil, which should never take the life of any man—least of all one of the greatest. Though he still breathes, I send my heartfelt condolences and prayers to your family for this unspeakable tragedy. I know you detest being told what to do, but be there for your mother. She will need you.

That brings me to the primary purpose of this letter. You must leave Haighdlen. Go wherever I helped send you before. Perhaps what you seek is still out there, for I doubt what lies ahead during Richard's reign will satisfy you. As my closest friend and future king, I shall not smear his good name. Nevertheless, I will caution you. Knowing your spirit, should you stay, I could never forgive myself if I sat idle to watch them kill it.

The contents of this letter are to be strictly kept with you and you alone. Richard will encourage the queen, yourself, and Prince Ian to flee the kingdom as war approaches. Preparations are underway for your sister in the case of his death in battle given he has produced no heirs of his own. While it vexes Richard that you carry the only heir to the throne at present, he has voiced on many occasions the child must be protected at all costs—even more reason to leave when he commands it.

As for the expected heir in question, any man would be fortunate to father such an extraordinary child. I am ashamed of my cruel, impulsive manner towards you this afternoon. It shall haunt me the rest of my days.

I advise you to burn this letter upon receiving it, though I know how unlikely you are to take orders from anyone, least of all myself. Protect yourself, my darling, and the child. No matter the cost. Forget me, forget what could have transpired, and be satisfied in what has been. The stolen moments we've shared will never be enough to cure our inevitable torment, but your security and aspired happiness will soon overshadow any selfish urge on my behalf.

I will end with this. Truly, there shall never be another who loves you as I do. My life's regret is never knowing you the way my heart and body desires. Whatever you may encounter in your life, Ruby, you must never underestimate your worth, for to me you shall remain as you are this day—passionate, beautiful, and vivacious, with a tenacity and brilliance all your own. This is how I shall choose to remember you.

Eternally Yours,
Charlie

CHAPTER 7

Silence enveloped the room as everyone finished the letter. Elise felt as if an elephant were sitting on her chest.

Mitch let out a slow whistle. "Man, the guy's got skills. Sure could've used some of that language on my essays."

"Poor Charles." Darcie sighed and crossed her arms. "Why can't they be together?"

Gavin rubbed his hand up and down Elise's back before pulling her into his embrace. Kissing her temple, he rested his cheek on top of her head. "Sorry."

Elise stayed quiet, finding comfort in Gavin's gesture. *I thought I would know what to do after reading the letter, but I'm even more torn.*

"Your mom's not going to want to leave," Mitch said. "Especially if someone's telling her to."

"I know." Elise scanned the letter again. "But maybe this was always supposed to happen to get them into our world. He probably found a different way to deliver it, but it would make sense of why my family left."

"Except this is eighteen years too early," Darcie pointed out. "Hadn't the rest of your family just arrived at your grandma's when we left? Why is Rona trying to take over now?"

"Do you think it's something we've done?" asked Gavin.

Elise nodded. She was sure their meddling altered the timeline more than Rona, but they still needed to find out how much. Elise had heard about Rona's prior failed attempts, and perhaps this was one of those times, but Elise was determined to make it the last. Their ultimate mission comprised of finding the spy, saving Ruby, and finding all they could about Rona to prevent her family's catastrophic fate. *Two out of three isn't bad, but it's not good enough to go home yet.*

Unable to suppress a yawn, Elise tried shaking herself awake. She caught her reflection in a nearby mirror, realizing that not even the maids had been able to cover up the dark shadows beneath her worn heavy eyes. *I don't know how we're going to do this, but we can't let everyone down. I have to be strong no matter what.*

"Lay down on the couch. Try to nap," Gavin offered.

Elise shook her head as half of her words were muffled in a yawn. "There's no time. We have to decide what's safe to tell the council." Careful to fold the letter the same way that Charles had delivered it, she placed the paper in the front of her gown since Ruby's drawing was no longer there. Her infectious yawn spread throughout the group as Darcie and Mitch walked towards one of the crimson couches while Gavin and Elise claimed the other.

"What do you think they'll want to know?" Mitch leaned back to make room so Darcie could rest on him.

"Probably the same dumb questions," said Darcie with a yawn as her eyes closed. "Why did we choose now? What do we know? They always think we're conspiring against them anyway. Why would this time be any different?"

Weren't they the ones who wanted to plan what to say? Elise agreed with Darcie though. If it was going to be another back and forth of pointing fingers with false accusations, was there any point in preparing? The truth was as farfetched as anything they could come up with. She let the moment pass when no one else answered Darcie.

Feeling the weight of exhaustion, Elise pulled Gavin's arm around her before nuzzling his chest. She idly watched the crackling fire in the grate on the only wall not lined with bookshelves. After visiting the castle so many times, this was without a doubt her favorite room. The family portraits and antique maps gave the library an aged yet sophisticated warmth. Elise realized with a heavy heart that she only recognized two portraits of her living family compared to the handful that showcased deceased members. *I still wish I knew who these people were.* As she gave in and closed her eyes, she was startled by Gavin's voice.

"What's Vaughn like?"

I thought he was asleep! Elise bolted upright. "What?"

Gavin stiffened his shoulders but managed a small shrug. "That's definitely him in there. I just want to know what he's like."

Elise sighed. "You mean what he means to me?"

A long pause passed between the two. Goosebumps prickled her arms under Gavin's expectant stare. *How do I convince him that Vaughn doesn't mean anything to me?*

"It's going to come out one way or another," he pointed out. "We may as well be honest with each other."

Elise nodded but didn't speak right away. It was difficult to say Vaughn meant nothing, because she had come to care about him—the imposter at least. Had she been falling in love with him? Never. Elise doubted she could even see a reality where she dated Vaughn. Her feelings were more complicated than that. While she couldn't deny an attraction, her feelings revolved more around gratitude. Vaughn proved on several occasions to be a leader and protector, often risking his life to save them. It may have been the actions of a fraud, but Elise doubted she and her friends would have made it half as close to Gavin as they did without his interference.

"There's something else you want to ask," Elise said. She forced the rising tide of nerves within her stomach to settle. *Spit it out, Gavin. Do you not trust me?* "You mentioned back at Nana's that you 'saw plenty'." Elise paused to see if he would react. When he didn't, she drummed her fingers on her lap. "What did she show you?" *Maybe it was a trick.*

Pulling his arm from around her, Gavin scooted away as he sat up. He leaned forward, clasping his hands together as he considered what to say first. "Rona has some of Vaughn's hair. It's how she communicates with him. It's what causes the headaches." Elise nodded before he continued. "I only saw her use it a couple of times, but. . ." Gavin cleared his throat before looking down at the carpet. "The way you touched him, and. . .the way you let him touch you—"

"Gavin, I—"

He held up a hand. "I saw the way you looked at him, Elise."

Elise frowned, unable to think of a response. *What must he think of me? He probably wants to break up. This is all so messed up. I don't want Vaughn. I want Gavin. How can I show him that?* She was momentarily distracted by Mitch's snoring on the other couch before focusing on Gavin's guarded expression. Elise folded her hands with a defeated sigh. "There was a lot going on. I was worried about you, Mitch and Darcie were fighting constantly, and Vaughn. . .well, he. . ." She shook her head to try again. "It didn't mean anything, okay? I want to be with you. He distracted me. Whether he used magic or not, I don't know. I'm so embarrassed. I don't know what to say." Warm tears stung the back of her eyes, but she managed to whisper an apology before they fell. *He hates me. He probably just wants to go home. Maybe he thinks he made a mistake coming back.*

"Don't cry. You're not the only one who needs to apologize."

His unexpected reply made her look back up. Sniffling, she swiped away another tear before asking what he meant.

"I almost gave in to Rona."

Elise felt like someone had punched her in the stomach. Whatever ill-controlled nerves were circling within her came bubbling to the surface. Wiping her cheeks and nose on her sleeve, Elise put on a brave face. *I can do this.* "What did she do to you?" Up until now, Gavin had refused to answer her burning question. Though it caused her mouth to dry and heart to flutter, she needed to know what *really* happened to him while he was missing. *Whatever happened, I can forgive him. That woman is capable of anything.*

As Gavin recalled the prison cell and field training, her heart broke with each mentioned injury. When his story took a darker turn, involving a bathtub, arousing touches, and kisses, Elise found herself twisting the fabric of her dress until both knuckles were white. Her toes curled with repressed rage, thinking of the hold this woman had on Gavin. *Have I ever made him feel that way? Probably not. I can't compare to someone like her.*

"You okay?" Gavin asked when he was done. When Elise nodded without a word, he shook his head. "No, you're not." He leaned across the couch to release her tight grip of the dress. Taking her hand, he drew circles along the back of it with his thumb. "I think we both struggled."

She nodded again, flattening her lips, but let him speak. *He had it so much harder than I did. I wouldn't blame him if he acted on his feelings.*

"I could've killed her, you know."

She looked up, unable to hide her confusion. *What? How could he do that?*

"I had this dagger." Gavin held up his hand as if still clutching the weapon but froze with his tightened fist in midair. He punched the air as he lowered it. "It was pointed against her chest, I could've—but I choked. . .just like she said I would." He rested his forehead against his clasped hands. "All this would be over."

Elise felt a lump form in her throat. She didn't know if she had ever seen Gavin so broken. It was her turn to comfort him as she returned the favor of massaging his back. *He's gotten closer than I ever dreamed of. Will I feel the same way if given the chance?*

"She was right about everything," he continued from his hunched position, making it difficult for Elise to catch every word. "I wasn't strong enough to kill her. I wasn't able to save those boys like I promised." Gavin scoffed before pulling the medallion from his pocket. "I don't even know if it was even worth it to get Tristan's medallion back."

"Who's Tristan?" Elise asked. She wanted to ask him about the medallion ever since he got it back from the fairies.

Gavin closed his fingers around the trinket, letting the chain dangle freely. "Probably the best soldier out there. Not the nicest guy, but a good friend. He deserves better. They all do."

Elise grasped his shoulders to pull him back against the couch. Taking his hand in hers, she waited until he met her gaze. "We'll get it back to him."

He shook his head. "I doubt it. I'll probably never see him again. Or any of them."

Elise pulled him into a fierce hug, clinging to him as if the tighter she squeezed, the more pain could be released. *I want to fix this. I don't want to see you hurting.*

Gavin buried his face into her neck. For several moments they held each other in a silent embrace.

I hate she hurt you.

"You can't face her," Gavin whispered.

Elise released her hold on him so he could sit up. "What do you mean?"

Returning the medallion to his pocket, he looked at her as if it were obvious. "She's *too* strong. There's nothing she won't do to get what she wants. I know you keep hearing that, but I've *seen* it. The stories I heard in that prison, the prisoners themselves, everything about that place is dangerous because of her."

She bit her tongue before proceeding. "What do you think we should do?"

With a shrug, he turned his face towards the fireplace instead of her. "Maybe leave when your mom does."

Elise blew a loose piece of hair out of her face before she stood. *Is he serious?* Pinching the bridge of her nose, she paced back and forth in front of the fireplace. Seeing Darcie stir in her sleep, Elise lowered her voice. "Look. I get you're scared. I am too. I don't know what all you saw, but I trust that she's evil. It's why I need to take care of her before anyone else can—"

"Dmitri's dead." Gavin rocked back and forth on the couch. "He's been dead for years. He's *supposed* to be dead. Did you know that?"

"Dmitri?"

"Yeah, you heard Ballard when he delivered that letter. *King* Dmitri of Lockesbarrow. He's Rona's brother. Supposedly, he's the only person she ever cared about, so when he died, she went crazy and started all this takeover crap." He wiped both palms back and forth along his thighs. "I think Rona used the diary to bring him back, and if that's the case, we're screwed."

"I don't understand." Elise shook her head as she tried processing what he was telling her. "You said the diary was blank."

"Yeah, it was," Gavin said. "It still didn't stop her from grabbing it from me. It's the only explanation for why her brother's back and Vaughn was able to get himself on that council. Not to mention your uncle's trying to pull us into one of his power trips. Don't you see how messed up everything is? We need to get out of here before it's too late."

Elise took a shaky breath. Every time she felt like the situation was becoming under control, something else came along. Although Rona grabbed the diary, deep down Elise had hoped it wouldn't give the sorceress what she wanted. She sank back down on the couch, feeling as if concrete walls were closing in on her. It was difficult to breathe, let alone try to formulate a plan. "But we can't leave."

"Why not?" he asked. His crazed stare unnerved her. "If we stay, Vaughn will eventually lead Rona here."

"She's altered too much to go home," Elise replied. "What do you think *home* looks like? Think about it. It wouldn't be what we already know. I may not even have a family in this timeline's future." Elise tilted her head back against the couch, releasing a heavy sigh. *How am I going to fix this?* "I have to put it back together."

"Elise, be serious for a second," Gavin said, twisting his body to face her. "You already decided to fight Rona. Now you're going to take on Rona *and* her brother? Plus fix every *single* change in the timeline? You can't!"

"But I have to." Her voice was devoid of emotion as she talked towards the ceiling rather than look at him.

"Then we have to figure out how we—"

"I already told you," Elise said. "*I'm* going to do it."

"How?" he pressed.

"I don't know!" she snapped after the third time he asked. Given what happened to Darcie, there was no way Elise could let her friends put themselves into any more danger. She winced as her sharp tone woke Mitch and Darcie, who stretched and sat up.

"Is everything okay?" Darcie asked in the middle of a yawn.

"Yep." Gavin pushed himself off the couch. "Elise is going to defeat Rona and King Dmitri, but don't worry. She doesn't need our help."

The sarcastic bite of his tone tugged at Elise's heart. She wasn't trying to hurt his feelings. *I have to protect y'all and this is the only way. I can't lose you again. Don't be angry with me.*

Darcie walked over to them. "Elise, why—"

Everyone jumped as Ballard swung the door open as if trying to catch them off guard. He checked the room to see if anything was out of place before informing them Richard was ready to meet.

Although Gavin's words stung, Elise knew better than to speak in front of Ballard. While he did the right thing sometimes, the steward was usually only looking out for himself. One whisper of gossip was sure to reach Richard within seconds, or worse, her grandparents, whom she had yet to see.

Give them the truth. It's all they want. Don't let Vaughn intimidate you either. While easier said than done, Elise felt an immense relief when Gavin took her hand. *Here goes nothing.*

CHAPTER 8

Elise hadn't known what to expect when Ballard led them out of the library, but it wasn't a full escort comprised of five armed guards. Being taken to the council this way felt like a death sentence. Elise's mind was filled with memories of the time she spent in the castle dungeon. *Gavin must be feeling it worse than me. He's been in two dungeons.* If Gavin was unnerved, he hid it well. Mitch and Darcie kept quiet, too. The only interaction came from the passing staff, who regarded the group with a combination of pity and apprehension. Besides a momentary glance over his shoulder, Ballard took no notice of Elise and her friends. She preferred it this way until he led them down a different corridor away from the study.

"I thought we were meeting Richard," she said. "Why aren't we going to the study?"

"Formal council meetings take place in the assembly chamber again," Ballard replied.

"Assembly chamber?" Mitch asked. "We watched the members come out of the study earlier."

The steward took a calming breath, continuing forward past a series of windows overlooking the garden. Dusk was approaching, already casting shadows throughout the courtyard below. "King Derek has held meetings in there, but the study is intended for His Majesty's private use. Prince Richard takes a more traditional approach and prefers for official kingdom business to be conducted in the assembly chamber." Spinning on his heel to face them, Ballard gestured to a closed door on his left. He knocked only once before the door was opened by a servant inside.

"Do *not* embarrass His Majesty," Ballard warned.

"Which one?" asked Mitch, to which Ballard merely rolled his eyes before stalking away.

Elise shivered upon entering the stale assembly chamber. Though not as cheerful as the ballroom, it was far grander than she initially imagined. Her eyes were immediately drawn to an exquisite chandelier centered over an elongated table that took up most of the room. Every corner boasted ornate marble columns while the remaining space was comprised of iron sconces, oil paintings of former kings, and embroidered tapestries. The elegant multi-paned windows on the exterior wall reached the ceiling and were partially covered by lush burgundy drapes that matched the velvet table runner and chair cushions.

Has this place always been here?

Richard beckoned them forward from his seat at the head of the table on the opposite end of the room. Above his hand hung a formal portrait of King Derek. Elise hesitated upon seeing her grandfather's imperial figure. Fortunately, despite the regalia, the artist captured the kindness behind his eyes. *I wonder where they're keeping him. He should be here.*

Elise took a tentative step forward while scanning the faceless sea of intimidating blue coats on either side of her uncle. She tried to concentrate on anything else besides the ringing in her ears and weak knees. Knowing she was seconds from hyperventilating, she swallowed a wave of nausea before trying to stabilize herself. Elise stilled when she felt Gavin's hand on her arm.

"You've got this. We're right here," he whispered.

Although she heard his words, she took another moment to process them until she no longer felt lightheaded. *I'm not alone. Gavin's here. My friends are here. We're going to be okay. Don't panic. Don't panic.*

"Are we to believe these children have insight into Rona's plans?" asked the man closest to Elise from the end of the table.

"We have no time for games," a younger man said from the center.

"We can!" Darcie called out over the growing rumble of disapproving commentary.

The men looked towards Richard, who nodded towards the clerk near Elise.

"This assembly is in session," announced a clerk standing by the door with the servant who let everyone in. "First order of business, introductions. Please step forward and state your name for the council."

I can't give them my name! You need to get out of here now. Elise searched for other exits, but found the only one to be how she entered, which was now blocked by guards. She ushered Gavin in front of her before finding a place behind Darcie and Mitch.

"Gavin Striess," Gavin stated.

As each of her friends introduced themselves, Richard nodded with approval until it was Elise's turn again.

"State your name, Miss," the clerk repeated.

"Elise. . ." *Say something. Anything. Lie. Make up a random last name already!* She stood frozen, unable to think of a scenario where she wouldn't have to share too much. *Why didn't I think about this part?* Elise opened her mouth, but nothing came out. *Come on, Elise! You look stupid! Smith, Johnson, Williams, Baker. Pick one!* She searched the council more carefully before locating Charles and Vaughn a few seats away on Richard's right. *They already know I'm here to help the family and have a connection. Making a false name won't do anything now. I look too much like Joranna and Ruby to get away with it. I have to face the consequences.* Twisting her hands, she looked at her friends' tense expressions. *What do I do? What do I do!* Abandoning any chance of redemption at this point, Elise closed her eyes. "Laurille."

As expected, the room erupted with gasps, groans, and the collective buzzing of inquiries amongst the members of the council demanding to know Elise's connection to the royal family.

"Did you know about this?" one member called out to Richard.

"Their unplanned, dare I say, *hasty* invitation doesn't account for such a revelation. Why are we only learning of this?" cried another.

Before the prince could reply, a third gentleman stood. "There is something sinister here, dare I even say something treasonous in our midst. Perhaps even too grave for only a crown prince. I move for Her Majesty, Queen Joranna, to be present at this hearing at once. If not, the king himself!"

A unanimous cry of approval rang out amongst the table from most of the members until Richard commanded for all to take their seats.

"What else are we not being told?" demanded a voice above the raucous.

Elise compared Vaughn to the other distressed men. Studying him, she saw the faintest of smirks cross his lips while he scribbled something down on the paper in front of him.

"I *will* have order amongst the Council of Lords before we proceed!" Richard bellowed, glaring at the most vocal of members. "I am perfectly capable of overseeing this business. My mother shall *not* be made aware of this hearing, and my father's health will not allow it. Now, I can assure each of you here that I am unaware of any possible connection this young woman has to my family. Let us add the subject in question to our interrogation and proceed beyond introductions." He waited until the room fell silent again before nodding at another clerk responsible for writing the proceedings.

"Are all those in attendance aware of the punishment for committing treason to the crown?" the first clerk asked, waiting for the majority to nod or mutter in the affirmative. "Very well."

"I should like to start, if I may," said a frail older gentleman near the middle of the table.

"Proceed, Ambassador Heathcote," said Richard.

It wasn't until that moment that Elise realized this gentleman and the elf she had seen before were not wearing the traditional blue uniform. The senior man tapped his fingers along the edge of the table as he collected his thoughts. Pursing his lips, he scanned a list of documents in front of him before examining the group of teenagers.

"According to castle records, you were present when King Derek voiced his intentions to declare war on Lockesbarrow, were you not? And that you understood Vynchia's intent to aid Haighdlen in this?"

How does he know that? She reasoned it had been months to these people since Derek was attacked rather than days.

Elise thought back to the morning they discovered Gavin was missing. The council had just finished meeting with only the elf opposing the decision on behalf of Leafbrooke. She located the elf ambassador, who keenly watched her along with the other councilmen.

"Yes, we were there," said Elise, not sure where the man was going with his question.

"Well, according to the prince," he said, gesturing towards Richard, "that was the last time any of you were seen in the castle until this afternoon."

Elise remained silent as her heartbeat quickened.

"Considering you carried such sensitive information before King Derek formally announced it the following day, please explain where you've been these last months."

Elise felt her throat constrict as she met Vaughn's gaze across the room. *How do I answer that?* Shortly after Ruby helped them leave the castle to find Gavin, Vaughn turned up instead of their arranged guide. In possession of the safe passage letters, she followed him along with Mitch and Darcie. The journey ultimately led to the shores of Lockesbarrow where Derek was injured before they were sent forward in time only hours earlier. *They're going to put us back in the dungeon for sure.*

"Answer the question," Richard commanded.

Elise looked over her shoulder at Gavin. *Help me.*

Sensing her distress, Gavin called out to the ambassador. "We didn't tell anyone if that's what you're asking."

"But how can we be sure? There are spies everywhere," the elderly ambassador responded.

"Yeah, there's one sitting in this room." Mitch said, pointing to Vaughn.

Another roar of surprise rippled down the table as the councilmen looked between the teenagers and Vaughn.

Vaughn sat motionless, unphased by Mitch's outburst. Given the twinkle in his eye, Elise wondered if he was enjoying the attention.

"Sir Rodrick, I apologize again for these baseless allegations." Richard's eyes furrowed as he addressed Mitch next. "You need to quit deflecting your answers and speak the truth."

"And *you* need to listen!" Darcie piped up. "We are telling you the truth. He's your spy. Whatever you're saying in here is getting back to Rona!"

"Enough!" Richard bellowed as he smacked the table with his fist. "I'll not have you making a mockery of this council."

A heavy silence followed until Charles spoke up. "I think we should heed their warning."

Elise watched as her own shock was mirrored among the seated gentlemen, including Richard.

"Charlie, you can't be serious—"

"Forgive me, Your Highness, but I am." Charles met Elise's gaze before turning to Richard. "We can't risk ignoring any threat, regardless of its credibility."

"Lord Fenton makes an excellent point," said the elf. He held up a pale hand when another member tried to interrupt. "We must consider this issue beyond Haighdlen's border. There have been multiple port closures, border disputes, and more unexplained kidnappings from all neighboring kingdoms. Perhaps Sir Rodrick should be dismissed until a proper investigation is conducted."

"I agree," Charles said. "After all, I was put under an investigation based on a mere rumor, and you wouldn't want there to be any discrepancies in *your* handling of council matters as Crown Prince."

Elise watched her uncle carefully. She knew Charles made a good point, yet judging by Richard's glare, the prince didn't appreciate having his authority questioned.

"Sir Rodrick has taken great care to strengthen our ranks in preparation for battle," Richard said.

"You put him in charge of *soldiers*?" Gavin exclaimed. "You're setting yourself up for an ambush!"

Richard's face reddened as he fought to keep control. "Mr. Striess, your outbursts will cost you if—"

"My outbursts are trying to save you!" Gavin said. "*I* was one of those people kidnapped. I can tell you exactly what's going on."

"Pray, tell us then," Ambassador Heathcote said.

Gavin glared across the table at the speculative gentlemen. Elise watched as he clenched both fists by his side. "Not until he's gone."

Richard made to argue, but Vaughn stopped him with a wave of his hand as he stood. "There's no need, Your Highness. I shall remove myself for the sake of the council. I hope you're able to come to an agreement as to what's in the best interest of Haighdlen. The kingdom is in excellent hands. Good day, gentleman."

Elise watched his movements carefully as he made his way towards them. She didn't know what to expect, but she froze when he winked down at her as he passed. As if that wasn't enough, Elise thought she felt his hand brush against hers before his figure disappeared into the hall. Only when the door closed behind him did she feel safe enough to speak. "He's not here to help you," she said. "He works for Rona and is very dangerous. More dangerous than Brahm."

"Rona's training all those who are kidnapped to create a large army. There are kids over there being forced to fight," Gavin said.

Richard held his hand up. "You've been gone too long. Let me inform you that Rona is no longer reigning over Lockesbarrow, nor is there any evidence of such an army or any imminent threat of war. We're only interested in building strength in the case that changes. Our priority is the king's health and maintaining good relations among the remaining kingdoms while we weed out the spies."

"No threat of war?" Elise asked with an incredulous stare. "Did Vaughn tell you that? Oh, sorry," she added with a roll of her eyes. "Did *Rodrick* tell you that? Because he's lying to you!"

"If it were a lie, then why would Lockesbarrow retreat from the prior battles that did occur?" asked a councilman. "There hasn't been an isolated attack in several weeks!"

Gavin stepped in front of Elise. "Look, I don't know why she's been quiet, but Rona wouldn't give up control. She's power hungry, manipulative, and too self-centered for that."

"Be that as it may," Ambassador Heathcote stated, "we are here to decide how to proceed with this supposed war. Your Highness, given Lockesbarrow's lack of action and your father's health, I am inclined to remove Vynchia from it."

"You can't do that!" Darcie said. "That's what she wants!"

"You're going to get yourselves killed if you do!" Mitch added before addressing the prince. "Think about the family before you decide something you might regret. You don't want to do anything else stupid to get more people hurt."

"What are you talking about?" asked Richard.

"That time you shot me in the forest," Mitch said. "Remember now?"

"Okay, okay, Mitch. We get it. Your Highness, this is what she wants," Gavin continued. "Her brother may be in charge, but he has to be a front for something. He's the only one Rona cares about, but she's trying to throw you all off the scent. The fact she got Vaughn on your council only proves it's something big."

"Sir Rodrick has been found guilty of nothing and remains innocent at this time," Richard said before addressing the ambassadors. "Now, I can understand the hesitation to engage in warfare alongside Haighdlen, but I do agree we need to remain ready for anything."

"Leafbrooke remains as it did before and will not be sending aid at this time," said the elf.

"I am disheartened to hear that, Ambassador Vailweyn, but I respect your position on this." Richard sighed, turning to the elderly man. "Ambassador Heathcote, I beseech you to please reconsider your alliance. Together we may stand a chance. Isolated, we both fall."

"I'm afraid I don't detect a threat," the Vynchian ambassador replied. "However, given the delicate situation with your father, I shall refrain from a definite decision until more evidence is presented."

Richard nodded. Elise supposed her uncle's lack of a response meant the offer was better than nothing. "Next, we need to discuss what steps Haighdlen will take to protect itself."

Elise met Charles' tentative gaze. *This is what Charles was talking about in his letter. Richard's going to try separating the family. I have to stop him.*

"Wait, before you do that, what about more help?" Elise suggested. "Are there any ambassadors from the fairy kingdoms?"

The answering chortles and laughter answered her question. Wishing she hadn't spoken up, Elise curled her shoulders inward and missed the days she felt invisible.

"That will be all from you," Richard said to Elise and her friends. "We must proceed. Now, despite your lack of propriety, I see no reason why you can't continue with your usual accommodations."

"Please don't send anyone away!" Elise blurted out. "We only want to help. Don't ignore us!"

"I suggest you get a hold of yourself, young lady," Richard said. "You are a friend of my parents. Nothing more. Don't embarrass yourself further and subject yourself to more guarded quarters during your stay."

Elise made to argue again but felt Gavin's hand around her arm. "Drop it," he whispered. "Wait."

She fought every urge to pull away from him and march up to her uncle. She knew that would be a one-way ticket to the cell he was already hinting at.

Before the guards could lead them out, a servant burst through the doors.

"Sire!" the man panted.

"What is the meaning of this?" Richard fumed. "Are we not to have a moment's peace?"

It's scary how much he looks and sounds like Derek sometimes.

"It's the king," said the servant.

The room waited with bated breath for Richard to reply.

The prince lowered his gaze. The muscles in his neck twitched as he swallowed. Suppressing his emotions, giving the illusion of the perfect leader, he softened his tone. "Is he. . .has he passed?"

"No, Sire, but the queen beckons you to his chamber." Richard sighed in relief before the servant continued. "The king is lucid as of now and wishes to speak with you."

Take us with you! What he wants to talk with Richard about? We need to get up there to talk with him too.

"I must conclude this session, gentlemen, if you'd be so kind as to stay this evening. Guards, have a maid escort these visitors to their respected rooms at once." Richard didn't wait for a response before passing Elise and her friends on the way out.

The four were not given another chance to speak to the councilmen before being ushered out of the assembly chamber. There was no sign of Richard anywhere, but Elise's heart skipped a beat when she found Ruby waiting for them in the main hall.

"Finally!" Ruby exclaimed. "I've been sick with worry ever since you left. Richard just passed in a hurry, refusing to tell me anything. What happened?"

Ignoring the flanking guards, Elise shook her head. "They won't listen to anything we tell them. Ruby, you're not safe here."

Ruby scoffed. "What are you talking about?"

Before Elise could respond, Ballard made his grand entrance into the conversation. "There you all are! I have assigned maids to take you to your rooms after dinner. Please follow me to the dining hall."

Elise bit her tongue before she got herself into too much trouble and followed the steward. Her bad mood improved along the way as the aroma of chicken and freshly baked bread reached her nostrils. She felt her stomach twist in knots and rumble no less than five times between sitting down and being served.

She was not shocked by Richard's or Joranna's absence, but she did wonder at her other uncle and aunt missing dinner. "Isn't anyone else coming?" she asked a servant.

"Only members of council who feel inclined this evening, my lady. The remaining family is otherwise engaged."

Elise frowned.

"Don't look into it," Ruby whispered. "I've eaten the last several meals alone."

"How come?" Darcie asked.

Ruby shrugged. "Sarah and Ian keep to themselves lately, and Mother never leaves Father. Eat. You must be famished."

Elise's stomach replied before she could. Giving into her hunger, she and her friends ate in silence. It was hard to get a word in with Ballard listening only feet away.

"Don't lose heart, Elise," Ruby said when they reentered the main hall. She yawned before suggesting they head to bed until any updates came about her father. "It's taking every ounce of control I have not to demand more information, but I'm a bit fed up with doors slamming in my face."

"Right then," Ballard announced when he joined them. "You'll be shown to your rooms at once. As before, I will arrange for a guard to be posted outside your doors and—"

"Oh, no, I see no reason for that," Ruby argued. "Leave them alone this evening."

"But Princess—"

"Honestly, Ballard, they've nothing to warrant such treatment, and if Richard didn't bother to order it, I see no reason to reinstate it." She held her chin high, meeting his challenging stare for several moments until he tightened his lips with a sneer.

"Very well, Princess," he said before slinking away.

"Disgusting man," Ruby muttered under her breath.

Elise chuckled in disbelief. "Wow, thank you." *I can't believe it. We won't feel like criminals anymore.*

"Get some sleep," the princess said with a smile. "You won't be scrutinized this evening. A meeting with the council is punishment enough."

They chuckled before Ruby turned to leave. It was only then Elise remembered the letter hidden in her gown. She called out to her mother before her eyes fell to Ruby's belly. *Is giving her this letter the right thing to do? She's already going through so much. I don't want her to hurt anymore.* Seeing the maids approaching, Elise went with her gut feeling and retrieved the letter. "Please read this."

"What is it?" Ruby eyed the letter warily as she took it. When Elise revealed who it was from, Ruby gripped the middle of the paper between her fingers as if to rip it.

"No!" Elise exclaimed, startling everyone in the main hall. Whispering a quick apology to the nearby staff, she nodded towards Ruby's hands. "You'll want to read it."

"Why, have you?"

Elise saw the familiar fiery rage flash across her mother's eyes. Ruby was an extremely private person. One hint of prying and the letter would be burned. No questions asked. "No," she lied. "I could just tell when he gave it to me that it was important. You should read it."

Ruby's shoulders relaxed as she considered Elise's words. The princess looked at all four travelers, assessing their reactions, before flattening the paper out. "Very well. Good night."

As they were led to their rooms and changed for the night, Elise's mind raced with all the possible scenarios that could arise from Ruby reading the letter. *I hope she reads it. Please read it, Ruby.*

Would her mother burn it after reading? Would she be convinced of Charles' feelings? Could this bring them closer together? What would happen to the timeline if they married? As usual, the other side crept in with doubts. *Knowing Mom, it could be crumpled up or in pieces. Poor Charles.* Ever since Lord Fenton vouched for Vaughn's removal, Elise's heart had softened towards the other man. Despite his questionable actions and words, she truly did believe he loved her mom. She knew Ruby loved him in return. Whatever happened later between them would be up to their own stubbornness.

By the time everyone went to bed, a storm developed nearby. As a round of thunder rolled in the distance, Elise groaned as she covered her face with a pillow. Despite everything that happened, she couldn't bring herself to fall asleep. Her mind wouldn't let her rest. *We haven't seen Derek or Joranna yet. This is so different than all our other visits. Something doesn't feel right. Vaughn is also somewhere in this castle and that scares me.*

She was startled out of her unending thought cycle by the sound of the doorknob turning. When the door didn't open right away, Elise broke out into a cold sweat as she was flooded with worst-case scenarios. *Please don't be Vaughn. Please be Darcie. Please be Darcie. Ugh, why was I so excited not to have a guard earlier?*

Elise's heart thrashed around inside her chest until she saw Gavin's face peek around the door. She closed her eyes and collapsed back against the pillows. "You scared me."

"Sorry," he whispered. "I couldn't sleep, so I came to check on you. You okay?"

Elise nodded, realizing a second later he probably couldn't see her well in the dark. It dawned on her this was the first time she and Gavin had been truly alone since reuniting. *There's no chaperones, friends, fairies, or guards. We're finally alone.* "Yeah, come in."

Despite the heavy covers, Elise shivered when she heard him turn the lock. Her breath hitched in anticipation as his dark figure crept closer to the bed. *I need you.*

CHAPTER 9

Elise slid over to give Gavin room on the bed. *Is he really here right now?*

"I didn't wake you up, did I?" he whispered. When Elise shook her head with a smile, he leaned his forehead against hers. "Good. I wanted to tell you how impressed I was earlier." Elise must've shown her confusion, because he quickly followed up with, "The way you spoke up to the council. I know that was hard for you."

She nodded. "I don't think I breathed the entire time." A breathy chuckle left her lips before she looked into his eyes. "You impressed me too, but that shouldn't come as a surprise."

"Why's that?"

Elise shrugged. "You're always confident. It makes me jealous. I mean, *look* at you. You survived being captured by Rona, and then hearing what happened to you. . .you're not afraid of anything."

"That's not true," he replied, holding up a hand when she tried to argue with him. "I've never been more scared than I was these last few days."

"You thought she'd kill you, right?"

Gavin nodded. "*That*, but. . .I kept thinking about you guys. *You* especially, and how I might never see you again." He reached down to intertwine their fingers. "I drove myself crazy knowing that Vaughn guy was so close to y'all. I kept thinking of the two of you together."

Elise felt a stab of guilt in her chest. *I hate he got the wrong idea.* "He doesn't mean anything to me."

Gavin shrugged. "It was still hard to watch though."

"I know what you mean," Elise admitted. "I worried about you and Rona. I can't compete with her beauty or power, and all I kept hearing was nobody says no to her." When Gavin didn't answer, she bit her lip. *Is that what happened between the two of you?*

"I said it before," he said. "We both messed up, and we can keep rehashing it, but that's not why I came in here."

Then why did you? Elise didn't feel the need to ask out loud, so she watched him carefully.

Gavin opened his mouth two or three times without forming any words before hanging his head with a frustrated sigh. He squeezed their connecting hands tighter until Elise could feel a thin layer of sweat forming against his palm.

Is he nervous? It wasn't often Gavin let his nerves show. At that precise moment, Elise couldn't think of *ever* seeing him so flustered. *What's going on? Did I do something wrong? Is he breaking up with me?* The longer his silence stretched, the more Elise convinced herself he must be upset with her.

"Whatever it is, I'm sorry," she apologized before more desperate words began spilling from her mouth. "I mean it. I only care about you. Please don't hate me. Let's forget everything that happened while you were missing. I can't do this without you." *You have to believe me.* She was caught off guard when his shoulders began to shake. *Is he. . .laughing?*

Sure enough, thanks to a patch of moonlight shining through the window, she could make out a wide grin across his face. "It's not funny. I'm being serious!"

"I know." Gavin took a moment to contain his amusement before looking up again. "I can't believe you thought I was breaking up with you."

Releasing his hand to cross her arms, she glared at him with an indignant scowl. "Well, why else would you be acting all weird like this?"

His voice softened. "Because I realized something while I was away." Gavin reached up to tuck a strand of hair behind her ear. When Elise raised her eyebrows expectantly, he licked his lips before taking a deep breath. "I think I'm in love with you."

What! Struck speechless, Elise unfolded her arms and searched his eyes. *Did he really just say that?* With a quavering laugh, she sat dumbfounded, feeling as if her heart would burst. A growing warmth spread along her entire body until it settled in the form of a lump in Elise's throat. *I can't believe this.* Cocking her head, she regarded him with a lopsided grin. "Really?"

Gavin nodded before his eyes widened. "I mean, I don't know why I said, *'I think'*," he added quickly, rubbing the back of his neck. "I'm an idiot."

He's so cute. Elise giggled as tears pricked the backs of her eyes. *Is this really happening right now?*

"What I should've said was. . ." Gavin inched closer until his face was a breath away from hers. "I love you."

Elise flickered her gaze between his eyes and mouth before leaning forward. "I love you, too." As their lips met, she still couldn't shake the fear that he would vanish any moment and she'd wake to find it was all a dream. Breaking the kiss, Elise dipped her head back as Gavin's mouth found the tender spot at the base of her neck.

At first, his soft familiar kisses released the usual butterflies in her stomach, but within seconds, it was as if a switch was flipped inside him. No longer did familiar Gavin's touches feel like simple caresses, but an unhinged, raw need to explore every inch of her.

Elise had never known desire like this. She didn't have a clue what she was doing. She became increasingly aware of their panting, mutual groans, and the quivering ache deep within her that pulsed like an itch waiting to be scratched.

Remembering his sensitive spot being similar to hers, she returned her attention to his neck.

'You don't want to do that', he had once warned her.

Yes, I do. Cupping a hand around his neck, she inhaled his soapy scent before nibbling the tender skin until eliciting a moan from him that awoke something within her. *I want you.*

She tugged on his shoulder until he rolled on top of her. Elise's mind ran away with thoughts of what could happen. As much as she wanted more, the risk was too high.

"We need to be careful," she said. "It feels strange to finally be alone like this anyway." When he didn't respond, she panicked. *He's going to get the wrong idea.* "I want you. You have no idea how much I want this, but. . .we should wait."

Gavin dropped his head onto her shoulder with a heavy sigh. "Yeah, you're right." He rolled over onto his back until their breathing returned to normal before pulling her into an embrace.

Elise rested against his shoulder as their legs tangled together. The thunder had ceased, and all that remained was the steady pitter-pattering of rain against the window. *This is still nice.* It may not have been how she imagined their first night alone together would turn out, but it was an intimate connection between them, nonetheless. She nuzzled her face against his chest, admiring how well she fit against him.

"Will you stay for a while?" she whispered.

"Mmhmm," Gavin hummed before adding with a chuckle, "I doubt you want us found together in the morning though."

She giggled again. "We'd never get a break from a chaperone."

He yawned. "We'd never get a break from Mitch and Darcie."

He's got a point. Darcie would whine and beg until she had every private detail. Closing her eyes, Elise focused on Gavin's heartbeat drumming against her ear. The steady rhythm, coupled with the steady rise and fall of his chest, threatened to lull her to sleep. It could have been for ten minutes or an hour. Elise couldn't be sure. They rested in their comfortable silence until Elise felt her body jerk involuntarily a couple of times. She fought against it until Gavin kissed her forehead.

"I better go."

"Are you mad?"

"No. I just wish I could stay longer. Who knows when we'll get another minute alone?"

He's right. Elise nodded, doubting he could see.

Gavin paused at the door. "I love you," he whispered.

"You too." When the door closed, Elise waited for any sounds of him being caught. Hearing none, she hugged close to her the pillow he had used and shimmied back beneath the blankets. *It still smells like him.* Although the feverish sensations were long gone, she squeezed the pillow tighter before burying her face into it to muffle a high-pitched squeal. She kicked her feet back and forth, wishing she could shout at the top of her lungs. *Gavin loves me. He really loves me!*

Despite their shortened night, Elise felt relieved when Gavin smiled at her upon entering the dining hall the following morning. *Good. He doesn't look upset.* She yearned to talk to him about the previous night but was unable due to the large party sitting amongst them, including Mitch, Darcie, and Elise's aunt and uncles. Besides pleasantries, little was said until Ruby joined them.

"Any news on Father?" the princess asked her eldest brother.

Richard rolled his eyes before stabbing a fork into his food. "How many times must you ask? He's fine."

His agitated answer wasn't good enough for Ruby, who quickly followed with, "Considering you're the only one you've allowed in his room besides Mother, I'm left with no other option." Ruby ignored Richard's glare and turned her attention to her two other siblings. "How odd to see the two of you here. I rather wondered if you both left."

"Not now, Ruby. We're not in the mood for your sarcasm," muttered Sarah.

"Speak for yourself," Ian replied with a smirk. "I rather enjoy Ruby's wit. *Someone* in the family should have an engaging personality besides me."

Will they ever get along? Elise rolled her eyes, relaxing as Gavin drew lazy circles against the small of her back. The two exchanged coy smiles before she rested her head against his shoulder.

Sitting across from them, Darcie narrowed her eyes at the sappy gesture before pointing her fork in their direction. "What's going on? Something's different."

Denying anything had changed, Elise felt the telling rush of heat seep into her cheeks.

"Spill it. Why're you two acting so weird? Do *you* know?" she asked Mitch when Elise and Gavin shrugged.

"No clue." Mitch couldn't help but smirk under the weight of Darcie's stare.

"You *do* know something!" Darcie hissed, tugging on Mitch's sleeve. "Tell me. I can't be the only one out of the loop. I'll go crazy!"

Mitch met Gavin's eyes across the table, clearly enjoying his girlfriend's momentary insanity.

Sitting up, Elise swallowed convulsively as she met Gavin's gaze. *Did Gavin tell him what we did, or almost did?* She sighed with relief when he shook his head to indicate that nothing was shared.

Darcie huffed. "If someone doesn't tell me *something* soon, I'm going to lose it." The tips of her ears had already turned red as she slumped back with her arms crossed.

She's such a drama queen. Elise couldn't suppress a smile as she shook her head.

Darcie softened her expression as she regarded Mitch before trailing a hand across his thigh. "It sure would mean a lot if you'd tell me."

Mitch froze with a mouth full of food. His cheeks quickly became the color of Darcie's ears before he swept her hand away. Once he was able to swallow, Mitch chuckled at Darcie's pouty expression. "It's not that big of a deal. I went to ask a maid for a glass of water and thought I'd stop to talk to Gav for a bit." Mitch scooped another bite of eggs on his fork with a wink in Elise's direction. "Only he wasn't in *his* room."

Darcie's eyes widened as her mouth hung open. Glancing between Elise and Gavin, she felt as if she was seeing them for the first time as she studied their body language for incriminating evidence. Checking to make sure no one else was paying attention to them, she fanned herself with both hands. "Oh my gosh. You didn't! Did you? You *did*, didn't you? I can't believe it!"

"Darcie, shh," Elise hissed, also checking to make sure her family wasn't listening. "No. We didn't."

"Liar," her best friend gushed. "You look guilty and happy at the same time. You both do."

Gavin squeezed Elise's hand under the table. *Part of me wishes we had, but we made the safest choice.* She didn't know how she'd handle any what-if scenarios while trying to save Derek *and* take down Rona. Her trail of thought wandered to Ruby. She glanced down the table at her young expectant mother, who was still bickering with Sarah and Richard. *By my age, Mom was in a strange land with a one-year-old. I can't imagine. . .*If that wasn't motivation enough to control her urges for the time being, she didn't know what was.

"Well, *something* must've happened," Darcie pressed.

"Yeah, something did." Gazing down at Elise with a lopsided grin, Gavin intertwined their fingers. "I told Elise I loved her last night."

Darcie gasped before clapping her hands. Bouncing in her chair, she nodded towards Elise. It looked as if it took everything in her power for Darcie to whisper. "*And*? Did you say it back?"

I could watch this for hours. There was something comical about Darcie's theatrics. Deciding to put her friend out of her misery, Elise nodded with her own face-splitting grin. She suspected if they hadn't been in the company of the royal family that Darcie would've broken into a song and dance routine.

"Okay, you have to—" Darcie cut off as Joranna's entrance was announced to the dining hall.

The guards and servants stood at attention as Elise's grandmother walked to stand near her children, barely acknowledging the four travelers apart from a brief nod. Joranna's bloodshot eyes were worn and sunken against her pale tear-stained face. Although remaining the epitome of royalty, draped head to toe in fine jewelry and fabrics, her mind was clearly far away from the room.

"Do you think something's happened?" Mitch whispered. "Or will happen soon?"

"Definitely," said Gavin. "I know we didn't use the diary this time, but we've always landed right where we need to be. I don't think we came to this time by coincidence, but if we don't do something soon to get to Rona, we won't stand a chance of helping."

"Mother, you look so tired." Sarah stood to hug Joranna. "Won't you join us and eat something?"

Joranna shook her head. When she spoke, her voice was hoarse and unrecognizable, as if the words being spoken were not her own. "No. I've come to. . .the doctor feels it's time for the family to. . .and I think he's right."

What is she talking about?

"You should go see him. Now," Joranna managed to blurt out as she wrung her hands together. "I fear I've have been gone too long already."

What!

"Absolutely not." Richard dropped his fork in disgust. Elise watched Ruby jump when it clattered against his barely touched plate. "Mother, I'm sure the doctor got it wrong. Again, there's no need to create havoc upon the—"

"*Richard*," Joranna snapped, holding up a hand as he tried arguing back. The room was engulfed in a palpable silence. Even Richard appeared to yield at his mother's tone. With a shaky breath, Joranna turned to leave without waiting for anyone to follow her. "The four of you need to come with me."

CHAPTER 10

Watching her family leave without being included felt like someone punched Elise in the gut. Drawing inward, it was as if she heard herself screaming without anyone noticing.

We have to see Derek! I can't let anything happen to him.

By the time all four reached the hall, however, Ballard was already in place to apprehend them. His signature strained smile of forced politeness was firmly in place. "Well, well, well. And where would you be off to in such a hurry?" he asked.

"We need to get to the king," Elise said tersely, growing more infuriated by the second as he regarded them with a smile one might reserve for small children. She wasn't in any mood to argue with the steward, and the amusement he clearly got from preventing them access to Derek only provoked her more. When he blocked Elise's next attempt to step around him, she groaned. "You *don't* understand! We need to make sure he's okay. Tell him to let us in!" She looked around for any other staff to help, but the remaining maids and servants merely stood watching. Some even acted as if they couldn't see or hear her.

"I'm afraid you wield no power here." Ballard looked down his nose as he spoke, a gesture that made Elise want to punch the smug expression from his face. "Now, I shall be glad to escort you to the drawing room. Or the library, perhaps? Trust that the king is in excellent care. There is nothing to worry your pretty little head about."

"They're calling in the family!" Darcie argued. "We need to talk to him before anything else can—"

Ballard held up a hand to shush her. "You'll merely vex the family, which I am ordered to prevent at *all* cost." Puffing out his chest, he tugged at the hem of his vest with a haughty sniff.

Richard really is out of control.

"We're not going anywhere *except* the king's room," Gavin stated. "And you're going to lead us there."

Ballard stared at the finger Gavin pointed near his face. "My, my, how bold you've become since your capture. Nevertheless, you forget your place, sir. I take my orders from the royal family, and the last time I checked, that does not include any of you."

Elise longed to say she *was* a family member, since Ballard wasn't present during the council meeting, but she knew it was a losing battle either way. They would have to find a way to get to Derek's room without the steward knowing. *That's easier said than done. This guy's got his nose in everything.* Then it dawned on her. She could try using her magic. It worked at odd moments here and there. It was worth a try. When she was certain her voice wouldn't come out as a stutter, she stepped in front of Gavin.

"Take us to the king." Elise spoke with an air of authority, careful to keep her posture strong, while at the same time feeling as if she could become sick at any moment. Feeling her stomach churn from nerves, she regretted having so much to eat. Closing her eyes, Elise willed her breakfast to stay down before she opened them and focused on what she wanted Ballard to do. *Take us to the king.*

The steward scoffed, unable to hear the internal battle Elise was fighting to control her magic. She continued repeating the command in her thoughts, imagining a force leaving her mind and entering his own.

Ballard looked as if he was ready to hurl another condescending insult her way, but no words came out. Instead, his mouth simply opened and closed without a sound.

"Keep going," Darcie whispered in her ear. "Just focus. You've got this."

Elise felt Gavin grab her hand with a squeeze of encouragement. Their support meant more than they knew. Tightening her mouth into a flat line, Elise concentrated on a spot in the middle of Ballard's forehead so as not to lose her nerve. *Take us to see Derek. Turn around.* She watched as Ballard turned his back to them. *Yes, that's it. Now, take us to the king.*

"Come this way." Ballard's brows creased with confusion, as if he couldn't believe what he agreed to do, before ascending the grand staircase without another word. His steps were uneven at first, prompting Elise to focus all the more on the direction she wanted him to go. *Don't mess this up. This has to work. Go faster, Ballard!*

Gavin, Darcie and Mitch quietly cheered her on as they followed the steward to where the royal bedrooms were. Elise instantly recognized Ruby's bedroom door as they passed it, but she felt a twinge of concern when Ballard continued walking past all the doors without stopping. Even her grandparents' room was unattended. Fearing her magic might be backfiring, that perhaps Ballard might be deviating from her influence, Elise scrambled to form new commands. Any hope of concentrating disappeared, however, when they rounded the last corner.

A large crowd of servants, footmen, and maids were gathered outside of a closed guarded doorway.

Elise only managed to follow Ballard halfway down the corridor before a shrill cry pierced the air around them that turned her blood to ice. *That's Joranna.* She broke out into a sprint, nearly pushing Ballard out of her way. Before Elise could reach the king's door, however, it burst open as Richard stormed out. In his own haste, he bumped into a maid, knocking over a towering pile of folded linens in the startled young woman's hands without apologizing. *I can't let him see me! He'll try to stop me.* To her surprise, however, Richard *did* see her, but rather than exert his authority, he merely brushed past her without a word.

She made it to the front of the disorderly group of onlookers, who were busy griping about the spilled laundry, with half a second to spare. Only able to catch a glimpse through the crack in the door,

Elise jerked her head back as one of the guards promptly shut it, but the damage was done.

Gavin, Darcie, and Mitch caught up in time to help the maid pick up the fallen linens while Elise stood facing the severe-looking guards, but she wasn't paying attention to them. Her mind was occupied with what she saw inside the bedroom.

Upon Richard's exit, the door was left ajar enough for Elise to make out a frail-looking man propped up on the four-poster bed. While she realized now that it was Derek, he looked nothing like the strong king she had come to know. His wrinkled face grimaced weakly as his chest heaved, each breath sounding painful, and his wispy gray hair was plastered against his sweaty forehead. She couldn't make out much more. Not only due to the sickly nature of his appearance, but the drapes had been closed, giving the impression it was much later in the day. The candlelight from a nearby table cast the large room in dancing swirls of orange light and shadows. The only other person she could make out in time was Ruby standing by his head with a wide-eyed expression while Derek's hand rested against her rounded stomach.

Another round of wailing from inside, this time from Sarah, sent a cold chill down Elise's spine. She closed her eyes against the gut-wrenching sounds coming from her grandfather's room.

"Disperse at once!" Ballard hissed to everyone standing in the corridor, clearly free from Elise's powers. The crowd broke apart, many weeping themselves, until Elise, Gavin, Mitch, and Darcie were the only ones left. "Out of my way and do as you're told!" He stepped around the four teenagers and into the room. The door remained open just long enough for a guard to allow him access. This time, Elise tried to get a better look. Standing on her toes, she caught a glimpse of the rest of her family. Joranna was now draped across Derek's chest, sobbing uncontrollably as Ballard and the doctor tried pulling her up, while Ian hugged Sarah as she wept into his shoulder. The king lay motionless with his arms by his sides on the mattress. Elise gasped when she realized Ruby, who hadn't moved, caught her staring. The door slammed shut even harder than before. "You heard the orders," growled one of the guards. "Disperse!"

"Come on," Gavin said, holding his hand out for Elise to take. "Let's give them some privacy."

"I can't." Elise's voice cracked as she spoke, yet she was desperate for one more look. "There might still be time. If I could just get inside—"

"Come back!" screamed Joranna from inside the room, making Elise jump. "Derek, darling, please. Please no. Not yet." There were deep, masculine voices, but Elise couldn't make out what they were saying. "No! I won't leave him," Joranna cried. Her anguished voice sounded unrecognizable from the composed woman the four travelers usually encountered.

Elise broke out into a cold sweat as another cry was ripped from her grandmother's throat. She felt her knees buckle but caught herself in time to hear Joranna plead with the others in the room. "Leave us alone. Don't touch him! Derek, you must wake up. It's me. You must wake up. Don't leave me. I can't—I c-can't be here without you!" Her words quickly slurred into incoherent mumbling. It sounded like she might be speaking into Derek's shirt.

"Let's go," Darcie urged, pulling on Elise's sleeve. "We shouldn't be here right now. It's too private."

"I'm not leaving," Elise choked out, determined to gain any access she could. *It's my family.*

Everything around her felt as if it were paused in time. Was this how it had played out before she interfered in the timeline? Was Derek supposed to die from this curse? Elise bit the inside of her cheek to keep from screaming. Derek wouldn't have been on that beach if it weren't for them. This could've been avoided. Her mind was bombarded with flashbacks of the diner where she met Derek, to the time they spent together preparing for his and Joranna's engagement ball, before her heart wrenched at the memory of his proud smile as he shared the news of Richard's birth in the bakery during their tour of Clara. While only a few days of Elise's life had passed since then due to the diary, Derek's entire lifetime was now threatened to feel as short.

Elise was unable to move from where she stood. It sounded like Joranna quieted down as a series of footsteps crossed the room.

Elise could make out Ballard's voice, followed by who she assumed was the doctor. Feeling the adrenaline building inside her, she ignored her friends' pleas to leave, instead choosing to listen intently with bated breath. She knew in her heart what the outcome was sounding like, but she wasn't prepared for it all to become a reality. When the door opened one last time, allowing a distraught Ruby to step out, Elise felt numbness spread throughout her entire body as the doctor's voice flowed into the corridor for all who were close enough to hear the truth.

They were too late.

Derek was gone.

CHAPTER 11

The days following Derek's death were lengthy and solemn with little opportunity to interact with members of the royal household. Elise wanted to mourn *with* her family, but they were well protected, kept away from prying eyes, to grieve in private.

The only perk was that any further thoughts and attention towards chaperoning were practically nonexistent now, allowing Gavin to visit Elise's room each night in secret. While their passions hadn't resumed from the first night, Elise found herself eagerly anticipating the sound of her bedroom door creaking open after everyone went to bed. Truth be told, *he* was the only reason she hadn't completely broken. Being isolated from her newly found family, whether *they* were aware of the relation or not, was threatening to drive her insane. Gavin's comforting words were all that soothed Elise enough to sleep. He would simply talk and rest with her, sometimes for hours, as well as stretches of time when neither spoke that she found equally consoling.

On the morning of the king's funeral, even the clouded sky evoked a certain somberness as people arrived from near and far to pay their respects to the late ruler.

From the guestroom window, her forehead pressed against the cold glass, Elise watched the endless line of carriages pull into the courtyard.

So many questions still swirled in her mind surrounding Derek's death. Despite the declaration that his passing was curse-related—spurring outrage throughout the kingdom and a cry to increase war efforts—Elise couldn't shake the gnawing reminder that it could have been prevented. The king wouldn't have traveled to Vynchia if it hadn't been for them. She clenched her eyes against another bout of warm tears. How did she have any left to shed? Swiping a hand across her cheek, Elise peered over at a black dress on the bed.

At Joranna's request Edith, the fabriwitch in charge of dressing the royal household, had provided Elise and her friends with funeral attire. While lovely— probably one of the *most* beautiful gowns Elise had ever seen—she couldn't help but think how grim it looked compared to the bright luxurious ballgowns from their past visits. Stepping closer to it, Elise brushed her fingertips along the dark silken trim. It would be a perfect fit, no doubt, yet she dreaded putting it on. Wearing the gown meant admitting this was all real. She also knew, however, that if she didn't hurry, the maids would have to help her. Elise hated when that happened.

Fortunately, Elise was dressed when the maids arrived, so they only needed to fix her hair and makeup. *I can deal with that.* Those were the two areas she often didn't bother with at home anyway.

Elise's mind wandered yet again as she studied her dolled-up reflection. At some point, she would need to address her plan to face Rona with the family. There wasn't going to be an ideal time, leaving her to ponder which options were less likely to get her and the others thrown in prison.

"You ready to go?" called Gavin from the doorway.

Elise jumped. She hadn't heard him come in. *When did the maids leave?*

"Sorry." Gavin closed the door behind him before approaching her vanity table. "I knocked, but you didn't answer."

He knocked? I really was *distracted.* Elise turned back to face the mirror as he came to stand behind her.

Gavin rested his chin on the top of her head, being careful not to mess up what the maids had styled. Black suited Gavin, she mused, as she took in his polished appearance.

"Do I have to go?" Speaking scarcely above a whisper, she wondered if Gavin had even heard her when he didn't immediately reply.

"No," he finally said, kissing her hair. Meeting Elise's eyes in the mirror, he lowered his mouth near her ear. "We could stay here, but I know you. You'll hate yourself if you don't go."

He's right. The funeral would happen whether she went or not. The least she could do was be there for the family, even if they didn't know she was one of them.

It was an odd thought, she realized. After everything she and her friends had been through, Elise still didn't feel like a princess. There were often moments at night, particularly when she was alone, when Elise imagined what would've happened if she hadn't accepted her grandmother's offer. Would she have ever seen Gavin again? Were they destined to be together, or was this a coincidental fling that would die out when they got back home? Since the first night he told Elise he loved her, the words had been uttered between the two of them many times. She loved Gavin, too, but a part of her feared he only loved the idea of who she was during this journey. If she survived facing Rona and was lucky enough to make it home alive, would his feelings change? *Home.* Home, the very thing she was fighting so hard to reach, felt incredibly far away.

Taking Gavin's hand, she followed him out. That was going to be a difficult conversation, but it would have to wait. Coming down the staircase, Elise was surprised at how crowded the main hall was. Scanning the sea of faces, she met Darcie's eyes.

"There you are!" Darcie stood on her tiptoes and waved them over to where she and Mitch were standing. "Where have you been? It doesn't matter." She was talking so fast, Elise couldn't get a word in. "Bad news, guys. The funeral is over already."

"What?" Elise shrieked, causing a handful of guests nearby to jump. She would've apologized had she not been so lightheaded as a flood of nerves attacked each limb. *This isn't happening.* "W-we missed it?"

Darcie shushed her as a couple of people looked in their direction before continuing in a whisper. "Mitch and I overheard some people talking. The burial was a private event for the royal members only."

"Yeah, everyone else is here for some kind of memorial service," Mitch added while scanning the room. "Your uncle's supposed to give a speech soon."

Elise felt the blood drain from her face. Not only could she not mourn with the family, but now she had missed the burial? *I wanted to see him one last time.* Her head swam until Mitch's voice pierced through the numbness to alert them that the family had just arrived.

A bizarre sensation flooded through Elise as everyone else cleared a path for the approaching Laurille family. It wasn't until Darcie hissed, reminding her to curtsy along with the rest of the crowd, that Elise realized the feeling pulsing through her was no longer heartache or grief. In that moment, she felt nothing but pure rage.

I am family! I should've been there! Why didn't they include me?

Joranna knew they were related to some degree, so why wasn't Elise told the burial would be earlier? *I wanted to say goodbye, too. I need to tell him I'm sorry!* As the family's arrival into the hall was announced, it was as if Elise were floating above her body watching everything unfold. Countless scenarios came to mind of what she wanted to tell her relatives, but as the procession started, Elise felt her rage slowly dissipate.

They look so broken. Elise had been so preoccupied with how *she* was grieving, how betrayed *she* felt, that it was jarring to witness those closest to Derek being forced to face everyone without him.

Richard was the first to pass through. *No doubt, his idea.* Joranna came next, followed by Sarah, Ian, and Ruby. All wore matching pale expressions, bloodshot eyes, and stoic statures. Their movements were synchronous, rehearsed, and void of emotion. *Everything a royal is supposed to be, I guess.* The mere spectacle of it all made Elise want to cry all over again. She didn't know if she could ever hide her emotions like that. *Maybe that was why they didn't invite me.*

Richard's lengthy speech was as expected—assertive, cordial, yet inspiring. He told tales regarding Derek's devotion and bravery, of his wisdom and leadership, but Elise couldn't help but tune out the prince's incessant droning. She was too busy watching Joranna. The queen's eyes were glassy, distant, but more than anything, lifeless. She was a picturesque figurehead, staring at nothing while her eldest attempted to rally everyone's spirits. *I need to talk to her.*

Her wish was easier said than done. Once the service was concluded, guests were allowed to approach the family, who waited in a receiving line at the front of the room. What Elise didn't expect was that it would be over an hour before she could get even a glimpse of her relatives.

"Elise?" Joranna looked at the four teenagers as if seeing them for the first time. "How nice of you to come."

"Yes, how wonderful to see you," Sarah echoed from beside her mother.

Ian simply nodded in their direction while Ruby accepted a hug from Elise.

"So glad you could pay your respects. Thank you." Richard's curt tone sliced through what little resolve Elise had managed up until that point.

"I would have liked to have gone to the burial." Elise glared into her uncle's eyes, praying her weak knees didn't buckle.

"Family only, I'm afraid," Richard said. "You understand."

"I am fam—"

"I believe you are the final guests, and my dear mother needs her rest." Richard held a hand up when Elise tried arguing once more. "There is a delicate matter I'd like to discuss if you'd be so kind to meet me in my study in ten minutes." With a dismissive nod, Richard turned to lead the family out before Elise or her friends could reply.

Wiping a fresh layer of sweat off her hands, Elise whispered Joranna's name until her grandmother paused in the doorway. Elise closed the distance between them before peeking over her grandmother's shoulder for any sign of Richard.

"I really need to talk to you," she whispered.

"I sense what you are feeling. Richard thought it best that only immediate family attend," Joranna said. She hesitated when Darcie, Gavin, and Mitch joined Elise. "I know you're related in some way or other, Elise, but it doesn't make a difference now. Please don't press the issue any further."

"No, it's not that," said Elise with a wave. "It's about Richard. I think the king thing is going to his head. He's completely power hungry—"

"Elise—"

"And Rona did something else after hurting the king. We think she's messing with the past and plotting something. I mean, *why* would she just stay quiet for months? Wouldn't a kingdom be weaker and easier to take over if its king was sick? Why didn't she act? Aren't you suspicious? I'm telling you, something is going on!" Elise took a much-needed gulp of fresh air after finishing her hurried rant.

Joranna shook her head at an approaching guard before folding her hands delicately with a sigh. "Enough. No more, please."

She can't be serious!

"But—"

"Richard is Haighdlen's future. He will protect it."

"But there's a spy!" Darcie added.

"Children, I'm thankful for your loyalty to Haighdlen. Truly, I am, but my heart can't carry anything else at this time. I beg your forgiveness, but this needs to be put to rest and left in the very capable hands of the council."

"The spy is *in* the council!" Gavin countered.

"And the prince won't listen to us," Mitch argued.

Joranna took a shuddering breath until she could control her tone. When she spoke again, it was barely above a whisper. "Do you see these people?" She waited while Elise and the others looked around the room. "They knew what an excellent ruler Derek was. They honor us with their presence. Don't create a scene. They're here to help us mourn." Taking a step closer, Joranna held a handkerchief over her mouth before continuing. "But, one by one, they will all leave and return home. In a matter of days, they will go back to their lives, but *I* am burdened with remembering every memory, every laugh, and he won't—" She clutched the soft cloth against her face to stifle a sob.

Elise's heart shattered as warm tears streamed down her own cheeks. She regretted saying anything now.

"He won't get to see the birth of his grandchild." Joranna wiped the corners of her eyes before checking to see that no one noticed her losing control. Clearing her throat, Joranna regarded each of them one more time. "So, please forgive me if I can't humor any conspiracy theories at this time. Richard told me there have been no recent threats to the kingdom's security and I believe him. You should, too. Thank you for attending, and I wish you a safe journey home, wherever that may be. Goodbye."

"You'll see what we mean," Elise called after her. "He's not listening, and unless someone does, Rona wins." She huffed when Joranna proceeded out of the room without answering. "I am so sick of being ignored about this."

"They're grieving," Darcie said. "They're not themselves right now."

Elise nodded. *She's right.*

"We better get to Der—Richard's study," Gavin said.

I almost forgot. With a heavy sigh, Elise led the way out for what she was sure would be their final visit to the royal study.

CHAPTER 12

Elise was shocked to find her mother standing outside of Richard's study.

"I came to eavesdrop, naturally," Ruby replied with a smirk before Elise could ask what she was doing there. "Richard's hardly spoken to any of us. I'm curious what he's up to."

I bet she wants to find out if what Charles said about Richard sending the family away is true. Elise bit her tongue. She couldn't ask if that was her mother's motive. If Ruby found out anyone else read Charles' letter, she'd erupt. Elise glanced down at the princess's rounded stomach. *Nobody needs that right now.*

Ruby took a step back and pressed her ear against the door. "I can't tell who is in there right now. All I hear is mumbling."

Knowing time wasn't on her side, Elise changed the subject in hopes of getting an answer about something she had seen moments before Derek passed.

"I know now might be bad timing, but can I ask you a question?" Elise licked her lips, fighting the urge to twist her fingers together. "And if you don't want to answer, that's okay," she added quickly. *Spit it out, already!* She watched Ruby's eyebrows raise expectantly. "When. . . right before your dad passed," she began, rubbing her sweaty palms along the sides of her skirt. "I thought I saw him put a hand on your stomach." Elise flickered her gaze between Ruby's eyes and stomach, hoping the other woman got the hint without making Elise say it. "Y-you just looked scared."

Ruby's brows furrowed before realization dawned on her features. The princess looked at Gavin, Mitch, and Darcie, as if gauging whether she and Elise should be having this conversation privately. Finally, she answered, but her voice sounded hollow. "The family believes Father transferred his magic to my child."

Elise's breath hitched. *Is that why I have magic?*

"We were fortunate to see the real him for a few moments," Ruby continued. "He remembered mother first. It was—" She trailed off as her eyes became unfocused. Swallowing convulsively, Ruby blinked several times before getting control of herself. "Anyway, we all got to say goodbye."

Elise desperately wanted to know what Ruby was going to say, but judging by the shakiness of her mother's voice, this conversation was about to end whether she wanted it to or not. *I need to act fast.*

"And he died right after he touched your stomach?" Darcie asked before Elise could.

Ruby nodded. "It was the briefest of moments, but I can see it so clearly. When he reached out to touch my stomach, I thought he would admonish me, but there was silence. I felt a warmth spread through me before the baby kicked. Father smiled, and then. . .he was gone." Ruby sniffed, brushing a stray lock of hair back into place. "Sarah thinks Father's magic is what helped him live as long as he did, so when he—" She tucked her chin downward, caressing her stomach. "Anyway, Richard hasn't looked at me since. I can't help but think he blames me for what happened."

"But you didn't do anything," said Gavin.

"Yeah," Mitch agreed. "It's not your fault."

Ruby smiled. "That's sweet of you."

"Hang on. Back up a bit." Elise took a deep breath. "What happened right after he was cursed?" *We missed all of this. Maybe something can point us to where we need to go.*

The princess sighed before slumping against the wall. It was as if discussing such an idea would not only drain her emotionally but physically as well.

She looks pale. Maybe we should do this another time. As concerning as her mother's condition was, Elise knew that Ruby would be the only member of the family to share with them such intimate details surrounding Derek's death. Elise pressed her mouth into a thin line, secretly wishing her mother could humor them a few minutes longer.

"It's all a bit hazy, to be honest," Ruby confessed. She checked to make sure no one was eavesdropping, including on the other side of the door. Continuing in a whisper, she leaned in closer. "When he first arrived, he was in so much pain. There were several nights he suffered these horrific fits. Hallucinations. Nobody knew what to do. Sarah tried to heal him, and for a while it was working, but then nothing she nor the doctor did seemed to help. It became harder for him to speak. His speech, it. . .turned into these broken phrases, almost as if it took every ounce of energy to speak. And when he did, he would have lapses in memory."

"Then it *is* the same thing," muttered Gavin. "I knew it."

Elise looked up at him. "What do you mean? The same as what?"

He licked his lips before raking a hand through his hair. "When I was locked up in Rona's castle, there was a storyteller in the dungeon named Horace. I learned from another prisoner that Rona placed Horace under a terrible curse. He said it was one of her favorites."

"That's sick, man," Mitch said.

"She wanted him to suffer." Darcie shook her head. "And while he was suffering, *she* took the opportunity to steal the diary from Gavin and chance altering the time—"

Before Elise could elbow Darcie's ribs to shut her up, the door opened abruptly, making their entire group jump. *I hope Mom didn't hear any of that.*

It didn't appear that Ruby heard Darcie's slip. Ruby clenched her eyes shut, inhaling sharply as she clutched her lower belly.

Expecting Richard, Elise was surprised to see Charles on the other side of the door. He looked equally surprised to see Ruby with them.

"I'm sorry. I wasn't expecting—*Princess*! What happened?" He was at Ruby's side in a moment. Using one arm to hold her up, he took her hand with his free one. His distressed eyes searched hers, but she immediately straightened her posture.

"Don't worry, I'm not staying," Ruby said breathlessly.

"Are you ill?" he inquired. "Would you like me to arrange an escort for you? Fetch the doctor?"

"Charles? Is everything all right?" called Richard's voice from inside the study.

Ruby shook her head. "That won't be necessary. I'm perfectly—" She winced before exhaling slowly.

"Is the child coming?" Charles asked. Without waiting for a response, he turned to lead her away. "Come, we've got to get the doctor."

"*No*," Ruby insisted, pulling against him until he stopped. "The child doesn't come for at least a couple of months. I've just exhausted myself these last few days. My body needs to rest."

"Let me take you."

"And let Richard see us together? No, I'm capable of getting to my room. Now go before he comes out here." Ruby did her best curtsy before walking in the direction of her room.

Once her mom was out of earshot, Elise looked at Charles, who was still watching the princess. "You're going to get the doctor, anyway, aren't you?"

"Of course."

"You know she's not going to like that." Elise could already picture her mother's face when the doctor arrived. "But thank you."

Charles bowed before leading them inside the study.

"What on earth took so long?" Richard asked from behind the desk.

While he was unaware of Ruby's pain, Elise still felt irritated at the prince's relaxed disposition behind the desk as he perused documents. He only looked up from them when Charles turned to leave.

"Where are you going? I thought you were staying for *this*." Richard gestured between Elise and her friends with one of the letters that were folded in his hand.

Charles shot Elise a tentative glance. "Ballard asked me to oversee the room assignments for the council members while they're all here. I'm going to check in on their progress."

Richard wrinkled his nose. "Ballard's never needed help like that before." For a moment, Elise held her breath, panicking at the thought of being caught working together. Fortunately, Richard shrugged and looked back at the papers on his desk. "He's losing his touch. Very well."

Charles bowed his head once more before exiting into the hall.

The deafening silence threatened to make Elise scream while they all stood staring at the studious prince. *He's doing this on purpose.* It was taking her uncle twice as long to do mundane things—stacking papers, signing signatures, and even leafing through a reference text. According to the grandfather clock by the door, a full five minutes passed before he acknowledged them.

"Right then." Richard set the quill down so he could fold his hands in front of him, "I called you here to thank you for your service to Haighdlen. My father spoke highly of you." Clearing his throat, he continued in a stern, authoritative tone. "But now that he has passed, I'm afraid your services are no longer required."

Elise's mouth went dry as her brain tried to process what he was really saying. *He's kicking us out?* By the looks on her friends' faces, they were also having a tough time processing what Richard said.

"B-but why?" Elise managed to squeak out.

"Your longtime friendship with my parents is commendable, but I have surrounded myself with *qualified* advisors and councilmembers. We can handle any threats going forward. And out of respect for my honored father, I will provide each of you with travel pouches with enough money between you to cover any expenses to get you back to wherever you came from."

Elise didn't know what frustrated her more, the fact that they were being forced to leave or her uncle's dismissive tone. In that moment, she felt equivalent to the crumbled wads of papers that had been scattered on the floor around Richard's desk.

"You can't do that!" cried Darcie, finding a firmer voice than Elise could.

"Yeah, you need us," said Gavin. "We can help, and if the queen were here—"

"You are to leave my mother alone." Richard stood so abruptly that a book fell off the desk, making Elise jump. A menacing scowl darkened his features. "She can't bear to look at any of you. It only reminds her of him."

"We're not leaving yet," Mitch said, flailing his arm around for emphasis. "You can't discuss war one minute, and then turn around and say there's no need to worry because the threat is gone. Rona's either coming, or she's not."

"And she *definitely* is," Elise answered.

"Listen, you *little*—" The door creaked open, and Richard's face paled when Joranna entered the room.

The sight of her grandmother made Elise sigh with relief. *Maybe she does believe me after all!*

Richard adjusted his coattails before taking his seat once more. He nodded for a nearby servant to tidy up the floor. "Mother? What a surprise. You should be resting."

Joranna strolled across the room, inspecting the clutter with a raised brow, until she stopped between Gavin and Elise. "Something told me I should be present for this meeting given our history together." She regarded the four travelers warmly, though her exhaustion was betrayed by an ill-suppressed yawn. "I beg your pardon. What have I missed?"

Darcie wasted no time catching Joranna up with little thought of how it affected the prince. "He's kicking us out and won't let us help."

Joranna's eyes widened as she regarded her son. "Richard, is this true?"

"Our business with them has concluded. There's been no immediate threat from Rona—"

"But she's not dead yet, is she?" Gavin challenged. "I agree with Mitch. You can't hold a council meeting to discuss allies and then turn around and say it's peaceful."

"It is all being handled." Richard locked his jaw, refusing to meet Joranna's eyes while he drummed his fingers together.

"Is it?" Joranna questioned. "Could you share your developments?"

His mouth tightened to contain his rising temper. "Mother, with all due respect, I don't wish to threaten the kingdom's security by discussing our intent, nor do I have the time. I am scheduled to meet with the lieutenant about Sanders's murder investigation following Brahm's escape. It's been delayed for months as it is and—"

"Then what's a few more hours?" Joranna asked. "Honestly, I don't understand why you can't allow them to stay a while longer. They can give us information from the last few months."

"We don't need it, Mother," Richard all but shouted. Collecting himself, he shuffled through the pile of letters in front of him. "It is not merely the investigation demanding my reply. I have several unanswered letters requiring my attention with regards to the ambassadors' decisions to join us, coronation plans, statue placements, portrait sittings, the festival. . .take your pick."

Joranna's brows furrowed while Richard listed off his mounting engagements. She opened her mouth, closed it, then tried again. "The festival? Darling, surely you don't mean the Harvest Oak Festival." When Richard nodded, she scoffed. "In light of our loss, there's no chance we can host such a celebration at a time like this. Simply cancel it."

Richard had moved on to signing more documents while his mother protested what sounded like a fun event.

Elise was intrigued by the sound of a festival. She had attended one in Vynchia while searching for Gavin the previous week. However, she also understood Joranna's point about it being an inappropriate time for such an occasion.

"Are you even listening?" Joranna huffed.

Richard glanced up, not bothering to hide his annoyance, choosing instead to simply say, "Father loved the festival. He would have wanted us to host it. Let it be a celebration of his life." His clipped tone left little room for argument before a knock at the door announced Ballard's arrival.

Oh no.

"A letter for you, Sire." The steward made his way hastily across the room, but not before Joranna caught sight of the folded envelope.

"Thank you," said Richard, reaching for it. "Was Charles able to assist you with the room assignments?"

Before Elise could come up with a lie to cover for Charles, the queen's body stiffened as she gasped. "Is that the Lockesbarrian court's seal?"

Everyone looked between the envelope and Richard with bated breath.

I don't understand. Is he selling Haighdlen out, too? There was no way Richard could be a spy. *Why would he be in contact with Rona's court?*

"Mother, perhaps you should leave before you're taken over with hysterics." Richard grabbed a small knife from a drawer to his left before slicing the seal delicately.

But Joranna had lost all maternal warmness as she glared at her eldest. Her eyes flashed in suspicion as she awaited his answer. When he provided none, she repeated the question with a stern tone. "Is that the *Lockesbarrian* court's seal? Answer me this instant!"

Elise's blood ran cold watching the two standing at odds with one another. It was a battle of wills that ultimately ended when her uncle threw his hands in the air.

"Yes! If you must know," Richard groaned. "Let us not create a scene in front of these guests. If you wish to speak privately—"

"No, I wish to speak *now*," she hissed. "Crown prince or not, what are you thinking? Does the council know about this?"

"This protects all of us, so they need not be involved," Richard assured her.

"Please, enlighten us," Joranna scoffed, reminding Elise of the fiery young woman she met in the diner rather than the composed queen her grandmother tried to be at all times. "Surely, if it is to protect us all, there's no problem having an audience. What are you planning?"

Richard lost a fraction of resolve under his mother's intimidating stare. He, too, reminded Elise of a previous encounter, namely the scared adolescent prince who accidentally shot Mitch with an ill-aimed arrow in the forest. When the prince hesitated to reply, Joranna stomped her foot before pacing in front of the fireplace.

"Mother, there's no need to berate me publicly like this. I only wish for my plans to remain private until the right time. There's no need to raise any alarm until the details are sorted out."

"I am entitled to these details," stated the queen. "You may be taking over as King, but don't forget that it was at the discretion of your father and I. It wasn't a day I ever wanted to come, but your handling of these matters makes me second guess our decision."

"I don't wish to hear anymore." Richard slumped back in his chair, massaging the bridge of his nose. "Haven't you anything else to do? Guests to entertain?"

Elise felt as if someone wrenched her heart out on behalf of her grandmother. She wanted nothing more than to walk over and punch her uncle in the face. All Joranna was trying to do was protect everyone, including her son. Why couldn't Richard see that? *Why does everything have to be a fight with him?*

Joranna closed her eyes until her bottom lip stopped quivering. With a shuddering breath, she looked up at him with moistened eyes. Her voice was barely audible over the crackling embers in the fireplace.

"I have visited this room more times than I can count, but no matter the case or situation, I was included. I was never made to feel so unwanted until today. If your father were alive—"

"But he isn't, is he, Mother?" Richard spat. "All this falls onto *my* shoulders! Not yours, not Sarah's, nor Ian's." He scoffed. "I shudder to think what Ruby would do in my stead."

Joranna approached her son slowly, like a lioness creeping towards her prey, until her gown touched the desk. She glared down at her son. "At least they would have honored Derek's wishes to rule fairly. Furthermore, everything would be handled by now. Ruby could be married, an alliance formed—" She paused when he stood abruptly to cross the room.

Everyone watched as he bypassed an offering servant to pour himself a glass of something from a decanter. The way he tossed back the drink made Elise wish she and her friends had already left. *This is getting really serious. He has no idea what she's been through, and he just keeps adding onto it.*

Joranna took a deep breath before continuing. "Perhaps he wasn't as present with all of you as he would've liked to have been, but he knew the importance of family. He made it his top priority to provide for you and this kingdom's future."

"Which is *exactly* what I'm doing, Mother," Richard said. "I am trying to do what I think he would want me to do."

"You're putting too much pressure on yourself trying to be him. Richard, you don't have to be your father—"

"Yes, I do!" he roared, making Elise jump again. She didn't like the crazed look in his eyes as he raked a hand through his hair. It was his turn to pace. "I can be like him. I *will* be just like him. Perhaps even better."

Impossible.

Richard hunched over his desk, squeezing the edges until his knuckles were white. His shoulders and arm muscles were tense as he almost failed to control his emotions.

"If you would just tell us, dear—" Joranna began before he cut her off.

"I'm getting married," he ground out between clenched teeth. Pouring himself a refill, not bothering to aim nor caring about the overspill, he held up his glass as if to make a toast. "Are you satisfied, Mother? Have I made you proud?"

We really shouldn't be here for this, but I can't look away. Is this really happening right now?

"Hardly." Joranna wiped the corner of her eyes. "Richard, what would possess you to make such a life-altering decision while mourning your father's death? You're stricken with grief! This isn't the time to be making these sorts of choices."

"It's for the best."

Elise scowled at his uncle's nonchalant reply. "Please, let us help you."

"Like you helped my father?"

Elise felt as if the air had been sucked from her lungs. She must have looked like a gaping moron, standing there with her mouth wide open without making a sound. Her skin prickled with dozens of goosebumps as heat enveloped her face.

"Richard!" Joranna shrieked. "You are out of line. This outburst only proves you're not in your right mind. They have done nothing to warrant such treatment."

"I will not yield, Mother. Nor will I apologize. We can all agree whenever anything disastrous occurs, these four are present. Rodrick has overseen matters regarding the engagement, and the details are settled. There is a lovely maiden, Iris, from the Lockesbarrian court whom I shall wed to help ease growing tensions. Perhaps even come to some sort of peace treaty agreement with King Dmitri."

He's crazy! And what about Aunt Gwen? That's *who he married. What's going on?*

"Rodrick?" Elise exclaimed. "You mean Vaughn? The guy the council kicked out? *That's* who you've been trusting to handle your business?"

"He was the newly-appointed Ambassador to Lockesbarrow before his dismissal. I still trust his loyalties." Richard took a sip from his glass. "With any luck, I'll sire a new heir within the year, and I can avoid the scandal involving Ruby's illegitimate child ruling."

Elise felt Gavin's hand wrap around her arm before she realized she had taken a step towards her uncle.

"I can't hear anymore," Joranna said. "I wash my hands of this. You certainly don't have my blessing."

Richard collapsed into his seat, reclining until he could cross his feet over the desk. Swirling the contents of his glass, he took a long sip before meeting Joranna's eye. "Well, then it's a good thing I don't need it, isn't it, Mother?"

Elise paled as her jaw dropped open. *He did not just say that!*

A muscle twitched in Joranna's cheek. She opened her mouth, paused, and stormed out without a word.

Elise jumped as the door slammed shut behind the queen.

"You're crazy," Darcie said to the prince. "You're going to destroy this kingdom."

Again.

"It's treasonous to insult a king." Richard drained the rest of his second glass.

Composing herself, Elise sneered down at him. "Then I guess it's a good thing you're not king yet." Her stomach tightened as she willed both knees not to buckle.

Richard's eyes darkened. "Careful. I doubt our relation is strong enough to save you should you tread too close where you don't belong. Now," he pointed to the door, "as I said before. It's time for you to leave Haighdlen. For good this time."

This is worse than I thought. He's not supposed to marry someone else. Especially someone from Lockesbarrow. Now there's even more stuff to fix before we can get home. We can't leave Haighdlen now!

Elise waited until they were far enough out of earshot, and away from lingering stares, before she beckoned her friends to follow her. Once they all reached the top of the stairs, Elise broke out into a run with the other three following close behind. Praying they didn't encounter any guards, or unwanted stewards, she took the familiar path to the one person who could help them. Out of breath, time, and options, Elise bent over to catch her breath before pounding on Ruby's bedroom door.

We have to find Gwen.

CHAPTER 13

Elise continued knocking, growing more flustered with her mother for not answering.

We don't have time for this! They're going to escort us out any minute.

"Ruby?" Elise called, catching a maid's attention at the end of the hall before rolling her eyes. "I mean *Princess* Ruby? We really need to talk to you." Three more knocks and there was still no answer. Elise had half a thought to kick the door or have Mitch run into it. He probably would if Darcie suggested it.

"Elise, I don't think she's in there." Darcie pulled her away from the door into a hug as Elise released the tears she had been holding in. "This wasn't your fault. Your uncle's just being a jerk. Nothing he said was true."

Gavin came closer to rub her back. "Even if they do kick us out of there, we'll find a way to get home."

Elise eased out of Darcie's embrace to dry her face. "Don't you guys realize how hard this has made everything?" When none of the others replied, she shuddered before explaining the consuming fears circling within her mind. "Lockesbarrow now has two rulers. One is supposed to be *dead*. Not only does that mess up the timeline, but Richard is about to marry someone from Rona's kingdom. If he does, he doesn't marry Gwen. Then my cousin isn't born. Who knows how his marriage will affect my mom, aunt, and uncle? What if *none* of my cousins are born?" Elise placed her head between both hands, as if she could block out the world if she kept her eyes closed. *Is it possible for someone's head to actually explode?* "I already failed to save Derek."

"Hey, you didn't fail anything," Darcie assured her.

She's only saying that because she's my friend. No amount of comforting was going to help her feel better.

"Elise, no one could save Derek," said Gavin. "I think, regardless of timelines, he was always meant to be killed by Rona. It's just how the events unfolded." He wrapped a tentative arm around her until she melted against his side.

"There's still time to fix everything," Mitch said. "Your grandma had been living in that house back home a long time before they needed to send you here, right? That means Rona attacks later if we don't stop her now. Even with your grandfather gone, there's still something to save."

They're right. Elise thought back to the first trip she and her mother made to Joranna's house after Haighdlen was overthrown for good. Ian's persistent texts caused Elise to check Ruby's phone only to find out the texts were threatening to reveal the truth about Haighdlen, something Ruby was adamantly against. In the end, it worked out for the best, since Elise probably would've never gotten the chance to see Haighdlen if it weren't for the threat Rona posed. All of this was happening for a reason, she reminded herself. While painful, she needed to accept the fact that Derek was always going to die.

However, there was still time to prevent more sacrifices. If they didn't stop Rona now, she would go on to take over Haighdlen, killing Sarah's husband Liam and. . .Charles. Closing her eyes, Elise relived her first confusing moments in Joranna's house when her estranged family arrived.

"But it wasn't my choice," Richard recalled about fleeing. *"I wanted to stay there. . .to die for my kingdom. For my people."*

Elise's aunt, Sarah, assured her brother that Liam and Charles pulled him out before he was killed.

Richard had only replied with, *"And now they're dead. They're both dead."* Although Sarah tried to convince him they were doing their duty, Richard remained inconsolable. *"They were my best friends. . .I could've been there to save them. I should have stopped Rona before she ever grew to be as strong as she is now. The people are doomed now. She finally accomplished what she set out to do all those years ago when she killed Father."*

"Y'all are right," Elise confessed to her friends. "This would've happened anyway, but it's still up to us to make sure Rona doesn't win. As bad as my uncle is acting now, seeing how he ends up is worse. I met my family when they were the worst versions of themselves. They deserve better. It's what Derek would've wanted."

"Now you're sounding like yourself," Darcie said with a beaming smile.

"Thanks guys," Elise said, joining her friends in a group hug. "We need to introduce Richard to Gwen. Then they can fall in love before he gets married. After that, we can focus on Rona."

"I wish it were as easy as it sounds," Mitch said with a playful pout.

"How can we get them to meet?" Gavin asked.

"Oh!" Darcie squealed, jumping up and down on the balls of her feet. "The festival thingy they were talking about. They can meet there!"

There's the old Darcie. Elise smirked.

"Watch out, guys. She's matchmaking again." Mitch rolled his eyes with a smile. "Is it sad I feel bad for Richard now?"

Darcie slapped his arm playfully as they chuckled.

Elise's smile dropped as a nearby door opened. Caught with no place to hide and her adrenaline spiking, she froze. As if by fate, she saw her expectant mother come out of another room followed by Sarah and Ian.

"Elise?" Ruby called upon seeing them. "What're you all doing up here? I thought you were meeting with Richard."

"We already did." Elise sighed with a hesitant glance at her mother's stomach. "How're *you* feeling?"

"Much better. Sarah and Ian kept me company while I rested. Are you all right?" Sensing Elise's unwillingness to elaborate in the hall, Ruby beckoned her siblings and the four travelers into her own bedroom.

Hurrying inside, Elise took in the familiar sight of her mother's room. She was once again captivated by the domed ceiling, painted to look like the sky. The white drapes were tied back this time, and the furniture remained as they were the day Elise first visited her mother seeking answers after Ruby's last trip through the portal.

"We were about to head downstairs for tea," said Ruby, "but you look distressed. What is the matter?"

It's now or never.

Elise spent the next ten minutes recalling the tense interaction between herself, Richard and Joranna in the study, including the prince's betrothal. The following silence only managed to spike Elise's growing anxiety. *Did I share too much? Am I making things worse?*

"Why didn't he tell us he's getting married?" Ian asked. "And to a *Lockesbarrian* woman? You're sure about this?"

Elise nodded, detecting the skepticism in her uncle's eyes, before Gavin added, "To make a peace treaty or something."

"That can't be right," said Sarah as she paced around the room. "King Dmitri wouldn't be so quick to agree to peace. Not with what Rona did to Father. It's taking too long to seek retaliation. Do you think Richard's being forced into something somehow? Blackmailed perhaps? What does the council say?"

"The council's being lied to," said Gavin. "We're pretty sure one of them is a spy."

"I can believe it," Ruby muttered.

Sarah clicked her tongue. "I wouldn't put it past Dmitri nor Rona to do such a thing." Sarah frowned. "We must tread carefully. Does Richard suspect any treason on your part?"

"I hope not," Mitch moaned. "All we've done has been to help Haighdlen, but he's still kicking us out."

"You're leaving?" Ruby exclaimed. "When?"

"As soon as the guards find us," Darcie replied with a hollow chuckle. "So, probably any minute now."

Elise crossed the room to stand in front of Ruby. "That's why we came to find you. There isn't much time left. Can you help us get to Gwen?" *Please, Mom.*

Ruby's eyes doubled in size as her gaze flickered first to Sarah and then Ian. Blushing, she shook her head. "What does Gwen have to do with any of this?"

"I. . .I can't tell you that," Elise said, biting her lip. "But if we don't, things will get worse." *A lot worse.*

"I'm afraid I don't understand. Who is Gwen?" Sarah looked at her sister expectantly.

Ruby shifted from one foot to the other under her older siblings' attentions like a two-year-old sneaking dessert before dinner. Scowling at Elise, Ruby answered. "Gwen is a girl I befriended in town. She helped me get the fairy magic to travel."

Elise blushed under her mother's scrutiny. She hadn't meant to get her mom into any more trouble, but they didn't have time to waste.

"She sounds fun," Ian said with his own playful smile.

Sarah, as expected, rolled her eyes. "I should be more surprised." She wrung her hands with an exasperated sigh before turning to face Elise. "What exactly is your plan?"

I can't tell them I'm trying to get Richard and Gwen together. They'd never help me. She had to think of something safe to tell them. "We would like to be allowed to stay for the festival and meet Gwen."

A silence engulfed the room.

"That's all?" Sarah finally asked with a raised brow, looking remarkably like Joranna as she searched Elise's face for the truth.

"We'd also like to not get arrested," Mitch added.

"If we can secure some fairy magic while we're at it, we should definitely try," said Gavin.

The other three friends nodded at his request, unable to suppress their own smiles.

"Can you take us to Gwen in time for the festival?" Elise asked Ruby. "If we can get her to give us some magic, and listen to what we have to say, we may be able to stop anything worse from happening."

Ruby hesitated. "There is no chance of Richard allowing me to leave the castle grounds, much less attend the festival."

"You've broken the rules before," Elise teased. Her heart warmed at the sight of her mother's smile. *Please take us. Please.* Deep down, she willed her magic to convince Ruby, but nothing seemed to be happening.

"Yes, but I'm not as energetic now. Staying in doesn't sound too bad these days." Ruby chuckled along with everyone else rather than appear irritated by her limitations. "But on a serious note, Gwen is not likely to acquire fairy magic for strangers. I *could* send you with a letter explaining your visit for Father's funeral and inform her that you need a place to stay during the festival. She may take you in."

"Couldn't we just stay at the inn?" Mitch asked.

With what money? We can't ask them to pay for something like this.

Sarah shook her head. "If you're planning to stay in Haighdlen after Richard's ordered your departure, you're not going to want to be caught or reported. Even more so if you're dabbling in kingdom affairs. You're sure you can help our family?"

Elise nodded.

Sarah bit her lip, clearly at odds with the proper way to handle the secretive situation. At last, she nodded towards her younger sister. "Better write the letter to your friend now, Ruby. Be discreet but include the necessary information about the situation."

This letter is better than nothing. We just have to hope Richard shows up to the festival and not catch us beforehand. Elise forced herself to remain calm as she accepted the decision.

Ruby sat down immediately at the curved writing table to draft her letter.

Fed up with pacing, Sarah walked over to the window.

It was only then Elise noticed it had begun to rain.

Sarah fiddled idly with a locket around her neck as she stared at the raindrops pelting against the window.

Elise studied her aunt's profile, feeling a sudden sense of déjà vu. It took another minute to recall why. During one of their first visits, she remembered her late great-grandmother, Queen Avalyn, staring out a window in a similar ominous fashion during a storm.

"I'm surprised Richard is hosting the festival at a time like this. I can't say I'm in a very *festive* mood. Come to think of it, it's rather vulgar, don't you think?" Sarah tossed an assertive sneer in her younger brother's direction.

Ian shrugged. "Perhaps he only wants to rally everyone's spirits. You know how much this festival meant to Father."

Sarah only responded with a reluctant nod before moving to stand behind Ruby. She stayed there for a considerable time, watching her sister write, while the rest of the room sat in an uncomfortable heavy silence.

Once Ruby had concluded the letter—careful to check that Sarah agreed with its contents—and signed it, she folded the paper and sealed it with wax.

"*No one* is to inform Mother of this," Sarah commanded. She waited for everyone to agree, including Ian and Ruby. "I've tried to not leave her alone for long periods of time already. This would surely throw her into hysterics."

"I wish we could talk to her more," Darcie said.

"That isn't possible," Ian replied. "She barely realizes when *we* are sitting with her. We try to take turns keeping her company, but she is often found sleeping anywhere but the bed she and father shared or scribbling away in her diary. I imagine it's good for her to get those feelings—"

"What did you say?" Elise interrupted.

Ian looked puzzled as he analyzed what he had just shared. "She can't bear to sleep in their bed. I mean, it's understandable since—"

"No, no. . .you said she's been writing in a diary?" Elise's heartbeat skipped a beat. *Why do I keep forgetting there's another diary that Joranna would be keeping in this timeline? Maybe if we get the fairy magic from Gwen, we can link the two diaries and get us straight to Rona instead of guessing!* "Can you get it for us?"

Her mother, uncle and aunt reacted like she feared they would. Each one looked at her as if she were crazy, even dangerous. She had to admit her question sounded suspiciously unhinged. Even her friends hadn't quite followed her line of thinking yet except Gavin.

"We can save Haighdlen," Gavin said. "We'll stop Rona and her brother, and if we succeed, Richard won't marry anyone from Lockesbarrow either. Everything can be like it's supposed to be."

Elise was thankful for his rescue and discretion.

"Richard isn't going to like this." Sarah regarded the four travelers one last time. Her usually controlled demeanor was replaced with one of fear and trepidation. She wrung her hands, much like Elise did before a panic attack, before stealing another wavering glance at the sealed envelope. Sarah's trembling fingers sought out the locket around her neck once more, squeezing it to the point Elise feared it would break. The older princess's shoulders slumped before she realized and straightened her posture. Clearing her throat, Sarah shook her head as her icy exterior resumed. "Right then. We'll contact Edith and Ruby can help have your costumes delivered to this Gwen person's house." Sarah cocked her head towards the door for Ian to follow her out.

Elise looked at the mirrored expressions of confusion on her friends' faces. *What costumes?*

Pausing in the doorway, Sarah caught their apprehensive glances before addressing her sister. "They *do* know about the festival, don't they?"

"I'll inform them," Ruby promised before her brother and sister left the room.

"Okay, please tell me *costume* doesn't mean what I think it does," Mitch whined once the door shut.

"Oh, I hope it does!" Darcie gushed as she stepped closer to Ruby. "I've always wanted to go to a real masquerade party! Please tell me that's what's going on."

Elise secretly sided with Darcie. She had always been fascinated with masquerades and ballrooms. This would be her first time, though she was surprised it was being held in Clara.

Ruby closed her writing desk and stood to push the chair back into place. She chuckled at Darcie's theatrics. "On the first night of the festival, there is a masquerade ball held in the town square."

"And. . .the royal family goes, too?" Gavin asked.

I'm glad he asked. I feel stupid thinking balls only happen at the castle.

"I've never missed it. Well, until now." Ruby looked down at her belly. "I'm sorry I won't be able to help you."

"You've done plenty. Thank you," Elise said before being startled by a knock on the door.

"Your Highness?" came Ballard's obnoxious tone through the door. Elise rolled her eyes. "The doctor is here to see you."

"The doctor?" Ruby looked warily at Elise and her friends. "I never sent for—" Realization dawned on her features before she quirked an unamused brow in Elise's direction. "Did Charles do this?"

Elise nodded, trying not to smile. "Don't be mad."

Ruby moaned and opened the door.

"There you are, Your Majesty, I—" Ballard froze upon making eye contact with Elise over Ruby's shoulder. "Ah, I see you're entertaining our soon-to-be *departing* guests. The prince tasked me with escorting them to the carriage. I'd be happy to send them on their way while helping you. I'll speak to the coachman about—"

"*I* will speak to the coachman." Ruby tucked the letter behind her back in such a way that was hidden from Ballard but easy for Elise to casually walk up and take. The exchange was subtle and quick, so much so that the steward didn't take notice.

Ballard spluttered before forcing his temper down with a frustrated sigh. "Your Highness, your brother *insists*—"

"Yes, you do so much for him, and I thank you," Ruby interrupted with a feigned smile that Elise imagined was difficult to pull off, "however, I'm perfectly capable of seeing them off on their journey. It's the least I could do. You have so much to prepare for the festival."

A tense moment passed between the two before he scowled in resignation. He pursed his lips as if tasting an overly sour piece of candy before choking out the words, "Very well, Princess."

Deep down, Elise knew Ballard was a good man. He had risked his own life to protect theirs when they encountered Brahm and his sister, Ingrid, in the castle library. However, that didn't mean he liked them. Judging by the stacked lines forming in his forehead, Elise suspected he didn't.

Ruby waited for him to leave before she rested her forehead against the doorframe with a sigh. "I suppose I better go see the doctor. Was there anything else you needed?"

"Seriously?" Gavin asked when everyone else shook their heads. "Okay, was nobody going to ask where Gwen's house is? I mean, we have the letter and that's great, but last time we were there it was the middle of the night. Does anyone know which house it was? The princess can't go this time. What happens if we pick the wrong place?"

Elise looked at her mother expectantly. *I'm glad he thought to ask before she left.*

"I'm so sorry," Ruby apologized before reopening her desk to retrieve a piece of paper to scribble down directions. Handing the note to Gavin, she bid them farewell and wished them good luck. "I'll speak with the coachman. He can take you directly. I've circled which house just there." She pointed to a circled rectangle on the drawing. "There's no need to worry."

Except there was *every* reason to worry. Although the traveling arrangement was simple enough, and the ride itself uneventful, Elise couldn't shake her growing paranoia as Gavin led their group through the residential area filled with small cottages a couple of hours later. Elise idly tapped her hand against the pocket of her cloak where she kept the money Richard provided. If this plan didn't work, maybe they could barter with a fairy for some magic or at least pay for a boat ride to Lockesbarrow.

"I think we're almost there," Gavin whispered, holding the directions closer to his face. It was nearly sunset, and if they didn't find Gwen's house soon, they'd be forced to sleep outside. The cool autumn night was already proving to be quite chilly as a shiver ran down Elise's arms. After scanning the surrounding homes, Gavin pointed to his right. "I think it's this one."

Elise followed the path of his finger to a quaint cottage. There was nothing about it that stood out from the others, but Elise couldn't remember the last time they were here well enough to pick it out for certain.

"Ready?" he asked.

Not at all. In fact, her hands were trembling, but it had nothing to do with the cold. This woman they were about to meet didn't know she was Elise's future aunt. She didn't know she was destined to be Haighdlen's next queen. Elise couldn't even share that much with her. Not only that, but Gwen was also going to be asked to help them find fairy magic while simultaneously being set up with Richard. *How did this sound like a good idea a few hours ago?*

Wiping two sweat-soaked hands along her skirt, Elise stepped in front of Gavin, and at the urging of her friends, tentatively knocked on the door.

CHAPTER 14

If it weren't for the letter clutched in her hand, Elise imagined Gwen would've slammed the door shut on them. Not that Elise would blame her. Their half story, since they couldn't very well give the whole one, was highly suspicious. Elise doubted *she* would have even opened the door at all had someone come to her door with such a proposition, yet there they stood begging for a place to stay.

Please. Elise stared back at Gwen's unamused expression, attempting to use whatever magic would work on the young woman. "I have the letter from the princess right here. You can read it." She handed the envelope to Gwen, who kept her gaze on them as she reluctantly opened it. Elise held her breath, waiting anxiously while watching Gwen's eyes scan the contents of the letter.

"Gwen? Who is that?" asked another woman who soon approached the door behind Gwen. *They could almost be twins. This must be her sister.* Mr. Archer, the falsely imprisoned farmer, and Gwen's father had mentioned he had a wife and two daughters. "What's all this? Did you tell them we have no more handouts to give today?"

"Oh, no, it's not like that," Darcie said. "We just came to—"

"To hide from the prince." Gwen sighed as she folded the letter closed once more. "They've been asked to leave the kingdom, but the princess writes to please offer them hospitality until the festival is over."

Gwen's sister looked between the two parties, obviously detecting the tension. "Well, if the princess requests it, surely we can honor her wishes." Stepping around Gwen, the younger woman smiled warmly. "I'm Talia." She pulled the small towel hanging on her apron free to dry her hands before shaking each of their hands. "It's awfully nice to meet friends of the princess. We're honored. . . however, I'm afraid there's not much room. You'd have to share one."

While all four friends eagerly spoke over one another to accept the arrangement, Elise couldn't help but focus on the way Gwen's mouth tightened into a thin line as she squeezed the letter until it crumbled within her fist. Talia had yet to stop talking at this point, already sharing their plans for the festival, until Gwen could take it no longer.

"Tal, this is absurd! Not only has Mama not given permission, but they're *fugitives*. Remember what happened—" Gwen paused as another woman carrying a rather large basket approached the door behind Elise and her friends. "Mama, there you are."

Mrs. Archer regarded the travelers with an alarmed expression, silently gauging a reaction from her daughters to make sure the situation was safe. "Is something wrong?" she finally asked when it appeared no one was in danger but remaining alert, nonetheless.

Talia ripped the letter from Gwen's grip before handing it to their mother. By the time Mrs. Archer flattened the letter back out, Talia had already shared its contents out loud with great flare and animation. Ending with a dramatic twirl, Talia slumped against the doorframe with a breathless smile. "We not only get to host guests for the festival, but they're friends with the royal family! I'm almost finished sewing my costume. Isn't it exciting, Mama?"

Mrs. Archer didn't reply until she finished reading the letter for herself. She smiled briefly at the visitors, and Elise was immediately put at ease by her presence. Giving them permission to stay, she then sent a stern maternal look at her youngest daughter. "Perhaps we should cease entertaining our neighbors for now and continue this discussion inside. Can you put on the tea, Gwen? I've got to unpack all of this." She gestured towards the food in the basket.

"Mama, I don't think this is a good idea," Gwen protested as Elise and her friends stepped into the main living area of the cottage. By the time everyone entered, there was barely room to stand. "Besides, I'm going out. Remember?"

Mrs. Archer clicked her tongue. "Oh, rehearsals are tonight. That's right. Talia, tea." She hoisted the basket onto the dining table with an exasperated sigh before emptying its contents, including bread and various vegetables. "Make it strong, please. My poor nerves need it."

Gwen locked the door before approaching the table to help unload the basket. Her brows furrowed as she examined her mother's rattled state. "Is something wrong? Did something happen in town? Come sit over here." She helped the older woman get situated on an oversized chair covered in blankets. "If I need to stay, I can—"

Mrs. Archer waved off her daughter's suggestion. "No need. It's nothing, really. I was only spooked." She paused to thank Gwen for putting the food away in the pantry and reminded Talia to pour enough tea for their guests before continuing. "As I was leaving the square, I thought I saw someone."

Elise noticed the woman's trembling fingers and pale complexion, not to mention the way she kept glancing out the windows as if someone was watching them. Unable to stifle her own superstitions, Elise also checked, but no one was there.

"Was someone following you?" Gavin asked, taking Elise by surprise. She hadn't expected him to pry, but she was also thankful that he had spoken her thoughts aloud.

"I don't think so. It looked like someone I thought I'd never see again." She reflected before correcting her statement. "Someone I never *want* to see again."

Elise felt the hairs on the back of her neck stand up as she imagined a looming figure spying on them.

Gwen kneeled by her mother's side. "Mama, you're absolutely shaken. Who did you think you saw?"

Mrs. Archer shook her head. "It doesn't matter, because there's no chance it was really him."

Him? Who would've scared her like this?

Frustrated and flustered by everyone's eyes on her, Mrs. Archer changed the subject by redirecting her attention to a different target. "Talia? Are you sure you swept in here today? The floors look dreadful."

"I did!" cried her youngest daughter from where she stood in front of a small stove. "Honest."

"She knows you did, Tal," Gwen called out, shooting a knowing glance in her mother's direction. When she spoke again, it was barely above a whisper. "Mama, what is really the matter?"

Mrs. Archer shifted under her eldest daughter's scrutiny, casting uncertain glances at Elise, Gavin, Mitch, and Darcie before deeming it safe enough to answer. "It was. . .it was that *boy*."

Elise felt the contents of her stomach churn. *Who is she talking about?*

Gwen's eyebrows rose as her mouth dropped open. "The one who stayed *here*?" When her mother nodded, sending an uncomfortable glance in the travelers' direction, Gwen huffed. "Let's not make this more complicated than it needs to be. I'm sure you saw someone with a strong likeness, but I doubt it was really him. He wouldn't come back to Clara, Mama."

"That's what I keep telling myself," said the older woman as Talia handed her a steaming cup of tea. Inhaling its rich scent, Mrs. Archer took a delicate sip. Her lips quivered as her mouth adjusted to the temperature. "Yet, I can't seem to put it out of my mind."

Gwen looked up at Elise from her kneeled position. "The last time we showed the hospitality you are seeking, our family was torn apart."

It was Vaughn after all. Elise thought back to the first night she met Vaughn, who had infiltrated Ruby's letter and pretended to be their guide while delaying their attempts to reach Gavin. During an uncomfortable cart ride, he had relayed a tale from his past. *"By the time I reached Haighdlen, I was weak and starving. I met a farmer who told me I could stay in his barn. By that point, gossip had spread about a dangerous Lockesbarrian fugitive. The farmer asked me to leave, which I did. I later heard he had been arrested, so I stayed hidden a while longer."* Yet it wasn't the story itself that bothered

Elise. It was what Vaughn had said next. *"I kept an eye on his wife and daughters—from a distance, of course. I felt I owed him that much. They're making a decent living selling their crops in Clara."* Mitch and Darcie had been in the cart with her, so this must have been news to Gavin, who had only heard Mr. Archer's account when they were all locked up in Haighdlen's prison. Derek had assured them he would look into a pardon, but Elise doubted he ever got the chance before being cursed.

"Oh, you can't go and say a thing like that without telling them the whole truth," Mrs. Archer fussed, resting the teacup on her covered lap. "But I'm sure they have better things to do than to listen to us prattle away like a bunch of gossips. But she's right. Our farm was taken from us, and my late sister took us into this cottage while we worked on local farms for a share of their crops. We manage, though. Anyway, Gwen, you had best be off."

But I want to hear more!

"Are you sure?" Gwen placed a hand on top of her mother's. "You look pale. I can cancel."

"Hold your tongue," Mrs. Archer fussed. "After the king's death, the kingdom needs this festival now more than ever. You were fortunate to be considered again this year."

Gwen rolled her eyes. "Mama, it's only a dance routine."

"Yes, but one on the opening night of the ball! That is when the most people will be in attendance, including the royal family." Mrs. Archer scowled before taking another sip of tea.

Perfect. That's when we'll get her to meet Richard. We just need to arrange it and find a way to Lockesbarrow. Elise made a mental note to speak with her friends the next time they were alone.

"She doesn't sound too excited about it," Gavin said.

Elise agreed. Gwen's movements were languid and unhurried.

"She did this to herself. I told her we were fine." Mrs. Archer tipped her head back as she finished what was left in the cup.

"What do you mean?" Darcie asked.

Mrs. Archer studied Gwen through the window. "She's been asked to join the opening dance for a couple of years but only now accepted. Gwen won't admit it, but I know she thinks we need the money. Since my husband and sister are gone, it's getting harder to manage everything."

"I'm so sorry," said Darcie, reaching into her own pocket to retrieve her portion of travel expenses. "We can pay you to stay."

Mrs. Archer waved it away as if it revolted her. "Absolutely not. We are honored to host royal guests."

"Are you sure we can't do anything to help?" asked Mitch.

Elise was surprised by his offer, and judging by the impressed expression on Darcie's face, she was as well.

"You're sweet, but there's no need." Mrs. Archer's eyes lit up. "Oh, that reminds me! Do you all have costumes? There's not much time, but—"

"The princess is sending some for us," Gavin replied.

Mrs. Archer opened her mouth but paused when Talia returned carrying a tray with four more steaming cups. The slightest blush colored the young woman's cheeks as she handed Gavin and Mitch theirs first.

Elise and Darcie exchanged a knowing glance. Thanking Talia, Elisa suppressed a chuckle inside her cup when Darcie did not do the same.

The rest of the evening passed in much the same way, with a great deal of small talk over a light supper. Unfortunately, the opportunity to speak privately didn't come until the middle of the night after Gwen returned and everyone went to bed.

"So, if we get your grandmother's diary, you'll combine your magic with some fairy magic—which we also have to figure out how to get—you want to go to Lockesbarrow and stop Rona?" Gavin's skepticism extinguished what little faith Elise still possessed.

"Don't forget she wants to get her aunt and uncle together first," Mitch chimed in.

"Gav's right. Are you sure this plan is a good idea?" Mitch whispered. "Derek just *died*. I doubt Richard will be up for being set up with anybody."

"If he even shows up at all," Gavin grumbled.

Maybe this isn't a good idea after all.

Picking up the candle holder, Darcie stood with a groan.

Candlelight illuminated Darcie's face, and Elise instantly recognized the growing, meddlesome excitement play across her best friend's features.

"Come on, y'all," Darcie whined. "Haven't you seen the movies? A ball is the *perfect* place to fall in love! Especially a masquerade! The romance, the mystery, the music. . ." Swept up in the moment, she performed a dramatic twirl in the middle of the small, darkened room the four occupied. The flame flickered violently, threatening to go out as shadows bounced across the walls, until Darcie slumped with a sigh.

"I'm thinking this is *your* fantasy," Mitch teased.

Elise nodded with a smile. "Except the part where she catches herself on fire."

"And *if* they're destined to fall in love anyway," Darcie added, ignoring them both, except to hold the candle out away from her body, "then this can't fail."

Mitch's audible yawn killed what little superficial energy Darcie had left, leaving the latter to suggest they get some sleep.

Except, Elise's anxiety often reared its ugly head the most when things quieted around her. Before everyone even got situated on their blankets, she knew she was going to have a panic attack. It started with a tingling sensation in the tips of her fingers followed a weakness in her kneecaps that made her question her ability to stand upright without falling. At least she wouldn't have to prove that one since everyone was stretching out on the floor.

Forcing her eyes closed, she focused on her breathing. Despite her best efforts, the ideal pattern of inhaling and exhaling soon quickened to a shallow rhythm that left her chest feeling constricted.

Darcie blew out the candle and the windowless room felt like an empty void imprisoning Elise's rapid imagination.

For the first five minutes or so, Elise consoled herself with the fun memories from the afternoon, but the meek attempt at preventing the impending attack only pushed her closer until she felt as if her mind were screaming. Feeling as if an electric shock bolted through her, she was on her feet in an instant. Unable to decipher where exactly her friends were, Elise decided it would be best if she didn't pace, but the lack of movement only fueled the rapidly embellishing thoughts.

I have to get out of here. How can I get out without them noticing? Crap, here it comes. I can't stop it. I can't. Stop, Elise. Stop! You're fine. Enough. What is wrong with you?

She swallowed convulsively, gripping two handfuls of the nightgown Talia had let her borrow.

What are we doing here? In my future aunt's house? This is getting too close. We are definitely messing something up with the timeline. We're meddling too much. And what if Vaughn is really out there? Could Rona be here as well? Her pleas for the madness to stop were ignored by her own crazed stubbornness. *Let's hope this works. We can't get to Lockesbarrow without magic. We can't get magic without the diary helping me. We won't get the diary if Sarah and Ian can't get it, and what if Richard doesn't allow the royal family to come? And if they don't come—*

"Stop it."

Gavin's deep, assertive voice—thick and hoarse from drowsiness—pierced through her thoughts like a needle into a balloon. The weight in Elise's mind evaporated. She lowered her gaze towards the area near her feet where she knew he was.

"What?" Elise whispered, trying her best to sound nonchalant. In that moment, she was thankful for the darkness, because he couldn't see the hot tears welling up. She wiped her eyes furiously with the back of her trembling hand while bouncing on the balls of her feet. Anything to release the adrenaline.

"Lay down, Elise."

Before she could reply, Elise jumped at the sound of Mitch snoring. She held her breath, hoping Gavin would also drift off to sleep and forget she was standing there, hyperventilating like a lunatic.

She waited.

All was quiet.

Good. Maybe he fell asleep.

Elise gasped as he wrapped a hand around her wrist and pulled her down to the floor. A pathetic choking sound escaped her lips when she felt his thumb brush across her hand, still wet from her tears, before he stilled.

"Are you *crying*?" Concern laced his voice and he no longer sounded half asleep. "Hey, if I hurt your feelings, I'm sorry. I was trying to help."

She shook her head before realizing he couldn't see. "No, it's not that."

"Then what's wrong?" When she didn't answer, he scooted closer until she felt his knees touch hers. "Tell me. What's up?"

Elise heaved a heavy, exhausted sigh and was thankful when he grabbed both her hands again. His touch grounded her, bringing Elise back to reality. She hung her head. *He shouldn't feel like he has to constantly take care of me. I feel like such a baby. I'm so embarrassed. He's going to get tired of this and break up with me. I know it. He gets kidnapped and acts like everything's okay now. He's so strong. My friends turn the lights out, and I freak out over things I can't control.*

"It's nothing. I'm fine," she lied. "Go to sleep."

"Come here." The impatience in his tone made her feel guilty. *He is sick of it, after all.* He pulled her into his lap. Immediately, she fit perfectly against him and felt the remaining energy leave her body as the panic attack finally subsided. "Are you cold?"

Elise shivered uncontrollably, an unfortunate side effect she suffered after intense panic attacks. She allowed him to ease her into a lying position and pulled her close before covering them both with his blanket. While it didn't immediately stop her trembling, she welcomed its warm embrace. They were an entanglement of limbs, giving Elise another reason to be thankful for the darkness. She pressed her back against Gavin's chest, feeling his breath against the back of her neck. The two lay there until the final tremors faded and her breath steadied.

"Better?" Gavin whispered, placing a kiss behind her ear.

She nodded.

"What happened?"

"I don't know," she replied.

"Liar."

She smiled despite herself. He really did know her better than that. "It's just that—"

They both jumped as Mitch let out a lone, offensive snore, which was followed by Darcie mumbling in her sleep. Gavin and Elise broke into fits of stifled laughter.

"A perfect match," Elise whispered between giggles.

Gavin agreed before running a hand up and down the length of Elise's arm. "Don't change the subject. Spill it."

"Okay, *Darcie*," she teased, leaning her head back as he trailed kisses down her neck. Elise stretched to grant him more access. "Let's just drop it."

Gavin moaned his disagreement before kissing her shoulder.

Although Elise couldn't see Gavin's face, she could almost hear an arrogant yet knowing smirk curving the corners of his mouth.

"Do you want me to stop?" he whispered, grazing her earlobe between his teeth.

Never. She shook her head against his chest. When he abruptly ceased his attentions, she rolled onto her back and pulled him on top of her. *I need more. Don't leave.* Elise's hungry lips sought out his as she drowned all her worries into the kiss. Only when he leaned back did she attempt speaking again. "Do you think our plan will work?"

"*That's* where your head still is? Man, I need to up my game."

She kissed away Gavin's playful pout before meeting his eyes with a sheepish grin. "Sorry."

Gavin stilled when Mitch mumbled something in his sleep before rolling over towards them.

Elise thought Gavin might continue his attentions to her aching body, but when Mitch sat up in the dark, Gavin rolled over to lay beside her.

Both Gavin and Elise shook with nervous, silent laughter. By the time Mitch resumed his snoring, the moment had unfortunately passed.

Gavin groaned into Elise's neck before he leaned over to kiss her. "I love you."

Elise smiled. *I'm disappointed, too.* Sometimes she still couldn't believe it. It was one thing to daydream in school about him loving her. It was another thing entirely for it to be a reality. "I love you, too." She brought a hand up to caress his stubbled cheek. "Since Mitch ruined the mood, I better go back to my spot, so they don't think anything in the morning."

They bid each other a good night, and Elise wasn't surprised to hear Gavin's breathing even out within a few minutes. Yet, Elise's anxious feelings didn't return. Once again, he had saved her from herself. Whatever was going to happen would happen.

She needed to be ready when it did.

CHAPTER 15

Fortunately for Elise and her friends, the days leading up to the festival passed swifter than those preceding Derek's funeral. During that time, not only had Elise received two letters from Ruby confirming the details of their plans, but she also found herself having *fun* again.

The Archers were incredibly generous hosts. When they weren't busy working on a local farm, each showered the four travelers with some sort of hospitality. Mrs. Archer was a fantastic cook and spent each night entertaining them with stories about their family and the town. Talia taught them popular local dances, and Gwen showed them all around Clara, including some shops Elise hadn't noticed during their previous visits. She enlisted their guidance with flower arrangements and last-minute details to help those organizing the festivities.

On more than one occasion, Elise was settled down for bed before realizing she hadn't obsessed about Rona that day. The liveliness of Clara was the only thing keeping her sane until the festival. In the meantime, she tried learning all she could about Gwen in hopes it would make a romance between her and Elise's uncle more feasible.

"Do you ever think you'll get married?" Elise asked on the morning of the festival as she strolled along the crowded streets of Clara with her future aunt. She held her face up towards the sun, enjoying the unseasonable heat wave that had rolled two days prior. It was all anyone in town could talk about apart from it coinciding perfectly with the opening night masquerade. The energy amongst the people was electrifying and infectious.

It's no wonder it was Derek's favorite place to be.

Gwen paused, taken aback by the question, before continuing in the direction of more shops. "I'm supposed to want to, but I can't imagine leaving Mama and Tal. They need me."

Elise understood that. If only she could share with Gwen that she'd be queen of Haighdlen. Her family would be set for life, but Elise knew to let it happen naturally. Suffocating under the growing pressure to break their silence, she steered the conversation to Gwen's ideal husband. Elise inquired what Gwen sought in a potential husband, and more importantly, what she hated.

Before Gwen could answer, the two women stepped apart as a group of children ran between them playing. She watched them with a wistful smile. "I want a family."

Good start. Richard wants an heir, and they'll have my cousin, Madelyn. Check. Elise pictured her freckled-faced cousin from her first visit to Joranna's house back home. Madelyn's small, angelic voice rang through Elise's memory.

"We don't want you to do anything you don't want to do," she had stated, *"but. . .Haighdlen is our home. We'd really love if you'd help save it."*

"A family's good," Elise agreed. "Anything else?"

Gwen shrugged. "You're asking me to create a fantasy, Elise. This is my home. A foreigner would want to take me to his kingdom, and a local man would need to support my desire to remain active in the town's growth. Not many men are like that. They'd prefer I sit idle at home, but I need a purpose."

This is getting better and better. Those are great qualities for a queen. No wonder Richard fell for her. This is going to be so easy.

"But he couldn't be arrogant," Gwen added. "I find arrogance detestable and could never give myself to someone like that."

Crap. Well, we tried.

Elise conceded it wouldn't be as simple as she hoped, but maybe Gwen would see another side of Richard.

Even she rolled her eyes at that possibility.

"So, you see I shall remain a maid." Gwen chuckled as she swung her basket back and forth by her side. "It won't be so bad, though. Talia is *immensely* popular. She'll be married soon enough and have lots of babies. Mama will get her grandchildren, and I can help focus on bringing in money so that she won't have to work anymore."

Elise's heart wrenched. Gwen's selflessness was admirable— even endearing, yet the more she talked, Elise realized there would have to be meddling after all. Her aunt wasn't going to approach a haughty prince, and Richard was close to signing a wedding contract as it was.

A silence fell between the two as they turned onto the next street near the square.

Elise's overactive brain considered multiple scenarios for her aunt and uncle to meet that night. Watching the multiple shopkeepers setting up tables and signs for the evening, she tried staging the perfect meeting place that would set the mood.

"Have I upset you?" Gwen's voice pierced Elise's focus, causing the latter to shake her head.

"No, why?"

"You've grown very quiet. That's all." Gwen looked at her expectantly, forcing Elise to put her plotting on hold.

Elise looked around for an excuse until she caught her reflection in the nearest shop window, which happened to be her favorite hidden gem. It was a simple pawn shop, yet each time Elise entered, there were always subtle changes.

Elise nodded towards it. "I was just thinking I'd like to go into that shop if we have time." It wasn't a complete lie. Elise was sure if she went in, something would pique her interest.

Gwen followed Elise's line of vision before chuckling in disbelief. "Did you not visit it yesterday? Come to think of it, even the day before?"

Elise blushed, unable to think of a proper response. She averted her eyes, catching a glimpse of Gavin coming towards them.

Gwen also spotted him. "Ah, I'll leave the two of you to it, then. Go on in." She gestured towards the basket of linens in her hand. "I must deliver these for last minute alterations, anyway. I'll meet you both at the house." Before Elise could reply, Gwen was already out of sight, lost in the growing crowds on the street.

Gavin greeted her with a quick kiss. "There you are. Talia wanted me to tell you the costumes are ready, and—" He looked up at the sign above their heads before rolling his eyes. "You're not going back into that old dump, are you?"

"I won't be long." Elise shot him an innocent smile, but his raised brow and tucked chin suggested he didn't believe her. "Come with me." Not bothering to wait, and ignoring his answering groan, she tugged on his arm to join her.

While slightly larger than Gwen's house, the pawn shop felt cramped due to its cluttered floorspace, poor lighting, and dust-covered shelves. The first thing Elise always noticed upon entering was the stale, musty fragrance of aged paper and candlewax. Reminded of a used bookstore back home, she paused to see if anything caught her eye from the door. Gavin's second attempt to leave went ignored as she pulled him over to a crooked table full of trinkets.

Elise picked up a porcelain teapot, one she had already held half a dozen times, before moving on to a comb and tarnished spoon.

"The festival starts in a couple of hours," Gavin complained. "Where *you* want to pull off this elaborate plan. . .and you're playing with a spoon."

Elise rolled her eyes. "I'm not *playing* with it." Setting it down, she brushed her fingertips across a collection of old worn shoes and quills. She didn't know what it was, nor could she explain it, but there was something enchanting about this place that stirred something within her. *So many stories.* Elise didn't expect Gavin to understand. She didn't even fully understand her own obsession with the store, but once she stepped foot inside, it was always much harder to leave.

"Back again, I see."

Elise jumped as the shopkeeper poked his head around the corner of a shelf. *I didn't even see him there.*

"*This* is why I hate it in here," Gavin whispered into her ear. "This guy's crazy."

While Elise doubted any ill will on the shopkeeper's part, the older gentleman certainly made no effort to give a good impression. Elise usually found him lurking in corners, making little eye contact, and avoiding people altogether unless he could detect a transaction worth his while.

"Y-yes," Elise stammered, watching the elderly gentleman limp across the shop to stand on the other side of a glass counter. She offered him a smile that was not returned. "I was just looking around to see what was new."

"Since *yesterday*?" Gavin hissed before she elbowed him in the ribs.

A sinister smile cracked the shopkeeper's otherwise stoic and sunken features. "I might have something. Acquired it this morning."

Ignoring Gavin's objections, Elise stepped forward as the ghoulish salesman retrieved a small velvet box from the top shelf beneath the glass. *I can't leave now.* Eager to see its contents, she fought to ignore the nagging voice screaming for her to walk away. Even Gavin was nodding towards the door. Peering over the counter, Elise watched as the shopkeeper lifted the delicate lid to reveal a bottle necklace. Elise's breath caught in her chest. She immediately recognized it as her mother's lost necklace. *Is it really the* same *one?* She had a flashback to the shores of Lockesbarrow where Rona spilled the remaining fairy magic before striking Derek in the chest. *How did it get here?*

Gavin rolled his eyes again when she waved him over. She suppressed her temper watching him shuffle his feet to take as long as possible. As he approached the counter, he looked at her expectantly with a hint of annoyance.

Elise ignored his moping and cocked her head towards the necklace. She waited for his eyes to widen, a statement of shock, or for him to say. . .*anything*. His facial expression remained neutral as he stared at the jewelry. When he didn't react the same way, she reminded herself he had only seen the necklace during the brief time Rona had it. There was no way for him to truly understand the time and dedication she put into wearing it up until that point. *Not to mention I can give it back to Mom.*

Feeling the weight of Gavin's disapproving stare burning into her cheeks, Elise chewed her bottom lip before ultimately inquiring about the cost.

"Elise! What're you doing?"

She winced at the bite in Gavin's tone.

"Twenty pieces," the old shopkeeper croaked with a toothy grin before removing the necklace from its box. Dangling the chain from a single, bony finger, he held it up in front of a nearby window for a better view.

Elise shuddered when the sunlight exposed layers of dirt beneath the shopkeeper's overgrown fingernails. The lines of his cracked wrinkled skin of his hands were equally smudged and unclean. She couldn't blame Gavin's reluctance to stay in the shop any longer than necessary. *This guy gives me the creeps, too.* Still, Elise knew this wasn't a mere coincidence. She was meant to come in and find this necklace. Her initial excitement to have it back was overshadowed by the impending realization that it could have only come from one place. *Vaughn is still here.* Mrs. Archer hadn't imagined him earlier that week.

"What'll it be?" he prompted, pulling Elise out of her thoughts.

Gavin shook his head at her, silently pleading for her to walk away. Yet, a nagging curiosity gnawed inside her to possess the necklace again. *We are looking for fairy magic after all. It would be the best place to hold it. I can give it to Mom later.* Pulling the small change purse from her cloak pocket, Elise poured the remaining coins from Richard onto her outstretched palm. *Fifteen.*

She slumped her shoulders with an apologetic smile.

"Bit short there, Miss." The shopkeeper frowned, twirling his finger so that the chain twisted and teased Elise even more.

She stared longingly at the dangling piece of jewelry. *I'd do anything to have it back.* She licked her lips. "Hey, Gavin—"

"No."

"Come on, it's just—"

"No," he whispered, keeping his eyes on the shopkeeper. "I don't want to waste any money on this junk. We need to save what we have to help get us home."

Elise wilted. She couldn't blame Gavin for being reluctant. He hadn't carried that necklace day and night around his neck, protecting it at all costs. Although he, too, watched Rona pour out the fairy magic it once carried, Gavin couldn't possibly understand the gut-wrenching wound it left within her. When Elise opened her mouth to speak again, it was towards her shoes rather than to the shopkeeper's face. "Maybe some other time."

"Pardon me?" the older man asked. "I couldn't quite make out what you said."

"She's not interested. Thanks," Gavin quipped, grabbing Elise's hand before leading her towards the exit.

"*That* is a striking piece you have there, Sir." The shopkeeper nodded towards the medallion swinging around Gavin's neck. "Might fetch a good price if you're interested."

"Yeah, right," Gavin scoffed, yanking the door open. "Not a chance."

Elise waited until Gavin slammed the door shut before finding the courage to speak. The last thing she wanted at that moment was for him to see her cry. *Don't lose your nerve.* "I only needed five coins."

"Come on, Elise. I already told you I don't want to. We might need that money later, and you're going to wish we had it."

Elise bit the inside of her cheek before pressing on. "But I really think there's something we're missing. Plus, it's not *all* your money. It's only five coins. If we could just go back—"

"Do you know what *I* think?" Gavin spun so fast on his heel she almost ran into him. "I think you're trying to juggle too much. What if this is a trap to distract us? Let's stick with our plan. We still have to introduce Richard to Gwen, find fairy magic, stop Rona, *and* get home. Going broke over some stupid necklace—"

"But it's *not* stupid!" she cried. "You don't understand. *You* weren't there when we got it!"

"And that's *my* fault?" he snapped. A tense moment of silence followed as his breathing quickened. "You think I'd rather be where I was?"

Elise's heart softened at the sight of pain in his eyes. He was practically shaking, but it wasn't out of rage. This was something else, but when she attempted to approach him, he quickly wiped his face with his sleeve and walked away.

Elise hesitated, taken aback by his rare vulnerability. *This isn't going the way I hoped. It's only getting worse, but I can't back down. I'm only trying to help, but I don't want to hurt him.* "Gavin, Mrs. Archer wasn't making it up the other day. Vaughn left this necklace. He must've picked it up that day we saw Rona, and—"

"That's it, isn't it?" He froze, casting a dark glare over his shoulder. "It's from *him.*"

"What? No!" she shrieked. *That's not what it is at all!* "I told you he doesn't mean anything to me, but if we could figure out why he's hanging around, it could give us a clue. Why would he leave it here for us to find?" *Is he even listening to me?* "He might be spying on us. I need to get to the bottom of this."

Gavin hung his head before chuckling in disbelief. "Guess I'm an idiot then. I thought we agreed to do this together."

That's not what I meant. "Don't be like that," Elise pleaded, catching a couple of people watching them as they passed. *Great. Of course, there's an audience. Why is he acting like this?* "You're not even listening to me!"

Gavin's sullen expression soured further as he dug into his pocket. Shaking his head, he silently closed the distance between them before taking her hand.

Elise watched as he placed five coins into her palm with a resigned sigh.

"Buy the necklace," he whispered. "I won't stop you."

"No, this isn't what I wanted," she argued, feeling unwanted tears welling up in the corners of her eyes. "If you'd let me explain—"

"I'll see you at Gwen's."

She watched him cross the bustling street as guilt stabbed her chest like a thousand knives.

Gavin ignored her calls until he was out of earshot altogether.

Elise dropped the coins into her purse with a huff. Her brain screamed to run after him and return the money. It would be simpler to forget the necklace and patch things up, but the gnawing suspicion of Vaughn's unknown intentions outweighed her better judgment. *Gavin doesn't understand. I have to figure this out. I can apologize later.*

The door creaked open as Elise entered the pawn shop again. She shuffled her feet to where the shopkeeper still stood.

Polishing a silver goblet, he cocked his head and smiled at her.

Without a word, she pinched the bottom of her purse and poured all twenty coins out onto the glass counter.

He inspected the payment. "Talked some sense into him, eh?"

Elise didn't reply except to nod towards the necklace, which was now back in the small velvet box.

He praised Elise's excellent choice before handing it to her. "Seems only fitting that you also get to wear a beautiful, exotic piece."

Elise ignored his flattery as she brushed her fingers along the ornate details of the Elven bottle necklace. She clenched her eyes shut, reliving the moment on the beach where Rona dropped it. Elise could hear her own guttural scream ringing through her ears as if it was all still happening. She saw Derek get struck over and over, crashing more violently to the ground each time. The nagging voice returned to remind her since Derek was dead, they really couldn't fix anything. Suddenly, she wasn't in the mood for a festival anymore. *This is so much bigger than us. How can we possibly hope to fix the timeline?* Not to mention Gavin was mad at her now, too. Everything was getting worse.

"Can you tell me about the man who brought this in?" she inquired.

The shopkeeper sniffed, staring warily at Elise before peering down at the box holding the jewelry. "Not much. He said it was royal business."

Royal business? What does that mean? "Are you sure there's nothing else?"

The shopkeeper declined to elaborate, causing Elise's mere frustration to escalate to rage. *He's no help.* She replied with a curt nod before hiding the box within her cloak and exiting the shop.

Gwen's house wasn't far, yet Elise felt as if she couldn't reach her friends fast enough. So many questions were swirling through her mind, and she wanted desperately to hear their thoughts on what she had found out.

In all her excitement, Elise didn't prepare herself to face Gavin following their argument. Upon entering the cottage, the air turned cold as she found him sitting at the table with his back to the door. He was listening to Mitch complain that Darcie already planned on making him dance that night, but as soon as Gavin's eyes met hers, Elise immediately regretted going back into the pawn shop.

It was the briefest of glimpses over his shoulder before Gavin turned back to Mitch without so much as a greeting.

Darcie beckoned her into their shared bedroom. *Great. Now I have a fun interrogation to look forward to as well. This day keeps getting better and better.*

"What did you do to Gavin?" Darcie pursed her lips. "He's acting weird. What did you say?"

Elise shared the details of their argument outside the pawn shop before crossing both arms across her chest.

"Can you blame him?" Darcie offered. "I see why he's hurt."

Elise scoffed. "You're my best friend. You're supposed to take *my* side. Plus, you know there's nothing going on with Vaughn."

Darcie held up both hands with a shrug, her nose pointed high in the air. "It's not me you have to convince, it's your boyfriend, and right now it sounds like you're putting that necklace and this mission before him."

Elise pinched the bridge of her nose. *Did she hear Gavin say that?* "I don't have time for this. I know you love it, but you know I *hate* drama."

"All I'm saying is you should probably apologize. He went through a lot, too."

Releasing a heavy sigh, Elise peeked out the door and saw a glimpse of Gavin's back. "I need to straighten this out before the festival."

"Good luck," Darcie said, slumping against the wall with her arms crossed.

I know we have a ton to do tonight, but if we're not on the same page, it's going to make things ten times harder. I didn't think it was such a big deal for me to get Mom's necklace back.

"Gavin?" Elise called out. She held her breath until he leaned back into her line of vision. "Can you come here, please?"

He and Mitch mumbled something to one another Elise didn't catch. The tips of her ears burned when Mitch chuckled, sending Elise's paranoia skyrocketing.

Gavin rolled his own eyes before he languidly stood to walk her way. An awkward moment of silence passed between the two girls before Elise gestured towards the door. "Out."

"But why?" Darcie whined. "I'm going to make you tell me everything, anyway."

Elise pointed a finger towards the other room until Darcie left.

As Gavin entered the room, Elise stepped around him to close the door. When he tried to speak, Elise held up a finger to stop him before leaning close to the door again. "Goodbye, Darcie," she said, waiting until she heard her best friend's footsteps fade from the other side.

Gavin put both hands in his pockets and leaned back against the door. When she didn't talk right away, he lifted his brows expectantly. A lock of dark hair fell across his chocolate eyes, momentarily robbing her of breath.

Though it couldn't be more ill-timed, Elise did her best to ignore the fluttering sensation pulsing through her stomach at his brooding appearance. Her thoughts began distracting her with what she *really* wanted to do while they were alone. Elise's gaze followed the line of his collar down to where his shirt hung partially unbuttoned. *Why does he have to look so good when he's upset? I'll never get through this.* When he called her name, she forced herself to look up at his face again.

"I don't want you mad at me." Elise fiddled with her fingers before tucking a strand of loose hair behind her ear. "The necklace doesn't mean anything."

"Oh, it means *something*," he corrected her.

She rocked back and forth beneath his heavy-lidded stare. An awkward silence passed between them before Elise realized she was chewing her bottom lip. "What I mean is. . .Vaughn doesn't mean anything. I wasn't choosing him over you or anything." When Gavin didn't reply, Elise removed the box from her cloak as a rising tide of guilt spilt from her mouth. "I wore this the entire time we searched for you. It carried fairy magic. I kept it safe and protected, hoping to use it to get us home. When Rona dropped it. . ." Elise's eyes glossed over as she stared at a tile in the floor, but her mind once again played out the events on the beach. "We found out who Vaughn really was, and I thought I lost everything." She sucked her lips into a thin line as she awaited his response. *You have to believe me.*

The silence between them grew so intense, Elise felt as if she would collapse from the weight of it. *What's going through his mind?*

Gavin looked as if he *wanted* to say something, but before he could utter a single syllable, the door opened and pushed him forward.

Elise gasped from the sudden intrusion, and only calmed when Mrs. Archer poked her head in.

"Oh, I'm sorry to interrupt. I didn't realize anyone was in here." Mrs. Archer bustled about the room before burying her head inside the closet. "I need to sew a small tear in Talia's sleeve. She's practically inconsolable. I believe I put it in here somewhere. . ."

Gavin and Elise shared an aching stare while the older woman muttered to herself about the unusually warm weather outside, not realizing she was causing the palpable unspoken tension between them to mount.

"Aha!" sang Mrs. Archer, holding the sewing kit up in the air like a trophy. Her triumphant smile faded when she looked between the two teenagers. A flustered, disapproving scowl colored her features as a line formed between her brows. "My goodness! Don't you know what time it is? You both must get dressed! The sun is nearly set, and Gwen's already left. Her performance will be early.

Hurry, hurry!" She tugged on Elise's sleeve with an offer to help with her hair.

Casting a disheartened glance back at Gavin, she mouthed an apology before Mrs. Archer once again closed the door.

CHAPTER 16

"Are you sure it's a good idea to wear this thing tonight?" Darcie asked as she clasped the bottle necklace around Elise's neck. "I thought we were trying to be discreet."

Elise centered the bottle against her chest. "Vaughn wanted me to find it, and if he shows up, I want him to see that I'm not afraid anymore."

"Is that true?"

Elise shook her head. She was terrified, but she would have to conceal her fear if their plan was going to succeed.

"Are you and Gavin good?" Darcie glared when Elise nodded. "Liar."

Elise fidgeted in her chair. "We're as good as we're going to be for now." She and Gavin hadn't made up the way she wanted to yet, but time was slipping away from them. Using a finger to adjust a smear of lipstick, Elise inspected herself in the mirror.

Edith's design was more daring than Elise was comfortable with, but she had to admit it suited her curves. Turning towards Darcie, Elise peeked back over wavy shoulder straps to inspect the low-cut back of her sparkling emerald gown. Goosebumps swam along Elise's naked arms as she trailed a trembling hand up the equally revealing front until she grasped the bottle necklace for comfort. *I can do this.*

As it turned out, Mrs. Archer was a skilled hairdresser like Darcie—who wasn't offended, but who also didn't pass up the chance to tease Elise about being replaced.

Elise tilted her head, admiring her elegant updo from all angles. She was thankful Mrs. Archer was able to incorporate the matching silk ribbon that arrived with the gown. The color stood out as it weaved in and out of her dark red hair. Settling her gaze on the necklace again, quavering doubts churned in Elise's lower gut as she ran both clammy hands down the fabric of her gown. "It's time to go." Readjusting the accompanying ornate mask for comfort, Elise turned around to see Darcie tying her own. "Wow. You look great!" *How does Edith make these so perfect?*

Darcie's plum-colored gown hugged her form like a glove except for a billowy feather skirt. Oversized matching feathers lined the top of her solid velvet mask. Against the lush, deep purple fabric, Darcie's pale skin practically glowed.

Elise chuckled when her best friend was unable to resist the urge to twirl.

A huge smile split Darcie's face as she squealed. "Thanks, but shouldn't we wait for the guys?"

Elise shook her head. "Gavin promised he'd find me since Mrs. Archer asked the boys to stay back and escort her once she's ready. I don't even think *they're* ready yet."

"And they complain about *us* taking forever."

Their excitement only grew as they followed Talia to the town square before the latter excused herself to join another group of friends. Although Elise had spent the better part of a week in town, nothing could have prepared her for its finished transformation.

According to the Archer family, the Harvest Oak Festival was a highly anticipated event, and Clara took its hosting duties very seriously. Nothing was left to chance and no detail went unnoticed.

Countless torches and lanterns lit the unseasonably warm night, sending an array of shadows dancing along the busy streets. Stringed flags and banners bearing Haighdlen's crest waved from shop rooftops and carts. It was nothing short of impressive, and Elise struggled to take it all in.

Proud vendors lined the main square with their most successful fruits and vegetables of the season on full display. Vibrant colors and scents attacked Elise's senses as she soaked in the rich sight and aromas of plump pumpkins, onions, fresh corn, sweet potatoes, apples, carrots and plenty more. Other carts showcased jewelry, wine, spices, perfumes, and painted canvases. Laughter, shouting, and buzzing conversations overlapped with lively music coming from a band of musicians playing near a makeshift dance floor.

Above the crowd, half a dozen performers dressed as masked scarecrows paraded by on stilts. As one passed, Elise stepped out of the way before gazing beyond the dance floor where a guarded dais awaited the arrival of the royal family. She dared to hope after counting the empty cushioned chairs. *There are five seats. Maybe Mom will get to come after all!*

"Elise, look at this." Darcie pulled Elise over to a lone decorated cart beneath a flower-covered arch. In the middle sat a magnificent crown-shaped corn dolly centerpiece. Around it lay intricate straw-woven hearts atop a bed of hay and fallen petals. Beside the cart stood an easel supporting an oversized oil painting of Derek.

Elise's breath caught in her chest. Taken aback by its likeness, she studied her late grandfather's eyes, marveling at the artist's ability to capture both Derek's assertive features and compassionate stare. *The people loved him, too.* Elise could still hear Derek's voice the day he led them through Clara as a young father.

" 'I hope my children grow to love it here as I do. As you can see, we enjoy most of these products in the castle and have come to know these wonderful people well.' "

Elise swallowed convulsively when Darcie asked what she thought of the display. Without taking her eyes off the canvas, she whispered, "It's perfect."

Darcie wrapped an arm around Elise's shoulder before pulling her into a hug. "I know you miss him, but let's try to have some fun."

Elise pulled away to survey the crowd. She couldn't shake the feeling they were being watched. "Where are the guys? They should be here by now."

Darcie rolled her eyes. "They probably stopped at the first food cart they came to. Let's go back there and check."

Shifting her eyes, growing more unnerved by the minute, Elise licked her lips. *Something is wrong. I feel it. I need to get Darcie away from here until I can figure it out.* "You go ahead. I'll wait here in case my family shows up."

Before Darcie was out of sight, Elise was well on her way to having a panic attack. Anxiety was already a crippling endeavor but experiencing it in public was like wearing a mental straitjacket. Every nerve in her body pulsed with anticipation while her mind fought to sedate the swarm of unwanted thoughts. Nothing about her surroundings gave Elise cause for alarm, yet the hair on the back of her neck rose, nonetheless. Instinctively, she reached up and squeezed the bottle necklace as her head swam. The once roaring crowd was now muffled as if she were underwater. *Where's Gavin? I need him. I need to know everyone is safe. Something's definitely wrong.*

Her thoughts cycled through the same erratic pattern until an offending trumpet silenced the crowd and her thoughts to announce the arrival of the royal family. Elise smiled, relief washing over her as she took in their masked faces. Among them, Joranna's handheld mask was the most impressive. Even the stick it was attached to was covered in jewels and pearls. Elise suspected the mask alone was worth more than anything she had ever worn. Cheers erupted as each member entered the dais and acknowledged the people. Wiping the sweat from her palms, Elise stepped closer to get a better look. *I wish I could join them.* Her smile dropped, however, as the applause dwindled.

Gasps and murmurs rippled through the crowd when Richard took the largest seat in the middle, leaving Joranna the place next to him.

Why isn't she in the middle?

Sarah and Ian hesitated before following their mother to fill the remaining seats at Richard's left.

Elise's heart fell as she stared at the lone seat to Richard's right. Rather than Ruby, Charles entered the dais to join the family. Elise didn't bother listening to Richard's welcoming speech. The few triggering words that did manage to reach her ears left her fuming. *Family, gratitude, honor, loyalty, dedication, love. . .* She couldn't help but think his speech was written *for* him rather than by him. The prince's recent behavior certainly did not model these ideals. Elise hoped to catch Joranna's or Sarah's attention with a subtle cough, even going as far as to bounce on the balls of her feet, but it was no use. Richard finished speaking so another performer could approach the dance floor and Elise still went unnoticed.

The Master of Ceremonies thanked the royal family before introducing a masked young maiden. Though she wore a bold, voluptuous white gown, reminding Elise of a delicate swan, the singer's shoulders slumped as she awaited the musicians to play. The maiden fidgeted with her hands as her credentials were read aloud, including her popularity across borders, namely Lockesbarrow.

Elise craned her neck to see over the other bystanders as the woman initially sang towards her feet. At first, it was difficult to hear her, but as the song progressed, the singer's voice displayed incredible range. Her raw, natural talent and ethereal tone mesmerized the crowd, the royal family included, and Elise couldn't help but hang on to every lyric.

> *Hold steadfast,*
> *Dear lover,*
> *For the thrills of life lay ahead.*
> *Dwell not on the past,*
> *Dear lover,*
> *For time chases no immortal bed.*
>
> *Cease fleeing this moment,*
> *This one aching moment,*
> *Alas, it is all we may share.*
> *Seize your moment,*
> *Our lone stolen moment,*
> *Kiss me now while I am still fair.*

As the song reached its climax, the young woman switched to simply vocalizing. *This sounds like something out of a fairy tale.* During one particularly high note, Elise felt her chest swell as tears pricked the corners of her eyes. This voice was hauntingly beautiful, as was the singer herself, and for a few precious seconds, Elise's worries vanished.

Until she felt someone watching her. Elise barely managed a clap as the young woman finished before gazing into the sea of masks around her. Cheers and whistles erupted as another jig began. Within seconds, couples reappeared, and skirts once again swept across the dance floor. Elise stepped back, putting as much distance between her and the dancers as possible. *I want Gavin. And where is Darcie? She should've found the guys by now.*

With one last desperate search, her heart fluttered at the sight of him. *Gavin!*

A masked figure emerged from the crowd with a subtle wave and made his way towards her. Elise's breath hitched as heat rushed to her face. *Wow, Edith's outdone herself again.* Elise didn't know why she continued to underestimate the fabriwitch's good taste in fashion. Gavin's costume was certainly tailored for his body only. She couldn't tear her eyes away from the way the solid black fabric hugged his athletic frame. Even the satin mask Edith chose, which covered almost his entire face, was complimented with a stylish hat. As if the fit wasn't perfect enough, the final embellishment was a dapper cape that hung over one shoulder.

He looked incredibly dangerous. . .and it excited her.

Gavin paused to let a group of people cross in front of him, giving Elise another moment to admire his mesmeric physique. She chuckled at the fact that even the way he rested a hand in his pocket got her hot and bothered. Her abdominal muscles tightened beneath her gown as he resumed his steps. All she could think about was ripping his costume off in a secluded alleyway somewhere away from prying eyes. *I'll happily let him return the favor.* Blushing from the direction of her own thoughts, she chuckled as he closed the distance between them with a series of goofy steps timed with the music. *Oh, good. He's forgiven me.*

"I didn't think you liked dancing," Elise said as the musicians finished another piece.

He replied by offering his hand before leading her towards the dance floor. As Gavin pulled her body against his, awaiting the next song, Elise felt a shiver course down her spine. As if their embrace wasn't sensual enough, he trailed a gloved hand along her jaw, tipping her chin up towards him. Goosebumps trailed along the exposed skin of her arms. *I love him so much.*

The first soft notes from the band sent the surrounding couples in motion around them, causing Elise to look down at her feet before Gavin lifted her chin once more. He tightened his hold, guiding her back and forth until she felt comfortable with the rhythm. Melting against him, she closed her eyes to soak in this fleeting moment. She doubted there would be any masquerades once they returned home. *Never in a million years could I have imagined a night like this.*

All her anxieties vanished when his hand slid further down her lower back. When Elise lifted her head from his chest, she saw the playful smirk that sent an exciting rush of adrenaline through her.

"Kiss me," she whispered, snaking a hand around his neck before crushing her lips against his.

It took only a second for Elise's excitement to come to a screeching halt. She could no longer hear the music over the deafening sound of her heart beating in her ears.

This wasn't Gavin.

Elise ripped the mask from Vaughn's face, inwardly screaming and berating her own ignorance. *How could I not know?*

Then came the stifling guilt. She thought back to the erotic dream she had experienced involving Vaughn during their journey to save Gavin. Deep down, she was convinced Vaughn manipulated her dreams with some sort of magic. It still didn't make it any easier to stomach the amused smirk on his lips.

What have I done? Gavin's going to kill me!

"What are *you* doing here?" she hissed.

She made to pull away, but Vaughn grabbed the mask before holding her flush against him. "Now, let's not draw attention to ourselves, shall we? Besides, *you* kissed me."

Gaping in horror, Elise watched him readjust his mask. "I-I thought you were Gavin!"

"I still can be if you wish." Feeling as if her knees would buckle from his arrogant smile, she composed herself long enough to stomp a pointed heel into his foot.

He bit his lip to stifle a groan yet kept a firm grip on her arm. "Play nicely," Vaughn warned, almost songlike, into Elise's ear before inhaling the sweet scent of her hair. His appreciative, primal moan vibrated against her own cheek. "I've missed you."

Elise attempted to jerk away again but was held still. She fought against the seductive effect his voice had on her body, but he was right. If she screamed and created a scene, it would do more harm than good for their already jeopardized plans.

"What do you want?" Elise's mind became keenly aware of the lazy circles he drew on her exposed back. *Stop it, Elise. Ignore it.*

"You look stunning," he said, ignoring her question completely before nodding towards her chest. "I see you found my little gift."

Elise glanced down at the bottle necklace. *I knew it was him.* She bit her tongue to control her nerves before grounding out her next words. "What're you planning?"

He clicked his tongue three times with a shake of his head. "All in good time," he purred before twirling her. "The night is young, and *you* are breathtaking."

Sucking her lips into a thin line, Elise increased her self-awareness, desperately searching for a familiar face or an escape.

"Word on the street is you've befriended the Archer family." Vaughn's breath tickled Elise's ear as he pulled her close.

Elise felt her blood turn cold.

Vaughn's eyes flashed from beneath his mask. "I often consider paying them a visit. They were such gracious hosts, as you know."

Elise pushed against his chest enough to meet his gaze. "Stay away from them!" she spat. "Tell me what you're planning. Why plant the necklace where I might not have found it?"

"I knew you'd see it." He threw a casual shrug in her direction. "Like all Laurilles, you couldn't satisfy your curiosity if you tried. After spending these last few months at the castle, I have found it to be a family trait."

"I'm warning you," Elise said, feeling the initial terror in her veins melt into a searing rage. She dug her fingers into the back of his arms when he prevented her from backing away again. "Stay *away* from my family. They're on to you."

He had the nerve to chuckle, sending what little gumption she possessed plummeting. "Is that so?"

If he weren't holding her up, she might have stumbled. *Focus, Elise! Don't let him see you weak.* She cocked her chin up at him. "You were already kicked off the council."

"Dismissed for an *investigation*," he corrected. "An investigation, I might add, that has yielded no evidence against me. In a matter of hours, I'll be restored and carry on with business."

"Which is?" Elise asked. She gritted her teeth when he didn't reply. "And why return the necklace at all? Is Rona here?" *Only hours? What's he planning to do?*

Vaughn used the climactic swell of the music to catch Elise off guard and spin her one final time. Feeling him release her hand, Elise caught her balance and whirled around, but Vaughn was nowhere to be found. As the other couples stepped away to mingle, she stood there, dumbfounded, convincing herself she hadn't imagined the whole exchange. When the initial shock wore off, only one clear thought remained in her head.

The family's in danger.

Elise ran frantically towards where her relatives sat. Gritting her teeth, she was convinced the population in Clara had doubled since she arrived. Elise lost count of how many people she pushed past, and even gave up apologizing when her own frustration piqued. *Can anyone move? I'll never reach my family at this rate.* At one point, all she could do was stare at the wall of people ignoring her attempts to get through. *If Richard sees me, I'll get arrested, but if I don't warn them, Vaughn or maybe Rona, might attack. Something is about to happen. I can't just sit here and wait!*

Out of time, and options, Elise peered around for a way to get Sarah's attention. Her aunt was positioned in the seat closest to Elise, but the eldest princess was invested in a hushed conversation with Ian. Reaching down, Elise picked up a small pebble near her shoe. She checked her surroundings to make sure no one was watching before nonchalantly tossing the pebble towards her aunt's feet. Elise stomped her own foot helplessly when it bounced off the edge of the dais.

Four stones later, one finally skipped along the wood panels before landing on Ian's shoe.

Close enough.

Elise crouched with bated breath as the prince inspected the stone before warily surveying the crowd. The moment Ian's gaze roamed close enough, she lifted her mask only long enough to wave him and Sarah over. Ian whispered something into Sarah's ear before the princess also glanced in Elise's direction.

Now to just get them here without too much attention. Richard had thankfully missed the subtle interaction, bouncing between conversations with Joranna and Charles, giving Sarah and Ian ample time to use discretion by excusing themselves one at a time.

Elise beckoned them away from the guards.

"Did you get it?" she whispered, feeling breathless as her uncle retrieved the diary from his vest and offered it to Elise. It took everything in her not to snatch the book from Ian's hands. Elise scanned the worn cover, brushing her fingers across it. She toyed with the corner, itching to open it. *I want to go home and forget about what I'm supposed to do.* "Does anyone else know about this?"

"Just Ruby," Sarah replied. "Ballard almost caught us, but Ian was able to escape using his invisibility."

Elise chuckled. She had almost forgotten her uncle's unique superpower. At the mention of her mother, Elise twisted the bottle necklace between her fingers. Checking over her shoulder, Elise asked Sarah to hold the diary momentarily while she unclasped the chain from around her neck. She held it out towards the princess. "Please give this back to Ruby. Tell her thank you."

Before Sarah could take it, however, Elise froze. There it was—that nagging, tugging feeling—the same one that prevented her from following Ruby through the portal that she couldn't explain before. It wasn't a panic attack, yet it left Elise paranoid all the same.

Whether it was magic, or plain intuition, she had learned to listen to it. Ignoring her aunt and uncle's inquisitive stares, Elise took a step back as an unnerving barrage of thoughts swarmed within her mind.

Vaughn put this where I would find it. He knew I'd get it back. What if he did something horrible to it? It could be tracking our location. I can't put Mom in danger, too. Quick, think of something!

"On second thought, she wanted me to keep it. I don't want to hurt her feelings."

While Sarah nor Ian looked completely convinced, neither questioned her decision apart from sharing a dubious glance.

"What will you do now?" Ian asked.

"Stop Rona," Elise said, hugging the diary close to her chest. *Open it. Open it right now.* Heat rushed to her cheeks as she idly stuck a finger between the pages before pulling it out again. "For good this time."

Ian lifted a skeptical brow, but Elise couldn't blame him. Her plan did sound farfetched, particularly coming from an outsider.

"And Mother's diary is going to make that happen? Is it charmed or something? Perhaps Sarah and I could awaken its magic."

Elise stepped away from his reach. *If they open it while I'm this close, who knows what will happen?* "No, really. I've got it from here. Thanks for your help, but there's more."

Ian scoffed before cocking his head towards Elise. "Why do I feel like we've just made a grave mistake?"

Elise scanned the crowd as if Vaughn could appear out of thin air. She squeezed the necklace in her fist, praying he wasn't eavesdropping somehow through it. She curled her toes before forcing herself to stand taller. *Spit it out! You look stupid.* "There's a man here. A spy. His name is Vaughn Garthorne, and he's going to—" She and the other two jumped as fireworks erupted above them. The cheers from the crowd were so deafening, Elise's warnings could not be heard until she repeated herself a moment later.

Sarah stared intently into Elise's eyes, as if trying to gauge if she were telling the entire truth. Over the whistles and applause amidst another booming display above them, the princess shouted, "I'll only ask you this once more. You're absolutely sure you can use *that?*" She nodded towards the diary. "Because if Mother finds out we—"

Before Sarah could finish, Elise was pushed aside by other guests making room for Joranna, who made her way off the dais towards the decorated carts for a better view of the illuminated sky. Sarah and Ian used the opportunity to wish Elise luck before excusing themselves back to their seats undetected.

Cursing the bad timing, Elise dug her foot into the ground and bit her lip to stop from screaming. She felt her frustration evaporate, however, after watching Joranna congratulate a few vendors before slowly approaching Derek's portrait. The queen stared at the gifts atop the hay and flower petals in silence. Despite the merriment around her, Joranna remained somber and introspective. Elise didn't know what was going through her grandmother's mind, but the mourning widow painted a truly heartbreaking scene that few even bothered to notice apart from her attending butler and the Master of Ceremonies. Hovering behind the queen, awkward and eager, the second gentleman approached with a jovial greeting and bow.

"How do you like our festival, Your Majesty? I believe the late honored king would've approved."

Elise held her breath at the mention of her grandfather. *I don't know if she's going to like that.*

Joranna, ever the perfect model of a queen, took a moment to compose herself before offering him a poised smile. "I believe you are correct. You truly have outdone yourselves this year. Derek would have certainly enjoyed himself. Please take care to return this to the castle after the festival." Lowering her mask, she gripped the stick and pointed towards the canvas. "I expect it to be in the same condition as it was loaned."

"Of course, Your Majesty," replied the Master of Ceremony with another bow.

Casting one last longing glance at her husband's portrait, Joranna nodded and excused herself to visit other vendors and members of court.

She's so broken. I still don't understand why he had to die. Why couldn't we save him? Maybe I could find a way to talk to her.

"There you are!" Darcie's voice was a welcome interruption from Elise's wistful thoughts.

Elise's excitement was short-lived, however, as Gavin and Mitch appeared beside her best friend. Her first thought was how handsome Gavin looked in his similar black costume, which sent another crushing wave of guilt pulsing through her body. *I can't believe I didn't know it was Vaughn before. Gavin won't understand. I really thought it was him.*

"You okay?" Gavin's brows furrowed as he studied her distressed state.

Elise swallowed convulsively. *He knows me too well. Even with a mask, I can't pretend I'm okay. Here goes nothing.* She shuddered under her friends' scrutiny.

"We need to get close to Richard. . . a-and tell him Vaughn is here." She let out a steadying breath, careful to speak to the ground rather than their faces before feeling cramped by the surrounding crowd. Elise led her friends behind the dais, careful to put enough distance between them and the guards as not to raise any alarm. They allowed a few stragglers to step in front of them while remaining close enough to overhear the royal family.

"So, you *actually* saw Vaughn?" Darcie whispered.

Elise finally met Gavin's eyes, feeling her throat constrict from his darkened stare. Eager to suppress her returning paranoia, she turned to Mitch before holding out the diary. "Here, hang onto this, will you?" She waited for him to hide it beneath his vest before nodding at Darcie.

"But why bother Richard? He's been brainwashed by Vaughn. Will your uncle even care that he's here?" Mitch asked while fidgeting with his shirt. "I get the feeling he'd be more pissed off that *we're* here."

"Maybe we tell Joranna," suggested Darcie.

Elise shook her head. *I can't bother Joranna right now.*

"Did you talk to him?" Gavin asked.

His abrupt question cut through any attempt Elise might have made to change the subject. Hesitant to anger him, she nodded.

"What did he say to you?" When she didn't answer right away, he stepped forward with more urgency. "*What* did he say?"

Elise winced at the bite in his tone. Seeing equally expectant expressions play across her friends' faces, heat rose to the tips of her ears. *How can I tell them the truth without sounding unfaithful?* After three attempts to speak, she faltered.

"Can you guys give us a minute?" Gavin's request, while soft and reserved, sent an icy chill plunging down Elise's spine. There was nothing in his voice to warrant her response. . .

It was his eyes.

Whether from the flickering torchlight or the costume, there was a subtle shift in their depths. Though masked, his fierce brown stare bore into hers, and she felt every silent dagger pierce her skin. Again, Elise questioned how she could ever mistake the effect they had on her.

Rather than wait for privacy, Gavin grabbed Elise's hand before pulling her away from Mitch and Darcie.

His swift stride made her stumble to keep up until he swiped a discarded lantern off a cart and led her into an alleyway between two shops. Elise gasped when he guided her to stand against the stone wall.

"Okay, what's going on with you?" Gavin asked, setting the lantern down near their feet.

Elise imagined her eyebrows getting lost in her hairline as she stared at him, dumbfounded. "*Me?*" She scoffed, not bothering to hide her disbelief. "*You're* the one leading me into an alley!"

"*You're* avoiding the question. Just please be honest with me. What happened with Vaughn?"

"Nothing!" Elise fidgeted with the necklace she still carried. When he noticed it hanging from her hand, she cleared her throat. "Okay, you were right. I should've left the necklace in the store. It *was* from him." She ignored his feigned surprise. "He wanted me to find it and knew I wouldn't be able to control myself."

Although he made every attempt to hide any reaction, a twitching muscle in his jaw betrayed him. "Then what?"

She shivered when he took a step closer. "What are you talking about?"

"You heard me," he said softly. He untangled the chain from her fingers and dangled it in front of her face. "How was he able to get so close to you? Did he hurt you?"

Elise shook her head as hot tears threatened to spill beneath her mask. *He's going to kill me.*

"What aren't you telling me?" Gavin groaned at her continued silence as he clutched the necklace and backed away from Elise. "Who knows what he did to it? He could be spying on us right now!" Without warning, he chucked it into the lantern.

Both jumped as the dancing red and orange flames spat and fizzled, burning bright green before burning out completely.

Elise gaped at the smoke, feeling as if she had swallowed a brick.

Gavin lifted the lantern up between them, but there was no sight of the necklace inside.

Vaughn really did use magic on it. I almost gave that necklace back to Mom. What if something had happened? I'm an idiot.

She glanced towards the square at the end of the alley to make sure no one else witnessed what just happened. In that respect, it appeared they were safe. Elise knew the only thing left was to tell Gavin the truth. He deserved that much. Coughing to clear her lungs, she willed her heart to steady and found the nerve to meet his gaze.

"You're right," she whispered. "I should've listened to you. About everything." She flattened her lips into a thin line. "I've been so blind to everything, and I understand if you're done with me."

Gavin rolled his eyes. "Done with you? Elise, you can tell me any—"

"I kissed him!" she ground out.

CHAPTER 17

Gavin set the lantern down carefully before lifting his mask off. He quirked an inquisitive brow.

"You kissed him?"

Elise licked her lips with a tentative nod. "I didn't mean to."

He scoffed before tossing the mask back and forth between his hands before glaring down, giving Elise the impression he might kick the lantern.

"I thought he was you."

Gavin didn't bother hiding his confusion.

Elise continued. "You said you would find me, and while I was waiting around, he came up to me."

"So, you assumed it was me and kissed him?"

"Well, he didn't tell me he wasn't," said Elise, realizing how lame her excuse was.

"Must have been difficult with your mouth on his." Gavin crossed his arms and leaned against the wall beside her.

Elise wished there was something she could say to make the weight of his stare lighter. The last thing she ever wanted to do was hurt him, but every word out of her mouth made the situation worse.

"I'm so sorry. But as soon as I did it, I knew it wasn't you and tried to get away," Elise offered, knowing it was a weak argument after the fact. When he didn't reply, her voice cracked as she pleaded for him to say something. His disappointed silence always broke her more than words ever would. Pretending to pick some lint off her dress, she continued. "He's expecting to get back on the council, and there's definitely something else going on, but I couldn't figure it out before he disappeared."

"What a shame."

Elise rolled her eyes as she stepped away from the wall to face him. "It was an accident, and I said I was sorry! I would *never* cheat on you. Now, I'm going to find out what he's up to and stop it before we try using the diary. You can stay here and pout if you like." As she made to walk away, Elise's empowerment was cut short as Gavin took her hand. In an instant, she was flush against him, pinned between his body and the wall.

"Careful," he warned, gazing at her mouth. "I'm not the same guy I used to be."

Elise's breath quickened as his hands wrapped around her waist. Although impossible, Gavin appeared taller as he towered over her. The heat of his body created its own sense of danger that concentrated itself in Elise's stomach. The power he had over her body was electric, plain, and simple. He tilted his forehead down to meet hers.

"I definitely messed up," Gavin whispered.

It was Elise's turn to be confused. *How did* he *mess up?* He turned to replace his mask as a drunken group of people passed by the alley.

Elise pulled him into a hug. Caressing his back, she felt Gavin relax against her until the two silently swayed to the distant music. She didn't know how long they held one another, but when he made to speak again, Elise placed a finger over his lips and kissed him.

Easing back, Elise felt rather than witnessed his eyes roam across every inch of her trembling body. Feeling naked beneath his gaze, she secretly longed for Gavin's hands to follow the same path. The familiar trail of goosebumps lined Elise's arms. What frightened—no, *excited*—her most was not knowing what he would do next. A lump formed in her throat as she accepted that her childish crush was over. She knew what he said was true. Gavin wasn't the same boy now, but a man. Something happened when he was taken from her, and now she hardly recognized him at times. . .or his touch. Yet, she craved more.

"If you don't know what you do to me, then I've definitely messed up," said Gavin.

Before she could respond, Gavin cut her off with a searing kiss. It was as if her thoughts were washed away by a storm. Elise buried a hand in his hair, but he quickly gripped her wrist. She gasped when both of her arms were pressed up against the wall as his lips began their journey down her neck.

"Are you still confused about who can make you feel like this?"

His breath was hot against Elise's collarbone.

Clutching a handful of her skirt, he paused until she managed to nod her head. Satisfied with the silent invitation, Gavin lifted Elise's gown enough to hoist her legs around his waist and swallowed her gasp in another kiss.

Elise's arms wrapped around his neck to support herself as she eagerly found his mouth again and deepened the kiss. It lasted another moment or two before he pulled away.

"You drive me crazy," he purred into her ear. "Do you know that?"

Her legs quivered as she hung onto his every word.

"All those nights we were separated, this. . .*this* is all I could think about. D-did you think of me?"

"Yes," she panted.

"And no one else?" He paused for her answer, making Elise whine with need until she met his eyes.

"Only you. I promise," she gushed against his soft experienced lips. She craved his kiss like oxygen and was rewarded when his tongue met hers.

"Good," he said, "because if I'm going to keep risking my life for you, you better not confuse me for someone else. Got it?"

Shuddering, Elise tilted her head back, this time giving him easier access to place kisses down her throat. Her thighs tightened around him as she used her heels to bring Gavin closer. The cold brick wall scraped against her exposed back, but there was no way she was going to make him stop now. Elise never knew love could be like this. Gavin somehow managed to freeze and scorch her skin all at once.

Each time she thought her breathing was returning to normal, he found a new place to touch that stole it again.

"I have to know you want this," he said. "That you want only *me*. Do you?"

Maybe it was the menacing edge in his voice. Perhaps it was the masks or the distant music and risk of being caught. Whatever the reason, Elise was absolutely consumed by her love for Gavin. Never in her life had she felt this way about anyone. Her desire for him was insatiable. How could *one* person simultaneously make her so elated yet frustrated? It made no sense, but she was determined to chase it until the end. She wondered if Gavin truly comprehended what he meant to her. If not, she feared he never would.

A layer of sweat broke out across her body, making her shiver wherever his breath touched. She softly raked her nails across his own heated skin and managed to choke out a response. "O-only you. There's only you. I only want *you*."

Elise heard the piercing, shrill calls of Mrs. Archer nearby in the square. Next came Talia's voice before her mother continued fussing.

"Have you seen Gavin or Elise? They're going to miss Gwen's performance. Help me find them!"

Gavin's hold on Elise faltered and she felt herself slip down as he sucked in a sharp breath. Gripping the fabric of his coat, Elise lowered her feet to the ground before they parted. Gavin muttered something indiscernible under his breath and slammed his fist against the wall while Elise adjusted her gown with unhinged frustration.

When their breathing and tempers calmed, she searched his equally aggravated eyes for the hundredth time. Would there ever come a day where she didn't find herself hypnotized in their depths? Tracing the edge of Gavin's mask, Elise moved her fingertips to his lips again before caressing the side of his face. As eager as she was to satisfy his body, Elise knew it was more important to soothe Gavin's mind and heart.

"One day we won't be interrupted. . .Again, there's no one else I think about." Elise rested a hand against Gavin's chest until his breathing evened out. "For the last two years, I've only wanted you. I convinced myself before all this that you'd never know who I was. There's still a part of me expecting to wake up. I'm really sorry for everything that's happened, but I'm in love with *you*," she whispered, desperate to hear it back. It didn't matter he had said it before. She needed to hear it *now*.

Gavin regarded her in silence before adjusting her mask with a playful smirk. Elise wondered if he stalled as long as he did to purposely unnerve her. He already knew how flustered she was.

"Okay, you can say it back now!" Elise pushed him until he stumbled back with a laugh. She couldn't stop a chuckle from escaping her own lips. Digging a heel into the ground, she crossed her arms with a playful pout. "You're enjoying this. Aren't you?"

"Only a lot." He shrugged before interlocking his hands with Elise's. His expression grew serious once more as he leaned down to kiss her. "I love you, too. You're forgiven."

Lifting Gavin's hand to her mouth, Elise kissed his knuckles before the two walked back into the square.

The royal family was seated once again, including Joranna. Everyone faced the Master of Ceremonies, but it wasn't until they got closer that Elise heard him introducing Gwen's group. A movement out of the corner of her eye caught Elise's attention before she noticed Darcie and Mitch waving them both over behind the dais.

"You guys good?" Mitch whispered as they approached.

"I'd say they are." Darcie chuckled as she fixed a loose strand of Elise's hair. A nearby lantern illuminated a bejeweled bracelet dangling from her wrist.

"Is that new?" Elise asked with a knowing smile.

Darcie blushed, smiling at Mitch over her shoulder. "I told him not to, but he caught me looking at it and used his coins."

Elise suppressed a chuckle when Mitch tried hiding a red mark with his collar. "I'd say you thanked him enough. Looks like we weren't the only ones who needed a minute."

Both girls giggled as Gavin nodded in approval.

"Have we missed anything?" Elise asked once she composed herself again.

"Your family's not saying much. Especially Joranna. Gwen should be coming out, though." As soon as the words left Mitch's mouth, the abrupt bang of a drum and crash of cymbals cut through the crowd's chatter.

They craned their necks in time to see two lines of masked, scantily clad women approach the dance floor amidst lewd whistling and calls from the surrounding audience.

Though their identities were hidden, Elise recognized her aunt's infamous red updo and loose twisted tendrils. Oddly enough, Elise noticed Gwen was the only one wearing gold bands around her upper arms.

Ignoring the carousing onlookers, Gwen led the second line forward before pausing in a practiced pose to await the music. Gwen's glassy eyes, coupled with a lackadaisical posture spoke volumes until a fellow dancer snapped her fingers. Gwen straightened her posture before blowing out a slow breath as the first lone whining note left a violin.

"She needs to watch herself," said a voice behind Elise, causing her and the others to jump until they saw Talia standing behind them with Mrs. Archer. The older woman chastised them for worrying her sick about their whereabouts before rambling on that at least they made it in time for the dance. Talia apologized on behalf of her mother with a hearty chuckle before turning their attentions back to the dancers. "As I was saying, this is the opportunity of a lifetime, not to mention good money, and she's going to throw it all away! I would've been such a better choice." Talia clicked her tongue, shaking her head as she continued critiquing Gwen's performance. "Why didn't they stick her in the back?"

"She'll do fine, Love. Just watch," Mrs. Archer said.

Elise had a suspicion Gwen's selection had everything to do with her beauty, which was certainly a sight to behold. Not only was she the only red-haired woman amongst the dancers, but her fair complexion and long limbs made her stand out. It was even more impressive since each of the women wore the same crisscrossed halter top with dangling beads and exposed midriffs. Though their skirts swept across the floor, the high-cut slits and sheer fabric left little to the imagination. Elise rolled her eyes. *A man designed these costumes.*

As she studied her aunt's provocative movements, Elise couldn't help but be proud of Haighdlen's future queen. If put into Gwen's position, Elise would have skipped the whole event altogether. She smiled to herself as she remembered the time Gavin experienced the same scenario when he didn't initially show up to Derek and Joranna's engagement ball, leaving Elise alone on the dance floor. Given all that had happened since then, it felt a lifetime ago.

The sound of laughter broke her reminiscing as she turned to see Charles and Richard clinking their glasses together from a few feet away. Elise took care to stay out of their sight but inched as close as she could without drawing attention from the guards. It was almost impossible to hear over the music, but fortunately for Elise, there were moments when the drums weren't pounding in her ears.

"I imagine the princess would have enjoyed the festival," Charles muttered into his cup before taking a long sip.

Richard sighed. "Think not of her, Charles. There's plenty of beauty in front of you. Besides, I will not have my sister's *situation* paraded around as if we condone it. The funeral was enough exposure for her."

Elise fumed. *Was he always this hateful or did something change after we meddled?* A small, yet spiteful part of her considered *not* setting him up with Gwen. Her aunt deserved better than this pompous, unsupportive hypocrite. *Why is it okay for* him *to end up with someone from the town but Charles can't be with Mom? Mom's shut away like a criminal while he parties and flirts with anyone he chooses. Is being queen worth putting up with a man like that?*

She knew better than to jump to conclusions, since there were times when even Derek came across in a bad light despite good intentions. Deep down, she knew Richard was only looking out for Ruby's well-being. . .but it didn't change the fact she wanted nothing more than to wring her uncle's neck.

"Don't do anything stupid," Gavin whispered in her ear, making Elise jump. She hadn't realized he followed her. "Just ignore them."

Elise was thankful when he squeezed her hand. It was difficult, but she was finally able to tune them out and focus on the performance again. The music swelled, and the slow steady rhythm of the hypnotic drum created a sensual beat as most of the dancers performed a series of choreographed steps. Elise hoped she was the only one to notice when Gwen fell out of sync two or three times behind the other ladies.

Elise could barely suppress a laugh at the sight of Darcie's glare. Not that Elise could blame her. Mitch was practically drooling. Gavin would be stupid not to join him. Despite Gwen's reluctance, Elise couldn't argue how talented she and *all* of the dancers were.

As the song neared its climax, the performers pulled matching sheer scarves from their tops and completed a series of synchronized twirls.

"What I wouldn't give to have a man look at *me* like that someday," Talia said with a dream-like sigh.

Puzzled, Elise followed the young woman's line of vision to the royal family. Ian was mesmerized, of course, but it was Richard who looked the most invested.

"Who is *that*?" he inquired with a nod. "The red-haired woman in front." He peered over the brim of his glass as he took a long sip. Sure enough, his feral, brooding stare followed Gwen's every move across the floor before he summoned the Master of Ceremonies to the dais to inquire about her.

"That is Ms. Gwendolyn Archer, Your Highness. Her father was a prominent farmer before his scandalous arrest. This is her first performance, I understand."

"It appears *you* are quite captivated," Charles told Richard with a drunken smirk as the music ended. "Not that I blame you. She is exquisite."

Elise looked between both men and the dancers as Gwen led the other ladies away from the dance floor amidst whistles and applause.

Gwen was soon joined by Mrs. Archer, who had slipped away from Elise's group and pushed through the crowd.

Charles chuckled at his friend's darkened, possessive stare. "Do you see something you like, Sire? Shall I summon her to your chamber tonight?"

I doubt she goes for that, but at least he's interested! We need to keep his attention on her no matter what if they're going to fall in love.

Elise stared at her uncle's face, hoping maybe her magic would extend to him. Although details of Richard and Gwen's original meeting were still unknown to her, a little magic couldn't hurt to push him along since it was clear he liked her. *It's not meddling if it was meant to be.* At least that's what she told herself to justify her actions. Crouching lower to avoid being seen, she focused on Richard's tense expression.

Ask her to dance. Talk to her. Charm her. Come on, ask her. All he needed to do was ask Gwen to dance and then they would fall madly in love. Their engagement would work itself out and they could convince Richard to help them get to Lockesbarrow. He wouldn't be mad at them being there once he knew they were friends with Gwen. Everything would be perfect. It was simple. *Ask her to dance.*

Richard stood. *Yes, good. Keep going. Talk to her. Sweep her off her feet.* Yet, as he took a step forward, Charles rested his hand on the prince's shoulder.

"Are you so eager?" Charles' knowing smile widened. "You'll be devoured by the mob of eligible maidens if you go out there unattended. Allow me to go or send one of the servants. Surely, there could be no objections from a farmer's daughter."

Richard shook his head as if to clear thoughts that were not his own and nodded. "You are right, friend. Have her brought to me." The prince called for his glass to be refilled before taking his seat once again.

This ought to go well. Elise held her breath as the same footman trotted down towards where Gwen and her mother were talking. *I've got to get down there.* She motioned for Gavin, Darcie, and Mitch to follow closely behind her, careful to avoid Richard's line of vision. Glancing back over her shoulder, Elise noticed only the prince and Charles remained in their seats. Joranna, Sarah, and Ian were nowhere to be found.

Hoping the others could keep up, Elise weaved in and out of the bustling crowd. She kept a close watch on the footman ahead of her since numerous couples were approaching the dance floor after the musicians began another set. The group of friends were detained at least twice by clusters of people moving in the opposite direction, not to mention the double take Elise did upon seeing Ian flirting with not one, but two dancer girls beside Derek's portrait. By the time Elise got close enough to Gwen and the footman, Richard's invitation had already been extended.

"This is a tremendous honor, Dearest," Mrs. Archer whispered to her eldest. "To be singled out by the Crown Prince himself? Many a girl has dreamed of such an invitation."

"Mama, you cannot be serious," Gwen replied, locking eyes with Richard. She swallowed convulsively. "Our situation is not so dire that we need to move this way to advance our status. My reputation—"

"Will only be questioned if you refuse," warned her mother. "Seldom does a woman in your position deny a future king."

As tempting as it was to push the timeline along, Elise did not even dare use her magic on Gwen for a decision. This was too personal, and her future aunt had the right to choose for herself without any interference.

Elise watched as Gwen checked her surroundings before continuing in a lower voice. "Mama, what if I were to become with child? His Majesty could already have any number of illegitimate heirs running around this festival he does not acknowledge. Do you honestly encourage me to satisfy this sinful invitation?"

"Of course not!" Mrs. Archer hissed. "But what if more could come of it? If he only got to know you—"

"Forgive me, Mama, but it's out of the question," Gwen said, meeting Richard's eyes again over the crowd. "I doubt he took the time to know those who previously accepted his advances." She turned her attention to the footman. "Please thank the prince for his offer, but I must decline."

The two women waited for him to leave before speaking again.

"You are right." Mrs. Archer sighed. "Forgive me. I just fear for you and your sister since your father's arrest. I'm not getting any younger, you know. I only want you two taken care of."

Gwen leaned forward to hug her mother. "I promise I will always care for you two. We will be fine, but there must be a different way than being used and cast aside by the prince." Glancing back towards the dance floor, she waved her sister over. "But it is getting late. I think you should take Talia home before she gets into any mischief of her own."

Mrs. Archer's reply was lost amidst the applause that followed the end of another song, but it appeared she took her daughter's advice as she waited for her youngest to approach.

However, Elise was too preoccupied watching the footman return to the dais. She held her breath as the servant leaned down to whisper the news to Richard.

"Do you think he'll be mad?" Darcie whispered, making Elise jump.

I forgot they were following me. Elise watched her uncle's expression darken before he stood up. "I'd say so."

Richard made his way off the dais. Except for a momentary delay created by a swarm of eager, eligible ladies, he never took his eyes off Gwen, who had already left her mother to browse the food carts.

"Something tells me he's not used to hearing the word *no*," Mitch muttered with a low whistle.

"Should we distract him?" Darcie offered. "Or get Gwen out of there?"

Elise's breath hitched again when Richard reached Gwen. "Too late," she choked out.

"Gwen's pretty tough," said Gavin. "I think she'll be able to handle him."

Let's hope so.

Darcie clicked her tongue. "Look at how he's looking at her. It's not Gwen's fault the costume is so revealing." She shook her head. "I can't *stand* his arrogance. If it wouldn't get her arrested, I'd tell her to slap him across the face. Am I right, Elise? Elise?"

It took two more attempts from Darcie for Elise to hear her name. She was too invested in studying her uncle's primal expression as he conversed with Gwen. Throwing Darcie an apologetic smile, Elise inched closer to the whispering couple. *At least I have a mask to help. If I'm not careful, they're going to see me, but I have to know what's happening!*

Elise held up a hand to keep her friends at a distance before sliding behind an adjacent cart. It was a tight, awkward fit, but as soon as she picked up Richard's deep voice complimenting Gwen's dance, Elise stilled with her eyes closed. It wasn't until Gwen thanked him that the prince continued.

"I will not insult you by pretending you did not understand the meaning behind my invitation." Richard paused, and though she couldn't see the two, Elise imagined Gwen nodded. "Yet you declined?"

"I did, Your Highness." Gwen's voice was steady, much more confident than Elise could ever hope to achieve if put in the same situation.

"Do you not think I deserve an explanation? Any other woman here would accept without question."

Elise chanced a peek around the curtain shielding her from view. She had to admit, despite her aunt's objections, the two shared unmistakable chemistry with one another. She could cut the fiery tension with a knife, yet Gwen squared her shoulders with a defiant chin.

"I certainly meant no offense, Your Majesty," Gwen said with a brief curtsy, "though it sounds like it will be the only time. You will no doubt succeed with your next choice, and *if* your men are unable to advise you, I would be happy to make a few suggestions."

"Do you deny me on purpose?" Richard took a slow step forward, but Gwen stayed put. "Does it excite you to make men chase you?" He brushed the back of his knuckles down the length of her arm. "I detect you are well worth the pursuit, so I will ask again."

Gwen's gaze followed the same hand as he lifted a finger to trail a path from her lips to the center of her exposed cleavage.

"I can guarantee you the most *erotic* pleasures." His finger continued down the center of Gwen's body before pausing at the waistband of her skirt. "A night to fulfill your darkest fantasies. The way you tremble at my touch, for example, betrays your aching need to be satisfied. You will not be disappointed."

This time, Gwen stepped back from his touch. Although her breaths came quicker, she found the courage to meet his eyes. "*That* is where you are mistaken, Majesty. I seek to satisfy my heart first, not to mention have a man's affection continue longer than a single night. Since I am convinced you can provide me neither, I will repeat my offer to point out a replacement. If not, then I bid you goodnight." With another curtsy, she turned on her heel and proceeded to disappear into the crowd, leaving a rather disgruntled Richard to stomp his way back to the royal dais in silence.

Elise remained in place a few more minutes to insure she would not be spotted before finding her friends.

"How did it go?" Darcie asked first.

"We've got work to do," said Elise with a sigh. "Honestly, I'm frustrated at what's going on, but I'm also proud of her for sticking up for herself. He definitely didn't like that."

"Should we go find Gwen and ask her about the fairy magic then?" Gavin offered. "Maybe she and Richard can get together some other time."

Elise reluctantly nodded before furrowing her brows as the Master of Ceremonies was summoned back to Richard. "What's he up to now?" she asked.

Before Elise and her friends could get closer, the Master of Ceremonies raised his hand to demand everyone's attention and request the royal family take their seats.

"It is my honor and privilege to continue the evening's celebration with an exciting announcement concerning His Majesty, Prince Richard."

The restless, carousing crowd pushed forward, eagerly prattling away about the upcoming declaration. While most focused on Richard, who straightened in his chair, Elise studied Joranna, who appeared as confused as everyone else.

"I must say how thrilled I was upon receiving the prince's letter yesterday," continued the Master of Ceremonies, pulling on his jacket fondly, "that I have scarcely rested in anticipation. Could we have our lovely songbird join us on the dais please?"

Elise gritted her teeth as the drunken crowd blocked the view. She caught a brief glimpse of the singer from earlier in the evening as she made her way up to the dais with the help of the footman.

What is going on? Why is she up there?

Elise's blood froze when Richard stood to greet the woman with a kiss on her hand. She immediately turned around to see if Gwen was watching. Elise found her aunt standing by the jewelry cart with crossed arms and a wary expression towards the beautiful swan-like stranger beside Richard.

"This lovely young nightingale, who blessed us with an angelic performance, is none other than the one who has captured our own prince's affections!"

What? But he was just trying to get Gwen into bed with him. Is this who he was talking about when he mentioned getting married? Who is she?

There was a collective gasp amongst the group before whispering and gossip started to radiate throughout the onlookers.

Richard intertwined his fingers with the lady's before facing the town.

The Master of Ceremonies took a glass of champagne off a nearby tray. "Let us toast to the future king and his future queen, Iris Brahm!"

CHAPTER 18

"Did he say *Brahm*?" Elise shrieked. "As in Brahm, the spy?"

"They have to be related." Mitch's face twisted in disgust. "Does he have a daughter? What woman would want to—"

"I doubt *he* has a daughter," Gavin said, "but his sister, Ingrid, does." Gavin described one of his encounters with Rona when Brahm mentioned Ingrid and her daughter. "There were arrangements after they escaped prison for Brahm's sister and niece to go back to Lockesbarrow."

"Then that has to be her," said Elise. "Ingrid kept her family name, too, it sounds like." She released a heavy sigh, surprised that a rush of anxiety did not follow. This sort of news would normally have sent her spiraling, but she was pleased with her ability to remain calm. "We'll have to add this to the list of messes to clean up on the timeline."

"But there's no way Joranna's going to accept this," Darcie argued. "Look at her trying to hold it together for the crowd. She's furious!"

Sure enough, Joranna wore a trained, plastered smile as she greeted the young songstress.

"I thank you," Richard announced, holding up a hand for the town to quiet down. "My beloved Iris and I are thrilled to be able to share this wonderful news." There was a hushed set of whispers amongst the crowd. "I sense your uncertainty, but I can assure you that such an alliance will only benefit Haighdlen."

"An alliance with who?" called a man standing ahead of Elise. "Is she Lockesbarrian?"

The gossip increased as many began shouting disgraceful objections towards the young woman. The remaining outbursts accused the prince of everything ranging from insanity to treason.

"How else do you explain such a slimy union? What exactly is her connection to our former Captain of the Guard?" called another, igniting a passionate uproar until the guards advanced on the townspeople.

Richard looked to his mother, but Joranna offered no response. In fact, Elise wondered if the queen was having the same thoughts. The prince locked his jaw and silenced the men with threats of imprisonment. "I will not hear of anyone besmirching my betrothed's honor or ruining our engagement. It is our wish to avoid war, and I am certain such an alliance will smooth any further entanglements with Lockesbarrow."

Elise glared at her uncle, uncomfortable with Iris's silence. *He's had this planned, so what was he doing chasing Gwen? We can't trust him. He could be working for Rona.*

"Let us celebrate. It is why we are here. I also wish to take advantage of our gathering to announce we are to wed in two days, prior to the coronation where we will *both* be crowned. Preparations have been underway for quite some time. That is all. Congratulations on yet another productive harvest," Richard said before leading Iris away amongst an explosive outcry from the crowd.

Two days? Why so soon? That's crazy! It doesn't make any sense.

"Did you sign our death warrants along with your marriage contract?" a third man accused.

The Master of Ceremonies tried to intervene, but he was drowned out by the distressed partygoers.

"Let's get out of here!" Mitch shouted. "This is going to get ugly."

"Wait, look over there!" cried Elise, frantically pointing to the side of the dais. "There's Vaughn! He's still here."

Richard and Iris stepped down to greet him, further increasing Elise's suspicions about her uncle's motives.

"I don't like this, guys," said Darcie as Vaughn nodded and bowed before the couple walked out of sight. "Something dirty is going on."

"Vaughn is definitely orchestrating everything," replied Gavin. "But he isn't the one we need to be worried about." Checking over his shoulder, he led the others away to a more secluded area. "Rona has a lock of Vaughn's hair. Whenever she wants to spy, or see what he sees, she uses it to create a connection with him," he reminded them.

"Which causes his headaches, right?" Mitch asked.

Gavin nodded.

"Then there's no doubt she's sitting back watching her little puppet manipulate Richard into practically handing the kingdom over," said Darcie with a sneer.

"While making it look like a peace treaty." Elise sighed. "There won't be a need to wait years to take over the kingdom like before. She'll be able to do it now if we don't stop this."

"Mitch is right, though." Gavin scanned the crowd before ushering them forward. "We need to get out of here."

Spotting Gwen, Elise called out multiple times, but the other woman continued without stopping. *Can she really not hear me?*

"Should we be yelling her name if we're trying to lie low?" Mitch asked.

I guess he has a point.

Elise felt heat rush to her cheeks but pressed on. "We need to follow her. She's our only hope to get magic and use the diary."

She checked over her shoulder once more in time to see the royal family being ushered to their carriages while the Master of Ceremonies worked to ease the crowd by calling for more music.

Before Elise and her friends could make their way through the sea of restless onlookers, a familiar voice called out to them. She froze when Charles walked into view. Feeling her heartbeat quicken, Elise searched for anyone else in her family who may have followed him. *What is he doing here? How did he see us?*

"Do not be alarmed," he began, "I have not shared your attendance this evening with His Majesty."

Elise leaned away from the offensive scent of ale on his breath. *How drunk is this guy?*

"Were you able to deliver the letter?" Charles hesitated, failing to suppress a smile when Elise nodded. "Good. Thank you. Please tell her I miss her, will you?"

The five of them stood in an awkward silence another moment or two before Elise took advantage of his inebriated state.

"Charles?" She waited for his eyes to focus on her. *Here goes nothing.* "Why was Vau—Sir Rodrick here tonight?"

Tensing his shoulders, Charles' features darkened at the mention of Vaughn's fake name. "It was not by my influence, I can assure you. In fact, it would seem my advice has gone *unnoticed* as of late. It would not be surprising if I were soon dismissed altogether."

"Why is that?" Elise asked.

"It is no matter. Forget I spoke of it."

Elise clenched her teeth as she focused on his face. Willing her magical energy forward, she proceeded to ask again. "*Why* is Sir Rodrick here?"

Tell us. Now.

Charles furrowed his brows as he leaned against the nearest cart for support. "There was. . .a meeting."

"What kind of meeting?" Darcie asked.

"Who was there?" Gavin pressed.

Charles shook his head with a shrug. "I do not know."

What else do you know? What do *you remember?*

"Richard. . .His Majesty, forgive me. He and I stayed up late one evening about a fortnight ago," Charles mumbled. "We both had incredibly too much to drink, but instead of going to bed, he called a meeting."

"A council meeting?" Mitch shared a confused glance with Gavin. "In the middle of the night? Does the prince even remember doing that?"

"It is difficult to say," said Charles before belching. "Forgive me. What was the question?"

"Well, weren't *you* there? What did he say?" Elise hissed. She bit the inside of her cheek to avoid screaming and grabbing his collar. His intoxication made this even more difficult.

"I. . .I was not invited."

What? But he just said it was a council meeting.

"But you're part of the council," Darcie said, echoing Elise's thoughts. "Why weren't you invited?"

Charles looked at all of them before clearing his throat. "I never said it was a council meeting, yet even then I doubt he would have had me join. I am not exactly in good standing with His Majesty."

Elise thought she would explode when Charles grew silent again. *Then what? Keep going!*

"Elise, maybe we should talk to him later," Gavin suggested.

"No!" Elise snapped.

"But he can barely stand," he continued. "He probably doesn't know anything."

"He does," Elise said, glaring at the royal advisor. "He's just not trying hard enough. Why else would he have risked coming to talk to us?"

"He already said," Mitch replied. "He asked if we got the letter to Ruby. That's it. Let him go already."

Elise felt that there *was* something else. She could not put her finger on it, but Charles was hiding something. Perhaps he did not want to keep hiding it, and that is why he followed them. She pondered his motives during another stretch of awkward silence.

"Are you going to ask him about Vaughn?" Darcie whispered.

"Not yet," said Elise, gauging Charles' ability to follow the conversation. "But his guard's down. This is the only time we're going to find out anything he might know. Charles?"

"He looks like he's going to be sick any minute," Mitch muttered to Gavin. "You better ask him quick, Elise."

Elise contemplated her list of questions before proceeding to wear Charles' resolve down further.

"Why did you come up to talk to us?" she asked.

"It. . .it is imperative the princess read my letter," he said.

Elise waited to see if he would continue on his own. When he did not, she pushed forward more energy as she stared deeply into his broken eyes. It took a moment of studying his countenance before Elise relaxed her shoulders and changed strategies. Unclenching her teeth with a deep breath, she could see him for the lost, lovesick man he truly was. Demanding anything from him would be useless. This would take a softer approach. *You can tell us. It's okay. We only want to help.*

"She received your letter," Elise whispered slowly. "Ruby is fine, but how is Richard?"

She flattened her lips into a tight line. Feeling her heart swell, Elise willed the rest of her resolve to convince his mind. *What do you really want to tell us?*

Charles opened his mouth, but no words came out.

Tell us.

"I fear. . .I fear he is in danger," Charles choked out. His face twisted in agony as if the words were spoken against his will. He wiped his face with the back of his hand before making eye contact with them again. "I warned him. I warned him not to make this announcement. I advised him to reconsider the decision." Charles grimaced as if his confession made him feel nauseas. "I told him as a friend that it would only bring about rioting and protests, or worse, attempts on his life!"

"And he wouldn't listen to you," Darcie said, gazing at Charles as if he were a wounded puppy in need of rescuing.

"Did that Rodrick guy put him up to this?" Gavin asked. "Was he in the meeting?"

Charles nodded before belching again. He swayed a moment before Mitch propped him up.

"But if he's so mad at you, why were you allowed to sit with him tonight?" Elise asked.

"To keep up appearances," Charles slurred. "He did not want the princess to come, but anyone else would have looked more suspicious."

Before Elise could ask any more questions, Charles cut her off with a piercing stare that broke her heart into a thousand pieces. *What is it? Tell me. What do you want from me?*

"Please," he whispered.

Please what?

"Please save him," Charles managed to choke out. "Please save the prince. He is not himself. That man is not my friend. I do not know what has come over him, nor how to stop him, but something occurred in that meeting that forever changed his course of action."

Darcie glanced over her shoulder at Elise. "I'll give you one guess."

"Do you think Vaughn cursed Richard? Or hypnotized him somehow?" Elise asked. "Could he be doing all of this without knowing it?"

"The prince is in his right mind. That much is certain," Charles said. "But he is closing himself off from his family, which is not like him. I suspect it to be a threat or ultimatum."

"Like what?" Elise asked.

"I know not," Charles said, "but if anyone can find out, it is you four."

"Well, let's just tack that onto our to do list," Mitch groaned. "It's not like we're strapped down with anything else."

"Please," Charles said, "Do not mention we have spoken, for I fear of who to trust any longer, but I will do what I must to protect my friend. . .and the princess."

Elise took her focus away from his face, removing any pull she still held on him. *He's exhausted.*

Charles blinked a few times as if waking from a dream before he looked at all four of them with a peculiar expression. "Have you seen my drink?"

"I think you've had enough," Gavin said before he and Mitch each took one of Charles arms to guide him towards the carriages. Keeping a distance, they watched and waited for Charles to stumble his way back to the dais before a guard helped him into a carriage.

"Once he sleeps that off, I doubt we get that kind of confession again," Darcie said. "What do you think happened in that meeting?"

Elise shook her head, scanning the crowd until she spotted Gwen tasting an assortment of delicate bite-sized cakes. "I don't know, but I think it's time to get us some fairy magic."

Waiting for a crowd of people to walk past, the friends made their way over to the dessert cart before standing around Gwen.

She looked warily at them, with a mouthful of cake, before shaking her head. Only when she swallowed did she walk away. "Whatever it is, the answer is no."

They caught up to Gwen at the end of the street. After the fourth or fifth time Elise called her name, Gwen finally turned to face them.

"No more, please," she begged, holding out a hand until they stopped approaching her. "I have been humiliated enough for one night."

Elise understood her future aunt's frustration. Not only was she not comfortable in her clothing, but she also turned down the offer to spend the night with Richard. Despite Gwen's wishes, Elise and the others could not afford to waste any time. Throwing caution to the wind, Elise took a direct approach.

"I'm sorry about how things turned out tonight," Elise began, taking Gwen's hand to lead her away from the crowd, "but there are bigger things happening right now. Can you get us some fairy magic?"

Gwen's mouth opened, as if she were already ready to argue or toss out a witty response, but Elise's unexpected question made her pause. Her expressions fluctuated so quickly that Elise had difficulty sensing what Gwen's reaction might be.

"Why on Earth—"

"We know you helped the princess all those times," Elise blurted out. "And I have magic, but not enough for what we need to do."

Gwen collected herself before steadying her voice. "And what might that be?"

The teenagers took turns filling Gwen in on everything that had happened they deemed safe to share.

"And fairy magic is the only way we can make it to Lockesbarrow," Elise finished. She knew the other woman was not entirely convinced given the tightness of her shoulders and guarded nature.

"I wish I could help you, but—"

"*Please*." Elise's voice broke as she desperately tried to wield her magic again, but it was weakened from forcing Charles to confess only moments earlier.

"Come on, Elise," Gavin whispered, gently pulling Elise away. "We can try by ourselves in the morning when we have daylight."

Elise reluctantly followed her friends away, suddenly too tired to put up a fight. *Gavin's right. We're not getting anywhere here.*

Mitch clicked his tongue. "As long as we don't run into that Horanis guy again, I'm good."

I agree.

"Did you say Horanis?" came Gwen's voice from behind them. Her entire body froze as if she would be enveloped in pain should she move. "As in, the King of the Fairies?"

"You know him, too?" Though they were isolated, Mitch scanned the area for any bystanders. Fortunately, they were well out of earshot of anyone else.

The muscles within Gwen's neck quivered before her unfocused gaze met theirs. "I. . .I *belong* to him."

CHAPTER 19

Elise parted her lips but made no sound. Silenced by a strangling numbness that managed to seep down to her fingertips, she studied Gwen as if meeting the other woman for the first time. An odd, aching sensation tugged at Elise's heart. All this time, she felt proud of the progress being made regarding growing closer to her family. Yet, as she stared into Gwen's glassy, fearful eyes, it was as if facing a stranger again.

The urgency of their escape halted as they processed the confession.

Looking at Elise, Mitch patted his vest and released a long, deep whistle. "I take it *that* didn't make it into your grandmother's diary."

Elise took a tentative step forward and felt relieved when Gwen did not move away.

Things just got way more complicated. At least ten questions popped into Elise's mind—all vying to be answered—yet in the end, she decided on one. "Does anyone else know?"

Gwen shook her head.

Let's keep it that way.

The same rational approach did not apply to Darcie, who—after finding her own voice—paced around Gavin, Mitch, and Elise. "But when? And how does *nobody* else know? Not even your mom or Talia? How exactly *does* King Horanis own you? What does that mean? Do you know where to find him? Is he close by right now?"

"Darcie, breathe." Mitch planted both of his hands on Darcie's shoulders to calm her. "Relax, will you? This is probably why she hasn't told anybody."

"Indeed," Gwen replied. "If *you* are in hysterics, imagine how my own family would receive the news."

Gavin joined Elise's side. "How does that work? I mean, how can a *fairy* own you?"

Grabbing a lantern from the nearest vacant cart, Gwen nodded towards the forest. "I suppose there is no use trying to deny anything, but we should move somewhere more private. Come this way."

"But it's the middle of the night!" Darcie objected when Gwen pointed towards the vast wall of trees ahead of them. "We can't risk getting lost out there again."

"You will not get lost," Gwen assured them.

"That's what *you* think," said Mitch. "We have a natural skill for getting ourselves in trouble. Especially in the forest."

"And the one time we *did* have a guide, he was purposefully leading us the wrong way," Elise added, reliving the moment they found out Vaughn was sent to prolong their journey to find Gavin.

Gwen dropped her shoulders and smiled. The type of patient smile one might give a small child. "This time will be different," she promised. "This time you have *me*."

The confidence with which Gwen spoke should have reassured Elise, but it only made her more hesitant to reenter the forest at this hour without protection.

Nevertheless, Elise and the others reluctantly followed Gwen away from the festival. Within minutes of entering the forest, wandering down the winding path, the only visibility came from Gwen's lantern. The flickering light bounced along thick trunks and overlapping vines, creating fleeting shadows that only lit a few feet ahead.

Elise's paranoia ran rampant, tricking her into thinking she could see movement in the darkness. Even the breeze whistled in ways that sounded like someone whispering. A cold sweat formed along her brow, making Elise grab hold of Gavin's arm as she became acutely aware of Mitch's breathing behind her. The four took turns jumping at random animal calls, crackling leaves, and insects flying too close. The chirping of crickets and frog croaks were deafening in Elise's sensitive ears. Yet, Gwen never slowed or faltered as she led them forward.

"How far are you taking us?" Gavin asked. "Do we really need to go this far?"

"I guess we could look on the bright side," replied Mitch. "At least it's not raining."

Darcie made a strange squeaking noise. "Did you *really* just say that? That's like people saying things can't get any worse! I swear, Mitch, I'm going to kill you if it starts raining."

For a brief moment, it felt as if things were back to normal. Hearing Mitch and Darcie bicker playfully back and forth lightened the mood for a short period of time until it became too difficult to ignore how deep into the forest they truly were.

Okay, I think we're far enough from people. She can tell us now. . .why are we still walking? I can't see a thing.

Elise cried out as she tripped over an overgrown tree root, but Gavin caught her.

"Are you okay?" Darcie asked. "Maybe we should stop now. We're nowhere near the town."

"And something just crawled across my foot." Mitch whimpered. "Can you please tell us what we need to know so we can get going, Gwen?"

Gwen took a few more steps forward before wincing and turning abruptly to face them. The lantern she carried swung back and forth, creating a haunting effect as it lit their pale shadowed faces. Each of them had discarded their masks at different times along the path, and all but Gwen wore the same petrified expression.

"I do not need to remind you how dangerous King Horanis is," Gwen replied with a grimace. Staggering, she looked down at her arm before regaining her balance. "Are you sure you want to face him again?"

Is she okay?

"No!" Mitch cried. "We can talk to another fairy. Any other fairy. Call one of the small ones."

Why is he doing this now? We're all scared, but we need to get moving. There's no time to stand here and argue like little kids!

The teenagers began to overtalk one another as the argument heated.

"I understand if you would rather go back," Gwen replied.

"Uh. . . hello? Did you hear me?" Mitch asked. "*Something* crawled across *my* foot, and we're walking around in the *dark*. Why would we have followed you into this creepy forest to turn around and go home? Just get one of the small ones out here already."

When the disagreement continued, Gwen huffed before setting the lantern down by her feet. Her voice rang above the others. "I thought you were in a hurry."

"We are," said Elise, giving Mitch a pointed look to quit arguing. "How do you contact the fairies? We've always found them by luck."

Expecting Gwen to call out or gesture, Elise watched as the other woman reached for one of her armbands.

Gwen's lips tightened as she pulled against the snug fit, but as the accessory loosened, they could make out a mark on the inside of her upper arm. In the weak lighting, it looked nothing more than an oddly shaped bruise that had not completely healed, perhaps a birthmark, but as Gwen lifted the lantern again, it proved to be something else altogether. The tender flesh was blemished with a combination of blue, green, and yellow swirls woven together like a knotted rope.

"It's called a Fairy's Kiss," Gwen informed them. "And if I am caught being marked, I could be exiled from society."

"So, it's like a curse?" Gavin asked, sharing an anxious glance with Elise when Gwen nodded.

"But it's only a mark," Mitch pointed out. "What's the big deal? Especially when you can hide it like you do. Tell everyone it's a tattoo."

Gwen's trembling hands forced her to set the lantern down again with a solemn expression. "Being marked by a fairy allows me to communicate with them at will, but it is often associated with a loss of virtue. Horanis spared mine, but the town would never believe me if word got out."

Communicate at will? Loss of virtue? "So, that's how you were able to help the princess get fairy magic so easily," Elise replied.

Again, Gwen nodded. "The princess happened upon me speaking with Horanis one evening. The price of her silence was access to magic when she requested it."

Blackmail. Elise shook her head. *Yeah, that sounds like Mom.*

"Horanis found out and forbade me from giving her anymore. Not to mention the visit from Lord Fenton."

"*Charles* came to you?" Elise's breath hitched. Every inch of her body froze as if drenched in an ice bath. *I never knew about this.* Rendered speechless, she was thankful when Darcie inquired as to why Charles visited.

"When pressed, Princess Ruby disclosed everything to him before his brief dismissal from court. Lord Fenton tracked me down and urged me to stop helping her, but it was too late. The princess was already with child and restricted to the royal grounds. I suppose I was fortunate both protected my involvement from spreading any further. After my father's infamous arrest, I believe another scandal would have killed my poor mother. Not to mention tarnished Talia's reputation by association."

One detail plagued Elise's mind more than any other. "You said it's associated with a loss of virtue, and that he spared you. I'm glad he didn't force you into anything, but do you know why he did that?"

Gwen let out a hollow laugh. "It is so odd to be speaking of it after all this time." She paced back and forth, caressing the mark as she walked. Gwen did not meet their eyes as she began to finally tell her secret. "He said I was to remain pure for another but would not disclose a name. My purpose was to be much greater as I would play an important role in a secret prophecy."

The feeling of Gavin's hand grabbing hers was the only thing that thawed Elise's stiffness, allowing her to think clearly once more. She squeezed his hand back, remembering why they had sought out

Gwen in the first place. She darted her gaze to Mitch's vest where the current diary was still hidden.

"What kind of prophecy?" Darcie asked before Elise could find the words.

When the other woman spoke again, her voice sounded distant and dreamlike as she recited the message by heart.

> *"My lips shall mark you,*
> *'til I see fit,*
> *Retain thy virtue,*
> *Shield this secret.*
>
> *Come, lure those here,*
> *Who first speak my name,*
> *Reveal to them your kiss.*
>
> *Though danger be near,*
> *A coveted game,*
> *Be crowned in forgotten bliss."*

Watching Gwen come out of her reverie, Elise wondered how many nights the other woman must have mulled over the prophecy's meaning.

"So, Horanis knew we were coming?" Gavin asked. "Then why not tell us when we met him before?"

"It wasn't time I guess," Elise said.

"Yeah, he wanted us led here like bait." Mitch glared at Gwen as he spoke. "Did you know when you met us?"

Gwen took a long, deep breath but did not cower. Holding her chin up, she met his gaze. "Not at first, but over time, I grew suspicious of your secrecy and involvement with the royal family. It was not until tonight that I knew for certain." Gwen rolled the sheer fabric of her skirt between her fingers. Chewing on her bottom lip, she studied each of them in turn. "And now here you are, speaking the name I've held in my heart all this time, but is it enough? Can I be rid of this shameful curse? Can I stop lying to my family?"

Elise sensed her future aunt's uncertainty. The questions weren't directed at them, but she knew Gwen longed for the answers. "I promise we're going to fix all of this and help your family. Go ahead and call Horanis."

"Elise!" Mitch stepped between Gwen and Elise. "Are you crazy? He kidnapped Darcie! Why would you want to face him again?"

"We need strong fairy magic to travel," Elise argued back. "Why *not* go directly to the source?"

"No!" he ground out. "I can't go through that again."

"Mitch, I know he's scary, but—"

"I *won't* let him near her!"

The desperation in his voice tugged at Elise's heart as she met Darcie's gaze behind Mitch's towering figure. She did not want to risk any of their lives, but Gwen was their only ticket to getting fairy magic to find Rona and end all this. It was a risk they would have to take. "Mitch—"

"You're really okay letting your friend get taken again?" he challenged.

Wiping the sweat from her palms, Elise lowered her gaze before responding. "I understand why you don't—"

"No, you *don't* understand," Mitch hissed, taking an involuntary step back when Gavin moved between them. Yet, he continued. "I've been shot at, nearly drowned, and chased across this awful place more times than I care to remember. . .but nothing, *nothing*, has been as bad as thinking I lost Darcie. I would take all those other scares fifty times over if it meant I didn't have to relive believing she was dead. Do you want *her* marked, too?"

Elise opened her mouth, but no words came out.

A stifled, agonizing silence followed that was only broken when Gwen cleared her throat. "She may already bear the same mark if she was taken once."

"Yeah, well, believe me. She doesn't!" he snapped.

Even in the near pitch-black darkness, the flickering light was enough for Elise to catch Darcie's blush and embarrassed smile.

Mitch's expression softened as he sent her an apologetic smile.

Elise chuckled in spite of herself. *Looks like Gavin and I are not the only ones sneaking off.*

"She'll be okay, Mitch," Gavin promised, meeting his best friend's glassy stare.

Looking between Gavin and Elise, a muscle twitched in Mitch's cheek as his hands curled into fists. "You don't know that. Besides, Sage is the smallest fairy, and he was able to send us before. Why bother with Horanis?"

"Because I want to know what he knows," Elise said. "He's the only reason we found out about the timeline and the prophecy. He made sure Gwen led us to this exact spot. I think there's more he's not telling us."

Mitch jumped when Darcie touched his shoulder before turning him to face her. Cradling his face between her hands, Darcie searched his eyes. "This is the only way. It will be okay. *I'll* be okay. . ." She kissed him gently before resting their foreheads together. Pulling him into a tight embrace, Darcie met Elise's eyes over Mitch's shoulder with a reluctant nod.

Elise took a deep breath, squeezing Gavin's hand tighter to keep her own nerves calm before addressing Gwen. "Call him."

Gwen raised her arm high enough to kiss the discolored skin. As her lips made contact, the mark began to glow with a searing light that nearly blinded them. With a brilliant flash—eliciting a cry from the teenagers—all went dark, including the lantern by Gwen's feet.

Elise scanned the void in front of her as she tried to gauge what happened. If not for her hold on Gavin's arm, coupled with the aroma of smoke from the extinguished lantern, she would question their whereabouts. Yet, there was no sign of fairy lights anywhere.

"Are you sure you did it, right?" Gavin called out. When there was no response, he asked again. "Gwen? Gwen?"

"She's passed out!" Darcie shrieked.

Elise's heart thrashed so rapidly within her chest that she could hear it drumming in her ears. Releasing Gavin's arm, she staggered blindly towards Darcie's voice. "Are you sure?"

"Yes!" Darcie cried out. "I heard something hit the ground over here."

Elise crouched down, sensing rather than seeing where Darcie was.

"This is bad," Mitch said. "I told you not to call him. Now he's killed her."

Elise ignored him. She could not bear to consider he may be right. Crawling on her hands and knees, Elise rummaged through the fallen leaves and twigs until she felt Gwen's soft hair. Elise trailed her fingers until she felt the lines of her aunt's nose and chin. "Gwen?" she whispered, sliding both hands down to shake Gwen's shoulders. "Gwen, wake up."

"Let's get out of here," Mitch whispered.

"Mitch, we're not leaving her here!" Darcie hissed. There was a rustling sound as she slid her hands amongst the forest floor. "I can feel her breath on my hand."

"Then maybe it's like what they did to you," Elise said to her best friend. "So, she's not dead."

Mitch groaned. "Yeah, but there's no one here to wake her with a true love kiss. Do you think Richard's just going to appear out of nowhere and save the day?"

Elise wished there was such a chance of that happening, but the longer they sat, the more paranoid she grew of Horanis's tricks.

"I can carry her on my shoulders," Gavin offered. "Help me lift her. We can try again later."

"That will not be necessary," echoed a familiar, silky voice around them.

Elise leapt to her feet, eager to find the fairy king, only to be met with the same confusing darkness. Turning in slow circles, she tensed her muscles in anticipation of him possibly jumping out at them. "Does anybody see him?"

The other three replied they did not.

"How fickle you are," Horanis chuckled, before Elise heard his voice lower to a mere whisper that tickled her ear. "Can you not sense my presence?"

Elise gasped, turning in the direction of his voice. She was suddenly aware of her own breathing as a layer of sweat formed along both palms. Taking tentative steps backwards, she cried out when she bumped into something.

"Hey, relax. It's only me," Gavin said. "You okay?"

"He's *here*," she whimpered. "He-he's talking. . .can't you guys hear him?"

If they shook their heads, she could not see them.

Mitch mumbled from somewhere to her right. "Isn't this what you wanted?"

"Shut up, Mitch," Darcie snapped. Her voice indicated she was still on the ground by Gwen. "Everyone, keep your eyes and ears open."

If there was one thing Elise truly feared, it was hearing voices others could not. First the scarf, and now this. Both tied back to the fairy king.

Panicking won't solve this. I've been through too much to let my anxiety control me any longer. I need to get a grip and face him. It's the only way we'll find out anything. You've got this, Elise.

Elise straightened, dried her palms along the fabric of her skirt, and took a steadying breath before calling out into the void. "We're here about the prophecy. We don't want any tricks. Now, come out!"

The surrounding crickets and frogs provided the only sounds with no sign of fairies.

They must think I'm crazy. Maybe I finally have lost my mind.

"I didn't make it up," she whimpered. "I really did hear him." Elise felt Gavin pull her into a warm embrace as tears stung the edges of her eyes. She replied with a sniff when he kissed the top of her head. An amused chuckle, accompanied by a bright light, made the hairs on the back of her neck stand.

"No need to appear so crestfallen."

Before them, gallant and enticing as ever, was King Horanis. Floating above Gwen's sleeping form, he gazed down at them from an illuminated orb that only went out once he touched the ground. Rather than be cast into darkness once again, dozens of small hovering fairy lights proceeded to dart out from every direction until Elise could see clearly again.

Mitch locked his eyes on Horanis, remaining silent and pale. Darcie gaped at the giant fairy while bringing herself to stand.

Looking up at Gavin, Elise saw his shoulders tense as he squeezed her hand while also staring at the king.

Good. They see and hear him this time.

Elise wiped her eyes with her free hand. "Let's get this over with."

"My, my, and skip the formalities? Very well. You are here to fulfill the prophecy, are you not?"

Elise bit the inside of her cheek, willing herself not to lose what bravery crept beneath the surface. "That depends." She paused to swat at a fairy flying too close to her face. "Have we heard the whole thing?"

A smirk snaked across Horanis's lips as he knelt beside Gwen. His wings curled as if to cradle her on either side. "She is stunning, is she not?" He trailed featherlike touches along her arm, ribs, and hip. "Poor little thing was on a horseback ride through the forest, no doubt troubled by her father's infamous arrest. So much anger and pain for such a fragile heart to carry. Vulnerable to my advances yet declined my offers to help."

You're trying to distract me. I doubt help is what you really offered.

"Why did you mark her?" Darcie asked. "And why—"

"Not *you,* too?" the king replied wryly.

Darcie's features grew small and the zipping lights around them betrayed her tinted cheeks.

Horanis stroked Gwen's hair. "You were merely a ploy to pass the time, but *she. . .*she was my masterpiece." The long fingers of his hand curved around her head as he turned Gwen's face towards him. His other hand grazed the mark on the inside of her arm. Without another word, he lowered his head and placed his lips atop of it as Gwen had done.

An audible gasp left Gwen's mouth as she arched from the ground, yet her eyes remained closed. A blue light, similar to the magic Elise once carried around her neck, danced along Gwen's skin, outlining the mark. Only when Horanis separated his lips from it did the light skip about the surrounding trees before disappearing altogether. Twinkling laughter rang out amongst the floating balls of light. The king scanned every inch of Gwen's face with sheer adoration before placing a chaste kiss on her lips. "You have done well."

"What will you do now, Father?" came a familiar, raspy voice as Hemlock landed on the king's shoulder. "Does she come live with us?"

"No." The king's indignant expression softened as he beckoned a group of fairy lights to come closer. "She has served her purpose. Erase all memories of us."

"*All* memories?" Thicket, the king's eldest, landed on his other shoulder. "Must it be all?"

"It is best," Horanis replied with a sigh, watching the lights close in around Gwen's body before it was magically lifted higher and higher.

"You're not going to hurt her, are you?" Elise asked warily.

"Certainly not," he replied, rising to his feet so that Gwen floated near his chest. Waving a hand across the length of her body, a bluish smoke encircled Gwen's head. A crease appeared between his brows as Horanis eased her gently onto the grass with a forlorn gaze. "A deal is a deal. She is free."

"And what exactly was the deal?" Gavin asked. "What is she free from?"

"Simply to play the messenger in my plan to vanquish Rona once and for all. No one should be allowed to mess with the fabric of time, let alone rise one from the dead. I knew I needed to intervene." The four teenagers remained silent. "Do not think for a moment you are the only ones out to see her demise."

It had not occurred to Elise that others were plotting as they were. Perhaps that made her foolish, but at least Horanis was including them.

"Can this not be the last time we speak to them, Father?" Thicket's whiny, mouselike voice droned as she sneered down at Elise. "She has that stupid look on her face again."

Elise was not sure what look Thicket referred to, but she attempted to change it, nonetheless. Scratching at the back of her neck while avoiding eye contact, Elise inquired whether Sage was nearby.

"Ah, yes, her favorite. No wonder she's curious," Hemlock grunted with an impressive rolling of his eyes. "She always gets her way when it comes to him."

"Do not get any ideas!" Thicket snapped at Elise. "There are to be *no* deals this time."

"Now, where is the fun in that?" Horanis inquired.

"Father, you can't!" Thicket continued. "It's one thing to part with the *one* human who means something to you, but it's another to—" The tiny fairy cried out as Horanis flicked her off his shoulder into the nearest bush.

Elise fought hard not to laugh at the high-pitched squeal that followed. Meeting her friends' eyes, it appeared they were struggling to do the same.

Quirking a brow at his son, Horanis waited for Hemlock to fly away on his own. "Let them not speak for me," Horanis continued as one of the hovering lights lowered to his shoulder, revealing Sage's poised, dignified face.

Feeling her chest swell, Elise wished she could be alone with him. The most level-headed of them all, Sage saw something in her that often led to assistance of some kind.

"But how can Gwen's part be done?" Gavin asked. "She hasn't married the prince yet."

He's right.

"Tell us the prophecy again," Elise requested. When Horanis obliged, ending at the same place as Gwen, she scrunched up her face in confusion. "And that's all?"

"Of course not." He chuckled. "But it was all Gwendolyn needed to know to be of service. Apart from being influenced by a spoiled princess, she proved quite useful."

Elise ignored the slight against her mom, not wanting to take the attention away from the prophecy. She asked again for the rest of it.

"She must know, Father," Sage replied. "It is time."

Horanis regarded Elise, looking her up and down several times before stroking his chin.

She watched his wings flex on either side of him and swallowed. Her throat grew dry under the watchful eyes of the remaining fairies and her friends.

He's wasting time on purpose and getting a kick out of it. Enough with the theatrics!

Once it appeared Horanis was satisfied, he nodded when Sage offered to recite the remaining portion.

Elise held her breath as his small mouth parted.

"For time moves on,
Masked in deceit,
If left unchecked,
Will not repeat.

Among those led,
A blooming descendent,
The bond estranged,
One must mend it."

"There you have it," said Horanis, applauding his son before turning to face Elise with a renewed solemness. "One cannot argue your lineage with the royal family. You all have two days to put an end to Rona and correct the timeline. For if another queen is crowned, this shall be our only reality."

"What does that mean exactly?" Mitch asked.

Elise took a deep breath. "It means if we don't stop Rona before Richard's wedding and coronation, Haighdlen will be attacked for good. . .and *we* won't exist anymore."

Mitch spluttered before finding his voice. "But we're not from Haighdlen, and *you're* not Gwen's kid. So, how does another queen affect you being born?"

"It's not that," Gavin replied, his eyes darting back and forth as he put the pieces together. "If Richard doesn't marry Gwen, the family history automatically changes."

"Makes sense," Darcie agreed, catching on. "And if, for some reason, Joranna doesn't bring Ruby and Ian to our world in time. . ."

"Then *I* won't be born there, and *we* never meet," Elise concluded, gesturing between them. She could no longer imagine a lifetime of not knowing the other three as she did now. Especially Gavin, whose gaze bore into hers with the same unspoken truth. "It's a chain reaction. Rona and her brother will destroy all of this if their plan works."

This is more than avenging Derek, saving Mom, or getting back home. Everything we know is at risk of not existing.

"I won't let that happen," Elise vowed before stepping forward in front of the fairy king. Lifting her chin, she narrowed her gaze and quieted the unwanted thoughts creeping below the surface. "We're ready to face Rona in Lockesbarrow. Just tell us what to do before you send us."

CHAPTER 20

"You will not be going to Lockesbarrow. Not yet."

Horanis's unexpected response left Elise and the others floored in confused silence.

"But why not?" Darcie finally asked. "You spent all this time telling us it's Elise's destiny to stop Rona, but now she can't go to her?"

Horanis hummed. "I said *not yet*." His languid, carefree way of speaking unnerved Elise. With every drawl and nonchalant movement, the king demonstrated a sense of boredom.

Is this honestly his idea of fun?

"We only have two days," Elise pleaded. "I'd like to get there as soon as possible."

"You will not stop the wedding if you are in Lockesbarrow," Sage replied, his voice the same lifeless tone it had always been, only now it made Elise grit her teeth. "Besides, the Lockesbarrian armada is sailing towards Haighdlen at this very moment."

"*What?*" they cried.

"Sage, you meddle too far!" Hemlock bellowed, flying to his brother's side. "You treasonous git! Father, rip the wings from his body this instant. Denounce his actions, dismiss him from your court, and let him be publicly disgraced!"

"Calm yourself, Hemlock," Horanis commanded.

"Father, it is known he is a favorite of yours, but—"
Hemlock's words were silenced as Horanis clutched him out of midair

within his grasp. "*That* is enough." The king released his son when he was certain no more arguments would follow.

Elise and the others watched a resigned Hemlock fly off without a word into the same bush Thicket had disappeared into.

Horanis's relaxed, unphased demeanor made Elise conclude that this sort of behavior must be commonplace on his part. None of the other fairies made a sound as Horanis turned back to address the teenagers.

"Is she really sending an army here?" Mitch's strangled voice mirrored the tightness in Elise's chest.

Elise waited with bated breath as Horanis shared a hesitant look with his youngest son before nodding.

"Then go tell my family that!" Elise shrieked, sending many of the fairies hurling backwards from the sheer force of her outburst. *I'm going to be sick. I'm definitely going to be sick. They're all sitting ducks.* Her strained voice cracked as it left her burning throat. "People are going to get hurt!"

"It is not for *us* to warn them." Horanis brushed a fallen leaf from his shoulder. He spoke of the impending attack as if it were nothing more than a minor account of the weather. "They have lookouts and such. Word will get out soon enough." His wings flexed as he yawned with a wide stretch, reminding Elise more of an alley cat than a fairy. "We tend to side with the Elves on these matters and stay to ourselves."

"The cowardly way," Gavin spat. "It's just a sick game to you."

Horanis had the nerve to laugh, but he did not deny it.

"Maybe, we can prevent it," Elise muttered, more so to herself than the others.

"How?" Darcie asked, her own voice already an octave higher. "We don't have a clue of how to stop Richard's wedding, let alone an entire armada!"

Elise looked back up at Horanis and Sage.

"Your family can do nothing," Sage chimed in. "That does not mean all hope is lost."

Elise made to argue but paused before words left her mouth. It occurred to her Sage always found a way to help her figure out difficult decisions. *He wouldn't say something like that without a reason.*

Gavin, who had not made the same connection, kicked at a pile of leaves with a frustrated groan. Mitch declared their situation hopeless, and Darcie slid her back down the nearest tree until she sat in a huddled ball of despair on the forest floor near Gwen.

"Why. . .why did you word it that way?" Elise asked, staring knowingly at the tiny fairy.

"You really must learn to censor yourself." Horanis glared down at his son but showed no sign of forcefully removing him as he had the other two. Elise thought she even detected a hint of a smile on the youngest fairy's lips.

"Magical creatures are not limited to land."

"Yeah," Mitch scoffed before the color drained from his face, "but that would only leave—no, no way. You can't be serious."

Merpeople.

"I believe you have helped enough, Sage. You had best be off now." Horanis nodded before the youngest fairy followed his father's orders and flew off.

Elise watched Sage's light drift until it went out altogether once he got too far away. *Does he even know what he's suggesting?* So many conflicting thoughts filled her mind until she felt lightheaded.

"You're seriously expecting us to get help from mermaids?" Gavin gaped at Horanis's stoic expression. "They don't trust anyone!"

"Neither do we, and yet we find time to strike deals with humans often enough. You should give them more credit," the king replied.

"No way. There is *no* chance I'm stepping foot near another lake. I'm not getting pulled in again," Mitch vowed.

Darcie had likewise paled, and Elise suspected she too was remembering the time they almost lost Mitch to the merpeople in Lake Mirage. She could not blame either for being against such a plan.

Elise chewed on her bottom lip, mulling over everything she had learned about the secretive creatures.

Then it occurred to her.

"Maybe we won't have to." Seeing confused expressions from the others, she clarified. "The bowl. Remember the crystal mermaid bowl? I saw it at my Nana's house, and we even went with Derek to pick it up for her when Richard was born. Queen Eugena said Joranna could use it to communicate with her."

Understanding dawned on their faces.

"That's right!" Darcie's face split in a beaming grin as she clapped her hands together. "So, we only need to convince Joranna to use it and ask the mermaids to stop the attack! What're we waiting for?"

Mitch shook his head with a scoff. "Why are you saying it like it's an easy journey? Let alone an easy task? What happens if Richard sees us first?"

"Mitch is right," Gavin agreed. "All it takes is for one guard to recognize us, and we're back in the dungeon. For good this time."

"We'd be safer in Lockesbarrow," Mitch grumbled.

Both boys had valid points. The odds of them waltzing up to Joranna were slim, but this was their best chance to stop an attack by sea. Elise doubted Rona herself was on one of the approaching ships, but the sorceress would be sure to send a deadly number of soldiers. Haighdlen would be surrounded and overtaken in no time if not properly warned. Elise felt deep down Rona could even find a way to sneak in undetected. There was no telling what the limits were to her magic. She herself had only encountered Rona in person for mere moments, yet it was enough to instill the same fear that plagued everyone else who met her.

Elise looked down at Gwen's sleeping form sprawled out across the forest floor. Her peaceful expression made it easy to see how much Elise's cousin, Madelyn, favored her mother in the future. Madelyn's innocent plea replayed in Elise's memory from her first night at Joranna's house upon meeting her extended family and learning about Haighdlen.

"We don't want you to do anything you don't want to do," her cousin had said, *"but. . .Haighdlen is our home. We'd really love if you'd help save it."*

An entire generation could be wiped out if she failed. All her cousins, not just Madelyn, deserved to live without fear of fleeing their home. Horanis was right. They were not needed in Lockesbarrow.

They were needed here, in Haighdlen. The biggest obstacle was going to be convincing her family of that. Not only did Elise possess magic, but she was also the fulfillment of a prophecy sent here to complete this very task. She would be naïve to ignore that. All of Gwen's suffering would be for nothing if Elise fled now. Clearing her throat, she squared her shoulders and faced the fairy king.

"Elise, what are you doing?" Gavin whispered, but she ignored him.

"Give us enough magic to go to Haighdlen Castle," she demanded. "My blood will get us through the protective barrier."

"Whoa, slow down," Mitch warned.

"Yeah, be careful," Gavin piped in. "You can't say something generic like that. What if he plays one of his games and drops us into a dungeon himself?"

Horanis failed to hide an impish grin, yet Elise stood her ground.

"We have to take that chance. Mitch, pull out the diary. We're lucky the fairies have helped us this far. Are you with me or not?" she asked.

Darcie took her hand, gesturing for Mitch and Gavin to do the same.

Elise understood their unwillingness, but ultimately, it would take a risk to pull this off. She searched Gavin's eyes, begging with her own for him to agree with her plan. A sigh of relief escaped her when she felt his fingers intertwine with hers. Not one to remain the odd one out, Mitch pulled on his collar before placing a hand over Darcie's. He used his other hand to retrieve the diary from his vest. Elise felt her heart swell with affection and hope.

If they failed, they failed together. If they succeeded, they would succeed together. Nothing could change that.

"Please also change our clothes!" Elise squeaked, realizing how conspicuous they would be arriving in their formal festival clothing.

Darcie nudged Elise before nodding towards their feet where Gwen remained asleep.

"Oh, right. And send Gwen with us! We need Richard to see her again. Gavin, grab her hand so she gets through the barrier, too." Elise and the others adjusted their footing so he could bend down to take her hand.

In all the commotion, she had almost left her aunt stranded in the middle of the forest with a possessive fairy king. That would haunt her for a long time, she mused. Elise mouthed a quick thank you to Darcie, feeling heat envelope her neck and ears. *Here we go.*

A little less than a minute passed before Elise realized the king had yet to move.

Horanis's impish grin only widened. "You are forgetting one important fact. *I* am not Sage."

I don't understand.

The fairy king chuckled to himself. "I am not swayed by human emotions and trials. It will take more than a sentimental drawing to gift you with magic."

"You can't be serious!" Gavin argued. "You set all this up so Gwen would bring us here. You're really going to make us pay?"

So much for Thicket's no deal approach. If Sage were still there, Elise and the others would already be on the castle grounds.

He is wasting our time. "What will it take?" Elise ground out.

"That is more like it," he replied with a melodic drawl. The only thing more menacing than his smile was the glint in his eyes as he focused on Darcie. "*Such* beauty."

"Forget it!" snapped Mitch, returning the diary under his vest. He stepped between Darcie and Horanis.

"Calm yourself, hero," Horanis replied with a condescending click of his tongue before nudging Mitch aside. The other three released each other's hands as the king lifted Darcie's with his own.

The bejeweled bracelet dangling from her tiny wrist glistened in the surrounding fairy lights. "This should do nicely."

"No!" Darcie quipped, yanking her wrist away from his grip. She caressed it with her free hand. "It's special."

"That's exactly why he wants it," Gavin pointed out without taking his eyes off Horanis. "He knows it'll hurt. It's part of his fun."

Elise proceeded carefully. "Darcie. . .maybe you should—"

"No!" Darcie repeated, clutching the bracelet against her chest. "Mitch spent all his money on it. He was so charming and thoughtful to do it. I even got to pick it out. I've only had it a couple of hours. No, I won't give it to you! Find something else."

Elise sucked in a breath, looking between Darcie and Horanis. Expecting the king to respond with wrath, Elise was once again blindsided when he answered her outburst with a calm smirk.

"Something else. . .or *someone*?" He let the threat hang over their heads before continuing. Darcie visibly gulped under his scrutiny but did not reply. "Five is rather a large party for traveling, indeed. Unfortunately, the balance of time has deemed it impossible for me to claim my beloved Gwendolyn or your precious savior here." He looked pointedly at Elise before returning his attention to Darcie. "And I have no use for these sidekick gentlemen. But you. . .as I have stated before, *you* would make a perfect wife to one of my lords. . .or myself." He cocked his head as he regarded her warmly. Darcie's eyes welled up with tears, prompting Horanis to click his tongue once again. "A mere bracelet is not so difficult to part with *now*, is it?"

Mitch closed the distance between himself and Darcie. Tipping her chin up to look at him, he wiped a tear away with his thumb. Both looked down as he reached to unclasp the bracelet, eliciting a sob from Darcie.

"Come now," Horanis called with a dramatic roll of his eyes, "It is not as if I am requesting a wedding ring or life of servitude. Show some dignity. Honestly, humans are exhausting."

Although the temptation was palpable, Mitch said nothing to Horanis. Instead, he handed the bracelet to a fairy waiting nearby. He and Darcie watched as it was carried to Horanis, who inspected it fondly.

"Listen to me," Mitch whispered to Darcie, waiting until she met his eyes. "I don't care how many bracelets, diaries, or vials we lose while we're here. . .I'm not losing you. Do you understand?" When Darcie nodded, he leaned down to kiss her before pulling away with a lopsided grin. "It was Richard's money anyway, so it's kind of his loss."

Darcie chuckled through her tears. "He does deserve it at this point, huh?" Taking a deep breath, she wiped her eyes and thanked Mitch.

Mitch replied with a kiss to the inside of her now bare wrist.

"How touching," Horanis said. Tossing the bracelet into the air, the four teenagers watched as it disappeared into a cloud of the same bluish smoke as before. He feigned disappointment by placing a long, bony finger against his chin. "However, *one* small bracelet is not sufficient payment for such a request."

He's joking, right?

"After all, you asked me for three favors—travel, garments, and a companion." He considered each teenager before focusing on Mitch. The king narrowed his eyes. "Give me the diary."

How does he know about the diary?

"What!" Elise shrieked. "You can't take that!"

"Collect yourself, you silly girl," he admonished. "I have no need for the entire book. . .I desire something much more important."

There's no way I'm letting him anywhere near the diary.

"Give it to him, Elise," Gavin whispered. "It's not the original. Maybe the one Rona has will show up later. We can afford to gamble with this one."

"He's right," said Darcie. "We don't even know if this one works."

Then why would he ask for it?

Elise weighed their options carefully. Unable to think of an excuse or counteroffer, she sighed with a resigned nod.

Mitch scoffed with a few whispered words of his own before holding the book in question out for Horanis, who swiped it with one dramatic sweep.

The pages, filled with all the memories and events Joranna deemed important enough to document, flipped before Elise's eyes as she swallowed a cry. It never became easier to watch others flip through the diary, something she had been unable to do since first accepting her family's mission.

By the time Horanis came to the end of Joranna's eloquent writing, less than a handful of blank pages remained. The king's eyes glinted with a hint of amusement when he reached the final entry. Expecting him to make a spectacle of the written words, Elise's jaw dropped at the gut-wrenching sound of paper ripping from the spine.

"What are you doing?" she cried, watching him tuck it away after folding it eloquently as Gavin blocked her with his arm. Elise did not even realize she had taken a step forward. Feeling as if her heart would leap from her throat, she grabbed Gavin's arm but remained still. *Something made him tear out that particular page.* Every nerve in her body ignited. "What did it say?"

"That is for me to know."

"But you can't do that!" argued Elise.

"On the contrary," he calmly pointed out, his even tone a stark contrast to her unhinged one.

A heat spread across her skin as she contemplated pushing Gavin out of the way to reach the king. Knowing she would never stand an actual chance of reaching him, she concentrated on his face, willing him to reconsider. The familiar electric sensations warmed her fingertips. *Read us the entry. Tell us what it says.*

The smaller balls of lights bounced with glee as Horanis laughed. The alluring sound reminded Elise of musical notes as it skipped about, echoing throughout the blackened forest. The muscles in her stomach clenched when he met her feeble gaze.

"Your weak magic is no match for mine, child," he said between breaths. "It is inexperienced at best, but I admit your meek efforts have livened up the mood."

Gavin lowered his arm to squeeze her hand. "There has to be something on there that makes it valuable to you," he countered. "Just tell us what it is."

"Come now, enough of this nonsense," Horanis announced with a clap of his hands. All hints of mirth vanished from his features, and though impossible, his youthful handsome face looked tired and worn somehow. "Time to get to work." With another grand sweep of his hand, Horanis pointed in the opposite direction from which they had come. "I need not remind you the importance of utmost discretion as you move forward."

Elise nodded.

"But we don't know what to say," Mitch interrupted. "We came out here to get magic to Lockesbarrow. How are we going to convince Joranna to use the mermaid bowl when everyone there knows we were sent away? We won't get through the front doors."

"Not without a disguise," Darcie added.

Elise looked expectantly at the fairy king. "We can trust you to help with that, can't we?"

Rather than a twinkling laugh, Horanis chuckled deep in his chest as he shrank to the same size as the others with a brilliant flash. The diary, which he had been holding, fell open onto the dirt path. The pages flipped wildly as his voice radiated around them. "Never trust a fairy."

As he hovered above their heads, the same blue smoke rained down onto each of them, prompting Elise to act quickly. "Grab onto me! Gavin, hold Gwen's hand. Mitch, get the diary! Take us to Haighdlen Castle!" An intense, warm wind picked up, whistling at a fever pitch as it circulated leaves and twigs around them until it felt as if they were in the middle of a vortex. Elise watched each fairy light extinguish one by one, with Horanis vanishing last before she succumbed to darkness.

CHAPTER 21

An incessant knocking pulled Elise from her already unsettled sleep. As reality hit, she sprang up in a cold sweat and assessed her surroundings.

Are we in the castle?

She did not recognize this room. It was by no means as grand as the guest room she normally slept in when visiting her family. It did not even have a window. The only light came from a mostly melted candle on the dresser. Elise looked over at two more beds close to hers where Darcie and Gwen slept.

Where are Gavin and Mitch?

Standing up, she also noticed she no longer wore the elegant emerald gown. It had been replaced with a simple, unflattering brown dress. Elise clutched a fistful of her skirt at the sounds of distant voices and footsteps outside.

Where did Horanis send us?

Leaning down, she shook her best friend awake. While Darcie reacted in much the same fashion as Elise, both of theirs paled in comparison to Gwen, who awoke seconds after.

"What is going on?" Gwen's voice lifted an octave higher than usual as she sprang from the bed. Planting herself against the wall, she looked between Elise and Darcie as if they were ghosts. "Where am I? What is happening?"

Elise took a deep breath, unsure of where to start. "That depends. . .what's the last thing you remember?"

"We were at the festival. I danced, spoke with the prince, and left." Gwen's lower lip quivered as her face paled. "Where have you taken me? And what are we wearing?"

All three jumped when an assertive female voice boomed from the other side of the door, ordering to be let in. More knocking ensued.

"Elise, look! It's the diary!" Darcie kneeled to pick it up off the floor. "What do you think this means?"

"Hide it!" Elise turned to Gwen. "We'll explain everything in a minute, but just play along and stay quiet until we can."

"What are you saying?" Gwen hissed, watching with an apprehensive eye as Darcie shoved the diary beneath a pillow. "What happened at the festival? Did you—"

"Fine. I have no choice. You had your chance," grumbled the voice. Upon hearing the jingling of keys, the girls stared in horror as the lock clicked before the door sprang open.

Light from the hall leaked into the tiny room, causing the girls to shield their eyes until they could focus on the woman looming in the doorframe.

"*This* is what I have to work with." The woman clicked her tongue, muttering under her breath while bustling around the room. "You will call me Ms. Persimmons. I am one of the housekeepers for the royal family. I will oversee all your duties during your stay." Collecting three aprons and bonnets from the dresser, she threw a set towards each of the girls. "I was told Lady Iris would be accompanied by her own staff, but I was not told they were such a lazy bunch. You couldn't even be bothered to snuff out your own candle. Were you planning on burning the castle down? Honestly."

She doesn't seem to recognize us. So, that's a good thing, I guess. A hint of guilt tugged at Elise's heart. With everything going on during their visits, she never took the time to get to know the servants. Perhaps it worked in their favor in this instance. If Ms. Persimmons did recognize her, she said nothing.

"Lady Iris?" Darcie asked, sharing an anxious glance with Elise. Gwen's own dubious expression only managed to make them look further ignorant.

"The prince's betrothed. You *are* here to tend to Lady Iris?" Her mouth tightened as she raised her eyebrows expectantly.

Elise stammered on the spot, suddenly feeling as if she were back in high school under the discerning stare of her chemistry teacher. *They even look alike.* Enough silence passed that Elise could feel the housekeeper's suspicion growing. She needed to act fast. "Of course," Elise finally choked out, locking eyes with Darcie and Gwen. "We are here. . .to tend to Lady Iris."

Darcie nodded fervently, and after a moment of hesitation, Gwen did the same.

The housekeeper hummed with disapproval. "Count your blessings you are not on *my* staff. If I ever caught such laziness, you'd all be flogged immediately. Now, there's a tray of biscuits and tea just outside. Ready yourselves, have a bite, and report to Lady Iris's bedchamber before the steward makes his rounds this morning. I'll not receive a lecture on your behalf. Get on now."

Yikes. Yeah, we don't want to see Ballard. He'll recognize us right away.

Half an hour later, the girls were washed up and fed. Fortunately, Ballard had not crossed their path, but Elise did not want to press their luck. It unnerved her further they had not seen or heard from the boys yet. *I hope they are safe.*

"We're going to be arrested," Gwen repeated over and over as they wandered the third-floor corridor. "Why did you bring me here?"

Having been watched and followed all morning by Ms. Persimmons, Elise had yet to fill Gwen in on everything. Peeking over her shoulder, Elise pulled Darcie and Gwen into a corner.

I can't mention the fairies, but I can tell her enough to keep us out of trouble. "I am close to the royal family, and right now there is a fleet of ships headed this way to attack Haighdlen." Gwen's eyes widened in horror, but Elise pressed on before her future aunt could interrupt. "The queen has a way to communicate with the mermaids. We have to convince her to ask them for help."

"B-but. . .why am I here?" asked Gwen.

So, you and Richard can fall in love. Elise cleared her throat, desperately searching for an excuse.

"In case Ruby sees us," Darcie piped in. "We're less likely to get in trouble if you're with us since you are both friends."

"We can only trust Ruby, Sarah, and Ian at this point," Elise continued. "Maybe Joranna and Charles, but it will depend on what Richard's been up to."

"Not to mention we need to stop the wedding," Darcie added.

Elise inquired if Darcie brought the diary with her just in case. Darcie replied by tapping the pocket of her apron with a smile.

"But why?" Gwen's brows furrowed. "Why can't the prince marry the singer from last night? If the prince has forgiven her family's connection, I do not see why we should interfere."

Elise and Darcie shared another strained glance.

"Are you lost?" asked a meek voice. They turned to see another maid carrying trays. Elise inquired where they could find Lady Iris before the maid replied, "Her room is just there. Second door on the left. This one is for her."

"They're not eating in the dining hall?" Elise had always had breakfast in the dining hall with the family during all her visits.

"Prince Richard is in with the council and requested no formal breakfast this morning," said the maid.

Darcie took the tray and thanked her.

The three girls waited for the other maid to round the corner before proceeding to the correct room.

"I do not like this," Gwen whispered. "We will be found out immediately. I will end up like my father! What will happen to my mother and sister?"

"Calm down!" Elise whispered. "The only way we get through this is if we act like we belong. I'm freaking out, too, but if we panic, we're dead. Now, we need a game plan. She will need to get ready. What do they normally do for us when we're here?"

"They help us dress, do our hair, and make our bed," Darcie offered. "They do so much more, so I don't know."

"Then we'll start with that," said Elise. Her heart pounded, hoping their attire would be enough to shield them from being found out. "Gwen, you help her dress. You're more familiar with the laces and corsets. Darcie, you'll do the hair since that's your area of expertise."

"I don't know if I can do it as intricately as they do here," said Darcie.

"It will have to be good enough," Elise said with a sigh. "I'll make the bed. Let us hope that is enough for us to slip out undetected and start looking for the guys and Joranna."

Pulling on the bonnets to cover their hair, the girls lowered their heads and knocked on the door. When they were granted entry, they found Iris sitting up in a four-poster bed.

"Good morning," muttered Elise before opening the drapes to allow a flood of sunshine into the luxurious room. She held her breath, feeling as if she were walking on eggshells. *Get in, get out. Get in, get out.*

"Good morning," answered Iris with a delicate yawn.

Elise suppressed a smile when Darcie set the tray down onto the bed, narrowly avoiding a spill as a spoon fell onto Iris's lap. When Darcie returned, blushing, to her side, Elise took a moment to study the young woman.

She certainly was a natural beauty, like her mother, Ingrid. Fair skin, soft cheeks, and impeccable manners. It was going to be tough to talk Richard out of marrying this one.

After an excruciating wait, Iris finally finished her breakfast and requested to be dressed. Darcie removed the tray, setting it on the nearest dresser with a clatter before waiting with Elise while Gwen stepped forward.

Elise was relieved Gwen was with them. She would not have stood a chance fastening all the hooks, buttons, and laces involved in the voluptuous gown Iris selected from her wardrobe.

Everything is going smoothly. Now, just make the bed and get out.

All was going according to plan until Iris sat down at the vanity table. As Darcie took her place behind Iris's chair, a soft knock at the door announced Ingrid's arrival.

"Good morning, dearest," she practically sang before her eyes flashed with disappointment towards the three maids. "Are you not yet ready for the day?"

Elise squeezed her hands into fists as her cheeks grew hot, yet she kept her face lowered. All the memories came flooding back from the night Ingrid and Brahm were arrested, and yet, here she was. Parading around like the queen herself. Elise could kill her uncle for allowing such an embarrassing display to happen in front of her family. *If Derek were here. . .*

"Almost, Mother. The maids are helping. They were only a few minutes late. Do not be angry."

"We shall see," Ingrid mumbled, entering with a great flourish. Her classic beauty reminded Elise of an old Hollywood actress. "There seems to have been much confusion over the staff I requested. I hardly recognize half of them."

Thank you, Horanis. That certainly was the fairy king's doing to gain them access. Elise knew they would not have stood a chance to blend in otherwise.

Elise busied herself with making the bed while listening intently to the mother and daughter.

"You sang magnificently, my dear," praised Ingrid, looking over Darcie's shoulder at her daughter's reflection. "No doubt your little prince will be ill in love this morning."

Iris looked down at her lap, fiddling with her fingers. The only sound came from the brush Darcie held as she tried to gently untangle the girl's soft dark hair. "I'm afraid his attentions may be pulling elsewhere. I was told by a footman he was quite friendly with one of the dancers last night."

Gwen froze by the door and met Elise's gaze. Elise shook her head. *Not now. Don't say anything.* She sighed in relief when Gwen collected herself long enough to prepare the makeup on the vanity.

Ingrid waved off her daughter's comment. "He is a man. *And* a king. Do not expect any different."

"Was his father not loyal to the queen?" Iris's voice was so quiet, Elise questioned the young woman's desire to marry Richard at all. "Every account I hear is that theirs was a passionate love."

Gwen proceeded to put on Iris's makeup, and Elise could not help but see the irony of the two women sitting so close to each other, secretly foes. Fortunately, Iris barely gave them two glances. She was too completely distracted by her mother.

"A rarity, to be sure," continued Ingrid, pacing back and forth, "but I'm afraid the prince is not favoring his father as of late. Best to take his faults with the strengths. So long as you quickly produce an heir, it matters not whose bed he shares."

Iris frowned but did not reply.

Elise found it odd to feel pity for someone she was supposed to hate. Deep down, Iris struck Elise as any normal girl with ideas of marrying for love. Perhaps she was not the villain, but Elise knew she needed to remain firm in their plan, nonetheless. She also prayed the subject would change, as the idea of her uncle's bedroom habits was enough to make her want to gag.

"Your itinerary is quite full." Ingrid beamed with pride. "There is the cake testing, your dress fitting, not to mention the flower arrangements and color scheme." Inhaling deeply, Ingrid released her breath with a blissful smile. "It is so good to be back." Not one to be caught too long in an awkward position with everyone's eyes on her, she diverted everyone's attention away by fussing at Elise, Darcie, and Gwen. "Are you not finished yet? How long does it take to dress someone anyway? My daughter will be queen tomorrow night! Enough of this nonsense. You are dismissed. Go clean something."

Already eager to leave, the three girls shuffled out of the room and down the staircase to the second floor where a group of servants searched the corridor.

"It is not here," one called.

"Not over here, either," said another.

"I've checked all the bedrooms. There's nothing," replied a third.

"That is unacceptable!" snapped a familiar, strict voice.

Elise tensed as Ballard, the overbearing castle steward, walked into view. While he had his moments, like saving Elise and her friends from Brahm and his sister, he also found pleasure in getting them into trouble as well.

"Her Majesty requests her diary. It shall be located and returned immediately or else," he barked.

Elise swallowed convulsively, watching his every move to avoid being spotted. She ducked into an open doorway, pulling Darcie and Gwen with her. "Leave it on a table or something. Then, let's get out of here."

"But they'll see me," Darcie argued.

"Let us cross the corridor to that other room," Gwen whispered, nodding ahead. "There is a table just outside of it. Elise and I will cover you, so you can set it down without anyone noticing."

Darcie bit her lip, unconvinced, but nodded and waited for Elise and Gwen to step out first. Hyperaware of Darcie's crouched, careful steps beside her, Elise stared forward and tried not to bring any attention to the group. Her paranoia spiked as others commented on the missing diary. Whispering ensued, even a couple of laughs, until Ballard ordered everyone to keep searching.

Almost there. Keep your head down. Elise's heart skipped a beat when Darcie retrieved the backup diary from her apron pocket. *Drop it. Drop it, now. Just drop it.*

As soon as they were close enough, Darcie tossed the diary onto the table. At once, the three quickened their steps into the room and waited with quivering breaths.

"Here he comes!" whispered Darcie. "Duck!" She closed the door only enough for them to peek around.

"Who is coming?"

Crying out, all three girls whipped around to see Queen Joranna behind them.

I didn't know she was in this room! Why didn't we pay more attention? She wanted to find Joranna, but she did not want to be found by Joranna. Elise's breath hitched as four guards burst into the room in response to the commotion.

"Step away from the queen!" one barked.

The sound of swords being pulled made Elise's blood run cold. Clutching her bonnet tighter, she avoided Joranna's eyes.

Elise, Darcie, and Gwen stared at the floor as they pressed their backs against the nearest wall.

"Show your faces," came another order. This time from Joranna herself.

Once again, they obliged.

A pool of dread settled in the pit of Elise's stomach when Joranna's face fell. This was not how their plan was supposed to go, and now they would be arrested and end up in the dungeon.

"Are you hurt, Your Majesty?" a guard asked.

"No," replied Joranna, her tone reflecting disappointment rather than fear. "These young women are no threat to me. You may stand down. Thank you," she added when they hesitated.

After a long silence, the guards sheathed their swords and filed out of the room just as Ballard appeared breathless in the doorway.

"Why are they leaving? I heard shouting," he panted, looking back and forth. "Are you quite all right, Your Highness? Is there anything I can—"

He caught sight of Elise first, then Darcie, and finally Gwen. Ballard's shock ran so deep, it looked as if he had been bewitched to remain frozen. At long last, his expression did change—this time, to rage. "The *insolence*!" Inching closer to the ladies, he practically spat through his teeth. "Never, *never*, would I ever expect you to be so stupid as to return after direct orders from—"

"Ballard," Joranna called, waiting for the steward to look at her. "That is enough. I shall handle this."

"But Your Majesty, this cannot be allowed—"

"Except by *me*," Joranna corrected. "Leave us, please."

While she feared for her own fate, Elise was always amused when Ballard got put in his place. This time his face resembled a deflated balloon as he stalked out into the hall. He perked up, however, when he saw the diary sitting on the table. Inspecting the cover, he lifted a suspicious brow at each young girl.

Elise gulped.

"I believe you were looking for this, Your Highness." Ballard held out the diary for the queen to take. After she thanked him, he sent one last sneer in Elise's direction before closing the door behind him.

Slumping against the wall, Elise, Darcie, and Gwen sighed in relief.

Joranna, however, wasted no time berating all three for their reckless behavior. "You know you are not supposed to be here," she added at the end of her lecture. "I expect a good explanation, and quickly, for he is probably reporting to Richard at this very moment."

Gwen and Darcie pushed Elise forward.

Glaring at her friends, Elise took a deep breath and met her grandmother's concerned gaze.

"Rona and her brother. . .are about to attack Haighdlen. There's an armada on its way, and we need to stop the wedding from happening."

CHAPTER 22

As soon as the words left her mouth, Elise wished she had found a different way to share the news. Had she bothered to look at her grandmother closer, she would have seen the queen was already pale and thinner. An assortment of used handkerchiefs and empty glasses with lipstick stains littered the table. Random pillows were discarded on the floor and the drapes remained closed, allowing only a sliver of sunlight to peek through. A pitcher and basin rested on a dresser in the corner, and an oversized blanket was thrown across a lone chaise positioned in the center of the room.

Has she been sleeping in here?

"This is grave news, indeed." Joranna spoke barely above a whisper. "You are absolutely sure?"

Elise nodded.

"I do not need to remind you what a serious allegation this is, Elise. You still stand by what you say?"

Again, Elise nodded.

Joranna walked over to the window, pulling the drape only far enough to peek out of it. "Where did you hear of this?"

"A fairy," Darcie said, ignoring Elise's tight-lipped glare in Gwen's direction.

Gwen doesn't have any memories of the fairies anymore.

Joranna's bewildered expression matched Gwen's as they both stared at Elise and Darcie.

"A fairy?" Joranna asked. "Honestly, Elise, you could not have picked a more unreliable creature."

"You both dragged me here because of a fairy?" Gwen asked incredulously. "I'm risking my life here today on a wild goose chase started by a *fairy*?"

You were the one who led us there. Elise held her tongue, although every fiber of her being wanted to lash out at the allegations. Yet, she waited for the women to finish.

"And who are you?" Queen Joranna asked Gwen. "I do not recognize you."

Gwen introduced herself, adding she was nothing more than the daughter of a farmer whose family housed Elise's party for the festival. She made no mention of her friendship and dealings with Ruby, which Elise agreed, was best for everyone. Especially the princess.

Joranna scrutinized each girl before shaking her head. "I must alert Richard immediately."

"Wait!" Elise cried out, blocking the door. "Not yet!" Sucking her mouth into a thin line, she searched for the right words to say. "We have a plan."

Joranna raised a skeptical brow. "*You* have a plan to aid in warfare and stop an entire armada?"

Elise paled at the sound of it. *Well, when you say it like that, no.* Licking her lips, she stammered on the spot.

"I thought not." Joranna attempted to sidestep Elise but was stopped again.

"Eugena!" Elise blurted out, wincing as the doorknob pressed against her lower back. "Ask Eugena."

Joranna took a step back, allowing Elise to alleviate the pressure from the door. Looking at Darcie and Gwen, she nodded towards Elise. "And you two are in on this plan?" Once the other two girls reluctantly nodded, Joranna took a deep breath. "That is out of the question."

"But *why*?" Elise pressed. "Is it because they live in a lake? Because I always assumed with their magic they could visit any area of water—"

"It is not that," Joranna said. "While you are correct, this sort of request simply is not done. Perhaps you do not remember visiting, but they are not known for their hospitality, nor do they cater to the favors of others—least of all, humans."

Elise opened her mouth, but Darcie beat her to it.

"Yes, but *you* are different," she said. "They gave you a bowl to communicate with them whenever you needed."

A crease appeared in the center of Joranna's forehead. "How do you—" Realization dawned on her face. "That is correct. I forgot you were there the day I received it." She wrung her hands before pacing back and forth in front of the chaise. "But what does all this have to do with Richard's wedding? Apart from the reports of protests occurring throughout the kingdom?"

Protests! This was more serious than Elise even realized. Even the people of Haighdlen were not going to sit around and accept a traitorous alliance. Maybe it would work in their favor.

"We can't let him marry her," Elise said, shooting Gwen a quick glance. *Spin the truth.* "Iris isn't the one for him."

"I agree with you there," Joranna said, heaving a sigh. "But it is out of our hands. He will not be convinced otherwise."

"What if we could prove it to him?" Darcie asked. She waited until all eyes were on her. "Her mom is here, and she was helping Brahm. What if we tricked Ingrid into giving away their plan? Richard might be brainwashed, but we all know she's probably acting for Rona."

"That's true," Elise said. "There's no way that woman wants to make peace. Not after she was thrown in prison here."

"She even escaped and is walking around freely in front of your faces. You know she's laughing at this whole thing," Darcie finished.

Gwen's eyes widened.

"You share my thoughts exactly," Joranna said. "In a matter of days, Richard has stripped most of our legacy from us. He is going to run this kingdom into the ground one way or the other."

"Which is why he must be stopped," Darcie finished.

It was Joranna's turn to widen her eyes.

"She doesn't mean kill him," Elise jumped in. "We think he's been hypnotized. I bet if we could get Iris alone, we could break her down for information. Part of me doesn't think she's completely on board with everything."

Gwen and Darcie nodded their agreement. If they were not successful in convincing Joranna, at least they provided a united front. Elise was surprised when Gwen spoke up.

"She's the weak link. In the short moments I saw her, there is room to infiltrate for sure, but it will be dangerous."

Joranna scrutinized each of them for the fifth or sixth time, as if waiting for them to admit this was all a ruse. Deducing their sincerity, she scratched the back of her head and began pacing frantically again with a huff. "Do you honestly realize what you are asking me to do?"

Elise felt it best to remain silent as her grandmother processed their plans. She herself had drafted multiple mental lists of pros and cons, but everything led to following through with contacting Eugena.

Only when Joranna slumped across the chaise, her eyes glistening, did Elise choose to join her.

"Hey," whispered Elise, waiting for her grandmother to meet her gaze. "You can talk to me. I know I'm asking you for a lot."

Gwen and Darcie stepped closer to the doorway to provide them privacy, but Elise lowered her voice, nonetheless, as she encouraged her grandmother to speak.

Joranna pulled out a fresh handkerchief from a nearby drawer, wiping her eyes delicately. Her voice was distant, sorrowful, and so incredibly meek it tugged at Elise's heart. "I am wondering how we got here. Everything Derek and I built together, everything we instilled in our children, and it is all about to be taken away in a matter of hours." She sobbed into the handkerchief as Elise rubbed her back. "I miss him so much."

Elise never knew a sound could destroy her as deeply as the sound of her grieving grandmother weeping.

"Forgive me," the queen said with a steadying breath. "No one should see their queen this way. If only Avalyn could see me now. She would call me an utter disgrace."

Derek's mother was always a stickler for the rules. Elise only spent a matter of days with her great-grandmother. Joranna spent years being coached how to be a queen with her as a mother-in-law.

"If Derek were here—" Joranna continued. "None of this would have happened. I blame that toxic council. Derek always hated holding those meetings. They will waltz my boy straight to his own grave."

Elise wilted. *Was there anything else we could have done to prevent this from happening? Was this always supposed to happen in one form or another?* Things did seem dire. Whether Rona attacked at this moment or in eighteen years, was the kingdom always meant to be overthrown regardless of interference? She shook her head. *No, I can't think that way anymore.*

"That's why we have to do this," Elise reasoned. "It might not work, but we have to try." She waited until Joranna dried her face and looked at her. "Yes, to save Haighdlen, but we need to save Richard, too. Even if it's from himself. Isn't he worth it?"

Joranna sniffled, but ultimately nodded. "Always. I would do anything for my children." She paused, scanning the room as if seeing the mess for the first time. "Good gracious. I have been withdrawn. My children also lost a father, yet I have only thought of myself." She stood to collect the handkerchiefs around the room. "If we are going to contact Eugena, I will not have her see me living in squalor."

Elise perked up, beaming at Darcie and Gwen across the room. "You'll help us?' she asked Joranna.

"Absolutely. I want to thank you girls. While I will never stop mourning my beloved Derek, I still have a duty to my family and this kingdom. Both of which Rona is planning to steal from me, and if I do nothing, I am essentially surrendering everything to her." Smiling warmly, she hugged Elise and nodded towards Darcie and Gwen before crossing the room to the door. She pressed her ear against it, listening for movement, before continuing in a whisper. "I do not want to trust anyone with the bowl. I shall retrieve it and return. You three stay here where it is safe."

Nodding, Elise added, "If you see Gavin or Mitch, could you let them know we're in here?"

"You got separated *again*?" she asked. "Are you sure they are here?"

Darcie shrugged. "Well, not exactly, but we hope they are."

Joranna frowned. "Let us address one problem at a time. I shall be back shortly."

Twenty minutes later, Elise concluded she and her grandmother had different definitions of the word *shortly*. It did not help the queen left the diary sitting on the table nearest to the chaise where all three girls sat. The temptation to rip it open, regardless of if they had a plan, was tantalizing. Surely, if needed, she could find some magical object to help boost her own powers like before.

"I have always wondered what the castle looked like on the inside," Gwen said, breaking the painful silence. She scanned the entire room, admiring the details down to the subtle woodwork. "I never actually thought I'd get to see it. It is incredibly beautiful."

You'll live in it one day. . .if we don't fail.

"I'm sorry we got you caught up in this," Elise apologized. She meant it. Now that things had slowed down, she felt selfish to forcing Gwen to tag along in hopes of falling in love with Richard. Maybe it was a mistake rushing it this way. He certainly was attracted to her, but Elise did not even know if Gwen felt the same way about him.

They shared a collective sigh of relief when Joranna entered the room, but stared in horror when Sarah and Ruby followed her inside. Only when the door was secured did Joranna pull the bowl out of her sleeve.

"What's going on?" Elise asked, looking between her mother and aunt.

"Should anything happen to Richard, Sarah is next in line," Joranna shared. "I summoned for Ian, but he appears to be out at the moment. No one has seen him. We could use his invisibility powers right about now."

That's right! I forgot he could turn invisible. It was a trait Elise envied, but at the same time, joked that she already possessed.

Gwen and Ruby stared at each other but said nothing.

"And I am not going to keep Ruby in the dark," Joranna continued. "She carries an heir of her own should the worst come to pass."

Elise never considered the possibility of ruling on the throne, and hoped she never would. It was one thing to know she was a princess. It was another to play the part formally. She loved Haighdlen, and prayed there would be a chance to visit should they fix the timeline, but she could not imagine a scenario of leaving her world. . .of leaving Gavin. She considered a world without not only him, but without Darcie, her mom, and even Mitch. The thought alone lit a fire under her to fight no matter the cost to preserve all their futures.

"Mother, should you not be resting? And are you sure striking a deal with the merpeople is the safest plan?" Sarah inquired.

"It is the *only* plan," replied the queen, setting the bowl down on top of the diary.

"Shall I open the drapes for better lighting?" Ruby offered.

"Best to leave them closed, dearest. We never know who to trust or where they may lurk." Joranna cleared her throat and asked Gwen to carry over the pitcher on the dresser. Thanking the young girl, the queen poured water carefully into the bowl. Setting the pitcher down on the floor, she touched the engraved crystal mermaids one at a time.

"Isn't that the coolest thing you've ever seen?" Darcie whispered in Elise's ear.

Nodding, Elise watched in amazement as the carved mermaids stirred and swam around the outskirts of the bowl. Small ripples appeared followed by rapid bubbles that splashed over the rim onto the floor. Joranna set the bowl on the diary once more and urged everyone to stand back.

All but Joranna gasped when the water took on a life of its own. It swirled, lifted, and threaded like clear ropes before coming together to form not one, but two individual heads. The heads were followed by shoulders and torsos. One male and one female. While their features were completely comprised of water, they were detailed enough for Elise to recognize them as Queen Eugena and her intimidating right-hand-man, Erumann. Despite the number of times she had heard of and seen them, Elise was no less mesmerized by their regal presence.

"Queen Joranna." Eugena's voice was distorted as the water that formed her mouth sloshed in time with the words. "This is an unexpected summons."

"Yes, I am so sorry to disturb you." Joranna's hand twitched against the side of her gown as she fought to keep her resolve. "But there is news of a Lockesbarrian armada headed this way. I thought perhaps that—"

"That perhaps you would sacrifice *our* queen instead of yourself?" Erumann accused, causing water to drip along the table as he lifted a fist.

This was a bad idea.

"I assure you that is not it," said Joranna.

"Why do you not send your own ships?" Eugena asked, echoing Erumann's thoughts. "Do you think us more prone to violence?"

"Of course not," replied Joranna. "I fear I have put off this request too long. I should have sought aid long before now. There is reason to believe Haighdlen is under a severe threat."

Eugena looked to Erumann before nodded. "We have received similar reports." Eugena's form rippled as she leaned to the side and stared behind Joranna. "Is that the girl? The one who accepted this bowl on your behalf?"

Elise froze. *Why does she always look at me? She's not even really here, and she's singling me out.*

"Indeed," said Joranna. "Do you wish to speak to her?"

Elise waved both hands in front of her, mouthing several objections as the stares of everyone standing nearby heated her skin. Darcie nudged her forward until Elise stood in front of Joranna looking down at the miniature water mermaids protruding from the filled bowl.

"She is weak! Let us leave her out of this!" Erumann growled, the water sloshing against Elise's dress before Eugena placed a hand on his shoulder. The water instantly calmed as she turned back to Elise.

Talking to heads made of water unnerved Elise in a way she could not put into words. Let alone being insulted by one.

Is this really happening right now? Why does she want to talk to me? It's not my bowl. Elise gulped, suddenly regretting her idea to contact them.

"What is your plan?" Eugena asked calmly.

"Me?" Elise squeaked. "Why me?"

"News reaches my ear one way or the other," replied the queen, "and *you* always find a way to be in the center of it."

Elise blushed.

"The king's recent passing, followed by a scandalous engagement *and* an incoming armada?" The queen's water form shook her head. "These are not by coincidence, and I am not a fool. Neither are you. So, I ask you again, what is your plan?"

Can I trust them? Elise glanced over her shoulder at Darcie, who nodded back with encouragement.

"Enough of this," Erumann bellowed. "My Queen, she is as ignorant as the rest of them. There is no plan, and they are willing to put everyone in danger on a whim!"

"Silence, my love," Eugena muttered before looking back at Elise. "Speak, girl."

Elise's body flared into a full hot flash as every inch of her burned under the pressure. She asked for this, and yet, in that moment struggled to even form words. Looking at each member of her family, Gwen, and Darcie, Elise settled her gaze on Ruby's stomach. *There's too much at stake to chicken out now.*

"I want to stop the armada before it reaches Haighdlen. I want to stop the wedding. Maybe even the coronation," she added. "And then I want to find Rona myself."

A deadly silence followed as Elise's answer was processed by everyone. *I hope I can trust all of them not to share it with Richard or anyone else.* It was too late either way.

At long last, Eugena nodded. "Quite ambitious. . .and noble. However, what you described is not a plan, child, but a mere goal."

Looking at Erumann, who shook his head, Eugena ignored him and nodded once more. "However, my army will locate and put a stop to that armada." She paused while everyone in the room smiled and cheered. "However, I caution you about seeking out Rona."

"I know she's dangerous," Elise said. "But I can't let her keep threatening everybody I love."

"And while that is commendable," added Eugena sternly, "it is worth noting that she is protected beyond her stolen army."

What is she talking about?

Erumann lifted a watery fist to his chest. "Whoever takes the life of Rona is also doomed to a most painful death."

What! Elise stammered on the spot, looking helplessly at her family's equally shocked faces. *Did they really not know, either?* Suddenly, Elise's lungs felt closed, her throat too tight.

"So, I ask you again," Eugena continued carefully, "Do you still believe in carrying out your mission?"

Elise did not know how to respond. There was always a chance she would not survive facing Rona, but it had also come with an opportunity to succeed and go home.

Now, everything had changed.

In that moment, Elise felt separate from her body. She heard whispering behind her, but she could not focus on who was speaking. Numbness spread throughout her body as the price of their mission came down to her willingly sacrificing herself.

Possibly dying is scary, but knowing *I would die. . .how can anyone expect me to be okay with that? Did my family know this before they sent me?*

Whether the present-day Laurilles knew or not, Elise felt utterly betrayed. *What will happen to my friends? Will they even be able to get home if I die?* Meeting Darcie's eye, the girls seemed to be sharing the same line of thought. This time, Darcie did not nod.

"We cannot ask her such a thing," Joranna argued. "She's just a child!"

"Rona's army is comprised of children," Eugena countered. "There will be unfortunate casualties regardless of our decision here today. What I need to know is if she will do what is necessary when the time comes, for no one else has been brave enough to take on the task."

"Elise, don't do this," Darcie pleaded. "We can figure out another way. We'll find the boys and do more research. There has to be a loophole somewhere."

While tempting, Elise knew deep down someone would have to be willing to kill Rona and *be* killed in order to save everyone. Never in her life had Elise stood up for anything, nor did she think she would ever have to. Rubbing the rough fabric of her skirt between her fingers, Elise took a tentative step forward.

"What are you doing?" Joranna asked. "Elise, you cannot—"

Elise shook her head to stop Joranna's interference as warm tears spilled down her cheeks. She faced the two water figures again. "So, if I agree, you stop the armada and save Haighdlen, right?" The queen nodded. Elise licked her lips and stared at the ceiling, unable to bring herself to look anywhere else. Short of breath, she curled her hands into fists. *This is worse than any deal with a fairy, but Richard could never get a ship there in time.* "Could you use your magic to send me to Lockesbarrow afterwards?"

"All four of us!" Darcie called over Elise's shoulder in spite of not having located the boys yet. "She's not going without her friends."

There was nothing Elise wanted more than to protect her friends, but Darcie's immediate support meant more than she would ever know. *Thank you.*

Elise waited with bated breath as the two mermaids whispered. Several droplets spilled along the cover of the diary, yet Joranna did not make any attempts to disturb the bowl.

After an excruciating period of deliberation, Eugena nodded. "You have my word. *If* all goes according to plan, and the armada is defeated, we shall meet you near Lake Laulie at sunset."

Wow, their magic is *fast.*

"Let us hope your bravery remains intact," Erumann sneered.

Eugena moved her attention to Joranna. "I would advise you to ready soldiers along your eastern border to be safe."

"Of course," Joranna answered.

Both dipped below the surface and the water calmed as the crystal bowl froze in place once more.

All was silent.

What have I gotten myself into?

"I did not expect that," Sarah whispered breathlessly. "Mother, surely there has to be another plan."

Joranna opened her mouth, closed it, and repeated the motion before shaking her head in shock.

"You don't need to say anything," Elise said. "I know what I have gotten myself into. I had to do it to save Haighdlen. An armada could kill so many *and* start a battle on your land. If we can get to Lockesbarrow in time, I can try to stop her."

"Doubtful," Ruby muttered under her breath.

Elise fought the urge to roll her eyes. *Thanks, Mom.*

Joranna admonished her youngest daughter before addressing the room. "We have until sunset to know for sure. You will need time to travel to the lake."

Wiping another falling tear, Elise sniffled and cleared her throat. "What will you do?"

Joranna squared her shoulders. "Well, after your selfless act of heroism, I can hardly stand to mope around here any longer. You will need reinforcements."

"But, Mother," Sarah quipped, "I commend her bravery as well, but you heard Richard earlier this morning. The Ambassador to Vynchia denied aiding Haighdlen after the protests began."

Joranna poured the water from the bowl back into the pitcher. "Then I will not speak with the Ambassador. I shall write to Queen Arymei herself. Between her magic and Eugena's magic, they could get the Vynchian fleet and our fleet to Lockesbarrow's shores by tomorrow."

"So soon?" Ruby asked solemnly. She crossed her arms. "The perks of magic, I suppose."

I need to tell her what happened with the fairies in case she tries to talk to Gwen about it.

Judging by the looks on Sarah's and Ruby's faces, neither had much confidence of their mother's chances.

"We keep this between us," Joranna said, settling her eyes on Gwen, who had paled during the whole mermaid conference. "Do I have everyone's word?"

Despite palatable doubts, each person nodded.

"Good. Sarah, would you fetch me my stationery? Be discreet."

Sarah nodded and left the room.

Joranna pressed a hand to her chest and began pacing again. "There is so little time. Magic will be as necessary as complete discretion on this matter. Richard cannot know until the letters are already sent out."

Sarah returned with the stationery before sitting beside her mother.

As the room quieted, it dawned on Elise that Gwen was still in the room, no doubt confused and filled with questions.

There was still the matter of what to even do with Gwen before Elise could leave for Lake Laulie. They could not simply send her home as if nothing had occurred. Elise took advantage of Joranna's involved conversation with Sarah to warn Ruby. "The king of the fairies wiped Gwen's memories. I don't have time to explain everything," she whispered into the princess's ear. "Gwen still knows you, but she won't remember giving you fairy magic. Keep it that way, please. Can you keep an eye on her? Keep her safe while I'm gone?"

Easing back, Ruby shuddered and nodded her understanding. It was apparent the princess's head was rapidly filling with questions but she remained silent.

"Yes, I'm sure you're lonely. A princess should be allowed to have friends," Elise said louder with a knowing smile, before continuing in a whisper so that only Gwen and Ruby could hear. "No one has to know when you two met."

"Well, that is ironic, because I am not sure I even know myself," Gwen chuckled. "I feel like it has been forever though. It all blends together really."

Ruby nodded with a bittersweet smile. "We have shared many talks, often late into the night." Cradling her rounded stomach, she raised her voice. "I would be honored to extend your visit here as my close friend if you accept. I could sure use the company during this time."

Gwen smiled. "I should like that very much, but I will need to write to my mother. Am I able to?"

Joranna paused her conversation to nod. "I see no reason why not, but we must proceed with caution. Please avoid any details you have overheard here today. Simply inform your mother the princess has invited you here for companionship. News will reveal itself in time, I am afraid. It will be best to let it occur naturally."

Gwen agreed before Ruby took her hand and led her out. "But first, we must get you some finer clothing." Their laughter carried into the corridor before Sarah suggested they also disperse to avoid suspicion.

"This is great!" Darcie whispered into Elise's ear. "Now, Gwen will be here and have more chances of running into Richard!"

At least something good might come out of this. Elise wanted to be happier. The idea that Richard and Gwen were under the same roof would normally be enough to put Elise over the moon. However, she could not bring herself to feel anything but existential dread as the plan was set into motion.

The following ten minutes passed like an hour.

Joranna drafted a letter for the current Captain of the Guard and one for Queen Arymei. She was able to make jokes about the legibility of such hastily written notices, but Elise did not join in the anticipation.

You wanted this. You asked for this. You can't be so surprised it happened this way. While logical, Elise could not get on board with her rationalizing train of thought.

Darcie did her best to comfort Elise on the chaise while they waited, but Elise was not paying attention. Her mind was far away from this room. All voices were muffled as she stared ahead in a daze. It was as if she were wandering lost around in a dense fog. The world continued turning, but she was immobilized within the confines of her own mind.

Trapped.

Paralyzed.

It dawned on Elise as she recounted the many panic attacks in her life, that she never truly understood fear until that moment. She was thankful to be sitting as the thought of standing made her knees weak.

Everyone here was willing to depend on her, but when the time came to act, could she rely on herself?

How am I going to tell Gavin?

She needed to find him, and Mitch, yet it was only when Joranna finished the letters that Elise was pulled out of her reverie.

"Sarah, take this letter to the captain." Joranna handed a piece of paper to her eldest daughter before turning to Elise and Ruby. "We need to get Arymei's copy to her ambassador."

"I thought you said you wouldn't talk to him?" Darcie questioned.

"I simply meant to try and negotiate. Only he will have magical access to communicate with her instantly, but Richard would never allow such a thing from our family." Tapping the letter against her chin, Joranna pondered how they would transfer it safely.

Darcie's eyes lit up. "What about Charles?"

"Richard's closest friend?" Joranna released a hollow chuckle. "Are you mad?"

Elise came to her friend's rescue. "No, she's right. I think we could trust him with this. He's made it known Richard hasn't been himself. He would want to do everything he could to make things go back to the way they were."

Joranna sighed. "We have no choice and are losing precious time. Let us hope you are right."

Before they could leave, however, shouting could be heard coming up the corridor.

"What on earth?" Joranna stepped closer to the door before Ballard knocked and entered.

"Forgive the intrusion, Your Highness, but there is a groundskeeper in the main hall who requests an audience with you. Prince Richard is not seeing anyone at present and there is a growing concern around Lady Iris's *staff.*" He glared at Elise and Darcie. "What shall I tell him?"

"For goodness' sake," Joranna huffed. "Richard wants to take over, yet will not take care of simple staff disputes." She instructed Darcie and Elise to stay with her as Ballard led them down the staircase.

All thoughts of hiding her identity were far gone when they entered the main hall to find Gavin and Mitch standing behind a shaggy, disgruntled-looking man.

Elise's breath caught as her heart threatened to stop beating.

Darcie had the same reaction as both girls ran past Joranna into their respective boyfriends' arms.

Elise tightened her embrace as tears streamed down her face. *Thank you, thank you, thank you. Thank God you're safe.* Ignoring the stunned audience, Elise kissed and hugged him once more, inhaling his scent.

"You probably don't want to do that," he chuckled. "We've been in the stables."

"I don't care," she wept into his neck. "I don't care. I'm just glad you're here. I love you."

If she were going to die, moments like this were sacred and numbered. The pure joy on his face and hearing him tell her he loved her back was what she wanted to remember. He would find out when the time was right.

For now, she was content with holding him.

CHAPTER 23

"Are you going to allow this?" complained the groundskeeper to Joranna. He sneered at the two couples. "Like I told Mr. Ballard here, these two are the most *incompetent* stable boys I've ever seen. They should be dismissed immediately!"

Joranna fought to suppress a smile as she folded her hands delicately in front of her. "I hear your concern, and I shall handle it personally. Thank you."

Whether or not he believed her, the groundskeeper bowed and stalked away muttering under his breath.

Once he was out of earshot, Joranna addressed the steward next. "Mr. Ballard, please arrange for any further disruptions or issues to be handled during court. I should like it if others do not get the idea to parade their problems through the main halls on a whim. We do have a level of decorum to protect."

"Understood, Your Excellency, but Prince Richard has suspended court gatherings."

"Honestly! He is being such a child." Joranna pursed her lips with an impatient stomp.

Ballard regarded the reunited teenagers. "Will *they* be remaining on the staff?"

The queen chuckled. "Goodness, no. I have business with them. See that proper garments are prepared for them before we go to the dining hall."

Stumbling over his words, Ballard pinched the bridge of his nose. Elise noted his eye also began twitching. "With the utmost respect, Queen Joranna, the prince has made it quite clear that they are not to be on castle grounds and—"

"And yet here they are," Joranna pointed out with an overly sweet smile. "*My* guests. Have five place settings added. Princess Ruby also has a guest who will remain with us for some time. Please also instruct Ms. Persimmons to have a room prepared for her."

Ballard bit the inside of his cheek. "Shall any other rooms be required for tonight?" He stared point blank at Elise, who glared back with the same level of disdain.

"No, one will be all. Thank you. You all stay with me while we wait for everything to be prepared." Joranna ushered them towards Richard's study.

"Your Highness!" Ballard squeaked, sweeping a strand of oily hair across his forehead. "Prince Richard was *most* insistent he be left alone this morning. I should caution you—"

"Ballard, that is enough," Joranna quipped. "Now, open the door."

The steward grimaced, his skin a sickly shade of green. Hanging his head, he opened the door and stepped out of the way. "Yes, Your Majesty."

Elise shivered under the steward's disdainful sneer. His eyes narrowed as she passed him, making her pause as Joranna stepped up to the doorway. "Maybe this isn't a good idea." She fiddled with her fingers. "We can wait out here. This really doesn't concern us."

Joranna smirked. "Since when has that ever stopped the four of you?"

She has a point. Elise held her breath as they filed into the familiar study.

Not once had Elise entered this room with enthusiasm. Often, she resembled a dog with its tail tucked. Goosebumps lined her arms as she caught sight of her uncle behind the desk. There would never be a time where she did not initially mistake him for Derek. The resemblance was uncanny, making her miss the late king even more. Richard was now the third generation of Laurille rulers she had encountered. If they did not get through to him soon, he would be the last.

Ballard cleared his throat. "Your Majesty—"

"Are you familiar with the word *privacy*, Ballard?" Richard groaned without glancing up from a document. "Perhaps we should discuss the definition of *dismissal* next."

Joranna cleared her throat, making Richard lift his head at last. "Mother! I was not expecting you."

"It appears not," Joranna agreed, narrowing her eyes on the empty glasses that had yet to be collected. "I thought we might discuss—"

Elise felt her knees buckle when Richard's demeanor stiffened and witnessed the seething fury behind his eyes.

He rose from the chair, sweeping his hand along the desk's edge. Inhaling sharply, he blew out an exasperated breath. "I do not have time for this. Ballard, dispatch the guards to arrest them this moment. They will be dealt with after the coronation."

"Not so fast," Joranna argued. "They are my guests."

Richard had the audacity to roll his eyes with a hollow laugh. "*They* have been your *guests* my entire life and yet have not aged a day. *They* claim to come in peace yet wreak havoc wherever *they* go. What a coincidence *they* should return prior to my being enthroned. I take it *they* have a problem with it?"

"Not at all," Joranna replied before Elise could answer. "I do."

Elise did not hide her surprise at Joranna's bluntness. All thoughts of the plan vanished as the air in the room chilled. She met Gavin's equally tense gaze, wishing they could return to the hall. *I thought she was just coming to fuss at him about not meeting with the groundskeeper. We shouldn't be in here right now.*

Richard smiled politely. "Perhaps we should speak in private, and if I recall, you gave your blessing for me to be crowned early before secluding yourself in mourning." He checked the clock. "Is it not a bit early for you to be out and about?"

Joranna did not take the bait but remained composed, something Elise knew she could not have done so easily herself. "At one time, I trusted it was in the kingdom's best interest for you to be crowned. However, in the past weeks, you have become quite corrupt."

"Careful," he warned.

Yet, she pressed on. "How long has it been since you held court? I had to handle a minor grievance in the main hall, of all places, because you are not receiving anyone. If this is to be the common practice, then we may as well leave the front gates open."

Richard closed the distance between them and took his mother's hand. "You are upset. Naturally, it will take time to grieve father's death—"

"*That* is another point I wish to make," Joranna added, pulling her hand away. "*You* have not taken the time to mourn *at all*. You have all but barricaded yourself in this study, avoiding your responsibilities—"

Rolling his eyes again, Richard turned on his heel and walked over to the window. "I am taking respon—"

"Oh, really?" she challenged. "Then where is Ian? Why are there reports that you have ceased your morning briefings? I even caught word from the servants of violent protests occurring in Clara following your announcement last night. Richard, do you not understand the severity of this decision? There could be attempts on your life! Have you even sent out guards to address it?"

Richard opened his mouth, reconsidered, and closed it again. His eyes flashed with calculation as if withholding information.

What is it? Spit it out!

"Are you finished?" he asked her before nodding towards Elise and her friends. "You have created quite a spectacle to undermine my authority. Spreading false narratives of my corruptness will not prevent the ceremony from proceeding."

Joranna held up a finger when Mitch tried to interrupt. Glaring at her son, the queen browsed the letters on his desk. "This group seeks to protect Haighdlen and learn the truth. Something that has been elusive as of late."

Richard shook his head. "I knew I would have those who doubted me. I feared they even sat on the council. Never would I have guessed my own mother would have such little faith in me." He asked her to step away from the desk, waiting until she finally obliged. "Allow me to put your conspiracy theories to rest. Tomorrow night,

Lady Iris will be crowned Queen of Haighdlen. *You* will lead the family in welcoming her *and* her mother. A united front is the only way to prevent war, which is all I seek to do."

"You can't prevent it. It's already here," Elise blurted out. "Everything we've warned you about is happening now."

Richard continued as if he did not hear her. "The council can continue speculating, but once we are wed, Lockesbarrow will be an ally."

"Yeah?" Darcie challenged. "Then why do they have an armada headed this way?"

I don't know if we should have told him that yet.

Hearing it for the first time along with Richard, Gavin and Mitch wore matching shocked expressions.

The smugness faded from Richard's face. Narrowing his gaze warily, he looked between each of them as if waiting for a practical joke to come to light.

"Perhaps you would have known if you received your morning report," Elise offered with a quizzical brow.

Rather than respond to her, he bent over his desk in a panic, shuffling the disorderly pile of documents. "I must meet with the captain."

"It is already done," Joranna replied calmly. "The situation will be resolved by sunset."

The prince stared at his mother as if she spoke a different language. He scoffed in disbelief, as if convinced their entire exchange was a satirical prank. "You have been so incredibly sick with grief that you can barely lift a spoon. I hardly think you need to have a hand in foreign policy. What is next, Mother? A coup against me?"

"Enough!" Joranna snapped. "You will not belittle me or your siblings any longer. If a rebellion occurs, it will be self-induced."

He slammed his fist against the desk. "*I* am being a strong leader!"

"*You* are being a spoiled tyrant!" she corrected. "You have completely abandoned your late father's priorities."

"Such as?" he demanded.

"What about investigating the prison?" Darcie offered.

Joranna made to calm Darcie, insisting she could handle the matter, but Elise felt compelled to support the argument.

"That's right! Gwen Archer's father is in there, and he's completely innocent. King Derek promised to look into it before he was cursed. Her family has even lost their farm over it."

"Who?" asked the prince.

"From last night," Mitch reminded him. "The dancer who turned you down."

"I can't blame her," Gavin added.

Elise suppressed a chuckle as she met her boyfriend's eyes.

Realization dawned on Richard's face before he shook his head. "How do you know—"

"We are getting entirely off the point," Joranna announced. "What I want to know is how you could collude with Brahm's family after what he and his sister did. Who initiated this arrangement?"

Elise bit the inside of her cheek so as not to scream when there was a knock at the door before Richard could reply. Ballard poked his head in long enough to announce breakfast was awaiting them in the dining hall. He bitterly added that enough places were set to accommodate every guest.

Richard looked down at the floor as the door closed. "Let us not quarrel, Mother. We both know this kingdom needs strong leadership, particularly during this vulnerable time. That is all I seek to provide. You need to join me and convince the people this is the right path forward. It is that simple."

Joranna sighed with a shuddering breath. Shaking her head with a glassy stare, she turned to face the door. Glancing over her shoulder, she added, "A strong leader would know the simple path is not always the correct one." Without waiting for a reply, she beckoned the teenagers to follow her.

The door was opened for them by a guard, and Joranna waited until they were all in the main hall before retrieving a handkerchief. She took a moment to compose herself. "I must agree with you. That is not my son. The difficult decision will be how to rescue him in time."

Luck, perhaps fate, was on their side, however, as Charles rounded the corner at that precise moment. Elise suppressed the urge to cry out as he greeted them with a mixture of surprise and ingrained manners.

Beckoning him to her, Joranna retrieved the letter from her sleeve and whispered important directions into his ear.

"It's to Arymei. Don't say anything. I'll explain later," Elise said when Gavin asked her what the letter was about.

"I need that delivered before he sets back for Vynchia today," Joranna finished.

"The Ambassador has planned to stay until after the ceremony," Charles replied to Joranna. "However, I do not believe any of the councilmen will be dining with the family. They have requested an emergency session with Richard, but I will deliver this immediately." Charles bowed before retreating up the staircase.

"Does someone want to tell us what's going on?" Mitch asked.

Elise and Darcie were prevented from informing the boys yet again as Joranna suggested they all freshen up for breakfast.

Ballard approached and ushered them upstairs to be bathed and dressed.

"How are you always around, man?" Mitch whined. "For someone so busy, you sure know how to pop out at the right moment."

Agreed.

Ballard tilted his chin haughtily. "The family relies on me to be available and oversee daily operations. Not to mention, just this morning, you four impersonated staff to gain access to the family and have added to my duties. I have been instructed to tend to your needs rather than your deserved arrest. You have no one to blame but yourselves."

I can't believe this guy actually saved us once. Sounds like he would've been happier letting Brahm win. I guess I should be happy he's so loyal to my family.

By the time they were ready and entered the dining hall, Ingrid, Iris, Gwen and the royal family—save for Richard and Ian—

had already begun eating. Elise and her friends took the seats opposite of Ruby and Gwen.

"Why are the maids eating with us?" Iris asked her mother, who had not yet looked up from her plate. "I thought I recognized one sitting with Princess Ruby, but now all three of them are sitting here."

Without the bonnets to conceal their identities, Elise and Darcie were instantly recognized. Ingrid's eyes widened as she choked into her glass before subsequently giving way to a coughing fit.

Joranna studied the woman before smirking at Elise and Darcie. Her voice was calm and unbothered. "Are you quite all right, Lady Ingrid?"

Ingrid looked between Elise, Darcie, and Joranna, opening her mouth repeatedly without actually speaking. At a loss for words, she finally dabbed the sides of her mouth with a cloth napkin and released an awkward set of polite giggles. "I am q-quite well, Your Majesty, thank you."

Suppressing a laugh around a mouthful of food, Elise chewed in silence. She basked in the opportunity to watch the other woman squirm in her chair. Given the devious glares she sent their way, Ingrid most likely recalled Elise and Darcie pinning her to the floor the night of her arrest. Elise still longed to know how Brahm and Ingrid escaped prison that ultimately led to Gavin's kidnapping. As her mind ventured down that unwanted path, Elise reached out and squeezed Gavin's hand under the table.

From that moment, any exchanges between Ingrid and Iris were whispered, further fueling Elise's suspicions. The only part of breakfast more frustrating was the series of looks Darcie kept sending her to speak to Gavin.

If she winks or clears her throat one more time, I'm going to kill her.

"You got something in your eye, Babe?" Mitch finally asked, prompting Darcie to roll her eyes.

"I think she wants Elise to tell me something," Gavin said with a laugh before turning to her. "So, what's up?"

Not here. Not like this. Instead, she kept it brief. "When the mermaids return, they're going to meet us at Lake Laulie and send us to Lockesbarrow."

"Does it have to be mermaids?" Mitch groaned. "I hate mermaids."

"I can't say I'm excited to get back there," Gavin confessed. "But at least they're helping us. Why do you sound so uneasy?"

When the doors were opened for Richard to enter, Elise watched the prince stride across the room to his seat at the head of the table without so much as a nod towards anyone. When his food was plated, he proceeded to stab at the contents with a fork, unbothered by everyone's stare.

Joranna played off his rudeness with an uncomfortable chuckle. "You must excuse my son. There are many preparations to attend to. He forgets himself."

Only when Joranna cleared her throat, did Richard look up and notice Gwen's presence. His eyes darted between her and Iris before he leaned back in his chair.

"Were you not supposed to meet with the council?" Joranna inquired.

"I cancelled it," he snapped, irritably whipping his cloth napkin loose on his knee rather than unfolding it.

Joranna offered the others at the table a polite smile before carefully proceeding. "Do you think that wise?"

Richard ignored her.

Determined to ease the tension, Lady Ingrid switched the topic of conversation to wedding preparations and the lace on Iris's gown. As Ingrid and Joranna prattled on, and everyone else settled into their own conversations, Elise ignored Darcie's insufferable attempts to get her to tell Gavin the whole truth by watching her brooding uncle.

Expecting him to be annoyed with the idle gossip, Elise watched as he feigned interest in what Iris was saying. Humming politely during pauses, he stroked his chin and nodded at whoever was speaking.

However, his eyes frequently landed on Gwen, who was too engrossed in her own talk with Ruby to even notice.

"I am told you excel in horsemanship, Your Highness," Ingrid said, nodding towards her daughter. "I am constantly encouraging Iris to improve her own skills, but I am afraid she would prefer to tend to her watercolors and singing. In those areas, you will not find anyone as accomplished."

"Yes, Iris, we were quite taken with your beautiful voice last night," Joranna agreed. "Like an angel. Is that not right, Richard?"

The prince redirected his attention away from Gwen as Elise met Sarah's eyes. The eldest princess looked between her brother and Gwen before realization dawned on her features.

"I must extend a compliment to Ms. Archer as well," said Sarah, nodding towards Gwen. "Your performance was quite captivating. Would you all not agree?"

Ingrid straightened up and wiped the sides of her mouth with a frown. "I must confess I found it a vulgar display. Is that what they are trying to pass off as art these days?" Shaking her head, Ingrid tittered into her glass.

Richard cleared his throat as he swallowed a bite of food. "I was not aware you were a renowned critic of the arts, Lady Ingrid. Perhaps you can enlighten us to a suitable art form that would insure Ms. Archer's protection against future scrutiny."

Joranna frowned at her son's impertinence while Iris hunched forward to make herself appear smaller.

"I should have liked to have seen it," said Ruby.

"It was nothing special," Gwen said to Ruby before looking at Richard. "And I require no protection but thank you."

The prince's eyes lingered on her long after everyone else returned to their meals.

Ingrid drained her glass before groaning. "A fierce migraine has come over me, I am afraid. Perhaps I should rest. Iris, will you not join me?"

Elise shared an anxious glance with her friends.

How convenient. She is up to something.

"Is there anything we can give you? A glass of wine perhaps?" Joranna offered.

Ingrid declined the kind gesture and ushered her daughter out of the room.

Another tense silence followed before Richard realized his family's eyes were watching him.

"What?" he asked.

"How long do you plan to act in such an impetuous manner?" Joranna demanded. "I am not in favor of this misalliance, but your mistreatment of those ladies cannot go unnoticed."

Richard rolled his eyes and popped a grape into his mouth. "What mistreatment?"

"You all but ignored poor Iris, who is meek as it is," Joranna explained. "And as for her mother—"

"Lady Ingrid insulted a young lady's reputation," Richard said.

"Please do not consider my reputation," Gwen interrupted. "I am perfectly capable of taking care of myself."

"I would not be doing my duty to you as your future king if I allowed such slander against your name."

Gwen scoffed. "It would benefit everyone if you did your duty at all."

There was a collective gasp around the table—except by Ruby, who laughed—but before Ballard or anyone could address Gwen's insult, the doors burst open. Charles ran in accompanied by another young man with blood splattered across his face and shirt.

"Lord Fenton! Honestly, what is the meaning of this?" Joranna demanded.

"Prince Ian was just attacked at one of the protests in town!" Charles informed them.

"What on earth was he doing there?" Joranna stood abruptly and made her way towards him. "Where is he? Is he alive? Who is this? He is also injured." She regarded the man beside Charles.

"The prince is alive, Majesty," Charles replied. "He was rescued and safely delivered here by guards and this young man."

"I am greatly indebted to you, sir," Joranna said. "You have saved my son's life. What is your name?"

The man in question bowed before the queen, wincing as he clutched his ribs. "Liam, Your Highness. Liam Faerse."

The blood ran out of Elise's face. *Liam? That's Sarah's future husband.* She chanced a look at her aunt, but Sarah had already made her way over to Joranna, who met Richard's eyes across the room.

"Well, Richard, here is the result of your peace treaty." The queen gestured towards the injured man before turning towards Charles. "Please take me to Ian at once and have Mr. Faerse treated by the doctor as well. Sarah, come with me. You can begin healing their wounds while we wait." Without another word, the two women exited with Charles and Liam.

Gwen cleared her throat, staring between the door and Richard. "Are you not going to go with them?"

Richard shrugged. "My mother and sister are capable of tending to my brother's needs. He hardly needs me to add to the chaos."

Gwen scoffed before looking at Ruby. "Is he serious?"

"Sadly," Ruby muttered miserably into her cup.

"Do you not want to go see him yourself?" Gwen inquired.

"And leave you?" Ruby asked, sending Richard a disapproving glare. "Unlike my brother, I possess a fraction of manners."

"I will manage. Go," Gwen urged, standing as Ruby stood to leave.

The doors opened before Ruby reached them as Charles returned. Sharing a tense silent exchange, he stepped out of the way to allow her into the hall.

"I think that's our cue to leave, too," Darcie whispered.

Gavin, Mitch, and Elise agreed and excused themselves as well.

"We can wait in the library," Mitch suggested. "They usually don't mind us hanging out in there."

"You guys go ahead," Elise said. "I'll be there in a minute."

Gavin paused and turned around. "Are you okay?"

"Yeah," Elise said. "I just want to hang around and make sure Gwen's okay."

Gavin hesitated but nodded when Mitch tugged on his arm.

By the time Elise hid behind the dining hall door, Richard was standing with Charles in a hushed discussion about what happened. She could only make out what he was saying once the prince called out to Gwen as she passed them.

"Would you care to take a turn around the courtyard with me, Ms. Archer?" Richard asked.

Gwen shook her head.

"Is that all the reply I get?" He smiled at Charles. "I suppose I should not expect more from a commoner."

Did he really just say that? What a jerk!

The men's laughter subsided when Gwen approached them.

"This commoner has plenty to say about His Highness," she corrected him. "Whether you are capable of hearing it is another matter entirely."

She appeared unfazed to their mockery and jeers.

"By all means," Richard laughed, regarding her with amusement. "Let us hear it. Do you worst."

Uh oh. He should not have said that.

Gwen narrowed her eyes at the arrogant prince.

"The crown may influence others to shield you against such censure, but I believe it will benefit Your Highness to hear the truth from someone who lives outside this castle." Gwen tipped her chin up towards him, a menacing flash in her eyes. "King Derek put his family and this kingdom first while you are busy pandering to a known enemy. In the few minutes I just spent at your table, it was made clear you ignored the wishes of your mother, the council, and ultimately the welfare of the people protesting by proceeding with such an engagement."

"You think I picked the wrong bride then?" he chortled, nudging Charles to join in before letting his eyes roam over her body.

Elise swallowed convulsively, debating whether she should step in with a diversion.

However, Gwen remained unimpressed as she squared her shoulders and stepped closer, careful to maintain a safe enough distance as to not alert any guards. "Until you can think of someone other than yourself, your subjects will sink into poverty, and Haighdlen will be vulnerable to attacks similar to the one made on your own brother." It was her turn to look him up and down. "Not a promising start for a king. Now, if you will excuse me, your sister is expecting me."

She spun on her heel and stormed off, not taking notice of Elise standing speechless gaping behind the door.

That was awesome! He needed to hear that.

Peeking through the crack in the door, Elise suppressed a laugh at Richard's stunned expression.

"Why does she keep doing that?" he asked Charles. "That is twice now she has berated me and stormed off."

"Why do you allow it?" Charles challenged with a knowing grin. "You have arrested others for less offense."

"I do not know." Running a hand along the back of his neck, Richard sighed. "Intoxicated as I was, I could not sleep last night from thinking of her. Now, she is a guest in my own castle. What have I done to deserve such torture?"

Charles shrugged and patted Richard on the back. "Would you like the short list or the long?"

Both young men laughed and walked out, leaving Elise to wait until the hall was clear to join her friends in the library.

CHAPTER 24

When the doctor allowed Ian to have visitors outside of family, Elise and her friends found Joranna holding her son's hand. The prince was asleep, and Ruby—who sat on the other side of the bed—informed them he had lost a lot of blood, evident from his deathly pale complexion tainted by various cuts and scrapes that accompanied a black eye. Sarah stood at the foot of the bed trying to heal large bruises on his calves with her magic.

"Did you find out why he was out there?" Elise asked.

Sarah nodded grimly. "I have been talking a great deal with Mr. Faerse, who is being treated in the nearest guestroom. Ian snuck out first thing this morning to join the protestors."

"But why?" Mitch asked. "Why be a part of the violence against his own family?"

"Supposedly, it was scheduled to be peaceful," Sarah continued with a skeptic shake of her head, "but it got out of hand and quickly escalated into a full riot."

"And Ian is not one to lie down and quit," Ruby added.

"It was foolish of him to be out there in the first place," Joranna snapped, wiping Ian's hair out of his eyes. "Completely reckless."

It must be so hard to see her son like this after just losing Derek.

"Did that Liam guy say anything else?" Gavin asked. "Anything about Rona or how they escaped?"

Sarah shook her head.

"The important thing is that he is home with his family," said Joranna with a sad smile. "After tomorrow, I fear I will not recognize our family any longer."

"What do you mean?" Elise asked.

"We may be separating for a while," she mumbled. "Richard spent the better part of an hour explaining it was for security reasons. Sometimes, I think he just likes to hear himself talk."

Crossing her arms, Elise scoffed and leaned against the wall. "Yeah, well, Gwen found a way to shut him up." Encouraged by their curiosity, she went on to share what was exchanged outside the dining hall.

"I love her." Ruby chuckled. "I wish I could have seen his face."

Despite her best effort, Sarah failed to suppress a smile of her own. "I cannot say he did not deserve it."

The lighthearted humor vanished, however, when the door opened to allow Richard and Iris entrance.

"How is he coming along?" asked the prince.

"Ah, Richard," Joranna tossed over her shoulder. "So good of you to finally visit."

Iris remained behind the prince with her head lowered. A silken purse Elise had not noticed at breakfast dangled from her gloved hands. As lovely as she was, the young woman stood like a porcelain doll that would potentially shatter.

Sarah cleared her throat. "I must check on Mr. Faerse now. Ruby, would you please join me?"

Ruby stood. "You go ahead. I should like to find Gwen."

As the princesses exited, the room was enveloped in a suffocating silence until the door closed again.

"Lady Iris, it is kind of you to visit my son," Joranna said.

Iris merely nodded her head, prompting Richard to clear his throat. "My darling Iris actually requests a private meeting with the travelers."

"Oh?" Joranna stared at Elise, Gavin, Mitch, and Darcie, who shared the same shocked expressions. "Whatever for?"

"I believe that would fall under the perimeters of *private,* Mother. Could you give us a moment?"

Joranna scoffed and met Elise's apprehensive gaze.

Elise shook her head. *Please don't leave us alone with them.* There was something brewing between the prince and his grim fiancée, who looked equal parts skittish and ill. Despite her wishes, Elise watched her grandmother exit the room.

"Tell them, darling," Richard said. "Whatever it is."

"Before you tell us whatever it is you came in here for," Elise said with a bite to her tone, "answer me this. Does your mother get those headaches often?"

Iris paled even more, which Elise did not know was possible. At this point, she was ghostly white. "Y-yes. I have urged her to be seen by a doctor, but she refuses." Seeing their unconvinced expressions, Iris lowered her eyes to the floor and cleared her throat. "However, that is not why I came. My mother cannot know I am here. Not yet anyway."

Spill it! Elise could not stand the building tension in the other woman's unspoken message.

Iris lifted the small purse and removed a velvet-lined box.

Gavin inhaled sharply, taking Elise by surprise.

"What is it?" she asked.

"I've seen that box before," he answered, keeping his eyes glued on it. "Rona used it to connect with Vaughn."

Elise's brows drew together. "Where did you get that?" she asked Iris.

"It was delivered to me this morning," Iris said before retrieving a folded piece of paper from her purse. She held it out for Elise. "Along with this."

The note simply read, *Deliver this to Elise. She will know what to do with it. Do not open outside of Lockesbarrow.*

Iris handed Elise the box. Despite the warning, Elise tried to open the box anyway. When it would not budge, she groaned. *He spelled it.* As irritated as that prospect made her, Elise considered the risk he took to get it to her.

"Can you hold onto this for me?" she asked Gavin before approaching the frightened young girl. "I want to know what you're really doing here."

"I-I just told you," she stammered. "I wanted to deliver that to you. Now, I'm done. I can go."

Darcie and Mitch blocked the door.

"You're not going anywhere," Elise said.

"This is treason," Richard argued. "Guards!"

"She has you under a spell," Elise continued. "I'm sure of it, and I want to hear her confess as to why." Elise targeted Lady Iris with her thoughts. *Tell us why. What is really going on? Why are you here?*

Trapped against the wall, it took less than three attempts from Elise's powers before Lady Iris fell to her knees in hysterics. "I cannot take it anymore. I w-was sent to marry the prince for a forced alliance. Rona said she w-would kill my mother if I didn't. . .and me."

"So, you have no desire to take over and be queen?" Gavin asked.

She shook her head and looked at Richard. "I am sorry, Your Highness. I have tried to play the part, but I am not strong enough. I cannot take the guilt any longer. I am a mere singer tainted by the wrong family line."

Keep going. How do we end the curse? Elise put all her strength into keeping Iris talking.

"I am an embarrassment to my mother and uncle," Iris wailed, "and now to Rona, too."

Vaughn must have known she would do what she was told and hand over the box without question. I still question his motive.

Elise repeated her request for the curse to be broken. "End whatever control you have over him. Turn him back to his normal self."

Iris stood, sobbing, and tugged on a ring she wore. "Richard was given this during the contract meeting. It was tampered with beforehand, cursed, so that Richard would be convinced to give it to me and make me his bride." She placed it into Richard's palm and closed his fingers around it. "Use your magic to destroy it, and you will see the truth."

Richard looked from Iris to his fist. Hesitating, he squeezed it until a light appeared from his powers. When he opened his hand again, it vanished, and he fell to his knees unsteadily. Before anyone could help him, he was able to stagger into a standing position while using the wall to hold himself upright. When the effects of the spell completely left him, he was able to correct his posture.

"There, you are back to normal now," Iris whispered, sniffling without meeting his eyes. "I am so sorry."

"I have to go," was all Richard said, waiting for Mitch and Darcie to move before opening the door and slamming it shut behind him.

What do we do about Iris? Elise's question went unanswered as the young woman fled the room in a fresh bout of tears.

"That was crazy," Mitch said, looking at Elise. "Did you make her confess or did she give up that information on her own?"

Elise sighed. "Honestly, I think it was a little of both. She never wanted to be a part of any of this. I believe that."

The doctor returned at that moment, insisting they had stayed long enough and to let Ian sleep in peace.

Now, we just have to wait until our meeting with Eugena.

A few hours later, Elise lounged at a table with her friends in the back courtyard just outside the ballroom. Invited to play croquet with Joranna, Gwen, and the two princesses, Elise and her friends opted to watch instead. It was a perfectly decent way to pass the afternoon, given they had no other plans, yet every chime of the grandfather clock inside the castle reminded Elise of what was coming.

"Do you think we'll even make it to Lake Laulie?" Mitch asked out of the blue. He tore a piece of cake off his plate and plopped it into his mouth. "I'm just wondering. Mermaids hate humans after all. Who knows if that was really Eugena you talked to. It could have been bewitched separately or something."

"It was really her, Mitch," Darcie groaned, pinching the bridge of her nose. She tilted her head back on the chair. "Is it sunset yet?"

Gavin squinted up at the perfectly positioned sun as its rays warmed their faces. Not a cloud appeared in the bright blue sky. "I'd say not," he replied sarcastically as birds flew in and out of the garden ahead.

Elise sat upright in her chair as Richard walked towards the ladies' game. "Guys! Guys, look!" Shielding her eyes to get a better look, she ushered them out of their seats. "Come on. Let's see what's happening."

Royal etiquette thrown aside, Elise sprinted down to the lawn with the others on her heels.

Joranna was taken aback by their hastiness. "Elise, my goodness. You should really slow down, my dear."

The other ladies, engrossed in a whispering exchange, giggled excessively until Richard approached.

"I did not realize so many of you would be out here. Do not pause your merriment on my account," he pleaded. Clearing his throat, Richard paused to collect his thoughts. "I have done a great deal of thinking about what you all have shared. In light of the recent acts of treason, I have ended my betrothal and wedding to Lady Iris. I will not have her defamed in all this, but I thought it best to send her and her mother home. It was a mutual decision between Lady Iris and myself. Her mother's temper I cannot vouch for."

He shifted from one foot to the other and folded his hands behind him. "First, I should like to apologize to you, Mother. Ever since Iris was kind enough to withdraw her control over me, memories keep flooding back of my latest actions, and I cannot help but be appalled by them. You of all people deserve the utmost respect, and I will do whatever is needed to remedy that." He kissed his mother's hand and faced Sarah and Ruby. "I should next direct my apology to my siblings. Ian will need to hear this later, but you— come to think of it, Elise, the four of you as well—all tried to warn me about the path I was taking. I would not listen. It appears my stubbornness was present before the curse, so it only intensified its effects. It was still not fair to—"

"Is that my mother?" Gwen interrupted, squinting to gaze across the courtyard.

Following her line of vision, Elise was also shocked to see Ballard was indeed escorting Mrs. Archer and Talia towards them. *What are they doing here?*

"Ahh, good." Richard nodded. "Right on time." He ignored Gwen's confounded expression and greeted the two women upon their arrival. "Thank you for coming on such short notice."

Mrs. Archer blushed as Richard kissed her hand. "The honor is ours, Your Highness." She darted a motherly side glance at Gwen. "I do hope Gwendolyn has been conducting herself accordingly."

"Of course," Richard assured her. "In fact, the kingdom could do with more strong women like her."

Talia tossed an unconvinced glare in her sister's direction as Richard continued. "I am afraid I may have offended your daughter last night at the festival, and to my utmost embarrassment, this morning as well. My manners were abhorrent, but her quick wit challenged my arrogant ideals and put me in my place, rightfully so."

Talia broke out in an unflattering fit of laughter. "She told him off. Now, that I can believe."

Mrs. Archer sighed hopelessly at Gwen before addressing the prince. "Your Majesty, please excuse any impertinence on my daughter's part." For good measure, she also slapped Talia on the arm to silence her, too.

Richard chuckled. "There is no injury to report, madam." At this, he met and held Gwen's gaze. "But I am disgusted to have given such a poor first impression that I believe only a most sincere, grand gesture can atone for it." He checked over his shoulder before returning his attention to Gwen. His eyes softened with a brief smile. "I only hope this is enough of a token to prove how truly sorry I am and to beg your forgiveness."

Richard stepped aside, and in the distance six guards were escorting someone behind them. Only when they entered the clearing could the group see a frail older man shuffling to keep up, his clothing reduced to rags that hung off his bony frame. His hair, gray and stringy, blew ever so slightly in the breeze as a layer of sweat formed on his brow.

"Is that. . ." Talia trailed off, her eyes widening in shock. "Is that *Papa*?"

Mrs. Archer and Gwen grabbed each other's arms with a gasp.

"I have issued him a full pardon," Richard informed them. "Not that an innocent man, which he clearly is, needs it. However, he is the first in a long line of false arrests made under the last Captain of the Guard." He held out his arm.

Mrs. Archer, unable to wait a second more, lifted the front of her dress and hurried towards her husband. Gwen dropped her mallet, grabbed Talia's hand, and the two trotted closely behind their mother.

I don't believe it. After all this time.

Elise choked back a cry when she watched Mr. Archer lift his head and recognize his family running towards him. He quickened his step as fast as his feet and legs, though weak and shaky, could carry him. Mr. Archer hunched forward with outstretched arms as his openly weeping wife threw herself into them. They rocked back and forth in the tightest of embraces, only parting long enough to envelope their daughters upon their arrival.

"Thank you," Richard said to Elise's group as he watched the sentimental reunion. He smiled as the crying elderly man placed kisses on his wife and daughters' heads and equally soaked cheeks. "For not giving up on me."

Elise wiped away a tear of her own and leaned into Gavin's embrace. "I'm so happy for them."

The reunited family slowly made their way back to the royal family and teenagers. After bowing to Richard and the others, all but Gwen chatted happily with Joranna and her daughters while Gwen stepped aside to approach Richard.

Swiping a hand across her face, she could not help but break out in the most genuine of smiles. Her voice broke in a choked sob and her smile widened. "I cannot believe you did this."

"Indeed, Mr. Archer is a free man," replied the prince. "You will also be contacted about reclaiming your lost farm, including compensation for wages lost for the duration of your father's imprisonment. I hope you will find this to be enough to forgive me."

Closing her eyes, Gwen tightened her lips to suppress another sob as more warm tears streamed down her cheeks. When she opened them, it was as if to see the prince for the first time. "More than enough," she whispered. "Thank you."

Kiss her. Come on, kiss her.

From where Elise stood, her uncle and future aunt were certainly close enough. The sun's rays bouncing off the castle could not have created a more romantic ambience, and yet neither gave in to the temptation.

"Are you feeling well?" Gwen inquired. "I imagine being cursed to have your free will removed could be quite taxing."

He chuckled. "My pride is wounded, as expected. I have not only disgraced my late father, but nearly ruined the legacy of my family, and almost waltzed my kingdom into a hostile takeover."

Gwen rocked back and forth, her lips drawn into a thin line. "That is quite a long list of achievements."

"Indeed," he replied. "I only wish I can gain the respect and trust of my kingdom before it is too late."

She stared at his profile while his attention was on her family. "I know you will do the right thing. It appears you have a heart in there after all."

His chest rose and fell with a laugh.

Catching herself staring too long, Gwen cleared her throat and pretended to straighten out her dress. "I must tell my family the good news."

"Please extend my invitation for dinner this evening to your family. I hope they will accept." He lifted her hand and planted a tender kiss.

It's better than nothing.

The sappy, lopsided grin returned to her face. The sun lit her eyes perfectly as she regarded him warmly. "Thank you."

He stayed a moment longer, watching the family laugh and cry together before another guard rushed up to him out of breath.

"There is news, Sire," he panted. "An armada was reported not far off our coast. It was intercepted by the merpeople, but not without casualties on both sides. Erumann has been slain. Eugena has sent word she will still meet with the travelers." The guard sent a pointed stare at Elise, who looked back in shock.

"Poor Eugena," Joranna said. "What a devastating loss. I shall need to reach out to her."

"Can you contact Edith first?" Elise asked. "It is almost time for us to go. I'm worried we're already going to be late, and we'll need something we can run in." She whispered for Gavin to make sure he kept track of the box even after changing his clothes.

"I can help you get to Lake Laulie in time," Richard promised.

Joranna ushered Elise, Darcie, Mitch and Gavin inside to be properly fitted prior to their meeting with the mermaid queen.

CHAPTER 25

One key advantage of having Richard on their side again was his ability to transport them to Lake Laulie faster. Not only did they get the luxury of a carriage, but his willingness to use magic easily cut their travel time in half. Elise was particularly thankful for that last part, since they managed to arrive shortly before sunset.

"I don't like mermaids," Mitch said as the carriage lurched to a halt on the path. His face fell as he gazed at the water through the thin line of trees. "Have I mentioned that before? I *feel* like I have."

Pecking him on his cheek, Darcie pulled Mitch out of his seat.

Elise could not blame Mitch for his distrust of the merpeople. He nearly died at the hands of mermaids, and every encounter usually carried some form of a threat. Despite that, Elise had no choice but to trust them. Especially after all they sacrificed just that afternoon to help her family.

Six guards followed them to the lake while maintaining a safe distance. Already, the drifting clouds had taken on rich red and orange hues. The water itself, quiet and still, resembled a sheet of glass as it mirrored the breathtaking sight.

It would be difficult to look Eugena in the eye after losing Erumann. Deep down, Elise knew the relationship between the two was more than the queen let on. However, when the time came to call them, and Elise stirred the waters as Derek previously modeled, the queen was not present among the dozen or so who did rise above the surface.

A familiar mermaid, Lanai, beckoned them into the water. Gavin, Mitch, and Darcie ventured only as deep as their ankles while Elise stopped when the water reached her knees where Lanai waited.

Elise wished it could have been Eugena who greeted them, as planned, but with Erumann's death, she could not blame the queen for seeking solace in private.

"Please tell Eugena I'm so sorry," Elise whispered. "I never meant for anyone to get hurt, I. . .I was only trying to protect Haighdlen."

Lanai gave a solemn nod and held out a folded wet blade of seaweed for Elise to take. "As promised."

Elise paused, her gaze flickering between Lanai and the slimy offering. *What am I supposed to do with that?* Nevertheless, she reluctantly took it from the mermaid. Once her fingers touched the thin layers, freshly coated with grains of sand, Elise felt something moving inside. She tilted the clump of seaweed until what resembled four small oyster pearls rolled onto her palm.

As Lanai watched her expectantly, Elise's bewildered demeanor resulted in an awkward silence. Chewing her bottom lip, Elise tried seeking a response from Gavin, who only sent back a slight headshake.

"Eugena promised to send us to Lockesbarrow. What are these supposed to do?" Elise massaged the pearls around with her thumb.

Laughter and whispers spread among the surrounding merpeople, causing Elise's face to immediately flush.

What did I say? Is this a riddle I'm supposed to figure out? I don't get it.

Lanai's widening grin further intensified Elise's humiliation and bafflement. "We travel fastest *under* the water."

"You mean. . ." Elise touched her lips as her brain processed what had to be done.

Lanai nodded.

"No," Mitch called out. "Absolutely not. This falls under what they taught us in health class. There is *no* way I'm taking drugs from a mermaid."

Darcie scoffed. "No one is offering you drugs, Mitch."

"Well, what do you call it?" he challenged her. "They look like pills, don't they? Plus, I'm not good at swallowing pills. I can barely manage a vitamin."

"They're pretty small," Gavin reasoned. "It sounds like it's to help us not drown. Would you like to drown?" He waited until Mitch finally shook his head. "Then let's get this over with."

Wading back to the water's edge, Elise placed a pearl in each of their hands. Blowing out her cheeks, and releasing a breath, she counted down from three. They took turns swallowing, chasing the pearls down with a swig from a nearby guard's canteen.

Bracing herself for an immediate transformation, perhaps fins or even a tail, Elise could not help but feel underwhelmed standing and staring at her circle of friends while nothing happened.

"Have I mentioned I hate mermaids?" Mitch grumbled. "Not to mention, look around. It's a secluded lake. It doesn't lead any—" He trailed off, his voice growing hoarse. Mitch took a couple more shallow breaths before clawing at his throat.

"Are you choking?" Darcie shrieked, leaning down to check his face from where Mitch was bent over. "He's choking! Somebody do—" She lifted a hand to her own throat. Panic flooded her eyes.

Then Elise felt it.

What first felt like a tickle at the base of her throat soon grew until it felt like a wire comb scraping the sides of her esophagus. The sensation moved downward, clawing its way into her lungs until she was wheezing. She watched as Gavin fell to his knees beside her, splashing water against her leg. Mitch and Darcie also fell, gasping and shuddering to breathe. Somewhere within the depths of Elise's mind came a strange, instinctive plea, urging—no, *demanding*—she go underwater. She submerged herself, and within seconds, her friends also responded by dipping below the surface.

Going against human nature, Elise took the risk of inhaling a much-needed breath of water. Rather than drown her, it soothed the burning and tearing of tissue, and she felt her lungs swell to accommodate and filter the water rather than trap it. Bubbles scattered in all directions as she released another breath. Once her brain processed what was happening, convincing the rest of her body she was safe, Elise was able to fully open her eyes.

Despite its murkiness, she was able to see several feet in front of her. Not only could Elise make out her friends, who floated close by, but she could also see a distant light glowing below. Waving her friends on, she kicked hard enough to propel herself downward. Gavin passed her within a matter of seconds, and Elise kept him in sight. Darcie stayed at a similar pace with Mitch bringing up the rear. Water rushed in her ears, and all sounds were muffled. She was faintly aware of nearby merpeople passing by to guide them. One in particular waved impatiently for them to quicken their pace.

I'm so glad I'm not in a dress. I'd never make it. I'm not sure I'm going to make it. She briefly wondered if Mitch experienced anything like this when he was taken under before. Lake Laulie was much deeper than Elise ever imagined. There was no telling how deep Lake Mirage was when they saved him. The light grew brighter, closer, and compelled her further. Elise was not a particularly strong swimmer, and her heavy limbs ached by the time she reached the bottom where the light was coming from.

It was Eugena's staff, and Elise gasped when she realized the queen herself was waiting for them. She had come after all. Next to her, two enormous shells—Elise questioned if they belonged to some sort of magical sea turtle—rested, overturned, for them to board like underwater chariots.

This is insane! There is no way any of this is real. Elise opened her mouth to apologize, but Eugena held up a hand to silence her. The heartbroken queen nodded towards the shells, ushering them in. It was an awkward climb, but Elise and Gavin managed to board one shell while Mitch and Darcie took the second.

Elise turned around to attempt speaking one more time, but Eugena shook her head. The light from her staff brightened until all four of them had to shield their eyes from an intense flash.

All at once, the shells quaked beneath their feet, and a rumbling sound shook and disturbed the water. Surrounding fish scattered away in fear. Elise grabbed Gavin's arm with one hand while the other gripped the shell. Bits of broken rock and swirling sand further clouded the water around them before a deafening crack pierced their ears.

Crying out, Elise witnessed a whirlpool trail form ahead of them as the rocky barrier parted.

It's a portal!

Gavin wrapped an arm around her waist as they were pulled forward by a powerful current.

With one last desperate attempt, Elise opened her mouth, but all that escaped was a horrific scream as the queen pointed her staff forward. The two shells, illuminated in the same light, lunged forward into the spiraling path as if from a slingshot.

Elise did not know if it was water or wind rushing across her face, muffling all sounds except a deafening roar. Everything grew hazy until they were plunged into darkness, yet the shell twisted and turned as if they were on a rollercoaster. A sudden dip made Elise scream and reach out for Gavin again. The two clung to each other while trying to stay inside the surging shell. It moved at such a high speed that Elise struggled to move. She did not know how they would survive this. A high, screeching sound reached her ears next, reminding her of a train whistle, and within moments she felt the shell lurch out of the swirling current. Tremendous pressure built in Elise's ears as she watched Mitch and Darcie get spit out of the portal next. With only a minute to gain their bearings, the shells lifted upwards.

Higher and higher they climbed, until at last, there was a hint of shimmering light above them.

Is this thing speeding up?

They were indeed gaining speed, and the surface was approaching at a rapid pace. She could hear Mitch and Darcie yelling behind them.

"Brace yourself!" Gavin gargled into her ear, covering Elise with his own body.

With only half a second to respond, Elise ducked down as the shell broke through the surface with the force of a breaching whale. A wall of ocean spray burst all around them, landing in the shell and submerging their feet.

She and Gavin bobbed up and down on the choppy water, unable to see anything except what little light the full moon above provided. Pulling him forward, Elise crushed her lips to his, clinging desperately until it felt like they were joined. They parted when Darcie's and Mitch's shell erupted into view with a similar gust, creating more uneven waves.

"Is everyone okay?" Gavin called out, wrapping his arms around Elise.

Darcie hollered back from their own rocking vessel.

Elise breathed a sigh of relief until she realized Mitch was leaned over the side, retching into the water. *Poor thing. I'm surprised we all didn't get seasick after that wild ride.*

A sinking sense of dread settled in her stomach as Gavin and Darcie quickly followed.

What's going on? No sooner had the thought crossed her mind, Elise also lurched over the opposite side as Gavin. Initially, she could only dry heave, praying for whatever was causing the excruciating cramps coursing through her body to exit. *I don't want Gavin to see me like this.* She winced at the sound of him expelling the contents of his own stomach. Longing for the same release, her wish was granted when her muscles seized, and she vomited into the water. Out popped the pearl, still fully intact. It plopped into the water with a brilliant glow before sinking into the depths of the sea in which they found themselves stranded. Elise spluttered and wiped her chin with her sleeve before falling to her knees in exhaustion. Gavin followed suit, and both sat with their backs rested against each other.

"I'm with Mitch," panted Gavin, his voice weak and hoarse. "I hate mermaids."

"Can't blame you. That was miserable," Elise mumbled, tipping her head back against his shoulder. "Do you still have the box?" She felt him adjust behind her as he checked his pocket.

"Yeah," he said. "Do you want to try to open it now?"

Elise inhaled a fresh breath of air, held it, and blew out over several seconds. "In a minute. If it requires magic, I don't have the strength yet."

They continued riding the gentle waves in silence. Elise drifted in and out of sleep, losing track of time. Given the gentle rhythm of Gavin's breathing when she did open her eyes, he had also fallen asleep.

"Hey!" cried Darcie from the other shell, startling them both. "Look over there!"

Gavin and Elise rose to their knees. While difficult to see very far, they managed to follow the direction of Darcie's voice and finger pointing to a massive spread of mountainous land. Tiny lights, emitting from lanterns and shops, sent a surge of adrenaline through Elise's fatigued body.

Leaping to her feet, Elise bounced with excitement, causing the shell to rock back and forth unsteadily. "Gavin, look! She's right. That's Lockesbarrow, isn't it? It didn't take as long as I thought. We won't have to float in the middle of the ocean all night." When he did not reply, she did a double take over her shoulder and kneeled in front of him. "Gavin?"

"Yeah, great," he snapped, raking a hand through his sopping-wet hair. "Can't wait."

"Should we jump out and swim to the shore?" Mitch called.

Elise watched Gavin close his eyes and lean against the edge of the shell as if to make himself smaller. Crossing his arms, Gavin's chest rose and fell in quick succession until he was practically hyperventilating.

I know that look.

"Just a second!" Elise answered Mitch without taking her eyes off Gavin. Elise was then careful to make her voice as soft and soothing as possible. "What's going on?"

"Nothing."

"Gavin, it's *me*. You've talked me through more panic attacks than I can count, so I know how to spot one."

He flinched when she first took his hand but slowly yielded to her touch. Releasing a series of shallow breaths, Gavin managed to find his voice again. "Sorry."

"Don't be," Elise whispered. "Just tell me what's wrong. Are you hurt?"

He shook his head. "I can't explain it. S-seeing the coast, being back here. . .something flipped inside me. I d-don't know if I can go through it again."

She wilted. Never had he appeared so broken, or scarred, like a little lost boy. Elise empathized with the fear, having learned it was always worse inside the sufferer's mind than outside of it. Knowing words would not be sufficient, she pulled him forward into a hug.

He melted against her, squeezing Elise until she was short of breath. Rubbing small circles along his back, she waited for Gavin's heart rate to regulate, supporting him until he felt calm enough to let go of her.

It occurred to Elise in the five minutes or so it took to calm Gavin down they had not moved any closer to shore.

Did we stop?

The ocean swayed around them, but it was as if an invisible shield prevented the shells from floating closer.

"Guys, we're not moving anymore, and the waves are getting rougher!" Darcie yelled out at them. "I don't know how much longer we can stay in these shells before they capsize!"

Gavin scrambled to his feet. "Okay, we have to go. I think this is as far as Eugena is willing to help us."

"Yeah, but what about you?" Elise asked as he scanned their surroundings. "I can't ask you to go back if it's scaring you this much."

He scoffed with a forced smile. "Don't worry about me. Darcie's right. We're close enough now to swim and let the tide carry us in."

Gesturing for Mitch and Darcie to follow, Gavin grabbed Elise's hand as both leaped into the dark water.

If there was a protective shield, it vanished once they all plunged into the water. Almost immediately, many approaching waves doubled in size, rising and falling around them. Every time Elise could get a deep enough breath, another wave would crash and send her reeling in the dark underwater. More than once, she crashed against the ocean floor. Clawing at the sand, she kicked off and steadied herself again and again while barely managing to suck in enough air above water.

When the waves calmed long enough for her to tread water, Elise was relieved when the others popped their heads up as well.

Thank goodness, they're still alive. I don't know how much longer we can survive out here.

"We're almost there!" Mitch yelled over the breaking waves. "We've come too far to get eaten by sharks now."

Beaten, exhausted, and heavy under the weight of the tide, Elise floated on her back while there was a reprieve to conserve her energy. Would they ever catch a break? Why did everything have to be life-threatening, one right after the other? It was enough to make giving up more tempting than ever.

"We can't quit," Gavin warned her. "You have to keep trying. Rest when we get washed to shore. It's not that far now."

Alternating between swimming and treading, they finally approached the shore. Elise said a prayer of thanks when her feet touched the ground and she could walk.

Dragging themselves from the ocean, the friends choked and spit up the water they ingested before collapsing in a heap on the sandy beach.

Elise checked on everyone, unsure of her own ability to stand now that she was resting. She wrinkled her nose as she bit down on grains of sand between her teeth. Numbness spread through her sand-covered arms and legs. Yet, an even bigger part of Elise was just thankful to be on land again.

Once recovered, she asked for Gavin to hand her the velvet-lined box. "Please tell me you still have it."

He fished inside his pocket and retrieved it, looking as shocked as her that it remained intact. "Vaughn said wait until we were in Lockesbarrow, so let's hope it still works."

Elise took it from Gavin, gasping when the lid opened with ease. *He must have spelled it to only work here.* Her brows furrowed when she gazed down at the light brown locks of hair. *It's completely dry inside.* Pinching pieces of hair between her fingers, she looked expectantly at Gavin. "How did Rona use this?"

He hummed in thought as he tried to remember. "She talked to it."

"Excuse me?" Elise asked.

"No, not like that. Like an incantation. Then it started to glow and showed a sort of live feed in Vaughn's head. I couldn't make out what she said, but you could probably use your powers to activate it."

"It's worth a shot," Darcie said. "We've come this far. It's our only chance to make it work."

"We didn't go through that portal of death for nothing," Mitch added. "And you got that other diary to work."

"Yeah, but I had fairy magic to help me," Elise countered.

"Vaughn wanted you to have it for a reason," Darcie pressed on.

Elise shook her head. "Which doesn't make any sense. Whose side is he on?"

"Who cares?" Darcie snapped irritably. "Now, hurry up. It's driving me crazy!"

Elise lifted the hair near her lips and focused on finding Vaughn. *Where is he? Show us.* This went on for ten minutes, all the while making Elise feel more foolish with every attempt.

"Ugh, it's no use!" she growled, tossing the hair back into the box.

"You're not trying hard enough," Darcie accused. "Vaughn wouldn't make it easy in case it got intercepted. Now, try again."

Elise glared at her best friend with an indignant huff. *Who does she think she is? How would she know what it takes? I don't see her with any powers.* "I'm doing my best!"

"Guys, relax," Gavin said. "We're all exhausted but turning on each other isn't going to help. Now, Elise, please try again."

After apologizing, both girls quieted as Elise sat up straighter and brought the box up to her mouth. *Show me Vaughn. Take me there. What does he want me to see?*

She jumped when the hair began to glow. In her mind, Elise was immediately transported into a throne room with four figures talking in secret. Gasping, she opened her eyes and relayed it to the others.

"It's working!" Gavin leaned closer. "Keep it up."

"You can do this, Elise," Darcie encouraged.

Elise clenched her eyes shut, willing the vision to show more. This time, a different light flickered from the hair, creating a winding trail towards the ocean. Crawling closer to the water's edge, enough for sea foam to wash over her hands and knees, Elise gasped as the light hovered over a small collection of shells. She brushed the shells away to make a hole. As the water washed into it, the same vision came to life before them in the small pool. At first, only the dark figures could be seen.

"Concentrate, Elise," Gavin groaned, waiting eagerly for the rippling image to focus.

Elise pinched the hair again, forcing her mind to think of nothing but finding out where Vaughn was. It mentally took a toll on her, but she could not let her friends down after what they all risked to get there. With a brilliant flash, more details came into view, including another approaching figure.

"Who is that guy?" Mitch asked, watching as a man entered into view.

"That has to be her brother," Gavin said. "We're seeing what Vaughn is seeing—or saw. Who knows when this actually happened."

"Okay, I see Rona!" Darcie exclaimed. "Who is she talking to?"

"Why can't we hear anything?" Mitch also questioned.

Slowly but surely, the figures grew closer as Vaughn moved throughout the room. As he neared, Elise's heart sank when Iris glanced at him over her shoulder.

"This happened today," groaned Elise. "Iris is wearing the same gown she was this morning. I'm guessing that's Brahm and her mom with her."

"What?" Mitch shrieked as sat up on his knees. "How does Iris and her mom get an instant trip while we had to be dragged through Poseidon's butt to get here?"

Elise covered her nose as an unexpected snort escaped while laughing. Darcie tousled his hair with a giggle of her own before pointing at the scene for him to pay attention.

"Mitch, you're not helping," Gavin laughed. "We had to make it without being detected."

"Forget being detected." Mitch dusted the sand off his hands. "That settles it. I'm about to work for Rona. If nothing else, for the benefits."

As Rona came closer into view, following Vaughn's movements, Darcie shushed the others. "Wait, I think I can hear something!"

They crouched down closer to the small pool.

Elise heard Vaughn groan, assuming she had tapped fully into his head, creating the inevitable migraine.

"Are you ill?" Rona called out to him.

Vaughn hesitated. "N-no, My Queen." His voice took on an echo as the rest of his message came in the form of his thoughts. "*Stay silent. Do not speak, no matter what happens.*"

Elise shivered in response, exchanging an anxious glance with her friends. She knew better than to ignore Vaughn's warning. *He knows something is going to happen.*

"Forget him, Rona. What do you mean the engagement is cancelled?" Dmitri demanded of Ingrid.

"The crown prince had a change of heart, Your Majesty," Ingrid informed him. "I can assure you, there is nothing wrong with my daughter."

Elise noted with a grateful heart that Iris remained silent about her involvement.

"Well, there is something bloody the matter with her!" Dmitri snarled. "Has she been compromised?"

Straightening her posture, Ingrid placed hands on Iris's shoulders. "Certainly not!"

"My niece's honor remains intact," Brahm assured the king. "We are still investigating what caused the sudden shift."

The king paced back and forth before facing his sister. "Rona, this man and his family came highly recommended. You assured me keeping the Brahm family close would secure an alliance between our kingdoms. The prince's public display of forgiveness and the peaceful union was to call Prisha out of hiding. I was promised all these things!"

"Careful of your tone, Brother," Rona warned. "For it was *I* who disrupted the fabric of time to deliver you to the throne." She took a step closer to him, her voice falling to a whisper. "You have missed much over the years, Dmitri, including all my hard work to claim this kingdom for us."

"I wish to rule with Prisha by my side," Dmitri argued. "You promised me she would reign as my queen."

"Forget your childish fairy tale life, Brother!" Rona hissed. "She is old, lost, and forgotten—conceivably dead, as you once were. I said what I needed to forward our plans." The sorceress spun on her heel to glare at the three onlookers. "And all was going according to the plan until this morning. *Why*!" Her voice echoed around the chamber, making Iris visibly jump. "Was it you? Did you suddenly grow a brain and try to sabotage me?"

"I can assure you, Highness, my daughter would never interfere in your plans."

Rona rolled her eyes. "I am getting quite tired of you speaking for her. Is she mute?"

"Leave the girl alone, Rona," Dmitri growled. "We have our own business to settle."

Rona's face split into a wide malicious grin. "I believe I stated our business is concluded, Brother. We will go on ruling as we are."

"You killed her. Is that it?" he accused. "Did you murder her as you did her parents? All for the sake of some pathetic power trip?"

Rona pinched the bridge of her nose. "I forgot how insufferably righteous you could be."

"If I may," Brahm spoke up, "in light of the recent defeat of your armada, and the return of the travelers—Elise in particular, perhaps the cancellation is a blessing in disguise. Erumann's death is a victory in and of itself that speaks volumes of your power."

"But it is not enough!" Rona huffed, her veil of composure dwindling as she turned her temper on Iris. "All this idiot had to do was distract the prince long enough for Haighdlen to begin destroying itself from the inside."

Silence followed.

"That reminds me," offered Ingrid timidly. "The youngest prince was critically injured during one of your desired protests. Does that not count for something?"

"But he did not die, did he?" Rona challenged. "If nothing else, without his eldest brother under our control, their insipid little family is stronger than ever since Derek's death. Considering how meddlesome those parasitic travelers are, they were involved in this somehow. I know not Elise's full relation to the Laurilles, but Laurille blood flows through her veins, nonetheless. Speak girl!" Her cold, severe stance towered over Iris's cowering form. "I demand you tell me what you did to ruin this."

Tears spilled from Iris's eyes. She looked between her mother and uncle.

"She's only a child," Ingrid reasoned. "Iris could hardly bring such ruin upon your Highness's legacy."

Rona took a step back and regarded Ingrid with indifference. "I thought I made it quite clear to let this spineless excuse of a woman speak for herself."

"But she—"

Whatever Ingrid planned to say was cut short as Rona gripped her neck. A jolt of light shot out of Rona's fingers, rendering Brahm's sister speechless. When the sorceress released her, she was already dead before her body collapsed on the floor.

Brahm and Iris cried out, falling to Ingrid's lifeless form with desperation and shock.

"How could you?" Iris screamed, attempting to lunge for Rona before Brahm grabbed her arm.

Rona quirked an unimpressed brow. "Oh, now find your voice. I confess, I preferred you silent."

"My Queen," Brahm spluttered, releasing Iris to hold his sister's hand. "After all my loyalty. . .everything I have done. . .what threat did she pose to you?"

"None, whatsoever," Dmitri admonished. "Rona, cease this tantrum, immediately, or—"

"Or what?" Rona chuckled. "You are not the brains nor the power behind this war. You are a puppet, brother, meant for nothing other than to bait the other leaders."

"You do not mean that," replied the king. "Love is in your heart, despite what your sinister mouth spews."

Rolling her eyes, the sorceress ignored her brother and sneered down at her feet. "Save your blubbering, Brahm. She served no real purpose." Advancing on the two mourning souls, with Iris's weeping nearly drowning out the queen's words, Rona glared down with contempt. "I want this to serve as your warning. A great deal rides on your unwavering allegiance. I have no doubt the Laurilles are concocting a plan, and I will not be a sitting target when they strike. Now, get up. We have work to do."

"I cannot," Brahm sobbed, watching his niece cover Ingrid's body with her own. "Oh, sister."

"Brahm, honestly, this is path—" Rona stiffened, sniffing the air suspiciously. Ignoring the bizarre looks the rest of the occupants gave her, she spun slowly around and scanned the room. "Someone is watching us."

Elise's blood ran cold when Rona's eyes landed on Vaughn. Panicking, she thrust a hand into the pool, disturbing the connection until it vanished completely. She asked Gavin to put the box back into his pocket.

The teenagers sat staring at one another in stunned silence.

"Do you think she knows it was us?" Darcie asked.

Elise shook her head and shrugged. *I don't know. I hope Vaughn is okay.*

"Poor Iris," Elise said. "I didn't like Ingrid, but having to watch her mom die like that. . ."

Gavin groaned and stretched his neck. "At least some good came out of watching that. It doesn't sound like Rona and Dmitri are as close as we assumed they were."

Mitch scoffed. "Yeah, the guy actually has a conscience."

Darcie clicked her tongue. "But he's still alive at a time he shouldn't be. That complicates things. I mean, it's one thing for Elise to want to save Charles and Liam from dying in the future, but Rona just plucked Dmitri out and placed him randomly on the throne without making sure everything else was stable."

"Yeah," Mitch agreed. "I doubt she considered him opposing her methods."

"She stopped his death, but not what led up to it." Gavin massaged his eyes. "If we don't stop her, then we risk the same thing happening. Even if we manage to protect Charles and Liam from dying during a future attack in our present time, every day Rona rules increases the odds of it happening sooner. We can't leave Lockesbarrow until she's stopped."

Elise's heart sank as she realized they were out of time. When the moment came for her to kill Rona, she could only hope her friends would not interfere.

"I don't think we're leaving Lockesbarrow anytime soon," Mitch whimpered.

Elise and the others gasped as a group of hooded figures surrounded them with swords and bows pointed in their direction.

CHAPTER 26

Elise's heart thrashed wildly inside her chest. Blindfolded, her wrists bound, she stumbled aimlessly at the mercy of their captives. Would they be taken to the castle? Or worse, prison? Elise's intrusive thoughts spread through her mind like a virus, conjuring up gruesome images of torture and warfare.

She did not know how long or far they walked, but when the blindfolds were removed, Elise, Gavin, Mitch, and Darcie saw that they were deep inside a forest at a campsite. All the soldiers were young, similarly dressed in torn, ragged uniforms, and many were crowded around the fire talking. Others trained with swords in the distance. As they were led forward, Elise sensed more and more eyes on her by the second until the surrounding soldiers all but trapped them in a large circle.

"Is this where you were?" she asked Gavin. "In one of these camps?"

Gavin shook his head. "No, this is different. This is something else." He scanned the area. "There aren't any officers and not nearly enough tents or weapons."

"We captured some prisoners for the captain," announced one of the soldiers flanking Elise and her friends.

A lone figure emerged from the assembled bystanders. He could not have been much older than Elise, yet she felt intimidated by his muscular presence. With a struggling mustache and overgrown shaggy hair that fell past his shoulders, the young man narrowed his eyes at them one at a time.

"You're a captain?" Gavin asked, eyeing the same rips and tears on the young man's shirt and trousers.

"Honorary captain." The boy shrugged with a menacing smile. "What do we have here?"

"We found them by the ocean's edge, sir," reported the soldier holding Darcie. "We think they're royal spies."

"It's been a long time since I've seen a girl this close." The captain leered at Darcie until Mitch pulled at his restraints. He laughed. "Taken, I see."

Elise scoffed. "We aren't spying for Rona."

"What little we did hear says otherwise," said the boy holding a fistful of her tunic. "They were deep in conversation about the queen's plans."

A disapproving murmur radiated through the crowd of soldiers with many calling for their deaths.

"That's because we're trying to stop her and save the boys in her army," Gavin said over the commotion. "It's the only reason I'd ever come back here. Believe me."

"Wait a minute," said the captain, raising his arm for silence. "Bring me a torch." Flexing his hand impatiently, he snatched the nearest one offered. Lifting his arm, the captain inspected Gavin closely. So close, in fact, that Gavin had to lean away and still the torch remained mere inches from his face.

What is he doing?

Elise watched as the captain's expressions transitioned from skeptic to shocked, and finally jubilant as recognition dawned on his face.

"I cannot believe it," said the captain. "Is that you, Gavin?"

Gavin's brows furrowed as he regarded the other man. "Do I know you?"

"I certainly know you," the captain laughed before addressing the crowd. "How fortunate we are, men! Gavin Striess is among our number again!"

The once hostile crowd erupted in cheers and shouts, taking Elise off guard. "What's going on?" she asked.

Gavin shrugged. "I don't know."

"'I don't know', he says." The captain laughed, amping up the other boys around him.

"Are you famous or something, Gav?" asked Mitch, wary of the surrounding soldiers pressing in around them.

"He's more than that, mate," jeered the captain. "Gavin's a legend among our ranks. He could barely hold a sword, but I have yet seen anyone stand up to Rona the way he did. A true hero, he was, and vowed to save us all. Now, he's returned among us vigilantes."

"Vigilante?" Gavin surveyed the campsite. "So, you're not part of Rona's army?"

"Some may call us runaways, deserters, or rebels." The captain winked at Elise, who stepped behind Gavin. "I prefer defiant militia. Long live Queen Prisha!" Chortles and murmurs rang out amongst the group, escalating to shouts of allegiance and battle cries as the captain pumped his fist in the air.

"Quite the poet," Darcie quipped.

"Call me Drebson," said the captain. "I was also a member of Isaac's unit while you served here." He shook Gavin's hand and clapped him on the back.

"Isaac?" Elise asked.

"He's one of the commanding officers," Gavin informed her.

"*Was*," Drebson corrected. "He was killed in a local raid about ten miles from here."

Elise paled as she studied Gavin's unreadable expression.

"What about. . ." Gavin swallowed a lump in his throat. "What about others from that unit?"

"Many of us belong here now," boasted Drebson. "We have lost a few, but that's the price of war. Am I right?"

Gavin's face fell, and Elise wondered if he was thinking of specific members. Yet, he did not ask for them by name. Perhaps he did not fully trust the captain.

"Forgive my manners, mate," continued the captain. "Release them. Any friends of Mr. Striess are friends of ours, and you must stay with us tonight. I can offer you no better protection or company in all of Lockesbarrow."

There was little reason to turn down a hot meal and a place to sleep while they formulated a plan. Within the hour, the four friends were given seats closest to the fire to get warm and dry.

Mitch poked at the contents of his dinner. "I don't want to be rude, but what's in this?"

With a polite smile, Darcie took a tentative bite. "It's very chewy."

"Leftover squirrel stew," said a boy about thirteen years old.

Darcie released what was in her mouth back into the bowl.

"It's an acquired taste," agreed a slightly older soldier beside him. "Sometimes we get spare potatoes and biscuits from sympathetic locals. Our supply is low, I'm afraid."

Elise fell into despair, trying to find joy with her company, but all she could think about was facing Rona. Magic would not be enough. She needed fighting experience. Regardless of Rona's unspeakable atrocities, there was still the matter of Elise having to willingly take someone else's life. Elise groaned with nausea as she forced herself to eat. Choking down the stew, her attention was drawn to Gavin, who absentmindedly twisted the medallion between his fingers as he stared into the fire deep in thought. "You're thinking about your other friends, aren't you? The soldiers."

Gavin nodded, his own stew forgotten. "If Isaac could get killed so easily, anything could have happened to them."

"They could be here," Mitch offered as someone brought him a second helping.

"We had a large enough introduction," Gavin argued. "They would've heard or seen us. I've lost sleep over it—seeing their faces at night. . .I promised to help. It was the one duty I took seriously."

Elise ran her hand along his back. "You can't beat yourself up, Gavin. Whatever happened is not your fault."

"She's right," Mitch said. "And you did something right. These guys hold you on a pedestal. If we don't make it home for some reason, you could have a future here."

Gavin drummed his fingers together and hung his head. "You joke but being stuck in this place made me start taking my life more seriously." His eyes glassed over as he stared into the flames. "I've decided when we get home to go talk to a recruiter."

What!

"That's deep, man," Mitch replied. "Your dad will be proud."

What about me? Elise silenced her selfish thoughts. She had no right to be mad at Gavin for not disclosing his plans to her sooner. After all, she still had not told him the truth about what would happen to her when she killed Rona.

Sensing the growing discomfort, Gavin shifted the conversation to include the others. "What about y'all? What are you guys doing after graduation? Darcie, I know you're getting your license for cosmetology."

Elise only half listened to her best friend list the places she was thinking of applying to with plans of opening her own salon one day. It wasn't that she didn't care. She had already heard it from Darcie several times already. Instead, she watched Gavin, who she felt like was avoiding her gaze on purpose. Did he expect her to be upset? Hurt? The truth was that his news was painful to hear, but not one part of Elise wanted to dash his dreams. She could not expect him to choose her over a lifetime of security, duty, and honor. In fairness, hearing the way he spoke made her respect him all the more.

"Mitch?" Darcie asked. "Did you decide yet?"

Mitch shrugged. "For the longest time, I assumed I'd go into engineering, but the last year or so I started considering culinary school."

"You'd be a great at that." Darcie smiled. "I bet my dad could let you shadow him in his bakery this summer. Maybe even an intern."

"I'd like that," said Mitch, taking her hand before looking at Elise. "What about you?"

Elise normally shied away from discussing futures. Truth be told, the future frightened her. Since it was only her and Ruby, she often felt obligated to stay near home to help out. She had held little jobs here and there to bring in some extra money, but the idea of college and careers always seemed limited. Now that she knew Ruby had family closer to home, including Joranna and Ian, and hopefully a brighter future if their mission succeeded, it broadened Elise's possibilities. Taking a moment of reflection, she considered what she wanted to dedicate her life towards.

"I don't know, really," she confessed, drawing lines in the dirt with the toe of her boot. "I want to help people and make a difference, but I don't have the stomach to do anything in the medical field."

"That's okay. What are some hobbies you enjoy?" Mitch offered.

She thought long and hard about her life back home. "I really like working with people. I volunteered in Darcie's mom's classroom a couple of times and really loved it. Something about being with the kids and seeing them learn was really fun."

"Sounds like you'd be a great teacher," Gavin suggested with an encouraging smile.

Mitch nodded around a bite of stew.

"And you have the patience for it," Darcie praised. "I know I sure don't."

If things were different, I think I could really like teaching. She feigned excitement about her career choice, not having the heart to break the news to Gavin despite Darcie's pointed look across the fire. At least Darcie was playing along for now, but Elise knew it was a matter of time before the truth came out. She did not want to spend what was most likely her last night alive fighting or persuading. Elise just wanted this—to sit with her friends and laugh. More importantly, to trick herself into thinking this is how things would always be.

They continued talking late into the night. At one point, a group of soldiers and Gavin helped teach her to hold a sword along with some basic moves. Elise's favorite part, however, was snuggling and making out with Gavin alone by the fire after many, including Mitch and Darcie, had gone to bed. Elise studied every curve of his face, each freckle, and made sure she told him every chance she got that she loved him.

"We should probably get some sleep," he murmured against her ear from where they lay spooning.

She opened her eyes and stared into the fire, much like Gavin had done earlier that evening. Never in a million years did she think they would get as lucky as to have this chance together to relax and enjoy one another's closeness. Being invited to spend the night in a safe campsite with a fun crowd was not on her radar for the evening, yet it was precisely what she needed. Elise nodded at his suggestion and stretched as Gavin planted soft kisses along her neck. After all, the real world had to come first at some point. She prayed Gavin's dreams would come true and accepted the harsh reality that she would have to give hers up.

He deserves a happy life, even if it's not with me.

A tent was pitched for the girls and one for the boys. Stopping by Gavin's first, he rolled his eyes as the sound of Mitch's snoring was already protruding from inside.

Elise giggled. "I love you."

"I love you, too."

They bid one another good night and crawled into their tents.

The night passed peacefully enough, but it felt like only five minutes passed when cries and warnings pulled her out of sleep. It awoke Darcie as well, who pulled the flap of the tent up and peered out. The fire was extinguished, apart from smoking embers. "What's going on?"

A soldier stopped in front of their tent. "Our watchmen just delivered the news. There are approaching fleets with Haighdlen and Vynchian flags. We are dispatching some of our members to greet them, but we've lost contact with a few rebels and the Masked Lady was spotted in the forest."

"Masked Lady?" Elise asked.

The soldier nodded. "She looks after us, leaving food and weapons, but no one's met her. If she's been seen, it means there's trouble from—" He lurched forward as an arrow pierced his back.

Darcie and Elise screamed as he fell to the ground. As they exited the tent, they witnessed a horrific sight. Pots and pans were thrown and kicked, tents burned, swords clashed, and cries filled the air as young formally uniformed soldiers ravaged through the camp.

It's an ambush!

Clamoring out of the tent, Darcie and Elise came face to face with Gavin, Mitch, and Drebson.

"Get away from here," said the captain, who already had blood running down the side of his face. "Head into the forest! Go as deep as you can!"

Whirling around to follow orders, they halted as a group of soldiers carrying swords and Lockesbarrian flags entered the burning campsite. Elise and the others stared in horror as Rona and King Dmitri followed with Brahm and Vaughn flanking them. Even further back, one of the uniformed guards gripped Iris's arm. The young woman was dragged forward with a petrified stare, bound and gagged.

We need to save her.

Elise's breath hitched when she met Rona's stare. Gavin squeezed her hand, which was the only thing keeping Elise from passing out.

Rona remained poised, as if unaware of the mayhem occurring around them. "Elise," she said sweetly. "I wish I had known you would be here, dearest. So good of you to visit. Have you met my brother, King Dmitri?"

"He's not the real king!" Drebson snarled. "A brother and sister both trying to be king and queen at the same time is disgraceful. Prisha is the rightful queen and always has been."

Rona nodded at the closest guard standing by her, who closed the distance and skillfully disarmed Drebson with little effort. A true assassin. Elise turned her face into Gavin's chest as the soldier slashed the captain with his own sword.

"Are these the travelers?" the king asked casually, as if they were nothing more than spectators at a sporting event. "The ones you told me about?"

Elise paled, recalling the scene she witnessed the night before.

"Yes, brother. They are the ones I told you about. The ones responsible for Prisha's disappearance."

What? "We had nothing to do with that!" Elise shrieked. "We haven't even met her!"

"Quite sad how they lie so easily. Especially Elise." Rona shook her head and feigned disappointment. Clicking her tongue, she clapped her hands together. "Do you not see, Dmitri? She will not be satisfied until she takes the throne for herself. We cannot allow that."

As Gavin, Mitch, and Darcie were apprehended, and forced to watch, Elise was left standing helplessly alone as the king's face hardened with rage. She found his eyes devoid of emotion as he nodded for Vaughn to step forward. *He's going to kill me. I can't breathe.*

CHAPTER 27

"Kill her," Dmitri ordered.

Gavin fought to free himself from the guard's hold, but it was no use. Also held against their will, Darcie and Mitch cried out, too.

"Elise, use your magic!" Darcie insisted.

"Yes, use your magic," Rona mocked with a chuckle before encouraging Vaughn to follow the order.

Elise's head swam as she swayed off balance, watching Vaughn saunter forward to kill her. She suspected his aid was only a ploy to lead them here. This is how she would die. Everything they had worked towards would all end here. Rona had won. Elise braced herself, inwardly spiraling at the thought of never seeing Gavin, Darcie, or Mitch again. Of never seeing her family again. It was all for nothing. The prophecy, Derek's untimely death, her family's estrangement. . .none of it would change. Rather than succumb to an expected panic attack, Elise took a shallow breath and met Vaughn's eyes. *Will it hurt? Will it be quick?* All these questions raced through Elise's mind along with memories as her adrenaline spiked. Try as she might, Elise was unable to sustain her external resolve. Warm tears burst through her brave facade, cascading down her cheeks without any sign of stopping. Elise made a few feeble attempts to muster her magic without success before falling to her knees.

A cry caught in her throat. Through burning eyes, her vision blurred, Elise could make out his boots inching closer. Hanging her head, she jumped when the toe of one of his boots lifted her chin. He gestured with his gloved hands for her to rise. *He's really going to draw this out. I am going to suffer so much. It's going to hurt so badly. I want it over with. Please get it over with. I can't take it.*

Without an ounce of hope, she pled with bloodshot eyes for him to spare her. Rather than reach for his sword, Vaughn took a few steps back. His gaze darted back and forth.

He looks distracted. What is he staring at?

Elise did not bother to hide her confusion, nor did Dmitri and Rona, who shared a wary glance behind him.

What is he going to do?

Releasing an embarrassing sniveling sound, Elise wiped tears away with her sleeve. Her arms were anvils, every muscle ached, and her legs felt unsteady as she willed herself to stand.

Facing her killer, Elise took a deep breath and closed her eyes.

And then. . .

Nothing.

Elise peeked to find Vaughn still watching her. Only when she opened both eyes did she see his mouth form one single, silent word.

Run.

Was he really trying to save her? *What about my friends?* Knowing she could not help them if she were dead, Elise did not stop to ask or focus on anything except getting away. Turning on her heel, she raced toward the forest amidst cries from her friends to run as fast as she could. A blast of magic shot to her left. Dodging right, she headed deeper into the cover of trees.

"You fool!" Rona shrieked.

Elise chanced a look over her shoulder as Vaughn blasted similar magical blasts at the guards holding Gavin, Darcie, and Mitch, who all took off running in the same direction as her.

"Out of my way!" Rona commanded, slamming Vaughn into the nearest tree with a burst of magic. However, as she reached the forest's edge in pursuit of Elise and her friends, a series of arrows shot from the top of the tallest tree at the guards. The closest ones ran to shield the king, who cowered under their cover. One by one, they were struck, until the final arrow came from the ground level, striking Dmitri in the back.

"No!" Rona cried, running back to her brother. The sorceress threw herself over him, repeating his name, and urged him to look at her.

Elise paused until her friends caught up.

"What are you doing? Go!" Mitch bellowed.

Is he really dead? Though she had gained a sizeable distance, Elise peered through hanging vines until she could faintly see Rona. Brahm was once again by her side.

"Show yourselves!" Rona demanded to the open silence around her, scanning the area for the slightest movement.

Dmitri's body staggered, redirecting Rona's attention before landing heavily at Brahm's feet.

Brahm kneeled to check his pulse, hesitated, and met Rona's gaze with a grim expression.

Throwing her head back, Rona let out a shrill, piercing scream. The unnerving sound echoed throughout the forest, disturbing birds and creatures who fled, and affecting all others who could hear. Surrounded by other dead bodies of her guards, she gave attention only to her brother. Reaching down, she lifted trembling fingers to close Dmitri's eyes before glaring at Vaughn, who limped into view. "Gather more guards. Find the travelers! I will make them suffer for this! I will deal with you after. Now, get out of my way!"

Gavin tugged Elise's hand to keep going. She heard Vaughn cry out, but there was no time to go back. They needed to get away.

Who attacked them? She searched the trees as they ran but could see no movement.

"Keep going!" Darcie screamed. "Someone's chasing us!"

Her cry made Elise check over her shoulder in time to see two soldiers appear from behind trees. They were gaining, yet all Elise could do was concentrate on not tripping and giving them an easy target. She became acutely aware of the wind in her ears as both knees threatened to buckle. It was no easy feat trying to keep up with Gavin, who now led the way past the jagged forest trees. Her chest burned, begging Elise to stop for air, but she did not want to be responsible for stalling them. It was difficult enough dodging sharp thorns and low-hanging branches without her slowing everyone down.

She gasped as a third lunged out of the bushes, taking Gavin down with him. "Gavin!"

The two men struggled, rolling around at her feet as Mitch and Darcie caught up. In less than a minute, Gavin was pinned to the ground.

Please, don't hurt him! Elise's breath hitched as Gavin braced for an attack.

"Is that really the best you can do?" the soldier asked with a lighthearted chuckle.

Gavin scoffed in disbelief as the other young man removed his helmet.

Elise stared at the soldier, who appeared to be similar in age to her and Gavin. She noted the disheveled forest green uniform and fresh cuts against his light brown skin.

"Everett?" Gavin asked.

"We feared you dead." Everett smiled with ease before leaping to his feet and helping Gavin to stand. "Looks like I just won a bet."

"Then that means. . ." Gavin trailed off, watching as the other two soldiers removed their helmets. One was noticeably shorter, and younger, with a mop of unkept hair, while the other was tall, poised, and more athletic despite a pale, sickly complexion.

Elise furrowed her brows, watching an initial calamitous moment descend into what she could only describe as some sort of reunion. *How does he know these guys? Who are they?*

"This is insane. I've been trying to find my way back here to help you guys." Gavin took the time to introduce Elise, Mitch and Darcie to his friends from when he was recruited into Rona's camp. Everett, Erick, and Tristan greeted them in return. "I can't believe you found us."

"The other rebels told us of their meeting with you," Tristan said. "We've been tracking you all morning with help from the Masked Lady, of course."

So, that's *Tristan.* She remembered Gavin telling her he was the best soldier, though not always the friendliest.

"It paid off," Erick beamed, raking a hand through his unruly dark hair.

"Masked Lady?" Mitch asked, sharing an uneasy look with Darcie. "Why don't I like the sound of that?"

The boys chuckled.

"She is a true legend here," Everett explained. "Rescuing soldiers, such as ourselves."

"How did you escape?" Gavin asked.

"You are not the only defiant soldier," Tristan replied with a smirk.

Elise marveled at the way Gavin's entire demeanor changed around these young men. It occurred to her that it had only been days for Gavin, but months had spanned in this timeline. She had no idea what they went through, but it clear to anyone with a pulse that there was a bond that ran incredibly deep. Not wanting to interrupt, she took a step back to stand beside Mitch and Darcie. When Gavin noticed, she waved away his offer to join them, but took the opportunity to point at Gavin's neck.

Understanding dawned on his face.

"Oh! I have something for you," said Gavin, pulling off the medallion and holding it out for Tristan to take.

Elise watched an array of emotions play across the soldier's face.

The little color that Tristan did possess vanished from his face as he froze. His mouth parted, but no sound came out. His eyes glistened with memories as his mind wandered far away from the forest. At last, he finally accepted and donned it around his own neck. "I did not expect to see this again." Twirling it between his fingers, Tristan cleared his throat and nodded at Gavin. "Thank you."

Warm tears pricked the edges of Elise's eyes as the two young men shared a brief hug and handshake.

"How sentimental." Rona's sarcastic, droning voice cut through the heartfelt moment.

Elise's heart stopped as she whirled around to see Rona, Brahm, and Vaughn flanked by a handful of new guards. Thankful to see Vaughn still alive, she was surprised to see him still standing given his haggard, beaten appearance.

Tristan pulled his sword from its sheath, prompting Everett and Erick to do the same. As the tips of their blades met Vaughn's and Brahm's in midair, Rona chuckled in spite of herself.

"Good of you to finally show some skill, but it is too late."

"Stand your ground, men," Tristan growled, digging the toe of his boot into the dirt.

"Cowards," Brahm spat. "All of you."

"Dishonorable they may be, but cowards they are not." Rona hummed with impressive interested, placing a fingertip on Erick's blade as she examined all three of Gavin's friends.

A bright, sudden flash of light made everyone jump. Elise doubled over and covered her eyes, afraid of what she might see if she looked. *Did Rona kill one of them?* Feeling her breath begin to return to normal, Elise finally opened her eyes when Darcie tugged on her sleeve.

Between Rona and the soldiers now stood Arymei, the Queen of Vynchia.

Elise stared incredulously at the magnificent presence of the queen, whom she had not seen since the day Derek was attacked. Three guards stood around her.

Joranna's letter worked! We're saved!

All felt right in the world for precisely two seconds until Brahm and Vaughn began backing away. Vaughn took it one step further, bolting out of sight into an even thicker area of the woods.

Elise fumed. *He's the true coward.* Surprisingly, Brahm remained still by Rona's side rather than chase after him. She also did not seem fazed by his absence as she crossed her arms.

"Queen Arymei, to what do I owe this honor?" Rona asked, her gaze fixated on the other woman's face.

"Let these children go, Rona," the queen commanded.

"Oh, but they are not children. Simply ask them," Rona replied, winking at Everett, Erick, and. Tristan, who glared as they brandished their swords towards her. "They're *real* soldiers now. In death, they may even earn the title of heroes."

Elise gulped at Rona's calm, collected tone. This moment called for anything else. Goosebumps trickled down her arms as she failed to see a way out of this scenario alive.

"You can give up now, Rona," Arymei announced. "You are no match for Haighdlen's *and* Vynchia's fleets, both of which are on your shores. You are outnumbered."

Rona answered with a shrug. "Let our armies face off. I anticipate a decent war." Rona smirked. "How many months has it been since we have seen each other?"

"This will not work, Rona," Arymei countered. "You will not distract me."

"Several months, at least," Rona resumed, ignoring the Vynchian queen's response. "Oh, I remember. We have not been in each other's company since the day I cursed the late king Derek."

Arymei did not reply.

Elise's stomach tightened at the mention of her fallen grandfather. Gavin stepped in front of her as if he knew she wanted nothing more than to charge at Rona herself.

How can she talk about it so lightly? Her brother just died, and she's already playing mind games. She's a psychopath!

"I relished watching you sob over his injured body, though." Rona circled Arymei as she spoke. "How humiliating it must have been returning with his cursed, aging mind to Queen Joranna." She stopped abruptly, inching her face closer to Arymei's before bringing her voice to a whisper. "The guilt alone must have been positively dreadful. Enough to drown you, I imagine."

Drawing his sword, Brahm joined Rona's side. "Shall I strike her now, my queen?"

Rona feigned a pout. "Do not be ridiculous, Thaddy."

Brahm grimaced. "Not here, Your Highness. Please."

Rather than oblige the disgraced captain, Rona rolled her eyes and nudged his blade away like a child. "Put away your silly sword, Thaddy. It is beneath you." She stared back at Arymei. "No, Queen Arymei came for a worthy fight, and a worthy fight she shall have."

The following moments were chaos. Elise, Darcie, the boys, Brahm, and even Arymei's guards were reduced to mere bystanders thanks to a barrier shield created by Rona to separate them. Although they all wanted to step in and aid the Vynchian queen, the soldiers going so far as to use their swords against the wall, they were forced to pray Arymei would prevail against the evil sorceress.

Magical blasts erupted from both women's hands. Back and forth, shots were fired. It was difficult to determine who was winning or losing as the queens appeared equally matched. They took turns delivering and receiving hits, yet neither was willing to yield to the other.

Helpless to break through, Elise focused on Arymei's tactics. She longed for her magic to make some sort of difference. The Vynchian queen was skilled in attacks and stealth. At one point, she even looked to teleport into the trees, sending a shower of leaves and branches down below.

Rona dodged, however, and the cat and mouse chase continued.

Arymei narrowly missed an incoming blow, ducking down and sweeping a leg under Rona's feet. Her victory was short-lived, however, as Rona's hands closed around her neck from behind.

I need to help her! She might not know about Rona's protection spell. If Arymei succeeded in killing Rona, she, too, would die.

Arymei arched backwards, twisting and trying to free herself. Rona's hold only tightened. Wheezing, Arymei clutched at Rona's fingers before teleporting again. Reappearing behind the sorceress, Arymei quickly connected her foot with Rona's spine, sending her forward onto the ground.

Rona rolled over in time to block Arymei's next attack. Their energies met in midair and clashed. Holding steady, the battle stalled as it took all their energy to keep their magic going strong against the other.

Rona finally gained the upper hand as Arymei tripped and stumbled over a root. The magical connection ceased, pushing both women further apart. Arymei landed against the trunk of a large tree.

With a wave of her hand, the sorceress caused the thick trunk of the tree to split with a loud crack. It creaked and twisted before toppling over.

Crying out in horror, Elise watched as Vaughn ran out from hiding and leapt to push Arymei out of the way, narrowly missing death himself as it shook the ground with a crash.

No one moved.

Elise's heart raced when she noticed Arymei's eyes were closed. Biting her lip, she waited for Vaughn to examine her.

"Don't worry," Darcie called. "Her chest is moving. She must've hit her head is all."

"You need to be more worried about yourselves," Rona replied from behind them as the wall barrier vanished. However, in the blink of an eye, Elise watched her friends, Vaughn, the guards, and Gavin's friends freeze as if tied by invisible ropes from the neck down. A second later, Elise felt as if her entire body was wrapped in chains that squeezed to the point of painful. Yet there were no signs of actual restraints.

Rona and Brahm inspected each of the captives.

"I am through with distractions. You have robbed me of the only person that matters in this world. I will handle you once and for all."

"But we didn't kill your brother!" Mitch called out.

"Shut it, will you?" Brahm spat before kicking Mitch in the leg.

"We clearly do not have much time," Rona said, flickering her gaze back and forth between those on the ground and the trees. "I need to act now."

Elise licked her lips and decided to address the sorceress herself. "You're afraid, but you don't have to do this, Rona!" Elise took a steadying breath. "I know fear. I *know* what fear can do. Not just in my head, but within my own family." Desperation tugged at Elise's heart, her eyes glossed over, and she used what last minutes she possibly had to look at her friends. "But it's a lie! You can't be controlled by fear. It won't last, but lo—"

"Do not say it!" Rona roared. She spat each word with disdain as she closed the distance between herself and Elise. "Do *not* say love will. It is overdone, pathetic, a *true* lie in and of itself. *Love* is what has failed me, and I will not be fooled again!"

"Rona—" Elise pleaded.

"Silence!" Rona's crazed eyes raked over Elise. A manic chuckle radiated from deep within her. "Save your little rehearsed, self-righteous speech. I have heard enough. Let me tell you about your precious love sentiment." She twirled a finger before poking the air in Elise's direction.

A searing, hot pain pooled through Elise's arm, as if the blood itself were on fire. Elise cried out, gripping the afflicted arm.

"What ultimately killed King Derek? What was he willing to die for? *Love.*" Rona jabbed the air again, sending a flash of magic into Elise's other hand that cradled her arm.

Elise fell to her knees as Rona moved closer.

"What is currently ailing the great, mourning Queen Eugena this very moment? Again, love. Or loss of it, rather. Take it from me, life is best when no one loves you. Only then can you know true strength."

"But you have someone who loves you," Gavin interrupted. "Brahm loves you, and he's been willing to do anything for you!"

"Hang Brahm!" Rona bellowed, ignoring the man in question, who frowned and remained silent. "He is no more use to me now than my dead brother."

She is completely detached of all emotion. How can she say these things? There's no way she actually believes what she is saying.

Welling up the courage, Elise kept her eyes fixated on Rona's every move. "From where I'm standing, you're the only thing those stories have in common. Love didn't cause those deaths. *You* did." She waited for the inevitable panic attack that normally arose when she spoke her mind, yet it didn't come. In fact, a quiet sense of calm steadied Elise's breath, and she relaxed her shoulders as best she could muster.

"And *you*, their weak-minded, anxious little savior. Behold what I have reduced you to, my dear, without a single touch. What has brought you here today? *Love*." She spun her hand around until Elise limply floated inches above the ground. "But, unlike your doomed little family, I refuse to lie to you." Rona dark red lips split into another grin as she sent Elise reeling in pain once more. The more bystanders, including Elise's friends, begged for her stop, the longer Rona watched.

I can't survive this. She's going to kill us all.

Writhing in agony, Elise screamed. Hot tears soaked her face. Her veins felt as if they would burst, her bones heavy and useless. She could not think. She could not move. Again, Elise desperately pushed for her magic to work. *Leave me alone. Let us go. Let us go.*

"Is that you doing that?" Rona chuckled. "Are you really trying to win? You see how well that worked for the queen."

Elise managed to turn her head enough to see Arymei's unconscious body on the ground.

"Do not waste your time," Rona purred. "My life lesson to you is simple. The root of all pain is love." She stroked a strand of hair out of Elise's eyes. "And I mean to cause you a lot of pain as love has given me."

Yanking Elise's hair, Rona forced her head back to look at Gavin, Mitch, and Darcie.

Elise gasped when Rona made the diary appear out of thin air. "Have you missed this?"

Elise longed to snatch it from the sorceress, but her scalding, hanging limbs prevented it. *Please don't.* She weakly uttered the same sentiment.

"Oh, but I must," Rona sang. "You see, I have spent many an hour with this blasted book, trying to uncover its secrets. Your own lover failed to help me, yet I prevailed in saving my brother with it. That is. . .until today."

The blistering, scorching pain swimming through Elise's veins all at once ceased. She felt her toes touch the ground, yet she remained frozen and breathless. Her brain remained numb with shock as was her ability to speak.

"Let me finish this story for you," Rona said, pointing the diary at each of the other three teenagers. "You shall not die today, dearest. For that would mean sacrificing your own life. I suspect you knew that."

Elise looked hopelessly into Gavin's eyes.

Rona followed her line of vision as understanding darkened his eyes. "Is your family worth all this trouble? Is *he* worth it?" she whispered into Elise's ear.

"Elise, don't," Gavin called. "Ignore whatever she tells you. I won't let you die! We can figure out another way."

Rona shook her head. "There is no need. Elise here will watch as each of you die one by one instead." Her chest swelled with pride as she fed on the panic, watching the blood flood from their faces. "Afterwards, Elise, you will open this diary and be sent back to whatever hole of a world you came from. Perhaps, their dead corpses will even follow you. Carry the burden of that loss." Pushing Elise to the ground, she advanced on Elise slowly as a lioness would her prey. Rona's soft, alluring tone then took on a terrifying, guttural hiss as she began speaking through gritted teeth. "Then, and only *then*, will you even get a taste of what I have been through!" Her words echoed around the forest. A flock of birds fled the trees around them as all parties gaped at the unhinged woman.

As Rona raised her hand to strike, Elise winced, clenching her eyes shut. *The pain is going to start again. I won't be able to handle it. It's too much. We've already lost.*

"Release the girl, Rona."

Elise opened her eyes in time to see an approaching hooded figure. The command was quiet, yet forceful, and when the hood lowered, Elise saw a masked middle-aged woman peering down at her. *She can't be much older than Joranna.*

The woman then removed her mask.

"Queen Prisha!" rang out the whispers from the surrounding guards and soldiers, including Vaughn and Brahm. Many hung their heads, lowering their weapons to kneel.

"Get up, you fools!" Rona whirled around. "You all answer to me! Me alone!"

"It is done, Rona," Prisha stated. "You have no power here."

Rona tipped her head back with a chuckle that made Elise's blood run cold. "Is that so? Pray, tell me who was it that fled in the first place, leaving her citizens to perish?"

"I intend to answer for my own crimes later," Prisha replied, careful to keep her voice even. "You, however, will answer for yours now."

"Do your worst, Prisha, but these are *my* subjects now. Lockesbarrow belongs to me. Now, if you do not mind, I am in the middle of something."

Turning her back on Prisha, Rona rolled her eyes when the rightful queen continued to push back.

"Release these children, Rona. *All* the children, in fact, that make up your so-called army."

"I do not take orders from you," Rona growled. "May Dmitri's soul haunt you until your death and beyond."

Elise grimaced as Rona shot another invisible force to immobilize Prisha, who remained calm with a stoic expression. It was Rona's turn to stalk towards Prisha one slow step at a time.

"You betrayed your people!" Rona exclaimed, her outstretched hand tightening into a fist. Her face split into a satisfied grin as the forcefield around Prisha squeezed harder. "And a traitor must *always* suffer in the end."

Prisha winced and hung her head. Her lip twitched as she released a distressed sigh. Composing herself, she met Rona's eye. "I apologize for Dmitri's death, Rona, and the pain it caused you. You may choose not to believe me, but I loved him, too. He was a good man, but the people deserved justice. The first time was a mistake, but the second was necessary."

Understanding dawned on Rona's face. "*You?*"

"Whatever version you chose to resurrect for yourself was not your brother. Altering time itself cannot truly bring him back. Deep down, you must know this. He was but a shell of his former self."

Rona glared into Prisha's eyes with such intensity, Elise felt it radiating off the sorceress. If looks could kill, Prisha would not be standing.

"This is my kingdom," Prisha continued. "I should have fought harder for it rather than be convinced otherwise by advisors. You have no power here. . .and it is time to stand down. Surrender."

"Says the woman who is currently captured," Rona pointed out. She leaned in until her nose almost touched Prisha's. "I commend your efforts, even admire your spirit, but you are too late." Rona turned back to face Elise with a dramatic turn. "It is also too late for you and your family. Now that I do not have to split the kingdoms with Dmitri, I can rule them both. You two ladies may have broken my heart, but you will never be strong enough to defeat me."

"You're wrong." The words left Elise's mouth before she realized what was said. "We are strong enough. Even if you kill us, we're strong enough because we tried." She felt adrenaline rushing through her where the pain once ran. Rona could kill her any moment, and probably would, but Elise held her head high, nonetheless. "The root of pain is not love." She held Gavin's gaze as she spoke. "Love is made up of too many elements to be the single root of anything. It can be whatever you make of it."

Gavin mouthed the words *I love you*. Elise did the same.

Rona clicked her tongue, staring between Elise and Gavin. "How poetic." Her sarcastic, mocking smile melted into a thin, strict line as her eyes narrowed. "What sentimental last words. Brahm!" she quipped, walking over to where Brahm and Gavin stood. The blade of Brahm's sword still rested against Gavin's neck. "Kill Mr. Striess first."

"No!" Elise wriggled and writhed against her invisible binds. *This can't be happening. This can't be real!* She could hear her heart beating in her ears. It pounded against her chest. There was so much she wanted to say to Gavin yet could not find words at the same time. Staring hopelessly, her own cries mixed with those of Darcie and Mitch. Prisha demanded Rona cease her theatrics and surrender, yet all objections were ignored. "Please, no! You can't. Don't kill him," she sobbed, thrashing against her holds. *He can't die. I can't lose him!*

Brahm lowered his sword before standing between Gavin and Rona.

Elise watched as every ounce of color drained from Gavin's face until even his lips turned white. His forehead glistened and his breathing was uneven. She desperately willed Brahm not to kill him, hoping a fraction of magic would leave Rona's forcefield. Brahm's inaction proved it did not, fueling Elise's manic attempts to free herself as the two men stared at one another. Brahm lifted the blade and rested it against the skin of Gavin's chest. *I've got to get to him!*

Then Brahm looked at Elise.

Every time Brahm put his eyes on her, Elise instinctively distanced herself. The hairs on her neck would stand and her thighs would clench. Elise did not trust this man or his intentions. He had done so many vile things.

Yet, this time was different.

Rather than repulse her, it stopped Elise's heart. It was as if she were seeing Brahm for the first time. He studied her face, clutching the hilt of the sword by his side, before inhaling deeply. Brahm bowed his head in Elise's direction before squaring his shoulders. "Forgive me."

Elise closed her eyes. *I can't watch.* "Brahm, don't!" she screamed, straining every muscle, before choking back a sob. Against her better judgement, she opened a single eye to peek.

In one swift motion, Brahm twirled the tip of the sword from Gavin's chest and sank it deeply into Rona's. Elise gasped, along with everyone else, as the sword pushed through her completely before protruding out of her back.

It was as if time stopped. The diary fell to the ground with a heavy thud. Rona's shivering body lurched over Brahm's shoulder, her expression one of genuine shock and disbelief. Her mouth hung open, quivering. "Thaddy. . .*Brahm.*" A look of utter betrayal flashed across her eyes as she regarded his own anguished expression. Perhaps, Elise suspected, even an ounce of regret.

All at once, the invisible shields disappeared, and Elise could move again as well as everyone else.

As Rona's body fell limp, Brahm pushed her onto the ground before falling to his knees with a painful groan. Panting, he clutched his heart.

"What is happening to him?" Prisha asked. "Did she strike him?"

Elise shook her head, rushing to Brahm's side along with Vaughn, who inspected Rona. "Whoever kills Rona also dies. It's how she's protected herself all this time. Brahm. Look at me." She took his face between her hands. "Brahm, stay with me. We can get you help."

"No," he wheezed. Doubling over, he gasped for air. "It has to be t-this way." With an awful rattling sound, he met her eyes with the same soul-crushing expression. "A traitor must *always* s-suffer in the end."

Brahm's eyes closed, his mouth drooped, and finally he fell forward, draped across Rona's lifeless body.

Elise looked at Vaughn, who nodded. *They're really dead.*

Nobody moved.

Nobody spoke.

The only sound came from the distant gulls, canons, battle cries, and the clashing of swords. As numbness spread over her like a blanket, Elise felt like she was watching and listening from underwater. The faces around her became distorted as she succumbed to the aftermath of everything. Before her brain could comprehend what was happening, Gavin scooped her up into an embrace. Inch by inch, Elise felt the numbness shatter until she could breathe again.

"Excuse me." Vaughn cleared his throat until Gavin and Elise parted. "I believe this is yours."

Thanking him, Elise reached out to take the diary, running her fingers over the aged cover. *I didn't think we'd ever get this back.* She smiled before looking up at Vaughn. "Were you really on our side the whole time?"

He shrugged with a charming, innocent smile. "Guess you'll never know, will you?" Winking down at her, Vaughn turned his attention to Gavin before holding out his hand. "The best man won. Take good care of her."

Gavin hesitated, looked at Elise, and finally shook Vaughn's hand. "It would have been more satisfying to punch you."

"Understood." Vaughn nodded before offering his arm to Prisha. "Might the rightful and beautiful Queen of Lockesbarrow have any openings in her court for a handsome, aimless philanderer?"

"That remains to be seen," Prisha chuckled, linking her arm with his. "Something tells me you will cause a great deal of scandal in my court amongst the ladies."

Elise and Darcie shared a knowing look.

"However," Prisha added, "I am in search of a new captain."

Vaughn accepted without hesitation.

"That reminds me," Gavin said to her. "I met a few inmates while I was kidnapped who are innocent. Now that I think about it, you may want to examine the whole prison."

Hopefully, Richard is doing the same for the remaining Haighdlen prisoners.

"Consider it done," said the queen. "That is, after I get this army dispersed and sent to their homes. I should like to recruit a proper army."

"So, what do we now?" Mitch asked, squeezing Darcie's hand.

Watching as the Vynchian guards helped Queen Arymei recover and stand, Prisha beamed. "We spread the word that war is over. Rona has fallen."

CHAPTER 28

Only after Prisha was restored as Queen of Lockesbarrow did she fulfill her promise by ordering the return of all surviving adolescent soldiers to their homes. They, as well as those who had fallen, were honored for their service. The next phase of her reformation plan consisted of investigating the prison, a task delegated to her newly appointed Captain of the Guard, Vaughn Garthorne, who—according to a letter sent to Joranna from Prisha—*"wears the uniform and title well, with the utmost dedication, and answers the call of duty in hopes of atoning for past wrongdoings"*.

Elise giggled in spite of herself as she finished the letter Joranna shared back at Haighdlen Castle. *There's a twist. I never would have pegged Vaughn for enforcing the law.* While his character was often shifty, this was an amazing opportunity for him, and she was thankful he was given a second chance after all his help.

"What are you reading?" Gavin asked as he, Mitch, and Darcie joined her in the library.

Elise held the letter out for him to take. "She sent Joranna some updates, mentions people she's hiring, and says she's sorry she can't make it to Richard's coronation with everything going on."

"That makes sense," said Darcie, reading the letter over Gavin's shoulder. "Anything about your friend? Travis or something?"

"Tristan," Gavin corrected her before his face lit up. "Actually, yeah. It says here she offered him the job of Ambassador to Leafbrooke. That had to have meant a lot to him."

"Why do you say that?" Mitch asked.

"When we were in the training camp, he told me lots of stories," Gavin explained. "But one of them involved his dad being the Ambassador to Leafbrooke and them traveling together. Rona killed his dad when she took over. It'll be a good fit for him."

It was Darcie's turn to giggle. "Not to mention that'll keep him in court to see more of Iris. Joranna said she's now one of Prisha's ladies-in-waiting. I doubt she'll be waiting very long."

Mitch rolled his eyes with a scoff. "You just can't help but meddle, can you?" He laughed at her feigned pout. "You're matchmaking across kingdoms now!"

"Hey, don't be jealous of my skills," Darcie teased. "*Someone* had to introduce them before we left. You could cut their chemistry with a knife."

"Well, if the hairstyling gig ever gets old, we know you'd make a great living planning weddings," Elise suggested with a playful smile Darcie quickly returned.

The door opened abruptly, interrupting their friendly banter, for Joranna to enter with a small white box in her hand.

"Oh, good, Edith has already dressed you all," she said, taking in their formal garments. "The coronation is about to commence. The last of the guests are arriving now."

"Yep, we're ready," Darcie piped up before nodding at the box. "Did someone bring you a gift? That was nice."

Joranna looked down at the box in question, turning it over in her hands. "Yes, rather unexpectedly. It was found among Richard's gifts, but no one saw who delivered it." Holding it up to her ear, she shook it lightly back and forth.

Elise prayed it was nothing dangerous and sighed in relief when Joranna lifted the top without any surprises.

The queen gasped as she lifted a silken pink scarf out of the box. "Oh, how beautiful!"

Elise's smile fell as her eyes widened. *Horanis's scarf!* She remembered the story of the fairy king gifting Joranna the scarf, but Elise never realized it was part of a coronation gift. "Let me see. There is a small note here." She lifted a piece of paper with elegant writing on it. *"To the mother of the new King of Haighdlen—may this scarf serve as protection wherever you reside. Sewn by the hands from my kingdom, may its magic cover you in yours and beyond. - Horanis.* Horanis? What kingdom is he talking about?" Joranna asked.

"King of the fairies," Elise replied.

Joranna looked back at her as if she had swallowed an ice cube whole. "I always thought he was a myth. The type made up to keep children from messing with fairies." Speechless, Joranna scanned the letter, rereading it many times. "But why would he reach out now? The wording he uses. . .it is as if he knows I am planning to leave, but I have not shared that. How would he know?"

"You're leaving?" Elise shrieked. "What do you mean you're leaving? The war is over. There's no reason to leave."

Joranna waited until Elise calmed herself before folding the letter with a sigh. "I was going to wait until after the ball tonight to share the news."

"I don't get it," Darcie said. "Rona's dead. Why leave now?"

The queen sat down on the nearest chair, careful not to wrinkle her gown, and rested the box on her lap. "Richard and I met with the council about our plan forward. Although the war is over, there may still be those loyal to Rona. Uprisings, those seeking revenge—all are possible. We have been too careless in the past, and we must move forward with a plan. As painful as it is to leave, it is also the best course of action to ensure our family's survival."

"Who's all going?" Mitch asked.

"We have not shared with everyone yet," Joranna replied cautiously, "but we will resume our previous plan for me to take Ruby and Ian. As I come from that world, it is in our family's best interest that I accompany them."

Elise scooted closer to the edge of the couch. Draping herself over the arm, she gazed at her grandmother. "Are you sure you want to leave?" She focused on Joranna's silent form, willing her magic to compel her grandmother to tell the absolute truth.

"I have done a great deal of thinking," Joranna assured her. She smiled at her lap. "If we take some of my jewelry and treasures, we can surely live comfortably. Ruby can deliver quietly there, and Ian is adventurous enough he will not fight such an opportunity. It will increase our chance for a safe future." She stared at the map on the wall depicting the four kingdoms. "It is funny. . .I have lived in Haighdlen far longer than I ever lived in the other world. You and your friends have longed to return, but it took a great deal of convincing on my part. In the end, it came down to be providing for my grandchild."

Again, Elise felt as if Joranna was not telling her something. She was quiet as she pondered her family's move. *It would make sure they are back in our world. If I'm born there, and Mom stays, I'll grow up and meet my friends. Everything will occur the way it's supposed to. . .but why do I feel so sad about it now?*

It was not that she wished things to happen differently. Elise certainly wanted to be sure she would meet her friends again in the new timeline. She shared a glance with Gavin, but her smile didn't reach her eyes. If all went according to plan, and the timeline was truly fixed, would he still be in love with her?

Gavin took her hand.

"Do you think Ruby will be okay?" Elise asked quietly.

"I do," Joranna said with confidence before her shoulders shook with laughter. "She has done enough visiting that world. Now, she will not have to sneak around anymore. Let us hope she has learned to be a bit wiser." When Elise did not reply, Joranna smiled. "She will be safe, and she has you to thank for that. I overheard her talking with Sarah that if she has a daughter, she is considering the name Elise. Is that not thoughtful? Such a wonderful tribute to you."

Elise laughed, but it was a hollow sound underlined with nerves. Unable to meet her grandmother's eyes, she still felt the uneasy weight of Joranna's knowing stare. *Maybe she's figured out who I am.* If she knew, Joranna did not hint or say anything. Elise looked up when Joranna hummed in surprise, claiming that there was something else in the bottom of the box.

"I seem to have missed something." Joranna lifted another folded piece of paper before her eyebrows rose in surprise. She pursed her lips before holding it out. "It is addressed to *you*, Elise. How odd."

Elise paled and glanced at her friends. *Why would he send* me *something?* She hesitated before finally taking the paper. Her name was written on the outside with the same elegant writing as Joranna's letter.

--Well done. The prophecy is fulfilled. Replace this and your involvement will be erased from their memories as the restored timeline resumes.

It was difficult to unfold the paper with her hands shaking like they were, but she finally managed and gasped when she recognized what it was. *It's the final entry he ripped out of Joranna's diary.* She was careful to hide it from her grandmother to avoid suspicion. Elise's eyes scanned across Joranna's original writing.

October 19, 1988

Dear Diary,

I am determined to write no more of my grief. The last several pages have served me well enough. As I enter another restless night, my thoughts have wandered again to the visiting travelers. Namely Elise. She is the most fearless young woman I have ever met. Despite the odds against her, I honestly think she is the key to saving our family. I know not her exact relation, but I am inclined to think we are closer than she lets on. If only Richard would take her more seriously. She has done so much already and shows a fierce loyalty. Even if we are forced to flee, and the worst occurs, Derek was right about her. She is a true Laurille, and we are indebted to her.

"What does it say?" Joranna asked.

Elise took a moment to compose herself as both of her eyes stung with approaching tears. "He wanted to tell me to take care of you all and make sure everything turns out okay."

For the first time in her life, Elise was thankful Ballard interrupted at that moment to inform Joranna that Queen Arymei had arrived. Elise waited for her grandmother to follow the steward out before she let out a trapped sigh.

Gavin scooted closer and wrapped an arm around her shoulders. "What happened? What did he say? Is something wrong?"

Elise shook her head before holding out the letter for him to take. Mitch and Darcie also took turns reading it from their stance behind the couch.

"That's deep," Mitch said an appreciative whistle. "I wonder why Horanis tore it out."

Darcie rolled her eyes and kissed his cheek. "Because she had to learn that for herself. Even if Brahm was the one to actually kill Rona, Elise was willing to face her and do what she had to do."

"Yeah," Gavin added, smiling at Elise. "If she hadn't shown so much stubbornness—" He referenced the torn entry with a wink. "I mean, '*fierce loyalty*', we would have quit a long time ago."

"I know I would have," Mitch muttered playfully. He patted Elise on the shoulder. "But you stuck with it, Elise, and now your family is closer. Only you could've done that."

It was difficult for Elise to take the compliment. She had not given much thought or energy to self-worth in the past, often seeking invisibility over notoriety. However, her friends were right. Since her return from Lockesbarrow, Elise also noted how close her family was becoming. While she could not say she was the one who ended Rona, Elise could accept that she helped end her family's estrangement.

"Thanks, but I couldn't have done it without you guys," she admitted. "And I don't know about you, but after this coronation and ball tonight, I just want to find a way home for good."

As soon as the words left her lips, they jumped as a puff of smoke appeared from the chair Joranna previously occupied. As the smoke cleared, Elise leaned closer and gasped at the sight of the diary—the *original* diary.

"Oh, finally!" Mitch exclaimed as he lunged for it before Darcie's arm stopped him. "Come on, I want to go home!" He tried again, but she prevented him once more. "Rona's dead. The family loves each other. Let's go home before something bad happens."

"And we will," Darcie answered with a laugh, "but we're all dressed up for a fun night, probably our last time at a ball like this, and I'm not going to waste it. Plus, you promised me a dance." The rest of Mitch's protest went unheard as Darcie pulled him out of the room to join the other guests.

Gavin and Elise shared a laugh.

"Poor Mitch," Elise teased.

Assuring her that Mitch would get over it, Gavin intertwined his fingers with hers before resting their joined hands between them. "That was really nice of Joranna to write down what Derek said about you."

Folding the entry into the front of her gown, Elise nodded.

"You got everything you wanted," he added before lifting their hands to kiss her knuckles. When Elise's smile did not reach her eyes, he inquired what was the matter. She tried to wave it off, but Gavin persisted until Elise chewed on her lip and sighed.

"I should be excited," she began, "because you're right. I did get everything I wanted." Elise squeezed his hand. "But, now that things have slowed down, I keep thinking about you wanting to join the military."

She felt him stiffen but continued in a small voice. "I wanted to be mad at you for not telling me, but that wouldn't be right since I didn't tell you what could've happened if I had been the one to kill Rona. I'm so sorry."

"I understand why you didn't tell me." He kissed the top of her head. "And I'm sorry, too, but please don't ever feel like you can't come to me with stuff."

Elise nodded and requested he do the same. "I hate you'll have to leave." She coughed to disguise a cry in her throat. "Will it be soon?"

That's a dumb question. We're about to graduate. Did you expect him to hang around while everyone else moves on with their lives?

He rested his head on her shoulder. "Sooner than later, probably. I have to talk to a recruiter first."

Don't cry. This is a great opportunity for him. At least you can enjoy the summer together. Rather than share her insecurities, Elise leaned her head against his and asked what made him decide to join.

Deep down, Elise wished she listened better. As he explained his upbringing, including his father's career, her thoughts wandered to the inevitable day when he would have to break up with her. *I can't expect a long-distance situation. He has to know what this decision means.*

She was not upset about the choice itself. The military was a highly respectable path. Realizing he was still talking, Elise forced herself to focus and return to reality.

"To be honest, I never really understood my dad until I was in Rona's training camp," Gavin confessed. "I know it was only a few days, but being out there with the other guys—let's just say my dad's old stories started making more sense. . .Is that stupid?"

Elise nudged his head up with her shoulder before kissing him softly. "Nope. It makes perfect sense." She attempted to stand up, but he pulled her back down to the couch.

"What is it?" he asked. "You're not telling me something."

Elise pretended to pick a piece of lint from her gown, taking a moment to admire Edith's flawless work yet again. She was going to miss these gowns and the royal treatment when all was said and done. Feeling Gavin's expectant stare on her, she forced herself to smile. "It sounds like your dad is going to be really proud of you."

He once again pulled her down as she tried to escape again. "And what about you?" His eyes searched her entire face before landing on Elise's lips. "Will you be proud of me?"

She detected a hint of uncertainty in his tone, which tugged at her heart even more. "Of course!" Elise intended to say more, but it became increasingly hard to concentrate when he trailed a finger from her lips down to her collarbone. The path continued until the same finger lowered the strap of her gown. Before she could react, he replaced the finger with his lips, tracing the same path back to her lips.

"Good," he whispered huskily in her ear before turning his attention to the sensitive skin behind it. "I thought you'd be mad at me."

"No." She moaned when his other hand cupped her bottom, which was a challenge given the volume of her skirt. "I'm just dreading when you have to leave." Clinging to him, she warned herself to enjoy every moment they had left together.

"Yeah, boot camp will be tough, but after that. . .Well, I kind of hoped you'd come with me."

His words cut through the desire pooling into Elise's lower belly, and she jerked forward as he slid down to kneel in front of her.

"Elise?"

What is he doing? Goosebumps covered Elise's entire body as he took her hand. She wanted to say something profound but was unable to speak as he drew small circles on the back of her hand.

He lifted his other hand to lift her strap back into place. The corner of his mouth twitched before he smiled and looked at her. "You look so beautiful. . .plus I'll never be able to plan anything more romantic than this. . .being dressed for a ball and everything."

"Gavin—"

Shaking his head, he cleared his throat. "I-I've thought about this a lot. I know I don't have a ring yet, and maybe it's too fast for you—"

"Do you know what you're saying?" She squeezed his hands. "Are you sure you want to do this?" Elise's thoughts swirled rapidly, her heart fluttered, and she laughed in spite of herself. Never in a million years did she think something like this was possible for her.

Despite the euphoric high she felt, a nagging part of Elise's brain reminded her of the challenges they could face, but she pushed them all away. Those could be dealt with later. She was not set on a particular college, and if she did pursue teaching, it was a career that traveled well. Marrying a military man would also come with many hurdles, but there was nothing she wanted more than to face them by Gavin's side.

"Let's do it," he said before breaking out into a smile of his own. The same charming smile that made her weak in the knees. "Will you marry me?"

Elise closed her eyes and sucked in a breath. Dreaming of marrying Gavin was one thing—she lost count of how many times she had scribbled *Mrs. Elise Striess* in her notebooks back home—but being asked to marry him was an entirely different situation. It did not feel possible. Things like this did not happen to invisible girls like her, and yet, here he was on one knee awaiting her answer.

"People are going to think we're crazy," she whispered, unable to control her smiling. *Or that I'm pregnant*, she added in her head. None of that mattered, however, and it was the first time Elise disregarded the opinions of others that she could remember. All that mattered was the two of them together in this moment. Feeling her eyes water, Elise nodded fervently and met his gaze. "Yes, I will."

Leaping to his feet with a childlike energy, Gavin scooped Elise into a tight hug before twirling her around. Before she could say anything, he crushed his lips against hers with such eagerness, the two shared a series of small kisses before Elise felt like she could breathe properly again.

"I love you," she whispered into his ear as he hugged her again. When he repeated the words back to her, she tightened their embrace. *I can't believe I'm engaged!* She suppressed the urge to squeal, choosing instead to clear her throat. "We should probably keep it quiet for now with everything going on, and it's probably better to have a long engagement."

He nodded in agreement.

"Not only for college, but maybe let us have some regular dates first." They shared a laugh before hugging again. She proposed a movie or dinner date when they returned home.

"That sounds pretty boring compared to fixing a magical timeline and saving the royal family together," Gavin whispered against her shoulder. He pulled back long enough to kiss her. "But a long engagement it is."

Pulling away to pick up the diary, Elise tossed a teasing smile over her shoulder at him. "Well, maybe not *too* long." She beckoned him to follow her. "You can go ring shopping if you want." Holding out her hand, Elise wiggled her fingers as if imagining one. Elise melted against him as he wrapped an arm around her. "After all, once I tell Darcie, she'll have the entire ceremony planned in a day."

Taking the diary from her to tuck into his vest, Gavin scoffed. "Probably an hour."

Wrapping her arms around his neck, Elise quirked a brow as she eased back. "You sure about this? I'm kind of a mess."

He shrugged with ease as his smile returned. "Yeah, I know. I've met your family." He laughed when she slapped him with a playful pout. "But just wait." He winked at her with a smirk. "You still have to meet mine."

Lowering her arms to link their fingers together, Elise's face grew serious as she searched his eyes for any sign of doubt. Finding none, she leaned forward and kissed him deeply before whispering against his lips. "I can't wait."

There was something thrilling about carrying a secret. Having Mitch and Darcie question their joyful smiles as they arrived to the throne room was worth every ounce of keeping their news quiet a little longer. Elise particularly relished catching Darcie glaring knowingly at her throughout Richard's speech. *You'll find out soon enough.*

The coronation proceeded as planned, with Richard officially being crowned King of Haighdlen in a lavish ceremony amidst cheers, applause, and fanfare. While the attention stayed on Richard, and rightfully so, Elise was especially moved watching Joranna, who was ever the vision of a proud mother and queen.

As the occupants of the throne room transitioned to the ballroom to celebrate, Elise reflected on the journey that led them to this moment. How many times had she feared the worst? How many tears and panic attacks occurred for Elise to finally find her self-worth? Watching everyone go through the motions of a toast, dinner, and later dancing, the evening felt as if it were passing in slow motion. Longing to bottle up the insatiable energy in the room, Elise committed the elaborate details of the music and merriment to memory, knowing it most likely could be her last time there.

Spotting Richard and Gwen sharing a dance as the Archer family happily observed from a nearby table, Elise thought back to the first ball she attended in the same ballroom when Derek and Joranna were engaged. Given the similarities of the two couples, if she squinted, Elise could almost see her grandparents again on the dancefloor.

With a heavy sigh, Elise rose and made her way to the royal head table. *I have to say goodbye sooner or later. I can't put it off any longer.*

Only Joranna, Ian, and Ruby were still seated. All three greeted her as she approached with Joranna asking if she was enjoying herself. Elise carried on with pleasantries longer than necessary as the pain of leaving felt too much to bear. . .and they would not even remember her visiting.

It's better this way.

"Where is Sarah?" Elise asked.

Ian nodded at the sea of couples dancing. "She is dancing with my friend Liam. I invited him, and it seems they have grown rather close since he saved me."

"I could not be happier," Joranna commented. "I have never seen Richard so happy either. Let us hope some good news comes out of these attractive pairings."

That takes care of Richard's and Sarah's futures. Ian will meet Aunt Morgan in our world at some point. That only left Ruby to be dealt with. Surely, their meddling planted a seed for a happier future. Scanning the crowd, Elise frowned. "Where is Charles?"

Ruby took a sip from her cup as Joranna wrung her hands. "I am afraid Lord Fenton is busy assisting Ballard with our traveling arrangements."

"That's too bad," Elise said. "I would have liked to say goodbye. It's time for us to leave."

Joranna stood from her seat and embraced Elise in a warm hug. "We are forever grateful for your help. We will not forget all you have done for us."

Unfortunately, you will. Elise inhaled her grandmother's sweet perfume. *I wish you of all people could remember me. I'm going to miss you so much.*

As they parted, Elise moved on to her uncle. "You healed up nicely. I hope you have a safe trip."

Ian winked with a smile. "You as well. Thank you for everything."

Elise nodded politely and paused in front of her mother.

Ruby met her eyes but said nothing as she stroked her stomach in lazy circles. *I know you can't say it, but I'm going to miss you, too. Hopefully, whatever future I return to is happy for you as well. You deserve it, Mom.*

Before Elise could say anything else, Ian asked his mother if she would like to dance. Joranna appeared shocked at the offer. After all, Elise suspected she had not done much dancing since Derek returned home ill. Staring wistfully at the dancefloor, Joranna smiled at Elise as her son escorted her away.

Now that it was only her and Ruby, Elise stepped closer to the table. "Good luck with the baby and your new home." Ruby nodded and wished her a safe trip. Yet, something still felt off to Elise. The spark had left Ruby's eyes. Elise could not imagine what anxieties preyed on her mother's mind about moving away and entering motherhood all at once. Licking her lips, Elise nodded toward Ruby's stomach. "Your child is lucky to have you for a mother. I know you're going to do great in the other world. You are strong enough, Ruby, even without magic. Don't forget that, even if things get tough."

Ruby looked taken aback by Elise's forwardness but thanked her and wished Elise well.

As difficult as it was to say goodbye to Joranna, it was twice as hard to walk away from her mother. Feeling a cry form in her throat, Elise caught Gavin's eye across the crowd and waved him, Mitch, and Darcie away from their table to follow her into the courtyard.

Given the crowd of people standing outside, Elise led them into the garden for privacy.

"Are you sure you're ready?" Gavin asked.

Elise sighed. "As ready as I'm going to be. To be honest, guys, I don't know what we're returning home to."

Darcie grabbed her hand. "It's going to be great, and no matter what, we'll always remember the truth of what happened."

Sucking her mouth into a thin line, Elise thanked her and pulled the piece of paper from her gown while Gavin did the same with the diary in his vest.

"I know this is emotional for you and all," Mitch said to Elise, "but I can't wait to get back and never look at another diary ever, ever again."

"I can't blame you there," said Elise as they all laughed. When Gavin handed her the diary, she took in one more view of the picturesque castle and braced herself. "Are y'all ready?" When her friends nodded, Elise slipped the final entry behind the other pages before fully opening the diary and welcomed the suffocating portal, for what she hoped would be the last time.

CHAPTER 29

Elise questioned the diary's magic when she woke up in her own quiet bedroom. Drowsiness consumed her, lulling her in and out of sleep. She watched the blades of the ceiling fan rotate at full speed eight or nine times before movement to her left made her scream and bolt off the bed. The sight of familiar red hair made Elise blow out a steadying breath. "Mitch, you scared me!"

"All I did was sit up." Mitch yawned and stretched from his position on the floor. As Gavin and Darcie stirred as well, he took in the details of the room. "Where are we?"

"Why did the diary bring us to your house?" Darcie asked Elise, who shrugged.

"Hey, what about my car?" Mitch scrambled to his feet and pulled on the blinds to peer out the window. His shoulders sagged in relief. "Oh, good. It's here."

"Do you think something went wrong?" asked Gavin. "Why wouldn't it have taken us to Joranna's?"

What business would the diary have to bring them back to her house? A diary, she realized, that was no longer with them. She could think of no reason her house would hold anything special. Nothing looked out of place or different. . .until she caught sight of the photo collage on the wall.

There used to only be four photos there.

Stepping closer, Elise counted eight photos strung together with clothespins on a makeshift board. Only now, instead of all being photos of her and Darcie, Elise saw a handful contain candid pictures of herself and Ruby. Some were recent, while others were old trips and birthdays. *Mom is smiling. Look how happy we look.* Elise pointed to one showing members of her family from Haighdlen. "What's going on?"

"Elise?" Ruby's voice called from downstairs.

Elise froze, looking anxiously between her friends. "I don't know if you're all supposed to be here. I'm not even sure which version of *here* this is." Grabbing Gavin's hand, she urged them all to follow her. "I doubt she'd want boys in my room. Let's go into the spare guest bedroom before she catches us." Tiptoeing down the hall, Elise led them to the next door and slipped inside. "Sorry for the mess. This room always gets used for storage, so—" Elise did a double take of the once cluttered space. Where stacked bins once rested against the wall, there was now a computer desk. The lumpy old mattress in the corner was now a full bookshelf. Various framed pieces of art hung on the walls and both windows now had matching curtains.

"Whoa," Darcie said, doing a full spin and whistling in appreciation. "If we fixed nothing else, your mom's improved interior design was worth it. This office is awesome!"

Elise said nothing as she approached the computer desk. Her attention was drawn to the framed college degree hanging above it. She smiled in disbelief at the decorative lettering spelling out her mother's name. Hearing her name again, Elise jumped when Ruby poked her head in before entering the office cradling a steaming cup of tea.

"Is everything all right in here? I heard screaming." Her eyes widened when she noticed the other three. "Oh, I am so sorry. I did not realize you had friends over. I would have made more tea."

Mom? This could not be her mother. Instead of a worn, wrinkled dress and stained apron, Ruby sported dress slacks and a silk blouse. Rather than a tangled mass of hair clipped on top of her head, smooth voluminous shoulder-length curls framed her slender face. She easily looked ten years younger and her once permanent scowl was replaced with an amused smile.

"Why are you all staring at me like that? Do I have something on my face?" She dabbed her cheek with the back of her hand before blowing on the tea in the other.

Yeah, makeup!

"I do not believe we have met," Ruby said to the boys. "I'm Ruby, Elise's mom."

Gavin and Mitch exchanged an anxious glance at one another.

Elise apologized as the boys awkwardly greeted her mother. "Mom, this is Mitch, Darcie's boyfriend." Licking her lips, she hesitated. "And this is Gavin. . .*my* boyfriend." *I can't introduce him as my fiancé yet.* Bracing herself, Elise stared in shock when Ruby beamed.

"You did not tell me you were dating someone! And Darcie, I am surprised you kept a secret that long," she teased before nodding towards the boys. "Well, you two ladies have done quite well for yourselves. I trust you are both respectful gentlemen?" There was a strict undertone in her voice that both Gavin and Mitch knew well enough to take seriously. Once both nodded, Ruby's cheeriness returned. "I wish we could all sit and talk more, but I am afraid I need to cut your visit short. Elise and I have some last-minute items to purchase for the party on Saturday."

Ruby set her cup down on the desk and shuffled through a pile of envelopes.

Furrowing her brows, Elise looked at her friends with a blank stare. She shrugged when Darcie mouthed the same question playing on repeat in her own brain. *What party?*

Gavin took the bait. "What party?"

They tensed when Ruby spun around. "Elise, you and Darcie didn't invite your boyfriends to your graduation party? We have been planning it for over a month!" She turned her attention to Mitch and Gavin. "You boys should come if you can. There will be plenty of food. Oh! That reminds me." Ruby took a delicate sip of her tea before addressing Darcie. "Am I still good to receive the family and friends discount at your father's bakery? I placed the order over a week ago, but I forgot to ask."

What is happening right now?

Darcie bounced on the balls of her feet with an uneasy smile. "Sure?"

"Thank you. Again, I'm sorry to ask you to leave for now. After we run our errands, Elise, I'll also need your help tidying up before the family comes."

The family? They're actually coming here?

"The whole family?" Elise did not hide her confusion. "Coming here?"

Ruby finished the rest of her tea before replying. "Well, they will stay at Nana's house, since we do not have the room, but yes. You do not think they would miss your graduation, do you?" She checked her watch. "I have to make a few calls before we leave. Darcie, always a pleasure. Boys, it was nice to meet you both. We will talk soon. Goodbye!"

As the door closed behind Ruby, a deafening silence filled the room as the group of friends stared at each other. The last five minutes had occurred at a whirlwind speed. If Gavin, Mitch, and Darcie were not there, Elise would question her own sanity. Shaking her head, Elise scoffed and pointed towards the door. "Okay, who was *that*?"

The oddities continued well after Elise and Ruby returned home from dinner and shopping. Not only did Ruby ask her questions throughout their outing, but she *listened* and seemed to care about Elise's responses. There were moments throughout the evening while her mother talked when Elise caught herself marveling at Ruby's transformation. It was simply incredible that this was the same woman.

Later that evening, while Elise lay on her bed texting Gavin, her mother's cell phone rang from the other bedroom.

"Elise?" Ruby called. "Can you please answer that? I am in the shower."

Elise pursed her lips and rolled off her bed. *Not sure that's a good idea considering what happened the last time I checked Mom's phone.* She would never forget learning about Haighdlen in the first place after reading a series of texts on Ruby's phone. Shuffling into her mother's bedroom, she peeked down to see Joranna's name and face on the screen.

Upon hearing Elise answer, Joranna excitedly went into a two-minute storytelling spree, sharing how excited everyone was to be planning a visit. Elise had to hold the phone away from her ear for the more animated parts. "I am tempted to go meet them at the portal."

How strange it was to hear Joranna speak of the portal so openly. Daydreaming while her Nana continued updating her on the other Laurilles, Elise absentmindedly fiddled with random items on her mother's nightstand. *I can't wrap my head around all these changes. Is this even real?*

"Elise? Elise?"

Hearing a pause, Elise realized she had yet to string two words together since answering. "Nana, I'm sorry. What did you say?"

Joranna chuckled on the other end of the call. "Can I get you to write down a message for your mother to call Ian at work tomorrow? Do you have a pen nearby?"

Hearing the shower still running, Elise agreed and sat down on Ruby's bed before opening the nightstand drawer. She shuffled through old papers and receipts before locating a pen. After scribbling down Ian's work number, something in the back of the drawer caught Elise's attention despite Joranna's continued talking in her ear. Checking one more time to make sure the water was still running, Elise pulled out a wrinkled piece of folded parchment. *Is this what I think it is? Would she really have kept it all these years?* The worn discolored edges gave away its age, yet Elise remembered seeing it— reading it—when it was new. Holding her breath, she unfolded and reread Charles' love letter to Ruby.

With every heartfelt word, her heart broke in much the same way as the first time reading it. Time was never on their side, yet something caused Ruby to keep this. Elise's mind immediately traveled back to Haighdlen Castle. The secrecy, the anxiety, and the urgency were so fresh in her mind. Since returning, Elise could not help but feel as if she were in two places at once. The idea that life was going on in Haighdlen at that very moment while she did mediocre things like go to the store with her mom and plan for a party felt unnatural.

Hearing her name repeated, Elise apologized to Joranna again.

"You sure are distracted this evening. Is everything all right?" Joranna waited until Elise replied before continuing. "I meant to ask you, is there anything specific you would like for a graduation present?"

Elise glanced down at the letter again. Running her thumb across Charles' signature, she cleared her throat. "Are you able to communicate with the family on short notice?" Elise knew she must sound incredibly suspicious, but her grandmother did not sound bothered and replied it was possible.

"Why?" Joranna asked. "Do you need to get a message to them?"

"Not *them*." Elise froze as the sound of Ruby's water stopped. She hurried to stuff the letter back into the drawer. Once it looked buried again, she slammed the drawer. "Hey, I have to go, but there *is* something I would like."

It was a stretch. Charles may have moved away or gotten married. Elise hardly doubted he spent the last eighteen years alone. Yet, it was a chance she was willing to take to give the one person who deserved it most her own chance of love. She had just enough time to make her request before ending the call as Ruby emerged from the bathroom in pajamas.

"Who called?" Ruby inquired.

"Ian wants you to call him at work tomorrow. The number is written down there. Goodnight, Mom." Without waiting for a reply, or a chance to lose her nerve, Elise returned to her room.

Please, she thought as her head hit the pillow. Within minutes, Elise was surprised to find herself already drifting off to sleep. *Please let this work out. . .Please, for Mom.*

The few remaining days leading up to her graduation passed in a blissful blur that included a real first date with Gavin. Elise's initial fears of him growing bored of her in their world vanished soon after she was invited to meet his parents. After that, the two of them were practically inseparable. There were moments Elise wished their graduation would not come, because that would mean time was passing and he would be leaving soon. She vowed to make the most of their summer. Yet, despite her wishes, time marched on and graduation day arrived.

Part of Elise felt silly knowing her entire family was attending. Her small high school graduation was nothing compared to a royal coronation or ball. Surely, her uncles and aunt knew that. Yet, there they were, waving and cheering for her as Elise crossed the stage to receive her diploma while her mother took pictures. She still considered them an odd group of characters who stuck out in this world, but Elise wanted to keep it that way.

The sight of them all lined up, her cousins included, on the school lawn to greet her following the ceremony filled a void inside Elise she did not know was there. Smiling down at her feet, she wove in and out of the crowd to join them.

"You did it!" Ruby exclaimed, handing Elise a bouquet of flowers. "I am so proud of you!"

Elise blinked away approaching tears as she hugged her mother. "At least I didn't twist my ankle in these heels. I was sure I'd fall on my face."

"I keep waiting for your mother to do the same," Ian teased, nodding at Ruby's own heels. After chastising his twin daughters for playing tag around groups of people taking photos, he turned to give Elise a hug as well. "I wish I could stay longer. Morgan also sends her apologies for not being here."

"Well, considering she just had a baby, I think I can forgive her." Elise laughed, thanking him for coming, and requested he send Morgan her congratulations.

"I will tell her, thank you. Congratulations yourself." He checked his watch. "I better get back home. It sounds like Mother will be driving the grandchildren to the party, so the girls will stick around here with you all."

Elise nodded, watching her other cousins Paul, Eric, and Madelyn joking and laughing near their parents. Richard and Sarah held their spouses' hands, and without realizing it, Elise had a wide smile spread across her face. *This is how it should be*. She said goodbye to Ian as Gavin walked up to her.

"Hey!" she exclaimed, wrapping her arms around his neck. "Where are your parents?"

"They're getting the car," Gavin said. "Dad can't stand to get stuck in traffic."

"Can you still make it tonight?" she asked. "Your parents can come, too."

He nodded and leaned in to kiss her as Ruby snapped a photo of them.

"Mom," Elise teased.

"Do you want me to get a family photo of everyone?" Gavin offered.

Without missing a beat, Joranna accepted the request and called out to Ian before he got too far out of earshot. Instructing Ruby to give Gavin her camera, she gathered all the children and ushered everyone into place with Elise in the center.

Once Gavin handed the camera back to Ruby, the family dispersed loudly, chattering over one another until Ian offered to drop off Richard, Gwen, Sarah, and Liam at Ruby's on his way home. Elise offered Gavin a sheepish grin. One by one, the adults wished her well and planned to meet up later until only Ruby, Joranna, and the cousins remained. "Sorry. They can be a lot."

Gavin waved off her apology and pulled Elise closer. "Don't worry about it. In fact, maybe the next time there's a family photo taken. . .I'll be in it."

Elise's heart threatened to leap out of her chest, and she kissed away his lopsided grin.

"Hey, get a room," Mitch called out as he walked up holding Darcie's hand. "This is a family friendly event."

Elise made to hug Darcie but stopped short when Ruby called out for them to pose together.

"Mom, come on," she laughed. "I think we have enough pictures."

"You will thank me later," Ruby replied.

"We will be here forever waiting for Ruby to take her photos. You poor dears are ready to get out of here, I am sure, but I would be happy to take one for you," said Joranna.

Darcie held out her phone to Joranna before posing with the other three. Once the last photo was taken, Mitch and Darcie said their goodbyes and planned to see them later that night.

"Oh, that reminds me," Joranna said. "Sarah wanted me to invite you to come stay with her for a couple of weeks this summer before you start college."

Elise suppressed a smile at her grandmother's subtlety. *Gavin knows all about Haighdlen, Nana. There's no secret.* Perhaps a trip would be exciting if she could convince her family to let Gavin and the other two join. While beautiful, Haighdlen was probably also a more enjoyable place now that it was not under a constant threat.

Elise lit up as a familiar figure emerged from the crowd and approached them. "He made it."

"Who?" asked Ruby.

"I can give you one guess," Joranna teased with a smile as she nodded over Ruby's shoulder.

Chewing her bottom lip, Elise watched her mother turn and come face to face with Charles.

"Hello, Princess."

Ruby stood frozen, staring at him as if he could not possibly be real. She opened and closed her mouth several times. "What are you doing? Who invited you?" she finally asked, glaring daggers at Joranna's and Elise's once she caught sight of their guilty grins. "Never mind. And it is just *Ruby* here."

"Forgive me," Charles said with an easy smile, taking in her full appearance before meeting her eyes. His own softened. "You look lovely as ever."

Time had also been generous to Charles, whose only sign of aging was the handful of silvery wisps of hair along his temples. Unlike Elise's family, he appeared to be made for the modern world's fashion, wearing a tailored dark gray suit that Ruby would have to be crazy not to notice. He turned to Elise. "I hear congratulations are in order."

"Thank you," said Elise.

Joranna patted Ruby's arm and nodded for her to introduce the two of them.

Rolling her eyes, Ruby stepped forward. "Elise, this is Lor—Charles. He is Richard's friend."

Liar. He's more than that.

Charles bowed his head. "Pleased to meet you, Elise. You may call me Charlie. At least, your mother used to."

A tense silence followed until a car horn honked nearby and Gavin's name was called.

Charles rested a hand in his pocket. "Please excuse me. I must go speak with your aunts and uncles."

"Let that be our sign to leave as well," said Joranna. "Ruby, you are good to drive Charles to the party, are you not?" Without waiting for her daughter's stunned reply, Joranna ushered the other grandchildren toward her van.

"Can you believe she did this?" Ruby snapped to Elise. "She knows better than to—"

"Nana didn't invite him," Elise confessed, biting her lip. "I did."

Ruby opened her mouth but no words came out. "Elise, how do you—"

"It's a long story, but I know you two are meant for each other," Elise said. "Don't be mad at Nana, either."

Ruby huffed.

"He's still crazy about you, Mom." Elise nodded to where Richard, Gwen, Sarah, and Liam were laughing at something Charles said. He tossed a smoldering smile over his shoulder at Ruby that would make any woman weak in the knees.

Ruby released a slow breath before shaking her head. "Elise, this is more than you realize. It would never work."

"Says who?" Elise challenged. She grabbed Ruby's hands with her own. "Mom, you have always had to put other people's needs first. I'm proud of your hard work and accomplishments, but it's time to put your needs first for a change. You had to stay away from Haighdlen for my protection and probably got settled here. Your degrees are not wasted, no matter what you choose, but I'm not a kid anymore. I have plans for my life. We can talk about them later, but it's your turn to live. . .wherever, and with whoever, that may be." Elise failed to suppress a devilish smile. "Not to mention. . .your legs look incredible in that dress. You're killing him."

Ruby laughed and tucked a loose strand of hair behind Elise's ear. "When did you grow up to be so wise?" She smiled as if seeing Elise as a woman for the first time. She cleared her throat and attempted a no-nonsense tone. "I won't make any promises, you know. He could turn out to be a complete cad now."

Elise chuckled. "I'm willing to place that bet."

Ruby kissed her cheek and nodded towards Joranna's van. "See you at home."

Gavin walked Elise to it before opening the passenger-side door for her. She thanked him with a kiss that was interrupted by the twins knocking and making kissing faces against the windows. Fortunately, the older three had enough sense to give them some privacy. Elise pounded the glass playfully and turned back to Gavin as his parents honked again.

"Will your mom be okay?" he asked.

"She's tough. I think so." A wry smile crept across her lips. "Plus, he's not wearing a ring. Fingers crossed."

Gavin chuckled. "Darcie will be proud of you."

"I think she will," Elise agreed. "I'll see you soon then?"

"Yeah, I can't wait. I love you."

"I love you, too." By this point, Elise could take a hint, as now *all* her cousins were fake retching despite Joranna's fussing. "I better go."

He waited for her to get settled before shutting the door with a wave and walked to his own ride.

Buckling her seatbelt, Elise stared at Charles and her mother through the window. "Do you think she'll be mad at me?"

Joranna lowered her head to peer out of the same window as Ruby softened her resolve and laughed at something Charles was saying. "I say she will thank you. . .just maybe not right away."

Elise chuckled.

"Richard gave him his blessing, I hear," Joranna said, pulling out of the school parking lot. "Goodness knows it is long overdue. Those two were made for each other."

I agree. Elise stared back at the passing school, realizing just how many changes were headed her way.

"I am proud of you, you know," Joranna called over the loud talking coming from the backseat.

Elise looked up from her bouquet and smiled. "Thanks, Nana." Her smile slightly faltered as a hint of mischief gleamed in Joranna's eyes. "What?"

Joranna offered an innocent wink and sweet smile in return. "Did you enjoy yourself?"

Elise glanced warily in response to her grandmother's loaded question. "Today?" *She can't mean what it sounds like, right?* After all, Horanis promised everyone would forget them. It had been one of the hardest things to get used to since being back home. Yet, there was a definite shift in Joranna's knowing stare. *There's no way she remembers.* "Sure."

Joranna drove in silence for several moments until her eyes lit up. "Oh! I almost forgot. I got you something." Opening the center console, she pulled out a gift-wrapped box.

"Nana, inviting Charles was your gift."

"Well, I wanted to give you another one." Joranna nodded for her to open it in the car. "I hope you like it."

Tearing the corner of the wrapping, Elise peeked at her grandmother for a hint. Encouraged to continue, she fully unwrapped and opened the box with a gasp. With trembling fingers, she lifted out a new diary and leafed through the blank pages, thankful it was not accompanied with a portal.

"Thank you," she said, leaning over to hug Joranna. "I love it." Lifting the front cover, Elise saw a small note written by her grandmother on the first page.

June 6, 2007

Dear Elise,

Your turn.

> *Love,*
> *Nana*

"Was it everything you wanted it to be?" asked Joranna.

This time, Elise did not question her grandmother's meaning. She closed the diary and placed it back into the box. Nodding, she imagined many more questions would follow when they were alone.

"It was," Elise replied with a wistful sigh. When Joranna slowed enough to make a turn, Elise thought she saw twinkling lights zipping in and out of the passing trees. She smiled. "It really was."

The End

Acknowledgments

I am incredibly thankful to God for giving me the gift of writing. His love, patience, and grace taught me that anything is possible with faith.

In 2007, Elise's journey began as an idea in a notebook. . .a passion project of a young girl scribbling away in class. Being able to share these characters with the world is a dream come true.

I wish to thank my editor, beta reader, family, friends, designers, and teachers. Additionally, I want to say thanks to my readers for supporting me. You are all an important part of my creative team. Words cannot express my gratitude.